"What should I bring you?" Emile inquired. "The body? The scalp?"

"No!" Le Clerc spat. "Do you need information on this man you hunt?" he asked, diverting the question he really wanted to answer.

"No, Monsieur Le Clerc," Sharpe said, a note of respect in his tone. "I know where they say this rendezvous is going to be. I will be there. And Josiah Paddock, too. You see, eh?"

"Yes. I see." Le Clerc removed the small velvet coin purse from his vest pocket. It was heavy as he placed it in the giant's hand. "For you, Monsieur, before you go."

Sharpe stuffed the coin purse into the wide sash about his waist. "I will see you in the fall, my friend."

"It is so long to wait. The fall." Le Clerc's words followed Emile Sharpe as the huge man disappeared into the shadows once more. "Bring me . . ."

Sharpe stopped and turned. Only the side of his face with the wide jagged scar showed in the firelight. "Yes, monsieur?"

"Bring me—his head!"

BorderLords

A NOVEL BY
Terry C. Johnston

BANTAM BOOKS
NEW YORK • TORONTO • LONDON • SYDNEY • AUCKLAND

BORDERLORDS
A Bantam Domain Book / published by arrangement with
Jameson Books

PRINTING HISTORY
Jameson edition published October 1985
Bantam edition / October 1986

ISBN 0-553-26224-6

Published simultaneously in the United States and Canada

PRINTED IN THE UNITED STATES OF AMERICA

OPM   16 15 14 13 12 11 10 9

For Rhonda and Joshua,
the two loves of my life.
They have been the wings
that have given this eagle his flight.

It has been demonstrated over and over again in the history of the West that the existence of laws, and the presence of lawyers to expound and of officers to enforce them, are not indispensable to just and orderly condition in thinly settled portions of a country. It was the universal testimony of those who were familiar with the life of the trapper, . . . that crimes of all colors were never so few, nor punishment for such as were committed so just and swift and sure, as in those remote localities where there were neither laws nor lawyers . . . Each man was in a measure a law to himself . . . Those rude men had a true sense of justice, and if they administered it in a rough fashion there was rarely a complaint that their judgements were wrong.

Hiram M. Chittenden
The American Fur Trade of the Far West

No court or jury is called to adjudicate upon his disputes and abuses, save his own conscience; and no powers are invoked to redress them save those with which the God of nature had endowed him.

Josiah Gregg
Commerce of the Prairies

Prologue

They had always come. Through all those years. And he knew, always knew, days before they showed up at the door. The ones who always came to barter for his services, to use his talents, to contract his time. Eighteen winters since the massacre at Seven Oaks. Eighteen winters since he had buried the body of his mother along with the remains of the others left behind by the wolves. All those years of carrying this burning fire within his breast. All those winters of moving in some way to right the wrong done him.

Those who came had always sat with him around the warm fire, while cold winter winds screeched along the logs of the hut. And always ate with him before they told him of the job at hand. He always wanted it that way. That they should eat together before the task was discussed. Matters of death.

This time there had been three men. They had come to bring him to St. Louis. The sounds of those words made a good taste in his mouth. He had never been to this St. Louis before. He had always worked north of that jumping-off point for the western fur trade.

But now three of them had come. Never had there been more than two. Perhaps these three men were as afraid of him as were the victims who were to be killed each time he took a job. The man who had hired him had also hired these three to come into this wilderness to seek him out. To ask him to take this job.

And all he had to do this time was to kill one man.

One

To escape the wind, Titus Bass headed them back toward the rimrock for their camp. It seemed somehow fitting, too, for above them, someplace along the rocky, castle-like walls bordering the west rim of the valley, lay the body of Josiah Paddock's Indian pony.

The immense cold slithering into the valley hand in hand with the deep purple shadows of early evening froze blood on a wound. Funny, to be thinking about all the blood freezing. He looked down at his own leg, wrapped tightly against the flow of the dark, red fluid. And he recalled the arrow that had bit at his flesh as he had torn it from the leg. Now the blood trying to escape from the jagged wound fought to flow in the dropping temperature. The improvised bandage and the leather of his legging showed no new spread of the dark fluid from the wound. Little comfort in that, what with the pain of hobbling along, using his rifle as a crutch under one arm, the other hand gripping the long rein tied to the one pony left to the two of them.

He turned slightly to look back at the travois and nearly stumbled over some sage hidden in the drifting snow. When there was sun, he could make out the small mounds over the rolling flatland of the river valley, was able to see the short shadows that warned of a clump of sage. But now in the dimming light, his moccasins had to be his eyes. And he told himself they would not make the shelter of the rimrock before the light was gone.

Bass's thoughts drifted to the young trapper, Josiah Paddock, suspended in the travois' sling behind the pony. He thought of the cold that had staunched the flow of blood from the chest wound, a gaping, ragged hole—and he shuddered. Perhaps from the cold, he told himself. Perhaps from his fear the boy would not make it back to the Crow village some six, maybe seven days away.

He thought back, too. Back to that very afternoon, when he

1

had made the crude litter. Bass lashed one buffalo robe across two lodgepole pines, then tied the poles to the saddle atop the only animal left to the two of them, the strong Indian pony. Then he carefully wrapped the boy up with the three remaining buffalo robes.

"Gonna cover your head, son. Warmer. Keep you warm."

"No," young Paddock whispered with trembling lips. "No. Wanna see the sun. Watch it go down. See it on the mountains. Please. Watch the sun on the mountains, Scratch."

Titus almost smiled, but the cold that bit and tore at his bare cheeks above the whiskers flecked with streaks and patches of gray froze his face to a stiff mask. Scratch. Long had he carried that handle.

Most call me now by a name I got hung with some years back. Ol' Scratch, it is. Give me that name when I was comin' to my first ronnyvoo—twenny-six, it were. Had met me three fellers outta Bayou Salade, down toward Wah-Too-Yar in them southern Rockies, an' they had felt sorry for this coon. Bud, Billy an' Silas felt sorry for me an' teached me what I would need to keep my hair. My clothes were store-bought'n, linsey-woolsey, they was. 'Sides, the seams was full of lil' graybacks by then. Had the graybacks bad, I did. Well, those boys come to callin' me Scratch on account of all that itchin' I was doin' all the time. Finally got me decked out'n a set of Yuta skins. Didn't scratch no more after that, but that damned name was stuck to me so hard that I couldn't shake it. By the time I left them three coons they was callin' me Ol' Scratch—on account of me gettin' the green wored off so's to be a regular mountain man.

The pony snorted and Scratch glanced over at the animal. The cold, blue frost billowed up from the animal's nostrils as the pony strained against the dead weight of the travois and its load. The boy needed warmth, and soon. There hadn't been that much Scratch could do for the wound back there in the pines where Josiah had fallen. The lead ball had passed through the chest so there was nothing to remove from the blackening hole. But, the young man needed warmth. And Bass would build a fire as soon as they reached the rimrock for the night.

Several times he had considered stopping for the night out here in the valley, along the river that flowed north into the Yellowstone. Stop somewhere in the trees and willows. But the wind would be too strong. The clouds told him that. High and stringy, blown out like a pony's tail on the run. They would have some bitter wind this night, their first on the trail back—after a day of death. His beard itched as it stiffened against the cold and he raised a hand. The dirty fingernail protruding from a hole in his mitten clawed at the frozen blood in his beard and then he remembered again the searing pain that had shot through the ragged, raw flesh along his face. The ribbon of torn tissue ran from the corner of his eye down into his whiskers at the cheek. The claw had ripped his flesh open.

But he chuckled to himself. Funny, now, to still be thinking it was the bear that had attacked him. It had not been claws. Only a crude iron hook that the white-haired Asa McAfferty had worn in place of a right hand that had been shattered to ribbons some years ago. Bass remembered now the tall Crow warrior who had challenged the white men's right to hunt the Whitehair down.

"It was I who first met the white-haired one winters ago, when his hand was cut off. I was the one who cut off the hand to save his life. It was this one who first knew the white-haired man when we had stolen trapper's ponies."

The Scotsman McAfferty had stolen much more this time, he thought. Much more than ponies. And lost much more than a hand for it. Not a claw at all. Only the crude iron hook. The mind plays some strange, desperate tricks on itself in a life or death struggle. But Scratch had won, even against the odds he had mounted against himself.

Every now and then he heard a groan of pain from the young trapper as the poles of the litter bounced and jostled over the scrub sage. Won't be long now, Scratch said to himself. Looking up at the rimrocks ahead, he thought of how long a day it had been for all of them. He turned his head to look behind him.

Behind Josiah's travois, dropping farther and farther away, stood the bare, lonely tree where McAfferty's body lay lashed across the limbs. Sharp thorns and brambles lay about the base of the trunk, where Bass had pulled them so that no dark thief of the forest would steal the cold flesh that was to remain forever in that place. Beneath the man lay the dark hide of the wolf. And wrapped over the lifeless form was the hide of the medicine animal, the great bear.

And Scratch remembered them pulling away from the tree at last. As the sun was running to find its bed for the night. Beneath the warm robes Paddock had held the scalp in both hands. He had taken the long, white tendrils into his fingers and clutched them tightly. Rocking gently in the travois, Josiah had watched the tree grow ever smaller behind him, then closed his eyes to sleep.

So much behind them now, as Bass turned his head to gaze forward once more. He felt so very old for this day. Behind him lay so much of his life. The man he had been sent to hunt down and kill, now secured high in a cottonwood. That had been a supreme struggle, what with his leg torn up by the arrow. And that feat of super-human strength had come after he had dragged the Whitehair's body up and out of the high-country bowl where they had fought to the death. And now the body rested behind them, high in a cottonwood, wrapped and bound against carrion-eating birds. But McAfferty's body was safe. Buried proper. He had done right by Asa at the end. And that was odd, too—to be thinking of doing right by the man you had just killed.

No. He shook his head and felt the braid brush across his cheek. The old man's hair was flecked and streaked with gray, with one single thick braid on the right side of his head, encircled with a piece of dirty, greasy red cloth. The hair that hung down from the back of his head, however, was not like the hair on the sides. Instead of the streaks of gray, it was coal black and hung straight down past his shoulders, unlike the gray hair that was curly and wavy except for the one, tight, red-wrapped braid.

No, it wasn't like the final fight had come as a shock at all. It wasn't sudden, either. He supposed he had known it was to come down to that for some time. But still, the feelings when that time came, slapped him across the mouth like a brutal blow delivered from the hand of reality. It ought to have been different, he told himself. But, who was he, after all? Merely a man doing what had to be done to buy himself another day, another season, perhaps another year in the mountains. Without running away. No, he could never run away. He had run headlong into this and had not cowered from it. But he had been afraid. Perhaps more so than Paddock had been. And he had dealt with that fear. This realization gave him a little more strength to struggle the last few yards across the snow-covered sage that fought to trip him up until he got them to the foot of the rimrock.

"You 'wake?" He stopped the pony and hobbled back to the travois.

"How you . . ." Paddock coughed, strangling on the fluid deep in his throat, ". . . how you 'spect me to sleep . . ." he hacked again into the cold air, ". . . when you're bouncin' me over every rock you can find?"

"Ain't rocks, son."

"Huh?"

"Sage."

"Ah." Then he coughed against the pain.

"We stopped now—for the night, Josiah." He felt like kneeling beside the travois, but knew he would only have to struggle to rise once more on the bad leg. If he got down, his tired body might not want to move again.

"Got me work to do." He started off toward the pony.

"Bass?"

"Yep?" The older man scooted back to the travois.

"We have us a fire tonight?" It was like pleading.

"We both need one," Bass replied. "Yes, son. We gonna have us a good fire."

"Thanks."

Titus hobbled up alongside the Indian pony, the Nez Perce buffalo runner he had traded for back to the rendezvous in Pierre's Hole last summer. He ran his hand down the animal's neck, stroking the damp hide along its withers. Then his hand wandered down and touched the medicine bundle's thick rawhide loop. It hung from the saddle's large pommel. Such a long, long day. Time to build a fire. Time to push away the darkness some.

Slowly, with the biting cramp in his fingers, his cold, numb hands loosened the knots in the rawhide thongs securing the travois poles to the pony's saddle. Moving back toward the litter, the trapper bent over to step between the two poles. He stood upright, took a step forward, bending his head down, so that one pole now sat on each shoulder. Struggling with the weight and trying to balance on the one good leg left him, Bass lifted the poles from the pony's back. Quickly he swung the rifle that was his crutch so the butt struck the pony smartly on a rear flank. Just enough to nudge him forward a bit, he thought.

The pony jerked and moved a few steps, clearing the travois poles before halting once more to hang its head in exhaustion.

"Good boy," he said quietly, feeling exhausted himself at the weight of the travois bearing down on his shoulders. Now he stepped back until the opening of the vee was wider than his shoulders and started lowering the poles to the ground. His rifle dropped, its muzzle slipping from under his armpit where he had tucked it.

"Damn!" he muttered to himself.

"What?" The frail question came from the bundle of robes wrapped over the travois.

"Nothin'," Titus replied. "Just clumsy of me, s'all."

When the litter was finally on the ground, he bent over to retrieve the fallen weapon. Snapping the frizzen forward, Scratch blew at the snow around the lock. With his right hand he brought up the pan brush that hung from his pouch and swept the pan clear of wet snow and powder. He dropped the brush and used the vent pick to probe the touch hole, clear it of any residue. Then he ran a small dusting of priming into the dry pan and dropped the frizzen down over it.

He wheeled around so that he could kneel at Paddock's head. "Gonna make us camp here, son," he said as he looked up at the darkening sky. The stars already were beginning to glisten across the growing inkiness. "Gotta get us some wood an' then we'll have us that fire we both needin'."

"Coffee?"

"Don't have none of that." He felt saddened somehow at not having what the boy wanted, perhaps needed. "Can fix you somethin' warm to be drinkin', howsomever."

"It'll do." Josiah hacked again to clear his throat.

It'll have to do, Titus thought as he rose and turned away from the travois. A few yards away a narrow creek ran down from the rimrock, headed for the river across the valley. There stood trees and brush where he would have to find some wood for their fire.

Against the pain in his tired leg, Titus bent again and again to pick up the branches of deadfall he kicked free of snow cover. Swinging his rifle, he battered the bigger limbs from their grips on dead trunks. Noisy, he thought. But who the hell would dare to follow them down this river? This be Crow country. And they were sent on this man-hunt by the Crow. Nobody save for a stray Snake, or Sioux, maybe—only them— would be anywhere near where they were now. No sense in being quiet anymore. And they were going to have a fire. So many days out of the Crow camp without a night fire to warm them. No hot food to drop in their bellies. But now they could have the warmth that would begin to heal the young trapper, the warmth that would take some of the gnawing fatigue from his own old bones.

When he had dragged the last of the large limbs over beneath the trees near the overhanging rock, Bass shuffled around in a wide circle, kicking at the snow with his thick buffalo-hide moccasin. He stumbled and fell several times before he cleared enough snow from beneath the overhanging rock shelf so that a lot of the fire's heat could be retained.

Kneeling over the pile of dry kindling, he pulled his striker and flint from his pouch before searching for some charred cloth. His numb, aching fingers shook so much that he could not hold on to either the flint or steel. He kept dropping them into the snow-dust. Finally, Bass set everything down on the pile of kindling and crossed his arms, stuffing a hand under each armpit. Soon his fingers began to tingle with renewed feeling. One at a time he brought them out of their armpit cocoons and placed them in his mouth where he alternately sucked and blew on them for warmth. When they began to ache enough so that he could move them, he once again picked up the flint and striker, searching once more for dry char in his strike-a-light pouch. This time he was able to hold on to the flint and char until a spark began to glow in the blackened cloth. Gently he moved the glowing char to his right hand and brought it close to his lips where he could breathe frostily on the ember while his left hand searched for the rat's nest of tinder he carried in a pocket of his shooting pouch. The fingers tore a section of the dry, ratted grass away, then laid the glowing char atop the tinder. Again he lifted the tiny pulsing spark close to his mouth and in an instant the tinder began to glow, then flared into a small tentative flame.

Quickly Bass set the tinder down atop some dry kindling and began to set more small twigs and wood shavings over the new blaze. Slowly he added larger and larger twigs and shavings until the fire burned on its own for a few minutes without his nursing it along.

He rose shakily, his one good leg cramped by the cold and the crouch he had been in during the fire-building. Without the rifle crutch, he hobbled over to the travois some ten yards away. Stepping into the middle of the vee above Paddock's head, he leaned over and scooped up the two poles beneath his arms.

"Where we goin'?"

"To get you warm, son." Bass pushed his chest against the narrow part of the vee where the two poles were lashed together. They creaked under the strain and he finally began to inch the travois poles forward. It was not a smooth trip for either of them. One step at a time, at the cost of extreme labor. Paddock moaned with each new step, with each new jerk. And Scratch groaned against the dead weight, against the almost useless wounded leg, against the sagging strength in the one good leg left him. His arms and shoulders gave out by the time he reached the fire and the travois dropped to the ground with a dull thud. He heard the exhausted yelp from the back of the litter.

"Sorry, boy." He turned around between the poles and scooted over to kneel beside Paddock.

"It be all right, Scratch." Josiah hacked some fluid up and tried to spit, but the liquid dribbled down the side of his mouth and chin. Bass took the sleeve of his elk-hide coat and wiped the chin dry. "I can feel the warm now. Th . . . ," Paddock croaked. "Thanks."

"You just stay put an' feel that fire," Scratch muttered cheerfully, feeling the warmth growing over himself, too. "I'll be gettin' us some vittles on. Maybe so, somethin' warm to drink, first whack." He started to rise shakily on the one good leg. "You just stay put 'til I get somethin' fixed up for you."

"Where . . . ," Josiah sputtered again. "Where you think I'm goin', ol' man?" He hacked as he tried to laugh.

"Ain't goin' nowhere fast, I s'pose. Neither of us. We do make a pair, don't we, boy? You ain't goin' nowhere an' me—why I ain't goin' fast." He fought against the clumsiness of the bum leg as he scooted around the fire to reach the pony tied in the willows.

Slowly he loosened the knots holding their remaining baggage on the pony's back, letting each bundle fall, plop quiet in the snow. He pulled the saddle free and dragged it over to the fire near the travois. Three short trips later, he had the bundles under the overhang of rocks where the heat from the fire radiated off the yellow sandstone into a warm shelter against the cold curtain surrounding them.

"Where you gonna sleep?" Josiah asked, slowly turning his head back to look at Bass.

"With you, boy."

"Like he. . . ." He coughed. "Like hell you are!"

"Ain't gonna lay a hand on your untouched body, son," Titus

chuckled at the sudden flash of spirit from his partner. "Onliest thing is, you got all the sleepin' robes for yourself. An' the best way we gonna keep each of us warm on this tramp back be to keep each other warm, sharin' them robes."

"Ain't never slept next to a man before . . ."

"Never split a robe, eh? An' don't you go gettin' any ideas, noways," Scratch snorted. "I'm figgerin' on saving myself for a squaw back to Rotten Belly's village. Some gal that's got her some tits. Last time I looked at you, shit—you didn't have you no tits to speak of. You ain't gotta worry 'bout me. I want me some tits to sleep with when we gets back home."

It hurt, but Josiah had to laugh softly along with the older man. He was only now beginning to feel some release from the thoughts of his own death. Every moment he had been conscious since they left the battlefield, Paddock had felt the depressive, gray veil of death settling over him. There was little he could do for himself during the jolting journey across the snow and sage to escape the grip of the dark spectre. But now the old man, his friend, was beginning the exorcism. He was feeling warmer.

Titus turned back to the younger trapper. "'Sides, you near had one of your tits blowed off back there," he commented, without much humor this time.

"I . . . I . . . ," Josiah stammered, in a fit of coughing, "I ain't . . ."

"Nawww," Bass interrupted. "You ain't goin' under." He turned away to fiddle once more with the fire. Leastways, you ain't gonna go under if I got any say in it, young'un.

"Got me medicines for that hole in you." And prayers that you last 'til we get back to the Crow, thought Bass.

"Gonna take us some time to be gettin' back to Rotten Belly's camp, what with me walkin' and Josiah Paddock layin' down on the job!" It sure as hell is gonna take us a lotta time to get back, he reasoned, too much time—and I hope we both got us that much time left us.

"Had me scared, you did," Josiah said finally, his voice muffled through the buffalo robes.

"'Tweren't nothin' to be gettin' spooked about, Josiah." Bass reached over for a second small kettle and began to scoop snow up into it as he had done with the first. "We been through too damned much together to be gettin' scary now 'bout a couple of holes in our meat. Now—ain't we?"

"S'pose . . ."

"Damned right."

The evening breeze that nudged them into the rimrocks had now grown in weight and bluster. It swirled headily around their camp before rushing headlong up the valley toward the Yellowstone. Bass looked out through the darkness, with his ears seeing all they had to tell him. When next he looked over at Josiah, Scratch saw that the young man was dozing again, his body demanding the rest the wound's healing required. He would have to wake the young trapper in a short time when supper was warmed. He went on with the preparations, humming to himself softly, moreso to keep the dark thoughts from pressing in around him as was the bone-chilling night wind.

"*Meself was begatted an' born in ninety-four,*" McAfferty had always told the story. "*I be a full-blooded Scot, descended from the border lords I am, an' most proud of that—though I was born this side of the east ocean. Me pappy come over, brung him his wife an' three boys over here then. Two girls an' me was to come 'long later on. Moved right out to get into the wild to be tradin' axes, blankets an' such as that to Injuns for skins.*"

Yes, Asa, Bass thought. You are the cause of much of this darkness about us. Fate always seemed to stalk you. An evil hand always held you in its grip. You never laid claim to your landholdings, so you were easy pickin's for the claim jumpers who threw you out of your home. And that was all your first wife Rebekka could stand.

"*By twenny-one I'd wandered back up close't the Missouri settlements. I heard of a man speakin' of a feller named McKnight, fixin' to lay beaver for the greaser country. Asa McAfferty was a lad ready for the West. By eighteen hundred and twenny-four I joined up with John Rowland down to Taos. We wandered some for a few seasons, endin' up in Aricara country by twenny-six.*"

That be when you earned you your white hair, ol' friend. Titus suddenly felt spooked, crawly and wormy inside, calling a dead man his friend—a dead man he had killed himself.

"*This ol' feller, a Ree medicine man, come up to me, sayin' he wants to talk with me 'bout Bible, personal-like. Feller just wants me Bible! Tolt me he'd have it by mornin' anyways— 'long with me skelp hangin' to his medicine bundle. I come down to havin' to part his ribs with me knife when he gone an' struck out at me with his 'hawk. Shakin' like the tremblin' earth come judgment day, I creeped back to them other white*" *fellers an' tolt 'em quiet what's happened. Them fellers just looked an' looked at me with the queer on their faces. Rowland finally tolt me what they was all seein' at on me. Said me hair was white. A sign 'bout killin' that Ree medicine man, it were."*

Seemed to be you always had your hand in the bad of things, Asa. Always had your hand in it stirring it up. Leastways, until you lost that hand of yours.

"Knave that shot me weren't much of a shot. Got me through the wrist—busted me rifle at that time, too. That right arm, it were of no earthly good, but that rifle still had a ball ready. Picked her up an' shot the feller shot me. Ended up havin' to cut me arm here. One of them Crow niggers took him a long buckskin whang, ran it over an' over the blood, then he went to rubbin' it in the sand on the bank of the stream. One of them Crow set to an' finished cuttin' on my meat with his knife, then set to the bone with that bloody whang. By that time the blood dried the sand to the whang so it made one devil of a saw! One of them Crow sewed best he could, as I was in 'nother mind by then. Them Crow give me one of them trade fusils an' a good bow with some fine cottonwood arrows."

After adding more and more handfuls of snow to fill the larger kettle, Titus finally pulled the waxy parfleche from his baggage and retrieved some pemmican and jerky. Crumbling and shredding both as best he could with the tired, cold fingers, the older trapper dropped the bits of food into the warming water over the fire. Then he added more of the limbs and twigs to the flames. Bass leaned back against the thick blanket he had draped over his saddle and sighed when the muscles of his injured leg finally relaxed.

"Put me an ol' iron fork I use to feed with in the fire an' let it set. Heated that iron devil up hotter'n the gates of hell, then I beat these two tines 'round from the hook. Carved me a chunk of wood to be 'bout like the end of me arm, then pounded the fork into it."

You done pretty with the hook, Asa. It were a good job with what you had to work with. I remember the piece of wood with the hook pounded in it. Remember it was held to the lower arm with leather straps tacked to the wood and tied tightly around the arm almost to the elbow. . . .

The colorful jig of the flames dancing around the kettles had a soothing, hypnotic effect on Scratch and he felt himself going forward into time, forcing away the emotional and physical pain of the recent past. There was a loss, no doubt about that.

But as he looked into the next few days, he thought perhaps longer than a week it might take them, on their journey back east along the Yellowstone. Just get through those days and everything would be all right. No. Just get through tomorrow. Then the day after would come. And the one after that. Yep. That was how it was done. Everything would be fine. We take the trip a step at a time.

He looked down at the leg, its dark bandage stiff now. His warming fingers touched the cloth and found the knots resistant to his first efforts to loosen them. Finally the frozen cloth gave way and he dropped the ends away from the wound. Bass pulled a knife free of its scabbard and used the blade to prick at the edges of one hole in the leather legging. Adjusting his leg so that he could move shadows away and replace them with light, Scratch peered down at the tear in his flesh. The one hole was barely an inch in length and looked like a frozen, dark band against the white flesh of his leg. The other hole. He pricked at the leather once more near the outside of his leg, finding he had to cut more leather this time. That's where the damn thing tore so much of the flesh. The wound was puckered and oozing still. He had pulled the coagulated, frozen blood away with the bandage. That's all right, he thought. Let her bleed, get opened up and bleed before I stuff it with medicines.

Rolling over on his side, Bass stretched out to pull another of his parfleches to his side. This one he had been sure to bring along on this hunt. The medicines. From the parfleche he pulled puffball and yarrow root, putting the latter in his mouth to chew. Grasping the knife by its blade, he smacked the shell of the puffball with the handle before cracking the shell in half with his stiff fingers.

Setting both halves between his legs, the trapper pulled the edges of the leather around each wound apart with his left fingers, using his right fingers to crack the coagulated blood loose from the wounds. Then he dipped his fingers repeatedly into the puffball halves, transferring the powder and dropping it into the wound before both halves were empty of their herbal dust. Painfully, he ground that dust into each of the two wounds with his fingers, clamping his eyes shut and gritting his teeth against the pain.

Bass rested for a few moments after the ordeal of ministering to his own wounds. Finally, the dizzying blackness subsided and he reached into the parfleche for the small clump of brown, waxed paper. When it was opened, he withdrew the mass of fibrous white threads, tore off a small chunk and placed it over the smaller of the two wounds. He tamped a bigger piece into the other wound. This web of the tree spider would aid in knitting flesh. He had never understood why, but the healing properties inherent in the spider's web hastened the body's own healing. He tore the yarrow root in half and placed a piece on each wound before wrapping cloth around his leg once more for the night. That leg would be sore, so sore and tender come morning. And they had miles to go.

So many miles since he had come out of the Ohio country of Kentucky. At sixteen, he spent little time in school, preferring to reach out into the forest on the hillsides freckled with bright color and light, blasting away at a squirrel now and then. Mostly dreaming of the day he would carve out his own future in the wildness around him. He had finally slipped away before morning light, leaving behind the little cabin where his brothers and sister lay sleeping, the chimney streaming a faint whisper of thready smoke from last night's fire.

The young boy had nearly starved to death at first, finally securing work loading the boats that plied the Ohio. The money he earned by the power of his sinewy muscles held him for a while before he drifted down the river to its junction with the Mississippi. And happened upon a settler's farm. And the settler's daughter who would love him before he was ready to return any woman's love. Then overpowered once more with the itch to move on. This time to St. Louis, where he found work as an apprentice blacksmith, sleeping in the livery, the frosty air each morning filled with the rich smells of animal musk and fresh dung.

And his first sight of a mountain trapper, an old veteran of the western spaces who found an eager audience in the young man for his stories of the high places. The young man lapping up the tall, windy tales of those distant horizons, the old trapper lapping up the cheap liquor that kept him talking.

Now Scratch was the old man. Gray-flecked whiskers and the salt-and-pepper hair that curled out from under the faded-blue bandanna knotted tightly at the base of his skull. Better than thirty-nine winters, the Crow would say about him. An old man in the mountains close to ten years now. And up here in the high country a man was judged to be old if he had passed that many winters by and kept his hair, or his sanity. Bass grinned slightly. He'd lost a bit of both through those long seasons. Yep. Up here a man's age was figured by how much he'd seen or done, rather than by the mere passage of time.

So old. So many miles behind him. Many more staring him down. He pushed the thought out of his mind quickly. He could not afford the luxury of self-pity right now, as he looked over at the sleeping man in the buffalo robes. And the pony, gnawing at twigs and bark at the edge of the light. Could it last the journey, carrying on its back that baggage he had not chosen to leave behind back there at the creek, and dragging the dead weight of the travois? Bass studied the pony, hoping the animal would find the sustenance and rest he would need to complete the trip. The firelight cast shadows on the animal, but the lightly spotted rump still shone brightly in the flames' illumination.

The crackling of the fire soon gave way to the bubbling of the kettles. He was brought out of his thoughts of the next few days and into the present. After removing the boiling jerky and pemmican broth from the flames, Bass dropped some roots and leaves into the smaller kettle remaining over the fire. There they would boil down into a medicinal broth. Better than coffee, he thought. Perhaps better than whiskey for what ailed them both. A quick search and he found two wooden spoons he had tucked away with his kitchen plunder. They were deep, almost small bowls in themselves. And when the medicinal herbs had boiled for a while, Titus removed the second kettle from the fire so that it, too, could cool down to a bearable temperature.

Leaning a little to his left, the older man reached out to nudge Josiah. "Gotta take me care of your wound, son." He shook the buffalo robe again and the sleeping man finally stirred. "Josiah. Gonna patch you up so's you can start your healin'."

"Don't take the robes off," the young man mumbled.

"Gotta, son. Onliest way I can get to them holes. Onliest way I can see what I'm doin'."

"Damn . . ." he muttered weakly. "Can't stand the cold . . . right now."

"I know." Titus dragged the parfleche over so that it sat between them. "Won't take me long, if'n you let me get started." He moved the buffalo robe back from Josiah's right arm and shoulder. Pulling the flap of the blanket coat back, then the flap of the leather shirt, he peered closely at the wound on Paddock's chest. With a free hand he then snapped off a piece of the yarrow root and brought it near the young trapper's lips. "Here, son. Chew on this." Then he slipped it between Paddock's lips.

"Sshiddd," Josiah exclaimed, his voice flowing around the piece of bitter root.

"Just keep chewin'—'til it gets good an' soft." Bass pulled another puffball from the parfleche and cracked the hard shell with the handle of his skinning knife in one swift whack.

While Bass took care of the bullet wound, the only sounds he heard were the plaintive whining of the wind, the faint crackling of the fire, and the stoic gulps Josiah made as he chewed the bitter-tasting root. Scratch gently ground the dust of the puffball into the chest wound, the coagulated blood and ragged flesh giving way under the pressure. Paddock flinched and jerked from time to time, but did not say a word. Bass looked up at his face occasionally to see the younger man's eyes narrowed against the pain. He continued to dip his finger into the puffball, then transfer the powder into the wound until the hard shell was empty. Titus then tore a small clump of the spider web free and laid it within the edges of ragged flesh bordering the wound.

"Lemme have it." He cupped his palm below Josiah's lips. Paddock spit the pulverized root into the hand and Bass scooped it up to place it between his teeth, tearing the root in half.

"Good . . . good to spit that out," Josiah hacked.

"Gotta chew some more on this," Scratch said, plopping the second half of the root back between Josiah's lips.

"Goddamn your ass," Josiah sputtered after he'd moved the root to the side of his cheek with his tongue.

"Cain't help the hurtin'." He pulled a piece of the root from his own lips. "Only help the healin'."

He set the soft, moist, lumpy mass over the spider web in the hole, then pressed it slightly into the wound. Josiah flinched once, then tried to pull away from the pressure. "You're half-some done, boy." He withdrew his finger. "Gonna roll you over now."

Helping the younger trapper roll onto his left shoulder, Bass then tugged and pulled at the coat and bottom of the leather shirt until he had moved the flaps away from the lead ball's exit wound. He continued pressing the powder and spider web into the hole. "Lucky, you were, didn't hit no bones goin' through you." The only response from Josiah was the moaning

against the immense pain. Finally Paddock's tongue pushed
the root to his lips and he spit it out to swear at Bass.

"Ain't you done hurtin' me . . . ?" He wheezed, forcing air
through the fluid in his chest.

"Got me somethin' take that bad taste out'n your mouth."
Scratch turned to the parfleches beside him. He picked up the
first small tin bottle and shook it.

"Ain't much left to that one," he muttered, rummaging with
his other hand to search for the second tin among his medicines. "I used a lot of that when you sewed my hand up last."

Then he found it. He took the cork from the top of the first
bottle, stared at the dull metal container a brief moment, then
drained what was left in it. Then he corked the empty tin and
tossed it back among the roots, herbs and medicine pouches.

"Part of my medicine for mendin' a man up." He smacked
his lips as he stared at the second bottle. "You be the skinned
polecat what's needin' the juicin' now, son. Trader's whiskey."
He put the cork between his teeth to pull it from the neck of
the tin bottle.

"Ain't . . . ," Josiah hacked wetly, "ain't gonna do me no
good now."

"Drink of it, Josiah. It'll be warmin' you from the innards
out. Fire here soon be warmin' your outsides what are froze
up." He helped Paddock pour some of the whiskey down his
throat. "Whiskey work to warm your innards. We just unfroze
you, you'll come back with some pluck." He kept dribbling the
diluted grain alcohol onto the young trapper's tongue until
Josiah finally shook his head weakly and fell back on the buffalo
robe. Scratch again began to press the root into the wound.

"Damn! When you gonna stop your hurtin' me?" Josiah
wheezed.

Scratch retrieved the piece of root Paddock had spit out on
the robe and set it on the edges of the wound. Every time he
pushed the root deeper into the hole, Josiah responded with a
fluid-laden cough that ended in a slow, rising moan. Thinking
of bandage, Bass finally pulled the sash free of Paddock's waist.

Paddock stared down at it while the old man pulled the sash
out from under him. It was the sash to his blanket coat. The
one he had worn since Charles Keemle had given it to him in
St. Louis so long ago.

Bass nodded. Yes. The sash would do nicely. Fitting it was,
somehow. The sash used to kill the old Crow woman. It had
been in the medicine bundle. But Josiah had broken into that

bundle, and defiled the magic. The circle taking form. Josiah had the sash back, and the medicine of the bundle had returned it to him. Now, the six-foot-long sash would bind up the wounds caused by the breaking of the medicine. The circle completed.

Over both entrance and exit wounds, Scratch placed a small piece of beaver hide before wrapping the sash around the chest and over the right shoulder. Pulling it tight, Titus tied the sash off in a square knot. Josiah, breathless from the squeezing, shuddered as the hacking cough seized him again.

"I'm done," he said, pulling gently on Paddock's right shoulder to tell him he could roll over onto his back once more. He saw the broken nose, and remembered the fight with the Crow warriors back to Arapooesh's winter camp. Over the days it had stopped bleeding, yet still there remained some of the dried blood in the brown-blond hair of the young trapper's mustache.

"When you took that fall off the ledge up there"—he gestured with a nod of his head—"you busted that nose real good, son. She's really bent over to the west now."

Paddock only nodded as he settled back against the soft robes once more. Then Bass saw it, in Josiah's left hand as the buffalo robe dropped away. "We put that to a safe place," he said firmly, slipping his fingers around the scalp.

"It . . . be in a safe place," Paddock said, struggling to breathe through the fluid in his throat. He yanked the scalp with the white hair back from Scratch's fingers.

"Gotta be givin' it to Rotten Belly . . . Arapooesh." Scratch withdrew his fingers, knowing. "Arapooesh waitin' for it." He paused for breath, fixed Bass with a hard stare. "I'm gonna be the one to give it to him."

"All right, son. You just take you care with it." He watched Josiah clutch the scalp against his chest all the more tightly. Bass pulled the robes back over the young man's arms.

"Got us somethin' warmed up for our bellies."

"It really be warm?" Josiah asked, already feeling the whiskey glow spreading out in radiant waves from his stomach.

"You can lay your set to that, Josiah." He leaned back over the large kettle and dragged it across the hard ground so that it would set between them.

"Got tired of cold food comin' out here, you know. . . ."

"Me too, son. Me, too." Bass dipped one spoon into the meaty broth and brought it out dripping with the thick juice.

"Here now. Drink you alla this you can stan'. Get your fill. Fire warm you from outside in—an' this here meat gravy gonna warm you from the inside out. C'mon now." He leaned over the buffalo bundle and pulled down the hide so that it was tucked beneath Paddock's chin. With the same empty hand Bass cupped the young trapper's neck and helped raise Josiah's head so that he could drink the broth from the spoon

"Wo-o-o-o!" he exclaimed, sucking in cold air with his lips slightly pursed to cool the heat of the broth in his mouth.

"Lil' too warm yet?" Bass dipped the spoon back into the kettle.

"Burn my mouth, why don't you?" But Josiah shut up as the old trapper forced him to swallow another spoonful of the hot gravy.

"Cain't be feelin' that bad—you cussin' at me now," Scratch chided back. "This here be what we both needin', hot as it be. Gonna do you no good cold. Drink it up, your fill, while it be warm. Won't take it long to be coolin' off real fast in this hoary air."

Bass repeated the ritual a spoonful at a time. Each mouthful blown on now before he put it up against Paddock's lips to drink. Every few sips some dribbled down the young man's chin. Then Titus wiped the chin clean with the thick hair of the buffalo robe.

"What you got settin' there?"

"In the other kettle?" Scratch queried. "That be some medeecin whiskey for you."

"Got more whiskey with you?"

"Nawww," he answered. "Just call the medicine my medicine whiskey 'cause it'll burn a bit goin' down, like Billy Sublette's finest. Gonna do you a whole helluva lot better mendin' you up on the insides than the whiskey you had ever could, leastways. . . ." He shoved another spoonful into the open mouth.

"Had 'nough of that now," Paddock protested as he gulped down the meaty broth. "Lemme try your medicine drink."

The older man set the spoon in the broth kettle and dragged the vessel back to the edge of the fire before grasping the bail of the smaller kettle to pull it to them. "You're gonna like this, son," he announced as he dipped into the herbal broth and fed Josiah the first drink.

"Arrr!" Paddock spat, spraying broth not only over the buffalo robe but on Bass as well. "What shit is that you're feedin' me?"

"Told you, it'll burn some, like the whiskey done . . ."

"Ain't never had no whiskey that bad, ever . . ."

"Or what'll do you this much good," Scratch interrupted. "C'mon, now. You gotta have the stomach for it. You gotta drink your fill of this here."

"I already had my fill!"

Bass shoved another spoonful of the vile-tasting brew into Josiah's mouth, then laid his fingers quickly over the lips to close them. He watched Josiah's eyes clench shut and his Adam's apple bob up and down as he swallowed quickly.

"You don't have to feed me like a goddamn baby!" Paddock protested lamely.

"'Til you drink what I think me to be your fill, I'll force it down you." To emphasize his point, he put another drink into the reluctant trapper's mouth.

"I'll drink it," was the answer. "Just . . . just don't fill up that spoon alla time. Not so much."

"I can set with that, son." He let some of the broth drip out of the spoon back into the kettle.

Scratch watched the level of the herbal mixture drop in the kettle until he finally spoke. "You best save some for this here nigger."

"Thought you'd never ask." Josiah eased his head back onto the robes as Bass withdrew his hand from behind his neck.

"Feel you like sleepin'?"

"Most of me does, that," Josiah answered. "Don't know 'bout my stomach, though."

"The warm feels good, do it?"

"Warm? No. Ain't warm. Burnin', more like it." He shut his eyes.

"Let you get you some sleep." Scratch dropped the spoon into the kettle before tucking the edges of the robe around Paddock's head once more. "I be to finishin' this up, then crawl in them robes with you. Most like you're warmer than I be right now, too."

He spooned mouthfuls from each of the two kettles until they were dry and then leaned back against the saddle once more. A pipeful of tobacco would taste good right now, he thought. But too much trouble to get the damned fixin's, and he was weary. He stretched his frame around the fire and dragged up several more of the larger limbs, snugged them up to the flames. The rock radiated the heat well at their backs. And they were out of most of the wind that rustled the branches of both cottonwood and willow, its dancing music growing and fading out there in the river valley. He would climb in the robes with Paddock and let sleep overtake him.

Dragging himself along by pushing with the good leg, Bass scooted over to the far side of the buffalo robes. He would let Josiah sleep next to the fire. The fire on one side and him on the other. That would help all the more to warm the young man. Scratch lifted the edge of the robes and slid within the warm cocoon beside Josiah.

"You sleep again?"

There was no answer from the other man except the soft snoring of sleep. Bass let out a sigh as he relaxed and ground his body into the softness of the buffalo bed. Looking out past the overhanging rocks at the dark sky, he studied for a few minutes the points of light in the dark overhead. Then he finally let his eyes close for sleep, a little fearful about the dreams that might invade his weary mind this night.

Two

The boy had been marked. The sign of the Hunter. Eagle's claw tearing strips of flesh from each of his arms. That was their medicine. The Crow. Arapooesh. An old chief's medicine. An old chief's words.

"You tell the young one, this night, what will be done with his flesh. You tell him one piece of his flesh will be burned each coming of the stars for the next four nights by our medicine seekers. They will say prayers for him as his flesh is sacrificed to the spirits. Tell him he will carry the scars of the flying pony for all his days as a blessing of those spirits. And you say to the young one that the ashes from his burning flesh, even the smoke—when it is finished—all is scattered on the wind so that our prayers will journey with him. You tell him this, when the stars come this night."

* * *

In the tangled landscape of dream, Bass heard the voices from that time ago—his own thoughts whispering to him as though he were not the speaker, but only a listener, the helpless watcher, seeing it all unfold like some crude map: with only those special landmarks evident to him, those special places where he alone must travel on that dark, lonely journey through is own mind's wilderness.

They were sending him and the boy after the man. The Whitehair. A foolish thing he had done, this Whitehair. Killing Rotten Belly's woman. The chief's woman. But McAfferty must have had him a good reason for the murder. Never knew him to do nothing without a good reason before. His Nez Perce woman had died in childbirth. The loss, the grief, the mourning had driven him to kill the Crow midwife.

"The Nez Perce woman, she was to die with the young one inside her. Perhaps. To pass to the Other-Side-Land without knowing her child in this life. She was to take with her Sleeps Before the Door, my first woman. To help on her journey to the Spirit Land, she took Sleeps Before the Door. Perhaps. This was all to be, what the dreamers had seen in their visions."

No. Not rightly. Asa McAfferty was mourning now, too. He knew exactly what he was doing when he had killed the old squaw.

"There was little breath left in Sleeps Before the Door when my brother's woman found her in the lodge we shared. My woman wanted me to be told of this man. That he had truly been here before. She had seen him the morning our enemy attacked our camp. This was the man from the north who shot at her to silence my woman from telling of him. This was the man from the north who killed my woman so that she would not tell of the blackness of his heart."

Yes. The Whitehair knew exactly what he was doing now, running west along the Yellowstone, then cutting south up the river drainage that would take him over the mountains and into the Land of Smoking Waters.

Paddock was the hunter, sent by the Crow to avenge the old woman's death. And the old trapper was the Spirit Helper to guide the way for the hunter. Medicine. And the bundle.

"He will not be without a medicine bundle to give him strength and courage for the time ahead, to bind him with the spirits who will carry his life in their mouths."

A medicine bundle, given to the hunter and spirit helper by the chief. Formed from the head of a coyote, its jaws sewn together with sinew, and from the jowls hung a few small locks of hair wrapped in red cloth. From the back of the head was suspended a round loop of willow, wrapped tightly in rawhide, to which was tied a fully stuffed war eagle. Sacred objects placed in the bundle by the chief. Powerful medicine from a powerful man. Powerful tokens of magic, held prisoner within the grotesque, shriveled head of the coyote, until Paddock had cut through the sinew one night and broken the medicine's spell.

Then they became alone in this circle. Rotten Belly's medicine had escaped the bundle. The coyote. Did not the old men of the tribe tell him their dreams of the coyote coming to help the Crow? To ward off the darkness from the other who had come to kill?

"The other white man was to wear the skin of the black wolf. Perhaps. He was seen by the dreamers, his head wrapped in ice, cold from the place of the Winter Man."

They had known the Whitehair was coming. The dreamers had told Bass he was to be the coyote who would also come, journeying to Absaroka to help the Crow. Was he to be the coyote? Or, was he caught in a trap like a terrified animal? One leg held tightly in the jaws of death, yelping and wailing until dark shadows overtook him? Was he the coyote?

"Arapooesh would be the one to drive the knife into the black wolf's heart. But, white man must kill white man. The one who brought the man with the hair like ice to us, the one who brought him here among us again, that one must go."

He felt close to the trap, but did not know when it would spring. Then the low blast of a rifle came echoing from up the canyon. He jerked uncontrollably with the roar, certain they were not being shot at, but feeling the jaws of the trap beginning to close about him. Asa McAfferty was letting them catch up to him now. The nagging doubts of his own strength, his own private power, his medicine. To be a warrior? He ought to quit now. To be a warrior, though, that was the incessant call to his heart. Yet, the nagging doubts would not let him escape. He was trapped in all those days gone by, days he would never hold in his grasp ever again. But being up in his mountains, that really was the crucible of it for him. The mountains belonged to the like of them—Asa and himself.

At the bottom of the cottonwood-lined draw they found the

carcass of the pony McAfferty had shot. And away from the hole in the animal's head led the tracks over the hill above them. But what bothered him was that he was not sure what the Whitehair had taken with him. The tracks led around the dead pony and something had been pulled loose from behind the saddle before McAfferty had scurried up the hillside. What had he taken with him on his climb?

"He's travelin' lean, Josiah. Real lean. Like a nigger what ain't gonna be on the trail long—come to think of it. He ain't fixin' to be by himself long out here. That, or he got himself somethin' else in mind."

There had been the matter of the plunder McAfferty had left back in the Crow camp—too much left behind. It had nagged at him only slightly until later, when Bass finally began seriously to consider just what Asa had on his mind. Too much left behind. Too little taken with him on this journey.

Now the man had deliberately slowed up, no longer trying to outrun his hunters. The nagging finally began to burn in Scratch's mind. The fire. Taking time to build one, for whatever reason—even smoking his clothes so Bass couldn't smell him.

The jaws of the trap were closing slow. The whole thing was out of control now. When a man finally chose his spot and was waiting for you to come to him—you had lost. That man, the one you were hunting, had finally gained the advantage, choosing the time and picking the place.

All too often a man had it sneak up on him. From behind. Out of the dark. Death usually came that way. After the time and the place had been settled, death was no longer an enemy. It could be your partner, and not the enemy that came stealing up behind you in the dark when you weren't ready, weren't looking. It was then that the man had taken the power unto himself.

Just who had become the hunted while he wasn't looking? Bass eased the hammer on his rifle back to full cock.

"Scratch?" the whisper echoed within his dream.

"Don't bother me!" he snapped back at Paddock, his voice a raspy bark.

"Scratch, damnit!"

"Said not to bother me." He sniffed the air, trying to catch a whiff of the man who had smoked his buckskins in sage the night before. He would head for the aspens. Those quakies would not be much cover, but there were a lot of them anyway.

From there they would move on foot, up the hill, after the Whitehair.

"Scratch! Damnit! Will you lis . . ."

The blast roared through the narrow draw, the sound bouncing around in the trees he had been hoping to reach for cover. They had been so close. He jerked around to watch the old mule pitch forward, throwing Paddock over her neck. His mule. Falling, falling into the snow in a dusty, white cloud. Above them a gray-white cloud hanging in the green boughs of the trees along the hill.

"Hannah!" he screamed, wheeling the pony around, kicking the animal in the ribs to give it flight.

The young trapper yelled for him as he came skidding up in a tight circle to put the pony between the position of the last shot and the boy. Bass reached out and yanked on Josiah's arm, pulling him up against the rear flank of the pony as they bounded toward the trees through the white powder billowing up from the ground. They came skidding to a stop and dropped to the ground. Bass slapped the pony's rump and sent it back down the draw to safety. Both men crawled up behind a boulder that had long ago lodged itself against two aspens. Below them lay the body of the mule. Hannah. The mule that had seen the old trapper through so much. Now her life oozed through the hole in her head.

"Damnit, Scratch! If you'd only listened to me! I was tryin' to tell you!"

"Tell me what, boy?"

"Goddamnit, ol' man! I saw him! I saw him movin' up there on the hill just . . ."

"You saw McAfferty?"

"Weren't him, not rightly. Just saw a . . . somethin' movin' up there—tryin' to tell you. I tried to say somethin'—an' then the nigger almost got me!"

Bass sighed as he stared at the carcass below them. "If'n he wanted you, son—you'd be down there right where Hannah's layin' now."

"He weren't aimin' for me then?"

"No. The nigger wanted Hannah." No longer could he whistle to the mule and watch her ears twitch as she trotted over to him. No more could he watch her snort when he laid a piece of cottonwood before her to chew. Asa had cut off his own chance of escape from this thing when he had sacrificed his pony back there. And now he was chipping away at Bass's chances, too.

His heart was small. Such a waste it was. McAfferty killing his pony. And now the old mule, too. But the man up the hill wasn't leaving any loose ends to dangle in the wind. He was cutting himself off from everything. And soon there would be no way out for either of them. If they weren't there already.

"This be where we part company, son."

"Wha-a-a?"

Arapooesh could have gone an' sent him out twenty braves to get the man, but this here's medicine," Bass had explained to Paddock earlier in the manhunt. "*Big medicine. Pickin' white man to go after 'nother white man what killed one of the tribe. An' you got your medicine from a chief. That be like it's come from the whole tribe.*"

"You're stayin' here, Josiah."

"Now wait just a goddamned minute here! I was the one as them Crow told to come after him . . ."

"An' I was the one he knew would."

"You're sure that's the way you want it to be then?"

"Yep," he answered. "That's the way it's to be." He studied the trees above their position and began to push off from the edge of the boulder.

Bass heard it more than feeling it at first. It was a dull clunk of a sound in his head. For a moment he imagined it might have been a ball hitting a tree. Same sound. Then he knew what it was as the sparks shot from his eyes and the black poured over him like a dark, liquid curtain. Time let go of him.

Through a crack in the curtain he heard the rifle blast. It seemed to widen that tear in the blackness. Slowly he opened his eyes and felt the scorching pain in the back of his head. He suddenly jerked himself up on one elbow. It came to him. Josiah was gone. The boy must have hit him over the head from behind, then headed up the hill. The tracks led up the hill to the pines. He eased himself over on his belly and crawled to the edge of the large boulder.

Above him there were brown patches of buckskin among the green pine boughs. "Josiah! You're a damned fool, boy!"

"This be mine now, Scratch!"

"Ain't none of your . . ."

"You just stay back now! You get back in . . ."

He saw the young trapper's body jerk violently around with the force of the large, lead ball. Spinning slowly, like a dance of death, the body spun into the thick green boughs.

"Josiah!" he yelled at the peak of his voice.

Bass tore his elkhide coat from his back and arms, then checked the two knives at the back of his belt. He was set. Grabbing the coat by the collar, he brought his left arm violently forward, flinging the coat to the right in front of the boulder where he was concealed. He was off as soon as he heard the lead clunk against rock. A moment later he heard the blast from Asa's rifle above him.

"Josiah! I'm comin' for you!"

He scrambled and clawed his way up the hill toward the stand of pines where the young trapper had been hit.

"Josiah! I'm comin'."

He finally skidded to a stop across the snow beneath the boughs. "Aw . . ." The rest of the word was caught in his throat.

The young trapper had been thrown and now lay face down in the snow. "Awww, boy." Bass yanked on the coat to roll the body over. He ripped open the flaps of the blanket coat and felt the wetness. He stared at his own fingers, wet with the faint, red film dripping down his palm. The bullet entered the right side of the chest. There was no heartbeat. And the chest did not move.

"You come . . . come so far, Josiah. Them squeaky boots of your'n an' that belt you had cinched up an' pinchin' 'round a empty belly. You come a long way, son. Long way with me." The terrible agony for his friend finally clutched at him and he began sobbing low, quietly, shaking with the release of it. "I was comin' for you. It were a damned-fool thing you done to yourself. I was comin' . . ."

"Mr. Bass!" The sharp voice cracked through the cold, still air to interrupt his mourning. "Mr. Bass!" The voice had moved a little, back along the top of the hill.

Spurred into action, Scratch reached inside the folds of Josiah's coat and pulled the fancy French pistol with its Damascus steel barrel free from the young man's belt and tucked it away in his own. The overwhelming emptiness and aloneness seared his senses. And now he felt that emptiness inside him make ready for McAfferty. He left the branches of the pine and began his climb up the hill.

He missed McAfferty with the first shot, saw the Whitehair dive down the opposite side of the hill before the smoke from the muzzle billowed out to obscure his target. Fingers tightened and clawed at his wheezing chest as he topped the hill.

Asa had moved south to this place instead of running on west to the Blackfoots. Why did the man have a thing, such a thing, with those red niggers? But then, Asa was ready to die. If not then, now. He was at peace with himself. And he was ready.

Bass stood to greet the rising sun as it crept over the top of the hill. He drank in the air, pulled it deep into his lungs. It was warmer in the sunlight. He needed that now.

"Bia tsimbic da-sasua," he said quietly to the sun. Almost like a prayer at first. Then, he said it louder, as if in praise, "It is a good day to die." He sucked in a deep breath, *"Bia tsim . . ."*

"'The heathen are sunk down in the pit that they made: in the net which they hid is their own foot taken!'"

McAfferty and his Bible-spouting. Man got him belief. Faith. If it ain't in himself, it be in something bigger than himself. *"Bia tsimbic da-sasua!"*

"Mr. Bass! There be little time left! *'Whatsoever thy hand findeth to do, do it with thy might; for there is no work, no device, no knowledge, no wisdom in the grave, whither thou goest!'"*

Maybe so. Wasn't much left behind anyways. Hannah and Josiah both gone. And now McAfferty pulling him toward the edge of that yawning chasm, that dark and gravelike abyss.

"I've come to take you, McAfferty!"

He dashed away, skidded to a stop in a small stand of pine. Looking down below him, Scratch could see that the narrow gorge grew into a box. The walls rose above him, like the yawning of those walls of the grave into which he knew he was falling.

"Was hopin' they'd be sendin' 'em some braves after me, Mr. Bass!" He paused for a few moments before continuing his hoarse address. "S'pose I knew it'd be you that would come."

"An' Josiah?"

"The boy?" came the answer from across the bowl. "Didn't mean to kill him. Truly didn't, Mr. Bass. An', before, I took me a bead on Hannah, thinkin' it was you as was ridin' her."

"Kill't her, too!"

"Had to be, Mr. Bass. Had to be. I had me somethin' took from me. The mule was . . . just to even up the score. Don't you see, Mr. Bass? Don't you see it now?"

Scratch watched in the direction from where the voice boomed at him and was only able to catch a fleeting glimpse of the buckskins against the dark background of the trees. Like a ghost flitting along—not real, of no substance. "No! I don't see it, McAfferty!"

"I wasn't worthy, Mr. Bass. I'd sinned against the Lord and had somethin' great in me heart took from me. The squaw . . . the squaw was took from me."

He thought Asa must have halted. At least he could not see or hear movement. "You took from me 'cause your God took from you, McAfferty? That it?"

"Man gets old, Mr. Bass, an' finds him a woman what loves him—a woman what he can love back. That man were ready to stay on the path of the Lord for her—an' she were took from him! With the baby! That man's baby!" He could hear the Whitehair crossing the snow. "It finally come down to just you an' me, Mr. Bass?"

"Just you and me now, McAfferty!"

"For the woman, Mr. Bass! This is for the woman!"

It was for more than that. He was here for more than that. He looked up to see the edge of the sunlight beginning to creep down the edge of the bowl. He would have to cross the bottom of the bowl, strewn with deadfall and boulders, to cut McAfferty off.

Then he saw him. Crawling up the side of the slope toward the top.

He pulled the wiping stick out and jammed it down into the crusty snow. He laid the forearm of the stock atop the end of the stick, and eased the butt into his right shoulder. The front blade crossed the target and he squeezed the trigger. Above the gray-white cloud of burnt powder he watched McAfferty slip and lose his grip on his rifle, then skid backward down the slope. He watched the Whitehair disappear into the brush near the bottom of the bowl. Bass reloaded, then heard the sounds. Asa was crawling up the slope once more. He felt old. His eyesight getting dim. Too late to pull out. The jaws of the trap over him were clamping down.

Finally he moved toward the last spot where he had seen the Whitehair. When he stepped into the disturbed snow where Asa had tumbled into the brush, he spotted the rifle. Picking it up, he knelt to his knees and pulled the hammer back. The lock was broken. His spirits lifted as he let the broken rifle slide once more into the snow. Man left his rifle behind. Broken. The odds might be improving.

The faint whistle in the air gave him no time to calculate, no time to act. He jerked as something bit into his thigh just below the hip. Staggering, tripping, falling backward, he began to roll down the slope. The burning sting in his right thigh tore at him again and again as he rolled.

"The bow-w-w!" he yelled.

He had forgotten the damned thing. He hadn't noticed it when he had looked over McAfferty's plunder left behind at the Crow camp. He hadn't put it together when he had seen that something had been removed from behind the saddle of the Whitehair's dead pony. The nigger was good with the damned thing, too. The air burst from his lungs as he thudded against a boulder, ending his slide. He felt lonely. His rifle was back up the hill, where the arrow hit him.

Bass finally had to look. Just below the bottom of the hunting shirt he saw the dark ring beginning to bubble, radiating out across the leather legging. And in the center, the ragged stub of the arrow's shaft where it had broken off during his tumble down the slope. He had to do something about it. Slashing fringes from his legging, Bass tied them together and circled his leg a few inches above the broken shaft before knotting the cord against the pain that clawed within his stomach. He took his knife handle and laid it across the first knots, then tied the handle down into the leather whangs. He turned and twisted until the blood's flow began to slow. And now he had to move.

Clawing to rise, Bass stumbled behind the big boulder just as another whistling shaft sailed past his arm. Behind the granite shelter, he collapsed. Scratch looked. And saw. The sun. Almighty sun. Its light was beginning to move across the bottom of the bowl now. It was coming for him. And all he had to do was to reach out for it.

"'*The wind goeth toward the south, and turneth about unto the north: it whirleth about continually, and the wind returneth again according to his circuits.*'"

The Whitehair's voice grew louder as he came closer and closer.

"'*The wind goeth toward the south, and turneth about unto the north . . .*'"

Couldn't see him. Only hear him. Just like a ghost. A spirit.

"'*It whirleth about continually . . .*'"

Forever. Coming closer. Forever is now. If he could make it to the edge of the light. All right. Everything would be all right. If he could make it to the trunk of the tree. On the other side. The light. He fell against the trunk, gasping against the pain in his ribs.

Bass brought his right hand up and began to feel the ribs. To count them. Then his fingers touched it. The cause of the pain. He hadn't remembered he had it with him. The boy's pistol. That fancy French dueling pistol. How many had it killed before? His fingers crept around the pistol butt and a thumb pulled the hammer back as he eased the pistol from his belt. The light began to touch his body. He would lie here. Revel in the warmth. Better with the pistol now. Better with the warmth.

"Mr. Bass."

The voice was close. He twisted his head around to look behind him. The Whitehair stood on the dead tree trunk. Staring down at him, the bowstring taut against the arrow's shaft.

"'He hath bent his bow and made it ready.'" He wasn't smiling; eyes narrowed; he glowered down at Bass. "An' the Lord's seen to it I have me one last arrow for what was needin' done." He shook the arrow a bit. "Didn't mean to kill the boy," he began. "S'pose I always knew you'd be the one comin' after me. An' when I seen the thing move in the trees, I had me no choice but what to shoot. This was somethin' between the two of us. Aye, Mr. Bass. Just you an' me. So it evened itself out, I s'pose—killin' young Josiah. Evened things up, like killin' Hannah for you." He brought the arrow down a bit. "An' now I'm headin' west, toward the big salt once more. Wind's blowin' me that way."

Bass knew it wasn't true. The Whitehair never intended on going any farther than here. But now he was to be the victor. The pain bounced around inside him with the confusion. He saw the bowstring inch backward. And the light reached McAfferty's feet as he watched the hook pull away from him slowly.

"I'll be the one what the Lord's chose to carry the wind . . ."

Bass rolled onto his right side and pulled the trigger. The blast bit at his ears and continued to roll back at him again and again as the echo resounded back and forth across the bowl. Within the deafening trance he watched the Whitehair's mouth open wider and move slowly up and down, forming no words, making no sounds. Gradually the hooked arm moved forward, slowly until the string was taut no more. The bow and its arrow sagged forward until it pointed at the ground. The arrow drifted to the snow. The hook climbed across the chest to the wound in the neck. McAfferty weaved a bit, then pitched forward, landing full weight on Bass.

Titus felt the searing at the side of his head, high up on the cheek. It ran from the corner of his eye in a stinging ribbon down into his whiskers at the left side of his face. It was dark again. The light he had waited for for so long was gone. And he fought to breathe. The weight of the monster upon him. He felt the medicine animal swallowing him. The bear!

He fought to breathe. Clawed for the light. He wanted to live! Bass wrestled and struggled against the medicine animal, whipping his head back and forth, tugging and tearing at the ground to pull himself free from the weight above him. His hand touched a wide leather belt. He pulled on it and the weight moved above him. He stopped and waited a long moment, not sure if the animal would rise to claw life from him once more.

Now Bass could lift the thing from his body, push it aside into the trampled snow. As the darkness moved from his face there came the light to flood over him again. The warm, yellow light suddenly splashing against his face. And air. Pure, sweet, glorious air. He crawled away from the body and dropped his head into the cold snow. The pain at the side of his face bit at him. He scooped up some snow and lightly touched it to the cheek. Bringing the hand back down, he noticed the white was stained with red—war paint. The color of revenge for the Crow.

He turned back now to look at the body of the thing that had fallen to smother him. McAfferty. Now he remembered. The falling bow. The mouth moving without words. There was a dark hole in the center of the chest. Around that hole spread the dark fluid against the buckskins. Now he pulled the White-hair toward him and rolled the body over. Quickly gathering the white hair into his hand before he might decide not to go through with it, Scratch twisted the long white locks into a tight strand and pricked the flesh with the point of his knife blade. He slid the weapon in a circle around the skull quickly until he returned to where he had started cutting the flesh. Bringing up the left knee to put down on the back of the neck, Bass yanked savagely at the hair until it began to rip free from the bone. Not just a topknot. The whole scalp he must take.

He struggled as he rose, then held the scalp up to the sun slowly climbing out of the east. He turned toward the light. Toward the warm, yellow light. "For you, this is done," he spoke in Crow. "For you, it is over now. No more. It is over now." He felt the yellow warmth wash over him.

"Arapooesh!" he yelled at the top of his lungs. "McAfferty!" His arms stretched in an offering to the sun. "Josiah! Josiah! Josiah!" He felt the warmth running over him in waves. Felt the warmth flooding from his eyes to flow down his cheeks.

"Bass! Bass! Bass! Bass! BASS!"

The echoes of the words came rolling back to him, swelling over the lone man in liquid waves with the warmth of the sun. Over and over he answered the hills as they called back to him. Again and again he yelled out to let them know who this man was who stood in their heart.

"BASS! BASS! BASS!"

"Bass!" Josiah coughed, the word emerging as a hacking whisper. "Bass! BASS!" He pushed against the body lying near him, out of the robes. "Bass!"

The older man jerked his head up off the cold snow, startled. He was cold and wet on the ground just beyond the edge of the travois where he had rolled when he had tossed and turned in his sleep.

"Wake up! You're . . ." Josiah sputtered a little, ". . . dreamin'."

Some of the robe still lay over him, but he had rolled away from the travois. And Titus felt clammy. The cold rushed in on him now. He shivered as he brought his hand up to feel his face, his forehead. Moisture poured off him. He was sweating in the cold.

Scratch stared down at the wet hands, and saw the thin lines of dried blood where his old flesh had been scratched by the thorns and brambles he had pulled around the base of the tree to keep the predators from the burial scaffold. Yes, he done it proper. The last thing a man could do for one who had died. Especially a warrior. A proper tree burial. The hands were testament to that now.

He looked over at Josiah and sighed with the deep exhaustion. "What the hell . . ."

"You was . . . dreamin'." He struggled to pick up the edge of the buffalo robe so that Titus could slip back beneath it. "You was yellin'—an' fightin' with me." The fatigue once more set in. "Ain't strong 'nough to be fightin' you yet."

"A dream?" he asked. "I was dreamin'?"

"Only."

Scratch began to crawl back into the robes. He shook his head. "A dream, huh?"

"Just a dream. A bad one. But just a dream anyways." Josiah rolled over to find a warm spot for his cheek against the thick, coarse fur.

"Ghosts."

"What?"

"Ghosts, son." He sighed and closed his eyes. "'Til I know why, them ghosts'll devil me. Gotta know why." He felt the beginnings of a fear of himself, of being alone with himself. "'Til I figure it out, them ghosts'll ride with us." He let the air out of his lungs and drew in a long breath. "An' I don't know why."

Three

Emile Sharpe turned one last time to look down at the thick icy fluid of the Wees-Con-Sin River flowing into the Father of Waters. And across this Wees-Con-Sin River sat the fort at Prairie du Chien.

Dog.

He smiled and turned to face the south, to push again into the forest. Dog. Some had called him a dog at times over the years. A mad dog at that. Perhaps he was not mad at all. Maybe only driven.

The man, his large bulk in momentum, moved quickly through the heavy forest, trotting along at an easy, half-loping gait. It was a comfortable pace for him, one he had grown accustomed to over all those years of moving from one place to another through the wilderness. Silent. Deadly.

Dog. Cousin to the wolf. He smiled again. Not so different from a wolf was he after all.

Last night's fire had been made back in the trees where it would not be spotted by the sentries. And he had rested a few hours there on the southern bluff where the Wisconsin flowed into the Mississippi. Three long, rain-sodden days before, he had camped within sight of Fort Snelling, a huge and imposing edifice to most men. A mere annoyance to this solitary stranger. With all its grandeur and military might, not a soul in that huge stone fortress had known this huge and imposing man had passed their way.

He liked that. There was no small pleasure in knowing he was the best. The best any money could buy. Slipping through the forest and the wilderness unheard, unseen, unknown by most. He liked it that way. And he should be the best, after all, he told himself. He had been at it all these years. Taking the victims one—sometimes two—at a time, before they even knew what shadow had loomed over them. But some, a few over the years, had come close to making their escape. He had liked that, too. Letting those few victims play out to the end of their ropes, enjoying the hope of escape. Then he had caught them once more, this time to read the panic, the bowel-loosening fear that comes when a lesser man smells the approach of his own death.

His one good eye crinkled up in the ever-present grin.

Bass gazed down at the shadow, his own long, dark shadow, watched it swing the rifle-crutch forward, then advance to merge with the weapon. He had followed the rifle, its rhythm that of pacemaker, for a week now. The first days had been no more than a string of beads, each bead another step eastward. He had not been able to think of the journey back, not even the day's own journey. But only each step beside the pony dragging the travois. That had been enough to keep him going. Each step a bead strung against the others until Bass had finally been able to reach this day, thinking of it as a certain time period, with its own boundaries and limits. Up to now he had pushed his own limits against each day's. But today they'd be home.

He had studied the bluffs rising to the south across the river. Their changing, the ebb and flow of red rock, had marked their own progress the last three suns. And now he could see the wisps of gray smoke rising ahead of him. The last rise was easier than he had expected it to be. Perhaps the wound high in his leg was beginning to knit. Perhaps it was the relief of returning that was finally healing his soul. He would not question it. Both were beginning to heal against their deep wounds.

He drew on the long rawhide rope and brought the pony to a slow halt. For a long moment Bass gazed below him to the east, and remembered his arrival at this winter camp late last fall. The old, gray-headed chief had explained why the tribe had moved its village to this new place from where the white men were to have found it.

"When the last moon rose full from the east, our enemy came to this our homeland," Arapooesh had explained. "They knew where we camped for the winter and rode down on us with a vengeance. Our people fought bravely, but there were many to sing over when the fighting was done. With struggle we have moved our winter camp to this place. With pain and heavy hearts we moved through the snow to this place where the two waters meet."

Yes, my old friend, Scratch thought now. With a struggle I too have come back to this place. Me too, my brother. With pain, yet. There was pain. But also more joy now that much of the pain could be forgotten, salved for a while. Mine is not a heavy heart, friend, the old trapper thought. I have labored through the snow to this place where the two waters meet. The meeting of two waters, rolling and tumbling together until they are one—just like two lives, two hearts—a man's and a woman's, mingling together to become one flow, one life.

Finally Bass pulled on the rope once more to move the pony in a wide arc across the snow so the animal now pointed to the west where the sun would begin to disappear within the hour. The buffalo runner hung its head in what seemed to be relief as its master hobbled back across the snow toward the travois.

"Now you can see," he said as he began pulling the robe down from the younger trapper's face, "see what I been waitin' to lay eyes on most of this day, son."

Titus bent forward and slipped his left arm beneath Josiah's neck to help in raising Paddock's head from the travois bed. He sighed as he looked down on the scene both could watch now.

Through the naked branches of the cottonwoods, he could see the dark, smoked-blackened lodges, their peaks releasing the drifting, lazy smoke up and into the breeze. South along the river that joined the Yellowstone at this place, where the women, bundled against the cold, stooping and bending, tying and hauling, gathering dry wood that would feed those fires of warmth and light. Children scampered through the wood-gathering party, chasing one another in mock battle with limbs for lances and rifles. He could almost hear their cries of joy and delight, the sounds of youthful happiness drifting up to him across the river, across time.

To his left, other sounds drew his attention. Below, horsemen were coming through the trees and down the rocky bank of the river to push their ponies into the ice-laden water. One by one, the riders forded the river and urged their animals up the bank, moving left up the rise toward the whitemen. Bass watched these young warriors approach until the eight braves had reined their snorting ponies to a halt. The air was suddenly full of sound. Silence had been the partner of the two men returned to this place for these many days. Now their ears welcomed the pawing of so many hooves, the snorting of the ponies, the grunts of approval from the young Crows. The air was full of the faint, blue mist rising from each animal and man that surrounded the trappers.

"*Maraxi'cekatu'we,*" the oldest of the young braves spoke.

"*Maraxi'cekatu,*" Bass responded, slipping his arm out from under Paddock's head.

"*Dak ake'ret, ba'wiky.*" The warrior still did not smile as he sarcastically congratulated the whitemen on their unexpected safe return.

"*Du'e.*" Scratch answered as if no offense had been given, knowing better. Watching the faces of the other young braves, he knew by their silent smiles that he had won the battle of words. "*Awa'xpewiky, a're-tatse'we u'a.*" He asked if the young warrior had come to welcome him home, as he did not have a family of his own among the Crow to welcome him.

There was a short grunt. Then, "*Kurutsi'm, kanda'kure ke'otem,*" asking if the Spirit Helper knew if the hunter wrapped in robes had the hair.

"Josiah." He looked down at Paddock. "Josiah, show 'em the hair. They wanna know if the hunter be comin' back with his hands full." Bass helped to pull back the heavy robe so that Josiah could bring out his left arm. In the hand hung the white hair attached to a full scalp. All the warriors but one yelped their praise and approval, their sudden cries startling some of the ponies which pawed and jolted against one another under their riders. The guttural sounds and high-pitched cries cut through the cold air for long moments until the large youth raised the one bare arm that was outside the robe draped over his body.

"*Du'a hu'kawe. I'axuxkakatu'we daka're watsa'tsk. Batse't ce'wiaruk.*" The warrior attempted to mask his rage with words of congratulation that the young hunter had been so successful, his Spirit Helper strong in medicine to bring about the raising of the hair.

"Batse' tsiri'katuac, bawiky." Bass repeated that their medicine was strong. *"Ciwi-ci'kyatawe. M'cgy iaxba'surake opi'rake, hu."* That the young warrior must never allow himself to think that these two men had anything but strong medicine between them.

The warrior glared back at the trappers while Scratch pulled the robe back over Josiah's arm and chest.

"No," Josiah protested as he moved his arm so that he could keep it on top of the robe. "Keep the hair out." He coughed dryly. "Let 'em see it." Bass nodded his approval, then looked back at the warrior.

The Indian pursed his lips tightly, his jaws clenched against the anger welling within him. He suddenly wheeled his pony around and shot down the slope toward the river. He had been bested and the cries from the other young men showed that they knew it.

Scratch turned also and pulled on the long rein to move the pony down the slope. The small party of warriors surrounded the travois, waving their weapons in the air, yelping their praise, singing their songs of war and boasting.

As they approached the north bank, dogs began to bark in answer to the cries and songs. Children ran through the trees, followed by adults, to form a growing crowd on the south bank. They waved and yelled, some singing their own songs, others yelling their praise, still more crying out in joy as they pulled their hair and raised their hands to the sky. The dogs raced up and down the bank between the rocks and the legs of those gathered there, scampering about, all the while barking and howling at the noisy throng. Bass stopped the pony at the edge of the icy water.

"Bi'bikme." He turned to the young warriors. *"Tsi'xe, mo'u'a bwa."*

Immediately three of the young men came forward. Two halted by the travois, one on either side, and leaned over to pull the travois poles off the rocky beach. The third warrior offered a hand to Bass so the trapper could pull himself up behind the warrior on the Indian's pony. Now the two whitemen would not get wet in the crossing. Slowly they inched forward again, Bass pulling on the buffalo runner's rein, the two young men on either side of the travois jostling against their heavy load to keep Paddock above the icy water until the party was safely on the south bank. There they lowered the poles carefully and Bass slid from the Indian's horse. He stumbled and fell against the rear flank of the animal and the warrior offered his hand again.

"*Wi'weaxki.*" Titus waved off the proffered hand. "*Bea'mi tsi'mu. Bikmo' tsaki.*" He told them he had been looking forward to this walk for many days now. He would walk into the village by himself.

The warrior who had reached out his hand to Bass now turned and waved his rifle at the throng, yelling at them to part. The crowd fell back to form a wall on either side of the party and moved forward as the horses entered the trees. Children ran alongside, laughing, and the adults trotted forward with them, yelling and singing their praise and songs of war once more. The crowd pushed and surged until the young warrior finally halted the party before the lodge where no smoke rose to the sky. Bass glanced at the empty smoke-hole, and knew of the mourning in this lodge.

Bass handed the warrior the rein to his buffalo runner and stepped forward tentatively. To the left of the lodge door stood the tripod as tall as himself. From its apex formed by the three straight limbs hung the skin of a large white wolf, the hide sewn together to form a medicine bundle. Beside it also hung a mountain lion quiver bulging with arrows. Atop both, over the rawhide shield, at the crown of the tripod, dangled a full scalp adorned with the tips of the loser's ears.

Bass stopped before the bear-skin covering at the door. With an open palm he slapped several times on the door pole to the left of the opening. "*Maraxi,*" he spoke loudly. "*Maraxi' cekatu.*"

He waited only a moment, feeling the play of the words across his tongue. Scratch liked the tongue of this tribe, their words being delicate yet sharp as the edge of a knife, without the guttural, clublike heaviness of so many other tongues. "*Awa'xpe, tatse'we.*" He had come home, proud, with his coup.

"*Kurutsi', kanda'ku ko'ot'tsi.*" He had returned with the hair. As Scratch heard sounds from within, he stepped back from the door, leaning on the rifle that for long days had been his crutch and pacemaker.

The large leather flap of antelope hide moved to the side and from the darkness within appeared the head of Arapooesh. He stuck his head out into the dimming light, squinting against the days of darkness in his lodge, days spent with no fire to offer light or warmth. He squinted and blinked, looking about him until he finally stepped out of the door to stand before Bass.

"*Tsa'xmi' u'a.*" Titus pointed the way for Rotten Belly to accompany him.

The pair moved slowly through the silent throng. The air hung heavy in the approaching twilight, the only sound now the pawing and snorting of the buffalo runner, the animal still weighted with the burden so long on its back.

The pair stopped beside the young trapper nestled in the buffalo robes. Arapooesh saw the trophy, but did not immediately reach for it. He glanced at Bass, then looked once more at the scalp. Titus watched the old man's eyes, studying the face and all the pain that was etched there. It ought to have been different, he thought. But the old man had been caught up in the jaws of this thing along with him. Now Rotten Belly could end his mourning. He would have the hair. The white hair. But Bass had no way to ease his own grief.

"Give 'im the hair, Josiah."

Paddock lifted his left arm and brought the white trophy up so that the long hair hung to its full length. There were quiet comments of surprise and awe and adulation from the throng gathered about the three men. Rotten Belly did not move forward at once, but, instead, looked around the group slowly, his eyes finally coming to rest on Bass.

"This is a day I watched the sun's path across the sides of my lodge. This is a day I knew you must come back. Or this is a day I knew you had found another trail, a trail into the Other Side. My heart was growing heavy with the light falling from the sky. My heart was getting small for me as the Fire Boy took his light into the west. My heart was growing small for you. I began to think of joining the woman on the Other Side. And my heart was on the ground, thinking I would find you on that same trail—to the Other Side. I was dreaming, and in the dream the People were singing of praise, the animals pawed the earth in excitement and the dogs barked their honor along with the People. And I saw dreams of sweats that pulled poisons from the body like dark clouds blown away by the winds from the west. I saw dreams of feasts that put the fire strength back into your bodies and healed your bellies. And I saw the white hair hanging before my lodge. The white hair dancing on the wind. Dancing on the wind before my lodge. And I heard you call out to me at the door. You are here. And the white hair will dance on the wind before my lodge."

Only then did he reach out to take the scalp from Josiah. Slowly he wrapped his fingers around the long waves of white hair, examining it in both hands. And, finally, he held it aloft. "*Pote Ani* has carried the wind!"

Arapooesh began to cry his own song of war, tears streaming down his face, his voice cracking against the lump that clutched at his throat. His song of joy, his tears of relief, were all answered by the tribe gathered tightly about the trio. The dogs set to howling once more along with the voices raised in shouts and songs. Bass felt his eyes smart, and the ribbon of healing flesh along his cheek burned with the salty tears as his eyes brimmed and overflowed. He blinked some of the moisture away and looked down at Paddock, feeling the lump rising in his own throat, a lump that grabbed at his words as he tried to speak to the young trapper. But he could not utter a word.

Paddock looked up at Scratch, his own lips quivering against the flooding emotion, tears streaming down his cheeks, past the broken misshapen nose. The moisture glistened and froze in his mustache and beard. The two friends cried together for the first time. And there was real joy in the explosion of this feeling. Their tears were for this place and this time, for what they had come through together, and for what they meant to each other.

Arapooesh had sent the trappers into his own lodge, then called forth his sister and her daughter to enter also. They were to build a fire and prepare a meal for the whitemen. The chief then watched over Josiah as several of the warriors lifted Paddock from the travois and carried him into the lodge as the fire was being built. They gently lowered the young trapper to the bed at the rear of the lodge, the bed where the chief had lain in mourning. Bass waited at the door for the old man to enter, but the chief stayed outside. The Indian told the older trapper that he would take up residence in the whitemen's lodge, turning his own over to the trappers. Few whitemen had ever had such an honor bestowed upon them. But then, few whitemen had ever had the honor of avenging a wrong done to the Crow, Bass had thought to himself.

Slowly the lodge came to life as the two Indian women prepared the meal over the warming fire. And then the young woman left suddenly, returning later with the trappers' baggage. She made another trip to the whitemen's shelter for the rest of their belongings. It was not long before the lodge became a home as possessions of the whitemen were brought in, hung alongside those belonging to the Crow chief.

Bass ate heartily, many times filling his bowl from the kettle that had steamed over the fire. And he watched the young Crow woman helping to feed Josiah in silence. He watched Josiah's eyes study the young woman. She wanted to nurse their wounds, but Bass told her that would wait until the next day. When the older man finally took his two pairs of moccasins from his feet, that was the signal for the two women to leave the lodge. When Scratch set a kettle of water near Josiah's bed, the young trapper looked up at him. "Who them two women?" Josiah asked.

"You 'member that young buck what didn't want us bein' the ones to hunt McAfferty down—the one what got his feelin's broke when Arapooesh sent Josiah Paddock?" He waited until Josiah nodded his head. Then Bass sat down on his bed near the door across the lodge before he continued. "That same fella what come up to meet us on the hill an' didn't like seein' you holdin' the hair. McAfferty's hair?"

"Yeah."

"That older gal be the buck's mama," he explained. "She be Rotten Belly's sister, that 'un. She's called Buffalo-Tail-Scares-the-Fly—an' the buck goes by the name of Strikes-in-Camp." He lay back into the robes and pulled several of the blankets over himself.

"The young gal?"

"Waits-by-the-Water. Her name. She be Strikes-in-Camp's lil' sister, Josiah. The fella what wants him a piece of your hide—she be his sister."

He watched the young trapper close his eyes. Then Bass put more wood on the fire against the frosty night air before lying back once more and closing his own eyes to sleep. And sleep came easily that night. The dream, the nightmare, the remembering, none came to trouble his sleep. They had returned to Absaroka.

Bass stirred, then pulled the blankets back over his head. It was cold in the lodge and he found it hard to doze. Finally he pushed the blankets away from his face and opened his eyes into slits. The light was gray. As he pushed the blankets down further, sounds drifted in to him from outside the lodge. A dog barked. Children's voices occasionally drifted through the air. Ponies snorted and whinnied as someone led them along outside. A woman scolded someone harshly. And there was laughter.

He smiled. It had been some time since he had heard such honest laughter. The sound was good to his ears. In the dim, charcoal light of the lodge, he looked across to Paddock and listened to the sounds of the young trapper snoring. It was good that he should sleep so well, so deep, so long. It had not been an easy journey for either of them. And now Josiah could sleep restfully, without the jostling, the bumping and jolting of the travois.

Scratch sat up and let the blankets fall from his shoulders. The air was frosty as he exhaled into it. He shuddered as he crawled from beneath the blankets and knelt by the door. Pulling the antelope hide door flap aside slightly, he peered out. The sun would break from the east shortly, yet the village was coming alive already. Bundled against the early-morning cold, the People scuffled along in the snow and called out to one another. A young boy shot by, chasing a young puppy that yipped its enjoyment of the game, while the boy giggled and shouted at the animal.

He let the door flap down and scooted over to the fire pit. There he took a short stick and stirred the coals among the ashes. He scattered some wood shavings into the small, glowing embers that were left. As they started to smoke, then burst into flame, Titus placed more small twigs on until the fire had grown enough for larger pieces of wood. He was startled as he turned to reach for a cottonwood limb. The door flap was pulled aside and the young woman entered.

With one leg inside the lodge, she crouched and waited, as startled as he. She looked down, then back at him as he motioned for her to enter. There was a hint of a smile as she dropped the flap over the door once more, then moved over to kneel by the fire. She set down a hide sack and a rawhide box, then waved him away from the fire. Bass returned to the robes without a word being spoken between them and pulled the blankets over him as he sat back against a willow backrest.

Waits-by-the-Water looked once at the young trapper, then went about her work. The older man watched her open the sack and rawhide box, pulling from them cooking gear and food with which she started preparing a morning meal for the two whitemen.

"We thank you," he began in Crow, quietly finding the words to use in speaking his thoughts. "Both of us, for helping." She smiled and nodded, glancing up at Bass only momentarily. "I know it is hard for you and your mother, caring for us, when your own brother does not wish us here."

With this she looked into his eyes for the first time. "He does not wish you well. I am sorry." Then she looked away, back to her work again.

"Why does he carry such a bad heart for us?"

She turned her head, staring at the door for a few moments before answering his question. "He is young. He fought well against our enemies those moons ago. He was proud that our People were proud of him. And he wishes to be strong and proud again. He does not yet know about you. Arapooesh tells us. But my brother does not want to listen. He does not want to believe. My father's brother tells him he cannot always have an enemy to fight. But my brother looks for enemies so that the People will give him praise once more. When you brought back the hair he said you would not come back with, you became his enemy." She turned her head slowly, looking down at her work once more.

"I am sorry for him," Bass finally replied.

"I am sorry for him . . ." she repeated, ". . . and for you." She nodded at both of the white trappers.

"Strikes-in-Camp is mean when he is angry," she continued, slicing on the cold meat before her. "He had blood to kill the day you were sent after the Whitehair. And he had blood to kill you—him—" she nodded toward Josiah, "the last sun when you had the hair. My brother believed it was his hair to lift, his hair to bring back to the People, to my uncle, Arapooesh."

"Now he wishes to kill us for bringing the hair back?"

"Kill?" She thought a moment, looking once more at the door. "I do not know if he wishes to kill. But his blood is bad now. His heart is small in his shame, a shame that you brought him when you carried the hair back. He is not simple. A man that is hard to know, for his blood is quick to turn bad . . ."

"He has swallowed a buffalo tail?" Bass interrupted.

She looked at him squarely for a moment, knowing that he knew of the belief, then answered, "Yes. Strikes-in-Camp has swallowed the buffalo tail. And it tickles the man within at times." The young woman dropped chunks of meat into the now-boiling water over the fire.

"Does he wish us harm?" Scratch began. "Does he wish *him* harm?" motioning toward the sleeping trapper.

She stopped and thought a moment. "Perhaps not your body. Perhaps. Your spirit maybe. He could kill a man and that man die a warrior, honored and proud. But, he could kill your spirit—like the day you went on the hunt—to kill your spirit would hurt a man for all time. To kill a man would make life good for him on the Other Side. But, to kill a man's spirit— then, that man would never rest, never rest on the Other Side."

"What you say is Crow, but we are not . . ."

"Crow?" She looked back at him to interrupt. "Are *you* not Sparrowhawk? Now? Were you not the Spirit Helper in the hunt? Did you not hunt down the enemy of the Crow? Does not the young one with the crooked nose bear the scars where Arapooesh marked him? Does not *your* soul bear the scars of the hunt? Are not these things Crow? Are they not?"

Waits-by-the-Water finally looked away, back to her preparation of the meal. There was some relief in those moments that followed, if only that she no longer studied his face for the answer to her question. He watched her for a few minutes, then turned to look at Josiah when the young trapper stirred. The pain of those scars was only beginning to grow. Last night, the first totally free of the haunting since the battle, there had been no nightmares. He had thought perhaps the ghost was releasing him, finally. But, now, with the young woman's words, he knew he was a fool to believe that. His own spirit hung in the balance now. His and Josiah's. They would feel their bodies mend and heal. But—what of their spirits?

Paddock stirred, then pushed the robes away from his face. He squinted into the light of the fire, glanced briefly at the smoke rising through the hole at the top of the lodge, then opened his eyes fully as he saw the young woman. He glanced at Bass quickly, then looked again at the woman.

"He is awake now," Scratch declared.

She looked up and smiled at Josiah, then spoke a greeting in Crow. The young trapper looked over to Bass for translation. "She's tellin' you . . . like, a 'good mornin','" he said quietly.

Paddock nodded to the woman, then coughed dryly as he clutched the right side of his chest. She moved toward him around the fire, but he waved her off as he finished hacking.

When he caught his breath again, Josiah leaned over and dipped a tin cup into the kettle of water Bass had set by his bed, tapping the cup against the film of ice on the surface of the water. He drank, letting the liquid soothe the dryness in his throat. Cold and dry this time of year, he thought. He leaned back again in the robes, looked over his head at the articles hanging from the poles and the dew cloth rope. Above him hung his own rifle. Near it were his belt, the two knives in rawhide scabbards suspended from the wide leather strap. He turned his head to the side and found his capote beneath him, rolled up to form a pillow for his head. He closed his eyes and sighed, sucking in a long breath of the frosty, yet warming air. The fragrance of boiling meat grew strong in his nostrils.

"Yeah. I am hungry," he said with a little enthusiasm. "Last night be the first fit meal for me since we last was eatin' here in camp."

"Maybeso you like squaw's cookin' better'n mine, eh?" Bass chided.

"Good chance of it, I'd say." He started to chuckle, then hacked against the pain tearing at his chest.

The woman looked up this time, but did not rise to try to help. "You will eat, then I will tend to your wounds." She nodded at both men, laying her hand on the painted rawhide box. "Every day, until your wounds heal, every day I will put medicine on you, to draw the poisons out." She looked over at Scratch. "It has been a long time since you lay in the robes of a woman. Both of you. Since a woman spread her legs, and offered her arms up to you. The poisons must come out. And you must release what is between your legs, deep within you."

He had known the Crow for many years. He knew how ribald, but how matter-of-fact about sex they could be. Yet, this morning it surprised him. Caught off-guard, he felt his face growing redder beneath the whiskers. The heat of embarrassment burned deep as he felt her eyes on him even as he looked away to her hands dipping meat out of the boiling water.

"Like the meat of the animals we kill to eat, some juices are poison to us. We must drain those poisons, then the meat will make our bodies strong. You must release your poison, for your body to heal quickly."

"What's she sayin'?" Paddock asked.

Scratch cleared his throat of the hot lump that threatened to strangle him before he stammered a reply. "She . . . she's talkin' 'bout tendin' to . . . our wounds . . . your wounds."

"Your face—it's red," Paddock said. "She say somethin' that make you feel funny?"

"Huh?" He hadn't really been listening to Josiah.

"She say somethin' make you feel funny—your face red an' all?"

Bass felt the burning itch from the neck up and across his cheeks. Bass swallowed slightly. "Just feel funny 'bout havin' a woman mendin' my leg, is all. That's all, son." He tapped the blanket over his right thigh close to the groin.

"Never knowed for you to be so scared, so skittish of such a lil' thing . . ."

"Woman touchin' me there," he finished as he watched the woman set a steaming bowl of meat and fry bread before Paddock.

"You might enjoy it now, Scratch."

"Don't know if I would." He instantly knew better. He watched the young trapper look the young woman over very carefully.

"Come to think on it, Scratch," he said, talking around a chunk of meat, "I think I'd enjoy it some myself."

Bass could not help it, but he felt stupid, childish even, for the feelings of adolescent jealousy over this young, young woman. He'd just have to cover up those emotions until the childish passions had cooled off.

"Just lookin' at her, I'd say any man'd want that'un snuggled up in his robes." He smiled at Josiah, almost assured that his act had been successful.

Titus watched her set a bowl before him, and leaned forward to lift it into his hands. The warmth spread across his palms, to match the warmth in his groin. He had grown hard there, rigid even. Bass squirmed to make himself more comfortable. He glanced up to find her looking at him with questions in her wide eyes.

"Your friend?" the young woman began. "You told him about the poisons he must release?"

He swallowed hard against the meat that was not fully chewed in his mouth, then coughed lightly. "Yes . . . yes, ah—you can work that—can get the, ah . . . poisons out . . . ah—work it out between yourselves." He nodded toward Josiah.

"What's that?" Paddock inquired.

"Just . . . she's gonna be mendin' you . . . your wounds, son. Be tendin' to what healin' . . . you're needin'." He stuffed another chunk of meat into his mouth with his fingers. The stirrings were there, and he had to admit them. There was desire.

He ate in silence, listening to Josiah chatter now and then from his bed, swallowing the dry bread and chunks of meat, forcing the food down past the hot lump captured high in his throat. His face no longer burned, but he felt the warmth elsewhere. It had been too long a time since he had been with a woman. He had often put such things out of his mind very easily, contenting himself with his work, its routine, its dangers, and the freedom of each day. And each year, at rendezvous, he allowed himself the luxury of feeling a woman wrapping herself around him, moving with him, and the explosion that often, all too often, left him feeling no better than before he had lifted the squaw's dress. Plunging inside her, their groins bucking, grinding until he was finished. It had been an empty exercise so many times, he could admit now. Would it—could it—ever be different for him, such an old man now? Perhaps she was right. It was poison. A man thinking of such things just poisoned his mind. Couldn't keep his head clear, keep his mind on living, on staying alive. And once a year, he had to flush those poisons from his body, from his mind—and from his soul. Then he could refresh himself, renewed for another year in the high lonesome.

Paddock finished before Bass. The young trapper lay back against his capote pillow. It was then that the young woman raised the lid of the painted rawhide box and pulled from it several small buckskin pouches. Waits-by-the-Water rose and came over to sit beside Paddock on the robes. Pulling the buffalo hide back, she spread apart the loose flaps of the shirt the young man wore. Quickly she untied the knots binding the ends of the bandage that was wrapped over the shoulder and around his chest. Carefully she pulled on one end of the sash bandage until she had pulled it free.

The small piece of beaver hide fell into his lap. She picked it up and examined it before turning to Bass. "The beaver?" The older trapper nodded to her and she looked back at the wound while he continued eating slowly, watching her examine the entrance wound.

Rising on her knees, Waits-by-the-Water looked over Paddock's shoulder to glance at the exit wound behind his shoulder. She poked briefly with her fingers around the hole on the back, then repeated the process around the hole on his chest.

With that done she peered closely at the coloring of the edges of the wound itself, both front and back. Finally she sat back and addressed Scratch.

"You did well?"

"You ask that?"

"No." She dropped her eyes a moment. "You did well. How long ago?"

He thought. "Seven." He swallowed a piece of meat he had been chewing. "Now, eight suns. Eight suns, now."

"The medicine is old, then." She dragged the small pouches into her lap, pulling the edge of her skirt up above her knees so that it would not bind her. The calves of her legs were hidden within a tube legging with no decoration, a legging that reached above her knee—but there, in a small border between the bottom of the skirt where she had pulled it and the top of the legging where it was tied, was the dark copper of her flesh, against it the short darker hairs lay sparsely against the deep brown.

After she had tossed aside the long sash, Waits-by-the-Water pulled at the thongs tying the top of one of the skin pouches. From this pouch she pulled a small wooden vial and yanked loose the stopper. Turning the wooden container upside down, she poured a small amount of the thick liquid on her fingertip, and then applied that liquid to her lips. That done, the woman replaced the stopper in the vial and the vial in its skin pouch. From the same pouch, she next pulled a small, four-inch-long sliver of buffalo bone. With the sharpened end of the bone sliver she began to probe into the entrance wound.

Josiah flinched now and then against the probing, not really experiencing pain but merely a tenderness. The young woman first pricked out the remains of the chewed yarrow root and threw it into the fire near the front of the lodge. Next, she probed and pricked until the remains of the spider web were pulled free. The web came out slowly, oozing with a thick, yellowish mucous. This mass, too, she flung into the fire where it sizzled.

Now Waits-by-the-Water peered closely at the chest wound once more, probing with a finger again directly around the hole. Then she leaned forward and placed her lips over the bullet hole and began to draw her cheeks in, sucking hard on the wound. She drew her head back and spat the mucous on the floor. She placed her lips on the wound again, drawing the fluids from the bullet hole until she was satisfied that the wound was cleansed. Josiah gazed down at the hole in his chest, now free of obstruction. The area immediately around the hole was almost whitish in color, having had most of the blood drawn from the tissues.

She looked up at the young trapper and nodded before pulling on his shoulder to roll him over. Waits-by-the-Water then repeated the process of probing, pulling and sucking on the exit wound until it, too, looked to be cleansed. Only then did she remove the thick liquid from her lips by wiping it free on the back of her hand and forearm.

She wiped the bone splinter clean on her skirt and reinserted it into the small pouch. From another pouch she pulled a small clay bowl, small enough to fit within the palm of her left hand. Into it she placed a small dusting of powder, then three different leaves. With a small, smooth, porous stone, the woman began to grind the leaves and powder together until all were well mixed. She set the stone pestle aside and leaned over the exit wound. Dipping a finger into the mixture, she brought that finger to her lips and tasted it, before getting a small, hollow bone from the same pouch. This she placed lightly between her lips, and stuck the other end of the bone into the bowl. She drew in a small amount of the pulverized mixture and then placed the free end of the bone inside the edges of the wound. She blew lightly, forcing the mixture into the wound. She repeated this process several times, until she had Josiah roll over on his back once more so she could blow the medicines into the chest wound. The only sensation Paddock felt during this part of the ministering was a slight tickle in the wound. Nothing more.

With the small clay bowl empty, she set it aside and took up another pouch. From it she took a small bladder with a thong tied around its top and dipped a thick, foul-smelling liquid on the tip of her finger. She smeared the concoction into the wounds repeatedly. Josiah tried to breathe through his mouth rather than his nose to escape its rancid odor.

After retying the bladder and packing it away, she pulled out a short, thin piece of pine bark, laid her finger over the chest wound as if to measure the diameter of the hole, then broke off a small piece of the bark. This she set within one edge of the wound, pulled the opposite side of the hole back, and pushed the bark down slightly into the flesh. Satisfied with its placement, Waits-by-the-Water repeated the same process with the wound in Josiah's back. She sat back and smiled first at Bass, then looked at the younger man, her face radiant with her accomplishment. She spoke softly to Paddock.

"What she say?"

"She said you was brave," he answered, "while she pushed an' pulled on you—where it hurt—where she knows she hurt you."

"Weren't much hurtin'." He coughed lightly before continuing. "An', 'sides, weren't 'bout to let her know she was hurtin' me."

The older man smiled and nodded his head, then turned his attention to the young woman. He asked why the small pieces of pine bark were in the wounds. She began to gather her pouches once more into her lap and scooted across the floor to sit beside Bass before answering.

"It is healing well. But now is the time to keep it open for some days."

"How long?"

"That I do not know now," she answered. "I will watch the wound for the days to come. It would be poor to have the wound heal over on the outside, and not yet be healed on the inside. If there are more poisons to grow inside, we must let them out, not let them be trapped inside. The poisons must be released, I told you before." The young woman laid her hand gently on Scratch's right thigh. "Now, it is time for you."

"What?" he asked, thoughtful of her earlier proposition. His leg grew warm where she placed her hand. He looked down at her fingers, each encased in a thin brass finger-ring. "The poisons?"

"No," she answered, her eyes measuring his before they began to twinkle in their dark depths. "Your leg, now. It is time for the medicine." She lifted the edge of the blankets and pulled up the bottom of his leather shirt. She began to untie the knot of his right legging.

"Hold it," he countered. "I . . . I'll do it."

She withdrew her hands and let him undo the knot. Gently he pulled the top of the legging down to expose the wounds near the top of his thigh. The woman shook her head and reached forward to grasp the top of the legging herself. She began to pull it down the leg when he reached out to grasp both her wrists. Waits-by-the-Water looked down at the strong hands holding her wrists, then up into his eyes.

"I must have the legging off," she explained quietly.

"Why?" he responded. "You can see the wounds now."

"But you have cut the legging. And I must repair it for you. I am to do everything I can to help you. Everything." She looked down at his right hand, then felt his grip on her wrists slowly loosen. The woman pulled the legging from his right leg, over the moccasin, then flung the legging aside on the bedding beside the door. Then Waits-by-the-Water went through all the steps in ministering to Scratch's wounds as she had done with Josiah. When finished she replaced the skin pouches back in the painted rawhide box, then withdrew a sewing kit from that same box. The young woman pulled the torn legging across her lap and was beginning to mend the holes in the leather when the door was pulled aside. Strikes-in-Camp stuck his head inside the lodge.

"Arapooesh would see the whitemen. Now." His tone was curt.

Bass answered first, by asking a question. "Where is Arapooesh? Are we to go to him?" He looked over at the woman and the younger man in the robes, seeing that Waits-by-the-Water did not lift her head from her sewing to look up at her brother. Josiah glared at the young warrior from his bed.

"No," he answered with a sneer, looking from his sister, past Josiah, and finally at Bass. "He is coming here. He is coming to his lodge to see you." He would not miss the opportunity to remind the two visitors that they were guests in another man's lodge. Strikes-in-Camp continued to stare at Bass, his gaze finally dropping once to the whiteman's bare leg, then back to glare into his eyes. Finally he withdrew his head from the door without another word and let the flap fall over the opening.

There were now sounds of many footsteps on the icy, wind-blown snow outside, and the flap pulled aside once more. The gray-haired chief came through the door. He moved to the left within the lodge and took a seat near the foot of Josiah's bed, across the fire from Bass. He looked for a moment at each of the whitemen, then saw Waits-by-the-Water preparing to leave, having pulled her belongings up into her arms.

He placed a hand out, palm down, and motioned the young woman to remain. "I will not be long here," he began. "These men need their rest, and what help you can be to them. You are to stay as long as you are needed." He turned now finally to look at the young woman. "For as long as you are needed, you are to sleep here. The healing will not only be by day, but also by night. You will bring your sleeping robes and remain in my lodge—here—so that they can call upon you for their every need, and want. You do understand?" His niece nodded. "But you must not lodge here during the time of the moon in your flow. All other times, you will bring them wood, water and food." He looked over at Bass. "And they are to call on you for all their needs."

After the young woman once more nodded, he looked at her again. "Have you dressed their wounds?"

"Yes. It is done." She spoke in reply to the chief for the first time.

"And?"

"They are not angry, their wounds," she answered. "There will be time, but they will heal. The young one, he will need to be in bed for many suns. In near a moon he might begin to walk. Longer to ride. But there is no evil in their wounds."

Bass listened intently to the Crow words and began to calculate on when would be the time for them to begin spring trapping. Surely it must now be the end of January, maybe February. Perhaps. He could not be sure. The cold came early, and stayed long, this far north. He dreamt of the Bayou Salade to the south in Colorado country. There he knew the winter winds would not blow so bitterly. There he would be able to trap much earlier in the spring. He knew if they were to have plews for trading come rendezvous, to add to those of the fall hunt, they would need to have a successful spring season. And the earlier they struck out from the Crow camp, the more profitable that hunt would be. They were talking now of Josiah needing more time to heal, but did they both have that much time? He could not know.

"It is good. The spirits have been kind," Arapooesh went on. "Your medicine has been strong." He nodded toward Bass. "The poisons of the journey, and your wounds, will drain from your body while you rest in Absaroka. So, we welcome you back. We must celebrate. There will be many feasts of good food that have been provided for the People. And ceremonies to welcome you back to our eyes. Your medicine is strong. And we are glad to have your medicine back with us now."

Rotten Belly then glanced over to the young man. "My sister, Buffalo-Tail-Scares-the-Fly, will come here after three suns have gone from the sky, when Father Sun has traveled halfway across the sky again. She and Waits-by-the-Water will prepare a feast of meat for us. Many of those with strong medicine like yours will eat with us, here, that night after the sun finally falls from the great circle of the sky. I have already given out the red-painted sticks to those who are to come. On that night my lodge will be a place of good food, laughter, and strong medicine once again." He looked past Josiah to stare at the rip in the lodgecover behind the young trapper.

It was there that the lodge had been cut so that the body of his murdered wife could be removed, along with the body of the young Nez Perce woman who had died in childbirth—the wife of the Whitehair. Now the ripped edges were sewn shut. Perhaps the lodge would heal itself also. "My friends," he said, looking at Josiah, then Bass, "we will eat that night to come, and celebrate. It will be good to laugh once more."

Arapooesh rose from the robes and stood, silent for a moment, then bid the trappers farewell. "My friends, I will see you again after the sun has journeyed across the sky." He crouched low and stepped out through the door. The flap slid back over the opening. Waits-by-the-Water resumed her sewing on the torn legging, quietly humming some light-hearted song to herself.

"Your brother will be here this night?" Bass asked.

"No," she answered. "It is not to be this way," she said, continuing her sewing without looking up at the whiteman. "He did not receive a red stick from Arapooesh." Then she glanced up at Titus and held his gaze evenly. "Arapooesh knows my brother does not wish you well, the both of you. Arapooesh knows this. My brother would bring bad feelings into this lodge. This Arapooesh does not want. And my brother is mad about this meat feast. It was a hard thing for Arapooesh to decide upon. He did not want the bad heart of my brother here. But, Arapooesh knows, too, that my brother has a bad heart about not being counted by Arapooesh for those to come this night. It is a hard thing. I have said enough on this already."

Scratch sighed and turned his head to glance over at the young trapper. "You sleepin'?"

"Tryin'." With that he rolled his head to the side toward the lodgecover.

"You do that," Scratch said. "Soon's the gal gets my leggin' sewed up, I be goin' out to see to the ponies. You get you your rest, son. Some big doin's comin' up—so you get you your rest."

Four

For most of the afternoon, the two women prepared the wild vegetables and roots they would use in the cooking of the meat and bones to be brought by the guests. Plenty of chopped and split wood lay piled to the right of the door just inside the lodge. Kettles of water and vegetables waited close to the fire that was fed steadily to take the chill from the late afternoon air.

The door flap moved aside and Waits-by-the-Water entered with another load of firewood cradled in her left arm. The wood clattered onto the top of the pile and she turned to kneel by her mother at the fire.

Josiah silently watched the two women in their preparations, mostly entranced with the young woman who had ministered to his wounds a few mornings before. Her long hair hung free of braids and ornaments. The eyes were oriental in their lines and above them rested delicate eyebrows. Her nose straight and small, unlike her mother's, which was larger and somewhat hooked near the top. The cheeks were well pronounced, giving a softness to the lines that circled the full lips. Those cheeks had been rubbed with a faint tint of vermilion to add bright color against the deep bronze of her face.

His mind briefly withdrew to the previous summer's rendezvous in the valley west of the Tetons where he first met the Whitehair. So many similarities between this Crow woman, and the young Nez Perce wife of Asa McAfferty.

"*A fine lady an' a beauty for the boot, she be,*" McAfferty had described his woman to Josiah and Bass. "*Princess of them people, as her pappy be one of the war chiefs.*"

Paddock felt the warmth of an inward smile flush over him. Surely this one, this young Crow woman, also had to be royalty.

Waits-by-the-Water untied her sash and let her arms slip free of the blanket coat she had about her. As her shoulders thrust backward to let the coat slip from her arms, the well-formed breasts pressed against the restraining buckskin dress. The soft contours of the mounds reminded him of the tavern maid who had given him the comfort of her body back in St. Louis. But the Indian's breasts seemed firmer. Perhaps she is younger than the blonde gal back there, he thought. He looked over at Buffalo-Tail-Scares-the-Fly. You could tell a lot about a woman by studying her mother. So he decided the large, firm breasts would soon become softer, sagging under the weight of age and many nursing children. What she would look like in the years to come—he knew. But, for now, she was very desirable, and he could dream about lying beneath the robes with her to warm away the ache of loneliness, a loneliness for another.

The women were—at least he knew the young one was—to stay with them, here in this lodge, until he healed. There would come a time when he could pull the leggings off her limbs and lift the dress over her head. Pull her down into the robes with him to run his hands over her breasts, let his fingers touch the smooth, flat, brown skin of her belly. Would she have known as many men as the Flathead gal? His thoughts flashed back. He never even knew her name. They had spent one night beneath the boughs with the Tetons looking down upon them. More than just a heated rendezvous coupling. More than fiery animal lust. She had been a comfort to him then. And now his thoughts drifting back to her were disturbing to him. There was something greatly unfinished with the Flathead girl, something that made his heart itch and ache in not knowing: how he had gone again and again to search those last days of rendezvous—never finding her. Never even seeing her after that one night of comfort and healing.

Looking now at a patch of skin he studied high on the Crow woman's thigh, Josiah felt unsettled. It had been a long time since his last woman. But that was not the reason for his confusion, for the contradictions in his heart. There remained something undone, something left unsaid within him for the plain-faced Flathead girl. The Crow woman was prettier in a way. She might even be beautiful with him beneath the robes, naked, willing and wanting the pleasure he knew he could give her. The Crow woman's body would give him immense pleasure, too, he was certain. But she—he could not remember her name! Had he ever known her name? She had given him more pleasure in the valley of Pierre's Hole than he had known before. Would he, could he, compare?

The door flapped open again and he watched Arapooesh enter the lodge. He stood slightly stooped near the door and nodded to Josiah as the women scooted back from the fire. Moving to the left around the fire and kettles, the chief came to the rear of the lodge to sit on the robes beside Josiah. He nodded once more to the young trapper reclining against a backrest, then turned to address the women.

"Where is *Pote Ani?*"

"He went out some time ago," the younger woman answered. "Saying he was going down to the river, in the trees, to see his ponies again." She paused a moment while gazing into the flames. "He goes to the animals often. I think he grows tired of staying in the lodge. His leg, it needs exercise and grows tired here."

"You must go now to find him," Arapooesh responded. "Bring him here now. He must be here before the others arrive."

Waits-by-the-Water rose and slipped the coat over her shoulders, tying the sash with beaded thongs at its ends about her waist. She nodded to Arapooesh and ducked low to step from the lodge, pulling the flap back over the door opening.

After pausing a moment outside the door, the woman turned to her right and moved through the lodges toward the river. In the fading light she reached the compound where many of the tribe's horses were kept. Making close to a full circle around the corral, Waits-by-the-Water did not see the trapper among the animals within the enclosure. Not far away, at the edge of the trees near the lodges, was the whitemen's shelter.

For a brief moment she stood outside the shelter before kneeling down to pull the entrance flap aside. It was dark inside. Slowly her eyes adjusted to the darkness. The trapper was not there. Letting the flap fall once more, the Indian woman rose back to her feet, considering where next to search. Now her thoughts led her to move through the cottonwoods toward the river. From the crowded tree-line she saw him.

Bass sat among the larger boulders on the bank near the ice-laden water. His hands were tucked up into his armpits for warmth against the chilly air that was rapidly becoming cold as the sun disappeared to the west. She paused a moment, standing very still, waiting in the trees, watching the man's back. It was then she became conscious of her own breathing. It was heavier. Not from the short walk in the snow. Could not be, she told herself. She tried to slow it, quiet it in the still, frosty air.

Through the thin blue clouds she exhaled before her face, Waits-by-the-Water watched as Bass first turned his head upriver, looking, as if searching, expectant of something. Then he turned his head slowly to the right and gazed downriver. She watched the whiteman look up and then down the river again. Until finally, Bass let his chin drop against his chest and shook it from side to side, his shoulders shuddering slightly. She moved across the rocks quietly.

Almost upon the man, with her left hand extended to touch him on the shoulder, the young woman came to an abrupt stop as Bass turned to her. He did not seem startled at first, and she let her arm drop to her side. He turned back to look once again at the river.

"You surprise me," he said quietly. "You were almost to touch me before I heard you. My thoughts were not with me."

The young woman moved around so that she could sit on the boulder near his knee, dusting the snow from the rock before positioning herself upon it. "And your heart?"

"Ah," he began, "my heart. It, too, may be far away."

"It cannot be here with me?" She looked steadily into his eyes, desiring them to say the words her heart had felt for some time now, those words her lips had been unable to utter.

He glanced at her face, seeing those eyes, then turned away just as quickly. "I . . . I don't know. Should my heart be here with you?"

She knew that she had said far more to this whiteman, the bearded savage who had come to her land from his home far away. The big mystery stirred within her, wanting to give rise to those things so long unsaid. To tell him they were both here together. To tell him that her heart could be as big as he needed and with him always. Instead, she could only answer with another question. "Where does your heart rest?"

He shook his head for an answer, his lips moving but no words coming forth at first. Bass looked at the young woman briefly, then gestured again.

There was a long silence between them, her heart searching out the courage to speak of the mystery, to fight the fear all her training, her people's ways—yes, her fear of him—that kept her from putting to words the song inside her now. Instead, she finally choked out a question. "Do you have a woman?"

"Each winter cold-time I come to the Crow, I have a woman who will visit to warm me in my robes. Last year's woman, she . . . now she is with a man. No—I do not have a woman."

There was the stab of pain in saying it. "And you know that."
He was not certain that she knew.

She immediately felt the apprehension that too much had
already been said. Yet there was still deep within her the fear
that unless she spoke out, this white man would pass from her,
too.

"Your eyes . . ." she finally began.

"What?" He turned to her once more.

"It is in your eyes, *Pote Ani*."

"What is that—in my eyes?"

She did not speak for a long time, continuing to stare at the
swirling mists dancing upon the river. Her heart danced, too—
wanting him to know, yet fearful of the vulnerability. At last,
she turned and softly laid a hand upon his wounded leg.

"Your heart is not big for a woman. In your eyes, they say
you do not have a woman to make your heart happy. And—I
am here to make you happy." She watched his eyes travel
slowly to her hand, then climb once more to meet the anxious
look on her face. "Can I not make our friend happy?"

"Our?"

"My people."

"I . . . I'm sure you can," he stammered.

"Then, it is good." She rose, pulling on one of his hands,
then circled her arms around his waist. For an instant she stared
up into his eyes before laying her head against his shoulder.

After a brief moment he raised his arms to encircle her
shoulders, pulling her closer into him so that their bodies were
fully touching, as he remembered the words he had so long ago
spoken to his young partner, speaking of the place a woman
had in the life of a man who belonged to the high lonesome.

"*A man gets lonesome for the sweet music of a woman's voice
after long seasons of hearin' nothin' but other coons 'round an
evenin' fire.*"

It was warm here with her in the dimming light and the cold
air rolling off the river with the mists. He felt her shudder
slightly, then wrapped his arms around her all the more
tightly. Slowly his chin dropped so that his cheek lay against
her hair. It was somewhat stiff from the chilled grease rubbed
into its strands, but still it smelled good to him. He rubbed his
nose lightly against the thick, black tresses and she tilted her
head to look up to him.

With a hand, Waits-by-the-Water pulled his head down so
that his whiskered cheek would lie against hers. His bristles

tickled, and she shivered slightly again. He put a hand up to grasp his beard. "My whiskers?"

"Yes," she responded. "They tickle my cheek."

"The Crow men you have held do not have beards," Bass said. "You are not used to holding a man with hair on his face."

"I have not held a man before . . . like this," she said softly and laid her head back against his shoulder.

He gazed out at the river before he spoke again. "You have . . . never been . . . with a man?"

It was a moment before the young woman pulled her head away from his shoulder to look up at his face. "Would that make you sad?"

"No. Not sad. You, you are . . . so . . . why are you not with a man now? Or before?"

"This will be my seventeenth summer," the woman responded. "My father would only then begin to think of a man taking me into his lodge."

"But, Crow women start . . . they hold men . . . have men in the robes before . . ." He sought for the words with desperation.

She pulled more tightly against him, despairing at his words, his wanting to know. After many moments she at last felt ready to answer him. "It is true what you say—many Crow girls play woman with the young men. My mother has taught me, winters ago with the first time of the moon flow, what a man would be like in the robes." That training too, she now thought, had also instructed her to wait on a man, to be there for his every bidding. And now she felt ready to respond to the lessons of the older woman. "Do you wish to be with me?"

"I am with you now . . ."

"To have our . . . to touch." She hesitated. "That is what I mean. Closer than we are now." She waited a moment again. "Do you not wish to be with me?"

"Yes," he began, then looked down at her again. "Yes, I do wish to be with you. But . . . where?"

"It is not for now." She pulled away from him slightly, feeling some pain in the parting, now taking his forearms in her hands. "Arapooesh sends me to find you. To bring you back. You must be in the lodge before the others come for the *iru'k-oce war-axu'a*, the Cooked Meat Singing. There is—will be—much time for us to be together now that we know we wish to be together." Then she started to pull on his coat sleeve. "But now I must take you to Arapooesh."

Bass began to walk slowly beside her, using his rifle as a crutch. They had taken a few steps when she stopped and slipped behind him to his right side. There she took his right wrist in her hand, slid the rifle away to his other side and lifted his right arm so that she could step under it and place the arm around her shoulder. He looked down at her strangely as she shouldered his weight. With her there to support his right side, he could now carry the rifle over his left shoulder.

He moved along with her. Swept up by her. Things had boiled down on him in the last few minutes as the sky darkened. He had not noticed the advancing dusk. She had drawn his thoughts and heart away. He did not feel in control of those thoughts, of his heart now. And there was something unsettling about it. This woman had so quickly invaded his thoughts over the past few days—was it more? There were rumblings of feelings that had not been with him for many years. He had pushed them back, so far back into his soul, that emotions could boil, erupt, overwhelm him if he did not struggle to gain some control. And there was confusion about this young woman.

"Most Crow women have been taken to wife by their eleventh, maybe twelfth summer." He looked down on the young woman walking at his side. "Why is it that you have not had a man before? And you are now sixteen summers?"

"You do not believe me." She looked up sideways into his face, scared—yet determined not to let shame expose itself.

"No . . . do not say that." He read something in her eyes and his face burned a little. "I only wonder why you have not chosen to be taken to wife."

"I wait," she answered simply.

"But now," he began falteringly. "But now, you wish to . . . ah," he again sought for the Crow words. "You said you wished to . . . ah, with me . . ."

"To be close with you?" Waits-by-the-Water looked up at him briefly once more. "Yes. And you ask so many questions. Let this one be for now." She looked forward again as they walked between the first gathering of lodges. "Besides, my brother has scared so many away from me before. Many before would take me to wife—he scares them. Like a crazy dog, sometimes." She shook her head gently.

He could feel it warming as it had not for so long. When last? Was it as long ago as Missouri? Longer? The settler's daughter. He had worked on the farm for a while, before moving on. Was it that long ago that he had felt the stirrings, the rumblings from within about a woman? Had it really been that many years? Ten winters? Was it more? His mind searched, but there was too much there right now to find the answer.

"Your brother," he finally remarked, "he will not like you with me. He does not like it—you . . . you coming to the lodge to help us. He will not be easy about you being with me." He searched for the word for *caring*. But there was not one to find. "It will be hard, because of him."

"I know, *Pote Ani*," she answered softly in the twilight mist, then said no more.

They circled from the back of the lodge. In front of the door were gathered several men, huddled against the cold and damp mist, who turned to give unspoken recognition when the trapper and the Indian woman drew close. One figure wrapped in a buffalo robe stepped forward through the handful of men.

"We have been waiting to enter until *Pote Ani* has come. Until he is in the lodge." The voice belonged to Strikes-in-Camp.

She stopped near the door and turned to look up at the white trapper. "My brother did not receive a stick." Crow etiquette did not allow her to address her brother, especially with such a rebuke. Instead, she had delivered her left-hand comment by addressing Bass. "I do not know why it is that he says *we*." She was aware of the seriousness of her words. The other warriors about them would also comprehend the gravity of her rebuke. Ultimately, she knew, her brother would recognize her meaning.

The young Indian burned at her words. Before the others, before the white man, his sister had reminded him of Rotten Belly's decision not to invite him to the Cooked Meat Singing. He glowered at the trapper, then turned the intensity of his gaze to the young woman before him. He burned within at the insult once more, feeling the presence of the others who were watching.

"I am to guard the door," he snapped.

"Then it is well for my brother." She spoke diplomatically to Bass, as if her answer would ward off the venom in her brother's gaze. She let go of Bass so she could pull aside the door flap. "I wonder if my mother is within."

"My mother has left," said her brother. "Only the whiteman, the young one, and Arapooesh remain within."

Scratch bent over to enter the lodge. Waits-by-the-Water studied her brother. She had spoken of their mother indirectly to him. And Strikes-in-Camp had answered of his mother. She had made him very angry to have spoken of his mother. They glared at each other for a moment, then she turned to leave as Arapooesh instructed the man at the door to allow the guests to enter the lodge. She said no more, but disappeared into the mist among the lodges nearby.

Arapooesh gestured with his right arm, inviting Bass to sit beside him on the robes at the rear of the lodge, near Josiah. Then the Indian commanded Strikes-in-Camp to allow the men gathered outside to enter. One by one they presented their red-painted sticks to the young warrior and stooped to enter the lodge, some going to the left while others slipped to the right until there were twelve men seated around the fire with the Crow chief.

"My heart is happy that each of you has come to sing this night," Arapooesh welcomed his guests. "We will sing in praise of these men who have honored us in their hunt of the White-hair." Then he motioned toward the kettles on the rocks at the edge of the fire. "Let each of you place your meat and the mashed bones in the kettles to warm. Soon, we will eat to nourish our bodies. But now, we sing to nourish our spirits."

One at a time, the older warriors and younger men moved forward to place the meat and bone meal they had brought into the kettles, along with the vegetables prepared by Buffalo-Tail-Scares-the-Fly and her daughter. The kettles steamed gently in the warming air of the lodge. When all had presented their portion for the feast, Arapooesh turned around to pull forward a small rolled hide that had been lying behind him. The small reddish-brown robe of a buffalo calf unfurled before the chief.

"*Baco'ritsi'tse*," he now commanded.

Beginning with the man closest to the left side of the door, each passed a small stone to *Pote Ani*. The white trapper handed the first to Rotten Belly. The chief then removed a piece of wild carrot root he had placed within the outer coals of the fire and held the stone aloft while letting the incense-smoke of the root drift and circle up to envelop the stone. As each stone was purified in the smoke it was placed before Ara-pooesh on the buffalo calf robe. The process was repeated for those at the right side of the lodge until finally all the stones sat in a circle on the reddish robe before the chief. He put out the

ember burning on the end of the carrot root and set it aside on
the rocks near the fire.

"We sing!" He nodded once to each side of the lodge. From
within his shirt, Arapooesh removed a small buffalo-bladder
rattle tied to a willow stick, its bark partially removed to create
a design along the handle. Once more Arapooesh took up the
carrot root, this time placing the unburned end in the coals to
catch fire. When it was burning well, he removed it and blew
out the flame so that only a smoking ember remained. Holding
the rattle aloft in his right hand as he had with the stones, the
chief proceeded to smoke the rattle in the incense of the carrot
root. This done to his satisfaction, the rattle was placed within
the circle of stones before him and the root extinguished.

Next he pulled a long rawhide box from behind him and laid
it across his folded legs. Bass remained attentive to the man at
his left although his wounded leg ached. The trapper shifted
position so that he could stretch out the leg to full length.
There was tenderness in the wounds kept open and seeping by
the small pieces of pine bark. He watched Arapooesh pull first
from the rawhide box a full marten, its paws and mouth decorated with colorful quills, twisted strips of leather hanging
from the same paws and mouth. Pulling the head up revealed
that the inside of the skin had been lined with red trade cloth.
From this pouch, Arapooesh pulled the stem of a pipe some
fifteen inches long, laying it on the robe outside the circle of
stones. He replaced the marten skin within the box.

Now he brought forth a muskrat skin that had likewise been
sewn into a pouch so that it lay back over itself, fur-side out. It,
too, was decorated with the quillwork and twisted strips of
brain-tanned hide. From this pouch he withdrew the pipe-
bowl. The deep brownish-red of the stone contrasted with the
dull sheen of the pewter inlaid on the bowl. This too was set
before him near the stem. Finally he pulled out a buffalo bull's
scrotum that was tied at the top and a small stick wrapped with
quillwork before placing the rawhide box behind him.

Picking up the root again, Arapooesh snapped it in half. Both
of the fresh ends were now placed in the coals before he untied
the thong wrapped around the buffalo scrotum bag. From it he
pulled a tobacco mixture and set fingersful of the mixture on a
flat stone before him. With one piece of the carrot root pulled
from the fire, the stem was smoked in the incense and then the
root's ember was extinguished. Both pieces were then thrown

into the flames of the low-burning fire as the guests muttered their approval.

Arapooesh placed the bowl on the stem before pointing the mouthpiece first to the earth, then to the sky above, and finally to the four directions. This done, he laid the pipe across his thighs and leaned forward to pick up the rattle that rested at the center of the circle of small stones.

He passed the rattle to his right. From there it moved man to man until it came to the Indian sitting immediately to the left of the door. That man rose so that he could face the whitemen on either side of the chief. Slowly he began to shake the rattle and weave his body in time to the rhythm he created. He sang a song of his own exploits in war and combat, a song of the many ponies he had stolen through the years. His song ended in praise of the whitemen:

I sing only as a warrior can,
A warrior who has struck many times.
My footprints cross the mountains,
My footprints cross the plains.
Many horses have I given away,
Many scalps have I taken.
I sing only as a warrior can,
To sing my praises to you.
Your footprints cross the mountains,
Your footprints cross the plains.
And you have brought us the scalp—
The Whitehair is no more of the living.
Your Spirit has struck him down.
I sing only as a warrior can,
To sing my praises to you.
It is a great thing you have done—
And you have brought us the scalp.

While the warrior sang and shook the rattle, Arapooesh filled the pipe with pinches of tobacco, gently tamping the mixture into the bowl until it was full. When the singing warrior completed his song of praise he stepped around the fire to stand before Bass. The whiteman rose with some difficulty to face the older warrior. Now the Indian pulled a small object from within his shirt and handed it to Scratch. Again, grunts of approval sounded around the fire. The warrior returned to his seat by the door.

Arapooesh nodded to the man at Bass's right as the white-man sat down. The Indian leaned forward so that he could pull a small coal from the embers with two small willow sticks. He picked the ember up between the sticks and stretched over to place the ember on top of the tobacco mixture in the pipe. Arapooesh drew on the stem until the smoke came easily through the mouthpiece. The warrior withdrew the ember and placed it in the fire. The sticks were laid before him near the rocks around the low flames.

The pipe was passed to Bass, then to the man at his left. From hand to hand it passed without being smoked until it reached the man who had completed his song of praise, who now passed the rattle to the man at his left. This warrior rose and faced the whitemen. His song of counting coups began while the first man sat to smoke the pipe in his own manner of prayer and celebration.

The second warrior moved forward to Bass when his song was finished. The whiteman once again struggled to rise upon his wounded leg. Then the Indian presented him with a small gift held in his outstretched palm. Scratch took it and sat down as the Indian returned to his place. He passed the rattle and took the pipe to smoke while a third warrior began his song. In like manner the warriors on the left side of the lodge sang their praises and smoked the pipe until it was finally passed to Ara-pooesh. The chief took the extinguished pipe and knocked all the remaining ash into his left palm, tossing the residue into the fire. He reloaded the pipe and lit it once again with an ember.

The Indian to the right of the door finished his song and moved to stand before Paddock. In Crow, a language the young whiteman could not understand, the warrior began, "I know you can not stand as *Pote Ani* stands to receive his gifts. Your wounds in this deed have been great. But our happiness for what you have done in this is greater than your wounds. The medicine of that happiness will heal those wounds all the more quickly and you will ride the mountains once more."

He pulled from his pouch at his waist a small present and handed it to the younger trapper who lay against a low back-rest. The process of singing and smoking repeated itself around the right side of the lodge, until the rattle came at last to Ara-pooesh, who laid it again within the circle of small stones. Likewise the pipe was passed to the Crow chief. With his palms facing upward, the old man held the pipe on outstretched arms and rose shakily on cramped, aged legs. He stood over the circle of dark stones and sang, his rhythm not from the rattle, but provided by the warriors who slapped hands against their legs in time with his song. He sang his story:

My heart was small and on the cold ground,
Something great had been taken from me.
In taking my wife from this lodge,
The Whitehair had robbed me of my spirit.
Pote Ani was the Spirit Helper to guide,
And the Young Man carried the medicine scars.
The medicine of Old Man Coyote carried my flesh.

Arapooesh held the pipe in his right hand as he raised his left aloft to show all those gathered in the lodge the stump that remained after he had cut off his left index finger. The wound still looked raw and dark from the crude amputation and the cauterizing on a hot stone, but new, pink flesh was showing. There were more grunts of approval from the warriors.

As my flesh heals, so does my spirit.
As your spirits are strong, so will your bodies be.
Strong spirits heal the body wounded in battle.
My strength has returned to me.
We have the hair of the Wolf from the North.
We have songs to sing in celebration now in his death.
We have the hair to dance over in happy feasting.
We have the hair!

With the last line of the chorus, Arapooesh reached into his shirt with his left hand and pulled forth the long, white-haired scalp Josiah had returned to him. Many of the warriors clamped hands over their mouths in astonishment—not for never having seen the scalp itself, but because it had been transformed. Within the heavy silence the old man slowly turned the full scalp from side to side, showing all that had been done with the trophy. Both Josiah's and Scratch's eyes widened at the sight.

From the crown of the white-haired scalp hung black hair braided within the long white strands, the longer strands of the bluish-black hair contrasting vividly with the snow-colored filaments. His left fist cupped under the scalp, Arapooesh now turned so that Bass could see what hung from the front of the trophy. Scratch quietly gasped at the sight of the crudely fashioned hook now tied to the long white strands of hair that McAfferty, when alive, had constantly pushed across his forehead, away from his eyes. The dark metal of the iron fork had been beaten into a crude hook, resembling the one McAfferty had worn in place of his right hand. On each side of the scalp, over what had been the temples, hung hair drawn up into bunches, wrapped with red trade cloth and with an eagle's claw suspended from the wrappings.

Arapooesh had sliced large circles around the flesh near the temple areas, one circle on each side of the trophy. The bunches of white hair wrapped with red cloth and bound with the eagle's claws were still connected to the whole scalp by a thin piece of flesh the chief had left intact. Now he brought his knife up and cut the strip on the left side of the scalp. He held the smaller scalp lock within the fingers of his right hand so all could see the bunch of hair.

"This brings my heart much singing," he continued, speaking now rather than chanting. "My heart is big once more. We have the hair. There is much singing within as I give back to you some hair, as you have given back to me my spirit!"

He leaned over to hand the bunch of hair to Paddock, who held up his outstretched palm to receive the gift. Arapooesh moved his knife quickly again and slashed at the strip of skin holding the second bunch of hair to the rest of the scalp. This freed, he now bent to his right to lay it across the two outstretched palms of the older trapper. Bass brought the small piece of scalp back against his chest, then nodded once to the Indian. There were shouts and whoops of joy from the Indians in the lodge.

"*Pote Ani* had one thing left yet to do to return my spirit to strength for me," Arapooesh began as the warriors quieted themselves. "The weapon which killed my woman. The weapon I placed in the medicine bundle for your hunt of the Whitehair. That weapon did not stay with the bundle. Is the bundle at rest with the Whitehair? Is it not?"

Bass only nodded. The cramp in his wounded leg hurt him in the long sitting. But there was also some pain in the lump choking him, an object caught in his throat that would have prevented speaking anyway.

"The weapon returned to Absaroka. The weapon is mine. The young whiteman will return it to me . . ." He stopped as

Bass started to lean forward so that he could address Paddock on the other side of the chief. "But, it is not to be returned now, at this time, *Pote Ani*. No." He watched Bass lean back once more. "It will be returned to me by the young whiteman after he becomes my son."

Again several hands went up to dark mouths in astonishment. Bass was startled at the sudden news. A great honor this was to be for the young trapper. Scratch himself had been adopted years before, by a warrior who had recently been killed in the tribe's battle with the Blackfeet. He well understood the gravity of this honor. To be adopted by the head man! Indeed, they were offering Josiah Paddock much from the entire tribe in the adoption ceremony. But, also—Bass was being honored again in the same stroke. He started to lean forward to award Josiah the news when once more Arapooesh brought his hand down to halt the whiteman's words.

"You will not tell him. It will be for another to tell of it to him. His name has not yet been chosen. So, he cannot be told until that time. There would be time to tell him of the coming ceremony when he takes his first sweat with the old men. To heal his wounds—and to prepare his spirit for the ceremony. My son!"

He brought his hand down to point at Josiah. The warriors yelped and cried out in joy. The suddenness of the Indian pointing to him, accompanied by the shouts from the others in the lodge, filled the young whiteman with surprise and bewilderment. He had hung on to most of the words, their meaning a mystery to him, while the chief had been speaking. And now he knew he had been singled out in some way. But for what, he knew not. He looked about him at the warriors who cried out, the warriors staring at him. He looked up to Arapooesh, who stood over him, a gentle, soft smile beginning at the edges of the old man's wrinkled lips, that smile softening the hard, chiseled lines brought on by age.

Finally he looked over to his good friend. Bass was smiling broadly, his yellowed, somewhat crooked teeth stark against the deepened tan of his face and the darker hair of his beard. It was not the smile he had inwardly feared—a smile that told him he had been the butt of a joke he did not understand. Instead, this smile radiating from the face of his best friend told him all was in place, all was well with the celebration, that the joy in this lodge was in some way in celebration of him. No more did he know. But, he was at ease now and settled against the willow backrest with a long sigh.

Arapooesh pointed to a man who rose at the left side of the lodge. Bending over to scoop up the rattle once more with his free hand, the chief gave the object to the warrior who had stood at the chief's command. The warrior took the rattle in one hand while the other pulled from a sheath at his waist a large, heavy knife.

Holding the knife aloft toward the smoke-flaps and shaking the rattle in time with the rhythm of his own medicine song, this warrior with the bear medicine now sang of the strength in the bear's spirit. That all should wish for such strength. That all would receive the prayer this night for their meal to give such strength to their bodies. This was a prayer-song that the strength of the bear would go with each of them into battle henceforth. His song finished, the warrior knelt over the kettles of meat and vegetables. With an elk-horn ladle he scooped up chunks of meat and various vegetables, placing them on flat pieces of wood that had been hollowed slightly. The crude plates were passed to his right until the first plate reached the warrior seated immediately to the left of the door. The process continued until all the warriors had meat before them. Then Bass and Paddock were given their share. Finally, Arapooesh was given a healthy portion of the meat and vegetables dripping with the bone-mash gravy. He nodded to the man with the bear medicine who had served up the meal.

"One Above," the warrior began, stabbing a piece of meat from the kettle for himself and holding it aloft over the fire with an outstretched arm, "grant that we may prove ourselves worthy of this feast." The only sound besides his words was the sizzle of the gravy dripping off the meat as it fell into the flames. "One Above, our Grandfather, grant that our bodies might prove worthy of the life you have given us. We thank you for this celebration. For bringing us together—in this time and at this place—to feast together as Crow have done for winters too many to count." He paused a moment, then spoke louder. "Grant us each this prayer, our Grandfather: That we live until next it is robe season again!"

There were yelps of joy and expectation as he sat down suddenly. All the Indians dove into their food voraciously. They scooped up chunks of meat and vegetables with their fingers, stuffing them into their mouths with ravenous delight, gravy dripping down bare chins while they licked fingers and slurped their enjoyment of the feast. Josiah was awed by the suddenness of the command to eat and stared for a few moments at the warriors about him stuffing food greedily into their mouths.

"Best be eatin', boy!" Bass hollered around the piece of meat in his mouth. "You ain't gettin' a feast like this'un all the time!" He pushed a chunk of wild carrot between his lips and licked his fingers clean.

Paddock nodded and smiled, grasping a piece of meat between the fingers of his left hand and stuffing it into his mouth. It was some of the best damned meat he had tasted in a long time, perhaps his whole life. He sucked his fingers clean of the gravy that dripped from them onto the robe. The juices, too, were delicious. Every man finished his supper and then cleaned his own wooden platter by licking it free of gravy and particles of food. The wood platters clunked against one another as they were stacked by the rocks that ringed the fire.

"We are finished?" asked Arapooesh.

"Not yet, my friend," stated the warrior with the bear medicine as he rose. The other warriors also got to their feet. "Come with us, Arapooesh. Your friends wish you to have something." He moved to the door and stooped to exit, followed by the rest of the warriors.

Arapooesh motioned for Bass to precede him, pointing toward the door. Scratch rose and went to the door, then paused, feeling that the Indian was not behind him. He watched the chieftain kneel beside Josiah at his backrest and reach out to lay a hand on the young man's shoulder. The Indian looked into the young trapper's eyes, not saying a word, then pulled his hand away and rose to join Bass. The cold air hit Scratch abruptly as did the dim light and difficulty of vision in the damp mist shrouding the lodges about them.

The group of men huddled near the door of the lodge for a few moments waiting until the dark forms began to take shape before them in the mist. The muffled sounds and blurred outlines soon took the definite shape of Strikes-in-Camp leading a strong, young pony toward them.

"This animal from my herd," the man with the bear medicine began as he put his hand on the pony's neck, "it now belongs to our friend, Arapooesh." He took the rawhide lead from Strikes-in-Camp and gave it to the chief.

The Crow chieftain moved down one side of the animal, then down the other, appraising the merits of the pony presented to him. He finally returned to stand within the semicircle of his friends. "I am very proud of this gift from you, my good friends," he commented at last. "The young animal is strong and will be fleet across the plains. My heart is very big now for this thing you have done for me."

"You have given much to all of us." The warrior with the bear medicine gestured with a sweep of his arm around the group of men. "For *Pote Ani* you give up your lodge and host him here. Too, you honor him with the Cooked Meat Singing that comes once a winter-time, should there be a man to honor. You honor each of us by asking us to come give praise to *Pote Ani* with you this night. And you honor the son of your sister by having him guard the door during our time of singing praise for *Pote Ani*. No, Arapooesh," he continued, "it is your friends who are to honor you. It is your friends whose hearts are big and filled with honor to see your spirit returned after so long a mourning. We welcome you home!"

Each man came up in turn to touch Rotten Belly's hand once before turning to leave, each to his own lodge in the quiet camp. Finally, only three remained: Arapooesh, Bass, and Strikes-in-Camp. There was a heavy silence between the three men, until the chief finally slashed through it with his words.

"Son of my sister," he said to the young warrior, "how is your heart this night?"

"What is it you ask, brother of my mother?"

"Do you not wish to celebrate? Have you not wished to honor *Pote Ani* and the young whiteman this night?"

"The young one you will adopt in a time to come?" he asked, and without waiting for an answer he continued, "Yes, the whole camp honors them for what they have done. As for me, my heart still burns with the shame you gave me the day you sent the whitemen to hunt down the Whitehair, instead of Strikes-in-Camp." He tapped his own chest with a finger. "No, I answer your question. I do not wish to honor these men. They are white. Their hearts are white. They will never be Crow. Their hearts will never be Crow. I will never honor them as you have." He spoke the words with an edge to them.

After a few moments of studying the young warrior's eyes in silence, Arapooesh finally spoke again. "Your heart is heavy, son of my sister . . ."

"Yes," he interrupted, "and it will lead the way." He abruptly turned and left, trotting into the damp mists that swirled through the camp.

"His heart is full of a need to take revenge on us for his shame," Bass commented. "I will need to be watchful of that one."

"Yes, *Pote Ani*," the Crow responded with sad resignation. "You will need to be watchful of him."

Five

The fog swirled, then lay still, only to move again after a moment's rest—as if it, too, were as restless as his spirit. Bass watched the moving, settling, shifting mist as it slowly blanketed the river. He finally sat on a boulder, on the spot where she had first touched him. It had not been that she had reached out with her hand. No. Not so much that kind of touch, he thought now. She had tapped within him something else, reaching inside him, beneath the skin now prickling with the numbing cold. That momentary physical touch had begun to loosen some old wound of its cancerous ooze.

Now he could look back, somewhat in pain, to a settler's daughter abandoned so, so many years before. Was the water in his eyes from the pain, maybe from the joy of long-ago-remembered feelings? No, he decided—the water in his eyes was from age. But he knew better. The mist brimming his eyes was from the cold that pushed itself within the folds of the elkhide coat. Just as surely the dark-skinned one had pushed herself into his being while he had been so careful, so very careful not to let such a thing happen to him.

He drew his mittened hand away from the warmth of an armpit and swiped at the stinging mist that began to pool and then run from the corner of his eye. Silly notion, me thinking myself in love with that gal, he chided himself and stood against the cold, rolling fog. Just that little stirring of his muscles, that little movement of his body had brought up some warmth. He began to walk down the rocky bench that touched the ice-laden river.

It was the movement that made him warmer, not the thought of her with him beneath the robes. Wouldn't need no fire in that lodge, he mused. She kindled enough of a blaze in him to warm them both and the lodge to boot. The hoarfrost on his mustache and the chin whiskers crinkled as he pursed his lips to spit, pushing out the remains of the tobacco quid on which he had been absently chewing. He turned back in the direction of camp, then stopped. Bass listened to the soft sounds of the winter night, muted as they were in the frost-bound, foggy air. The muffled shuffling of horses' hooves as the animals pawed the frozen ground—eating, perhaps, as a defense against the sleepless cold that made an animal ache until the new day's sun could warm its hide once more.

A dog barked once, then again, and next came a yelp of surprise or pain, as if it had been hit by someone whose sleep had been disturbed by the animal's nocturnal concert. The old man started up the slope, watching the ground before him in the faint, pastel-gray light so that his feet might not trip, his toes not be bruised against the rocks.

So careful was he that he cried out in surprise when a big toe snagged a large tree root laid bare by the last spring-time flooding. Bass knelt to massage the angry foot and as he did so there was a rush of motion to his side. She was there and touched him even as he was raising his head in surprise. She reached down to take his hand in hers as he stood back up. Startled—hell, yes, he was. To have her here with him now after those long, lingering and warming moments of thinking of her beside this river.

"Come."

She said no more as she let his hand go and gripped his left arm to lead him on up the bank. His steps were mincing, not from the wariness of his footing, but from favoring the nagging wound in that right leg. She shuffled beside him, every now and then looking up at him, only a glimpse of her face visible from within the shadowing hood of the blanket capote.

They came to the outer ring of lodges and he began to veer left, bumping her as she attempted to steer him to the right. Bass stopped and looked down into the full, upturned face that met his questioning gaze. Her closeness stirred him. "That way, woman. That way back to Arapooesh's lodge." He shrugged his head in the direction he thought he should go.

Instead, she gently shook her head and the hood slipped back slightly from her face. There was a soft smile, the smile he

had seen on the bank of this river once before. Then she nodded to the right and pushed him off in that direction. He followed obediently, yet not without some misgivings.

"Where is it you are leading this man?"

"Come."

It were as if all the explanation needed was encompassed in
that one word. "Come," he repeated softly to himself. *She says
to come and this old nigger just follows like some trained
mule.*

Suddenly she stopped at the doorway of a strange lodge,
leaning forward to pull back the deer-hide door flap without
letting go of his arm.

"You," she instructed. He looked quizzically at the doorway,
wondering whose lodge this was, and why they had come for a
visit at this late hour. "You. Me." The young woman nudged
him through the opening.

Inside, the fire was burning low and the lodge was comfortably radiant from its warmth. Smaller than Rotten Belly's, this
lodge tended to hold its heat much better. He stood just inside
the doorway as she came in behind him to stand at his side
while their eyes adjusted to the new light. It was then that he
noticed they were not late-arriving guests at all.

"Where are the others of this lodge?"

She pushed him to the left around the fire toward the bed of
robes piled near the rear of the lodge. "You will not tell me?"
he asked of her as she pulled him gently to the robes and sat
beside him. "Where are the others?"

"There are no others tonight, *Pote Ani.*"

"Who lives here?"

"Some relations of mine." She reached over to work on the
knot in the sash he had tied about the bulky hide coat. "They
will stay with my mother this night in our lodge. It is bigger
and they will like that. This is smaller. And I like that."

"And Josiah?" he inquired as she pulled the coat from his
arms. "Your mother?"

"Yes." She took the coat, set it on another bed of robes. "My
mother will be there for the young one if he needs her this
night." Standing, she dropped her own capote, then knelt to
begin work at the knots on his heavy moccasins. "It is you who
need me this night." She pulled the first buffalo covering free
from his foot. "And I need you."

As she bent over his other foot, he stared at the dark part in
her hair, now noticing she had dressed it with vermilion. For

special, he thought. Special doings. Almost imperceptibly, the twinkle returned to the corners of his eyes, as the deeply engraved crows' feet spread their claws slightly in his peaceful smile.

The young woman peered up at his face as she tossed the second moccasin away. For a moment he gazed into the soft beauty before him. The deep eyes shadowed by the firelight had within them a fire all their own, a fire that warmed him in parts long left cold.

He turned his gaze away from her face finally as she gently lowered him down into the rich, coarse softness of the buffalo robes. Her head came down to nestle into the curve of his shoulder and her left hand coursed down his body until it rested along his right thigh where the healing wound lay. His heart ached with the strong pounding that he knew she would surely be able to hear. Titus cleared his throat in his discomfort at the nearness of her warmth, the immediacy of her flesh.

"It still hurts you much?" she asked, rubbing the wounded flesh gently with outstretched fingers.

Bass cleared his throat again. His "no" was a guttural squeak. She smiled.

"Waits-by-the-Water?"

She raised her head to look over at him.

He felt the trickling run-off of frost turned to water in his mustache. "You brought me here . . ."

"To be alone with you, *Pote Ani*. As I have wanted to be since first you came to our camp When the Ponies Grow Lean." She continued to stare into him as if all that had to be said had already been explained. Then seeing the question in the eyes surrounded by wrinkles of age and weather, she reached up to touch the flesh healing beside his left eye. "The mountains have marked you, my man . . ."

"My . . ."

He started to speak but she quickly brought the fingertips down from the healing scar to touch his lips in an unspoken command for silence. "They have marked you, as surely as you are a part of them, never to be removed from them. Marked you as surely as you have marked me, from the first day you and the young one came to our camp, back moons ago." Now her fingertips returned to the scar near his eye. "You are slow to see what you have done to my heart, whiteman. I grow very impatient in waiting for you through these long days of your healing."

Waits-by-the-Water took her hand away from his face and laid her head once more on his chest. "I told my mother of my heart for you. She talked to our relations. And we have this lodge this night." She could feel his breath catch with the words she had spoken, then waited until he at last let the breath out of his chest before she continued. "It is this night I wish to become *Pote Ani's* woman."

This last statement was made without hurry, slowly and softly, like the tumbling of the fog outside the lodge. He waited for more as she rose to a kneeling position, between him and the fire, her body an outline and shadow in relief against the back-lighting. Quickly she untied both her moccasins and leggings and cast them aside. More slowly she inched the bottom of her dress above her knees, then pulled it up over her head. She shivered as she moved back against him and pulled at the robes near their feet, bringing the heavy weight and warmth over her naked body. He lay still for long moments until the involuntary shudders left his body. He then scooted aside to tear his own clothing from his body.

Their flesh now warming one another beneath the coarse hide, he asked, "Waits-by-the-Water wants me?"

She did not answer save for the movement of her head against his chest, the hair moving across his bare flesh with a tickling, a teasing anticipation. "To be *Pote Ani's* woman?" Again he asked a question answered wordlessly. "*Pote Ani* could live with this woman," he whispered into her ear as he rolled onto his side so that he could face her.

"To become your woman this night, it is what I want." She reached out to slide her hands gently over his chest.

Scratch inched closer to her and reached up to cup a hand around the smooth, soft mound. He felt her shudder as his palm crossed the quickly erect nipple. "My hands too cold?"

"No. Because my man is warm inside for life," she answered. "He causes me to be warm inside for him. My body waits for you." She took his penis in her hand and stroked it lightly a few times. Then she slowly turned away from him and rose to her hands and knees. "My body waits for you, *Pote Ani*. I am warm inside. Come mount me now."

Lord knows he was ready. Hot with the fever of this triumph now come this cold night. Without thinking, he rose and moved behind the young woman. Then he stopped, his flesh against the back of her thigh. Into his mind came screaming scenes of ponies in the rut, wild animals filling themselves with the lust man shared with all species.

Bass collapsed to the bed of fur, pulling her against him, the woman's back against his chest. He lay there breathing, for it seemed hard to do that—and not really thinking in any coherent pattern—yet trying to sort this out.

"You do not want to warm yourself inside me, to warm me inside with yourself?"

"No," he answered immediately. Then after a moment more, "No, that—that is more than I could ever want for, with you, Waits-by-the-Water." He caught his breath once more and continued. "You . . . you have had men before?"

It was a while before she answered softly. "*Pote Ani* has been with other women?" She moved more closely into him. "I have had two men."

He was confused. Thinking she had been with no man before. Yet she had never said that. Only that her brother had scared them away, those who would take her to wife. Perhaps . . . yes. That's what she meant. No man had taken her to wife because of the fear of her brother—but, two men had taken her. As the animals do. He understood now. And it did not matter.

"They have mounted you like this?" He spoke softly into her ear.

The young woman reached behind her to take his penis into her hand and held it there. "The way of the horses, they told me. It was . . ." She turned a bit toward him. "—it was not gentle their taking of me. But like the way of the horses I have seen in our herds." She turned the side of her face against his whiskers before she continued.

"But, I wish to be your woman, *Pote Ani*. It is not gentle, this that I have known in men. But, I am yours to take as the mare receives the stud in heat." Her hand left his penis and came to the other side of his face. "You have had other women. I have been with other men. And you can teach me."

He chewed on the words he would use, now that he understood all that she was telling him. Two others had taken from her roughly, leaving her little, perhaps, save for their relief, and some residue of bitterness within her. His heart swelled and reached out for her. His hand circled beneath her arm and cupped a breast once more. The shudder shot through her again.

"You have been touched there, before? By a man?"

"You are the first. To touch me where it grows warm beneath your touch."

"Has ever a man laid on top of you?" he asked softly as he rolled her onto her back.

"No," came the soft answer as she placed her hands on his shoulders. "Always like the ponies."

He reached up to pull one of her hands from his shoulder, guiding it down to his rigid flesh. "Help me into you," he whispered as his leg with the tender wound spread hers apart. "I am warm and ready for you," he stammered as she began to place him where he could enter. "We will be like people, you and I. Not like animals. All things for you, my woman, will be gentle. No more will there be pain."

With the last few words he inched into her waiting warmth. Bass paused, to savor the moment, the sensation. Then he looked down into her eyes. "Has a man kissed you before?"

"Once, it was. A trapper with many others came to camp near our village. When I was younger." Her hands returned to his back and pulled him closer to her face. "He caught me in the bushes by a stream, pulling water. Suddenly I was surrounded by his arms and his face was all over mine. The hair on that face—and his hot breath in my mouth before I could close my teeth on his lips." She giggled a little beneath him now. "He cried out in pain and I ran. The kiss, this thing, it was not good to feel."

Bass bent his head over hers and let his lips brush against the fullness of hers. He felt them part slowly, almost automatically. Whispering against her lips he spoke. "You have yet to be kissed, my woman."

Pressing his mouth fully against hers, he felt the young woman's lips open more widely. Her legs came up and circled his, pulling him all the deeper into her inner warmth. The trapper began to move in and out of the woman as he took his lips from hers, arching his back in the muscle spasm of need and desire.

"I want to move with you." Her words spun out short and hoarse.

He did not answer except for a couple of short nods. With him she began to move beneath the buffalo robes, pulling at his back, pulling at him to be all the closer, all the deeper within her warmth. Their dance grew in intensity, as they climbed ever higher until at last she finally spoke again.

"This is good. This is as it should have been for me—with you . . ."

The last was broken off as his warmth washed into her in a great flooding of sensation. Like tears too long kept pent-up within a bottle. Bass came rushing forth in a wave of relief he had never before felt. She answered his deepest thrusts with the rising of her own hips, moving with him so that he stayed deep with her, buried until he was spent.

But as his movements began to slow, she felt her own body almost separate from herself and move against him with an urging of its own. She mounted the urging and climbed upon the fear step by step, a fear of the separateness of her body from her heart and being. A climb until at the top, her body came back to her, to join once more with her heart and her very being in a great washing of warmth.

Waits-by-the-Water shuddered beneath him and gently rubbed his back with her nails. Bass slowed his rhythm to a gentle roll, then relaxed on top of her body, feeling their breathing beginning to return to normal.

"It is what I never had hoped it could be," she finally whispered.

Titus raised his head and gently kissed her lips before laying his head along her shoulder to suck in the aroma of the young woman's body. Yes, he thought, it was all that he had ever hoped it could be. Here, with her, beneath the frozen moon and the crying of the wild animals in their nearby wilderness— he had cried out in answer to their loneliness and found the answer to his own.

"You seen my coat?"

The older trapper ripped through their plunder and gear in a frantic search. Finally he dropped to his knees, threw his head back and closed his eyes, recalling when he had first been given the coat.

He had taken the three hides to the old Crow woman to be dressed and tanned. The bear and wolf had been done beautifully. Then she had come out of her lodge with the heavy bundle of the two elk hides. Gradually she had taken one arm away from the bulky hides and had begun to tug at the worn blue capote Bass had hanging from his shoulders.

Rather than merely dressing the two elk hides, Comes Running had tailored them into a crude coat. The woman's old hands had gone to the four thong ties after he had drawn the coat over his shoulders. The tiny, wrinkled fingers had fought to tie the thongs into knots. Then she had pushed up the wide collar, also of dressed elk and made from the cape over the bull's shoulders. On this piece of hide she had left the hair, sewing the collar into the shoulders of the coat so that the fur lay on the outside. In this way, she had said, the whiteman could turn his collar up and have the warm fur against his cheeks. Yes, it was a great coat—one that would cut out the winter winds and the wet of snows and rain.

When he opened his eyes at last, he sighed, then turned once more to Paddock, who lay covered at the rear of the lodge. "I said, you seen my coat, son?"

"What coat you talkin' about?"

"You know damned well what coat I'm talkin' 'bout!" he snapped back immediately. Then he thought better of it. "My elk-hide coat . . ." he said more quietly, ". . . you know it, son. The one I had me made here. Only got me two. One wool—my blanket coat. Other'n be the elk-hide coat. Where it be, Josiah?"

"I ain't had it."

"Just sayin' maybe you seen it—where I left it . . ."

"Said I ain't seen it!" he barked at Bass, then rolled his head back toward the lodgecover once more. "Didn't take it! And I ain't seen it!"

It was some time before Bass answered the angry reply. "Just thought me you might'n seen where I left it, is all. Didn't mean to rile you none. Didn't mean me to say you took it neither." He closed his eyes and sighed once more. "Just wanted to find my coat, is all."

Getting old, he thought. Now I'm forgetting where I put things. Damned fine, stinking shit mess you're getting to be, ain't you, Bass. Old man, that you are! Cain't even remember where you put a goddamned coat anymore. Old man—your brain's getting old and turning to shit!

He shook his head as the vision came into focus. A large, brown pile of fresh, still-steaming bear dung along the trail last fall. He had stopped to stare at it, tingling with the danger and challenge in the closeness of the animal, prickling with the fear of possible confrontation with the beast. Yet, he had stayed—and stared—transfixed by the pile, the steam gently lifting out of the mass to dispel itself into the shocking, cold air.

Turned to shit! And he chuckled to himself. At last! He could laugh at the vision of his brains turned to shit. Damn if he'd let that happen, he told himself. And finally smiled within the beard.

Getting older, yep. But not getting old. No. He was a man of the mountains—no, a child of the mountains. And he would go on. He was not done yet. Bass decided he was going to find that damned coat, wherever he had left it. Prove to himself that he could remember. Prove to himself that he was not yet old.

Scratch rose from the bed and turned. After putting several pieces of firewood on the low flames, he stroked the coals into the center of the firepit. He wrenched his old capote over his shoulders and arms before stepping from the lodge into the brightness of the winter morning.

He stalked through the lodges toward the edge of the trees where stood his whiteman's shelter. There he would begin his search for the missing coat. A young dog took up the walk, at first staying at the man's heels, sniffing at the footprints left in the new dusting of snow. Most of the previous snow pack had burned off in the last week or so, but the village was greeted this morning with a new trace of white on the ground.

At last he turned into the trees near the place where he had built the corral for their horses with the spotted rumps. Bass stopped momentarily to look over the animals, their heads bent low in the shadowy cold where the sun had yet to penetrate. He still dreamed that one day he would come down here to this place and there she would be. That old mule of his. She would be milling about with the other animals, showing the ponies who the real booshway was in that outfit. Hannah. He wished it so. Wished so hard, it just had to be. But he finally turned his head, then moved on. Such a thing was not to be. He carried the old gal's forelock proudly, like a scalplock taken in combat. Only this one was taken as a last gesture of love between two friends—the old mule and him.

As he came to the clearing there was the fragrant smell of a fire burning. Smoke filtered through the trees to diffuse the early light streaming over the ridge. The chief sat between the tent and the fire with several of his counselors. Here were the wise ones with Rotten Belly. Buffalo Calf, Moon That Dances on the Hill, Comes from Across, and Plays with His Tongue. The old ones. Advisors. And, dreamers.

Vividly he remembered the words of Rotten Belly just two short moons before as the chief had told Bass the old men had known the whiteman would be their guest this winter.

"Then it will be as our dreamers have been told. A white-man, a friend to Absaroka, was to come for the medicine dance. To fight alongside our people against the enemy who comes out of the north where the Cold Maker lives. Our old men have told us of the whiteman coming. Of the whiteman coming to help in our struggle."

Bass continued to watch the ancient warriors from his place in the trees. The council had not become aware of his presence. Again the trapper's mind moved back to the words of the old chief.

"The old men speak of one who comes with a hand wrapped in the fur of our brother the beaver."

Self-consciously, Scratch looked down at the right hand missing the finger, remembering the beaver fur he had used to wrap the hideous wound caused when the sow grizzly had ripped the tomahawk from his grasp.

"This is the one called on by the spirits to come to us. The dreamers know another is to come, one with the hair of white all about him. The hair of the Winter Man. The dreamers know this man has been here before. The dreamers know this man has been here, in this place, before. But, we know him not."

Bass knew who that whitehair was to be now. But, it still did not fit. Why had McAfferty led the Blackfeet down on the Crow winter camp?

"The second whiteman—he is not clear to us. We see him coming from the place where the north wind sends his breath down on us. It is cold."

It was cold, he had to admit. The air was blue with bright sparkling frost this morning. It was cold and he decided to move on to Rotten Belly's fire. Scratch stepped out of the trees.

One of the old men saw Bass and turned to the chief. Arapooesh raised his head in the trapper's direction, motioning him to come and sit with the men. Scratch kicked at the dusting of snow near the edge of the fire, clearing a place to squat before he plopped to the ground.

"Pote Ani," Rotten Belly addressed him. With the chief's acknowledgment, the other old men grunted their greeting to the whiteman. "I have not yet lit the pipe this day. So many guests this new day—and I am not a good host. But, there are many things of importance to speak of between us. My counselors, my friends here"—he gestured broadly with one arm—"they are here to talk with me of death once more. And it tires my heart."

The Crow chief looked again at the whiteman, then finally smiled. "It seems that my friends here are all old: many more winters than yourself, *Pote Ani*. All they wish to speak of is death. My friends, are they ready to die? This I ask them, for all they speak of is death. Not this one, their chief. I am still a young man, *Pote Ani*!"

He laughed, causing Bass and the others to chuckle along with him. "I am still a young bull, and not yet ready for the wolves to pull me down, to eat my flesh. Yet all about me are gathered these old men who spin tales of death. This thing—death—is yet a stranger to me in many ways. There is time still, before I will meet this thing, before I know death well."

His smile slowly faded and he turned his eyes away from the trapper to gaze into the fire once more. "Yet, my friend, *Pote Ani*, this death comes close from time to time. This, to remind me that I, too, am heading for the Spirit World one day." He shook his head, as if in search of just the right words he should use. "My friend, several suns ago a group of Lumpwood hunters left to go hunting. This morning before light, two of them returned with word that the rest of the party would be back before the light had fallen from the sky four times. The two brought word that the rest to follow would be bringing back three bodies to us."

Bass lifted his head and stared at Rotten Belly, his eyes flicking as he looked at a few of the other old men. "No," the chief answered the question he saw in the whiteman's eyes, "they are not our warriors. There was no ambush. Our medicine was not tested. The Lumpwood hunters had headed toward where the sun rises from its bed each morning, along the path of this river."

Scratch mentally plotted the course of the Yellowstone to himself, watching it flow to the east and north on its trip to the Missouri. "If the three are not your warriors—Crow warriors—I do not understand." He shook his head. "They would not bring back the bodies of their enemies."

"The three are not our enemies, as best we know, my friend."

"Then, who? Why this mystery? Why can't . . ." He let his voice drop off, then finally shook his head in utter exasperation.

"*Pote Ani*, my friend," the chief began. His voice softened, seeming to draw a person closer to him. "If the word of the two

warriors who came in before light is true, the three bodies
found by the hunting party were not Indian."

Bass jerked almost imperceptibly. "You do not know for
sure?"

The old chief shook his head. "No, our friend. We do not
know for sure that they are white, as yourself. We are told they
were found near the north bank of the big river we camp beside." He gestured with a wide sweep of his robed arm. "Some
suns' ride from this place, a ride toward the sun's coming-
up place, near this fort you call Cass where The Crane lives."
He pointed toward the yellow rim of the sun beyond the ridge
to the east. "The three were dressed as we—as you, my friend.
But there was hair, much hair, on two of the faces. Much
as yours has the hair of *Cirape*, our friend the coyote, on
it."

Rotten Belly looked around at his counselors before continuing. "The first, a man whose face was covered with hair—
his body carried many old scars of battle. The second one, this
man, he had a chest like the large kettle. But he was shorter,
shorter than you, *Pote Ani*. A whiteman, it seems, is he—he
wears hair only over his mouth." He drew an index finger
across his upper lip. "The last, he has the dark skin like the
stocks of our guns. Darker, my friend, than Medicine Calf's—
he who lives with Long Hair's band now—as he once lived with
us."

Bass was certain he knew this Medicine Calf, remembered
him from some place, from some time. Perhaps many winters
ago it was that he met this mulatto ex-trapper, at one time
called Antelope Jim Beckwourth. Ah, Scratch's mind flashed, a
strange coon that'un was: having been captured by the Kicked-
in-Their-Bellies band of Crows and brought before the Sparrowhawk mothers, women mourning the loss of their sons; Big
Bowl's woman had said there would be found a mole on one
eyelid of her long-ago captured son, a boy carried off by the
Cheyenne; then the discovery of Beckwourth's mole on one
eyelid and the subsequent tumultuous celebration in welcoming back to the fold this long-lost son. Bass had to smile at this
Medicine Calf's damned luck.

Arapooesh saw the hint of a smile on Scratch's face, mistook
it for recognition. "Perhaps you would know this one: the dark-
skinned one?"

"I know of only one such black-skinned man in the mountains," Scratch began, suddenly realizing there was another.

He closed his eyes as if in deep thought. "Ah, there is another I have known—many robe seasons ago—this one also lived with the Crow." He opened his eyes to stare at Rotten Belly. "This one, was he one who long ago lived not with the Many Lodges, but with the Kicked-in-Their-Bellies, your people?" Bass then shifted his gaze to the brilliant, early-morning blue overhead, as if in hope of finding the answers written there.

"*Pote Ani*, you find part of the answer to what might be a very difficult riddle. This one, his name of Cut Nose, you speak of—also called Five Scalps, he may well be the one whose life was taken on the frozen river. Perhaps. This one, he would be old now. Many seasons, many seasons this one has been gone from us—away to where the sun moves out of its bed each morning. It is said he has lived with our enemies, the—the Arikara." The last word was spoken as if spitting out something foul from one's lips.

"Who . . . ," Scratch began, then his voice trailed off into silence.

". . . killed these men?" Arapooesh finally spoke. "This is what you ask?"

Bass nodded as he tossed some small twigs into the low flames of the fire. "Yes," he answered quietly.

"The two who came with the news say they do not know, that the rest of the hunting party would be slower in coming home. One thing they would do is to look for those signs that point to who had killed these men, these trappers." The old chief finally sighed, the long breath making a frosty trail in the early-morning air. "Perhaps, only—it might have been the Minnetarees. Then, maybe—a band of the Sioux. These are not far away from the river we call the Horn. I do not know—only can I guess at the riddle's answer. Assiniboin, they might be . . ." His voice trailed off into silence.

Bass tapped at the crusty snow with a small twig, the only other sound behind the faint crackling of the limbs on the fire. He wondered who the trappers were, worried who their killers were—and the why of it all. They had been killed close to Fort Cass, a small fortress which stood about three miles below the mouth of the Big Horn on the east bank of the Yellowstone. Perhaps the three had been traveling upriver toward Fort Floyd, what was now becoming known as Fort Union. Where were they coming from—and where were they headed when the end came? With everything frozen up the way it was, it made no sense to him that these three were out trapping.

Headed somewhere—and caught in an ambush, perhaps. As Arapooesh would say. But the three were in Crow country. Cass was known as "Tulloch's Fort," named for Samuel Tulloch, factor and builder of the fort back in 1832, a fort erected to cater to the Crow trade.

He finally rose slowly from the ground to stand closer to the fire. "When will the Lumpwoods come in with the bodies?" Bass asked of the chief.

"They will be some four suns behind, this hunting party—so the two who came first have told us." Arapooesh squinted up at the whiteman across the smoky fire. "You move like a young man, despite the slow leg, my friend. Not like we who are old, we who have the cold settle quickly into our bones." He then lowered his eyes. "You will help us with this, *Pote Ani*? With this riddle?"

Scratch turned slowly and moved away into the trees, leaving behind him the old ones, those whose many years held countless riddles yet unsolved. And now, Bass could not even remember why this morning he had walked down to his old shelter.

He leaned over the small fire in the lodge to push another limb into the flesh-warming flames. After he had lain back against the robes, Bass finally sensed something different, something remotely out of place. It was like a tingling in anticipation of something unknown yet to happen. At first, he let his senses become aware of the altered atmosphere in hopes that he could figure it out. Yet he was not certain of anything until—he realized the camp had become very quiet outside the lodge walls.

Where before there had been the usual noises of the Sparrowhawk people going about their late-afternoon preparations of the evening meal, along with the excited voices of children, the yelping of running dogs and the lively chatter of women as they hauled water or wood back to their lodges—now the village had become quiet except for the sounds of many feet scuffling across the snow outside.

Titus had once again become sensitive to the rhythms of life in the winter village, and now this change in the routine troubled him. He struggled as he rose, the mending muscles of the upper leg and hip tight, agonizing when he used them. Pulling the blanket coat more tightly about himself and retying the sash about his waist, the trapper ducked through the doorway and stood outside. The people were hurrying toward the east.

He turned back and peered past the door flap he had pulled aside. Josiah seemed still to be asleep, so he let the flap fall back into place. His curiosity piqued by the mass exodus, Bass fell in with the Crow people as they walked toward the eastern edge of the camp. Eventually, he came to the edge of the trees near the bank of the river where stood the hundreds of spectators, each waiting in private, muted anticipation. And then he saw them.

The large hunting party was just topping the hill across the river, beginning to descend the slope of the north bank of the Yellowstone. They moved slowly, letting their tired animals set their own leaden pace. As the spearhead of the group arrived at the bank, the riders reined their ponies to a halt while one lone warrior rode slowly out onto the ice at the river's ford. The animal pranced nervously until brought under control and was made to walk slowly across the slippery frozen surface. When he had made it across the river near the waiting throng of quiet, murmuring villagers, the young warrior turned the pony and motioned for the other riders to follow.

As the next man began his crossing of the ice, the last of the riders broached the top of the hill and began their descent to the ford. One by one they crossed the flat, ice-crusted river, each warrior waiting until the rider before him had arrived on shore before he would venture out onto the ice. Bass noticed that each of the sternly quiet faces was painted—painted with the colors of war, red predominantly. But there was no black. If they had been victorious in battle, the riders would have painted themselves with the black of battle victory. Instead, those faces that were partially buried beneath the fur of robes and various cold-weather headgear were painted red.

When only a few riders remained on the north bank, Scratch could see that their cargo was more than just the carcasses of elk and deer. Beneath robes or blankets on three of the ponies were wrapped the frozen, contorted human bodies. Those stiff forms swung slightly as men led the three ponies cautiously across the frozen river.

When the last corpse was on its way across, the rest of the party began to move up the south bank into the trees toward the village. After all the ponies had passed by, the onlookers fell in behind the somber procession. Near the center of camp, the hunters positioned their mounts into two long lines, down the center of which rode those warriors pulling the animals carrying the three corpses. At last the old village chief moved down the center of the crowd to meet those three warriors.

Bass watched Arapooesh move slowly toward the hunters. He walked almost as if reluctant to complete this mission, as if wearily resigned to this ceremony. Finally the scuffling feet came to a halt before the first Lumpwood warrior, a proven veteran of many battles, one who now stood motionless in the quiet, still air waiting for his chief to speak the first words.

"My brother"—Rotten Belly's words cracked the fragile, crystalline air—"did not your warriors follow the murderer's trail?"

"We did follow," the warrior answered, "for more than one sun's ride across the sky." He sighed. "We turned for home when it was clear to us these murderers were too far ahead of us—moving too fast for my warriors."

Arapooesh moved down the side of a pony carrying one of the stiffened bodies. First he laid a hand on the blanket that shrouded the corpse and then he bowed his head. After a long moment of prayerful silence, the old chief raised his head once more and moved to the second pony's burden. Again, the old gray head bowed, almost touching the edge of the second blanket. Finally, the ritual was performed one last time with the third body.

Rotten Belly raised his head and turned toward the fourth horse in the procession. The animal carried what appeared to be the remaining possessions of the dead men. Not much property left behind by the murderers, the thieves. He reached out to touch the much-used snowshoes, then a battered, worn buffalo robe. "It is a strange thing—the murderers did not take much," the old chief finally said after the long silence. "My heart is small to see that these men did not have much of value to leave their killers. It seems their lives were worth far more than what could be stolen." He shook his head as if in disgust. "A shameful thing, this—men who gave their lives to thieves who wanted to steal nothing more than a worn-out, many-wintered robe. To have given their lives . . ." His voice trailed off into the frosty silence.

He turned and moved slowly toward the first pony. "You must have some idea, my brother, who their killers are." He addressed the hunting party leader and it was more of a statement than a question.

"The scum of the Big Water, my chief," the warrior answered

with a look of undisguised disgust spreading across his face. Arapooesh jerked his head to look at the hunting party leader, who spoke again before the chief could even ask his question. "Yes—Arikara. Carrion-eater." He spat into the snow. "The ones who take the scalps of women. The same ones who kill babies and children! Arikara. My mouth is dirty for speaking their name!"

Rotten Belly leaned toward the first pony, reached out and yanked back the blanket from the corpse. There was quiet murmuring from the crowd around the naked body. The man had been completely scalped, the whole top of his head covered with the frozen, coagulated blood. The eyes had been gouged out, their blackened holes staring grotesquely at the crowd, many of whom clamped hands over astonished mouths and eyes, shutting out the sight.

Bass stepped past one of the ponies in line to get a better look at the face, this face that bore only a mustache.

It was Menard. Yes, he knew the old Frenchman. A river trapper, one who had rarely ventured into the mountains. But this one had known the river tribes as one would know his own cousins. Bass raised his eyes from Menard's butchered face to find Arapooesh watching him. The old chief motioned slightly with his head, and Titus nodded in the affirmative. Yes, I knew him.

Rotten Belly dropped the blanket over Menard's remains and moved back to the second pony. Another blanket was pulled back and another bloodied, eyeless face stared out at the throng. Only this time it was more difficult to make out the features beneath the coagulated, frozen blood. Yet at the same time, it was easier to see where the scalp had been removed.

The killers had taken special care to ceremonially destroy this body. The tongue had been ritually pierced with a sharp stick, pulled out of the mouth, then nearly severed. A red, pulpy mass of tongue flopped uselessly from the mouth ringed with yellowed, cracked teeth. Against the ebony of the skin shone the purplish-white skull.

Slowly, some of the Indians came forward for a closer look at what remained of the corpse's features. Then they backed up and returned to their places in the silent crowd. Many of these people had known the man. In dreaded anticipation, Bass edged out of the throng once more and made his way to the chief's side.

It was Rose. That was his name, wasn't it? Yep—Rose, he

thought. Again Scratch looked up at Arapooesh and nodded. Hard to forget this nigger.

"Rose," he responded in English, then caught himself. "The Cut-Nose." He drew his fingertip across the portion of one nostril that had been bitten off in a water-hole brawl down to New Orleans.

Arapooesh spoke now in Crow. "The Five Scalps—the name he was given in his third year with the Sparrowhawk."

"The Five Scalps," Bass repeated in the Crow tongue.

"Such was the one we both believed it would be," replied Rotten Belly. "But—I would not have believed he could be killed . . ." His voice trailed off to a heavy, painful silence.

"We all must die," Scratch replied after a moment.

Rotten Belly looked over at the trapper. "My friend, I would not have believed he could be killed. There are many winters in him. He has many robe seasons riding with him to the Spirit Land Beyond. Older than you, perhaps. But, not as wise as you, *Pote Ani*. Maybe."

Ain't a wise man what's got his hair ripped off, Bass thought. "Do wise men live long lives, my chief?" he asked.

"Ah," the chief snorted quietly in reply and looked down at the ground while he dropped the blanket back over Edward Rose. "This one, the Cut Nose, he has lived with these Arikara. He has been some good friend to the Arikara."

"Murdered by the vultures of the Big River," Bass snapped.

"Their hatred grows hot as the coals of a sweat-lodge fire— enough hatred to kill one who has lived with them for so many seasons."

The old chief seemed suddenly more weary. He placed his hand inside Scratch's arm and clamped on with the tired, bony fingers. Bass was startled at the chief's sudden need for support. His eyes were full of questions as he looked into Arapooesh's face. "I grow tired. Death robs me of much of my strength. The cold does no good for me, *Pote Ani*." He led Bass on their way toward the last body. "You will help a friend again, maybe."

"I will help a friend, always," Bass replied as they scuffled through the snow.

The last body was wrapped in a well-worn buffalo robe, hairless in spots, the hide thin and ripped in other places. How many meals had been made from the animal it was taken from? How many sleeps had it kept the man warm? How many winters had it turned the icy winds from the north?

This time, Bass himself reached out to pull the thinning hide away from the face. This one was a whiteman, too. His small-pox-pitted face was covered with a beard. A thick scar ran from the collar-bone up and over the jaw, spreading the gray beard like a well-worn path, continuing up the side of the face to the temple where it ended against the skull. Other thick, white scars coursed across the shoulders and down the back, disappearing into the darkness beneath the old robe. The full scalp had been stolen here, too. Eyeless sockets glared out like black shadows at Bass, yawning with the nearness of violent, savage, merciless death. The open, frozen mouth gaped tongueless. But into it the killers had stuffed the dead man's penis and scrotum. The final humiliation of a hated enemy. He must have been some bad medicine for them, Bass reflected almost reverently.

"All of them scalped." Arapooesh looked away from the last face. His breath came hard, in gasps. "Full scalps. Medicine. Bad."

Scratch knew the last man, too. Now came the end of many chapters in the long life of the man some said had once worn a gold earring and pillaged beneath the skull and crossbones flag of a Gulf-coast pirate ship. Others said he had saved his own life by marrying into a Pawnee family, had even eaten human flesh to prove to his new-found family-captors that he was truly one of them.

It was him. The old gray-beard who had been left for dead by those as would have called him friend, back when Ashley was first pushing into the mountain fur trade. Left him for dead after the sow grizzly had butchered his old frame. Old? Shit! If he'd been old then—what would that make him now? Gotta be close to some sixty winters now, anyway. Bass continued to stare at the old, gray-beard's face.

"This one," he finally spoke to Arapooesh, "there was no big heart for him among the Arikara—if it was they who killed these three old warriors." He shook his head. "This one—he would have been one they would have wanted to kill, bad. They would have had black hearts for this one." Then he nodded toward the body of Rose. "That one, and this one here—the Arikara would have believed it to be some very big medicine to find them together: to kill them together at the same time."

Slowly he dropped the stiff, frosty buffalo hide back over the old, scarred trapper's face. "Cut Nose, the friend and member of the tribe, he later turned his heart against that tribe. As he did with the Kicked-in-Their-Bellies, he did with the Arikara. And he became their enemy. They did not become his enemy. He became theirs. A shame, my friend. And, this one," he rubbed his hand over the worn buffalo fur, "he had been an enemy of the Arikara for many, many—so many robe seasons. They knew this one well. It is good that he goes to the Other Side Land having been killed in battle by such an enemy worthy of his own hatred, the Arikara."

Good-bye, Glass. Four times them Rees tried hard to lift your hair. Farewell, ol' coon. Titus dropped his eyes to the snow as he felt the sudden tightening in his throat against an upswelling sob. Ol' Hugh, the grizz-scarred ol' salt, gone over to the Other Side now.

Bass turned away as the old chief's arm finally dropped from his. The white trapper strode off reluctantly, wanting to ask how the bodies would be buried or if they would be returned to Tulloch's care—but in no way ready to attempt to speak. Instead, he only stopped and turned once to look back at Rotten Belly. The chief nodded to Scratch before the whiteman continued to hobble back to the lodge.

Suddenly she was at his side. Slipping one arm around the bulky waist, she placed her other on his right arm. Bass slowed almost to a halt as he looked down at her in surprise. Then he moved off again across the crusty snow, wondering himself how an old, scarred veteran could be so attractive to this beautiful young wisp here in the wilderness. She, an embodiment of all temptation, the embodiment of the seductive lure of the wilderness—Waits-by-the-Water turned him warm with her closeness.

"I have something to show you—to give you, my man." She spoke without looking up into his face.

"You have given me much, much already, my woman."

"This I give you—you have not had before." Her eyes had a twinkling depth to them that spoke almost by themselves.

"Yes," Bass responded, "tell me."

"Your coat." The young woman glanced fleetingly at the trapper's face before looking at the ground again. "Your coat . . . I know you truly love quillwork . . . your coat . . ."

"You're the thief!" he roared.

"Yes." She favored him with a falsely injured pout. "I am the thief. Many, many suns have I had it."

"Why did you steal?"

"Only to return it greater than what I had taken," she answered quietly. "Your coat now has my gift on it, my quillwork for you." She looked at him long now before turning her eyes away. "That is as it should be, *Pote Ani*. To return something in greater measure than what we take for ourselves. My love, my love for you, I wish it to be so."

This girl-woman could cause him so much pain, yet bring him so much joy. She would bring pain if he fell in love with her. And it had been so long, so very long since he had allowed himself the luxury of being completely vulnerable. Bass glanced over at her. She was still there, as if she really did believe in him. As if she really did care for no other.

It seemed to fit. This thing with the girl-woman who said she wanted him. It seemed to fit even though he felt the scars on both his body and his heart that had marked every season in the high country—each scar yelling out to him now that he was not far behind McAfferty and the three frozen corpses. How much time was left to him? Who could say? Yet, this woman thing still seemed to fit with him. And there was more than small comfort in that.

Six

Yes, thought Emile, he had been at this a long time. How long? There were forty-six winters behind him now, back there in all those forests, those rivers, all that wilderness. It was out there, beyond the civilization of man that his life had begun north of Lake of the Woods, on north of Fort Alexander. Forty-six winters come and gone now. Winters spent warm within a cozy hut, with one or more of his women. A cheery fire, a little hunting, and always the stew bubbling over the flames. Until they came.

The scarred flesh that had sealed the one eye shut many winters before crinkled now as he smiled again. One man this time. So easy, yet so much money offered for his death.

To come to St. Louis to meet the rich one who was hiring him. From there to find the man he would kill. Then return to St. Louis a last time to collect his reward. Perhaps a scalp.

Sometimes they wanted a scalp. Sometimes other proof. Never once failing in his task. Only one time had he not been paid. There had been a second scalp hanging from his belt that day before he returned north. And from that winter on, everyone knew you paid Emile what he asked for his services.

But this one who was asking him to come to St. Louis had offered more money than had ever been offered before. So it must be that this one he was to kill must be very important. Very important to have this particular scalp. With as much as the three messengers had offered from their employer, the giant would not have to work again. He could live comfortably for the rest of his life. He would not have to run the woods in search of his victim ever again. Perhaps. But, there had always been something more than money, something more than the bags and purses of coins paid him. Returning to his hut and his women when the matter was settled. For more than the money he always waited for the messengers to come to him. Emile Sharpe's wrinkled scar rippled once more over his eye. Oh, yes, he grinned: it was for more than the money.

It was late in the afternoon when Bass pulled the ponies to a stop in the small grove of trees that served as the compound for their horses. Looking with only half a heart Titus knew that within less than two hours the sun would make its final slide behind the mountains to the west. Slowly, wearily, the trapper pushed himself from the cold, creaking leather of his saddle and rested against the side of the pony, letting the frozen joints become accustomed once again to standing under the weight of his body. With the rifle cradled in the crook of the left arm, he moved his right hand to stroke the animal's neck.

This pony had begun to endear itself to the old man—serving him as it did since the last summer of rendezvous and celebration, a warm season followed by cold and snow, and the chill of death. Involuntarily, the shudder shot through him and he turned. Bass would unload the animals later. Not long would it take to warm himself in the lodge, then return to the compound to free the animals of their burden of meat, supplies and much of his plunder from the hunt.

Smoke curled from the tops of the camp's dwellings, each lodge warm and busy with the preparations for the last meal of the day. Children and women swarmed back and forth bringing to their homes the fruits of the successful hunt. Warriors and old men were they, the ones who had once more filled the boiling kettles of the Crow camp.

Bass stopped and looked about him. Few of those who had been on the hunt were to be seen. Into the lodges for warmth and rest they had retreated. Yes—to be warm again in the lodge, and to rest against the strength-robbing cold of late afternoon. To feel her near once more would be enough for now, just to know she was so near. How easily satisfied he became as he grew older, he mused. Gone was the nagging itch of lust that drove him as a younger man. Instead, there was a much greater peace just in knowing she was near. An old man's priorities, he thought. To be warm, to rest within the robes, and to have his woman near for him. That was enough for now— and later, well, she would warm those too-long cold places he kept buried from the world. With the thought, Titus set off toward the lodge.

Only a thin, straggling wisp of smoke curled and lifted from the smoke hole of Rotten Belly's lodge as he neared. Surely she would have heard of their return to camp before now and built up the fire for his return. And the boy would be needing all the more warmth with the night coming on soon. Maybe not to blame her for his expectations, he told himself as he stepped toward the lodge door. But, that was silly—he had come to expect much from her in their few days together, expecting much for she had given him much.

Bass pulled the door flap aside and put one foot into the lodge as a sudden rustling of robes sounded near the back of the lodge. He dragged his other foot in wearily and let his eyes become adjusted to the dim light. The fire was low and would require building, yet his gaze wandered to the whisper of movement at the rear, across the fire from where he stood. There was enough light to see his woman as she pulled the blanket around her bare shoulders and sat up, drawing the edge of the thick, woven wool across her bare breast.

His mind was slow in making sense of it as he took a tentative step to move around the smoky fire. He saw Josiah draw a blanket and robe back over his bare leg where the woman's movement had pulled them away in her haste to sit up. She said nothing as his old eyes flickered, his gaze darting back and forth between the two young people together on the bedding at the back of the lodge. Her eyes looked up at his, then cowered when his met the embarrassed gaze.

"Scratch . . ." the younger man stammered.

His mind was beginning to warm with the retreating cold. It had been slow to move on this, just as slow as his eyes shifting now to stare at Paddock. She had been with Josiah in the robes and could not face the eyes that demanded an answer. But Titus knew.

"What . . ." Scratch began. But he knew. His woman—why had he let himself believe she was his woman? She had bedded down with his partner.

"Just what . . ." he started again, thinking how silly he was, an old fool, to think that she was really his woman, and that Paddock had truly been his partner. What an old fool he had been.

"Didn't know you was gonna be gettin' back . . ." Josiah started.

Bass dropped to the bed at the right side of the lodge, lowering his head as he began to shake it, side to side, in disbelief. Slowly, slowly as if not to shake loose what felt like ice crystals inside the skull. The cold, the numbing, shattering cold of it all. He shivered, trying to think—but could only feel the loss of them both now.

"I'm a fool, you thinkin' . . ." Bass whispered. Josiah shook his head. Bass just nodded. "Yep, I'm a fool—me thinkin' this was my woman—an' me thinkin' you was my, my . . ." He suddenly jerked up, pulling against the tight new skin over his leg wounds and kicked at the fire, scattering some of the burning embers and sending showering sparks toward the smoke hole. Burnt he was. All burnt up and consumed. He had to go.

"You, you got it all wrong."

"Have I?"

"Yeah," Josiah said.

"Don't think me so, Josiah." He turned and pulled a few of his belongings from where they hung along the dew-cloth rope. "Took me a few, it did that. But, I don't think I got it wrong at all." Bass threw the articles onto a blanket and wrenched around as if searching for more that he did not want to leave behind, knowing the rest would probably be in his little shelter at the edge of camp.

"'Tweren't like that at all." Paddock spoke a little louder, raspier. The anger he felt flowing from the older man raised the volume he used to push his words out. He glanced at the Crow woman. "She . . . me . . ."

"I know." Bass bent to fold in the corners of the blanket around his plunder. "You an' her—some fun whilst the ol' man gone to make meat—'pears to me." He grimly raked the blanket parcel into his arms. "Playin' with each other an' both of you playin' me the fool at the same time, you son of a bitch!"

He hurt inside now with the words, the cold and numbness gone, replaced with the nagging emptiness. It was the same nagging hollow hole that had eaten at the cavern within as he had stared down at his young partner's body beneath the pine trees in a lonely mountain bowl back there—so far away in miles, so far away in time. The loneliness had come home once more. Back there he had knelt over this young man's body, then stared down the hill to where his mule, that companion of years and trackless miles, lay dead on the trampled snow. And then his loneliness had led to an anguish and rage at the man he had seen bring down both the mule and his partner.

There it was again, that word he had been fool of—partner, friend. Now he laughed and stepped toward the doorway. He must get away before the same desperation drove him to kill again. Let the emptiness that grew moment by moment be enough to carry him through his days without people, for they were faithless and refused to bind themselves to him. "You old fool," he cried out at himself as he stepped from the lodge and limped toward the ponies.

"You dumb, stupid ol' man!" The voice broke through the doorway, following him as he moved away. "You ain't worth the trouble cryin' over, Bass!" The younger man's voice was now filled with a rage of its own, an anguished bleating of words. "I didn't take nothin' from you."

He had hobbled too far away to really hear the words behind him now, thankfully. There they would remain, behind him, as so much was now. Just when he had believed there was so much to move toward, it seemed that all that remained was to move away from what was to be left behind. He would put season after season behind him; the despair of loneliness was an enemy he had staved off before. He could do it again. By moving, and moving some more, he could keep it at bay. Yet the thought sobbed through him as he felt the nothingness of what was to come. It whimpered through his soul and he cried out against it as he reached the ponies.

"Damn him!" Josiah blurted out hoarsely as he shifted against the pain searing through his side. He turned his head to look at the woman who still had her eyes on the empty doorway.

"You." He threw the word her way and she looked back at

him. "You . . . go!" He brought the left arm out from the buffalo robe and pointed toward the door. "Go!" he commanded again, then shook his head in despair at his not knowing the language of the woman.

"Tell him come back!" He pointed his arm frantically, stabbed the air several times, hoping she would understand the gesture.

The young woman nodded and stood, letting the blanket fall from her shoulders. She stood naked save for the moccasins and soft leggings that reached above her knees. Maybe he was the fool, Josiah thought, sending her after the old man. She was a beauty and had warmed him so. Yes, he was a fool to send her away after the old man now when he could drink of her warmth with no regrets.

The other one. Another young woman. His mind was suddenly full of her and he did not feel comfortable with these first tickles of vulnerability. Almost unconsciously, he reached up to envelop the small buckskin pouch that hung from his neck.

But there were regrets. He had learned that much—there were regrets and there would only be more if Bass left now.

She knelt shivering against the cold to scrounge for her dress and capote, but Paddock threw her the blanket instead and motioned again frantically. "Bass!" What was the name?

"Pote Ani!"

She threw the blanket around her shoulders and looked into his eyes briefly before turning to leave the lodge. It was the look of one who did not yet know if she had won or lost. A look of awe and wonder, yet with some impending sadness.

When the door flap settled over the doorway, Josiah sighed and let himself fall back against the robes, the pain burning along his side. She would bring him back and they would have it out over the old man's stupidity. That was a laugh—all those months, all those miles, the old man trying to make him feel stupid. But he had learned so much from the old, stupid son of a bitch. They would have it out now, and when he was stronger, he would kick the old man's ass. He would kick it black and blue. Bass had been deserving of such for some time now.

Josiah closed his eyes against the pain that made the hurting of his wound secondary. She would bring Scratch back—then he would explain the why of the young woman, Bass's woman, being in his robes. He would explain all about his lust and his fever for her, and how she had answered his need—the young could be foolish, too. He would explain it all away and then he would kick some sense into the old man's head.

Bass quickly tied lengths of rawhide rope from the halter of each pony to the tail of the pony in front of it. Then he painfully vaulted into the cold saddle and drew the piece of buffalo robe around his legs and waist against the cold. He shifted in his seat to adjust the heavy elk-hide coat, then nudged the ponies forward out of the stand of trees. Forlorn, they reluctantly obeyed and moved away much more slowly than he wanted them to. Already the moisture from his eyes was freezing in the whiskers across his cheeks and the salt in those tears burned the healing wound at his left eye, causing the flesh to quiver with the sting of salt and cold. His nose dripped and he wiped it with the sleeve of his coat, yanking the arm brutally across the lower part of his face. He would try to wipe it all away as easily as that, he thought. He knew better than to believe it.

She hurried, shivering in the cold, struggling to keep the blanket wrapped around her nakedness. Scurrying through the lodges, across the cold ground, sending up little scuffs of snow with the toes of her moccasins. Her own eyes burned with the cold that whipped moisture at their corners and she realized she was crying—for this man, for what he thought of her, for her disgrace before his eyes.

Yes, she must catch him now. Before it would be too late—to explain to him what had happened, the reason she had gone into the robes with the young one. Before it would be too late to explain how she had grown lonely for him the last few days and wanted to be held by him again and again. The sob caught in her throat and she choked, gasped for breath. There was danger in this caring for another. She ran past the last lodge toward the stand of trees where the whitemen kept their ponies.

The animals were gone. He was gone. Only four of the ponies remained. The young one's animals. *Pote Ani* had gone quickly. She darted through the stand of trees toward the river, reading sign on last night's snow. He had led them this way toward the crossing of the water. She yelled into the falling night for him.

"Pote Ani!"

On she ran, through the trees toward the river, hoping against hope that she was not too late. She stubbed her toe and almost lost the blanket. Flinging it around her once more she took off, despite the pain in her foot, despite the anguish at being too late. Her feet skidded to a stop near the rocks along the bank of the frozen river. She saw him climbing the bench on the other side, heading up the rise, moving west.

"*Pote Ani!*" she screamed. What were the words he had taught her? Why could she not remember?

"Bass!" Why could he not hear her? Why would he not turn around?

"*Pote Ani!*" She fought the stifling despair.

"Bass! Bass! I love you!"

He had cluttered his mind up with too many things. And now it felt like his heart yawned empty and bare, echoing the shadowed fullness of his mind. There had been too much that he hadn't taken time for—for her. For himself. The neglected time, the missed opportunity to really tell her. It all seemed so far away from him now.

Bass swiped at the frozen moisture where it clung to his beard. He had fought on through the night and most of this day, refusing to drop from the saddle, unheeding of the protests of the animals he both pushed and pulled west with him in his own private torment. He had thought the movement would push him through the first, lonely grip of agony—just moving, just being busy with the physical torture. But it had not. The fatigue that wrestled to overpower him was now winning. And with the collapse of his body would come the emotional desolation he feared the most.

Of their own accord, the animals took him into a small grove of cottonwoods near the river. Then they stopped. Slowly he returned to the conscious world and the realization that the hypnotic sway of the animal beneath him as it had beaten through the snow now had relinquished its spell over him. Bass finally raised his head and opened his eyes from the slits they had become amidst the blinding glare of the sunlit snow. Only now the brilliant light had faded and his eyes were greeted with the gray-blue patina of the evening haze.

Letting out a long sigh, Scratch finally slipped to the ground. His legs quivered under the sudden change of position and the new weight upon them. They would have to hold up if he was to hold up, he thought. Can't get away if they don't carry me. He straightened and pushed himself away from the pony. The animal, released from the weight of his body, sidled away and Bass was left to stand alone on wobbly legs. His mind assessed his circumstances as he looked around him. Now he must decide where to make his camp.

Good cover over there, he thought, as he pushed his legs in the direction of some cottonwoods surrounded by willow and bramble, the brush blown clear of most of its snow. After surveying the spot, Bass turned and whistled low for the pony. He watched its ears perk with a twitch before it looked his way. The pony remained where it stood, as if cast in stone by its own fatigue. Finally Bass whistled low again, louder and more insistent. Then he cursed himself for the noise. The fatigue had made him careless. Any other time he would not have done such a damned, stupid thing. But the animal plodded over to the old trapper, dragging the other ponies behind it.

Reluctantly, he pulled his cramped hands, that had long ago formed themselves around the reins and his rifle, out of their mittens and set the weapon against a tree. With frosting fingers Titus pulled at the knots securing baggage to the ponies' back and let the bundles fall to the snow. Each animal blew and rippled its muscles as he cast off their burdens. On unforgiving legs he pulled what he needed within the willow and bramble shelter, then stepped outside one last time, finally yanking the woolen blanket mittens over his hands again.

"You're prob'ly too tired to be movin' far anyways," he murmured to the ponies as he began to run the halter ropes out to the willow branches. Too much trouble to dig out the picket pins. The animals would feed well on the twigs.

That chore completed, there remained one task before he could return to his haven for the night. In the fading leaden light, Scratch scuffled along through the snow, his numbed toes finding pieces of wood buried beneath the deep powder. Each new chunk of deadfall was added to the crook of his left arm until he finally stumbled back into his willow refuge.

"*He goes west, nigger's countin' on makin' it to Blackfoot country,*" he remembered having told Josiah as they had set out after McAfferty. "*A hard, cold trail starin' you down now.*"

Same now, Asa, he thought suddenly. It's the same cold, winter trail staring me straight-on in the face now.

Bass could read the signs. Unless he got his fire going soon, the night just might finish him off. The fatigue and cold were now crawling into him, pushing slowly, steadily toward his core. His hands fumbled with the large flap on his shooting pouch. Finally he brought the hands up before his eyes, inches away from his face where he could see them in the charcoal-like light.

"*With what I'm s'posed to sew you up?*" he remembered Josiah asking after the grizzly sow had ripped his hand up, leaving with a finger.

"*With the sinew!*" he had answered, now looking down at the battered, scarred right hand.

"*You want me to sew you up with one of these?*" Paddock had held up a piece of soft leather that secured two needles.

"*You get your sticker blade hot in the fire there, run 'er over real quick on them places you sewed up. Then put the root down over 'em an' wrap my hand up,*" he had instructed through each step of the surgery. And the young trapper had done well enough with what he had had to work with. A mess, the flesh torn and sliced and gaping around each wound. Paddock had drawn the heated knife over each of those wounds, smelling the seared flesh and hearing the faint crackle as the tissue and sinew burned.

"You gotta help me," Bass slurred now at his hands. "Help me. An' I'll help you." I can make them warm, he thought. But they've got to do what I want them to do. No other way. "Ain't no other way. We gotta do this together now, fellas."

The hands moved away from his face as if upon his instruction, with a will of their own. The fumbling with the pouch flap continued but they finally found their way into the mouth and one hand touched the small metal box he was after. Now the shuddering began, slowly rising as he drew the tinder box out of the pouch. Suddenly the shakes were out of control and the box went spinning into the white dust of his frozen refuge by the water. Bass dropped to hands and knees and frantically began to sweep the powder aside in a four-legged dance of frustration and fear.

After several minutes of furious probing he sat back on his haunches and looked up into the tree branches overhead as the last fragment of light slipped from the horizon. Bass began to cry.

He talked to himself through it, whimpering at times with the words he sputtered against the tears, until the sobbing grew and turned into racking spasms. Hopelessness was all he felt now. Damned near everything had been taken from him. All that was left was his own life. The spirit would soon be gone, its flame that had long burned within him now snuffed out with the cold and empty wind whistling through his soul.

The frozen moisture along his cheeks crinkled as he clamped his eyes shut, squeezing hard as if to blot out the pain at the left side of his face. His eyes burned with the tears and the muscles cried out in agony at the sudden constriction. When finally the sobbing stopped, Bass found his eyes frozen shut. Slowly he lifted a leaden arm and brushed a woolen sleeve against the frozen moisture. The eyes blinked open.

His head dropped backward to gaze at the dark canopy overhead, sprinkled with cold luminescent diamonds. He cried out from deep within his own despair.

"Aaaggghghghg!" The voice sounded loud to him although its volume stayed trapped in his head. "Grandfather! Old Man Coyote! I am not ready to die!" The words came in Crow.

"This is not my time. This is not my place!" He shook his head. "I must not die like this! You cannot let this be, Grandfather! Old Man Coyote can not have his way with me! We warriors must die the one, proud death that comes with the flash of the lightning! This is slow torture. You cannot let this be! Grandfather, I will fight this! I will fight Old Man Coyote in this death dance!"

Bass dropped to his hands again and began to move slowly about in an ever-widening circle. His left hand bumped into it, and the mittened fingers surrounded it. Then both hands cupped it and brought it out of the snow. The arms stretched upward, hands cradling the tinder box as if in offering.

"Grandfather, you play Old Man Coyote with me!" he whispered hoarsely, his voice clogged with the lump buried in his chest. "You test me to see if I am ready to give up to you, and when you see that I am not ready, you end your little joke with me." Bass brought the metal box against his chest. "Grandfather, I thank you for teaching me this again."

The spirit within him awakened from its embers of light. His frozen fingers clumsily lifted out char and flint and steel. Then the bird's nest. Soon there was a spark that glowed on the black char that gave way to flame within the dry grass. The numb fingers found it hard carefully to lay small twigs upon the burning nest, but soon he had the fire going and he could crawl over the bundles to unroll the robes.

The world around him now could scream it at him, telling him that he had nothing beautiful in him, nothing worth binding itself to—but the ember had never died. While the pain would remain to mock him, to chastise him for caring, its darkened hand could not quell an abiding hope that he would remain, remain as so much about him fell away.

On his left side, lying fetally around his small fire, Scratch finally let his eyes fall shut. Time would remain for him and he would try to forget those times past. Push on into the future and what it held for him. For more than a day he had torn his thoughts away from her. But now, as her visions came to interrupt the blackness beneath the fiercely clenched lids, Bass gave in. Not from weakness did he surrender. But from a sudden, self-realizing pain that told him this love he would have to deal with for many years to come.

"Can a man take fire in his bosom, and his clothes not be burned?" It was the voice of the Whitehair, McAfferty, trespassing upon the private recesses of his soul with its haunting, ghostly voice. *"Can one go upon hot coals, and his feet not be burned?"*

The huge place inside where he held her could not be denied. The ember remained alive. Its heat burned at him, but seared with less pain only when he finally admitted that he loved her.

The gentle, rolling, tumbling sobbing returned. The sounds caught in his throat. If need be, he would nourish his love, continue to hurt for her. But he hoped he would make it through. Bass was not sure now as he cried himself to sleep in the wilderness. A lone coyote screeched out in the distance as if in echo to the man's own solitude. He was not sure how he would make it, though. The uncertainty was sure to pass from him. Titus Bass at last wanted to pull through.

Seven

Titus sat, stared for a long time at the river that ran to the south. Calculating on why McAfferty had ever headed south, upriver, when Bass had believed the old Whitehead would buck directly for Blackfoot country. So, Bass had rested the animals at that spot for a couple of hours, feeding the ponies on some frozen cottonwood bark he had peeled for them. The old trapper had eaten sparingly of the pemmican purchased last summer. Little was left now. It had always been his trail food, when there had been little time to hunt.

So his studying, calculating mind remembered the cold, winter manhunt. Here this rocky river, strewn with boulders, came tumbling into the Yellowstone from the south in a springtime rush to the sea. But now the two were frozen sheets brought together as if two sections of a braided rawhide rope which sorely missed the third strand.

That was it. The three of 'em, he thought. Slowly rising on cold legs, the wounded thigh still biting at him with a dull, healing kind of pain, Bass mounted his pony and pulled the rest of the pack animals into action. The beauty of a sudden flash of memory struck him. Why hadn't he remembered the route before? Shit! Something else to remind him how old he was getting. Forgetting things again.

Long ago, so long ago. Memories crashed and bumped against his soul like dangerous chunks of ice thudding against the warmth he fought to keep alive within his being. Yes, some memories were cold.

"I can winter outta a robe season where I wants to," he had told Josiah so long ago. "Mostly take my cold bones up to the Absor'kees. Real partial to them Crow, I am. Thieves that they be, they still have the warmest lodges I've laid my robes down in. They likes the whiteman, that they do. Whiteman has horseflesh, you see—an' them Crow is squampshus over horseflesh. Them Crow bah-park. Yes, big medicine for this ol' coot."

Some warmth. He needed some warmth in his soul to grow and push against the chunks of ice. The days of youth. A young man having moved across the plains alone, not having known of the dangers of solitary travel. Maybe it had been his type of good fortune, or maybe just something silently answering his courage, but he hadn't seen an Indian during those weeks of pushing from water hole to water hole across the sea of buffalo grass until he had hit the river an old trapper had told him of— the Platte.

Bass smiled suddenly. The memory warmed the longing, cold place within him. The river, guiding him, taking him there. The river was it. And he remembered the way now.

The three rivers headed over the pass from the Yellowstone. The way he would go now, down to the three rivers. Hell, he had done this trip before. He was remembering pieces of the route now, scattered fragments of the landscape. He was going to make it over the mountains. It had been years before. How many? That he was not entirely certain of either. But, he had been that way on another trip west out of the Yellowstone River country, up into the high places, then down to the Three Forks of the Missouri.

"They will go up by the mountains; they will go down by the valleys unto the place which thou has founded for them."

"You for all time gonna keep talkin' to me, huh, Asa?" he asked the ghostly specter in his mind. "S'pose that be all right, too. Not so lonely, then."

If he kept the memories alive, even with their searing pain, he would not be so lonely. He liked the lonesome. It was the lonely he could do without.

When the Yellowstone finally took itself to the south, heading down the narrow valley between two ranges of hills that threw themselves up against the mountains, Bass left the river and struck out due west. The sun had been directly behind him that morning when he had left the comfort of the old river. It would run south to its place of birth in the land of the Big Smokes. And Bass, he bade farewell to the river where it turned south as he broke free of its frozen bond to forge a trail of his own making.

The climb up from the flats had not been that difficult, most of the landscape having been blown clear of much of its snow by recent chinooks on this side of the divide—squaw winds, he called them. Bless the Wind Man, he thought. He knew I needed to get over this pass. And it was Time he was always fighting. Now, in some small way, Bass had felt buoyed up by the fact that things were going his way. What snow the chinooks and Wind Man had left behind was hard and crusty. Not the surest footing in the world for the ponies, but a damned sight better than plowing through the deep stuff. And once over the top and headed down, Scratch knew why his skin had tingled with a muted excitement. Perhaps anticipation. He was dropping into Blackfoot country.

"Jest take your time, friend," McAfferty had told Bass and Paddock as he was leaving the pair late last fall. *"Use your time for trappin'. Be cold 'nough when you find them Crow fires."*

Scratch had not really understood back then what Asa meant. But the old Whitehead had meant to bring the Blackfoot down on the Crow winter camp, extinguishing those winter fires for good. Blackfoot. Ol' Asa really had him a thing for them Injuns.

If he was fortunate, them niggers would be holed up in their lodges north of where he was now. If he was lucky, he could stay to the flats now, where the wind had swept most of the snow clear and the sagebrush stuck their hoary heads up through small mounds of the white residue. Like starched collars on them as live back east in them settlements, he smiled. His neck was free of any starched collar and fancy silk necktie.

Some of them had already gone back. Lot more will be going back, too. Getting out of the mountains. They didn't belong out here in the first place anyway. Go on back east! Go on back to them people settlements. Get out of my mountains! My mountains. The sound of it rang good to him. Being free up here, in his mountains—far, far better than being back there where you were always safe. Safe and sane, maybe.

Yes, his neck was free of any collar and silk necktie. Not a damned thing to chafe his neck but the wind that always pushed at his back now as it came roaring down the western slope of the peaks behind him. Let them go on back east. He would stay. Far better to stay.

"I am Crow. I am not Crow. My heart is with the Crow," he had told Rotten Belly and the old warriors in counsel last fall. *"My skin is white. I am man-in-between. I am man many times in between. When first I came to your land, it was for the beaver alone. Now I return again and again for the land fills my heart."*

His mind turned to look at Josiah with the aged dreamers around the fire. *"Here is my strong friend. Together we are Crow for the winter. It is his second cold time in the mountains, this friend. He will spend it here with me so the Crow can teach him what he needs to know. Those things this old man cannot teach him. Those things that are Crow."*

Yes, he nodded now. Surely the Old Man Coyote, *Akbatadia*, had put the Crow people in the right place for them. But Bass was leaving that place. Leaving that people behind. Just as he had left his own family behind so many, many years before.

When he struck the Gallatin, Bass tried to remember the Indian names for the river. Troubled with failure at that, he continued west along its course, assured that he was not far from the Three Forks themselves. There he camped late one afternoon. He built a small fire to warm some water, then crumbled jerky and pemmican into the rolling, tumbling kettle, before moving on a couple of miles farther to make his cold camp for the night. Blackfoot country, after all. And a man with so much gray hair on his head had to take him no chances.

Bass moved up the Madison for part of the morning until he located a place to ford the river. It was running slowly, the water low, most of the winter's ice pushed against the banks like a white piping border on the dark waters. From the Madison he moved west again toward the Jefferson, finally striking the river where it rolled west along with him. The climb that late afternoon brought him to the top of the hill where he looked down into the valley. There a river from the north came running into the Jefferson. He moved up this hill from the river to get a better idea of the country that lay ahead. Something out there would shake his memory, something down there would push his mind into recalling the landmarks. And there was something else down there. Not at all what he had bargained for.

Damnit! he cursed. Goddamned niggers! He backed the ponies into the trees again and dropped to the ground. On hands and knees Bass crawled to the edge of the timber and lay on his belly to watch the dark forms below him. Damn! If he had stayed with the Jefferson . . .

That river to his right came around the base of the hill where it ran plumb into the river that tumbled into it from the north. And if he had stayed with the Jefferson, he would have come around that hill right smack dab into them niggers! It would have been too late to do anything but fight. And die, most like.

They was Blackfeet, wasn't they? He knew they had to be. Flathead farther west of here. Ain't far enough west yet for them to be Flathead. Snakes? Nawww. Not up here when they could be a lot warmer to the south in their wintering ground. It had to be Bug's Boys—had to be. And he continued to lie there, studying the distant camp below him at the junction of the two rivers. Nervously he glanced back into the trees, back into the pattern of green and white, to catch a glimpse of his animals waiting patiently for him.

Bass sighed wearily. Another cold camp for him this night. He studied the village below again. It wasn't a raiding party. Lord, too many of the red niggers for that. And them lodges. A raiding party wouldn't take 'em time to pack along lodges and squaws, kids and such. No, goddamnit! This was something else entirely. Them niggers was already moving to find buffalo for an early spring hunt. He looked at the sky. Maybeso. Spring might come early this year. Lord knows they'd probably had 'em their share of winter already. Wasn't no small doin's down there, neither. No, sir. That was a damned big mess of Blackfoot he'd walked himself onto.

His gaze shifted from the sky to the village once more. A mess of niggers that large had to feed themselves real regular. And the hunters would be combing the hills around the camp for game. He was in the worst spot he could imagine: fair game for a Blackfoot hunting party. Damnit! He found himself actually whispering the word under his breath. He'd been stupid enough to believe he could come into this part of the country without running into them niggers. Your brain's surely getting addled, ol' man.

Only one thing to do, and that was hightail it out. But where? Back to the east? He surely could not drop down to the Jefferson and head north. That's where the village evidently had come from. And there'd be more of them Blackfoot north of here anyways. East of here was no option, either. He wasn't heading back to Crow country. Too much left behind there along the Yellowstone. North was out. East he'd never choose. He needed to head west, but that took him right down into them niggers. South looked to be the ticket. South for a ways before he could finally skirt this part of the country and get back on the westward trail once more.

Bass studied the terrain off to the southwest. Down there a ways, maybe a day's ride, little more—a big river runs into the Jefferson from the west. He could cross the Jefferson and follow it west once more. With some luck he wouldn't run into any hunting parties trying to feed this village on their slow early-spring tramp.

He remembered the early days with Josiah Paddock along with the words spoken to the young, starving greenhorn.

"I come out alone 'long the same way you done. Lookin' back on it, too—this here child some lucky to get to the mountains without some red nigger liftin' hair off him. That way's crawlin' with Injuns most time. Sioux, Pawnee, too. They give no truck to a lonely whiteman travelin' through that land. Man as travels 'lone out here just get himself used for target practice, maybe get himself broiled over a hot fire like a stuck pig by them niggers."

Damn! Red niggers always spoiling a lonely man's getaway plans.

And so he slid back to his animals, coaxed them into moving with him through the trees near the top of the hills. He tied the pony's long rawhide rope to his belt, and took up the slack with his left hand. The rifle was ready in his right. He laid the robe back on the pack-animal's back so that the two other rifles would be handy enough if the situation arose, and struck out on foot. Funny to think of that now. McAfferty's rifle, the one the old Whitehead had discarded when the frizzen spring had broken—mainspring, too. Bass had repaired it back in the Crow camp during those long, peaceful days of mending his body. Of healing his soul—with her.

Now he'd done it. He had allowed himself to do it once more. Allowed himself to draw up the festering pain within his being.

It had been hard to push the remembering away for most of that day. But his mind kept working on two things. Keeping his soul alive with all the torment her memory forced upon him, and keeping his eyes and ears alive for Blackfeet. From up here along the top of the hills he finally saw the river's course as it wound its way down to the Jefferson. Would not be long now—few more hours at most, and he could head west again. But then his gaze caught the movement.

Something like black forms, almost indistinct, but visible enough to be seen moving across the patches of white to the south. Headed his way. Bass cursed again. Country was crawling with 'em. Coming back to camp with meat, he thought. Most likely. If he continued south, he'd run right into 'em. And if he stayed put, chances were that they'd end up pushing him back north into the village.

He'd have to strike out west from here. Couldn't take the chance of waiting for them to pass by him. Couldn't take that chance and hope that he could reach the river running out of that big hole of a valley. He'd had to move west from here, cross the Jefferson and strike out on his own trail.

He'd just have to head up into that rougher, higher country now. On his own. No river to work its way for him. Them Blackfoot would stay below with the easier footing, less snow, the warmer chinook winds. And he'd head back to the tough country, the high lonesome where only his kind could survive.

Scratch forded the river, finally locating a place where the animals could cross with some sure footing. He scrambled up the wide, soft bank and into the trees once more. Rarely looking behind him or to the left, he kept wondering what to do about the trail he'd made. Surely they'd run onto it, see it headed west, and wonder who had made the tracks. But he was getting too weary to think of any way to hide all the ponies' prints now in the snow and on what bare ground had been blown free of the white powder.

"Maybe you're just barking at a knot," he whispered to himself. "Still tryin' to do the impossible."

So, he pushed himself up the hill into the thick timber once more and then dismounted. He tied the animals off and moved back down the hill some hundred yards, dragging the coat he had taken from his back behind him. At places where the snow grew crusty, he had to beat his footprints with the coat to obliterate the tracks in some futile way.

"That's it, child," he murmured to himself. "Gotta blind this trail much as you can."

And finally he found the boulders wedged between the trees. Here he would make his stand. If them niggers find the trail, they'll come up the hill following the ponies. Then, he'd be behind them. If he was lucky enough, they'd take the horses and the rest of his plunder and would not find him. Things had gone bad enough this day. Could he count on luck? What if they did find the animals?

He remembered something he had told Josiah when his young partner was still new to the mountains.

"Horse critters that get to know the smell of whitemen don't like the smell of Injuns. Them red niggers smell differ'nt than we, you see."

Oh, Hannah. Why you, too? Why were you taken from me too? He felt the sob catch low in his throat.

"Hannah's better'n horse for smellin' somethin' that ain't right. Mules better'n horse for smellin' for that count. They hates the smell of Injuns more'n any horse I knows of."

Hell! Them Blackfoot find the animals. He'd be afoot then. Have to cross on over on his own hook. Had to have a robe, at least. Maybe them old snowshoes that belonged to Glass—Rose, maybe. One of 'em, anyways. Titus set the two rifles against the rocks and cradled his own into his left arm before moving quickly back up the hill to the ponies. There he untied the snowshoes and the thickest robe he had, and dropped them to the snow. He separated the ponies and took the first on up to the top of the hill where he tied it off. He returned panting to take the second around the brow of the hill where it was tied. Again and again he returned, moving each animal to its solitary refuge in the trees, trying to cover the tracks as best he could in those long, anxious, frantic moments left before the hunting party would run onto his trail beside the river below.

Finally the animals were all separated and he returned to the robe and snowshoes. Quickly, in the growing cold, Bass untied the stiff rawhide thong and unfurled the robe. Gathering up the snowshoes, he tucked them under the right arm that held the rifle. Scratch dragged the robe behind him, scattering the snow and covering most of his tracks before he crawled back into his private rock fortress. Made a fella feel a little better—maybe even right pert—what with having him some plunder and truck along if he did have to hoof it on foot over the mountains. He sighed, then took in a deep breath to let it out slowly again. He was beginning to breathe more normally now. The exertion had cost him a lot of strength there for a while, but the tingle of danger gave his muscles a renewed spring-like coil, making them ready for the Blackfeet.

"Though a host shall encamp against me, my heart shall not fear." Again came the voice of the Whitehair, again his specter welling up from within his own soul. *"And now shall mine head be lifted above mine enemies round about me. Deliver me not over unto the will of mine enemies."*

"I'm gonna do ever'thin' I can," Bass whispered to himself, "ever'thin' I can to be sure I ain't handed over to them niggers."

Looked to be there was a dozen of 'em, maybe some fifteen now. Each led at least one other pony laden with game. Some pulled along a couple of horses with the meat strapped to pack frames on their backs. He smiled a little—it had been a good hunt for them niggers. The minutes crawled by as he watched them moving down the east bank of the Jefferson until they reached his trail and stopped.

One of the Indians dropped to the ground to study the prints Bass had carelessly left behind. Then another came up to join the first. They knelt over the tracks and one pointed down to the river. He could see the shadowy figures leave the others and hop through the snow down the bank to the water's edge. There they seemed to study the other side of the river and the hillside leading up into the trees—up toward his refuge. One of the men turned and seemed to be talking with another who remained on his pony. The one on the ground waved his arms, gesturing toward the hill across the river.

Their arguing voices carried up the hill on the frigid, gentle breezes.

He could not catch all that was being said. Hell, he didn't know Blackfoot anyway. But what he did hear was the tone of the voices. The one by the river must be young and anxious to count coup. The leader of the hunting party who remained on his pony now gestured with his arm to tell the other warrior to get on his pony. The man by the river stood for what seemed like a long time before he finally began to climb the bank where he mounted his pony once again. While the rest of the hunting party again set out on their trail back to the village, the one lone warrior kept his pony's nose pointed south.

Another warrior dropped out to come alongside the rebel. They talked with each other, then moved their animals into the trees on the east bank. There they tied the pack animals off in the cover and emerged again to drop down to the water. The two warriors crossed the river and splashed up the west bank, heading along the trail Scratch's animals had made as they zigzagged up the hill toward the trees. His heart began to race, pounding the adrenaline through his veins, pulsing with a force that roared at his temples. It had been many moons since last he had been in battle—if you did not count hunting down a whiteman. Many moons, it had been, since last it had come down to his life, or a red nigger's.

"*Surely thou wilt slay the wicked, O God: depart from me therefore, ye bloody men.*" McAfferty's voice rang with an eerie echo in his mind.

"You gonna stay with me for this'un, huh, Asa?" Bass whispered to the ghostly specter. "Always knew you didn't run from a good fight."

Just as quickly his mind shot back to that winter day when they began the hunt for the Whitchair, when Bass and Josiah believed they were going to be killed by the Crow to avenge McAfferty's murder of Rotten Belly's wife. Scratch recalled turning to look at his young partner.

"*Was you to go under—had hoped it'd be . . . some other way'n this. Man's hands tied from him—ain't able to do nothin' 'bout it. Ain't no way for a man to die.*"

Suddenly Josiah's response pushed through his soul: "*Ain't 'nother man I'd choose to be dyin' 'longside, Scratch. Ain't 'nother one 'cept Titus Bass.*"

"Shit!" The old trapper scanned the weapons laid out before him. "At best—dyin' be a one-man job."

Bass quickly checked the powder on the three rifles. He pulled both pistols from the belt around his elk-hide coat and set them on a flat spot of the rocks in front of him. Should he take the chance of firing? The rest of the hunting party was slowly disappearing from view now as the two coup-hungry warriors continued up the hill. Surely that hunting party would hear the shots if he just made quick work of the two brash youngsters. Could he chance it? Not use the guns at all and take on the two of them at once?

He had him some time to figure it out, to make himself ready, to plan out what he was going to do. Some time, yes. But not a lot of it. The two warriors continued up the hill toward the trees, following in the path he had taken his ponies. Both men kicked at their animals' ribs, spurring them up the snowy slope, the hooves of the horses issuing brilliant sprays of white that came cascading down behind them on the hill. Bass watched them, fascinated.

As they passed to his right, Scratch got a closer look at the two braves. Shit! The boys were young. Not youngsters, to be sure. Probably counted many a coup. Maybe even lifted hair off a whiteman or two. But, by now, lot of Indian warriors looked young to him. He'd just have to show them two bucks a little about fighting—Injun style. Then the two disappeared into the trees, heading toward the place where he'd first stopped the ponies.

Bass stuffed one of the pistols, his own, into the belt at his waist and slipped over the boulder to drop to the snow. His right hand went around the belt and found the first of two knives. He quickly unsheathed it, turning it once in his hand to find a comfortable position for the handle in the palm. The palm was sweating. For a brief moment he stopped his scooting when he reached a big pine. Beneath the old, faded-blue bandanna he was sweating. This ain't like me, now, he thought to himself. Getting all riled up over a couple of young bucks. Just gotta take 'em one at a time.

He glanced around the tree and heard the warriors. He could not see them yet. They seemed to be arguing with one another. Probably got up there and can't figure out what the hell's going on. He smiled to himself and moved out. The braves continued to argue and then he saw them. Their horses were prancing around and around in an ever-widening circle. Finally one of the warriors pointed toward the side of the hill, in the direction the disturbed snow led. Bass knew they'd eventually find the ponies. He'd only kidded himself thinking he could get away from this without a fight. No sense in playing the joke on yourself. You're the one what's got the most to lose here, nigger.

The second warrior took off slowly into the trees, heading away from Scratch around the side of the hill. The first warrior, the one who had first argued with the hunting-party leader, continued to bow his head to look at the snow. He finally dropped to the ground and knelt to study for any sign of tracks within the tumbled, obscured spoor.

Bass slipped from tree to tree until he was within a few yards of the warrior. Suddenly the Indian raised his head, as if magically aware of the whiteman's presence. In a flash the Blackfoot glanced to his right to see if the second brave was close at hand, then back to where he had seen the whiteman. By now Bass had skirted uphill and slid to a stop behind a tree. Too close. Can't hide no more.

"*Pote Ani does not fear this thing, Arapooesh believes,*" the old chief had told him as the two whitemen were preparing to hunt down another whiteman. "*He knows there is no use in lingering in this life when one's time has gone. Why should a man linger, like the wildflower in spring holding on to hope of passing the heat of summer and the cold of the coming winter? Only the earth and the sky are everlasting. It is men that must die. Our old age is a curse. And death in battle is a blessing for those who have seen our many winters.*"

The warrior was too close now. Can't hide no more. Bass stepped out into the open.

"Ha'rs in the butter now, ol' coon," he muttered quietly.

The first warrior rushed toward him but came to a skidding stop in the snow when the whiteman moved out of the protective cover. The Indian saw that Bass carried no firearm in his hand so he brought his rifle up to his hip and pulled the trigger.

Titus wished he had been faster. He dove to his left down the hill. He heard the ball whistle by and thunk into a nearby pine. The warrior yelled out.

"*Nistoa nahtoya sacoay! Nahtoya ahghsee!*"

It wasn't so much to call back his friend as it was an exhortation to the spirits to protect him in battle. Bass didn't understand the words being yelled at him as the Indian rushed forward. But the meaning was clear enough. The boy wanted to raise some hair.

"Essummissa! Nistoa pehta! Cristoa kee pe tah kee!"

Bass snorted. "Fella looks to be mad as a bear with two cubs an' a sore tail!"

He rose to his hands and knees slow enough, then up on his wobbly legs a little more quickly. He glanced down at the pistol at his waist and saw that the muzzle was now packed with snow. Probably not worth a damn now, anyways, he thought. You gotta do this with your hands.

"For they shall soon be cut down like grass, and wither as the green herb."

"That's just what I'm figurin' on doin', Asa," Scratch muttered under his breath, "cuttin' him down some."

He flipped the knife around in his right hand, grabbing the blade, then quickly flung it with a side-arm motion. It sailed by the warrior, only grazing the Indian's left arm.

The Indian stopped momentarily to glance down at the wound, seeing that his own blood had been drawn, before continuing his headlong rush at the whiteman. Again he howled as if he were a bull in the rut.

"Now I got him in a real sod-pawin' fret," Bass said aloud. "Just wish he'd shut up an' let me die in peace."

He shifted the tomahawk in his left hand to the right just as the brave grabbed his rifle by the muzzle and swung it back and forth at the whiteman. Bass stumbled backward, dodging the lashing weapon. The young brave had a wild, crazed look in his eye now. He wore a silly smirk, as if thinking he was to make quick work of this whiteman. On he came and Bass tripped, but regained his balance in time to ward off the rifle by parrying it with the 'hawk.

Now the youthful smirk deepened into a sneer, a blood-lusting thing that painted the face wilder than any grease and earth paint could. Bass fell. "Deadfall, goddamnit!" He thought they'd be the last words he'd utter. He could hear the other Indian coming back through the trees, answering the first warrior's battle cry with one of his own. He threaded his pony through the trees toward the lone whiteman. The first warrior held the rifle muzzle in his left hand and began to pull the tomahawk from his belt. That was all the time Scratch needed.

In that brief instant the whiteman lunged toward his foe, plunging his head into the man's chest. As he collided with the Indian and felt the flesh give, he heard the sound gush from the warrior's lungs. Then he leaped on top of the young Indian.

They grappled for a moment until the brave finally dropped the rifle. The empty left hand now grabbed for the whiteman's head, the fingers digging into the blue bandanna and his hair. Bass felt the false topknot fall away as the fingernails scraped at his scalp. The powerful youngster pulled the whiteman off him.

Bass rolled, yanking the young warrior on over him so that the Indian fell beneath him once more. The Blackfoot tugged again at the bandanna and hair. Bass felt some of his hair rip free from the skin. He winced as the warrior's hand finally pulled loose from him. The Indian glanced at the bandanna and the long scalp-lock in his hand, then back at the whiteman in some disbelief. This man had already been scalped once. Bass felt the muscles in the Indian's right arm tense once more in an attempt to loosen the whiteman's grip on him. But the action came too late.

Already Scratch had his right arm arcing. The 'hawk smashed against the side of the warrior's head. The blade caught him at the temple and continued across the top of the left eye, burying itself in the man's skull as it slashed through the bone and drove on through the base of the brain. The body went rigid beneath him, then Bass felt the muscles go limp.

He was splattered with it. Blood and gore clung to his own face and his right arm was smeared with it. As if hypnotized with the adrenaline of battle, Scratch studied the tomahawk buried in the man's skull, watched the blood begin to ooze, then pour over the metal and wood. He tried to pull it loose from the wound.

It was locked. He yanked again, harder this time. The tomahawk would not pull free from the skull. Then came the sounds of the pony rushing at him and the cries of the second warrior. Bass looked up and saw the Blackfoot bearing down on him before he leapt to his feet. *Not gonna die on my knees, I ain't!*

He grabbed for the second knife and pulled it free of its scabbard as the warrior drew upon him. *Nigger's too close now to shoot me with his talking iron.*

"Cristecoom sah kits tah kee! Ah! Pah kaps shotta! Eehcooa pah kaps!"

And on came the Blackfoot in that long instant. This one, too, brandished his rifle as a war-club. Bass, with a sense of morbid anxiety, watched the frothing steam gush from the pony's flaring nostrils.

"Pohks a pote! Sah kee eneuh! Akeeha! Ohks kos moi nema, neetasta!"

They were upon him as he leapt aside, burying the knife in the only place he could reach to do damage. The Indian's leg. High on the leg where it joined the hip.

Bass felt the knife bite into the flesh, sinking quickly in that instant before the tip hit some resistance of bone and continued on into the left leg. The warrior screamed in pain. His pony danced stiff-legged to a halt near the body of the first Blackfoot. And the animal turned, its rider now quiet, as if resolved to the pain he must bear in the killing of this whiteman. He glanced down at his fallen friend, the one who had brought him to this place, then slowly raised his eyes to stare at the whiteman. Bass had no weapons now. He stood defenseless in the snow among the trees. Panting. Staring back at the big youth atop the pony.

"Now this nigger's pawin' 'round to get himself some trouble."

Then the warrior reached down and tugged at the knife buried in his leg. Scratch watched in awe as the Blackfoot yanked at the weapon's handle trying to extricate it from his hip. His body must be shut off from the pain, Bass realized as he stared at the young Indian. Again the brave yanked savagely but the knife would not budge from its hole in his upper leg. Suddenly the warrior raised his rifle toward the whiteman and pointed the muzzle directly at Bass.

"Blessed be the Lord my strength, which teacheth my hands to war, and my fingers to fight."

In that instant as the ghost's voice rang in his ears, Scratch crouched and began his dash. But it was not a run or leap to the side as before. This time he rushed directly toward the mounted warrior. Startled, totally surprised by his action, the Blackfoot jerked and pulled off his shot. Bass felt the bullet rip at the top of his shoulder. But on he careened across the final few yards of snow and blood and death to reach the pony and the warrior.

He grabbed furiously at the knife buried in the Indian's leg while the warrior frantically jerked at the 'hawk in his own belt. Bass pulled the Indian from the pony's back, the Blackfoot jolting down on top of him in the snow. The warrior sprang up, attempting to stand, but fell to his left on the weakened, useless leg. The 'hawk went spinning and skidded out of reach. Bass dove toward the tomahawk as quickly as the warrior's weight left his body. He scooped the weapon up into his right hand along with a fistful of snow and dove at the Blackfoot. He swung quickly, too quickly. The handle glanced off the side of the Indian's head.

Scratch brought the right arm back as the brave heaved him off with a powerful thrust of his muscular arms. The sweat stung his eyes and Bass was momentarily blinded, seeing through the fog that the warrior was crawling on his side toward the rifle. Titus lunged once more and this time the 'hawk found flesh in the shoulder where the neck began. He felt the skin give beneath the blade, heard the crunching resistance as the collarbone gave way.

He pulled the weapon free and plunged it down again into the same wound. A third time, and he felt the body shudder, then go limp. But still he struck, again and again, as the warrior's head slowly parted from the rest of the body. The gore splattered over him once more. His hand dripped with it. The 'hawk's handle was slippery with the warm, dark syrup of life. But still he continued to strike the body again and again in a slowing frenzy of butchery.

Finally his own left hand gripped his own right wrist. The weapon came to a stop. He sobbed, his own tongue stuttering something he could not himself recognize. Tears gushed and he coughed as pain suddenly seized his chest. It was often this way, he remembered. In the killing, there's still some pain for the victor. He fell to his side.

Bass lay there in the snow, feeling the icy crust warm beneath him until his skin began to turn numb. He didn't remember how long he had lain there, spread-eagled in the snow, between the two butchered, bloodied warriors.

Now his mind began to snap him back with the pain at the back of his head. The numbing cold burned into that part of the skull where he'd once been scalped. The first Blackfoot had pulled his replacement scalp loose along with the bandanna that usually held the old trophy in place on the back of his head. He rose to one arm, resting on the elbow. To his left the first warrior. To his right, the second. He got to his knees and wondered if the hunting party had been far enough away or had they heard the battle cries of the two warriors, heard the two smoothbores boom off the hillsides. In a way he didn't care anymore. But his body had its own will to live. Perhaps there was a spark still left within his core that could not be extinguished after all. A spark that drove him to his feet and forced him to walk on wobbly legs. He gathered up the first rifle and 'hawk. He yanked at the knife still buried in the second Blackfoot and discovered why it had refused to budge. It was buried deep into the hip joint.

Bass yanked at the dead Blackfoot's leg to work at the joint until he could tug the blade from the bone. He stuffed the bloodied weapon in the sheath at his belt without wiping the steel. Quickly he hobbled over to the first warrior and dropped the collected weapons in the snow. He gathered a second rifle, along with the first warrior's tomahawk. Then Bass placed his left sole on what was left of the Indian's face. He twisted the tomahawk handle down and away from himself with all his strength, slowly feeling the metal blade crunch against bone, then finally give way. The weapon was freed at last. He scooped the others up into his arms after taking the first Blackfoot's knife to replace the one he had lost. Then the whiteman staggered downhill to the refuge where he had left his own rifles. There, he dropped the Indian weapons into the rock shelter.

The old trapper took up his own rifle, checked the priming, and slid once more out of the rocks, heading around the brow of the hill to retrieve the ponies. One at a time he brought them together and hitched them to one another until he could finally lead them down to the rock refuge. He gazed down at his own hands and arms in the fading light. His buckskins were coated with blood, as if he had butchered an animal and dressed it out after a kill. Then he studied the river below him. The Jefferson.

He would not be able to follow it now. He would have to strike out due west into the high country. When these two warriors failed to appear in camp by morning, others would come looking for them. And when those who followed found the bodies, they would not be far behind him.

"Blown out their lamps, you have, ol' coon," he muttered. "Others be comin' soon to try an' cut your own wick short."

Now he wondered if he should have left the bodies without scalping them. At least take the time to bury them in the snow. No, he decided. It was best this way. Be some big medicine for those who come looking for the two warriors. Big medicine to mark this place.

Scratch recalled the memorial the Crow had erected at the site of the winter battle with the Blackfeet where McAfferty had brought the tribe down on the slumbering Sparrowhawks. There had been short tree branches stuck in the ground to form a circle of stakes some twenty to thirty feet in diameter.

"What's this here?" Josiah had asked.

"Medicine," Bass had answered.

His eyes had slowly pored over the crude circle of blood-stained branches. Tied to some of the stakes were skin pouches, to others dangling feathers, bounding in the breeze. A few of the crimsoned markers had been topped with locks of long black hair. One had held an old trade fusee, its stock broken, the barrel bent around a tree after heating in a fire.

"Medicine over a place they done battle," Scratch had uttered in an almost prayerful explanation.

"It say who they fought?" Josiah had inquired.

"Yep, it do, that. Blackfoots. See them burnt rings down the bottoms there—on the sticks—tells it be Blackfoots. The niggers the Crow got in a tussle with. You just don't go off an' leave a man without markin' where he's laid. Well, Crow don't go off an' leave a place they lost braves neither. Now that they marked the place where Crow blood was spilt on the ground."

Best this way. His way, after all. Leaving the bodies for the others to find. Like his own memorial. Not hiding the battle site at all. That was his medicine.

Maybe so. Let the wolves have the carcasses. If the rest of them Injuns do run me down, I'll die with these here scalps on my belt.

"Them niggers'll have their craws plumb full of sand an' fightin' tallow then." He shook his head with resignation at what he now faced alone.

"Thou has not shut me up into the hand of the enemy." The ghostly voice had a metallic, raspy ring to it now.

"They ain't got their paws on this child yet, Asa!" He spoke loudly enough that the volume of his voice surprised him.

The flesh on the trophies was beginning to harden at his waist where he had tucked the scalps in his belt. Likewise, the raw flesh at his shoulder had hardened and the blood had frozen, adding a stiffness to the movement of his left arm. After loading all the weapons and lashing them to the first pony behind his, he rose to the saddle at last. The two Indian mounts were tied along with the others in his pack string.

"Them Injun guns take extra patchin'." He was talking to the ponies. "Bigger bore, you see." As if they knew what he was talking about. But he smiled anyway, knowing the loads were down and seated in the smoothbores. He was ready and gently nudged the tired animals into motion.

Bass gazed back downhill, longingly, at the river—at the windswept sagebrush bottom land where the going would be so much easier. But his ponies did as he directed them. They took him up the hill, ever higher toward the peaks and the snowed-in passes. His body and mind yearned for the ease of fast travel down below as the river dropped farther and farther away behind him in the graying light.

But his heart led the way. The only way. And he wasn't sure if he was really running away from something now. Maybe . . . just maybe, he was finally running toward something.

Eight

It had been late fall by the time the three messengers had found Emile Sharpe and delivered their contract offer. A thick dusting of snow lay on the ground, and there was some color still in the trees along his path as he headed south and west toward the Assiniboin, the Minnetaree, and finally, the Mandan. There, the ones who cautiously called themselves his friends had told him what he needed for the job at hand. It was there along the upper Missouri that he had learned what he would need when the time came for him to kill this lone man.

When he finally made enough of the pieces fit, he turned due east and headed for the Red River of the North, then on to the beginnings of the Father of Waters. And turned south. The Missouri would have been a much shorter trip, perhaps an easier trip in winter. But easier and shorter was never something he had sought after. Too many posts along the muddy river. Too many people anyway. And someone might recognize him. Someone might realize why he was moving through the wilderness once more.

That was something he could not chance. Too much money riding on this contract. It would pay off to stay away from the muddy river, to stay far away from Bouis' Post, Primeau's House, Loiselle's Post and Fort aux Cedres. Vermilion and

Cabanne's Posts would know him too. Best the way he had come now. Just a few more days of running through the wet, frosty forests and he would be in St. Louis. Then he would send word to the rich man who had hired him. Early spring now, at last. And he had finally come, through the blistering blaze of winter and all those miles. But the days of cold and tortured travel would soon be worth it. Now he knew whom he was after. And why he alone had been called. The French in Canada had a word for his kind he could not remember. Only that the creature was considered half man, half wolf, a monster that always came out of the wilderness to strike.

Josiah heard the sounds of many feet scuffling across the snow outside. Suddenly the door flap opened and the bright, late-winter light burst into the lodge. An older Crow warrior he recognized hunched through the doorway and came around the fire-pit toward Paddock's bed. The whiteman watched another man behind the warrior pull the two lacing pins free below the doorway on the lodgeskin. Paddock was curious, and a little concerned.

The warrior spoke softly to Waits-by-the-Water. She pulled on her capote and ducked from the lodge. Now there was no one who could explain to him what was happening. Josiah rolled slightly and pushed himself up against a backrest. In this half-sitting position he could not stay long; his body had been telling him for the past week that he needed more movement, more activity. It was becoming angry with him at having to lie around the lodge all day, through the night.

Now two young warriors stooped to enter the lodge, one dragging behind him two slender poles with a dressed elk hide slung between them. The older warrior stood near Josiah's head, first speaking to the whiteman in Crow, then quietly directing the two others who approached the foot of Josiah's bed. The older Indian knelt down and pulled back the robes and blankets from Josiah.

"What the hell you doin'?" Paddock snapped, leaning forward to reach for the robes, the pain slowing him as he grew more anxious.

The older warrior continued to talk to him in soft tones, from time to time trying sign language to explain something to the young trapper.

"Don't know what . . . I don't know sign language, damnit!"

Josiah fell back against the backrest once more. "Don't know what's goin' on, neither," he grumbled. But he continued to watch the warrior who carried on his oneway Crow monologue.

The older redman pantomimed, showing Josiah that he needed to take off the trapper's clothing. First the shirt, then the imaginary leggings and breechclout. He moved his hands over his own body as if scrubbing the flesh. Again he knelt by Josiah and began removing the whiteman's leather shirt.

"Looks like you're gonna give me a bath, huh?" Josiah let his arms be raised and the sleeves be pulled from them. "S'pose that'll be all right. Yeah. Go 'head." The shirt slipped over his head and the cold midday air struck his bared flesh. Josiah shuddered.

The warrior knelt, began untying the strips that bound the leggings to Josiah's belt and pulled the leggings off. The whiteman's legs looked stark and milky against the rich darkness of the buffalo robes beneath him. Then the old Indian moved to untie the moccasins and slipped them from the young man's feet. Paddock wiggled his toes, glad to be free of the restraining footwear despite the freezing air.

Now the Indian moved toward Josiah's head and brushed the whiteman's bangs away from the forehead with his fingertips. Josiah was naked save for the breechclout, along with the bandages over his shoulder and at the side of his chest. With the quick hair-grooming completed, the older warrior rose and spoke softly again to the two younger men. They moved their pole-and-hide travois alongside the bed and laid it on the ground. One stood near Josiah's head, the other near the whiteman's feet. The older man chattered at him, then smiled and nodded.

"Guess you're gonna have to show me what you're doin' . . . what you want," Paddock replied.

The man nodded and shut up quickly. He stood beside the small travois and then lay down on the large elk hide that was strapped with rawhide to the poles. From his supine position, the old warrior turned his head to look over at the whiteman and grinned, as if to say there was nothing to fear. He got up and gestured for Paddock to slide onto the litter.

The younger trapper eased over, feeling the stiffness in his body, the cold in the air, the residual pain left high in his chest. Finally he swung his buttocks over the pole and rested on the elk hide. He lay back and let out a sigh of relief that the short journey was over. The warrior quickly drew a wool blanket, then another, over the whiteman and barked at the two young men.

They knelt and grabbed the two poles and carried Josiah out into the bright cold sun. Josiah squinted against the brilliance of the late-winter glare ricocheting off the white covering the ground. Then he recognized Rotten Belly's graying head at his side.

The young trapper studied the manner in which the buffalo robe was thrown over the Indian's left shoulder and under the right arm, the flaps held with the left hand to leave the right arm free for gesture. Then Paddock finally sorted it out. The old chief was decked out for some special occasion.

Josiah's gaze dropped from the Indian's eyes and ran past the smooth, whisker-plucked cheeks and chin to the bright, dangling ear ornaments. The rim of the ear had been punctured and brass wire passed through the openings. From the wire hung large pink shells and tarnished brass beads. The old Indian could tell him what was happening. Arapooesh would understand his uncertainty.

"Can you tell me what's goin' on?" Josiah inquired as he tugged to pull the two blankets more tightly about his neck.

The old chief placed a wrinkled hand on the young man's shoulder, smiling almost benevolently. "We take." He motioned with an arm across the camp.

"I know, I know," Josiah stammered. "What for . . . where?"

"We take," the chief repeated, his smile still apparent. "Lodge . . . our lodge . . ."

"I . . . I thought this was your lodge." Josiah felt suddenly stupid.

Arapooesh nodded. "Other lodge, we take you, Jo-Zee-Haw. Other lodge, now. You"—he pointed then to himself—"me . . . other lodge. Heal. Other lodge heal you. Heal me."

Paddock watched the old chieftain nod again, as if all had been explained. But he was still confused. Shaking his head in disgust, he remembered the old trapper's words.

"Ignernce is somethin' you don't know 'bout yet. Bein' dumb means a nigger forgot what he's found sign of."

Paddock grinned slightly. He wasn't dumb after all. He just didn't know what was going on. It was all right. He was going to be all right.

"Yeah," he muttered. "You're gonna heal me, is it." There

was an edge of quiet disbelief in his tone. "S'pose we're gonna have some fella sing over me an' shake his rattle, then I get up an' walk back here, huh?"

Rotten Belly motioned for the two young warriors to proceed and they moved out of a small knot of people who had gathered about Josiah and the chief. "Nothin' more to do than go along with it," Josiah murmured to himself as he swayed gently from side to side. The procession moved through the center of camp toward the trees by the river. "Nice day for a walk, fellas," he declared, looking first at one, then another, at all of the older warriors who moved alongside the litter. "Nice day, it is. Good one for some fresh air—sunshine, too."

He had to admit he was still nervous. His apprehension was stronger than the residue of anger and bitterness he felt for Bass for having abandoned him here. Still, he wished Scratch were here to explain things.

The movement stopped. Josiah cranked his head around so he could see where he was. The procession had drawn up at the edge of the lodges, and it looked as if the whole tribe had gathered to watch. The Arapooesh was at his side once more. "We heal. You . . . me. Now, Jo-Zee-Haw."

The bearers lowered the litter slowly to the ground. Paddock rolled over onto the healthy shoulder, feeling still the pull and pain at the other side of his chest. There were so many watching, so many come to see what he had yet to learn. Young ones, old ones, children. They formed two long lines that led away from the litter toward a small, willow dome. Now Arapooesh knelt beside the whiteman and pulled the blankets back. As they came off his body, the cold rushed at him once more, but Paddock was relieved to have the breechclout on in front of all these people, all these eyes, all these smiling faces.

"It's some joke, ain't it?" he muttered to himself as Rotten Belly rose again. "Gotta be, everybody smilin' like this."

The two younger warriors, strong men both, knelt beside the litter and raised Josiah to a sitting position. Then each placed one of Paddock's arms over his shoulder and brought the whiteman to his feet. The pain made him wince against the sudden movement. Arapooesh quickly motioned for them to be more careful.

"He is my son-to-be," Rotten Belly spoke in Crow to the two warriors. "You two take care of him as we enter the sun's dedication lodge."

The two nodded and eased Josiah slowly toward the small,

willow dome. Paddock looked to either side at the large crowd, and then at the willow structure as he drew nearer to it. The trio proceeded down the aisle of villagers until they arrived at the dome. They stopped momentarily at the edge of the structure while another, a very old man in a very old blanket coat, stepped through the willow framework to place a dressed elk hide on the snowy ground inside the structure. The two younger men slowly lowered Paddock onto the elk hide. A rolled buffalo robe was brought up so that the whiteman could lean back against it in a semi-reclining position.

More elk and buffalo robes were brought and spread across the snow by the older men in their woolen capotes, their bare legs evident beneath the bottom of the coats. As the robes were spread on either side of him around the circle formed by the structure, Paddock counted the twenty-four thick willow branches that had been shoved into the ground. Their tops had been bent over to form an arc before the other end of the limbs were lashed together at the top of the dome. Twenty-four limbs, each crossing the others at the apex of the medium-sized structure.

Paddock watched the older men who had laid their robes out on either side of his. They each dropped their capotes and quickly removed their moccasins. Beneath the coats none of the men wore any clothing. They moved naked in the cold winter air to seat themselves around the small circle of robes. Ten older, scarred, battle-honored warriors took their places around the empty hole in the middle of the structure. Some shuddered involuntarily at the cold, some gazed up at the sky as if in contemplation, and others watched Josiah with calming smiles washed across their faces.

Arapooesh came to stand at his side. He dropped to Josiah's left—naked like the other men. Swiftly, several young men began throwing blankets and buffalo robes over the domed limbs. Two others carried in rocks with forked sticks. Josiah watched the process for a few moments before the blankets were thrown over to block his vision. The rocks were brought in one at a time by the two warriors from a low, hot fire near the lodge. When all eight of the super-heated stones were in place in the pit at the center of the willow structure, the last blankets and robes were thrown over the lodge, completely shutting out all light.

He felt claustrophobia closing in about him as surely as the darkness had suddenly washed over the lodge. Paddock felt the old chief's wrinkled hand on his bare thigh, placed there to reassure the young whiteman. The edge of one of the blankets was pulled away and a cast-iron kettle with a dipper made from horn was shoved inside behind the bright shaft of light. Then the blanket was dropped again and it was pitch black inside once more.

Josiah felt Arapooesh pat his leg four times as he heard the kettle rustling to the right side of the lodge. He then felt the kettle being passed over him, on to Rotten Belly, then on to the warrior seated at the chief's left hand. It was quiet again, except for the heavy breathing in the blackened structure. Finally the chief began to speak in Crow, as if in explanation to the whiteman beside him. The quiet words were soothing, although Paddock did not understand them.

"The sweat-lodge is an offering to the sun, my young warrior," the chief began. "We do this for you, to offer to the sun— it is on your behalf, Jo-Zee-Haw." His hand searched in the darkness for the kettle nearby and he located the horn dipper. "The sweat-lodge is erected only for a very serious undertaking, only for the most important of purposes in Absaroka. For the Sparrowhawk people, this is a very solemn occasion—yet also a time of great joy, for I am taking a son. A new son . . . for one who has been killed in battle. Blood of my blood, he was. Now, this for you, Jo-Zee-Haw. This for the sun. The sweat-lodge, awu'sua, this for Father Sun."

Paddock heard the sound of the dipper in the water, the horn scraping across the lip of the kettle, then the hiss of steam as the water splashed on the super-heated rocks. Four times only did the hiss reach his ears, four times was the water in the dipper dripped on the rocks before the whiteman began to feel the growing heaviness of the air. The water-turned-to-steam made the air harder to breathe at first, and the atmosphere, closed-in, black as the bottom of a cooking kettle, began to warm with the heat of both the rocks and the rising clouds of new steam.

It was a warming relief at first, but soon the atmosphere began to turn unbearable. He itched to breathe fresh air once more. He yearned for the light outside. He wanted to be out to stretch his limbs, limbs that ached from many, many weeks of inactivity. Then it was Rotten Belly who began to speak again.

"Greetings! Small Sweat-Lodge!" he began in praise. "We are making this for you, Father Sun!" It was the first prayer of the ceremony, spoken in reverence, uttered in new joy and celebration.

"Mountains of renown, our place of glory here on the Earth-Mother. All places of Absaroka, the Sparrowhawk people. The true people. Big Rivers and Small Rivers—smoke. Beings all about us—smoke. You Beings Above—smoke. Beings in the Ground—smoke. Earth—smoke. Willows about us now, willow of the pipe—smoke."

Suddenly Paddock heard the voice beyond the structure, the one high voice of a woman who took up singing the repeated strains of a song. Slowly her voice was joined by many rattles and the thumping of small, hand-held drums. The voice rang clear, as clear as the air must be outside, he thought. How he yearned to have this over with and be back in the fresh air.

"When the leaves appear," Rotten Belly spoke again, addressing the seasons this time, "when the leaves are full grown, when the leaves turn yellow, when the leaves fall—year after year, I want to keep on seeing these times."

Others in the lodge grunted their approval of this fundamental hope of all men. "For this, I offer smoke," Arapooesh continued.

"Greetings, Fat! Wherever I go, I want to chance upon something fat!"

Again the men in the small structure offered their approval. Josiah felt his head beginning to grow lighter in the heavy atmosphere.

"Charcoal! Wherever I go, may I blacken my face in victory celebration. Return safely from taking ponies. Return safely from taking the scalps of my enemies. Safely I want to return to you!"

There were some quiet shouts from the older warriors around the lodge. Their approval was strong at the words of the old chief.

"You, Winds of the Four Directions—smoke," Arapooesh offered. "Wherever I go, I want the Wind to come toward me. Wind, do not send me there on my own account. It is you who brings the Father to me, you who brings the words of the Grandfather to my ears—and to my heart!"

Paddock was pouring sweat now. The rivulets of it were running from every pore in his body. Outside, the singing had been joined by others, answered by the chorus of joy from those within the lodge. Then suddenly several of the blankets were pulled back and the bright light burst into the humid shelter. With relief, Paddock sucked at the fresh air, as a new-born infant, hungry for nourishment, sucks at the teat of life. He watched the steam clouds circle, waver at first, then rush from the top of the willow branches that were now bared of robes and blankets. He could see that the village people outside had formed a large circle around the sweat-lodge, many holding rattles they shook, others beating on small drums, and still others waving fans of eagle-feathers.

"Sun, we are doing this for you!" Arapooesh cried out loudly. Outside the lodge, the voices of hundreds of the villagers rose as one in an answering refrain.

"This for you!" they cried out.

"Sun!" the old chief began again. "May we live until next winter-time!"

Again the village people shouted, their voices thundering in the midday winter air. "May we live until then!"

Suddenly the light began to disappear once more, and with the brilliance of the sun, also vanished Paddock's hope that the ceremony was complete. Finally the lodge was darkened again. Now another voice to Josiah's left was offered in prayer, then the voice of another to that man's left and finally a third as the offering of celebration went to the sun and the winds, both of which brought life and a change of seasons to the land. During the three prayers and into the fourth man's offering, the old chief sprinkled seven more spoons of water over the heated rocks. Josiah could again hear the hissing of the steam and feel the air about him growing heavy. Then all was quiet, as if the Indian men in the lodge were deep in their own silent meditation.

He heard Rotten Belly grinding something to his left. Then Josiah felt the hands, the open palms offered below his nose. From the old Indian's hands came the sweet fragrance of sage. The blankets were removed a second time. Paddock looked down at the old wrinkled palms that held crushed sage leaves. Their smell was a relief from the fierce steam that robbed the young trapper of his breath.

Josiah adjusted his eyes to the darkness and looked up into the chief's face and saw dimly that his eyes were merry, smiling. Arapooesh nodded toward the sage. He finally brought the palms beneath his own nose to show the whiteman what to do. He lifted his open palms to his face as if drinking handfuls of water. The old Indian sucked deeply at the fragrant aroma of the crushed leaves. Then Paddock nodded in understanding. The chief tossed the leaves onto the hot stones and took up another sprig of sage. This he stripped into Josiah's open palms, laying the bared sage twigs on the rocks to burn. Paddock rolled his palms together to free the aroma of the fresh leaves. Outside, the shouts of joy and celebration continued, backed up with the songs of the old women, the rhythm of both rattles and drums.

There came the sound of the dipper scraping against the kettle again, and now the hiss of steam reached his ears. Each of the ten times the water hit the rocks, Josiah stuck his face down into his wet, dripping palms to allow his nose to suck at the aroma of the sage leaves. His head was pouring with sweat; he was perspiring as he had never done before. Everything was wet but he was beginning to pass the miserable stage. Every pore had opened up. He felt the outpouring from his body, like a flushing of evil and illness from his flesh, if not from his soul. Again and again, as the ten dippers of water were poured over the rocks, Paddock sucked at the fresh aroma in his hands, savoring it to combat the stifling wetness in the blackened structure. Then the muscles of his body began to let go of him, began to release their grip of painful tightness.

He heard the others in the lodge repeatedly hitting something and remembered the buffalo-tail switches, the kind the old men often used to chase away flies in the summer. Suddenly he felt Arapooesh swatting him softly, all over his body, his arms and belly, his legs and his feet. Every part of him felt the snap and drag, snap and drag of the buffalo tail as it stimulated the flesh to perspire all the more. Even in the dark, the old chief knew where the wounds were and avoided them. Still he worked at the chest and the shoulder, his blows with the buffalo tail growing stronger as Josiah sucked at the sage leaves and found his soul loosened, his pain diminishing.

Finally the blankets were pulled off the willow limbs again and fresh air burst into the dank structure. The brilliance of the sunlight streaming into the lodge dazzled him. He was fading, his consciousness diminishing with the heat, the oppressive humidity, the power of the darkness that had washed over him. Paddock felt himself loosening from his body, as if his being were separating from the flesh. That newly freed being now realized the pain he had suffered, and continued to suffer, only served to remind him that growth comes not from avoidance of the pain, but from the recognition of it and the experience of moving past the torture to the joy and relief beyond. The songs and chants all about him rang within his ears, but dulled now by the voice of his own soul speaking to him.

The blankets were brought over the willow framework a last time and with it some muting of the sounds outside. Now the water hissed again on the hot stones, as he began involuntarily to count the times the drops splashed across the rocks. Surely if there were ten dippers last time, there would be only twenty this time, Paddock reasoned, sucking at the sweet aroma in his hands. But on past the count of twenty the water was poured over the stones. Soon Paddock lost count as his head swam, as the steaming heat became unbearable.

He considered reaching behind him around the wet buffalo robe and drenched elk hide to raise the edge of the blankets for some fresh air. He thought his stomach would heave, and he wondered where he should throw up. But Josiah choked down the feeling. A numbness overtook him then and the lightness in his head began to descend: working its way down his shoulders into his torso where the pain released its fiery grip from his wounds. Down and down, the light feeling washed over him, past his hips, which seemed stiff no more, into his legs and feet, which eventually loosened their resistance to movement. For the first time since that freezing morning on that snowy hillside many weeks ago, Josiah felt as if he were going to pull through.

And the darkness was an enemy no longer. He accepted its place into his soul for he realized that only in the darkness, where everything else was shut off from him, could he search deeply enough into himself to reach for and grasp onto that private power that would heal him. The healing would come from no other place, he realized. Only from within. That was the message of the darkness. It drove everything else away and forced a man to look within once more to his own wellspring.

His dripping head bowed once more over his palms as he sucked at the soaked, crumbled leaves. He heard the other, older men muttering to themselves. In prayer, he thought. Yes, I am thankful that I am here. For this, I can give thanks. You have shown me. Yes! You have led me to the dark tunnel to show me that I am truly the only one to lead myself out. Me! I will be strong once more!

The selfishness poured from him with every drop of perspiration that rushed out of his pores. A shaft of light burst quickly into the blackness as a blanket was removed from the structure's roof opposite Josiah. It was planned that the first light to break into the dark sweat-lodge's spell would fall on the young whiteman. No more than the one small shaft of radiance.

Then Arapooesh reached for Paddock's breechclout. The young trapper looked down as if in a daze as the old chief lifted the front flap and worked his fingers at the buckle. The belt was pulled away and then the breechclout slowly pulled from beneath Paddock. Dampness, water was everywhere. The elk robe he sat upon seemed drenched, but he was not uncomfortable.

Another blanket was pulled back now and more light streamed into the lodge. Outside, the singing and instruments had stopped. Only the breathing of the old men around him. Only their rhythms and that of the earth songs greeted his ears now. The old chief had something in his hands which he showed to Josiah, motioning to the young man to recline even more against the bulky buffalo-robe backrest. Paddock slid down until he was almost fully stretched out.

Rotten Belly took the pulverized wild-carrot root that had been soaking in water away from the young trapper's face and began to wash the whiteman's body. The Indian lifted an arm to scrub the flesh with the softened root, then laid the arm gently on the robe once more. Over all his flesh the root was rubbed, stimulating, tingling the skin. With help Rotten Belly rolled Josiah over. As the chief rubbed the root over his back, Paddock realized the relaxation his soul felt. His body responded only to what others did for him now, in preparation for what his soul would be called upon to do. These Sparrowhawks had shown him how to heal himself. And he would go on from here.

More blankets and robes were removed now, until the frame was bare. The steam had vanished and only the cold, midwinter air ran its fingers over his skin. He was naked before these people, but it did not matter. He was part of them. As much a part of these people as he could ever be. There was no embarrassment as the two young warriors stepped within the willow framework to lift him slowly from his elk-hide bed.

Paddock was surprised to see that no one stared at his genitals. As he looked about him at the hundreds of spectators, they all seemed to be looking only at his eyes. And those eyes smiled back at him. The other men in the sweat-lodge rose slowly and there were others who brought them large kettles of snow. The older warriors stepped off of their robes and knelt to stuff their hands into the kettles of snow. Handfuls of the white powder were brought out of the kettles and used to scrub at their bodies. The men began to move more quickly now as they scrubbed and rubbed at their skin with the freezing snow. Then Paddock was helped outside the network of willow limbs.

Two older women began to scrub him down with snow as he stood between the two warriors, supported on their shoulders. All over his body he felt the rush of sensation to his flesh, the tingling of cold, the numbing realization of newness scrubbed over his flesh almost as if that flesh had never felt anything before. As if being born. The cold was there, to be sure, he thought. But—it was not cold.

As soon as the others had completed their snow baths, they were brought their capotes. Finally Josiah felt the sleeves of his coat slipped over his arms and a sash tied to close the front of the woolen garment.

The two braves began to kneel with Josiah between them. Paddock felt them both drop away beneath his shoulders as he remained standing. He looked down as the two young men turned to gaze up at him. They started to support him, but stopped and backed away. Then he realized he was standing on his own. One of the Indians motioned for Paddock to lie down on the litter. Josiah looked down at the elk-hide stretcher for a long moment, then lifted his gaze to read into the young warrior's eyes.

Josiah slid a foot forward and stood still. He transferred the weight to that leg and brought the second foot forward. Slowly at first, agonizingly, he began to walk. He stepped off the litter and onto the snow before he stopped in front of the two young braves. Then Arapooesh was beside him.

"Hear me, O Sun!" the chief shouted to the blue heavens above. "I want him to be an old man. All you Above—let him live to be an old man! This is my prayer—for him who is my son! Awu'xtpe! Sun Runner!"

The old chief held out a decorated otter-skin bag, each of the four legs bound with beads and quillwork, brain-tanned streamers and red trade-cloth. Red-bound eagle feathers hung from the lips of the otter skin. Josiah finally realized he was supposed to take it. It was his. A gift from the chief.

"My son," Rotten Belly finally spoke, moving the otter-skin medicine pouch closer to the young whiteman.

Josiah was finally clear on it. He had been adopted by this old man. He was now a Sparrowhawk like Scratch. They had brought him here to adopt him, to heal him, to mend his soul. Then Arapooesh spoke in Crow once again.

"My people," he began. "This is my son. Our Grandfather approves. He makes him to walk again." There was a loud chorus of shouts before the old chief continued.

"Our father, the sun, approves—for there is no trembling in my son's step." He held aloft Josiah's hand that gripped the otter-skin bag. "He joins my society, my own—as one of my own. The Otter Society is richer for his presence." There were more cheers from the tight, crowding throng of celebrants as Rotten Belly turned slightly so that he could stand beside the young whiteman. "We go to our lodge now. No longer will I have another home. This one, my son, will stay with his father. He will go away like my brother, *Pote Ani*—but will return again to his people. He will return, yes—for his heart is here in Absaroka. Here it will stay. In my lodge, at the heart of the Sparrowhawk people, my son and I will live out our days. This is good, Grandfather!"

The cheers thundered in his ears. Paddock felt the old chief tug at his arm, and began to step forward. It was new, this walking once more after so many weeks. But there was a release of so much pain. His chest no longer heavy. His muscles and tissue no longer painful. And his soul had found its own release. He felt lighter with each step toward the old lodge. His new father, to replace the one he had never known, was at his side now. No one helping him. What he had found was the strength within himself to move past the pain. Through the tunnel of darkness that these people had presented to him, Paddock had moved toward the light. The happiness that came with that realization flooded over him just as the cold had, the cold so long ago on that hillside so far away now. That hillside that had ripped so much from his being, but only to prepare him for this renewal.

He was thankful for that ripping, tearing, shattering lead ball that had collided with his body so long ago. He was thankful for the darkness it had brought to his soul. He was thankful for the message of rebirth the Sparrowhawks had brought to him. And he was grateful once more for what Titus Bass had meant to his life.

* * *

Hours ago, he was not sure just how many, he had begun his long, all-night ride. He was rolling his own hoop now—alone and in a fine fix. Bass had to put some more country between him and those who would be coming after him, as soon as they discovered the two warriors had not returned to camp. When they went out looking for the two warriors and discovered the bodies, they'd be after him like bees after a bear that had raided the honey tree. So he climbed and dropped, climbed and dropped, ever moving upward toward the higher peaks that would lead him over and out of this part of the country. Blackfoot country.

Bass finally stopped sometime while the fat sliver of a moon was high. He went back to one of the pack animals and scrounged until he found the pieces of rawhide. He knew their hooves had to be hurting. So he finally allowed himself the time to stop and do something for the ponies.

"Man's gotta take as good care of his animals as he does himself," he had once told his young partner. You're right on that track, ol' coon, he told himself. Being afoot could spell the end for most men out here.

Beneath the pale winter moonlight he fashioned some rawhide boots for each of the animals. Crow always did it, he thought to himself. One hoof at a time was encircled in the section of rawhide, the corners of the square brought up, quickly trimmed with one of the Blackfoot knives he had taken, then tied off around the lower leg of the animal. The whole process did not actually take that long although he felt the pressure of time upon him. Even so, Bass enjoyed the brief movement the labor required of him. It was a chance to move the cold muscles that had grown stiff from being too long in the saddle. Lumbering back and forth around his animals got the blood pumping again, warming him now as the winter night found itself more than halfway through its long journey.

So he climbed back atop the pony and pulled the others into motion. They drifted out of the high meadow and into the edge of the trees once more where the skimpy light still shone brightly against the white backdrop, broken only by the dark soaring silhouettes of the forest trees. Yes, he was glad he had taken time for the animals—and himself, back there. The old snow, with its daily warmed, nightly frozen crust, had been scraping at the ponies' forelegs with each step. And with each step he had felt the animal beneath him beginning to hesitate in lifting a hoof and putting it back down to make a new hole in the crust. But now the pony was moving more quickly. He turned in the saddle and looked back at the animals trailing behind them. He had looped sections of the old rawhide rope from one pack to the neck of the animal behind it, then a section from that animal's pack to the pony behind it.

It was working. He was gaining again. Almost as quickly as he knew he had to, almost as quickly as he wanted to. Scratch looked behind him. The animals plodded obediently in their own bobbing rhythms. Behind them fell away the stands of pine that shone darkly, almost ominously against the pale background of the old snow. He was moving. Soon—maybe three, maybeso four days—he'd be out of this part of the country where he could once again drop to the rivers and the easier going. For now he'd just have to tough it out and push on through.

Hell—he'd been in tougher scrapes, he told himself. This ain't nothing to a child like me. He was cold—hungry too. A man could find it pretty damned easy to be feeling sorry for himself in such a fix. Could be without any fixings at all. What did he have to bawl about anyway? He had him all the fixings he needed right back there on those animals. Yep, he consoled himself. Things could be a lot worse. He could have been forced to cross over on foot, carrying a solitary robe and maybe a rifle or two. Maybe with the snowshoes. Maybe not. He'd done that before. Plenty times. When he was younger. And he'd made it then. What troubled him was the fear that he might not make it through such an ordeal now. Growing old.

His mind flashed back to Josiah. The boy. Hell, now, nigger. Paddock ain't a boy. He'd been growing into some fine man, yessir. And Bass was proud he'd had him a part in that growing process. Teaching. Showing. Helping. Keeping him alive, yes. Then damnit! The thought gripped him just as surely as the hot coal rose in his throat and forced tears of pain to cloud the corners of his eyes. Damnit! Why'd the boy have to go and take her from him? Why'd she have to go and fall for Josiah? He sniffled, fighting the flow of pain through his frame.

"For the lips of a strange woman drop as an honeycomb, and her mouth is smoother than oil; but her end is bitter as wormwood, sharp as a two-edged sword."

"Goddamnit!" he burst out and the words startled him. "Damnit, Asa!" He spoke more softly to the ghostly specter this time. "Why cain't you just leave me be with my mis'ry, with this load I'm carryin'?"

The scent of her came back to him on this late-winter night with no other smells to greet his nostrils. The remembrance rushed at him with every cold-air breath. The warm, musky odor of her body as it had heated beneath his own each night they had slipped away for their private time together. His cold, numb fingers tingled as he recalled the slight moistening of her flesh as it had begun to warm beneath his caress. The smell of her readiness rose to his nostrils now. She had been the best he had ever had. And, now, the lonely trapper had to fight to keep her a memory—a memory that he could not, would not allow to become something bitter from the past. He would fight to keep that bright part of her within him. Painful, yes. But he had lived with pain for so long. What was a little more to him? It only proved that he was still alive; proved that he had not been frozen here in the saddle during this long-night winter ride. Yes. It helped Bass prove to himself that he was still alive enough to hurt.

It must have been hours since he had begun thinking on them. Josiah. And her. Waits-by-the-Water. A long time had he been riding with the memories of them to force a warmth down into his center, to keep him warm with a flicker of life-giving pain at his core. The steady motion of the pony beneath him in its tired plodding had hypnotized him in a way, sending his thoughts into other regions. But now the animals had slowed on him and he finally recognized that they were stumbling to a halt.

Titus glanced back at the animals. They were all dragging their hooves through the deep snow. Then he looked down at his own pony's legs. There beneath the hooves the snow was balling up. The rawhide boots were causing the snow to bunch and roll and gather beneath each hoof, not allowing the hoof to glide over it as it would with fresh, winter snow. This late-winter stuff was softer, mushier, wetter beneath the hard crust. He had wanted to protect their forelegs from the icy crust. But once the animals broke through the crust with each step, the soft snow beneath each hoof bound itself around and under the rawhide boots. He pulled on the rein, then dropped to the ground.

Time for him to move around, too. He laid his rifle against a young pine that poked its head up through the deep snow. Then he beat his arms around his chest to start his blood pumping and warm his limbs. He stomped his feet, breaking through the crust. But eventually the legs began to feel warmer from the pure motion given them. And the feet. They felt heavy. But they were warm within the cocoon of the three pairs of winter moccasins. The innermost was cut for a snug fit; the ones he always wore. Over that pair he had slipped another pair made by a Crow woman from a deerhide tanned with the hair on, to turn the cold. Finally, Scratch's outside pair was made of the tough waterproofed buffalo's hump hide to turn the wet. It was a little clumsy, but warm.

It took him some time to get the work done on the ponies. He pulled his hands from his mittens into the shockingly cold air. He'd thought his hands were getting cold in the blanket mittens, but now they were blocks of ice. The suddenly protesting fingers had been warm in their woolen cocoons. But eventually they responded to untie the thongs securing the rawhide boots. One at a time, he re-wrapped the rawhide around the lower leg to form a sleeve to protect each leg against the flesh-gouging crust. Then with the thong re-tied, he brought his aching fingers to his mouth to be sucked on and warmed, or put beneath his armpits for warmth within the thick coat, or stuck down in his crotch where she had made him warmest of all. He pushed that thought away as quickly as he would push away something physical. The memory was something very tangible to him. He could feel the heft to it.

"To keep thee from the evil woman, from the flattery of the tongue of a strange woman. Lust not after beauty in thine heart, neither let her take thee with her eyelids."

"Both of you—you an' her—you won't let me be," he almost sobbed. Bass sniffled and rubbed his nose with a sleeve.

He could taste her, smell her, hear her voice in his ear as the moan began low, began deep in her being. It was real, this haunting he carried with him. The specter of what had been with her, of what she had made of him. The ghost of what could have been.

Soon enough he was finished and rose slowly on crackling knees that snapped out of their frozen, kneeling posture. He'd help the ponies. Only fitting. They were helping him move away. Bass gathered up the rifle and took up the long rein in his right mitten. He tugged and got the animals moving behind him. He stomped down with each step, forcing himself through the crust for them to follow. He pushed his body through the soft, mushy, clinging-wet snow that rose to his waist again and again with each plodding, exhausting step. Each new step seemed to take so long. His foot would break through the crust and the one leg would sink below him until his crotch finally banged to the surface of the icy crust. As he brought the trailing leg up from its captive hole, he would continue to sink more. Some of the icy crust forced its way past the long tail of his leather shirt, past the bottom of his woolen shirt, into the open gaps left between breechclout and leggings. He cursed the fact that the woolen longjohns had become so rotten, so rank, that he had finally thrown them into a fire last spring. He damned himself that he had not replaced them. But the shock of the icy crystals against his scrotum kept him awake for his own private ordeal. It kept his body moving. And the cold blasting against his groin helped to push away some of the tempting heat that tingled and rose there when he thought of her.

In the first graying light that told of the coming day, Bass ventured down off the ridges into the ravine where he hoped the going would be easier. He would have to rest awhile. The animals, too. Skirting the sides of these ridges on his way across the mountains—that had been the hardest path to choose. But, then—he'd always done things that way, it seemed. Found the hardest goddamned way of doing anything. Moving through the mountains. Killing a man. Finding someone to love him. Always the hardest way possible.

And now he was going to take it easier on himself. The new growing light gave the old snow a luster of day-old ash. Down across the gray he pulled and coaxed the ponies. Down through the stands of trees into the ravine where he would find the going easier, where he would find a place to rest for a few hours.

The snow down here resisted his efforts to break through it less than the icy, frozen stuff up there. Down here in the shadows where the low-riding winter sun could not reach, the surface of the snow could not be warmed each day and re-frozen each night. The powder here broke more easily. He moved better now. The snow was still deep but the crust no longer held the trailing leg prisoner, forcing him to sit and drag that leg forward for another muscle-wrenching step. He could plow through it, leaning forward to press his body's weight against the soft resistance. The ponies quickened their steps, they too sensing the new-found ease in this forced march of his down into the ravine.

The slope eased as he broke out of the trees into the more open country in the bottom. He stopped for a moment and calculated the path he would take. The long, wide bottom would lead him west by northwest if he was correct. He checked the sky at his back. The darkness was fading there. He needed to stay here along the side of the ravine, and not go all the way into the bottom where a stream might have cut a path. In the still air he thought he could even hear the gurgling of the water of that hidden stream down there, bouncing and bubbling across its bed beneath the ice and snow that gave it some respite during the long winter months up this high. He moved off again, his ears filled only with the efforts of his own breathing, the faint gurgling of the nearby waters and the whispered companionship of the early-morning breezes stirring the snow-laden branches. Suddenly the bottom slipped away from him.

"He sendeth the springs into the valleys, which run among the hills."

Bass shoved the rifle from the crook of his left arm, watching it slowly slide into the soft white. As he sank on through he released the rein and flung both arms out to his sides to try to stop or slow his descent through the snow. His feet broke through a thin crust of ice. The blast of freezing cold roared at his legs as they slipped into the water. Down, down he went, his head sinking beneath the surface of the snow until the buffalo-hide moccasins hit bottom and slipped. The rocks along the bottom of the stream tumbled against the soles of his moccasins. His legs flailed, trying to find a place where his feet could grab. His arms struggled frantically to regain his balance but on his body went, sending him down, ever down into the water. The old trapper finally plopped to the bottom of the stream.

The shock of the cold, frigid water numbed him for a few moments. He yanked his head back to look up toward the hole in the snow. The pale light struggling down into the ravine formed a darker, crude circle against the white walls imprisoning him. Slowly against the muscle-numbing, life-robbing cold of the water, he brought first one leg, then the other, beneath him and began to rise shakily. He was in water deep enough that it had soaked him up to the armpits.

At last he stood in the water that rose almost to his waist. Flailing wildly against the snow with his arms, Bass fought to climb out of the hole. It was agonizingly slow. His legs refused to answer his call to move. His arms had to do it all and they rebelled too. Finally the snow began to give way once more and he started to crawl out, beating the powder down before him with his arms before using them to pull himself forward a few inches. Then he beat the snow some more and pulled himself a little farther. At last his feet were out of the water and he lay on the bank, in deep powder, the water sluicing out of his buckskins and freezing.

He beat at the snow and inched himself forward and upward. Slowly rising until his head finally broke over the surface of the deep powder, Bass lay panting. Now with his muscles finally slowed, they began to shake. Slowly at first, his body began a low rolling shudder that grew into uncontrollable shaking. He had to move again. Goddamn! But the soaked elk-hide coat was heavy. Comes Running. The old woman.

"Never wanna get old like that," Josiah had commented, looking at the ancient Crow woman who had made the coat.

"She's lived many, many winters. Promise me, son, you'll shoot me when I get where I'm needin' help like that," Bass had almost begged his young partner. *"Promise me, boy. Pains my heart to see such a thing. Be painin' me to think of Titus Bass like that."*

Damned if he wasn't like that now. Feeling all the years, all the miles, all those cold winters etched upon his soul, etched so deeply they seemed to rob him of the last vestiges of strength he needed to pull through this.

A tree burial. Doing it up proper. The way he'd done for Asa. Proper. It showed respect for the one who had died. Help the dead one pass on the way to the Other-Side-Land. Last thing the living can do for the dead, that is. A proper tree burying.

No tree burying for him now. No one to bury him. No one to mourn his passing, save for the howls of the coyotes and wolves in the distance, as if singing his funeral song. He was a warrior, dying in a strange, foreign place, and dying alone. The greatest loneliness came from the fact that he was dying not of his own choosing. A proud warrior chose his place. He had to move. Now—against his own body and the will it exerted. He had to move again. Now, against the weariness of his mind and the part of it that told him it was time to give in. And now, against all of his heart and will—all except that solitary part at his core telling him there had to be more than this at the end, a meal for the wolves.

NO! He was not going to feed the wolves! No free meal on his old hide.

He struggled to pull the helpless legs beneath him through the soft powder, crawling, stumbling, crawling again until he could stand atop the snow once more. Half-crouched, his arms swaying at his sides as if in total, useless exhaustion, Bass slowly turned and saw the animals. They had not moved. Their heads were hung low in fatigue and they were oblivious to his temporary, premature burial. And they were on the other side of the creek now.

Scratch was not about to re-cross the snow that hid the rushing, freezing water. And he had to get out of the low, whispering wind that circled him, played with him, each gust robbing his shuddering, convulsing body of more warmth. He had to find some warmth. The trembling, stuttering lips tried to whistle. They were dry. His whole mouth was dry from the gasping, sucking, yearning-for-life breathing spent crawling out of the snow grave. The high, dry, moisture-robbing air gave his mouth no relief. He slowly looked down at his right arm and commanded it to move. But the useless log hanging from his shoulder refused.

Please, he began to beg of it. I need some snow. My mouth. Dry. Can't whistle. Can't talk. Please. Some snow. My mouth.

At last the fingers twitched within the mitten, then scraped against the snow. A small clump of the powder finally reached his lips where the arm quaked in front of his face. Most of the powder fell from the mitten, but his dry, swollen tongue managed to lick at some of the flakes. He let the leaden weight of his arm fall to his side again. He scraped at the surface again and again, each time bringing the shaking hand to his mouth to lick greedily at the wet flakes. The moisture gradually saturated the dry membranes inside his mouth.

He tried to call out to the animals. But he achieved only a guttural rasp. He tried to whistle. At first only a raw sound whispered through his lips. He licked at them with his snow-dampened tongue. Again he tried and this time emitted a low whistle. No response from the animals. He tried, louder this time, and his pony perked its ears and raised its head. Now he had its attention. Another whistle and the animal reluctantly began to step forward. The rest of the animals resisted, but soon followed. Slowly they tromped through the snow and down into the water, half-submerging themselves in the creek and the snow that buried the water. Then they clambered up the snow bank toward him and ground to a halt near the breathless, shuddering man.

His tired eyes half-closed, Bass scanned the broken snow for some sign of it. There was none. Another rifle gone. And with it the strength and will to search for it in the deep powder hiding the creek. His best. Damnit! It had made him many a meal to fill an empty belly. And kept what hair he still had firmly locked to his skull. *Ol' Make-'em-Come,* she was. The best he'd ever had.

The old trapper remembered how he had finally talked a shopowner out of the .54-caliber flintlock. It had not been the best Pennsylvanian he had put his hands on, but it had always done everything he asked it to do. It was a heavy Derringer with a slightly Roman-nosed stock, heavy flintlock with a flat, goosenecked hammer, and a cast brass patchbox with the top finial in the shape of an eagle's head.

The best he'd ever have. Such a loss, measured against all the other losses. An old friend. Like Hannah, the mule he had loved. Then his young partner and the woman Bass had finally allowed himself to love. So much lost. And now the old rifle that had become a part of him. But the cold numbed the desire to search for it. He gradually lifted his gaze to the top of the ridge. Soon the sun would climb high in the sky. But little light would reach him down here.

He would have to rest the animals now. He would have to rest himself. Try to stay alive. Keep from dying. Keep from freezing to death. Get out of the wind, he told himself harshly. The rumblings of real, genuine hunger began to paw at his belly. Been more than a day now, it has. And there was little of the pemmican left in his food pouch. No strength to hunt, even with one of the other rifles. And he could not start a fire. They'd be after him this new day. They'd be on his trail.

But a little sleep. Just to shut his eyes for a few minutes. Just to give them ponies a break, he convinced himself. Only for that, he believed.

Slowly Titus plowed toward the aspen up the slope. There he pulled each animal into a crude semi-circle around the spot he had chosen. They were cemented where he placed them, unmoving in their fatigue. They would nibble twigs eventually. He could not take the chance of a fire. The smoke rising in this thin, dry air would give him away. No fire to warm his freezing, soaked, icy skin. He was just going to have to make it out of this country the hard way.

Blackfeet. Niggers wanting his hair. Any whiteman's hair. His hair now. The little he had. No smoke in the high, thin air.

He wouldn't trade a fire for his hair just yet. Not yet, damnit! The core of him began to glow like an ember remaining in the midst of dead ashes. He would will himself to live.

Bass's trembling fingers fought the straps until the two robes finally broke loose and dropped to the ground. A pony snorted twin jets of steam in the cold, gray air. The trapper's soaked, ice-caked leathers and coat creaked and chafed at his raw, frozen skin. The hair around his mouth crackled as he tried to stutter and mumble some words of encouragement to the animals. Now he dragged the two robes into the center of the tiny circle he had made with the ponies and the trees, those boughs completing the make-shift shelter against the wind.

The ponies gave no response to his soothing, cooing, frozen ramblings. Their rumps brunted against the rustling breezes, their heads hung in exhaustion, they were too tired to paw for grass or nip at twigs and bark. The snow would soon make their muzzles too sore to root for something to chew on, their hooves too tender to paw at the frozen ground beneath the heavy white blanket.

Bass spastically pulled open the two buffalo robes and spread the two wool blankets out over them. Onto his makeshift bed he crawled, slowly bringing the blankets and robes around himself to form a cocoon-like tube of wet warmth against the cold, against the wind, against the world out there that had taken so much from him. Here was his refuge. If he was to fight the death that dogged him now, he would need his strength, Scratch told himself. Just to sleep for a while. Need it to fight back. To fight over the mountains. Put it behind. Go on.

"Prob'ly look as miserable as an ol' hog stroppin' himself up on a fence post," he muttered, gently trying to console himself.

He burrowed his head beneath the robes and blankets. The air around his face was beginning to warm now as his breathing gradually slowed and became more steady. Some sleep. The shuddering was not so violent any longer. His hands were warming within the icy mittens. His feet were miserable in the soaked, heavy buffalo-hide moccasins. All three pairs of moccasins soaked. Sleep.

Time had slipped on by him, stealing away each night as he slept. Another day stolen from him. Time he had wasted. And during the day while he knelt hunched and bent over the traps and the streams, it had crept up behind him to steal away from his grasp, slip through his fingers. The years might as well have been water one picked up in a bucket with the bottom rusted out. Right through the hands. Time gone now and never to hold again.

And he realized his eyes were closed at last. Some strength to fight back. Some sleep to fight back. As consciousness let go of him, Bass realized he was mumbling to himself. But it didn't matter any more. He had stopped shuddering.

Nine

The heavy iron gate clanked shut behind him as he sat atop his horse, measuring the weight of the night about him as one would heft something new and unaccustomed. When his second son had latched the gate and rode up beside him, the old man once again felt the strength in numbers. Rarely had he ventured at night beyond his walls into the city. His was a strange mixture of pride in family heritage, along with the gentle, musty arrogance of having a lineage in this city that dated back for generations. Yet this aloofness also caused him an unsettled fear of venturing into the growing, evolving city after the sun had disappeared.

These homes of the monied French were a combination of fortress and stately mansion. Most homes in St. Louis were small cabins that had been built during and after the colonial period, but the rich fur traders built their homes behind ten-foot walls, some of them two feet wide, with small portholes placed about every ten to twelve feet around the stone palisade. These walls most usually encompassed an entire city block, surrounding the main house, servants' quarters, a gazebo, barn and other smaller buildings.

Most of the houses were either square or nearly so, with the plastered, two-foot-thick log walls some fifteen feet high. This particular home was only one story but had a complement of both an attic and a basement. Atop the structure was the typically steep French hip-roof: a radical 52-degree pitch at the front and back, an almost vertical 72-degree pitch at the ends. The roof, which was formerly thatched, now lay under thick wooden shingles. Casement windows ran around the walls, each hung on swinging hinges. On three sides of the house stood a portico or *galerie* rising some five feet off the ground and some fourteen feet wide, supported by thick, whitewashed pillars on all three sides. On the back of the house this porch had been walled in so that the home now boasted two more rooms.

The old man nodded to the three other men with him, all younger than he, and together they rode across, then down, Fourth Street toward Walnut and the Auguste Chouteau home. The old man, his two sons, and a nephew—all leaving the familiar ground of their established part of the city. Past courtyards hidden securely behind the high whitewashed walls and immense iron gates they rode slowly, almost deliberately. Turning left on Walnut, the party moved past LaRue des Granges, now becoming known as Third Street, then turned left again on LaRue de l'Eglise, Second Street to most, Church Street to others. The riders stopped in front of the Green Tree Tavern, which lay in the shadow of the immense Catholic cathedral. The nephew dismounted and went inside, returned shaking his head. The group turned back down toward Elm.

Retracing some of their steps down Second Street, they turned on Elm to ride into the oldest, and most run-down part of the old city beside the muddy waters. Across First Street they pulled up their horses and dismounted in the muddy yard in front of the low-slung hovel. The three younger men gathered about the patriarch and decided that the eldest son would stay outside with the animals. That son unbuttoned his silk vest so that the two pistols stuck into the high waistband of his britches would be accessible to him. No chances were to be taken in this part of town. The reputation of this watering hole was not lost on the like of the monied French in St. Louis.

The graying old man placed a hand on his eldest son's shoulder for a moment, then turned toward the door of the Rocky Mountain House. A wobbling drunk just leaving stumbled into the doorway but hurriedly careened out of the way, surprised at the presence of the well-dressed, distinguished guest flanked by the two young men.

Just past the open doorway the trio stopped, allowing their eyes to become accustomed to the dim, smoky light. Their nostrils were assailed with the combined odors of stale smoke, fresh urine, and the dankness of unattended vomit in the room. The patriarch removed a silk kerchief from his sleeve and placed it over his nose until he had adjusted to the foul stenches present in the saloon.

Soon their ears grew used to the cacophony that battered them. The nephew, oldest of the man's companions, touched the patriarch's sleeve, then pointed to a corner table crowded between large, high-backed chairs to form a type of secluded booth. The nephew nodded toward the booth and led the way through the long, rough-hewn tables and benches, past the muttering, wondering toughs who turned to stare at the three who moved by them with such disdain.

"Get them Frenchies, will ya!" one customer snarled as he nodded at the newcomers whose dress made them conspicuous.

One of the two men at the corner table turned his head at the approach of the Frenchmen and tapped his mug against the arm of the man across the table from him. They slid themselves along the wide benches toward the wall to allow the three visitors a place to sit.

"Now, ain't this cozy," one of the drinkers commented as the guests sat down.

"Uncle," the nephew began his introduction, "this is *Monsieur* Redman." He nodded toward the man who had spoken. "And this is *Monsieur* Nutes . . ."

"That's Nute," the second man responded quietly with a low, whiskey-sodden voice.

"*Monsieur* Nute," the nephew corrected himself, somewhat nervously. "Gentlemen." He paused at the use of the word, then gestured toward the old man. "My uncle, *Monsieur* Josef Gabriel-Rene LeClerc . . ."

"Now, that be a mouthful of parley-vous!" Redman spouted as he rose slightly from his bench to bow and present a dirty hand, black grime crusted into the wrinkles like scrimshawed ivory.

The old man stared at the hand, then looked up into the American's eyes. He shook Redman's hand briefly, then presented his hand across the table to the quieter of the two. "*Monsieur* . . ."

"Nute," the man responded. "That's Hickerson Nute, sir."

There was a touch of genuine politeness in the sound of the second man's voice now as he extended another grimy hand toward the gloved Frenchman. LeClerc shook the proffered hand briefly, then returned his eyes to Redman as he removed his right glove. "My nephew says he told you I would be coming this night."

"That he did," nodded Redman.

"We were not sure to find you at la Green Tree—or *ici*, here." LeClerc's eyes flickered as his gaze swept the room quickly.

Redman held up his earthen mug. "Whiskey's better here—not so much water in it." He swilled a long drink. When the mug hit the table once more, Redman continued. "Don't think us two to not be thankin' you neither, Monsur LeClerc." He nodded toward the nephew. "He give us your silver this afternoon, sayin' you'd be wantin' to see us this eve'nin'." Raising his mug once more and emptying it before signaling the barman for a refill, he continued. "An' don't think we don't appreciate this chance to be drinkin' on 'nother man's money!"

"There is more *l'argent*—silver, that can be yours, *bien entendu*—of course," LeClerc began.

"An' I don't doubt that at'all," interrupted Redman once more.

"Much more silver," LeClerc continued. "My nephew has said the two of you were for hire." He looked up at the barman who clunked down another full mug before the American, picked up the empty vessel and then looked down at the older Frenchman.

"You havin' anythin'?" the barman inquired.

"*Non*," LeClerc answered as the barman began to move off, "*mais*—but, these two will have another, *aussi*—on me, as it is said." He reached into a pocket of his vest and removed a velvet coin purse, retrieving a coin from it to place into the open palm the barman stuck out at him.

"Why, thank you, sir," Redman responded with real appreciation. Nute raised his mug briefly in salute toward the French gentlemen.

"You are for hire?" LeClerc pressed once again.

"Your nephew, he tell you we done some work for him coupl'a times, eh?" Obahdiah Redman asked.

"*Oui*."

"He tell you we do good work?" He glanced at his partner, then back to LeClerc.

"*Oui*."

"Then, he told you we don't work cheap, neither." Redman brought the mug to his lips. After another long drink that drained the first mug, he wiped his sleeve across the stubble on his chin. "We get us one hundred dollars in silver for doin' such good work—'cause we don't get caught, neither." He took up the full mug. "So, what's this job you wantin' me an' my friend here to do for you?"

LeClerc cleared his throat slightly and glanced quickly about the room. "You have been west—*à lieu sauvage?*"

"Never," Redman garbled.

"You might think of a forthcoming trip, then?" LeClerc prodded.

"Wouldn't be for our health!" Redman answered. "We can drink to that!" He roared with a bass-low laugh.

"*A Dieu ne plaise*—God forbid! It is not for your health, this journey west," LeClerc continued. "Rather, for another man's health will you travel far away, *du pays sauvage.*"

Redman finally took his eyes off the old Frenchman and looked over at his partner. Nute merely raised his bushy eyebrows once and looked down into his mug to stare at nothing at all.

"A trip such as that gonna cost you," Obahdiah finally responded. When he saw that LeClerc sat quietly, he continued. "We can make us some good money here on the river, Mr. LeClerc." It was the first time he had tried out the Frenchman's name. He drank again before speaking.

"Gettin' us such good money here on the river—one hunderd dollars for our good work—you'd have to make it pretty interestin' for the likes of us two to be leavin' the ladies an' good whiskey for what you got planned out there," he stated flatly.

"Ladies and whiskey," Nute echoed as he cracked his mug against Redman's.

"Whiskey an' ladies," Obahdiah answered and drank. He drew his sleeve across his chin to catch the dribble. "Dependin' on the trip, it could take us a long time to . . . to do our job, you see."

"*Je comprends*—I understand."

"Where is it you be thinkin' of us takin' our trip?" Redman inquired.

"*Aux montagnes.*" LeClerc thought for a moment. "The mountains."

Redman whistled low as he glanced over at Hickerson Nute, who finally raised his head once more to stare at the old Frenchman. "That be a piece of travelin', ol' friend. Not like goin' up toward one of them posts 'long the river, up to Bell'view an' north."

"Yes," LeClerc answered with impatience.

"All the way to the mountains, eh?" Redman eyed the Frenchman. "What you thinkin' a job like that be worth, Hickerson?" Nute responded only by raising his eyebrows and screwing up his chin as if in contemplation. "Just as I thought, my friend," Redman continued. "Good job like that, takin' us a lil' journey—that oughta least cost you some . . ."—he meditated briefly—". . . some five hunderd dollars—plus supplies," he added quickly. Nute nodded his agreement.

"Five hundred, you say?" LeClerc asked dubiously, toying with the men.

"Plus supplies," Redman reiterated. "Might have to take us some friends along, too." He glanced at Nute for approval. "Goin' to them mountains, lotta folks feel better when there's comp'ny 'round 'em. I wants to make it back, you see."

"*Je compre* . . . I understand, *Monsieur*."

"We just might have to find us some friends to come 'long with us," Redman mused.

"*Monsieur*," LeClerc finally responded. "That will not be necessary."

"Now, how's that?" Redman asked testily.

"You will have plenty of . . . *ensemble*—friend, with you, *Monsieur*."

"Yeah?" Redman tilted his head. "How you mean? Some of your fellas comin' 'long with us?"

"That will not be necessary, *c'est vrai*," LeClerc answered. "You will be traveling to the mountains with many . . . friends. In two days, the Sublette-Campbell shop will open its doors to hire the men it needs to travel west toward the mountains. They need many strong men such as you to handle the animals that will carry the supplies to *le rendezvous*. *N'est-ce pas?*" he asked. "This is so?"

"I see your thinkin'." Redman smiled a somewhat greasy grin and swallowed some more whiskey.

"The man we hunt left two years ago with a group traveling to the mountains to trap *le castor*—beaver, we have discovered," LeClerc continued. "It was first thought that he had abandoned the party and returned to the city, at least along the river below us—hiding out to remain free of punishment for his crime."

"Yeah?" Redman wanted the old Frenchman to continue.

"*Oui,*" LeClerc went on. "But he did not return as we supposed. *C'est vrai*—that much is true. He cannot be found along the river. All the way down to New Orleans we have searched for some hint of this one, we have, *Messieurs.*"

"Why ain't you takin' them as you hired to look for 'im 'long the river?"

"The ones who look," LeClerc answered, "that is what they do. Only look. They are not ones who do such, such good work as the two of you. *Comprenez*—you understand?"

"I'm tryin'," Obahdiah said. "Them fellas find what you be after, an' then you send some others—like us here—to get the job done. That it, eh?"

LeClerc nodded. "*Oui.* I believe you have it, *Monsieur.*"

Redman again glanced at his partner. "Goin' out with one of them supply brigades, eh?" He chewed on the idea. "Not bad. Not bad, at all, monsur," he commented after a moment. "We do our job in front of a lot of folks, that be a mite dangerous, though. Them all are rough fellas 'round them rendezvooz parties."

"With much drinking," LeClerc countered, "and fighting . . ."

"An' killin', too?" Redman raised a questioning eyebrow.

"*Le mort, aussi. Sans doute.* And killing, too," the Frenchman answered. "*Oui.* The killing, too."

Redman sat back against the stone wall and stared at the old man for long moments before he spoke again. He finally glanced over at his partner. Hickerson Nute's eyes shone brightly beneath the thick eyebrows. His silence had become comfortable to the talkative Redman. And the canny look in Hickerson's eyes had answered Obahdiah's question better than any spoken words. He looked once again to LeClerc.

"Seems we best be askin' for more," he said. "What with this long trip we have starin' us in the face, an' havin' to do our work 'round a bunch of wild, mean rowdies . . ." He chewed on the cost. "Seems we best get us some seven hunderd fifty—apiece." Hickerson nodded.

"And supplies, too?" the young nephew suddenly injected, not quite believing the price.

"An' supplies, too."

"*Monsieur* Redman and *Monsieur* . . ."

"Nute."

"*Monsieur* Nute." LeClerc nodded to the quiet partner. "In

two days when you have signed on with the brigade, you will be taken to my family's counting house, and there allowed to deposit the money—pistoles, guineas, dollars, whatever—in silver, if you desire. My son here"—he motioned to the young man at his left—"will go with you to the counting house. Arrangements will be made so that only one hundred of your dollars can be taken out of the deposit before you leave. You can freely spend that money on your last days, the last days of *les mesdemoiselles . . . les* ladies and *les* whiskeys before you go on this journey."

"An' the rest be waitin' for us when we get back?" Redman inquired.

"*Oui.*"

"In that bank?" Hickerson wanted to know.

"*Oui.*" LeClerc nodded. He pulled the last remaining glove over his right hand and stood, allowing his nephew and son to slide off the benches behind him.

"We got us a deal, then." Redman looked up at the grayheaded man.

"*Oui. C'est entendu.*"

"You gonna tell us who we goin' after?" Redman asked. "How we gonna know him?"

"My son will give you all the help you need as the time draws near to your journey," LeClerc responded. "You will know him when you see him."

"Just like an old friend, right?" Redman grinned at Nute.

"Yeah," Hickerson answered. "We'll know him just like he was an old friend, monsur."

"I like the idea of travelin' west, I do," Redman said. "Like me the idea, too, of workin' for fellas what pays for good work bein' done for 'em."

"I pay," LeClerc stated. "I pay very well for a good job done for me."

"You rich 'nough to pay for the best."

"*Peut-etre*—perhaps. I will trust that you are the best at . . . what you do."

"We're the best, us two." Redman felt challenged. "You want us to bring you back somethin' to prove we got this fella?" He looked over at Nute quickly while he licked his lips. "We could bring his hand, maybe?"

"That will not be necessary," LeClerc answered. "However, *Messieurs,* the man might have a pistol with him." He saw how interested Redman got at the mention of the firearm.

"This pistol, it is the brother to this one." He pulled aside his riding coat, reached beneath his vest. From the waistband of his riding britches, LeClerc pulled the dueling pistol. Even in the dim, reflected light of the oil lamps, the beauty of the Damascus steel barrel was astonishing. Redman looked closely at the pistol. "It will be like this one, *exactement*. You will bring me its brother. Then I will know you have the man I want."

"You'll have 'im." Redman leaned back against the wall and picked up his mug. "An' the pistol, too, monsur." He drank briefly.

"Two days," LeClerc responded. "Two days until you meet my son at the counting house with your papers."

"Papers?"

"To show you have signed on for the journey west with this Campbell," LeClerc answered. "*Bonsoir, Messieurs.*" He turned quickly and left the table for the door, followed by the two young men.

"Have us a trip, Hickerson," Redman commented after the Frenchmen had left the Rocky Mountain House. "An' have us some money, too." He reached into his coat pocket to retrieve the skin pouch of coins. He jangled it in front of Nute's face.

"Some money, a lil' trip, an' more money," Hickerson agreed, almost whispering across the table. "Maybe, we just steal us the pistol, huh?"

Redman's face froze. "No!" he whispered harshly. "We gonna get that fella."

"Why can't we . . ."

"I want that fella, Hick," Obahdiah broke in. "Stealin' the pistol back just won't do for me. The ol' Frenchie gonna get him his money's worth from this boy!" He leaned back against the wall once more and his face relaxed. "Yeah, ain't gonna have to work for some time, then, my friend."

"We come back an' be rich, Obahdiah."

"We come back an' be rich, Hick." Redman grinned.

Across the foggy reaches of the dream, his hands slipped into the warm tissues beneath the buffalo ribs. The cold in his fingers was suddenly gone and the hands re-emerged with the slippery heart cradled in both palms so that it would not skitter from his grasp. He turned it up to his mouth, carefully juggling the slimy organ until he had it positioned so he would be able to drink from the aorta. And he remembered Josiah's first drink of buffalo blood. From the bull's heart.

"Go 'head, son. Take a horn. That's medicine water, buffler blood is."

The young trapper approached and took the heart to drink, squeezing the organ with a pumping action to drain it of the thick, warm syrup. Then without warning, blood gushed from Paddock's stomach and splattered to the ground. In one quick lurch he had vomited all the fluid he had taken from the heart. But the fluid had done its job. It had relieved a thirst. So his body could rid itself of the thick syrup.

With his huge knife Bass slowly cut a long slice in the bull's stomach, which measured almost three feet in diameter. He finished swishing the stomach's juices around and brought cupped hands to his lips. Slowly he poured the liquid into his mouth, some of the fluid dripping onto his chin whiskers and down his chest. Now he was ready for the humpribs roasting over the fire.

The fat popped and sizzled, dripping into the flames, causing the coals to flare. Fat, juicy humpribs—enough to feed a whole brigade. Broiling over the cherry fire. He lapped the juices from his fingers as the meaty broth dripped from the roasting animal flesh. He licked them clean, greedily, in anticipation of the blackened meat being done to a fine pink inside.

Bass licked his dry, parched lips and awoke with a start. He bolted upright. The wound at his hip was tight and cold. Worse yet was the missing flesh across his shoulder. It burned with a cold pain, bringing him to consciousness all too quickly. Yes, he was awake. Damnit! And from such a beautiful dream. Damn!

"I laid me down and slept; I awakened; for the Lord sustained me."

"Ah, shit, Asa!" he mumbled sleepily. "Ain't enough I see my dream ain't real—that meat ain't for me to eat. I gotta have you whisperin' in my ear all the time, too!"

He blinked his eyes again in the fading light of mid-afternoon. The light would be gone soon, especially down here, away from the tops of the ridges. Scratch shook his head and pulled the clammy blankets and robes more tightly under his armpits. He looked up at the ponies. Their hanging, sorrowful heads barely moved in the depths of their cold slumber. They sagged under their packs and had not nibbled the aspen. Should he move on? He looked again at the sky to the west up the valley where he had been heading. Wasn't too late to be thinking of moving on now. Maybeso. Any of them Blackfoot niggers coming after me by now, they ain't gonna be moving far from a fire tonight.

He gently touched the wound at the top of his shoulder. Not much of one. Just some flesh gone, a little blood. Not too bad. Hadn't bothered him much while the adrenaline had been pumping. He wasn't about to let it get to him now.

Damn, if his belly didn't pinch. A mite hungry, you are, he mused. Just a mite starved for fleece, ol' coon. Even if he could hunt way up here at this time of year, what would he find anyway? He hadn't seen sign since first light. After all, the bears had long ago taken to their dens for their peaceful winter's sleep. That's what he could use more of. Sleep. But his stomach demanded more of him. Goddamned belly—keep a man awake. Elk and deer long ago escaped this high country where he was now caught, the animals gone to range for forage far below. Maybe he was a fool, after all. Come so high just to freeze or starve. Maybe both. Shit, he shook his head in disgust with himself. Even the small rodents and game had the sense to stay in their snug, warm burrows. Scratch's stomach flopped at the thought of having to eat squirrel or chipmunk—maybe marmot this high. Nawww! He'd fared better in the past, going hungry for just as long, without stooping to eat the big rats that dug holes in the ground up above treeline.

Besides, he sighed, if he had some game to eat he could not build a fire. Did not dare build a fire now that he had slept most of the day out. He would have to skin the animal and eat the bloody meat raw. Maybe not even chewing—just sucking at the warm, thick juices and blood.

"Ain't . . ." He was startled to realize he had actually spoken; the voice seemed so far away from himself. "Ain't gonna trade my ha'r for some vittles just yet, I ain't," he completed the thought. "I'd only cure me of a empty paunch—then never live to eat 'nother meal again. No, sir. Not me, I won't. I ain't that stupid!"

He grinned weakly, recalling the time he had called Josiah Paddock stupid.

"Wished I was young an' stupid like you be, Josiah Paddock. If stupids was beaver dollars, why, I'd be back to St. Louie wearin' fine silks an' smokin' big ceegars, talkin' nasty to them red-dressed ladies right 'longside Ol' Ashley, Lisa an' Billy Sublette himself."

But he wasn't stupid. The boy wasn't stupid.

Titus struggled to rise, fighting his way out of the confining, warm cocoon of blankets and buffalo robes. His brain-tanned leather clothing had dried somewhat from his body's own heat. Now what residue of dampness remained in the skins began to chill in the air of the waning afternoon. He stomped his leaden feet a few times and slapped his arms at his sides. He would sleep some more, and his body fell to the robes before he realized it.

Once before in a walk on foot over the mountains, he had had to place a chunk of deadfall below himself on a slope to keep from rolling on down the hillside in his slumber. He had curled against the deadfall that night, sleeping against it as if he was snugged up to the warmth of a bang-tailed whore back to St. Lou. Well, at least the warmth of knowing he was rolling no further. Bass pulled the blankets and robes back over himself and closed his eyes. No more dreams of meat. Not now. Maybe think of them ladies in fine, skimpy underclothes back there in St. Louie. He'd be cuddled up with one now on some nearly clean sheets, feeling her soft, milky breasts fill his roughened hands. The air would be damp with the early-spring rain, the fresh breezes tossing the curtains at the window. He thought he could smell the rain, and the love-musty sheets.

"Man can always get such as them whore forkers to stick his poker in, plumb center," he had told Josiah an age or so ago. *"Any nigger can blow his whistle in any cache hole what comes along. Ain't no special 'bout that. What a change it be—layin' with a gal what loves you an' you feel like the whole damned Rockies is turnin' 'round on you in layin' with her. Man comes on such a feelin' maybe once't in his life—if'n he's a lucky child."*

"You been there, Scratch?"

"Once't, son. She were the kind that put the twinkle back in a ol' nigger's step, bring the dumb back to palaverin' an' naybobbin' again. Now that ain't to say there ain't been some as've turned my meat to stone an' my innards to grits for a spell—yessirreeee! But that gal was one to make your innards shine! But a man can play at bein' happy. But way inside he's gettin' et up with the lonelies. Down inside where he don't let no other man look—he's bein' chewed away."

"Scratch? Are you bein' et up inside?"

The memories of the heart could be a cruel trick one plays

on oneself. And he had allowed himself to do it. Another had grown so close to his heart that she had hurt him there. She was dark. And the smell of her skin was musky with the sweetness of the wilderness. Yes, he could almost smell the aroma of her body.

But all that assaulted his nostrils was the dank odor of wet buffalo fur. Bass closed his eyes all the tighter, squeezing them shut to push the vision away.

When he next awoke in the late afternoon, Scratch found himself quietly sobbing. He let it come, this crying for his hunger, his pain, his fatigue, and cold—the whole hopeless condition he found himself in.

He sat up and the sobbing ceased. No dream here. Only the nightmare of reality he had to face. The tears had frozen under his lower lids and the tops of his cheeks. He swiped a course, woolen mitten at the frozen film, and snorted to clear his nose.

"You cain't sit here bawlin' like some scared painter kit," he consoled himself. "Some calf without its mamma, now. You . . . you'd just better be gettin' on with the livin' . . . before your bones cain't move again."

He rose to his feet shakily and stomped out onto the snow. He sped up his movements, flushing his body with the heat of circulation and muscle activity. A couple of the animals were awake with him, their glazed eyes following his labors as he rolled up the blankets and robes once more. These he strapped back in their places aboard one of the tired ponies.

Inside those blankets and robes his leathers had thawed some more, but now they were freezing again in the frigid air, no longer protected from the dropping temperature by the heavy hides and wool. Bass looked to the east where the light had disappeared. It was surely dark east of the divide now. But he was, after all, west of the big spine. Then he looked to the west where he would head this night. The sunset lit the sky with a brilliant winter incandescence. But it was difficult to admire the beauty of the scene before him when he already felt halfway into the grave of his own making.

When he finished strapping the robes aboard the pony, Bass stepped back a few paces to look the animals over. He saw the rifles and was reminded of the loss of his favorite. It was down the slope somewhere. Near the hidden creek. Scratch pushed through the huddled animals and slid and stumbled down the snowy incline.

He found the place where he had crawled out of his white

grave and began to search the deep powder with his feet. Around and around in an ever-widening circle he marched, this time his ears atuned to the gurgling of the hidden waters. Now he stopped and tried to remember what hand the weapon had been in when he fell through the soft snow. His left. It would have to be over here, then. Again he searched for long minutes until the light was nearly gone from the sky. When the snow was finally gray with early night, Bass stood there and sighed deeply. The sigh grew into a soft, racking sob at his loss. He finally brought it under control and pushed back up the hill.

Once in the saddle again, Bass kicked gently at the pony's sides to move the animals along the side of the slope. He rode in the direction of the disappearing sun, watching the light band above the hills before him turn gray, then an inky black blending into the pitch of the rest of the sky.

It was not long before the cold became so intense once more that he actually began to fear he would freeze in the saddle. Either his body would lapse into a frozen, stone-like state until he did in fact freeze to death—or the wet buckskins would freeze him to the leather on the saddle. He reined his pony to a halt and the other animals behind them plodded slowly to a stop.

Bass dismounted, thinking it better to walk for a while now, to keep his circulation going until he would find another place to sleep again. Sometime near the middle of the night. Sometime after the large sliver of moon had passed mid-sky. In the saddle he might drop off to sleep and never awaken again. The movement kept his body warmer, kept it more alive. It also kept him from dreaming.

This night was darker than the last he had ridden through, but the white of the snow helped him a little. Best to get on west, out of this piece of country, on over these mountains, as quickly as possible now. The forge was struck. No doubt about that. And he had to live with it. So dark now. The sky like a dark blanket with millions of tiny flecks of frost thrown across it. There. His eyes caught the trail of the shooting star. What did Asa use to call a shooting star? Comet.

McAfferty had often told of the year he turned seventeen. The year of the earthquake where Asa's family lived back east. His mother thinking such was a sign that their son was to be a preacher.

"We had the big comet star come over. A big, burnin' star flyin' 'cross the heavens. To this here child that was sure sign,"

the Whitehead had always told the story. *"Sure sign. Best ye'd ever wanna read. Put up there by the Lord tellin' me He wanted me for His callin'. I set me stick right then an' there on preachin'."*

Memories, too. They were dark. Along with the night.

In the murky gloominess he began to stumble. His legs were not working well for him. He tripped over rocks and deadfall, picking himself up time and again, tugging at the animals behind him. They followed, dutifully. So dark he could not really see where he was going. Just looking up from time to time to read the stars overhead to keep some sort of bearing as the land rose and fell before him.

He and the ponies slid and careened over rocks they could not see until it was too late. Again and again he rose to dust himself off, knocking the snow out of the wet gauntlets, the mittens that hardly kept his hands warm. Repeatedly they blundered into stands of trees where he and the animals were lashed by branches. He cursed at himself, at the ponies, at the night—backing away from the tree limbs that slashed across his face and shoulders. It seemed he was wandering in circles, having to double back a ways before he could head west by northwest once more. His freezing, leaden feet failed him time and time again, too. They stumbled easily, unable to feel their way across the uneven, unseen, sometimes frozen, sometimes snowy-soft ground.

When the ground began to even out after several hours of knee-busting, snow-floundering travel, Titus finally gave in to the exhaustion and climbed aboard his pony. He had decided to ride for a while until the signs of freezing crept back into his bones. As he settled himself in the saddle he decided this time to take no chances: he would rope himself to the pony. He lashed one end of his buffalo-hair rope to the horn of the Santa Fe saddle and wove the rest over his thighs and around the cantle, tying the other end around his waist with a slipknot he could release in an emergency. He gently nudged the animals into action and they began to plod down the side of the slope.

The motion of the pony, its slow, almost hypnotic gait, along with the dark velvet curtain overhead, made it easy for an exhausted man to fall asleep atop his horse. He resisted the pull at his eyelids and the push on his mind to slip into a semiconscious state by attempting to concentrate on the bitter cold that attacked the flesh of his face. He pulled the fur cap down tighter on his head until his eyes were almost covered. He tugged at the collar of the heavy elk-hide coat so that he could hide his face behind it once more.

Just before he awoke, Bass had the sensation of falling, falling, never being able to stop himself in that descent. Then he plopped to the snow-covered ground with a thud. He was awake and lying in the snow on his right side. His hip hurt again, too. He realized he had fallen. And worse, the rope was taut and the pony was dragging him through the snow.

It took him a few minutes to sort it out, what to do, how to stop his being dragged across the snow, over the rocks and deadfall. Titus finally yanked hard on the buffalo-hair rope. He had to yank harder again as the pony continued to drag him. Then the animal stopped.

He sighed and let his head drop to the snow. The coolness felt good on his cheek. He remembered how good it had felt when the Whitehair's claw had cut his face from the corner of the left eye into the whiskers at the top of his cheek. How good it had felt to feel the sting of cold pain as the snow was pushed into the river of raw flesh at the side of his face. He had come out alive. And, now, the same relief washed over him with the cleansing cold. It was good to feel the cold. He knew he had not frozen to death.

Bass remounted and moved the ponies out. Close to first light he would make a temporary camp again and get some real sleep. But it was good that he was still alive to make these plans. He could draw himself out of the wind, wrap up in the robes, and close his eyes for real. But for now, Scratch realized what it meant to be among the living. And he was thankful.

He fell off five more times during that all-night ride, sometimes losing his balance, on others being lashed and whipped out of the saddle by tree limbs as the ponies stumbled in the dark through stands of pine, finding their own way around the boulders and rocks strewn across his westward path. And it had begun to snow. What started were the soft, fat, wet flakes of a late-winter storm, each fragment of white lifting gently on the breeze to flutter awhile before it swirled and settled about him. Bass was not conscious of the snowfall. Each flake tinked quietly on the hair of his face, the fur of the cap and elk-hide coat until it turned him ghostly white. Spirit-like, the white specter rode on into the night, oblivious to the cold flakes caking around him.

As the sky turned charcoal before dawn the snow turned to sleet and the wind wailed through his beard. He was lashed into wakefulness once more by the stinging needles of sleet that drove into every crevice of his clothing, as if seeking to freeze him to the saddle again. Chill rain dripped down his back, poured from his neck down his chest and to his belly where he felt the buckskins soaking up all the moisture until they could hold no more. He was drenched again. If it continued to rain like this for very long, the surface of the snow would again be frozen tonight during the next leg of his journey. Maybe the hard surface would this time make the going a bit easier. He consoled himself with that belief as his shudders grew more and more frequent, more insistent as his body heat was sucked through his chilled skin once again.

Near first light, the gentle, drizzly rain—now without the pain of the wind—brought out some small animals in the forest. First the rabbits and the squirrels darted about in search of food. And with the small animals came the predators. Hawks hunting for an easy meal darted through the open meadows and swooped back to the high places to feed their young. He could stand to feel something warm in his belly himself. Even raw, uncooked flesh, still warm with life, could be sucked on for its life-giving juices and thick blood.

Ahead in the dim light, Bass saw the hawk swoop and strike at the rabbit skittering across the surface of the snow. The hawk ascended again and came back a second time, but another strike was not necessary. He had done his job the first time. The bird settled over his kill. Bass drew up on the pony's reins and slid quietly from the saddle. He searched about him for something to throw, to drive the large bird away from the rabbit both he and the bird wanted to eat. Finally he found a small limb jutting out of the frozen snow. Bass expected he would have to break the limb off the deadfall hidden beneath the white surface, but was surprised when the limb came out of the snow with no resistance.

Now he crept toward the hawk. The bird had his back toward the man, was hunched over the dead rabbit, its wings mantling its prey. Closer and closer the man drew until he was near enough to be assured of a shot that would drive the large-winged hawk away from the meal both wanted so desperately. He cocked his right arm, fighting the wet, frozen coat, then heaved the stick forward with all his might. To his surprise, the limb struck the hawk on the back and the head, sending the bird sprawling across the snow. Scratch dashed forward before the bird could come back and snatch the rabbit in his talons and fly off with the meal.

"Men do not despise a thief, if he steal to satisfy his soul when he is hungry."

"Ah, shit, Asa! I ain't worried 'bout stealin' the goddamned rabbit from the goddamned bird!" Bass looked around to address the silent forest.

But the bird did not move. Bass slid across the surface of the snow and stopped by the rabbit. Tufts of white and red were scattered around the carcass. The red looked inviting but his stomach knotted, warning him to take the eating slow. Quickly he slipped out a knife and cut the rabbit up. He lifted a hind quarter to his lips and licked at it almost delicately. The warmth was good on his tongue. It had been a long time since last he had eaten something warm. Then his teeth sank into the resilient flesh of the huge muscle. He sucked at the juices breaking free from the flesh. Then he saw the hawk and the idea struck him.

Bass finished skinning the rabbit and washed it off with the crusty snow. He laid the butchered pieces down and moved to the body of the bird. He rolled it over onto its back, spread the two wings out and placed a sole of the heavy moccasins on each wing. He slit the bird open with the knife tip, from the neck down to the belly, then pried at the flesh so that he could tear back the skin, pulling it away from the thick, meaty chest muscles. Again and again Scratch slashed with the knife, until he had a heap of thin-sliced raw meat. He lifted the blade tenderly to his lips and licked at the dripping blood.

As he drew near the ponies once more, he felt sorry that there was no bark that he could peel for them to eat. But there were only pines. He found them gnawing on each other's tails in an exhausted attempt to put something in their bellies. The pony behind his had pushed its muzzle deep into the thick, coarse mane of his buffalo runner. Bass stopped to watch, fascinated that the ponies would try to nibble at each other in this way. His stomach lurched at the thought of eating the coarse hair—knotted, stringy, and gagging at best. Then his stomach heaved and the blood welled up to dribble across the white snow at his feet. Most of it stayed down, so he sucked once more at the flesh he carried in one hand, his glance darting back and forth from pony to pony, watching the animals chew on each other's manes and tails.

He finally climbed into the saddle, after wrapping most of the bloody meat in a small piece of old hide. Bass had to push and strike at the dulled pony who nibbled on his riding animal to force it back into line. Then he kicked his own horse gently into movement, sucking at the rabbit haunch cradled protectively, possessively, in his mitten.

The sun later rose over the ridge behind him, forming a brilliant band of color beneath the dark, watery clouds overhead. Its light struck the ground before him as far as he could see, causing him to squint. Blinding white as far as he could see, the dazzling light robbed him of the gift of vision. And with the warming air came the steam smoking from the ponies' nostrils. His own breath plumed out of his fur cocoon and froze around his face. The droplets frosted on his eyelashes, the fur of his cap where it was tugged down around his face, painting his mustache and whiskers with a ghostly glow in the new day's light.

"Lift up thine eyes on high, and behold who hath created these things."

"Yep, Asa," he replied quietly, "an' all this cold, cold white." The steamy cold made his face feel miserable, his skin plastered and drawn like a stiff piece of rawhide.

Bass finally pushed down the side of a small ravine as the hills began to drop away before him. Down here someplace he would find a suitable place for camp. Hell, wouldn't be no camp. Just grab some sleep and hope he awoke still wearing a little hair. A stream had cut itself into this gully. And down there he might hope to find some forage for the ponies. Scratch brought them to a halt. The drooping animals were so tired he wondered whether they would forage.

The juices and blood from the bird and rabbit had replaced a little of the warmth at his core. He slipped wearily from the cold saddle. He quickly tied a couple of the animals to the trees and hobbled away down the slope by himself. Down there he might find some willow, perhaps some bark to feed them.

By accident he came upon the dark form lying atop the snow. He stopped suddenly at the first sight of it. As soon as he could tell it was the carcass of an animal, Bass drew to a halt and looked about him. As alert as he could be in his weakened state, the trapper listened to the sounds of the quiet late-winter forest. He had not interrupted another animal's meal this time.

Finally he edged forward and stared down at the carcass. It had been an otter. From the looks of things, a bird had attacked it, begun to eat its meal, then left. But that had been many days ago. Nothing else had touched the carcass since. The body of the otter had lain out in the thawing sun, through the freezing nights, into the thawing air once again. On through the soaking rain.

Who was he to question it? Bass kicked at the stiffened body with a wet toe. The otter was left for him, for some purpose. His toe rolled the body over. Then he knelt down near the decaying carcass and grabbed one of its legs. He rose and began to drag it back to his temporary camp. Who was he to question, after all? Bass moved uphill, lugging his rancid prize behind him until he reached the ponies.

His nose dribbled and ran as he sliced at the carcass, stripping the bones of flesh. He carried handfuls of the putrefied, cold otter to each of the ponies. Only a few of the animals attempted to nibble at the flesh. He figured it would be better than nothing, letting the ponies suck and chew on the hard, rancid fare he offered them. But even so, he had to give them more.

Back down the slope Bass stumbled, across the frozen, slippery crust. In the bottom he slid to a stop and hacked at the willow branches there. He carried an armload uphill, then a second, and when he dropped a third in the middle of his camp, Bass knew he could not complete another trip. So he kicked at the willow branches, spreading them before all the ponies, giving each an equal chance to nibble at the frozen limbs.

Bass dropped the damp robes and two blankets to the ground once more and crawled into their welcome warmth. His hands trembled with the frosty cold as they knotted the buffalo runner's long lead rope to his belt.

"Shit!" he mumbled quietly. "Got me the tremblin' willies way down inside now."

He would sleep for a while, forage for some more in the afternoon, then sleep again. It made sense to him to get as much rest as he could. Even the frightening dreams of her could not keep his eyes open any longer. He ached for sleep almost as badly as he ached deeply inside for the touch of her fingers encircling him, gently kneading his flesh into a rigid readiness. But she was so far away. So very far away. And sleep was at hand. He had learned to live with the fear, to deal with it, to heft it as if it were a burden one had to carry. Already, as sleep tugged at his senses, he knew the load was lighter than before.

Ten

Emile had much to think on as he neared St. Louis, drawing closer to the Frenchman he was to meet. He already knew whom he would hunt. There remained only the matter of terms, the price on the young man's head.

The man he would seek was young, strong enough to kick a man to death. A fancy French nobleman had challenged Ezra Paddock's son, Josiah, to a duel over the hand of a rich French girl. Angelique, her name was. And young Paddock had killed the young Frenchman. Kicked him to death rather than used the priceless dueling pistols. So the family wanted Josiah killed to right the wrong. To even the scales somewhat. Never to have their own son back—but in some way to put an old man's heart at rest.

The giant smiled. Why should he care, after all? Why should he care so much why they were sending him after this young man in the mountains? All of this over the hand of a beautiful young French girl.

He just might have to take her for himself. Just once before he left St. Louis for the mountains. Yes, he would have to think on that. To smell of her perfume and powders as he spread her milky legs and pushed himself inside her writhing body. He would enjoy that. To find out what one man had already been killed for.

Josef Gabriel-Rene LeClerc passed through the small iron gate in the great stone wall. He stood upright, straightened his cape over his shoulders and turned to secure the gate with the large padlock. He dropped the key carefully into a vest pocket, felt the pistols beneath the vest, and moved off toward the river, skirting most of the large homes in the French part of town, staying to shadows and stealing through the trees. He was struck with the irony of it all—having to sneak through his own city like the common thieves his people watched for at night.

Reaching LaRue Royal, now more often called Main Street, the Frenchman stopped and backed into the shadows of an old building. An oil lamp shed its light down the street, in feeble competition with the nearly full moon. He gazed quickly up and down the narrow street before he began to cross the muddy cobblestones. The warning clank of iron-mounted wheels drawing near the corner gave his old legs speed to reach the shadows once more. Once there, the Frenchman withdrew into the dark recesses at the corner of a building and waited breathlessly as the large carriage passed. The dimly visible family crest on the side of the vehicle was easily recognized: Berthold.

Someone is working late this night at the Chouteau-Berthold warehouse, he thought.

Around the side of the building, through a narrow walkway, the smell of the river began to fill his nostrils. His feet felt their way through this passageway, the moon's light unable yet to penetrate the closed-in walls. As he emerged from the walkway, he trod the unfamiliar wooden planks that formed the terrace above the wharf. He halted after his first few steps. In the great silence of the night the hard-leather heels of his boots clattered noisily on the wooden boards.

He stopped and looked about him, studying the dark places, and those where the shadows loomed all the more ominous. Summoning up his courage, the Frenchman started to walk once more, this time treading more lightly, more quietly, more slowly than before. He glanced over his shoulder at the moon, then jerked around at the sudden sound in front of him. A small, half-empty crate clattered as a skinny, bone-bearing dog slinked away quickly.

The old man's heart raced. He calmed slowly, and removed his left hand from the pistol at his waist. He slipped toward LaRue des Granges, and when he crossed the narrow end of that street he saw the moonlight reflected off many of the tin-roofed buildings at the edge of town. Above them the coal-smoke pushed into the sky, crowding the lighter colored clouds out of the way in the moon's reflected glow. Then he stole back into the dark shadows again.

He glanced to his right, at the levee where the boats bobbed at their moorings. Both keel and steam, they plied the river:

south to the towns of Natchez and New Orleans, north up the Ohio, and north up the muddy waters toward the western mountains. Paddock was out there. But it was from here that his end was going to be assured. Tonight LeClerc would ensure that the man who had run away to the mountains would never . . . He had to smile. Tonight, he would seal the murderer's own death. It should be anywhere along here, he thought. *He is to meet me right along this stretch between LaRue des Granges and LaRue de l'Eglise. Here, under the hill.*

The boards underfoot were sodden with rain. He felt the dampness soaking through the thin leather of his boots. His stockings were wet. The two riverfront toughs had received their advance money and the rest of it was safely sealed in the counting house. They had signed up with Campbell and were now en route west. He smiled again. Their kind might be counted upon along the river. Yes. But it was a different breed of man who left for the west to trap its mountain streams and wander the high places. He could not be sure the two he had hired would make the kill. And, he had to be certain . . .

The shadow loomed out at him, quickly followed by the huge bulk of the man as he slid silently out of the night. The old man stopped suddenly, surprised and frightened. The man was actually larger than his shadow. Larger than he had been told the man would be. Some six feet seven inches of muscle and bone rose before LeClerc now. Each of the two hundred forty pounds, spread over the tall, muscular frame, made the man seem all the larger in the play of shadow and light beneath the moon along this muddy river.

LeClerc took a hesitant step forward but the apparition strode toward him and the old Frenchman shuddered to a halt. The man inched forward slowly, perhaps aware of the frightening effect he had on people. Shadows began to reveal his face, bringing to light the huge scar that ran down the man's forehead, across the brow. It continued across the right eye, almost completely sealing the eyelid, before it finally wandered on down the cheek to lose itself in the patchy whiskers.

Studying the monster before him, LeClerc unconsciously pulled the flaps of his riding cape farther apart so that the handles of the two pistols could be seen. He wanted the man to know he was armed. The huge man's scowl faded into a white-toothed smile that emerged from behind parted whiskers.

"Monsieur," the big man began, "you will not need your lit-

tle popping guns—if you are the one who has brought me here."

"*Vous . . .*," he began, then paused. "You are . . . Emile?"

"*Oui*," he answered. "I am he." His large hands sank to the hips where they rested in arrogant confidence.

"I am the one who brings you here," the older man began. "Josef Gabriel-Rene LeClerc."

The giant smiled widely again, evidently a man who enjoyed the easy humor in things. "You French, with all your money. You buy yourself a long name, eh?"

"Why . . ." LeClerc was not sure how to answer, nor sure of the shape of this challenge. "Perhaps you are right, in a way— *aussi*. *Mon pere*'s . . . my father's name, and his before him. They are mine now, *aussi*, too."

"Ah, you French," Emile responded with some disdain. "With all your money you control the big rivers—have the fur trade in your purse, eh? Lords—your money makes you. A Lord who controls the lives of other men, this I see. Eh?"

LeClerc, apprehensive, looked down at his boots, then quickly at the thick moccasins on the big man's feet before raising his eyes to the chiseled face once more. "So you, ah . . . *parlez-vous français*?"

"*Oui*," the monster answered, watching the sudden relief flow across the old man's face. "But, *Monsieur*, I do not like to speak it." He watched the gratitude disappear from LeClerc's eyes.

"*Je* . . . I was hoping it—we could speak French," LeClerc began. "I was told you were . . . part French—this English, it is so hard for me at times. To . . . remember the words . . ."

"Ah, and when you are scared, all the harder, eh?"

"*Oui*—yes, yes!" he answered excitedly, suddenly in no small way ashamed for admitting this truth.

"Emile has told you, has he not, you have nothing to fear from this one."

He watched as LeClerc eyed some crates near them. Sharpe nodded toward the boxes to show the older man it would be all right to seat himself. "*Mon pere*, he was French. A poor excuse for a man who came to my village near the Big Hook, took his fun, and left. What French I learned did not come from Papa. It come from the others, others since I was a boy. It has been long time since last I spoke the French to anyone. My mother"—he gazed at the river momentarily as LeClerc sat down—"she old woman when she die. Killed. At the Seven Oaks many years ago now it seem." He looked down at the seated Frenchman. "You know of Seven Oaks, eh?"

"Yes. Yes, I do."

"You know I survived the fight then, no?"

"Yes, this I am told."

"And, the rich Frenchman brings me down the big river, the father of all rivers, to this town for him." He turned his back on LeClerc to face the water once more. "You send good money to bring me down the river. I can be a man who kill the ones you send the money with to me. Then, maybe—I never come. Think you of that, LeClerc?"

"I did."

"Maybe I kill those men, too. Maybe, eh?"

"Yes."

"And you keep sending them with money for me to come down to visit you. All times, you send more runners to come for me, eh?" He chuckled. "Me, I could kill them, take your nice money, and never come see the man who so foolish with his silver."

"You . . . you could have done that, *oui*," LeClerc finally answered.

"But"—Emile turned to look at the Frenchman—"I did not. Do you know why, *Monsieur*?"

"*Non.*"

"Would you not come for me on your own self, eh?" Sharpe gazed down at the older man.

"Yes," he had to admit. "Yes, I would have come to you myself—if it took that to get you to come for . . . for me."

"Why you want me so bad?"

"You . . . you are the best, I have heard. All the way into Canada, Emile." He sounded tired, so tired. "I am told you are the best." His voice trailed off to a whisper.

"*Monsieur.*" He grinned again. "Please do not play the game with me now. I live far to the north. I like it there. You bring me here all this way, this trip, to tell me you say I am the best." Now he leaned his face a little closer to LeClerc's. "I am the best." Then he pulled the grinning, scarred face back. "Now, *Monsieur*, you tell Emile why it is you hire two others to do the job for you, along with Emile Sharpe?"

"How is it that you know of this?" The old Frenchman was startled, genuinely surprised that the giant knew of the two waterfront assassins he had already hired.

A low chuckle filled the night. "You would know of me without friends in this city, eh?"

"*Oui.*"

"You would know of me if your friends did not know of the northern country?"

"*Oui. Oui* . . . but . . ."

"Ah, Emile has friends, too, *Monsieur.*" He chuckled. "You pay these two some good, you do. Ah, but they are not what you really need, eh?"

LeClerc knew not only that Sharpe was good at killing, a demon in a fight, but that the man must also be smart. How would they say it? A fox, perhaps a wise wolf—cunning and playful at times, but always deadly. Yes, he decided, this is the man for the job. A good one for the wilderness, those mountains—a man proven in the wilderness.

"You have the best of me—*oui*, Emile." He gazed out at the river, then back up at the big man's face. "I have hired two to go to the mountains, this you know . . ."

"*Oui, Monsieur* LeClerc," he interrupted. "You pay them good, you do. Ah, for them to have their hair pulled, you have paid them good! They will not know me?" He watched LeClerc nod. "They get in Emile's way—argghh!" He ran a large thumb around his neck. "Emile not like." Then his face gentled once more. "You pay these two good to have their hair pulled!" He laughed, and each time he did so, it made LeClerc's stomach tumble. It was not a gentle laugh, rolling with humor. No, there was an underlying sinister edge beneath the affable roar. "I know how good you pay these two. So, I know how good you will pay a man like me." He pounded a fist quickly against the broad barrel of his chest. "Emile Sharpe, *metis*-blooded, to bring your heart rest once more."

"*Mon coeur* . . . my heart, yes—to have it at rest after . . ."

"It come close to two year now, *Monsieur* LeClerc—*oui?*"

"*Oui,*" he responded. "You know of this, my son—you know of him?"

"Yes." Emile nodded slowly. "I know of your son. The other, the one you send your two killers after, he is in the mountains. That much you know. Yes. This much I know. There are not so many that one cannot be found. We have the same friends on the river. Only, *Monsieur*, you see—my friends are everywhere on the river. Go farther than your friends, yes. So, it is how I know for sure that the one you seek must be far upriver, far to the mountains." He nodded once more.

LeClerc did not speak.

"Emile Sharpe know about a job, yes—he know all that job before he go do it." The giant man sighed almost sadly. "How much is it that you really pay me for this big job?"

"I . . . I . . ."

"You tell me!" Emile brought a fist close to the old man's face. "You tell me how much."

"I will pay you what you want before you go . . ."

"And how much the money when I come back?"

"What . . .," LeClerc stammered a bit, watching the big fist drop away from his face and return to the man's side once more. ". . . whatever you want."

Yes, it was true. The old Frenchman had already invested much in the search for the killer of his son. He had paid bribes to countless informants, sent his own spies out to gather a bit of information here, some remnant of speculation there—all to learn the killer's whereabouts. He would not spare one coin left to him to see this thing done to bring his heart rest.

"Whatever it is you want. You name your price." Now he bowed his head. "Anything."

"This I know, *Monsieur* LeClerc. This I already know," Sharpe responded, almost with a touch of softness, a touch of sympathy. This old Frenchman would pay handsomely, would pay almost anything, perhaps his own life ultimately, if he could be allowed to kill the murderer himself. The son— LeClerc's son—he must have meant much to this old man.

"Yes, I know, *Monsieur* LeClerc. But I will need very little before I go." He turned partway back toward the river. "There is little you can give me before it is that I leave here."

Then Sharpe thought of the girl. Angelique. He must see the young woman before he would leave. Just one night he would have to have her before moving toward the west. To spread her legs and drink in the perfumes and powders of the pretty French maiden. A rich man's daughter . . .

"You see, like you—I, too, am a lord. Of all that I see in the wilderness. It is there I am a lord. There is none over Emile Sharpe." He bowed his head slightly. "And, when I return . . ." He thought of the old man, and a man's love for a son—what he himself had never had from his French father. This old man before him, not much older than himself. Yes, I am getting old, too—some forty-six seasons it was now.

"What is it that I should bring you to show?" Emile eventually inquired. "Bring you the body?"

LeClerc's head snapped up. "No!" He spit the word out. "No," he answered again, more softly now. He knew what he wanted from Sharpe.

"Then, it must be this—his scalp, eh?" He watched the old Frenchman rise from where he had been sitting on the crates. "*Scalper*, eh?" Then he saw the old man shake his head. "No, *Monsieur*? No scalp, eh?"

"Do you need the . . . information from me on this man you hunt?" LeClerc asked, diverting the question he really wanted to answer.

"No, *Monsieur* LeClerc," Sharpe said, a note of respect in his tone. "I need me nothing more. Before I say yes to any job, I all time know what I need to do that job. Emile knows he will find the one we want at the rendezvous in the mountains. I know where they rendezvous for the trading fair this summer that comes. Each year the traders, they say where the trappers are to go for the next summer. I know where they say this rendezvous it is going to be. I will be there. And Josiah Paddock, too. You see, eh?"

"Yes. Yes, I see." LeClerc reached into a vest pocket and removed the small velvet coin purse. It was heavy as he placed it in the giant's large hand. There in the open palm, the coin purse looked so small, so dainty and out of place against the massive spread of flesh. "For you, *Monsieur*. For whatever, before you go."

"Yes." Sharpe stared at the coin purse a moment, then stuffed it into the wide sash about his waist. "I will see you in the fall, then, my friend. Maybe, eh?"

The old man sighed at first. "It is so long to wait. The fall." LeClerc's words followed Emile Sharpe as the huge man began to disappear into the shadows once more. "Bring me . . ."

Sharpe stopped and turned. Only the side of his face, the right side with the wide jagged scar, showed. The rest of the man was shrouded in shadow. "Yes, *Monsieur*?"

"Bring me . . . his head!"

Bass moved along the river after crossing over the mountains, striking the river's path as it flowed to the west. He smiled, knowing he was getting closer. Now the waters were flowing in the same direction his soul was leading him. The ground had begun to drop away from him, too.

He had left the high mountains behind. Up there it was still winter. Winter with a vengeance. He had made it through the cruelest, soul-robbing time of year the mountains threw at a man.

"*Just 'nother time of the year a man's gotta live out here,*" he had once explained to Josiah over a frosty-morning fire. "*Man just make himself a home wherever he is, best way he knows how. These here doin's all rustled up by the Cold Maker, what the Crow call him. Know him too as the Winter Man. Talk of him bein' white as the snow you're sleepin' on—comin' right outta the north lands in the smack-dab of a real winter white-out. Shakes his ol' buffler robe an' the sky fills with snow. A real blazin' blue norther. Ridin' over the mountains on his white pony, snortin' the snow.*"

"Ridin' over the mountains on his pony . . ." His lips fell silent as he turned and looked behind him one last time.

The old trapper stayed with the Clark's Fork River as it wound itself between two ranges of low mountains after leaving what had become known as Hell's Gates, staying with the river even as it had pushed temporarily to the northwest. When the river he had supposed to be the Thompson flowed into Clark's Fork from the northeast, Titus decided that it was time to see if he could locate the old post. He was in English country now.

From the hillside above the grouping of small, ramshackle buildings, Bass wondered why the inhabitants had never put up a stockade, much less a wall around the buildings. He pulled the animals across the bottom land still dotted with tufts of old snow. The sky was heavy, lonely. It made all the more intense his secret desire to have some human companionship. He rode up to the buildings rehearsing what he would say, what he would ask of these traders, only to find that the post had been recently abandoned.

He stared at the desolate outpost, remembering something he had said a year ago. "*Son,*" he had told Josiah, "*this coon ain't seen a whiteman in, goin' on nigh seven, eight moons now. Every now an' then I gets tired of hearin' the sound of my own voice.*"

No one was there. Disappointment washed through him. No one to welcome him. So the trapper made himself at home. He picketed the ponies around the trading house and pulled his baggage inside, one load at a time. He set about starting a fire for cooking what scanty fare the trail had provided him in the last few days. It would not be much, he told himself. But Bass had been looking forward to this meal for many, many days now. Just to have something warm, something actually cooked over a fire to put down in his belly.

He sat somewhat uncomfortably, nervous at first, within the trading house—four walls around him and a roof overhead for the first time in many years. The late-winter winds blustered about the structures, setting up a strange wail. A ghostly wail, a longing wail.

Over the cry of the wind he thought he heard the singing of the coyotes. Along with the pelting of the rain on the shingled roof.

"Ain't no good when them critters is out howlin' in the rain." He spoke aloud for the first time in days. And the sound of the human voice surprised him, almost raising the hairs along the back of his neck.

"Yep," he continued. "Heard tell a coyote comes out to howl in the rain is really a Injun what was taken whilst his medicine was still strong—taken by the gods an' changed into the coyote critter to revenge some wrong done to them gods."

The chill prickled the back of his neck now. Reminded of so many dark nights such as this one, he recalled hearing the sounds of rocks crashing in so many distant valleys, that crashing magnified over and over as their deathly cries echoed about him. And he remembered all the while those legends of the giants warring in those hidden valleys and canyons.

Those sighs of the wind around the buildings only made more real the fears hidden deep within his bowels. The quivering shadows as the air sank and blew through the room and muscled the firelight around only made those once-forgotten fears re-emerge deep in his very mortal being. He looked out the glassless windows, watching the rainy mists swirl on the winds, watching the mists as they seemed to take ghostly form, then dissipate. Over and over the ghosts moved about his small refuge of warmth and light, where other humans had been before.

Those ghosts along the parapets of the castle he had envisioned many times before on those countless nights when Josiah had explained the characters and the scenes of *Macbeth* to the old trapper. The ghost that haunted him was not so different from the ghost that had haunted McAfferty. And the Whitehair's ghost. What eerie, deviled haunting he must have suffered.

What would lead a man to kill another, a friend? Sure it was, them witches had greeted Macbeth as though he were the king. But Duncan was the king. Macbeth was only one of them fellers under him. Those old witches had deviled him, sure enough—maybe only because Macbeth had for so long wanted to be king himself. Yep, Macbeth had long time hankered after the power himself. So when he heard them old hags of belching smoke and fire hail him as king, he thought he might just hurry things along a bit. Them witches, after all, were the ones given to the telling of things to come.

Was it up to a man to push things along on his own? Or should he wait until things come his way naturally? Asa had pushed things right along, trying to make them happen. And Bass had been satisfied with letting things flow over him, around him. Not so itchy the way McAfferty was, but finally swept up in it all.

What was one to figure was real, after all, in a world where a man with his wits about him could not tell the difference between good and evil? How could he hold it against Macbeth when it wasn't the man's fault if he could not tell good from evil in a world gone upside down? How could he hold it against Asa? Perhaps it was the sadness he felt now inside, with all that anger, knowing McAfferty must have felt he was doing what was supposed to be done anyway. Maybe tortured in his own mind with ghosts of his own.

It always seemed to be the man easiest for the Devil himself to use who looked to be the man who thought he was a man of God. He'd start off doing one thing wrong in the name of right—and it just got all the easier each time the Devil called. More and more such a fella thinks he's only doing what's right, and he's getting deeper and deeper all the time in the Devil's own claws. Devil never does nothing to catch a man. The poor nigger just catches himself for the ol' red feller. And then there ain't nothing he can do about it.

He jerked his head around again, watching the swirling mists of spring rain. He'd just deviled himself again. Making his own mind conjure up the ghosts and the Devil himself. Sleep was hard to come by, until Scratch finally realized that the haunting, wailing sound whispering through the room was only the wind slipping around the building. It was something he was not accustomed to. Finally, he fell asleep.

The next morning he didn't hurry away, staying to re-heat some of the meager fare he had cooked the night before. While it was warming over the low flames, Bass moved the ponies to some better grass, then explored the buildings. Nothing much had been left behind. Only when he came around the western wall of the main trading house, did Bass see the sign. The letters had been gouged out long ago, the large wooden plank now hanging precariously in the wind under the eaves. He nodded and smiled. He had been right after all. This was the post that traded with the Flatheads. Bass put his fingers into the incised letters on the wood sign, trying to make sense out of them, trying to remember the sounds to be made for each letter. None of the letters seemed to spell the sounds for *Flathead*. His fingers moved through the snaking path of the *S*, followed by the pyramid of the *A*, then an *L*, until he had traced all the letters in *SALEESH HOUSE*. Bass shook his head and moved away. He glanced once more at the sign, then sighed as he continued back to the trading house, feeling as if he had forgotten more about reading and ciphering than he had ever learned.

He dug into a few tins, prying the lids off with the tip of his knife. None held coffee. What he would give to have some coffee! He thought how stupid he was to expect the British traders to leave something of value behind. Still, he hoped. And there was some small comfort in being surrounded by a place that had once held human life. He mused that he must surely be getting old. Must be, to draw some comfort from merely being where other humans, whitemen at that, had dwelled. Years before he would have found this post an obscene intrusion in the wilderness. But now he took that small, warm comfort just in being within the once-busy trading post.

So he finally loaded the animals after breakfast and pushed them along the river, heading northwest again. After climbing the low hills, he paused and looked back. He gazed down at the grouping of low-roofed cabins one last time before turning and pushing the ponies over the hill, leaving the post, a marker for British lands, behind.

The river fooled him a few days later, growing wider and wider, then blossoming into a lake. There he made his camp. The next morning Bass backtracked to find a place to ford over to the river's southern bank, heading once more to the north and west. At the shore of the lake he pushed southwesterly around the large body of water. Better to do this, he decided, than move north around the lake. If his memory was correct, if what he had been told was true, Titus knew he had to strike out almost due west from here to hit the next post. Just like them Britishers, he smiled. Put them way-stations along the trail for him.

That night he drew the ponies up into a small grove of trees and made his camp. Sleep seemed somehow all the sweeter here beneath the stars. But there was an edge to his mind, knowing he was plunging deep into the British-claimed territory where he would be unwelcome. An American trespassing deeper and deeper with each passing day.

By god! They had no right to this country neither. It didn't belong to no man. Those who could stay were those who could wrench a living from the land, season after season—not running back to some trading post, not pulling back to the power and the might of some huge fort when it came time to leave the outpost. Bass felt the inner sanctity that came with knowing he was one of the few. Oh, the others might put on airs of being superior to him in some way. But, he felt the tiny glow within his own, private self brighten in knowing he was one of the few to whom this wild land had been kind, to whom this savage wilderness had opened itself reluctantly.

The next day Titus awoke to the damp chill in the air. The sky once again looked heavy. The clouds were gray and leaden, ready to drop on him at any time. He stretched in the new light, then realized what was wrong. The ponies were gone. He jerked at the blankets and robes savagely, pulling them away from his legs, and then wrenched the rifle into his hand.

"Goddamnit!" he cursed. "Niggers got my horses!" He stomped his foot in anger with himself. And shuddered in the damp chill air.

He had let his guard down too early, he surmised, thinking these Indians were friendly enough with whitemen. Flathead were still to the north and east of him now. These, these Indians were another . . .

Bass knelt over the scrambled pony tracks until he made sense of the direction they had gone. He kicked his robes and blankets under a tree, covered them with some pine boughs and laid a branch over the ashes of last night's fire. Then he took off on foot across the islands of snow.

It did not make any sense to him. The tracks he followed did not show signs of man. There were no moccasin prints along the animals' trail. And the ponies' tracks did not show that they were being ridden. They were not deep enough to show the burden of a rider. The animals' gaits did not show they were being ridden, either. Damn! If he'd only been more careful. Know better than to tie his one pony off and let the others be. Took the easy way and lost the ponies. Figured they'd stay with the buffalo runner, the one with the spotted rump. But his own pony had taken off, too. Even if they weren't stolen, he thought, the animals might be on their way back to some village right now, having been discovered by some Indian who could boast before friends of wild horse-raiding. Nigger just got him some free ponies, is all. But it just didn't make sense, the animals heading back toward the hills to the east.

He topped the low hill and spotted the ponies below him. Yep. Goddamned animals! Goddamnedest animals he had ever pushed and pulled across all those miles. They were down there, grazing in the bottom as if they were pasture stock. Slick as could be. He pushed off the top of the hill toward the ponies. Heading back home, they were. They had 'em enough of this ol' nigger, he thought.

His runner came when Bass whistled, all but two following dutifully. He looped his belt around the neck of the runner as a crude bridle, eased onto its bare back, and then went after the two that had balked. Bass leaned off the wide, bare back of his pony to grab the picket ropes that hung from the necks of the two wary, freedom-loving animals. Then he headed back to his camp. Nearing the site, Scratch smelled something strange. He tried to place the odor. Tried to wrench something out of his memory to make sense of it. Perhaps only the coming rain, he considered. Wet country like this full of strange smells.

Back in camp he hobbled the two wayward animals and picketed the rest with the pins driven deep into the soft, moist earth. Bass yanked away the pine boughs covering his baggage and dragged it closer to the fire pit where he would prepare some breakfast. He didn't have much left. Just a couple of strips of some dried meat. As it lay in his weathered palm, the meat didn't look all that appealing. His belly was ready for some fresh meat. He would go out to look for fresh game.

Bass checked the hobbles and picket pins one more time, checked the priming on both pistols and the rifle, and then headed off to the north, straight into the stiff, freezing wind. He had to run onto something to eat soon. If things continued this way, he'd be forced to cut the old snowshoes apart. His stomach lurched at the thought of boiling the rawhide strings of the snowshoes, perhaps even the rawhide boots he had made for the ponies many, many nights before when he was running to get out of Blackfoot country. All of that to make a pasty, nasty-tasting gruel. Still, such a gruel would nourish him in a small way. The rawhide still held some small meaty nourishment that would allow his muscles to fight the damp cold. Or maybe he'd have to kill a horse. But he would try to find some game first before he settled for snowshoe soup or gave up one of his horses.

He killed two small rabbits before he turned to head back to camp. It seemed like over an hour, moving about on foot, before he finally started back down the slope toward his camp. Over the top of the next low rise he heard the excited braying, the frightened whinnies of the stock. Bass instantly dropped the two rabbits and bolted off headlong to the top of the rise. Niggers getting into my animals now, he thought, his mind racing along with his heart.

At the top of the low rise he looked down the few hundred yards to the scene of the attack. One of the hobbled ponies was down and thrashing, its legs clawing at the air. The other animals circled around their picket pins, dancing frantically, rearing up to paw at the attackers with their front hooves, then kicking at the attackers with the back legs.

"*Lots of pilgrims as come to these here mountains, wantin' to run 'way from somethin', 'spectin' the mountains to take care of 'em,*" Scratch remembered having told his younger partner what seemed ages ago. "*Wolves has et many a time on greenhorns as thought they knew these here hills. Them's the kind as have their bones scattered all over by such scavengers as wait for others to do their killin' for 'em.*"

Bass knew how the animals worked at killing horses. And he felt stupid for not having taken measure to keep the horses safe in his absence.

The wolves would at first follow the man and ponies, keeping to the trees, out of sight most of the time, downwind for sure so that the ponies would not smell the danger. While the horses were grazing, one of the wolves, usually a ringleader or the male just below him in the group's hierarchy, would approach.

This wolf would frolic and roll, twisting his body playfully, coming ever closer to the pony chosen for the slaughter. With his rollicking, the wolf would reduce the horse's anxiety. His playful actions would also serve to rivet the attention of the pony. While the horse was paying all its attention to the cavorting decoy, another wolf, usually the most powerful in the band, would approach the horse from behind and when the moment presented itself, both the wolves would act in concert. As if at some pre-arranged signal, both wolves would leap on their quarry. The playful wolf would sink his jaws into the throat of the pony, while the second wolf would slash away at the pony's hamstring. In this manner, the two wolves could bring down the larger animal very quickly. And when the pony was on the ground, it did not stand much of a chance as the other wolves in the group rushed in.

Bass did not have a plan of attack as he rushed down the hill toward the ponies. He had reached the crest of the rise just as the two larger wolves leapt on their prey and brought it down, the horse thrashing and kicking wildly in its death throes. The old trapper was at full speed by the time the other four wolves came out from hiding and rushed the downed horse. They each pranced carefully through the flying hooves and legs of the other ponies that had suddenly become aware of the danger to each of them.

At first his ears were filled with the whinnying, helpless cries of the animals. But then his ears began to pound with the sound of his own racing heart: resound with the rasp of his own breath that seemed to fill his whole body. He burst into the moving, flowing circle of animals. A pony's flying hoof sent him sprawling toward the downed horse. Bass rolled over on his shoulder, cradling his rifle, and tumbled back onto his feet, wincing at the pain in his hip. He was hit almost instantly by a large wolf that sprang from the dry grass and leapt on top of him.

Scratch rolled the animal off and swung an elbow at the wolf, catching it across the muzzle. The wolf backed up a few steps, smarting from the blow, but there was another wolf charging the trapper. Bass had an instant to slip his hands down the muzzle of his rifle and swing it like a club. The weapon was in the middle of its air-singing arc as the second wolf leapt from the ground toward him. Bass stepped aside and struck the wolf full-force across the ribs.

Bass grunted with the shock of the blow as the wolf yelped in sudden pain. Titus wheeled with the rifle still in motion to crack the butt across the head of the first wolf. The animal sprawled across the top of the crusty snow and brittle grass, the side of its head spurting blood and one eye hanging grotesquely from its socket. It lay still on the snow, its legs kicking in death spasms.

The second wolf limped toward him, but cowered as the trapper swung the butt of the rifle in his direction. Bass danced away from the wolf toward the downed pony, knowing the horse was done for anyway. The legs of the other ponies flailed the air, their hooves as much a danger to their master as they were to the attackers. Two of the smaller wolves tearing at the side of the bleating pony raised their heads and snarled at the man's approach. They began to slink back from the carcass, growling and snapping at the trapper. Then one of them suddenly feinted as if to attack. Bass drew up the rifle butt just as the rib-wounded wolf landed on his back.

The man went down on his face, rolling again to his side, this time crashing into the bloody, disemboweled belly of the wounded pony, its legs flying in the air and striking both the back-riding wolf and the trapper. Scratch yanked the pistol from his belt as the jaws came open and the wolf came leaping at him again, its mouth full of phlegm and blood, dripping and spraying with each of its own vicious battle cries. Titus raised the muzzle of the pistol to follow the wolf's path through the air toward him, firing at the animal in the middle of the wolf's arc. The beast instantly dropped to the ground as if its strength had suddenly dissipated in flight.

Another wolf leapt over the body of the downed pony behind Bass, overshooting its mark. It landed, rolled once, and sprang to its feet to take another leap toward the man. Scratch jerked the rifle up and fired point-blank as the wolf's paws struck him, knocking him back against the dying pony. He watched the rifle's muzzle sink into the flying wolf's neck and pulled the trigger. Blood and tissue exploded from the back of the attacker's head. The body of the wolf thudded painfully onto Bass.

The fourth wolf came in with his last friend right behind him. One grabbed for the man's arm while the second tried to pull at the trapper's wildly kicking legs. The pain bit into Bass. The wolf's teeth clamped onto his right arm. Scratch tried to reach for his second pistol, but the wolf ripping at his leg pulled him down. Again the man tried to pull the pistol free from his sash but the right arm was held in the ripping vise of the wolf's fangs. Frantically, Bass reached for the pistol with his left hand and pulled it free. He pointed it and fired at the cause of the greatest pain. The wolf gripping his right arm was blown backward from the close-range force of the lead ball; its impact sent the animal sprawling over the trapper's legs and into the other wolf.

Bass yanked his legs up toward his body as the other wolf released its hold on his leg and lunged for his neck. Bass wrestled with the animal, attempting to strangle it. But the wolf was winning. Scratch was losing his strength after the first rush of adrenaline through his veins. But he brought his knees up into the wolf's belly and kicked. The push was enough to cause the wolf to back off far enough so that Bass could get to his knees and lash out with the pistol. He swung again and again with the pistol muzzle, wildly striking the wolf a few times.

That was effective for the moment. The wolf yelped in pain and backed off. The smallest wolf of the pack had never ventured into the fray, but had stayed on the outskirts of the action, snarling and threatening, its hair raised, the hackles bristling along its back. It now backed away from the man as the other wolf retreated from the pistol's clubbing blows. Bass got to his feet shakily, the pain surging down his ankle and right arm, the adrenaline still pumping.

The two remaining attackers began to slink backward, snarling and circling each other, but never feinting an advance or closing in on the trapper. Soon they retreated into the edge of the trees where they sat panting, the one wolf licking its wounds. Bass crouched low, feeling his pumping lungs and racing heart beginning to slow. He waited those long, agonizingly long, moments watching the two younger wolves retreat to the trees. Then he dropped exhausted to his knees beside the dying horse.

Its body still quaked in its dying. Too much had been ripped from its belly. The wolves had made quick work of the soft tissue and flesh. Only one thing for him to do. Scratch crawled over the animal's back and brought a knife out of his belt. His left hand wrenched the pony's jaws upward as his right hand slashed quickly across the horse's neck. The blood gushed over his hand, warm and thick. He felt the animal give one last, spastic jerk before it finally lay still. Merciful anyway, he thought, as he rose and looked over his shoulder at the two wolves sitting patiently some twenty yards away.

"Don't care me a shit for such critters, Titus Bass don't. Not one consarn," Scratch had once muttered to Paddock about a

wolf that let a couple of coyotes do its hunting for him, then came in to drive the hunters away and enjoy the feast he had not worked for. *"Black devil let them other poor critters lead 'im to a free meal, then come in an' take 'way from 'em. Cain't set with that. Catches in my craw, it does—thems as'll let others do theys work for 'em, then come in to take what the gettin's got. Got me somethin' 'bout such doin's as sours my milk."*

What a mess. He kicked at the baggage tied to the dead pony's back. He knelt and reloaded the pistols, then the rifle, before setting them across the flat surface of the dead animal's rear leg. With much effort, he loosened the cinches and yanked the wide leather straps free from beneath the pony. Slowly he began to gather the baggage strewn about the site of the wolf attack.

First the books.

He lifted up the muddied volumes and tried to wipe some of the snow and thick mud from the covers with his sleeve. He remembered last summer's rendezvous, when he had traded Elbridge Gray for them. He smiled, recalling how the other free trappers had chided him for wanting to trade for the books when he could not himself read.

"Josiah here can read with the best of 'em," Titus had responded quietly. *"This here partner of mine gonna be learnin' me to read them books all over 'gain this here winter with them Absor'kees."*

The old trapper swiped once more at the snow on the biggest of the two books, a thick volume with a fading dark blue cover, once again caressing the collection of Shakespearean tragedies as gently as any man would touch something very special to him. Then he knelt to take up the other volume, *The Pilgrim's Progress*, and set it across his left thigh. Bass rubbed at the muddy snow on the white leather cover that had already become soiled over several years among Gray's own packs. Then he finally noticed he was smearing blood across the book's cover. Almost sobbing, Scratch wiped at the drips of blood.

He smiled when he saw that most of the blood came off. The books were precious. The books were important friends to him now. Now more than ever. The Rocky Mountain college taught men through practical lessons, but many of its students also enjoyed the learning brought to them through literature. Many a trapper, including those who could not read themselves, found others to read to them. Those few who were better educated than the others were the teachers in the open-air institution of higher learning.

Finally he arose with his two valuable possessions, wrapped them in scraps torn from his yellow calico shirt, and stuffed them in one of the scattered packs. He distributed the baggage among the nervous ponies left to him.

Bass looked at the two wolves lolling like shadows in the trees. He knew what they wanted. He drew his knife, strode to the dead horse. The wolves would not get the choicest cuts, anyways. He wrapped the thick, warm steaks and liver in an old parfleche and then stuck his knife into the ground a couple of times to clear it of blood. He lashed the fresh meat aboard his own pony behind the saddle, then climbed onto the animal's back slowly.

His muscles ached. His wounds were beginning to cry out in pain. His whole body seemed to dread what he now pushed it to do. Another long day's ride. He felt the warm, wet dribble down his ankle, the thick syrup running from his wrist down the back of his hand. He slung the right wrist away from him, snapping the clinging blood off onto the snow. Not that bad, he considered. Not so bad he couldn't let the wounds stop bleeding on their own.

It was not that far to the next post anyway. Maybe a week. Maybe less. Get him some mending done there. A damned shame that he wasn't any good at sewing up his right hand with his left, a right hand that already was missing a finger from an angry bear's raking claws. Be all right—he'd get to that Britisher post. In this country, only critters come after him probably be the wolves when they finished their meal on that pony. He looked down at the dead animal. Such a waste. Losing so much. A friend, and the woman he loved. Then the best rifle he'd ever owned. And finally one of the ponies from rendezvous. He and Josiah had traded a young Nez Perce for those horses. An old squirrel rifle and some squeaky boots traded off. Then the boy's big horse thrown in to seal the bargain.

Nez Perce. He had to be in their part of the country now. Maybe some other strange red niggers hereabouts, other tribes this side of the mountains. He'd just keep himself out of trouble, skirting any camps he ran onto. Keep on going to the ocean. See for himself. And keep on going.

Strength to keep on going. He turned slightly in the saddle. Eat the best part while it's still warm. The fingers fumbled at the rawhide until he finally pulled the liver free, sat it across his lap and re-tied the parfleche behind his saddle. Then Bass kicked his pony into motion. The other animals reluctantly followed as the lead pony's movement yanked out the slack in their ropes.

He bit down into the raw liver, tearing with his teeth to free a section from the slimy organ. It felt good, the warm, raw, healing flesh sliding down his gullet. The rest of the meat in the parfleche would not spoil, he knew. In this temperature his own wounds would not spoil. Bass smiled. Fresh meat. The pony's and his own. The blood and juices from the organ seemed to fill more than his belly as he pushed down the draw and up the next hillside. The fresh meat seemed to sate his soul. He would draw strength from the pony's liver, strength that he needed to make it on to the ocean from here. He was better than halfway now and there would be no turning back.

Perhaps he was no better than the carrion-eaters, vultures, those creatures that fed on the bodies of the dead. Already half-dead himself, Bass considered it only fitting that he should join their ranks. If the strength his body took from the dead animal's flesh allowed him to survive the final days of his journey, then the wolf attack had been worth it. His wrist and ankle stopped dripping. He would not bleed to death, at least. Only his soul continued slowly to pump away his life-force. Seeping drop by drop. Only his soul continued to bleed.

Eleven

When first the pain started in her belly, Looks Far Woman had been riding behind her father in the late afternoon sun. She was to ride in no other place. She had brought some small disgrace upon the family. To be with child and not have a man was looked upon by her people as a bad thing, yet carried with it a special shame for she was the daughter of an important war chief.

Her father had asked Looks Far many times since last fall when she finally grew big inside her skin dresses whose child she carried. Each time the young woman's eyes looked to the ground. At first her father had spoken angrily. In recent weeks he had become quiet with her, perhaps finally accepting the fact that his daughter was going to bear this child, was going to raise it alone—doing both proudly. Perhaps he had faced the fact that he should accept the child, too. It was too late for anything else. The family had stayed with the tribe, and he had begun to hold his head up once more as the others in their winter camp came to accept the woman with no man soon to have a child.

Now they followed the clan chief who would lead them to their new spring home along the river whose waters rushed on to the western ocean. They were migrating north and west, across a plain blown free of most of its snow by recent chinooks. It was a course others plotted. And Looks Far followed.

The first time she had felt the pain arrive as a teasing of what was to follow, a testing of her muscles for the work to come. The young woman who was a girl last summer had said nothing then. Perhaps it was nothing. But she had tried to count those long months since she had had her last bleeding. That was when she had begun to add a pebble from the ground to the tiny pouch hanging from her belt. With each full moon, Looks Far chose another pebble: a single, round, multi-colored stone to mark the coming and going of the full moon, without flow. For only four winters she had been bleeding and now she was to be a mother. Perhaps her man would be happy to know.

But as she looked over her shoulder to the south, where surely she believed he must be, she could only imagine how far away he was. The teasing pain rose slowly within her belly, low within her pelvis again, to remind her how long they had been riding this day. It seemed that they had been riding all their days together. Moons had come and gone since last she had suffered the sickness that filled her stomach, pushing it up her throat and into her mouth to splatter on the ground and choke her with its smell of rottenness. She had been glad to see this sickness leave her by the time her tribe made their winter camp close to the base of the mountains. Quietly she had carried the early-day sickness and her misery alone. It was not good for her family to know. They must not think she was weak. But her mother's eyes told her through those long weeks that the older woman already knew.

Looks Far gazed up at the hillsides and mountains framing this long, narrow valley. Everywhere white as she rubbed her belly beneath the robe draped from her shoulders. The little life had been kicking for over a moon now, and once he had even made her cry out in real pain. His legs must be strong, she had told herself when the pain had finally passed—legs that will kick and run, dodge and play with the other boys of their village. He would be accepted. The shame would go away. And she would learn to live without her man. The ultimate pain that stayed with her day and night came with the realization that her man would never know of the little life they had made together.

The little life had rolled and tumbled within her, and once she had thought the being there would choke itself out from the hiccups. But that, too, had passed. From time to time she had allowed her young sister to put an ear to her belly, to listen to the little life within, to feel the little life move and kick in her belly. Each time Looks Far had wished it was her man who put his ear to her belly, to talk softly to the little life within her.

Perhaps she had dropped a pebble somewhere without knowing it. One hand slipped beneath the robe again to count the stones in the pouch as she had counted so many times before. There were only eight, and she feared that was not enough. But maybe she had dropped a pebble somewhere and had not missed it until now that the coming pain made her count the stones more often while they rode. She looked over her shoulder once again, to the south. That was the trail her heart took each time it led her thoughts away from the duties at hand. So she would find another pebble to replace the one she had dropped. That would make her heart sleep softer in the nights to come.

Her father stopped when the signal was given as the sun began to fall behind the hills to the west. She rode up beside him to hear him say this was where they would camp for the night. The trail had been long since leaving winter camp, he said, but in two short suns' ride they would be to the place where the tribe would stay until the buffalo hunt was over. Then, her people would begin to travel to the whiteman's great camp.

A year it had been since last the people had traveled to the gathering of the hairy faces. Now they wanted to trade again with the faces hidden behind the hair, and join in the celebration. But first the hunting. And first the little life must come to meet her. All this before she could allow herself to hope against all hope that her man would meet the little life tumbling within her.

As the words came from her father's lips and he began to slip from the pony's back to the snow, she felt the little life within her push hard against something under her ribs, then at her back. The sudden movement took her breath from her and she could not get it back. Looks Far Woman's eyes grew moist and the tears rolled from them. She cried out. She had not meant to, but the sound had escaped her tongue before she could bite it to show that she was strong in her pain. This for her people. This for the little life to come. This for her man so far to the south.

Through the thick clouds over her eyes she saw her father rush back to her, look up at her and question in words that barely passed through the ringing in her ears. Is it the child, he wanted to know. She bit her lip and nodded her head. Yes.

Is this her time, her father asked.

How was she to know if it was her time! A few, fast-moving moons before she had been only a girl. But, yes—she knew. Her father asked again.

"Yes!" Looks Far cried out as the little life pushed hard against her under the ribs once more. The pains were hard now. They were strong and coming more often, like the bubbles in a kettle, preparing to boil.

Yes, she cried, then realized her father had not asked anything more of her. She bit her lip and lowered her eyes. This must not be, she told herself. Her father must not think of her as a girl. She was a woman, and she belonged to the man of the south. And a woman did not cry out with the birthing of the little life.

The light would soon be fading from the western sky. Women of the village bustled in tiny knots of fierce activity as they scurried to erect temporary lodges as shelters against the bitter night temperatures to come. Willow was quickly cut and dead tree branches stripped of small limbs to form crude frames over which blankets and hides could be thrown for cover against the night frost. These would not be warm shelters, but at least some of the damp frost would be held at bay. In the midst of each group there began to appear the tiny glow of firelight as younger children did their part to defend against the coming cold and darkness.

Near what seemed to her to be the center of this little whirling universe of her people sat Looks Far. She shifted her position from time to time to find a more comfortable spot with the robe wrapped cocoon-like about her on the ground. A younger sister brought her a thin broth made of crumbled pemmican in warm water. Looks Far sipped at it and found it disagreeable. She put it aside and pulled the robe more tightly about her as a protection against the night chill. The rolling pressure welled up once more within her to cut her breath short.

About the young woman the small fires began to dim until most were merely pockets of soft, blood-like glows across the meadow. When the moon came up Looks Far contented herself to look at it, to try to think of the white ball only. Soon it would be full, and she could then put another pebble in her pouch. She could add two now—one for that pebble she had lost and one for the full moon coming. Then she would have enough. Then, she would feel better about the pain between her hips.

Oh, how often she wanted to move closer to the glowing embers near her family's shelter—just to warm her hands, to warm her tiny, cold feet. And to warm the cold, tumbling, angry knot in her belly. But she bit her lip and held her tongue. And watched the sky. And tried to think of other things.

Everywhere white, she thought. Looking around her she saw that it was everywhere white with the snow. That same pale, bluish-white that the late winter moon gives to the night landscape. Even the sky resting so close above her looked flecked with the soft white flakes, but they did not fall. They were only stars and she had tried to count them once as a little girl. Now her pains were as many as the stars and she had lost count of them. Looks Far would count the stars now instead, and talk to the little life within her belly about the beauty of this winter night when he told her he was ready to come out to meet her.

There were lights in the forest, too—not like the stars so close over her head. These lights stayed on the edge of the forest surrounding the meadow where her people began to pull robes around them now and sleep close to other tired bodies. She knew these lights to be the eyes of the forest watching her, measuring her in this time of cold pain. She would not let them see her clench her fists against the belly and double over with the shaking work of the muscles—this she reminded herself. This she kept saying each time she saw the eyes of the wolves that shone like lights in the black forest.

Once she rose to get herself a drink from the kettle that

already had a thin crust of ice on the water's surface. She waddled like a fat buffalo cow heavy with calf. She knelt to dip a
cupped hand into the water. It felt good trickling over her dry
lips. She realized how thirsty she had become from the short,
raspy gasps that accompanied the rising of each wave of pain.
She bent once more for another small, cupped handful, but
pulled back. She closed her eyes with the rising push between
her hips and did not see the star racing overhead in its fiery
journey across the sky nor its fall beyond the hills to the south.
The little life jolted her violently as she squatted near the kettle, but this time it felt as if he were running a tight fist across
the inside of her belly. Looks Far wondered how much longer
it would take him to come meet her. And she knew it would not
be long.

It was good, she thought, rising slowly to stand on trembling, tired legs, with the dampness seeping between her
thighs. It was warm when it first came, as she knelt awkwardly
by the kettle to drink away the dryness in her throat.

And now the warm wetness between her legs turned cold in
the night and she knew the little life within her was ready to
come meet her. She must not squat again until she was ready
for him, she told herself as she waddled back to a soft spot near
the two shelters her family had erected. Squatting was the way
she would let the little life slide out of her belly.

She must not push. Not yet, she reminded herself. Then,
yes then, in the bright splash of day the lights in the forest
could not tell the Spirits of the tears creasing her cheeks and
the low moan she bit back in her throat. They could not tell,
for it was hers alone to know.

Ponies nearby snorted with exhaustion, blowing out against
the cold night, too trail-weary to paw through the snow for a
shoot of something green to eat. The pale light showed their
hanging heads haloed with the thin, disappearing vapor that
escaped from their nostrils. But her time was only the beginning of the much-work the women of her tribe had told her was
to be. She thought on those things, trying hard to remember
them, in order to push the crowding pain from her mind.

She forced her mind to drift away from the pain in her belly,
to bring to her ears once more the words of the old women
with her first one-time-a-moon bleeding. Over and over her
belly the women had rubbed their fingers to try to tell her
about the process to come. And now her mother was beside

her, pulling the edges of the robe apart and running her fingers over the young woman's belly, telling her little life it would not be long now.

Her mother's chattering and her sister's questioning words said nothing, meant nothing to her now as they helped her to one of the cold shelters thrown up against the night frost. She hoped her little life would know the sound of his mother's tongue with so many squawking around her now. Neighbors came to wag their tongues and add their own chatter to her mother's until all the voices blended into a cacophony.

Finally, there was only one voice that remained with her in the shelter. There was only one face she could dimly make out in the pale light, as she strained to see through the hot dampness that stung her eyes. Were these tears, Looks Far asked, or only the salty, bitter wetness that comes to stain my brow when I work so hard?

The older woman took up the young hand and squeezed it, as if to tell Looks Far to squeeze when the pain in her belly rose again. Looks Far answered and squeezed the old hand that held hers. Then the old hand left hers and went to her belly. There the fingers gently pushed across the wide mound that warmed the little life, trying to feel where the baby lay within her.

When the hands started to lift the bottom of her dress, Looks Far protested and started to rise to cover herself, pushing her mother's hands away from her. That was her private being: for her. And her man. And now her little life coming to meet her. No one else, she cried out to her mother who chattered back with soft, slow words.

Looks Far finally allowed the older woman to untie the soft leggings from the belt beneath her dress and slip them off slowly. The pains came closer together now. From the corner of her eye she could plainly see in the pale light that she had stained the light-colored leggings, with the warm wet when it had come earlier in the night. But she could clean them, to make them presentable when at long last she would show her man their son. She would brush her hair until it shone as deeply lustrous as a winter-kill hide. She would wipe her eyes, pushing from her shiny cheeks the stains of the tears that ran steadily across her face finally to caress the softness at the fold of her neck.

The older woman took her moccasins from her feet before pulling the light robe over the young one. The chills shook her daughter after every pain. Her mother was trying to tell her something. Looks Far blinked her eyes to push away the blinding tears and watched the old woman pantomime for her. She put one hand to her head, then pointed to her own belly, low between the hips, and nodded her head quickly to say *yes*.

Now the old finger pointed to her head again, then to the side of her belly. The older woman shook her head from side to side. She seemed sad to Looks Far. What was she trying to say? Why should she look so sad? The little life within her was coming to meet her now and everyone should be happy. Then the pain gripped her as never before. The long fingers deep in her belly slowly encircled her from the inside—tighter and tighter until the two hands formed one hard, tight, squeezing fist that shook itself within her being. She cried out.

When the fist loosened itself slowly, Looks Far called out weakly for her mother and her sisters. Her mother had had the little life come to her five times already. Her mother would tell her what to do now that the little life was wanting so much to come out.

The fist came and went again, raking the inside of her belly. Looks Far shuddered with the easing of the pain and her legs shook without control. Her mother called out to a sister to build up the fire once more. Looks Far turned her head to see the younger girl scurry to add kindling to the glowing embers. Then she closed her eyes and sought out a place within.

When next Looks Far opened her eyes, her sister was handing their mother a small kettle. Her mother offered her something in an elkhorn spoon that steamed like the trails of ghosts in the frosty air. With one arm she helped the young woman rise to her elbows and held out the spoon in her other hand.

Looks Far sniffed of the thick soup in the spoon and felt sickened at it. Her head began to swim and she felt hotter than before. She knew her stomach was crawling to her mouth again and turned her head. When it came there was not much to push past her tongue and spit out. Only the sick taste from her stomach that burned and made her choke. The older woman poured the soup on the ground and dropped the spoon. She cradled the young Flathead squaw in her arms until the convulsive vomiting had passed, then eased Looks Far back on the makeshift bed.

Again and again her mother tried to coax Looks Far to drink from the spoon, but it was of no use. Looks Far felt sickened by the smell of the broth. She wanted to let her stomach out of her mouth each time, but there was nothing left to pour from it.

Her mother began chattering excitedly once more, her words pouring out in a different pitch—her pleas now more frantic, more urgent than before. She showed Looks Far the two short staffs driven into the ground near the foot of the bed. The older woman squatted before them facing Looks Far. Then she gripped a staff in each hand and rolled her face up as if moving her bowels. Again and again, she pantomimed, repeating the urgent words, her pinched face swelling, the flesh pushing against, contorting, the deep wrinkles of many winters.

Looks Far finally remembered the telling in moons gone away of the grabbing of the two stakes and then pushing. If she squatted over the robe with her hands gripping the staffs, she had been told, she could push the little life out. Then the pain moved her remembering to the now as the rumbling tore everything away but the present. The fist was tensing within her more and more frequently, each pain coming on top of the one before it like beads strung together on a thong. It would be soon, she told herself. Then Looks Far cried.

Nute and Redman were both nursing hangovers by the time they arrived at the Sublette & Campbell store on Washington Avenue. This painful end to their last drunken spree in St. Louis made both men edgy, irritable, and full of nagging doubts about going through with this march across the prairies to the summer rendezvous in the mountains. There was the promise of money—dollars, guineas, pistoles—whatever it would be. All the same, it was money the two could spend upon their return to the city by the river, their mission completed, their assassination a success. During the past few days the two men had laid wild, elaborate, drunken plans to spend their new wealth upon their return. And that wealth would be enough to make life a lot easier for some time to come. Enough wealth so that both men could eventually ward off those self-doubts and fears, that anxious, nervous worry over the journey now facing them.

They stood in the slowly milling crowd of some forty men who jostled against each other in front of the shop on Washington Avenue that cool, damp, cloudy morning as the sun began to break over the horizon to the east. It was quite a collection of clerks, mule-tenders, general laborers necessary to transport the trade goods valued at some $15,000 west to the mountains. Nute remained sullen despite the muted, joyous mood of the throng at embarkation. Redman had to admit that he was finally finding the prospect of the journey across all the trackless miles a little less formidable, a little less frightening. He stepped toward a twenty-six-year-old man near him.

"You know what day this is?" Redman leaned close to the stranger.

The other man turned toward Redman, caught the foul stench from many days of whiskey and damp sweat on the man who had addressed him. He looked Obahdiah up and down before answering. "Looks as if to be the day we are leavin' for the mountains, friend."

"I can see that," Redman snapped. The man averted his eyes. "I ain't stupid," he tried to explain. "Just me an' Hickerson here, we had us a few days of celebratin' before we leave." He saw the stranger finally look over at him again. "Lost track, is all, my friend. I mean to ask you what date. We lost track, is all."

"Twentieth," the stranger answered, sympathetically this time. Then a smile came across his broad face. "April—in case you and your friend there been celebratin' for that long a time." The stranger saw Redman draw back now and turn toward Nute to laugh.

"Ain't been more'n a month, it ain't." He laughed along with Nute. "A few days, maybe. No longer'n that, eh, Hick?" They both laughed until the pain of aching heads ended the joke. "What day is it anyway? What day that make it—the twentieth?"

The stranger smiled almost benevolently. "That makes it Saturday." He turned to watch some activity near the two double doors at the front of the shop.

"Saturday, eh?" Redman answered. Then the inspiration to be civil struck him. "Name's Redman. Obahdiah Redman." He stuck out his grimy hand.

"Larpenter's the name," the stranger answered. "Charles."

"An' this here's Hickerson Nute." Redman finished pumping Larpenter's hand, nodding his head toward his sullen, silent partner. Larpenter withdrew his hand and offered it to Nute. Hickerson finally shook it briefly.

"First time?" Charles inquired.

"How you mean?" Redman answered.

"First trip to the mountains?"

"Oh, yeah," Obahdiah answered. "Our first. Goin' out to take us care of the mules for these fellas. Watch the stock for 'em." He stepped back from the edge of the boards that formed a low platform in front of the shop. "You gonna be tendin' stock?"

"No," Larpenter answered quickly. "A clerk for Campbell. Won't have much to do 'til we get out to the mountains." He stepped back alongside Redman. "My first trip, too, friend. It's new to most of us here." His arm swept an arc across the crowd. "Campbell and his partner, William Sublette, just last winter formed them this company for the mountain trade. Both been to the Rockies before. Came back last year and formed them a new company to supply the rendezvous where them trappers come to get 'em supplies. Sublette, he's goin' upriver with some goods for the posts in the upper country. Campbell, an' us with him, goin' across the flats toward the mountains."

Redman retrieved a bottle from his coat pocket, pulled the cork. He stared at the small amount of liquid in it before turning the bottle up to his lips and draining what remained. He brought the small bottle down from his face and smacked his lips.

"Be the last of that you'll have before you hit the mountains, friend," Larpenter commented.

"An' I'll be one to miss it on the trail—friend," Redman answered. He turned to Nute. "You got you any left?"

"Best you finish it now, if you have any more on you," Charles suggested. "Campbell don't like drinkin' on the trail."

Nute produced another small bottle that was still about half full. He took a slug of the cheap whiskey from it and passed it on to Redman. Obahdiah drank quickly, wiped the top with a dirty sleeve and offered it to Larpenter.

"No, thanks," he answered. "I don't often . . ."

"Larpenter!" a voice from the crowd at the door called out. "Charles Larpenter!"

"Campbell's callin' me now." Charles began to move away into the crush of bodies. "We'll see you on the trail." Then he was gone in the push of men at the door.

Redman watched as a man he supposed was Robert Campbell, just twenty-nine years old this spring, handed Larpenter some sheets of thick paper. The leader of the supply brigade gestured and the two disappeared inside.

Redman and Nute moved through the crowd of men toward the front of the shop, stepping out of the way of a number of saddled horses that were being brought to the front of the crowd. Down the street, turning the corner from Second Street, plodded the first of the horses and mules. They had been loaded with the heavy packs of trading goods by baggage handlers at the warehouse near the wharf and then led to the embarkation point at the shop. Within minutes more than two hundred animals pushed against one another along the narrow, muddy street. The sun was just breaking over the horizon, smearing a little light into the band of open sky beneath the heavy gray clouds.

The group of men boiled away from the doorway as several figures emerged from the shop. One of these well-dressed men stepped forward and addressed the assemblage. The long, curled mustache he sported moved slightly beneath the thin, aquiline nose as he spoke in a voice thick with a Scottish accent.

"Men, we are about to leave this city behind," he began. "Most of us will not see St. Louis again for many months, next fall at the earliest, perhaps." He pointed toward the stomping herd of mules. "Each of you will be given one mule to ride, and two more loaded with baggage and such to care for. They, these three animals, will be in your charge for the remainder of the journey. The two mules you pack along with you are carrying many pounds . . . let us say, much wealth in goods destined for the mountains. That wealth is in your charge. It will be your personal responsibility. Do not fail Mister Campbell." The man, who was slightly over middle-height, paused for effect. He was spare, but broad-shouldered, possessing a military bearing despite shoulders that seemed a trifle bent. His long, thinning, brown hair hung nearly to his shoulders, neatly combed and in place around the square face and the restless grayish-blue eyes that darted back and forth in their sockets with great intensity.

"I repeat: do not fail Mister Campbell"—the voice carried over the throng—"and each man will be paid very handsomely upon his return from the Rocky Mountains. Men!" He paused again. "To your animals!"

Nute and Redman joined the jostling, murmuring mob as

the men bulled their way toward the waiting mules. At last, near the tail of the caravan, the two partners found six mules not already chosen by others. Both men stood beside their animals awaiting further instructions as some cattle, both bulls and cows, were brought up by handlers and herdsmen.

"Shit!" Redman wrinkled his nose as one of his mules emptied its bowels onto the muddy street. "Takin' the whole goddamned farm, we are!" He watched the steam rising in the damp air from the freshly laid pile. "Just as long as you don't shit where I'm gonna lay my head every night," he said as he slapped the mule along its flank, "you an' me gonna get along fine."

"To St. Charles." The Scottish accent rose in the air as the stranger mounted his horse at the head of the caravan. "And the Rocky Mountains!"

There was some cheering, shoving, and cursing as the men climbed aboard the mules and took up the lead ropes for those mules behind them. Those in the lead plodded off down the street, crossing Lombard and heading west out of town. Eventually the men and animals in front of Nute and Redman began to move out. Redman let Nute come up beside him as the procession moved out of the narrow thoroughfare that was Washington Avenue toward the broader, rougher lanes leading them west into the wooded countryside.

"S'pose they got beddin' for us, don't they?" Nute inquired, looking over at his partner.

"Surely they do," Redman answered. "Couple of blankets apiece, under them canvases back there." He tossed his head toward the four mules following them. "They got us everything they said we'd need for the trip back there. And, Hick, all we gotta do now is find this Paddock fella, get 'im, an' bring back that pistol to Monsur LeClerc. Make us some money for our trouble gettin' to them Rocky Mountains with these mules here. Not too bad a deal we made, eh?"

He matched Hickerson's grin. "We might even have a good time, too—come this rendezvous out there. Have us a drink or two on this Campbell fella, fuck us some squaws like they say is always there to get your cock hard. They love us white fellas, they say. Right?"

Nute nodded his head.

"Everythin' two fellas could ask for on a lil' journey," Hickerson continued. "Drinkin', fuckin'—an' killin'." He smiled broadly beneath the many days' growth of whiskers. "Some

drinkin' first—then a lotta fuckin'. An' we do what's most fun
for us—the killin', eh? Some killin'."

Twelve

"It is so hard," she whispered, her voice a rasp deep in her
throat. Looks Far peered through misty eyes at her mother.
"There is more help needed for this . . ." She broke off as she
felt the tumbling pain begin to roll over her once more.

The older woman gripped her daughter's hand again as another muscle spasm washed over the young woman. Quickly
she threw back the edge of the blanket that hung over their
makeshift shelter and called out to her younger daughter.

"Grass Singing!" She waited the few seconds it took for the
girl to come. "You must find the woman your sister needs—
Dreams of Horses! Bring her here, now! She will bring this
child out! Go, now!"

Looks Far panted as the rippling seizure eased, giving her a
short respite. Her limbs quivered, her eyes clouded over with
the agony of labor. She shook inside as the tears flowed in answer to the pain. She tried to lick her lips to moisten them, but
her tongue seemed stuck within her dry mouth and failed to
respond. Knowingly, her mother helped raise her head again
and gave her liquid from the elkhorn spoon. As she dropped
the spoon again into the small kettle, sounds of feet shuffling
over the snow broke through the blanket and hide shelter.

Part of the covering flew back and a small shaft of light shone
behind the dark, skeletal shadow of the old woman. No one in
the tribe knew for sure how old the woman was, this Dreams of
Horses—for the old woman herself was not sure. It only
seemed as if she had been old when the present elders of the
tribe had been children. She lived on, through winter after
winter, the wrinkles merely growing deeper, the thinning skin
ever molding itself to the skeleton it still attempted to hide.

Years before, in a time before anyone in the tribe now living
had been born, the old woman had paid a handsome price to a
tribal visionary for those secrets she had used repeatedly in
cases of a difficult delivery such as this. Dreams of Horses now

hoped her medicine would be enough once more as she knelt beside the robe bed to touch the young woman's forehead with a skeletal fingertip. Her hand moved away and ripped open the front of her own blanket coat. From the belt that hung about her waist by what seemed to be only a promise, she drew a small pouch from among an assortment, untied it and probed its contents.

"Turn her." The old throat cracked out the words softly. She did not look at either Grass Singing or the young girl's mother. The two quickly responded by pulling a robe aside and rolling Looks Far onto her right side, away from the ancient woman. "Her dress," she crackled again. "Lift it." Looks Far did not protest as the skin dress was pulled up beyond her waist to expose most of her bare back.

The woman withdrew her hand from the pouch. Between two fingers were small particles that she began to rub into the small of the young mother's back. Again and again she retrieved more of the mixture of a secret root and dried ground horned toad from the pouch, then rubbed the mixture into the skin of the young woman who moaned with the coming of the next pain. Dreams of Horses continued her massage through the next several pains and then retied the pouch and stuffed it into her belt.

Looks Far could not remain on her side any longer. She let herself fall once more on her back. As the pain moved some distance away from her, the young mother opened her eyes to see if she could make out the forms gathered closely about her bed. As she stared at the ancient one, a bony finger came up to touch her lips into silence.

"The feathers." Dreams of Horses hissed. "The feathers," she repeated, this time looking at Goes Away Dancing. "Her man's feathers. They have been taken from this lodge?"

Goes Away Dancing understood. "She, she has no man. He . . . he has no feathers." When the ancient one looked down at the young mother again, Goes Away Dancing continued. "Her man has no feathers—no."

The ancient one drew her face very close to Looks Far's before she spoke, her short breath coming like puffs that stank with a foul odor in the young girl's nostrils. "Entrails, the entrails," she repeated herself. "Have you eaten," she said as she took another breath, "the insides of the four-legged . . ." Laboring for breath, she continued her questions, ". . . the entrails . . . of the walks-about?"

Looks Far turned her head, slowly shook it, not only in answer to the question, but also to escape the acrid breath.

"The flying one." More of a statement than a question. "Have you . . . eaten a bird in the last moon?" A thick cough rattled in the old woman's throat.

Again Looks Far Woman shook her head. Dreams of Horses merely nodded once and pulled the front of the dress up so her hands could slide over the swollen abdomen. She pushed and prodded from side to side, probing from just below the ribs down toward the groin. Then she held her hands within the young woman's pubic hair while another contraction shook Looks Far.

"This one," the ancient visionary began, "this life . . . it is big . . . for her." Dreams of Horses looked down at her belt again to choose from among the assortment of skin pouches. From one she took a pinch of fine dust and held her fingers beneath Looks Far's nostrils.

"This medicine . . . the old men say . . . old men . . . long ago, old men . . . into your nose. You sneeze . . . make you sneeze for the turtle. The turtle . . . will come to chase." She coughed again. "Turtle chase the baby out. He is . . . big to . . . chase out."

Looks Far sneezed twice as she inhaled the fine powder into each nostril. There was a strange sensation that came with the release of the sneeze, a lightheadedness that washed over her. She yearned for sleep, if only between the pains that were becoming an onslaught. The ancient one leaned over her and pressed down upon her abdomen just below the ribs.

"No despair," the old woman spoke. "This big one . . . will come to . . . his mother." She felt the tumbling of the baby within the young mother. Dreams of Horses took from her belt another pouch and drew a dried root from it.

"This . . . you chew." She offered the wrinkled object to the heavens, then placed it against the young mother's lips. A long-ago person had taught Dreams of Horses of this plant she could only call by the name "buffalo-do-not-eat-it." Perhaps it would put the young woman to sleep, so that the baby would come out at last. Perhaps the young mother could dream through her work and the pain would move away from her body.

As Looks Far chewed on the root, it made her think of things dead and dying, like the buffalo in the river when spring floods had drowned the shaggy beasts, their decaying, stinking bodies bobbing as they washed along the banks of the rivers.

She wondered if she were dying, in giving breath to the little life within her.

Was she passing over into that other land the elders spoke of when honoring the fallen warriors? Why should the passing be so hard? And still she chewed, feeling the numbness flow into her arms and legs, bringing them to rest from their shaking torment. Her breathing slowed.

Dreams of Horses watched the young woman's limbs relax and felt a hidden smile grow across her old heart. The root was working. Her own back ached from bending over the young woman. The ancient one straightened the crackling bones along her spine. She put old fingers to her neck, removed the thong around it. Dreams of Horses placed the thong over the young mother's head, then adjusted the charm between the young breasts. This was the gift of an ancient one, given many winters ago in a tribal meeting from a woman of the Crow.

The old woman released the charm and let it lie against the firm mounds, remembering the Sparrowhawk name for this special rock medicine. *Bacoritse*. A curious object of sacred charm, to the non-Crow merely a fossil of strange shape and color, now heavily wrapped with beads of purple, yellow and red. Perhaps this placement of the charm around the young mother's neck was the last thing the ancient one could do without help from One Above.

There had not been that much warmth escaping from the struggling embers, yet Dreams of Horses drew some heat magically from the bloody embers. Indeed, it was warmer inside the shelter with the young mother and those of her women, but this aged visionary needed to draw upon the wisdom of the night. She disappeared into the cold darkness.

Finally she pulled the shelter cover aside and slipped within once more, returning to kneel with painful creaking beside the young woman with the swollen belly. As she settled upon the edge of the blankets, Dreams of Horses took from her belt two charms suspended on solitary thongs. These she set beside one another near the top of the young mother's rounded belly. The old woman slowly stretched her hands, the right palm to cover the beaded turtle, the left to shelter the beaded lizard. Then the old one closed her eyes to shut out everything else, to close herself to the world now as she opened herself to the help of One Above. Through him she would bring this baby forth.

Through her he would bring relief to the young mother with the too-big little life within.

Dreams of Horses let all thoughts slip from her mind as the words came to her lips. Eventually she began the ancient song chanted over a mother in labor. This the old Flathead woman would sing for the young mother.

Kouk, kou u mi nin tchou min,
Sei-tklish ta po min.
Sow-ool k ats min,
Sow-ool k ats min,
Tiltco ta pai pahtoo.
Sin-ko-sow; kaw-muck er sno.
Tuh tuh pai ish.
Smai-cout sei-tsum tchin-pucki.

Her trembling voice grew in its intensity as she repeated the special song over and over, rocking to and fro beside the young woman, her hands continuing to shelter the medicine charms protecting the belly, calling out to the belly to give forth the little life.

High, upon the mountain top I flew,
My face grew hot.
The white cow buffalo,
The white cow buffalo,
Came running toward my hiding place.
The sky shows me; her old years talk to me.
Never do I ride stars.
She moves through my days without fear.

Still the fist was made and loosened in her belly. But the heaviness in her head had slipped away. Looks Far ran her tongue around the inside of her cheeks to again taste the sweetness of the broth. She would rest now and let the little life find its own way out to meet her. Constantly her nostrils filled with the smell of burning sweetgrass incense, twisted into a braid and lit with a coal from the fire. The shelter became strongly scented with the sweet fragrance. Looks Far drew the essence deeply into her lungs, feeling the smoke lift her body gently as if she were floating a few inches above her bed. She floated into sleep and sank into dusky dreams of snowy forests shrouded in darkness, of wolves tearing at her belly, and of her bearded man come to save her in the blinding whiteness.

Dreams of Horses kept the braids of sweetgrass lit and let the incense pour over the young mother. She continued to kneel beside the big belly and cup her hands over the turtle and the lizard, there to pray and sing the song of old.

It had started to snow, only gently though, with the big, fat flakes that silently spoke of a long-time snow. They fell and were now and again blown by the winds into the small shelter of hides. The woman of many winters hunched down, fatigued, at the young woman's side.

She wanted this girl to have this baby more and more as the hours wore on. Perhaps, she thought, she wanted it even more than she had wanted her own children: children she had seen born, grow and die—leaving her alone for years beyond counting. Yes! She prayed to One Above that this one would see her child born, grow and die of old age; offered a prayer for this young mother to be proud and filled with the joy that would make her forget this time of labor and pain.

All across the young woman's belly, pushed and disfigured with the signs of life within it, Dreams of Horses brushed the sprig of sage she had first held over the sweetgrass smoke. She knelt to pray once more to One Above, bowing the aged, white head over the swollen abdomen. Her old, misshapened body was shaken now with the slow sobbing that racked her frail frame. The old woman inched forward to peer at the young woman's face, the many tears falling from the aged, dim eyes to rain across the young mother's cheeks and brow. The ancient one fell atop the big belly in exhaustion, both of her skeletal hands still clutching the beaded charms.

The tremor beneath her hands and arms began as a slow rumbling, then grew in its intensity—a solid pushing, wave-like, as waters would lap at the shore of the river when it becomes swollen with the spring-time snow-melt and rains. The old, hoary head jerked up with a start. She shifted the beaded amulets so they would not fall with the movement. Her fingers sought out the depths of the contraction. And she smiled.

Dreams of Horses crawled within the cradle of the young mother's legs, pulled at the blankets and robes that covered the place from where the child would come. As Looks Far Woman's trembling legs were bared, there came from deep within the body of the young woman a sound to match the growing rumble of the volcanic contraction. From a groan it moved into a growl, which finally increased in pitch to emerge loudly as a scream of pain. The two other women in the shelter moved quickly to the young mother's side at this, the first sound emitted during the long hours of labor.

Dreams of Horses looked at the face of this young mother, then returned her watchful gaze to the moist opening where the child would first see light. There! As the scream ravaged the silence, there! The top of the head! Indeed, she thought. Now this young mother could scream—if not for relief, if not for joy, then a scream of respect for the separation that must come of its own will, in its own time.

The child's head moved toward the outside world, then withdrew as its mother's legs, trembled, drew up in a convulsive shudder. The young woman did as the ancient one had told her—she panted like a dog taken over with heat. Close to the opening of life the ancient one now placed her hands, touched the smooth flesh, felt the softness, warm and damp, under her own dried skin. Then, the birthing mother let out another moan that grew into the growl of the animal before it pierced the shelter as an intense scream.

The head came out to meet her. One old hand slipped from the young woman's leg to cradle the tiny globe. Slowly, agonizingly, the head turned, the rest of the body following, as the channel of life shifted in preparation for the final convulsion. More of the neck and then the top shoulder slid free of its confining shaft. The ancient one smiled, she could finally smile, as the second shoulder slipped free. Dreams of Horses then realized how right she had been—this new life was large, almost as big as a buffalo calf.

Its young mother panted quickly, then groaned again quickly. But this time there was no eerie scream to assault the ears. The child slipped free from the opening of life. Its slick body was pasted with blood and mucous in its long-time journey toward separation from its mother. The old woman turned the child in her hands, still cradling it close between the young mother's legs.

A son! She had a son! This truly was a part of his father! Tears rolled down the furrows in the old cheeks. She could not recall ever having cried before at the birth of a child, through all those countless winters that took her mind back beyond remembering.

"A son!" Her voice crackled with excitement, as she held the young life up for the younger women to view. Then she quickly drew the edge of a blanket about the boy's body to shelter him from the life-robbing cold.

The child's grandmother, Goes Away Dancing, laid a thin wad of sinew near the old woman. Dreams of Horses picked it up and put the end of the mass in her mouth, using what was left of old teeth to pull away from the rest of the wad a thin band of the animal tendon. This she left hanging from her lips. Drawing the edge of the blanket aside, the ancient one milked the long, thick cord of life toward the child. With the final drops of precious fluid left to remain within the baby's body, Dreams of Horses took the sinew from her lips and tied it around the umbilicus only inches away from the infant's fat belly. Around and around she wrapped the sinew, tying it on every wrap until the ends of the animal tendon were short. From her belt she removed a small knife, using it to slice at the cord just above the place where she had knotted the sinew. She smiled with a timeless glow. The child was now cut from this bond with its mother who had supplied it with nourishment for these past moons. Now the child and its mother could build another bond, one stronger than any flesh would be.

Looks Far's sister slipped quietly from the shelter, to return but seconds later with sections of trade cloth that had been soaked in hot water. She knelt beside the old woman and helped bathe the little body cradled between Dreams of Horses and its mother. Goes Away Dancing realized her smile was frozen, her eyes locked on the grandchild. She glanced down at her daughter's face. The new mother's eyes were half closed in fatigue, in relief at the absence of pain. Goes Away Dancing wiped her daughter's moist brow and cheeks with the corner of her capote. Then she reached beneath her daughter's shoulders and raised Looks Far.

With her upper body nestled against her mother's, Looks Far Woman slowly opened her eyes to gaze upon the two women huddled near her thighs. Dreams of Horses drew back, then turned slightly to move the child out of the shadows. The young mother gasped as the ancient one slid the blanket away from the child's body. Her gaze was drawn immediately to the member between the baby's legs. She smiled to see the tiny penis.

"A son . . ." she croaked against the shards in her throat.

And she smiled the deep, reverent smile at this wonderful event.

Dreams of Horses returned the smile, feeling her eyes brimming once more. Quickly she bowed her head as she turned away from the others' gazes, pulling the blanket about the young life once again. With the boy's head now covered, she presented the bundle to Goes Away Dancing, who took the baby into the crook of one arm while the other continued to cradle her daughter's head. Finally the new grandmother placed the young life against its mother's side and pulled a part of the blanket away from the baby's face.

"Feed him, my daughter," she whispered in the stillness where only the fall of tears and the soft padding of snowflakes were heard. "Give him the life of your body."

Looks Far gazed into the tiny coal-like eyes of her son. Quickly she yanked at the thongs along the side of her dress, then slid the leather away from her breast. The firm mound was almost rigid in its fullness and anticipation of suckling. Looks Far took the man-child's head and shifted it to rest against her upper arm as she placed her nipple against her son's lips. Slowly the lips parted, then opened in unknowing reflex. The mystery was just as quickly solved as the little mouth grasped the rigid nipple and began to suckle. Tentatively at first, then more steadily as he learned. The milk finally began to flow from his mother's body into his. His young mother gently rubbed the edge of the blanket back and forth over the tiny head, to dry it of the remaining blood and mucous. Even here in the dim light she could see the pale color of the short, bobbed curls. It was his head of hair, she thought.

Her eyes rolled upward to gaze upon the others in the small shelter, and all smiled back at her. "My man . . . ." she began, attempting to stifle the sob clutching at her throat. "My man . . . he has a son!"

Thirteen

Bass kept to his southwesterly path for more than a week, some nine days as close as he could recall. The afternoon of the sixth he had struck the wide, musclebound river and followed it as the waters raced westward. Scratch had never been this far west before. It was then that he wished he knew what river this was. His life so often depended upon knowing what rivers were where, the locations of mountain passes and the placement of those mountain peaks that could guide a man through otherwise unfamiliar territory.

He scanned the skyline constantly, watched the movement of shadows, getting information, and rapidly calculating his position. A man had to figure fast in the mountains, but this was not the arithmetic he used to chalk down on a slate board back in Kentucky as a youngster. This kind of calculating meant a future of staying alive up in the high country. The man who survived in the mountains had to understand everything those hills told him. They were his teacher now. Some men were just out and out lucky, nothing more than that. But most men couldn't stand to fail more than once in this school.

So Scratch stayed with the unknown river that nagged at him with its own sort of frothing familiarity. Bass had from time to time looked up to the northwest, toward the great mountain far in the distance, its shoulders mantled with snow. The great mountain reminded him of home, his own Shining Mountains.

The aches and pains of the trip threatened many times to overwhelm him, coming close to destroying him bit by bit, day by day—but still he pushed on. Driven, he seemed possessed to find the answers to the haunting of that one ghost which had so long pursued him this late-winter journey. If he could only put some questions to rest, Bass thought, then he was certain his own soul would be more at rest. The damaged, torn skin at his shoulder began to knit, although the wounds at his wrist and ankle still hurt, reminding him of their newness with cold, dull, constant pain. The scabs over the healing flesh each chill morning kept him longer within the warmth of his robes. But Titus pushed on, often spurred on only by the hope that his solitary trek would soon be over. He had to swim the animals across the river when it met another larger flow. At the shallowest, calmest place of early-spring runoff about two miles back up the smaller river, Bass untied each from the others, tugged, then pushed the animals into the freezing waters. One by one, they plunged into the current. As his buffalo runner's hooves lost the bottom Bass slipped from the pony's back, clung to the saddle horn and began to swim against the strong flow. He watched the other animals fight the current, hopeful that all the baggage would not take too bad a soaking.

He and the ponies reached the south bank of the river farther down its course, the boiling current bobbing man and animals almost half a mile downriver before their feet and hooves touched the sandy, rocky bottom. Two more times Bass plunged into the strong, musclebound current of the river to help pull the two Blackfoot ponies toward the bank. The last animal took some cooing, some coaxing, before it fought its way through the water toward the bank. Bass struck it hard on the rump to send it on its way, then clung to the pony's tail as it finally completed the swim.

As he stood on the south bank, Titus began to shiver in the whipping air. The ponies tried to shake themselves free of the water clinging to them, loosening their packs in the process. Titus pulled the animals into the trees and decided to make camp there.

After building a fire and nursing it into a welcome warmth, Scratch stripped out of his wet garments. He quickly wrung them out as he had done so many times before and hung them over tree branches. He retrieved the elk-hide coat from atop the packs strapped to a pony's back. It had stayed almost dry in the river crossing. Wearing only the quill-decorated coat and his thick moccasins, Bass looked to be some strange, bare-assed creature as he hobbled slowly around his fire, pulling baggage from the animals' backs and constantly stoking the flames.

The night came on and with it, the welcome closing of his tired eyes. The dream of the bear returned once more.

"First time to meet a grizz an' ye walked 'way from it to tell, youngJosiah. 'Twas the Lord's hands in it," McAfferty had commented after Paddock had a run-in with a sow grizzly.

And Josiah had wondered at the Whitehair's words. So Bass

had explained as best he could, from his own beliefs, his own fears, his own medicine.

"Then there be a reason for it. Meanin' you meetin' up with a grizz. Bears like that always mean trouble for a man—carryin' bad tidin's for him that crosses trail with Ol' Caleb. Man can walk away from a fight with the critter—why, may not even have 'em a tussle—but it carries bad tidin's for the man. Meetin' up with a grizz is the Great Spirit's way of tellin' a man there's some big doin's in the makin' for him."

Scratch had begun to take a mystical sort of comfort in the dream that came to press itself against his sleep over these many weeks of travel. Each night in the dream, Bass had felt the recognition of the bear as his brother—a mystical, silent omen that led him into the forest. The dream had each time found Bass following the animal into the dark forest, yet awakening before he could emerge from the dark canopy overhead. Each successive night found the old trapper moving into the darker and darker recesses of both his mind and the forest, the light growing progressively dimmer. From time to time the bear would turn and stand on its hind legs as if to attack. But it never had rushed the man. Instead, Scratch had watched each time as the bear had beckoned to him, as if wishing him to follow deeper and deeper still into the darkness. The dream grizz stared at the whiteman with only one eye. The other lid was scarred shut. Each time the animal dropped to all fours and continued his journey into the darkness. And Bass always followed the bear, followed the dim trail, the trail the bear cleared for him. He had followed almost reverently.

Scratch awoke in the chill gray dawn and pulled the coat more tightly about himself. He wrestled the robes from his body before laying some twigs over the embers he dusted free from last night's ash. He added more limbs and the flames grew to wash a warm radiance across the gray pallor of the early light. Then he struggled into his chilled, stiffened clothing. The brain-tanned leather began to loosen and warm quickly against his body heat. Only the trade-cloth breechclout took time to warm in his crotch and across his buttocks.

He would have to hunt again this day, he thought as he pulled the last of his venison near the fire and sliced thick strips of the meat from the haunch. He skewered these strips on shaved, sharpened sticks and placed them over the low flames, one end of each stick shoved securely in the ground at the edge of the fire. Then the old trapper began to repack the bundles he would strap to the ponies' back for another day's travel. Most of the baggage had dried reasonably well. What was still damp he would strap on top so that it might air out more easily, catching what sun it could during the day's ride. He finally leaned back against one of the bundles and stretched out his legs near the warmth of the flames, contenting himself with rotating his breakfast from time to time over the cheering blaze.

When his meal was over and washed down with the cold river water, Bass loaded the bundles on the well-fed ponies. The trapper led the animals along the southern bank of the river. There he turned left, heading almost due south along a well-worn path, a trail that had seen many moccasin prints over untold years. The travel was quick for the old trapper, Bass preferring to walk, stretching those muscles his body needed to exercise. The sunlight dappled the trail through the tree branches, and the heavy foliage at the trail's border allowed the ponies to nibble as they followed along.

Then Bass saw them. At first it was only movement along the trail up ahead. He jerked to a halt and heard the ponies plod to a stop behind him. The figures moved back and forth across the trail. From the river, into the trees, and back again to the river. Two men.

Scratch ground-tied his pony to a clump of brush. He crouched, began to steal quietly down the trail. As he crept closer, the indistinct sounds of the men's voices reached him. Titus drifted into the woods off the trail and approached the figures from above. Through the thick stands of trees and lush undergrowth, he crawled to within thirty yards of the two men, and watched.

The two hunkered at the water's edge, their backs bent as they wrestled with a pair of bundles. Both men lifted their loads and straightened, then turned. They moved to Bass's left, coming closer until the old trapper could see that one of the men wore a mustache, and the second—yes—he had a beard.

Titus rose to his knees, then slowly to his feet. His apprehension changed to a genuine joy. These were the first whitemen he had seen in many, many weeks. No longer was he careful not to make noise. Scratch blustered like a stormwind through the thick vegetation, bulling his way clear of the trees and swaggering down to the trail dappled with sunlight.

The two laborers were so intent upon their work that Bass was nearly upon them before they realized he was approaching on foot down the trail. One man reached for a rifle that leaned against some of the canvas-wrapped bales. The other stepped behind the stack and pulled out a pistol. "Ho, there!" Scratch called merrily, his spirits soaring as the burden of solitude and loneliness lifted from his shoulders.

The two men glanced at one another. The man with the drawn pistol moved around the bales warily and spoke first. "Who are you, friend?"

"Name's Bass," he answered as he came up to the two laborers. "An' glad this nigger is to be seein' some friendly faces." He stuck out a right hand toward the man who had spoken to him, a tall, muscular man who looked to be in his middle forties. "Titus Bass is the name."

He stood before them, dressed as an Indian from the northern plains and mountains—but he was obviously a whiteman. The first worker looked down at the scarred, scratched and bloodied hand and wrist that was finally healing from the wolf attack. He saw that the old trapper's right index finger was missing. Then the worker focused his attention back to the newcomer's face. He finally put away his pistol, grasped Scratch's offered hand. His partner set his rifle back against the stack of bales.

"You came on us by surprise, friend," he offered in explanation. "Coming up on us the way you did."

"Weren't tryin' to be sneaky," Bass apologized. "Saw you fellas from back there," he said, gesturing up the trail with his thumb, "watched 'til I saw me you was white folks. Sorry to s'prise you the way I did. I just was happy to see you fellas— got me a bit lonesome for folks to talk to, is all." He offered his hand to the second worker who stayed close to his rifle. "Titus Bass is my name."

"Guiomme Tardit," the second man answered, his accent thick, nasal, Gallic. He took the offered hand and pumped it happily.

"I'm sorry I come on you sudden like, too," Bass apologized.

The second Frenchman glanced quizzically over at his partner. The first worker explained: "He does not understand you, Mister Bass." Then he smiled. "In fact, he does not understand me most of the time. Very little English does this one know. French—out of Canada." He spoke briefly to Tardit in the man's native tongue, and the congenial Frenchman smiled and pumped the trapper's hand once more before releasing Bass's arm back.

"You have come over the mountains, I take it?" asked the English-speaking man, his voice tinged with a British accent.

"Yep," Bass replied. "This poor child starvin' most of the way. My paunch got so small it could've chambered a .64 ball!" He shook his head now with the sudden remembrance of all that he had been through. "Damn, it's good to talk to someone else ever' now an' then. My animals listen, but, I'll be damned—they don't talk back to me, you see." He threw a thumb back over his shoulder. "Maybeso I best go get them first whack. Then I be back an' give you fellas a hand with your truck here."

"Mister Bass," said the Frenchman's companion, "allow me to introduce myself, also. I am Jarrell Thornbrugh. And I likewise am glad to have someone to talk with." The smile on his face was genuine and wide. "You be off now to fetch your animals, and return straightaway. But you have no need of helping us, Guiomme and me. Rest yourself, I say. I am happy just to be able to wag my tongue again at someone who knows my own language. Seems most of the time I have French, or some blasted native I have to talk to. Does my heart good to have someone new I can talk to."

Titus nodded. "An' I'm one as can bend your ear, friend." He smiled. He turned once more to head up the trail.

"Mister Bass," Thornbrugh said and waited until the trapper stopped and turned around to face him. "Where is it you are going? If I might ask?"

Bass was more than a little confused at the question. "I'm . . . I'm goin' to get me my horses."

"No, I did not mean that, sir," Jarrell said. "Where are you and your animals headed? Why are you over here on this side of the mountains: in Hudson's Bay country?"

Scratch looked down at the toes of his thick moccasins for a moment before answering. "Headin' to . . . Van . . ." His voice trailed off as he looked up at the Englishman.

"Vancouver, you say?"

"Yep," he responded. "Knew I didn't remember the name of the fort. Vancouver."

"Why?" Thornbrugh inquired. "Why are you heading to Vancouver? You don't seem to be in need of provisions. Still have your animals and whatnot."

Bass looked back down at his moccasins again, then back up

to the Englishman when he had an answer formed in his mind. "Have me some questions what needin' answers, sir," he said quietly. "Got me a ghost or two to lay to rest. At this Vancouver, I think I can find me my answers."

Scratch turned quickly as if that were answer enough for the Englishman and headed back along the trail toward his waiting ponies. In and out of the rays of sunlight, across the tiger-stripe pattern of shade along the trail, Bass scooted quickly. The haunting would soon be over. The exorcism would soon be complete.

"For if a man think himself to be something, when he is nothing, he deceiveth himself. But let every man prove his own work, and then shall we have rejoicing in himself alone, and not in another. For every man shall bear his own burden."

The voice was at his ears once more, as surely as if the Whitehair were beside him. Bass stopped and looked around to be sure. He was alone. The voice had seemed so real, but once more the words had come from within his own mind, rumbling within his own ears. Asa's words. His Bible-quotin' again, he nodded briefly to himself. His ghost stayin' with my soul, feedin' on me. Bass knew his own soul was small now, providing the specter of his dead ex-partner all the more fertile a place to dwell.

"For all my life is spent with grief, and my years with sighing."

The loneliness of the journey that was coming to an end had made him all the more susceptible again to recalling the chatterings of the ex-preacher-turned-trapper. "Ah, McAfferty," Bass whispered as he drew near the waiting ponies, "when will you finally leave me be? When will you let go of me?"

"They will go up by the mountains; they will go down by the valleys unto the place which thou hast founded for them."

"No!" he said, startled at the loudness of his own voice in the quiet of the forest. "No," he said more quietly. "I found me my own way. No one showed me, McAfferty. Not you. Not your Lord. Me. I found me my own way here."

Bass swung up into the saddle and pulled the lead rope into his hand. "You cain't tell me any other way, now," he whispered to the ghost at his side. "Cain't tell me anythin' I'll be believin'. An' soon I'll be rid of you. When your soul's at rest, you'll quit devilin' me." He kicked gently at the pony's sides and moved down the trail. "When your soul's finally at peace, ol' friend—you can leave me be."

Yes, he had finally arrived. Or at least he was close. Vancouver was where he would find his answers to put the ghost to rest at last. Vancouver was where McLoughlin was. Josiah had told Bass how McAfferty had spoken almost in awe of the fort's Chief Factor.

"Told me all about him, Asa did. With his white hair hangin' down to his shoulders, and them piercin' pearls of eyes, he called 'em. Said McLoughlin commands both duty and respect from all those around him."

We'll just see about this McLoughlin myself, he thought. We'll just see for ourselves about the man.

"Then he said the Lord had set the man down in the wilderness," Josiah had continued, *"sayin' the doctor's made himself a haven of safety and settlement in that same wilderness, all to the credit of his own God-fearin' soul."*

"Just how God-fearin' a nigger s'posed to be what sets one man on another?" he asked out loud. "Just who can answer me that? Maybeso this McLoughlin got him a lot of explainin' to be doin' to Titus Bass here. Yessir."

"Then Asa said that was more than a fur-tradin' post. Said it was truly a community of God-fearin' souls, set in the wilderness of the heathen and the savage." Josiah had shaken his head in the telling. *"He must of been some taken with the man, 'cause he said that there be a man doin' the Lord's work out here. Said there be a man of medicine in these mountains."*

Shit! He spat on the ground at the thought. We'll be seeing just how much medicine this fella has. We'll be seeing if this here McLoughlin got him medicine enough to match up to Titus Bass and take the circle from him.

The workers came into view once more.

"Happen to know what day it be?" he asked as he slid from the saddle.

"Monday," Thornbrugh replied. "Monday, April twenty-nine."

"Don't much matter what day of the week it be, leastways to me." Bass came around the pony to lean his rifle against some of the bales.

"It does here, my friend," Jarrell commented. "Sunday's a day of rest, most of the time. Unless there is work to be done that cannot wait. The good doctor does not like work on Sundays, Mister Bass. But, if the trade requires it of us, then Sunday is like any other day. Yes. To be sure."

"One day like the one afore it." Bass smiled and moved down

the sandy bench toward the barge with its load of supplies. "Just like the one come after it. All the same—all the same it is to this here child." He hefted one of the bales into his arms.

Thornbrugh dropped his load at the stacks of baggage. "In a way, I envy you, Mister Bass. Yes, I do. For me, this is but a job. The days have meaning—what day it is, I mean to say. What day of the week, what day of the month." He shook his head before moving to the barge again.

Thornbrugh lifted the last of the bales and stepped off the wooden platform onto the soft, sandy beach lapped with ice-laden water. "I do envy you, friend. Not having to care what day it is. One day like the next. Each day like the one before it. Admirable, it is. The freedom—you see?" He looked into the trapper's face and smiled. "You do see what you have, don't you?"

"Don't rightly know as I do."

"It is so simple, so beautifully simple, this life of yours," Thornbrugh began. "If it is as I have heard it mentioned by others—Americans, that is." He snapped his fingers and smiled more widely as if struck with inspiration. "It is not a job for you, is it?"

Bass nodded in agreement. "No," continued Thornbrugh, "it is not a job for you as it is for us, Guiomme and me, and so many others. It is your life." He spoke the last word reverently. "I wait for the time when I can leave the service of the Company, return home, and have that which you have now, Mister Bass. This is my job, see?" He made a semi-circle of his arms as if carrying the bales of supplies. "I move things that are not mine from one place to another. From here," he said, picking up an imaginary bale and dropping it to the ground, "over to there. Over and over, Mister Bass. And you"—he shook his head as if with the weight of the newfound realization—"you climb over the mountains. Freedom. To come and go as you wish. Don't you see it?" He stepped closer to Bass.

"No," Scratch answered softly. "Never really thought me . . ."

"Come now," Jarrell interrupted. "You have it all. So much. So much more than any of the rest of us here, even at Vancouver. This is my work, Mister Bass. But this is your life!"

"My life?" Bass replied. "Starvin'. Gettin' ate by wolves. Fightin' an eagle for a piece of his meal . . ." His voice dropped off again in contemplation. "It don't seem all that great a passel of freedom to me." He wondered at Thornbrugh's concept, this manner of praise for the life the trapper had chosen.

"Mister Bass," Thornbrugh said as he finally sat down on a single bale beside Scratch, "unlike so many who have come to Vancouver—you Americans—they have come begging, needing. Our help, our supplies, our horses—all of it. You see, you have come without that need. Without that begging."

"I ain't beggin'," Scratch replied. "But I am needin', sir. I'm needin' somethin' what I feel I can find at Vancouver. That be all I'm after. I don't come to take nothin'."

"Ah, yes," Thornbrugh responded. "Your—how did you phrase it? Your ghosts? Yes. But, Mister Bass, we all have ghosts with us. The spirit of something we cannot shake free of. We all have them. There is no denying that fact, sir. Yet, with all of that, you are not imprisoned by your ghosts. Mister Bass, you are free to roam this country and make of your life what you will. You, sir, are lord of your domain. Those who come begging at our door, they are not of your cut, sir. You have risen above them, Mister Bass. My god, man—you have to know what you hold in your grasp! What you have in your hands!" His voice had an edge of desperation to it as he pleaded with Bass to understand his point.

"I ain't no . . . no lord," Bass finally commented quietly. "No man works for me—just like I work for no man."

"No," Thornbrugh cut in, "you fail to understand what I am trying to express to you." He shook his head a moment in search of the words, then slid closer to Bass. "You are a lord out here, in this wild land, Mister Bass." There was much enthusiasm in his voice again. "You are a lord of the mountains," he said, sweeping his arm around him. "And not only are you a lord in this savage, brutal place, having come to terms with this land and your place in it—but you are truly a lord over your own life. And that, sir"—he paused—"is what is of the utmost importance. Ah, how I envy you, personally." He leaned back now, as if appraising the American before him. "And you must surely see why it is that I envy you, envy your life—how you are master of it."

Bass looked down at the sandy beach again, considering the words this Englishman had been speaking to him. At first, it had galled him to be considered a lord. That was what he had tried to escape back east. Working for a boss, working for someone who thought himself better than he was. But it began to make sense, this Englishman's concept. What he had been escaping from, Bass now held in his own hands. Power. A power over one's own life. The power to choose where he would be, when he would work, where he would go next. Yes, it did come into focus for him now. It was a peaceful contentment that flowed from the knowledge of this power. It dawned on Bass that he was something above the ordinary, the commonplace. He had indeed taken his life into his own hands and had made it work for him. He did indeed control his own destiny. To live and die by his own choosing, by his own hand—that was power.

"I got me near all a man wants, Mister Thornbrugh," he admitted quietly. "I got me a good rifle what can shoot true." He hugged Asa's old weapon a little tighter to his breast for reassurance. "Best meat a man could ask of the good Lord brung him by that rifle. I got me whiskey when I needs a wettin'. Got me warm women in my winter robes, too. Out there." The place inside singed with pain as he swept the skyline with the muzzle of the rifle.

"God's prettiest sculpturin's to lay sign in, to live out my days in—an' all them nights full of blazin' sky." Bass shook his head from the wonder of it all suddenly rolling over him once more. "I hear them mountains talkin' to me sometimes. I can hear what they try an' tell me. Yep, Mister Thornbrugh, I think maybeso I know what you're talkin' 'bout now," he agreed, and saw a smile break across the big Englishman's face. "I s'pose I do got more'n most men just hanker for all their lives, right here."

Bass studied the broad, sturdy face, then added, "A lord, huh?" He clucked once. "Very interestin'."

"Yes, sir." Thornbrugh rose and faced the American. "I salute you, Lord Bass." He snapped his hand to the side of his head to complete the compliment. "Lord of all he can see, this one. And he has seen much! Lord Bass, I am at your service, sir!"

"Told you, no man works for me." Bass looked up and smiled.

"But surely I can be of some service to you, sir?" Jarrell inquired happily. The big, muscular Englishman had a disarming air about him. "You say you are on the way to Vancouver. Yes?"

He waited for Bass to nod. "Yes. Then we can take you there, Guiomme and me." He pointed to the Frenchman stretched out atop some of the bales. Tardit arose and slid off the baggage. "We are at your service and provide you with the finest in transportation this river has to offer," said Jarrell, extending his arm toward the barge.

"Float down on that thing?" Bass asked nervously.

"Why, of course, sir," Jarrell answered. "We must return to Vancouver on the 'morrow for more provisions. And your company would be most appreciated. *Oui*, Guiomme?" He turned to look at Tardit.

The Frenchman grinned dementedly, obviously in ignorance of all this English gibberish. Jarrell continued. "*Oui*, Mister Bass. We are at your disposal for the last leg of your journey to Vancouver to visit this other lord, his excellency, Doctor McLoughlin. Much like you, a lord of his realm. Much like you: at peace in this wild, unforgiving land."

Thornbrugh reached behind him, took up his rifle. "And my boss, *Monsieur* Pambrun, will be very unhappy with me if I should be late getting these supplies in before dark. Pambrun is the chief, the head factor at our post, this Nez Perce on the Walla Walla, sir." He headed off the beach down the trail toward the trees. "We must get our horses and load the first of these for the short trip back to the post."

Bass and Tardit followed the amicable Englishman toward the horses. "*Monsieur* Pambrun is a kindly soul, Mister Bass. A kindly man, that one. And he will be honored by your visitation, sir. One who has come not begging for a thing. He will be honored with your presence, Lord Bass." Then Thornbrugh started singing an old whaling chantey, his voice terribly off-key, almost grating to the ear.

> *As I was a-walking down Paradise Street,*
> *To me way, hey, blow the man down!*
> *A pretty young damsel I chanced for to meet,*
> *Give me some time to blow the man down!*
>
> *She hailed me with her flipper, I took her in tow,*
> *To me way, hey, blow the man down!*
> *Yard-arm to yard-arm away we did go,*
> *Give me some time to blow the man down!*
>
> *But as we were going she said unto me,*
> *To me way, hey, blow the man down!*
> *"There's a spanking full-rigger just ready for sea."*
> *Give me some time to blow the man down!*

Yes. To enjoy the music of another human's voice. Bass found himself humming along with the Britisher through the last verses of the chantey.

So I give you fair warning before we belay,
To me way, hey, blow the man down!
Don't ever take heed of what pretty girls say,
Give me some time to blow the man down!

Bass was almost there. Almost where he could grab for the answer. Perhaps a lord in some way, as this Englishman had said. Perhaps. Maybe so. But not totally free.

"Thou shalt preserve me from trouble; thou shalt compass me about with songs of deliverance."

In that dark, private place within himself, Bass knew there was a genuine haunting. And the ember of that spirit which refused to die within his own soul, that ember which had allowed him to cross over the mountains and reach this place, was alive and hopeful at the prospect of freedom. Soon he would be free of the haunting specter. Soon he would be rid of the darkness within his soul. Once more, at last, he would be lord. His life would be free to string itself back over the mountains. He would be free.

The mules had kicked up on their handlers for better than four days, finally settling down a few days before the caravan reached Lexington. This small frontier town was the last outpost of established civilization the men would see for months. Outside the scattered gathering of cabins, shops, and numerous watering holes nestled along the Missouri River, Campbell gave orders to establish camp. There the supply brigade stayed for several days awaiting William Sublette and his keel-boat, *Gallant,* to come upriver from St. Louis. It was Sunday, April 28. Campbell was hopeful when he told his brigade they would be leaving before the end of the first week of May. By now most of his handlers, clerks and mule-tenders were restive, ready for the overland journey. This calculated delay at Lexington wore heavily on some of the men who had mentally steeled themselves for the trip that lay ahead.

On Wednesday, May 1, William Sublette's keel-boat was seen coming upriver. From Lexington it would be pulled behind the steamboat *Otto* which was to haul Sublette against the Missouri's current as far as Fort Pierre at the mouth of the Teton River. That afternoon they docked the *Gallant* behind the *Otto*, which was already tied to the rough-hewn wharf. The next morning, unloading began. Muddy waters lapped at the dock as the men cursed and wrestled with the cargo. His brigade's supplies for the overland trip were taken off the boats and brought to Campbell's camp. The tins of hard-tack, bacon, and cornmeal were divided among the packs to be lashed atop the less-burdened mules. These supplies, along with the sheep and cattle, were to serve as trail food until the brigade reached buffalo country.

Out of boredom, Obahdiah Redman opened his mules' packs with the thought of repacking the baggage. "Hick!" he whispered loudly one late afternoon, "c'mere!"

Hickerson Nute ambled over to the scattered disarray that surrounded his partner. He kneeled before Redman, who sat on the ground among the various tins and oilskin-wrapped packages.

"You ain't gonna believe this, Hick. C'mere!" He gestured impatiently. "Look at this, will you? 'Sides all these traps here"—he waved at the piles of iron traps—"I got me some choc'late! Can you believe that?"

He held up a small, waxed-paper-wrapped parcel that had been torn open. Nute took it from his friend's hand and peered down at the dark-brown bar. He took a fingernail and scraped across the top of the bar, then stuffed the finger between his lips. He brought it away with a loud smack.

"Choc'late, all right," Hickerson replied. "Good, too."

"Take it, take it!" Redman insisted. "They won't miss one bar of choc'late."

He got to his knees and pulled a tin toward him. "You gotta look at this, too. Hick, can you believe they got us haulin' raisins to them mountains?" He glanced up at Nute. "That's right! Raisins. See? Look for yourself."

He held up the large round tin, its top pried off with the tip of a knife blade.

Nute stuffed a hand into the hole and pulled out a handful of the small, dark objects. He placed one on his tongue and began to chew. Then a smile grew across his face.

"Cain't believe it." Hickerson put more into his mouth.

"Nope," Redman responded. "Hard to believe, my friend. They got us haulin' fancy food like we was headin' to some fancy party." He shook his head in mock disbelief. "Them fellas out to the mountains s'posed to be so tough. Shit! What kind of fellas trade their beaver for raisins an' choc'late? Eh, Hick?"

Nute ate a handful. "Like they got 'em a sweet-tooth. Sure do."

"Nawww," Obahdiah objected. "Means them fellas ain't near as mean as we been thinkin' they is. Eatin' this fancy stuff! Vittles fit for dessert on a gussied-up French party table! Shit! Can you believe it, Hick?" He shook his head once more. "Fellas what eat this stuff—why, this job gonna be easier'n I ever thought. Yes, sir! Gettin' that pistol an' that fella out there, why—that's gonna be like takin' candy from a baby!" He grinned broadly up at Hickerson, proud of his own joke. "You see, Hick? Just like takin' candy from some baby." He snickered. "Let's see what you got in your gear, Nute." He rose and set off with Hickerson toward their small canvas tent that they had pitched upwind from the cattle and sheep driven along with the brigade from St. Louis.

Across the camp a runner burdened with a large leather pouch scurried toward the larger tents at the east end of the compound. "Stewart!" he yelled. "Mister Stewart!"

Out of one of the larger canvas structures emerged a man of middle height, some five feet, eleven inches tall. His dark brown hair was not as neatly combed as it had been the morning of departure from St. Louis many days before. The quick blue-gray eyes darted about in their sockets, scanning the crush of moving men and animals until he spotted the courier rushing his way. The runner held up a bundle of folded paper in his hand and waved it at Stewart. The Scotsman set the Manton rifle against the wall of the tent and stood patiently.

, "A letter, sir."

"I see," Stewart replied as he accepted the flat parcel. "And doubtless the last of these I will see for some time."

He turned on his heel and entered the tent, picking up the Manton rifle as he passed through the door flaps. Inside, he set it next to its brother. Two matched rifles, crafted in England expressly for this trip to the United States. He thumped down on a small canvas stool and turned the flat parcel over in his hands before opening it.

Sir William Drummond Stewart
in the care of.
Mr. Robert Campbell and Mr. William Sublette
St. Louis
United States

The words were written in the familiar, grandly expressive hand of his brother George, who had remained behind in Scotland. At last, Stewart ripped open the seal on the letter and began to read.

When at last he read the words, "Your loving Brother, George," William went back and quickly reread certain parts of the letter. Finally he let the pages sag between his knees and hung his head. He could believe it, and then he couldn't. He knew the words were true. He and George had a special relationship with each other. But the truth of it still clawed at him painfully. William had figured for some time this was the way things would turn out. But his heart had not been ready for the reality of it all.

Surely, he told himself, he should be saddened by the news of their mother's death many weeks before. Surely this should make any dutiful loving son grieve. But he was saddened not by her passing; instead, Stewart was angered at the injustices shown him by a mother who had been only politely civil to her son, with very little more added to their relationship. And now that polite old woman he had never felt close to had died—had died leaving their family estate of Longiealmond to his brother, John. Yes, John was the family favorite.

Stewart let his chin rest against his chest and sighed. It was a crushing blow to him. He had served well, distinguishing himself in His Majesty's Service as a military officer. He had done no wrong to deserve this burning slap across the face. Yes, he felt stung by the affront. To John—it all went to John: the pretty favorite; his mother's favorite.

Outside, he could hear the faint sounds of male voices carry across the compound on the early dusk air. Some good voices, a few discordant, drifted into the tent.

Will you come to the bow'r I have shaded for you?
Our bed shall be roses all spangled with dew.
Will you come to the bow'r I have shaded for you?
Our bed shall be roses all spangled with dew.
Will you, will you, will you, will you come to the bow'r?
Will you, will you, will you, will you come to the bow'r?

So be it, he finally decided. If that be the shape of things, so be it. He rose slowly from the stool and stuffed the folded papers into one of his small bags near his shaving outfit. He planned on keeping the letter long enough to read and reread the words over and over on this journey, perhaps as many times as it took until they were burned into his memory. William would have to work himself out of this bitterness. His family simply did not understand the woman he kept on his estate. They simply did not understand the depth of that relationship. So his mother had handed him bitter retribution from the grave. So be it, he thought as he turned from the small wooden folding table. I will go on despite them. I will go on.

"William?" Brotherton poked his head into the open doorway of the tent. He read the troubled look on his friend's face. "What is it?"

Stewart quickly turned away from his pouch where he had stuffed the letter. "One more. One more nail, dear friend," he replied. "Merely one more nail in the coffin of my soul." He shook his head and went over to a small wooden table where an open bottle of port stood. He poured two small cups of the liquor and handed one to Brotherton. Stewart clanked his own cup against his friend's. "A toast," he began. "A toast to a successful journey—and to each of us finding that for which we are looking in this new land."

They lifted the cups to their lips. Brotherton watched Stewart's face over the rim of his own cup. He was troubled at what he read in William's eyes.

Stewart downed the stout port he had brought for the journey, draining the cup. He swallowed slowly, then his face seemed to relax. "Ah, that is better. Much better," he commented and turned to pour himself more of the wine.

"Surely, you can tell me," Brotherton begged. "You can tell a friend what troubles you so."

It was long moments before Stewart answered. After he sat on the stool once more and stared out of the open doorway of the tent for some time, William spoke. "My dear mother . . ." He slammed the small table with his flat palm. "Why the hell do I say, 'my *dear* mother'?" He shook his head as if in disbelief. "This woman with whom I was never really close—oh, she had always made out to be close to me. But we all knew, her children all knew, she was close to but one of us—*John*. Dear, dear brother John. The favorite. Damn his hide!" Stewart's voice was harsh now. "Her favorite. Damn his bloody, everlasting hide!"

"What is this all about?" Brotherton moved a bit closer and squatted on the ground before the slumping body of his friend.

"He has it all, don't you see?" Stewart pleaded with Brotherton to understand. "Dear brother John has it all. The big estate—Longiealmond! It is John's!"

"Then . . . ," Brotherton began. "Then, your mother has . . . she has passed on?"

"Yes!" William roared. It took a moment more to compose himself, to allow some of the seething anger to drain away so that he could speak.

"Dear God," Brotherton responded. "God rest her soul." He sipped at the port.

"If, if it all weren't so damned, bloody laughable"—William fought the sob—"then I just might damn her soul to hell."

"No!" Brotherton snapped. "You must not say such things!"

"They are what I feel!" Stewart rose suddenly, tipped his head back and drained the port again as he stood. "And more of this will help me feel all the better." He went to pour another cup.

Brotherton went to Stewart's side. "It really will not help a thing." He put a flat palm across the top of Stewart's cup. "It is the port talking, my friend. Only that. And your grief. It is your grief, isn't it? Your great sadness at the loss, the passing of your dear mother—all this that makes you say these horrible things?"

Again Stewart took some time in answering, waiting too for Brotherton to remove his hand from his cup. He slowly poured more of the port into both of their vessels and sat back down. "Yes, my dear friend. Perhaps it is the loss. But the loss of so much more than my mother. It is the loss of Longiealmond, and all I dreamed of doing for the estate."

"But you still have your holdings," Brotherton injected. "You still have Murthly! That is no small claim, I must say." He shook his head. "That is a beautiful place! While perhaps not as large as Longiealmond—nevertheless, much more beautiful. And more private. You always loved the privacy it afforded you. Didn't you?" He looked Stewart in the eye. When William looked away he continued. "Well, man, didn't you?"

"I . . . I suppose you are right. It is much more beautiful than, than Longiealmond. Yes. And quieter." Stewart rose again and stood at the open doorway of the tent.

Brotherton came to stand beside him. Together they watched the late afternoon sun disappear to the west, the men moving slowly, ambling about the camp, others lounging around the evening cooking fires.

Stewart turned to look at his friend. "Dear, dear Brotherton. I am so glad you came along with me, to make some sense to this old horse soldier. This man you see standing before you has suffered the wounds of battle, he has commanded men in war—it was Waterloo at the peak!" His voice rose a little. "And yet—I allow myself to become defeated by this final blow from my family. The final wounding. Almost prophetic, wouldn't you say, dear friend? Almost prophetic that my brother's word reaches us on the eve of our departure across the uncharted wilds of this virgin land? To find that my hopes for my own land and all my dreams resting upon those selfsame hopes—are now dashed? To receive this letter here, at this time. Dear God, by the twists of fate!"

"William—"

"No," he interrupted, "I will go on. I must go on. You see, I could have ventured across this amazing wilderness—one more day and I would have missed the damnable letter. I would have blindly ventured forth, my friend. Equating all I was seeing with what would some day be mine back in Scotland. But now"—he paused a moment—"now, it is perhaps all the better this way. There is so much left behind that will never repair itself. Never, never to be mended. And better it is, believe me. Now I can go into this new land fresh and unfettered. No longer carrying the illusions of the gentry . . ."

"But you are, you are a lord, Stewart," Brotherton responded. "That is not an empty title."

"Ah, but it is in many ways." William sighed. "*Laird* Stewart. In so many ways, an empty title for me. My Murthly—yes. But out there, where few can venture, even fewer are the lords of that domain. I feel, and this might seem strange, dear friend, I feel much more kinship with those whose very life is spent out there." He pointed to the west, toward the disappearing sun.

He nodded twice. "Much closer do I feel with those *lairds* of the borderlands than to any so-titled *lord* back in Scotland. These men, these wild, far-seeing men we will meet, they are more worthy of this title than that which has been bestowed upon the like of my brother, John."

He nodded toward the west and brought his cup up as if in a toast. "To those wild and noble men, a breed like no other on this earth, I drink. I drink to those few, true lords of the borderlands. To those few who by their own nobility and wildness protect the vast wilderness across this border, a border few dare to cross. Those borderlairds who daily wrench their very existence from this savage, beautiful wildness." He brought the cup to his lips and this time sipped more slowly at the port.

"A border?" Brotherton shook his head. "You will have to explain these thoughts of yours."

"Long, long—a long time ago—when my land was first penetrated by foreign invaders, the lords along the borders were the warriors charged with repulsing the threat, pushing back the attack. Those lords of the borderlands were of necessity the strongest, the fittest for the protection of our lands. And they were of the mettle to take very seriously that for which they had been charged. It has always been thus in my native land of Scotland. Those most brave, those most noble—were the ones who always stepped forward to take up the gauntlet, to answer the challenge of all who would cross our borders. Yes—truly noble," he said as he sipped long again at the port.

There under the bow'r on roses you'll lie,
With a blush on your cheek but a smile in your eye.
There under the bow'r on roses you'll lie,
With a blush on your cheek but a smile in your eye.
Will you, will you, will you, will you come to the bow'r?
Will you, will you, will you, will you come to the bow'r?

"Come," Brotherton said, after the song died away and the silence settled around them. "Christy and Harrison will soon have the evening meal ready for us. Campbell will be eating this last night with Sublette. As will Vasquez and Jeunesse. Sublette will not see them for some many months now. And we ourselves will have many months to enjoy this noble wilderness you have dragged your dear friend along to see with you. Come now—let me drag you to supper. It will cheer you. Tomorrow we finally set out across the great wastes to those mountains they say dwarf the foothills we crossed to get to that great river and St. Louis. We will cheer you, William. Your friends are here, they are with you now. And the unhappiness is behind you."

"Yes," Stewart answered. "I am indeed among my friends, am I not, Brotherton? And you have quieted this old warrior's heart much this evening. There is, indeed, so much to experience now. And I wish to grab it." He clenched his fist tightly out in front of his chest. "Grab it all."

Fourteen

The small, sturdy man stepped from the doorway of one of the handful of buildings that was set out from the palisades of the fort. He stood beneath the small awning of the building and watched as a pair of laborers led Thornbrugh's pack animals to the warehouse. They came single file through the small gate. The Frenchman was surprised to see a stranger riding behind the procession. He stepped down from the low veranda to look more closely at the oddly garbed visitor who had followed Thornbrugh and Tardit into the compound.

Bass glanced quickly about at the scattered collection of buildings within the palisades. Made of cedar, they had been built with care, unlike many of the American posts along the upper Missouri which had been thrown together with unpeeled logs. Bass thought that these English did indeed intend to stay put. These were no temporary posts, built to last but a few seasons. The English truly had made a stake and would not easily relinquish their hold on this land.

Titus saw the stocky Frenchman approach. He pulled the reins on his pony and looked down on the short man who smiled up at him. Bass returned the smile and stuck out his hand as he leaned out of the saddle. "How do!" He grasped the small Frenchman's hand. "Name's Titus Bass. S'pose you be Pambaroon?"

"Pambrun, *Monsieur*." His eyes flashed with amusement as his tongue rolled the "r" sound in his name. "Mister Bass?" he asked, in a Gallic accent thick as Guiomme's. "Who are you with?"

Scratch's eyebrows arched. His blank look indicated he did not understand Pambrun's meaning.

"Who are you with, eh?" Pambrun finally let go of Bass's hand. "Ah, company you come from, eh, Bass?"

Bass slid from the saddle as Thornbrugh approached. Standing beside Pambrun, the pair almost dwarfed the Frenchman. "He wishes to know what American company sent you here." Jarrell smiled. "As fort commander, he is required to ask this."

"Hell, you know nobody sent me here." Bass snorted, with a smile in Thornbrugh's direction. "You tell him nobody sent me."

Thornbrugh knew that Pambrun understood Bass's reply.

"He is *Americain*. So, he get lost maybe, eh? Maybe his company not far away. Why he wander this way, to our lands, huh?"

"Now, damnit!" Bass answered, looking to Jarrell in exasperation. "You know yourself I ain't lost, an' from no damned company neither. An' you tell him I ain't just wanderin' 'round his country. You know where I'm headin'—that Vancouver fort. Jumpin' Jehosophat, Thornbrugh! You know I don't work for no man. Tell your boss I'm here on my own hook."

Thornbrugh spoke in precise French to explain Bass's presence to Pambrun, who from time to time looked over at the American trapper, sizing up the six-footer who towered over him. When Thornbrugh finished Pambrun again offered his hand.

"You are welcome." Pambrun grinned toothily. "Welcome to Fort Nez Perce on *le* Walla Walla." At a loss for English words, he turned once more to Thornbrugh and spoke with him before heading back toward his cedar building. Bass watched him walk away.

"Pambrun does not know if he should believe you or not. He is not sure of you," Thornbrugh explained, "not sure whether or not to believe that these answers you seek at Vancouver are answers for yourself only—not answers about the Company here for your American employers. He does not believe you do not have a boss. He says all men have a boss, Mister Bass." He grinned.

"Well, I ain't got no boss," Bass shot back in a hoarse whisper. "Ah, shit. No sense in lettin' that lil' booshway put me in a fume. What does it matter what that lil' Frenchy thinks of me anyway?"

"Mister Bass," Thornbrugh said as he and Scratch led the trapper's animals toward one of the low, cedar buildings, "it may matter much that these people believe you are here . . . how did you say it? On your 'own hook.'"

"Why's it so all-fired important that they believe me? You believe me. I think you understand what I'm lookin' for out here. Why's it . . ."

"I am afraid, my friend, that the answers you seek will not come your way if doors are closed to you." Thornbrugh stopped Bass near the doorway of the dormitory-type building. He watched the animals jog to a weary halt.

"Now I ain't understandin'," Bass commented.

"It would be best," Thornbrugh said, pausing a moment as if to collect his thoughts. "Yes, best indeed, if you would, if you *could*, convince these men of the Company of your sincerity. We . . . they are very suspicious of you Americans. The battle lines have been drawn in some of their minds, it seems. If you wish answers to your questions, it would be best to show there is nothing to fear from you."

Then he looked Bass squarely in the eyes. "If those ghosts you wish to exorcise are ever to leave you, this you must do first, it seems."

"I don't need 'em to like me—to get my answers." Bass replied after a moment.

"Perhaps you are right." Thornbrugh slipped back along the pack train and began to release some of the bundles from the ponies. "They do not need to like you, I suppose. But you must see, Mister Bass—these men must trust you, trust what you say, trust your motives, perhaps even respect you to a degree—before the doors will be opened to you. If you want to find answers, you must. . . ."

"Didn't know it would be this goddamned tough to get me some answers out here." Bass interrupted as he tugged at the lashings of a pack animal. "Sounds like you folks like to play your games, huh?"

"No, Mister Bass," he said, shaking his head slowly. "It is not at all a game with these men. Indeed, 'tis is very serious business—a very deadly business." He dropped the bundles to the ground and moved on to another animal. "There is a war being waged out here in this country—and that is no game to these men. They have seen over the last few years you Americans coming into this land, slowly encroaching upon their domain."

"This ain't their land," Bass snapped back angrily. Immediately he felt sorry for lashing out at Jarrell. "I'm sorry. But this land ain't theirs. . . ."

"I understand—at least, I think I understand what you mean. You have no need of apologies, Mister Bass. But these men feel it is theirs. And what is more, these other Americans coming in here from time to time feel it is their land, likewise. They don't look at things as you do, my friend. Neither side in this war, this economic war—a struggle of money and beaver, a war for the hearts and pelts of the native population; neither my people, my company—nor your fellow Americans who come poking around this land see things as you do. Don't you see how different you are from these other Americans? You must use that difference, you must gird yourself with your very difference so that confidence will be gained in you—so that those doors will be opened to you." The last bundle dropped to the ground and Jarrell bent over to gather it up into his arms. "Surely, you must see that you are quite different from these other Americans who have come here before you."

"I s'pose I ain't . . . ain't like no other of 'em," he began.

"That's right." Thornbrugh moved toward the doorway of the cedar building. Scratch followed. "And that is precisely your armor, Mister Bass. Precisely what you must use to convince these powerful men out here."

"Fellas ain't much differ'nt than them fellas back east, ones what control the fur comp'nies, are they?"

"Perhaps not."

"All of 'em thinkin' the lands belongs to 'em, leastways gonna be theirs afore too long now. An' it don't belong to no man—no man owns it."

"Perhaps. Again, you may be right." Thornbrugh dropped his baggage in the corner of the small room where six beds stuck out, three each along two walls. Then he turned to Bass. "But, what about the natives—these Indians? They believe it is their land. Yes?"

Bass shook his head. "Yep, you're right, friend."

"Oh, quite. They, too, feel it is theirs." The two men headed back outside for the rifles. "And they allow you to come and go through their land. . . ."

"Most of 'em, they do."

"Indeed!" Jarrell chuckled. "These two are Blackfoot horses, if I am correct." He slapped one on the rump. "You got yourself here through some nasty country, I presume."

Bass grinned. "Some of 'em get a mite touchy 'bout a fella trompin' on their ground."

"It is the same." Jarrell smiled and lifted another load. "The very same for these men here. You must understand that, Mister Bass. If you can see why it is that the tribes wish to hold on to their land against you—why they do not want you taking their furs from their land—then surely, you can understand why it is that these men in this land look at you with so much suspicion. Can you begin to understand why it is that they doubt your word?"

Bass did not answer until they had dropped another load of his baggage in the corner of the room with the rifles and returned for a final trip. "I'll have to think 'bout that, friend. The Injuns, they been here so long. An' these white fellas, yours an' them damned thievin' American traders, they all so new out here. Don't see me how they can be the same."

"But very much so. And the Company is not above using the natives' own territorial pride of ownership against your fellow Americans."

"In keepin' us outta their land," Bass responded.

"Precisely." Thornbrugh smiled at the American trapper. "Therein might lie part of your answer, Mister Bass."

Bass grinned and dropped the last load in the corner of the dorm. "This be all right here?"

"Yes, of course. No one will disturb it here, my friend. You will be protected here. Your property likewise is in no danger. Mister Pierre Pambrun takes great pride in caring for his visitors. And as his guest, you will be treated with the utmost civility. A real gentleman he is, that one."

"Hell, now—you're the nicest fella I've met me in a long time." Bass smiled as they headed out to the animals.

"Why, I don't doubt that at all." Thornbrugh slapped Bass on the shoulders. "I thank you for the compliment, my friend. But Pambrun, you are *his* guest. This is *his* fort. Why, he even gave a suit of clothes to one of your American fellows last year. A man named Wyeth, who came through here on his way to Vancouver. Pambrun liked that one, although this Wyeth was planning on establishing fur operations nearby. A suit of clothing for his visit to the good Doctor at Vancouver. Wyeth was in pretty bad shape when he arrived."

"Know of 'im, I do," Bass replied. "Fought us some Blackfoot back to last summer, we did. Hmmm, more of them fellas beggin' an' needin', huh?" Bass followed Thornbrugh as they led the animals toward the stables.

"It seemed that way, yes."

"Well, I ain't needin' no suit of clothes." Bass chortled. "Wouldn't feel right wearin' such foofaraw anyways. You tell this Monsur Pambaroon I ain't needin' no clothes from him. Get that 'cross to him, right off. Mine just fine. Done well by me long 'nough. An' this here Doctor, he's just gonna have to take me as I am." He gestured up and down his body with an open hand. "I'm all I got, an' I ain't dressin' up just for him—or for nobody."

"Ah, Mister Bass"—Jarrell smiled—"you are quite the way I first took you. You have confirmed for me the impression I initially formed of you. Lord Bass: he needs no finer raiment than that made by the natives of this fair land! He comes to visit Lord McLoughlin dressed as regally as any native lord of this grand wilderness!" He swept his arm low, bent over in a generous bow when they reached the stables. "And here we shall put up your horses while you are on your visitation to the good Doctor. Pambrun will see that your horses are well fed and cared for until you return for them."

"I don't plan on bein' at Vancouver all that long, friend."

"I wish you would call me by my name—either of them, Mister Bass. Either Jarrell or Thornbrugh."

"I'll do me that—only if'n you'll quit callin' me Mister Bass this an' Lord Bass that." He smiled as he saw the grin spread across the Englishman's face. "Just call me what most others do, will you?"

"And what is that, pray tell? Titus?"

"Nawww. Most don't use that to call me—leastways, if'n they's wantin' my attention."

"What is it then—what most call you, my friend?"

"Scratch."

"Scr . . ." He chortled. "Scratch?"

"Ain't so funny a name to me, now!" he said defensively.

"Please, please do not take offense, Mister Bass . . . er . . . Scratch, I mean. It is just an odd name, indeed, for someone such as yourself."

"Ain't odd a'tall," Bass replied. "Got me that handle some time back, first come to the mountains, I did. Had me the nits—skin-bugs—bad. Scratchin' all the time, I was. Name got stuck on me back then. Grown to like it quite some by now," he stated proudly.

"Then, Scratch it is!" Jarrell responded. "No more Titus. No more Mister Bass. Ah, no more Lord Bass for you."

He watched the trapper nod in appreciation. "Scratch. Yes. I see now. Truly you are a Scratch. Yes!" He snapped his fingers. "And that is precisely what you will cause these men to do. Scratch. You will cause them to itch to meet you, my friend. You likewise are a lord here, whether you take to the title or not. Ah!" He nodded his head and grinned. "You will cause them to scratch at the very core of their beings, at their very souls where they live, my friend. Scratch, you are!"

The old trapper's fears eventually eased and he became comfortable on the swollen river flowing swiftly to the sea. Tardit and Thornbrugh took turns steering the craft down certain parts of the river, a few times both men hanging on to the long-beamed rudder that was tugged this way and pulled that by the current.

Fort Nez Perce was quiet with few hands around. Thornbrugh had told Bass that with the coming of the spring brigades, for a few days the post would hum with activity. And Pambrun. The little Frenchman. Pierre had eventually grown to be more than merely civil to him. Pambrun had warmed up to him last night. It was as Jarrell had said. The Factor had evidently come to accept that Bass was not like the others; he had taken the time to discern that the trapper was there on a much different mission.

Bass had loaded one large buffalo-hide parfleche and shouldered the painted case from the pickets and bastions of the company post, carried it down to the barge. Jarrell pointed to a spot in the water some twenty feet from the bank and told Scratch that it was there one would normally find the wooden wharf where the barge could be tied. However, with the spring run-off swelling the current, the wharf was submerged. The snow was disappearing down here, and was beginning to fade before the sun in the high country where rushing little creeks and streams began their journey to the Pacific Ocean.

Feeling lazy in the warm sun as the barge floated along the river, Bass thought about how little sleep he'd had the night before. Pambrun had kept him up talking, with Thornbrugh as an impromptu interpreter. And now the heavy bobbing of the barge rocked and lulled him into semi-consciousness, where his mind wandered over the events of the previous night.

Some time after he'd finally fallen asleep the night before, he had been awakened by the voice. Slowly, he'd opened his eyes in the darkened room where he had spread out his robes on the floor rather than sleep on one of the beds offered to him. He recognized the voice as Jarrell's, who was some few feet away in a bed. Startled at first, Scratch realized that the Englishman was talking in his sleep. Bass eased back down on his elk-hide-coat pillow and was trying to slip back to sleep when the other man began singing.

It was the voice that had brought Bass back to being fully awake. It had not been the grating, off-key, scratchy, wavering voice he had heard Thornbrugh sing with earlier that afternoon. Instead, this voice was strong, clear-ringing, and baritone. Thornbrugh had sung and talked in his sleep most of the night. Singing songs almost without end, each a pleasure to listen to. Each time the Englishman had begun to speak, Bass had tried to go back to sleep, and each time he had just fallen off, Jarrell began to sing again. When morning came, Bass felt as if he hadn't slept at all.

Before boarding the barge that morning, Bass had inquired of Thornbrugh about the sleep-talking and sleep-singing. Jarrell had immediately bent over with laughter. "Surely you can't believe those stories, can you, Scratch?" He roared again with laughter. "They always tell me I talk and sing all night. And what's the biggest part of the whole bloody story is that I sing . . . 'pretty.' Can you fathom that? Me? Singing pretty?"

Bass had protested, saying that he had heard the songs himself. And he had somehow convinced Jarrell that it was indeed true that this big Englishman who could not carry a note for his life during the day, did indeed sing very well in his sleep.

Bass was now brought out of his reverie to hear Jarrell begin singing. He turned slowly to look to the rear of the barge at the Englishman.

I gave my love a cherry that has no stone.
I gave my love a chicken that has no bone.
I gave my love a ring that has no end.
I gave my love a baby with no cryin'.

He finally noticed Scratch staring at him. "Ah, dear friend, Bass. My singing not as good as it was last night?" He laughed merrily and continued his song as Scratch went back to watching the waves on the swollen river lap against the sides of the barge.

How can there be a cherry that has no stone?
How can there be a chicken that has no bone?
How can there be a ring that has no end?
How can there be a baby with no cryin'?

A cherry when it's bloomin', it has no stone;
A chicken when it's pippin', it has no bone;
A ring when it's rollin', it has no end;
A baby when it's sleepin', it's not cryin'.

The day moved slowly. As dusk fell, Guiomme and Jarrell struggled against the current to steer the craft to the northern bank. Thornbrugh jumped into the shallow, icy water and pulled at the two thick ropes to anchor the barge to trees for the night. They made their camp beneath the edge of the green canopy, lighting a fire for a quick meal, some welcome warmth, and to push back the darkness a little longer. Bass fell off to sleep listening to the rhythmic lapping of the waters against the sides of the barge.

The next morning he awakened to find Thornbrugh standing over him, nudging him with a toe. "Rise, my friend. We must be pushing off very soon to make Vancouver."

Bass sat up and scratched at himself as Jarrell went over to tap at Guiomme before kneeling by the fire and stoking it with more limbs. "You slept well, I trust?" he finally asked of the trapper.

He saw Bass nod sleepily, then continued. "Not at all like the previous night's rest, eh? My singing did not keep you up?"

"Don't 'member you singin' a'tall," Scratch replied wearily. "Needin' that sleep, I s'pose." He looked to the east where the sky was beginning to turn light, a thin gray border just beginning to grow beneath the dark canopy.

"You must be hungry, Scratch. You didn't have much to eat last night. Surely, the inner man is hungry."

"If'n you got somethin' else'n that pig-meat you brung you 'long," he snorted. "Rags my ass, it does—eatin' pig."

"I'm afraid that is all I was given by *Monsieur* Pambrun." Out of a thick bundle of waxed paper Jarrell speared thin slices of ham and began to place them on a small cast-iron griddle. "The best the good doctor has to offer." He held a slice of ham up on the end of a fork.

"Nothin' else, huh?"

"Would you prefer to hunt some game?"

"Nawww." He kicked at the robes and stood. Slowly he stretched, removing the kinks from his muscles. Lately his legs had begun bothering him, especially the knees. The cold, late-winter cross-country trek had not helped his joints at all. He supposed the pains he suffered were the curse of having to spend many of his hours in freezing waters setting traps and hunting beaver. "My heart tells me there be far better vittles'n that pig to eat—but my belly tells me it's ready to eat now. So, I'll sit an' have some breakfast with you, Jarrell. I will."

Bass was hopeful they would again continue to make good time moving downriver this day. Afraid to admit it, he still was more than a little nervous about being on the water aboard the flat barge, seemingly adrift and at the mercy of the swollen river. From time to time he would awake to realize he had dozed off with the rhythmic bobbing of the craft. He would stretch and rub his legs, and occasionally move to the rear to talk with Thornbrugh, studying the islands that infrequently dotted the river.

Toward the middle of the afternoon the sky clouded up and burst with a quick, terrifying spring squall. The water rippled, dotted with wind-whipped foam. Guiomme and Jarrell hung to the rudder beam together. The Frenchman crouched low against the wind while the Englishman stood upright against its temporal fury, singing out in his strident, nerve-grating voice.

I'm lonesome since I cross'd the hill,
And o'er the moor and valley;
Such heavy thoughts my heart do fill,
Since parting with my Sally.
I seek no more the fine and gay,
For each does but remind me
How swift the hours did pass away,
With the girl I've left behind me.

Bass felt the fear rumbling deep in his bowels. It was a fear of something he knew nothing about, a fear of something over which he had no control. Death, especially sudden, capricious death, had never been a stranger to him. But this was something entirely different. Now he could do nothing but go along for the ride. He felt helpless against it. Against the possible consequences of the brief, raging storm. Then, above the roar of the wind and the grinding rattle of the drops splattering against the wooden barge like hail, Bass heard the Englishman's voice. Forcing himself to let go of the railing with one hand so that he could turn, Scratch eventually wheeled around to stare disbelieving at Thornbrugh. Then the trapper smiled.

Oh, ne'er shall I forget the night,
The stars were bright above me,
And gently lent their silv'ry light,
When first she vow'd she loved me.

But now I'm bound to Brighton camp,
Kind Heav'n, may favor find me,
And send me safely back again
To the girl I've left behind me.

Perhaps the storm was not all that bad, after all. He couldn't help smiling at the Englishman. And finally Thornbrugh looked down at the American huddled against the railing near the front of the empty barge. Jarrell interrupted his song to laugh loudly, the water from the rain pouring down his face, the wind whipping at his garments savagely.

"My friend, Scratch!" he shouted above the strident whine of the fury. "Surely you cannot be afraid! This is but nature finally awaking in spring after her long winter's nap!" He laughed loudly again, letting his head fall back of his shoulders in merriment. "Or perhaps Mother Nature is but a critic of my singing, also!"

His laughter caused Bass to laugh along with Thornbrugh. The Englishman waved for Bass to come to the rear of the barge. On his knees the trapper began to crawl back toward Guiomme and Jarrell. Hand over hand along the wooden railing, his moccasins frequently slipping on the wet boards and sending him sprawling—Bass fought against the mighty tug of the wind at his body. At last he came up beside the Englishman and sat down in a soppy clump against the railing. Guiomme crouched on the other side of Jarrell.

"Now, gentlemen!" Thornbrugh roared once more, "We will sing together!"

In Scarlet town where I was born,
There was a fair maid dwellin',
Made ev'ry youth cry, "Well a day,"
Her name was Barb'ra Allen.

"Come on now, lads!" he shouted into the wind. "You must sing along with me this time! You must learn the words so you can sing along with Thornbrugh. Again—we will do it again!"

'Twas in the merry month of May,

"'Twas in the merry month of May," Bass and Tardit stumbled through the line.

When green buds they were swellin',

"When green buds they were swellin'," Guiomme mumbled around the unfamiliar English words.

Sweet William on his deathbed lay,

"Sweet William on his deathbed lay," Bass repeated, beginning faintly to remember the song from days gone by.

For love of Barb'ra Allen.

"For love of Barb'ra Allen." He knew he had heard this lover's lament before.

He sent his servant to the town,
The place where she was dwellin',
Cried, "Master bids you come to him,
If your name be Barb'ra Allen."

Well, slowly, slowly got she up,
And slowly went she nigh him;
But all she said as she passed his bed,
"Young man, I think you're dying."

She walked out in the green, green fields,
She heard his death bells knellin',
And every stroke they seemed to say,
"Hard-hearted Barb'ra Allen."

"Oh, father, father, dig my grave,
Go dig it deep and narrow.
Sweet William died for me today;
I'll die for him tomorrow."

They buried her in the old churchyard,
Sweet William's grave was nigh her,

And from his heart grew a red, red rose,
And from her heart a briar.

They grew and grew up the old church wall,
'Til they could grow no higher,
Until they tied a true lover's knot,
The red rose and the briar.

"Good! Good!" Thornbrugh exclaimed. "Let's go on!"

They sang on through the few hours of the storm, three men lashed by the wind, pummeled by the heavy drops. Two frightened men led by one whose voice rose above the fury. Two in chorus who became less and less frightened because of the bravery of the one. Bass looked from time to time at this big Englishman, feeling a genuine liking for the man as well as a mounting respect.

By the time the storm roared past them, Scratch was certain this Jarrell Thornbrugh must be a lord himself. Despite his claims to the contrary, despite his working for another man—this mighty Englishman was somehow at peace in the face of terrifying adversity. He might be accustomed to such rabid squalls on the river, but Bass nevertheless felt a real kinship with the Englishman. Indeed, here was a man who would stand beside him in a good fight, whether grizzly or Blackfeet. Here was a man far more worthy of a place in the Rocky Mountains than many others Bass had met through the years. And, here was a man who seemed to have made peace with his own ghosts.

The sun came out briefly before it began to sink to the west ahead of them. In less than two hours it would fall away behind the horizon, and the night would come. Another night of sleeping on the river bank. Then Thornbrugh slapped a large hand on Scratch's sodden shoulder. Jarrell pointed downriver about a mile. There on the flat plain that stretched above the mighty Columbia rose the fortress. Just beyond it, to the south and west, and closer to the waters, was a village, buildings huddled here and there across the plain.

Bass looked up at Jarrell and saw the Englishman nod once.

"You have come, my friend," Thornbrugh announced. "The castle of Lord McLoughlin awaits you, fair knight of the wilderness. Likewise, dear Scratch, the end of this ghostly, haunting pilgrimage you have undertaken. May you find what it is you seek."

Bass studied the approaching fortress. There on the northern bank of the Columbia rose this mighty bulwark of the English.

"Ah, look at it, Scratch! A fortress with north and south walls running some six hundred and forty feet, the east and west walls extending close to one hundred and twenty feet." Jarrell was exultant.

Bass drank it all in. Rough-hewn logs some twenty feet high rose out of the earth to surround the buildings, only the tops of which could be seen briefly before the river carried them on toward the landing. Every one of the four corners was bare of the normal, imposing bastion, that tower from which one could enjoy a commanding view of the whole countryside.

Scratch had heard of the American posts and forts on the Missouri River, most of which had been built since he had arrived in the mountains some nine or ten years before. The descriptions of those forts had seemed absurd, ridiculous, even outlandishly fanciful to him. Yet now the descriptions of those American forts seemed to pale against the reality of this experience. Truly, here was a fort that would dwarf any of those, he thought. If those wild descriptions he had been told were true, then this place was all the more amazing.

Weeks before, when he had spent that night alone within the four walls of that abandoned Nez Perce outpost, he had been impressed by the industry of his fellow men. Yet, until this moment, he had not felt the might of the English presence in this great northwestern territory. Not until now had he begun to understand the posture of strength from which the English Hudson's Bay Company dealt with its competition.

He had to duck and scoot out of the way as Thornbrugh and Tardit fought with the large rudder to steer the barge against the current toward the north bank. The barge struggled, pushed and bobbled, bullied by the mighty river, acted as if at any moment it might tip and slide on over into the rushing foam. Bass, suddenly apprehensive, sucked in a deep breath, then remembered some words of a song Thornbrugh had taught him.

I'm lonesome since I cross'd the hill,
And o'er the moor and valley;
Such heavy thoughts my heart do fill,
Since parting with my Sally.

He sighed and felt better for it now as the waters lapped

lower along the sides of the barge. They were out of the swiftest water now and making for the landing in a lagoon leading in from the river to facilitate the loading and unloading of river craft. He could see a small knot of people emerging from the fortress and moving down the wide path toward the wooden landing. Another small group of the curious was coming out from the orderly little village with its wide lanes and log cabins and huts to greet the barge. Nearer the bank a short, square Indian woman raised her blanketed arm and waved happily. Bass turned toward the Englishman when he saw Jarrell raise his arm to return the greeting.

"Someone you know?" Bass inquired.

"I should say, indeed!" Thornbrugh replied happily, tugging at the rudder. "She is my woman. To most, what would be a wife. It, it is not strange this . . ."

"I," Bass interrupted, "I have had me a woman—a wife—before, too."

Thornbrugh, along with Guiomme, leaned heavily against the rudder. Finally the Englishman grunted so low under his breath that Bass could barely hear him. "Then, dear Scratch, you must know how I feel about coming back to her."

"Yes, my friend," Bass answered as he rose from his knees to stand at the railing. More people gathered at the landing. The trapper's gaze settled on the hefty Indian woman. "Yes, I know how you must feel to be comin' back to her."

Fifteen

Bass walked up from the temporary landing, saw the large garden and cultivated fields that surrounded the fort on its west, north, and northeast sides. He stopped a moment to allow Thornbrugh and his Indian woman to catch up with him as he marveled at the extensive cultivation.

"Most times, you will see many workers in the gardens and fields," said Jarrell as he came alongside the trapper. He gestured across the well-cared-for property. "You will likely not see such greenery at your American posts."

"I ain't got me nary a idea if they do," Scratch answered.

"But, I 'magine you're right, friend. Real civilized this place is—just as you said. Just as I'd been told it were."

"From these massive gardens, the good doctor supplies the fort's own larder, besides those of many of the inland posts. The bread you ate last night at Pambrun's table—the wheat was grown right here. It must have been some time, Scratch— some time since last you had bread to eat."

He snorted in agreement. "It be many a robe season since I last et me bread."

"I mentioned this Wyeth, a fellow American," Jarrell continued. "Pambrun served this Wyeth his first bread since he came out from your settlements—some many, many months before. Such a simple fare—yet many a man would find himself endeared to another who gives him something so simple and mundane as a loaf of bread. Yes, my friend, here are grown timothy, oats and barley, besides Indian corn, peas, potatoes. The seeds for the wheat to make breadstuffs came to us directly from York Factory."

"A . . . factory?"

"Not really a factory, as such," Jarrell replied. "That is oft the term used to describe one of our larger posts where things are produced for a substantial portion of the trade."

Jarrell strode on, followed by his woman. Bass followed them up the wide path, once looking over his shoulder at those gathered near the landing. He saw Guiomme along with the others finish tying the barge off, then head for the small village.

"The Frenchy not comin' with us to the fort?" Bass inquired.

"No, that he is not," was the reply. "He himself lives in the village with his woman. I, likewise."

"You mean you don't live up here?" He nodded toward the tall palisades.

"That is correct, Scratch."

"Where you figurin' on me to be stayin', then?"

"Sir, you will be afforded very fine accommodations here at the doctor's post." He smiled over at the trapper. "Better than those accommodations afforded you the last two nights. Better it will be than our Walla Walla." He circled his arm around the shoulders of the short Indian woman. "I myself will have me a warm sleep-mate this night. And you, in turn, will not be kept awake by my nocturnal soliloquies—nor my poor excuse for singing!"

They entered the open gate at the southern wall, near the

western corner. Another stood open further down the wall toward the eastern corner. After he passed through the gate some ten feet wide, Bass saw two large, two-story buildings some eighty feet long by thirty feet wide. The ground rose slightly before him all the way to the northern wall of the fort. To his left he noticed a small wooden building.

"Whooeee! That be a big'un! If'n that be a big outhouse?" he asked almost tongue-in-cheek.

"No, Scratch," smiled Thornbrugh. "That's the powder magazine."

"Ah . . ."

"It's a big magazine," Jarrell finished. "Where the powder for this fort and other posts is stored. Stone reinforced for safety, I might add. Come. We will secure you quarters with the rest of the single men in the Bachelors' Hall, the big dwelling house."

Thornbrugh led his woman and Bass to the right, past the warehouses and into the massive, open courtyard. Ahead of them along the south wall were two small buildings and a larger one-story structure. Turning there, the party made its way toward a long, high, single-story structure some one-hundred-fifty feet by thirty feet, which Bass assumed was this Bachelors' Hall, the dormitory and apartments for the single men. Then Jarrell stopped suddenly. Titus looked back and saw why he had halted. Thornbrugh peered upward at a man of huge bulk. The man stood on the porch of a large house directly northwest of the dormitory. The man's long, flowing white hair contrasted starkly against the stately, full-length black frock coat he wore. His right hand gripped a stout cane, the molded, gold head of which barely jutted from his massive hand.

Thornbrugh saluted. Then the large figure on the porch lifted the cane in acknowledgment and turned to enter his house. Jarrell saluted again and caught up with Bass and the woman.

"Who be that?" Bass asked.

"Your benefactor."

Bass's expression went blank.

"The good doctor," Thornbrugh explained. "That was John McLoughlin."

"That be the ol' boy his own self?"

"Yes," he answered. "And surely someone had told him upon our landing that Tardit and myself did not come downriver alone."

"I gotta talk to that man," said Bass.

"Your ghosts, I take it?"

"Yep."

"I am sorry, but I do not understand what McLoughlin himself has to do with your haunting." They stopped outside one of the doors of the dorm where the Indian woman seated herself on a long, wooden bench.

"This is a real ghost, Jarrell."

"I am sure it is."

"Ain't no reg'lar hoo-doo now," he replied. "Kind that just devils you for the fun of it. I been followed by a real ghost."

"Is it that you mean the ghost of a real person, then?"

"You got it, friend," Bass answered, following Thornbrugh into the dorm and down a long row of beds and lockers. At the foot of many of the beds rested large chests: the cassettes of Hudson's Bay Company, in which a man's personal effects were kept. Near the north end of the long room the Englishman stopped and motioned toward a bed that had no cassette at its foot.

"Here is your bed."

"Don't like me any bed," Scratch replied, plopping his parfleche on the foot of the mattress.

"It is yours to use should you choose to do so." Jarrell smiled at his American friend. "Or, you may sleep on the floor if you desire."

"Use me them blankets?" He tapped the thick red woolen blankets at the foot of the bed. "Put 'em on the floor be all right?"

"Certainly. That is why I told you yesterday you had no need of bringing your buffalo hides along on this leg of your journey."

Bass fingered the clean blankets. "These be in lot better shape'n mine own, you know."

"I would not doubt that," Jarrell responded. "These are cleaned on a regular basis." He sat on the adjoining bed and brought his legs up as he leaned back against the wall in a relaxed posture. "You have no body lice?"

"Lice?" Bass asked. "Oh, them gray-backs? Nawww."

"Your name, how it was given you, is what I meant to make light of—to make a joke of such an infestation."

"Infes . . ."

"Infestation." He laughed lightly. "Having a case of the lice."

"Ain't had me that since I give up on wool, linsey-woolsey,

too. These here Injun leathers don't give them nits no place to roost, I s'pose."

Thornbrugh nodded at the trapper. "I suppose you knights of the wilderness have it all the better on us for that, too."

Bass sat on the cot and stretched his legs, wiped his open palms up and down the clean blanket spread across the mattress. He and Thornbrugh were quiet for some moments, each in his own thoughts. The Englishman pulled away from the wall, sat up straight on the bed when five men entered the dorm and went to their beds at the other end of the room. The look on Jarrell's face grew pensive for a moment before he finally looked over at the trapper.

"I do not know if McLoughlin will want to see you. He has recently been troubled by the Americans. Much more of late, it seems." He shook his head a bit. "It may be that he will harbor resentment for you, merely being an American."

"How he know I'm American, first off?"

"My dear Mister Bass"—Jarrell smiled widely—"none of our people dress in the custom of the wilderness." He gestured at Scratch's clothing. "You are dressed as one of these American trappers."

"I ain't nothin' else."

"I understand. And, so does he. McLoughlin could see that when he examined you from afar awhile ago."

"He were lookin' me over real good, huh?"

"As he will be doing for some time now."

"What you mean, some time now?" Scratch asked suspiciously. "Ain't I gonna get me a chance to see him tonight? Tomorrow, maybe?"

Thornbrugh leaned forward with his elbows on his knees and chuckled lightly. "Things had best take their own time, Scratch. It is better that the good doctor send for you rather than you request an audience with him."

"I need to talk with him."

"This is why you came to Vancouver?" Jarrell inquired. "How you wish to exorcise the ghost?"

"No exorcisin'," Bass objected. "Just gonna get some questions answered, then maybe the ghost'll be at peace an' leave me be, is all," he answered quietly. "Yes, to your question, Jarrell. Yes, it be the doctor I'm needin' to be talkin' to 'bout those things."

"It would be best to let things take their natural course, in that event. Give him the time to request you visit him."

"I ain't got the time!" Bass shot back. "I'm sorry," he went on. "I feel I ain't got the time to be waitin' for him to take a likin' to me, Jarrell. He's gotta have him some answers I'm needin'. I come all the way here to get me those answers, an' I can't be waitin' on this doctor to take a shine to me first-off."

Thornbrugh sighed, then the smile flickered back on his face. "Just . . . just what sort of information is it that you are needing of the doctor?"

"You mean you'll be goin' to 'im an' rushin' things a bit for me?" Bass asked, almost child-like.

"Yes." Again the Englishman sighed. "If it will serve us all in the end, I will do so, for you." He rose to stand beside the bed. "What is it you require of the doctor?"

"I'm needin' 'im to tell me 'bout a fella I knowed once," Bass began slowly. "More'n that—a fella what was a partner of mine some time back. This fella, he up an' left me two times. Fella was a ol' ex-Bible thumper—an' his God told him to take 'nother path from mine, twice it was. 'Specially this last time, some moons back now, he up an' took off from me an' . . . an' a partner I had me last fall."

"I am afraid I do not understand any of this." Thornbrugh stared at the American trapper.

"Maybe I can make me some sense to it all for you." Bass sighed. It was a relief merely to be talking about it now. "This ol' partner come back then last winter. I was stayin' with the Crow then—Rotten Belly's people, they was. An' this fella come back with his Nepercy woman to spend the winter with us. Then . . . then somethin' happened. Maybe made him go real crazylike." He looked up at Thornbrugh, hoping to impress upon the big Englishman the need for answers.

"I don't know why," Bass continued. "But he had led him some Blackfoot down on this same Crow camp couple of moons afore me an' this other partner—a young'un—got there for the winter. But this older fella led them goddamned Blackfoot down on the Crow . . ." —he paused to ponder his thoughts— ". . . for some goddamned reason."

Bass shook his head and stared down at his moccasins. "I know this ain't makin' much sense to you, friend. But—it all don't make any sense to me, you see? If'n it don't make sense to this nigger, just how can I be makin' it come clear to someone else? Can you tell me?"

Thornbrugh shook his head almost sadly. "Your affliction must be great, dear Scratch."

"My what?"

"Your affliction—your trouble. How you are troubled at this . . . this confusion you carry around with you." He thought a moment, then continued. "Have you thought that it is merely your own self that is causing this haunting to confound you so?"

"You mean I'm bringin' it on my own self?"

"Perhaps."

"You ain't hittin' center there!" he shot back a little testily, glancing over Jarrell's shoulders at the men down the long rows of beds. "You ain't gonna say I'm the one what's gone crazy now?"

"Farthest thing from it. I am sorry if you believed that what I meant was that you were the prime cause of your own confusion."

"You gotta know I ain't crazy"—the sob clutched at him. "It's . . . it's just that I cain't get this ghost of 'im to stop devilin' me."

"You say this old friend is dead now?" Thornbrugh wanted to be certain.

"Yeah," he replied sadly. "Leastways, his body's dead. An' I done me what I could for his spirit. Buried 'im proper an' such. Still, his goddamned spirit ain't at rest—so he ain't givin' me no rest, neither."

"He meant much to you, I take it."

"Was a time that he did." He shook his head sadly again. "I got me a trouble with people, howsomever. Just like yourself, Jarrell. I take folks to my heart an' then . . . then they, they sort of, well—it seems they do wrong by me."

"Is it that they betray you, friend?"

"I s'pose you could call it that," Bass replied. "Yes, I put my faith in 'em—an' they go an' do somethin' to destroy that faith I had. Always, always—damnit! It always happens. Should make a man like me not wanna have him any friends, shouldn't it?" He looked up at Jarrell with a look of genuine concern in his eyes, a genuine need.

"Then I must do what I can to merit your faith in me, my dear friend," the Englishman responded. "I will see what I can do to gain you an audience with the doctor. And with all expediency. Perhaps tomorrow. Perhaps the day following. I cannot promise for sure. But I will do what I can. Yes, Mister Bass. This is the least I can do."

"If you can do that—get me in to see the doctor, this

McLoughlin"—Scratch paused, sighed—"then maybe I can get myself healed up. I can be at peace if'n I can get Asa to be at rest himself."

"Asa?" Thornbrugh responded quickly, jerking his head up to fix his eyes on the American.

"Yeah," Bass replied. "Asa McAfferty. That be the ol' fella's name."

"Yes." Thornbrugh nodded, then lowered his head.

"You not tellin' me something?"

"Nothing. Nothing, my friend."

"Nawww," Bass injected. "You know somethin' you ain't tellin' me right off, Jarrell. I need me to know. Need me to know all of it. You knowed him? Right?"

"No," Jarrell answered too quickly. "No. I did not know him." He did not like the way the conversation had gone. "You must have trust in me, Scratch. You must trust me when I say I did not know him."

"But, you did know *of* him?"

"Some time ago, it was, perhaps," he finally answered. "Yes. Knew *of* him. And that was all. Strange it is"—he shook his head—"you bringing up that name out of the past. To bring that ghost with you to Vancouver now. After all this time."

"Why?"

"Are you hungry, my friend?"

"I asked you why?"

"I can bring you something to eat from the kitchen."

Bass quickly rolled his legs off the bed and stood before Thornbrugh. The Englishman's evasiveness made him testy. "I ain't that hungry. For food, leastways. Need me some answers. An' if you can give me 'em now, all the better."

"But you have not eaten since breakfast—the pig you say you do not enjoy eating." Jarrell attempted to make light of things.

"That don't matter—I can always find me somethin' to eat."

"Perhaps you should rest then. It has been a long journey for you over the mountains. And you have not actually rested well the last two nights."

"Damnit! I got me 'nough sleep! I gotta know what you're hidin' from me!"

"I am not keeping anything hidden from you, Scratch. I am merely trying to see what needs you have, as our guest. To feed you and see that you are well rested before your visit with the doctor."

"I got me other needs what need tendin' to," Bass broke in. "You're making this here child feel mighty squampshus 'bout this whole shitteree."

"Squampshus?"

"Huh," Bass replied, "found me a word I gotta explain to you now, huh?" He watched the Englishman nod. "Funny feelin'. Somethin' I cain't put my finger on for the life of me. An' that's just the way I'm feelin' 'bout how you're not answerin' my questions 'bout McAfferty."

Jarrell sat down on the edge of the bed and waited for Bass to seat himself on the one across from him. Scratch leaned forward with his forearms on his knees, waiting expectantly for Jarrell's reply.

"You must believe me," Thornbrugh finally said after long moments of thought. "I need you to trust that I speak the truth to you. As will the doctor. There will be no deception there. As there has been from others. This McAfferty, for sure. But I did *not* know the man. Believe me, Scratch. His name *is* familiar, yes. But I didn't know him. Do you believe me?" He looked the trapper squarely in the eye.

"Yep, I s'pose I gotta believe you, that."

"I am gladdened that you do—for it is the truth." The look of pain that filled his eyes slowly vanished.

"I'll have to take it for the truth, then."

"True it is," Jarrell replied. "And for that reason I will aid you in all ways to gain this audience with the good doctor." He rose to leave.

"This doctor . . . this McLoughlin," Bass began, "he know McAfferty?" He saw Thornbrugh stop and look at the floor, almost as if he were studying the wooden planks. "McLoughlin know him, Jarrell?"

Still the Englishman did not answer.

"McLoughlin knowed him, didn't he?" Bass persisted. He waited a moment more. "Didn't he?"

"Yes." Jarrell turned to face Bass with a look of some small relief on his face. "Yes. McLoughlin knew McAfferty."

Bass plopped to the bed. His body sagged. He felt close to the answer now. This pilgrimage he had undertaken—that was the word Jarrell had used: pilgrimage—was to prove itself worth the starvation, the blood, the fight with the wolves, the whole of it after all. Something buried deep within him, down deeper than he often dared to look in his soul—had told him here he would find the answers. And his guts had not steered him wrong again. No, sir, his intuitions had been right. He had long ago learned to rely upon his guts—what they told him about something, or someone. And they had not betrayed him now. It was worth it, all he had gone through getting to Vancouver now. Just as his guts had assured him months ago—this Doctor John McLoughlin held the key to ridding himself of McAfferty's ghost. And with the Chief Factor's help, Scratch would put Asa to rest with his own soul intact.

He felt his body sag a little more as some of the tenseness, the nervous expectancy was shed from both his body and mind now. He looked up to see the Englishman staring down at him. "I think I can use a little sleep now, Jarrell."

"Of course."

"If'n you can see to it that I can palaver with the doctor as soon as he gets the chance . . ."

"To be sure," Jarrell said. "I will, Scratch." He turned to go. "The small cabin with the red-painted door. Same color as the cassettes, the chests here. Spanish-red door."

"What? I don't understand what you mean."

"If . . . if you have need of me before the 'morrow," he began and paused. "Down in the village. Our place. The woman and I. Our place with the red door. Come for me if I can be of help to you, my friend."

"You've helped this ol' nigger much already," Bass responded. "An', an' you are a friend. A true friend." He closed his eyes at last and let out a long sigh."

Thornbrugh turned and walked down the long corridor between the rows of beds. He stopped at the door to look back at Bass. The American seemed to be falling to sleep now with the dimming light. And he was glad for it. The man needed his rest. Being haunted must surely take much out of the man. This American trapper felt things so deeply.

Thornbrugh sighed. He had not lied to Scratch. No, he told himself. He had not lied at all. But neither had he told the whole truth of the matter. McLoughlin would need to hear of this. He must hear of this at once. The doctor must be told who this American is—and why he had come. Who he had come to inquire about.

Thornbrugh's loyalties to McLoughlin were strong, forged in a special fire over the years. Yet, he felt some strange, new loyalty to this buckskinned mountain trapper, also. Perhaps to-

gether—the doctor and the trapper, McLoughlin and Bass—
they would each end their own private haunting. Together.
They would help each other put the ghost to rest at last.

"You do rise early." The voice sounded beside him.

Bass was sitting on one of the long benches against the dorm
wall, enjoying the early morning. He had been watching the
large Hudson's Bay Company flag catch and flutter on the
breezes from its flagpole near the warehouses at the south wall.
Now he saw beside him a tall, slender, clean-shaven young
man who looked to be about twenty-four years old.

"Howdy," Bass replied. "Ol' habit, I s'pose it be. Gettin' up
early, I mean."

"Soloman H. Smith." He presented a hand to Bass who
shook it. "The H is for Howard. I am recent of New Hampshire
by way of Vermont and the Newfoundland Banks."

"You . . . American?" Bass asked just as quickly.

"Why, y-yes." The man seemed startled that he had been
asked such a question. "As I said, born in New Hampshire. My
father was a doctor. After he died, my mother moved us to
Vermont. Tried medical school for a time. Just not cut out for
being a doctor, I suppose. Disappointed my mother, it truly
did. Dropped out and became a fisherman . . . oh, here I
am—really rambling on. But, American, yes."

"Didn't know there was any more of us here." Bass turned to
get a better look at the new acquaintance. "You a trapper?" He
squinted one eye, looking Smith's cloth garments up and down
with a discerning gaze.

"No, sir," Soloman answered. "Oh, I came out to this country thinking I would be. However, matters have a way of taking
us along their own course. I am schoolmaster here at Vancouver."

"Teacher, huh?" Bass squinted again.

"Nothing wrong with that profession, is there?"

"S'pose not." Bass grinned to put Soloman more at ease.
"How be it you come out to trap an' end up a schoolmarm . . .
teacher, that is?"

"Don't strike you as a schoolmarm, do I?" Soloman laughed.
"Well, sir—had been fishing on a schooner off the Newfoundland Banks. We were returning home when a British
packet rammed us in the fog. Our ship was sliced clean in half.
Not a soul lost, I'm lucky to say. We were taken aboard by the

British and brought into Boston. That's when I ran onto this fella called Nathaniel Wyeth—"

"That's him," Bass interrupted. "Seems he's poppin' up ever'where I go. Was down to Fort Nez Perce couple of days back an' he'd been down there, too. Made his first friend in months there with lil' French fella, name of Pambaroon. French booshway even give him a suit of clothes."

"Pambrun did that, yes," Smith agreed. "Got to his fort around the middle of October. The rest of us were treated well, but I had to wait until my arrival at Vancouver on the twenty-ninth of October before I could acquire some new clothes." He gestured toward his own cloth garments. "My other clothes were in terrible shape by the time we arrived here, the horrendous journey and all . . ."

"Country'll eat a man up, first whack, it will."

"And it came close," Soloman continued. "We were brought down the river here on a barge by two Canadians. But with all the troubles, Indians and all—by the time Wyeth got us all here to Vancouver, only twelve of us by that time, it was just to find out his ship had not come in. That was the crushing blow. You see, he had planned for a ship to leave from Boston loaded with trade goods and supplies to travel around the Horn of South America and meet us here on the Columbia. Wyeth would construct a post to serve as competition to the British here in this great Northwest. We also planned to catch salmon—have us a profitable sideline in the fish business."

"Son," Bass slipped in, "you makin' my head swim. You mean to say this Wyeth fella had him plans to get his fort outfitted with goods brung here by ship from back east?"

"Yes." Soloman nodded. "That's right."

"Why the devil didn't Wyeth just bring you all here on the ship?"

"Not sure why not." Soloman pondered the ground beneath his boots. "Perhaps to save room and passage costs on the ship for the essential goods and construction supplies for the post he had dreams of building out here. And well he didn't take us along." His voice became moody for a moment. "This ship, the *Sultana*, was lost in the south seas—wrecked, we received word. And with that wreckage came the end to Wyeth's plans. The doctor here, McLoughlin, he had to tell Nathaniel the bad news."

"Wyeth an' you boys all end up joinin' up with the Britishers, huh?"

"Oh, no, sir." Smith turned toward Bass. "The group that was left to Wyeth—not many of us, to be sure—after the journey west and after so many saw the reality of dying at the hands of some Indian, we disbanded for the most part. Some left with Nathaniel to go back east last March with a spring fur brigade. He pulled out for the east coast with the spring express the first of March. Nathaniel still entertains his illusions of re-outfitting himself and returning to become a thorn in the side of the British out here. Build that fort of his, set up trade, and drain some of the valuable fur business off from the Hudson's Bay Company. Grand plans they were."

He paused and shook his head slowly before continuing. "A noble effort. But he really had no idea, no conception at all, of what trouble it would be to estabish a fort out here—much less be able to compete with this mighty company." Smith grew pensive again. "However, I had to choose my own way at that time. I had had enough of the uncertainty and whims of weather, geography and the redman alike. I've been working around the post here, odd jobs for my keep. When John Ball— he was the first of Nathaniel's men to be the school teacher here at Vancouver, and started last fall—quit the doctor first of last month, March, to build a place of his own down in the Willamette Valley and try his hand at farming, I asked McLoughlin if he would want me to continue what Ball had started with the children. McLoughlin immediately agreed and here I have been for almost two months now."

"Traded your traps for a slate, huh?" Titus remarked. "Trapper turned teacher."

"I suppose it does sound a bit dull on the face of it, doesn't it?"

"Don't mean to be belittlin' your . . . trade, son," Bass apologized.

"No offense taken, sir," Smith replied. "I just had a choice to make. I didn't know for sure what Wyeth would ever put together for himself and the rest of us. However, I was certain of what I could put together for myself. And I grabbed for it. Something I could do, something which made me feel very good, on my own, to boot."

The young teacher chuckled. "There are times when the job has its own rewards, sir. As with bright students such as Dominique Pambrun and Ranald McDonald. The doctor let the rowdier ones know he will thrash them soundly if they do not behave. Why—young David McLoughlin was the first and only student who could speak English for a while; so if a pupil lapses into French on me instead of using English, that student has to wear a heavy leather medallion around his neck for the rest of the day. But by and large, I get to reward most of them daily with barley sugar as a treat for good behavior. It is just the few, the rascals." He chuckled again.

"Whenever I think back to fighting Indians—I often wonder what is really worse: fighting an Indian that wants to scalp you; or fighting the rambunctious, rowdy students in my class!"

"You fought Injuns, you say, son?"

"Only once." Smith nodded. "Not really fought them. We were told to stay back out of the way and leave the fighting to those veterans of the mountains. Some Blackfeet had cornered us down in the bottom of Pierre's Hole last summer . . ."

"You was at that ronnyvoo?"

"Why . . ." Soloman said, a puzzled look on his face. "Why, yes. Wyeth and the eleven of us left to him had hooked up with Milton Sublette to head for Snake River country and were heading out of rendezvous with Mister Sublette's brigade when we were surprised by this large band of Blackfeet . . ."

"Got pinned down an' the rest of the ronnyvoo camp come roarin' in to finish the fight. Never did get us that'un finished, howsomever."

"Why, yes." Soloman turned to face the trapper. "Sounds to me . . ."

". . . Like I was there," Bass said softly. "Saw many a good man go under that day. Good friend I lost there. Really never knew why we didn't take us the fort them Injuns built 'em in the trees."

"It was your kind I saw that day take over the fight, riding in from the rendezvous encampment, jumping from your horses, stripping your clothing for battle. In a sober, morbid way—it was yet a very grand sight to behold, indeed. I had to decide after we arrived here that I did not have a stomach for Indian fighting."

"Most of us really don't, son."

"I mean to say, I would . . . if I can, I would prefer never to have to go through such a thing again."

Bass put an open palm on the knee of the young American beside him. "I think you made you the right choice, son."

"You really do?"

"Yepper." He rose from the bench. "Each man's gotta find his own way—an' you ain't got nothin' to feel put under 'bout, givin' up trappin' for teachin' here." Then he remembered his manners. "I'm sorry, Mister Smith. Name's Titus Bass. Recent of Pierre's Hole, Three Forks, winterin' with the Crow, an' a mighty long walk here!"

"Pleasure to meet you, Mister Titus Bass." He stood up to shake the trapper's hand.

Bass looked around at the buildings of the compound. "You don't know where a fella might find him a bit of vittles, does you? I ain't et for 'most of a day now."

"Why, certainly," Soloman replied. "You can come with me to breakfast in the kitchen. I have an early breakfast most days, then wander back over here to Bachelors' Hall, where I hold classes for the youngsters. I have some quiet time to prepare my lessons for the day before the children show up. How about this morning after breakfast together, I give Mister Titus Bass, of the long-legged journey, a tour, a guided tour to be sure, of Fort Vancouver?"

"That . . . that'd be just fine," Bass said. "Yes, sir, that's somethin' this ol' nigger'd really 'preciate."

"Nigger?" Smith seemed to look at Bass's deeply tanned face all the more closely. "You don't look to be . . ."

"Jumpin' Jeho . . . I ain't a *nigra* if'n that's what you're askin' 'bout," Bass replied to ease the young man's sudden tension. "Just a way of talkin' for a lotta coons—lotta us trappers. Nigger don't mean a darkie—nigger don't mean somethin' bad, noways, neither. Just a way of . . . of sayin' somethin', I s'pose. Don't know how we all got to usin' the word . . ."

"An expression," Smith interrupted. "It's just an expression you and your kind are wont to use at times, then."

"I s'pose what you're sayin' is right."

"Interesting." He pondered for a moment. "Very interesting. I might use such a thing in class this day."

"Talk 'bout niggers?"

Smith laughed lightly. "Oh, no, Titus. I may call you Titus, may I not?" Bass nodded. "I will not talk about niggers. Not at all, in fact. The children have no idea what a nigra or darky is, for that matter. But sometimes the ones who are slow in English, learning good English that is, might be excited to hear some real earthy, homey expressions used in everyday speech. Those expressions real people use to describe things, those descriptions . . . those ways of saying things that are very, very descriptive."

"You ain't takin' me to class with you now," Bass protested.

"Why—I hadn't thought of that." Smith grinned. "But it would be a marvelous thing. Yes! You could talk to the children and I would translate for you. Yes! You have struck upon something good here."

"You just get that notion right on outta your head, son," Titus protested again. "Why, sir? Have you plans for this morning?"

"No. Well, no," Bass stammered. "Not as far as I know. Gotta talk with the doctor . . ."

"You have an appointment, then?"

"No, not rightly, I don't think," Bass replied. "But—you ain't gettin' me near no school house!"

"Ah," Soloman remarked. "McLoughlin does not see visitors until the afternoon, after lunch it is." He put a hand on the trapper's upper arm. "Then you have the morning free for me and the children. Oh, come on, sir. It is the least you can do. I am going to take you to break your fast. Can't you smell the aromas coming from the kitchen now?"

Bass could not help it. His nose filled with the savory fragrance coming to him from across the large compound. His mouth watered at the prospect of another warm meal pushed down into his belly.

"What do you say? Huh, Titus Bass? Pretty fair trade, eh?"

"Awww, shit!" Then Bass clamped his lips shut. "I'm sorry, sorry for cussin' in front of a teacher . . . in front of you, son."

Smith laughed heartily, squinting his eyes at Bass. "Oh, shit, Mister Bass. You have no need for apologizing to me. I have heard sailors all my life. Shit, I'm not offended at all. Come, let's get your belly full of hot food, now. Then, I'll give you the tour."

Sixteen

After a hearty breakfast in the kitchen, which was situated behind the doctor's house, Smith and Bass began their tour. By this time, the fort was itself beginning to come to life. The sounds of human industry floated on the air: the ring of an axe on wood, the clang of a blacksmith's hammer, oddly disembodied, floating on the morning air, the faint chime of a hammered nail driving into a whipsawed board, the whiskey voice of a teamster calling out to his mules, the whisper-snap of harness leather as the slack jerked out of the traces, the creak of wagon wheels rolling under the strain of cargo.

Soloman had explained that most of the clerks would take their breakfast with the Chief Factor in McLoughlin's house, in the dining room, while the twenty-three workers would eat in Bachelors' Hall. But Smith's own personal habit of rising early precluded having his first meal of the day with the doctor or in the main hall. Instead, the young American school teacher always arose early and went directly to the kitchen itself to request his breakfast firsthand, taking his meal almost directly from the many skillets that were warming.

The two men emerged from the passageway that connected the house with the kitchen and circled the back of the Chief Factor's house. Boards groaned under their weight, as the two men stopped for a moment.

"This place, the house, is called many names, Mister Bass," the teacher began. "Although the Chief Factor is not properly authorized to employ the title, the place itself is called the Governor's House or the Governor's Mansion. Then variously referred to as the Commander's House, the Manager's residence—even the *Ty-ee* House, which is the native word meaning 'chief.' Some simply call it the Big House. Any one of the terms may be used and it is readily known you mean where McLoughlin himself dwells."

From the outside it looked as if it were a single-story building. However, the manner in which it was constructed had made for several rooms in an attic area with no exterior windows or dormers. Near the side of the house lay a supply of lumber and tools covered with oiled canvas. Smith pointed out that workmen were still finishing the second floor of the house this spring. Along the south wall of the large house ran a wide front porch. It was elevated about five feet from ground level, with two central sets of steps that wound toward the main door of the house, located in the middle of the south wall. On either side of this front door were three large windows with their curtains drawn. On either side of the two staircases sat ancient eight-inch cannons, both mounted on naval carriages and pointed directly at the main gate at the south wall of the post.

"Perhaps you'll get a chance to see inside the Big House one of these days," Smith commented as they strolled around the southwest corner of the house. Somewhere a meadowlark trilled its morning song atop a palisade.

"That be one thing I'm countin' on, young fella," Bass replied.

Soloman pointed to his left at the Owyhee Church, just west and north of McLoughlin's residence. He explained that religious services were held there for the Indians. Between the church and the kitchen along the north wall was another fifteen-foot-wide gate that remained locked most of the time. Further west of the church sat a small, one-story structure, square in construction, its windows barred with straps of heavy, blackened iron.

"Looks to be a helluva lot like a jail to me," Bass remarked.

"Right you are," Smith said. "That's what it is."

"I'll be damned!" Bass said. "Even got a jail here. What—you get too drunk, maybe? Gotta spend a night in there?"

"No, no," Smith answered, "the jail here is reserved for much more serious crimes than merely getting drunk and raising a ruckus. The doctor himself doesn't take much to imbibing spirituous liquors, but the jail is not used to hold drunks."

Near the southwest corner of the jail another medium-sized building was under construction. Smith pointed out that it would be what they would call the *new office*. To the southwest of it, however, was the *old office* where the clerks did their accounting and handled the large northwestern operation of the company.

"I myself am not much of a church-going man, Mister Bass," Smith remarked. "But, I find that each Sunday I do enjoy attending one of the doctor's religious services. He is not Catholic as so many are—so he holds a service where he reads a portion of the Church of England prayer book, I suppose it is. We have the services back there at times." He pointed to the Owyhee Church building.

"It is not the rigid letter of religious creed that is so highly important to McLoughlin. Instead, Mister Bass, he is a man who often speaks of the need for a community of worship—a spirit of worship that remains utmost in the mind of the Chief Factor. The gathering of his people under his large wing—and he takes this chore very seriously—is something he genuinely loves to do. Sometimes we have held our Sunday services in the Big House, in the main dining room where the doctor will conduct our prayer and songs from a hasty pulpit following breakfast. Some clerks will read from the Bible, mostly the New Testament passages. Then McLoughlin might read from his Anglican service, followed by his son James finishing the morning with another short reading from the Bible before we sing a few more songs to conclude the service."

Smith nodded his head. "Sundays, traditionally a day of rest for most, appears to be the busiest day of the week for the doctor. Besides our own Anglican service, he also holds a separate service for the Catholic employees—French mostly. So he will read in their native French tongue. McLoughlin has requested the company to dispatch a priest to the Columbia on countless occasions. Although he is greatly distressed by the repeated rebuff, he keeps up with the services for the welfare of his employees."

Along the north wall, to the west of the jail, stood another small structure. Outside, more rough-hewn lumber lay stacked under oiled canvas. Soloman explained that this lumber was not for construction of the fort's buildings; rather, it was for the construction of furniture. This was the carpenter's shop. The rasping sound of a saw burred in counterpoint to the rhythmic tap of a hammer on soft cabinet wood. The smells of fresh shavings mingled with the heady scent of cut cedar and pinesap.

"There is a sawmill some five miles above here on the river," Smith explained. "Several workers are kept busy for about half the year cutting lumber down and hauling it here from the mill. Those same carpenters then build the fine furniture you saw in the kitchen—the fine furnishings you will see on your visit to the Big House. They also build furniture for many of the inland posts. Chairs, tables, desks, chests, beds and such."

Continuing west of the carpenter's shop, Smith pointed out the larger one-story structure some eighty feet by thirty feet that was known as the wheat store. Here were stored the wheat and other grains grown in the fields surrounding the fort walls. Bass sniffed of the musky scent of wheat, barley, oats and corn. A mule brayed in protest across the compound. A whip cracked, a man cursed. The mule whimpered one last time and was silent.

"Back in twenty-nine," Smith explained, "Governor Simpson—that's the doctor's boss . . . hell, the boss of the whole damned company . . . had McLoughlin build a new grist mill down on the falls of the Willamette. The river runs south of the post, its mouth pouring into the Columbia just a short distance west of here. I have been there myself once, and I must admit it is an ideal spot for a mill to grind the wheat into flour. But McLoughlin knew the natives were, shall I say sensitive, about having construction near the falls. Perhaps they were fearful of some gods or something. But, the doctor knew there would be resistance to the company building the mill there. Nevertheless, the governor ordered the doctor to build the mill and he did so in the fall."

He let out a long sighing breath. "That winter when the mill was abandoned for the season, after the harvest had been ground into flour, the natives came in and burned the whole of it down. I believe, as the doctor does, that it symbolized to the natives the worst of white intrusion into their land. And right on the heels of a terrible epidemic of ague among the Indians. But McLoughlin persisted. The next spring the mill was again raised on the site of the burnt and hacked timbers, and the mill race itself was finished just last year. Did you enjoy the sweetcakes you had along with breakfast?"

"Been some time, son," Scratch answered. "Yes, I did. Some time it's been since last I et so much bakin' goods."

To the west of the wheat store along the north wall stood a long, one-story structure called the beef store where the ground was hard, tromped and packed by many cloven hooves. There hung the butchered meats, both cattle and swine, some smoked. Bass's nose crinkled as he sniffed the heady scent of hickory, smelling like mulled wine, like the stale ashes of a cookfire. Behind the beef store against the north palisade was a well. In the event of a siege, the fort would not go without water. However, as Smith explained, such an attack by the natives on the fort itself was thought to be a very remote possibility. The Indians in the area had at least become aware of the Chief Factor's stern, yet benevolent hand in dealing with them. While the natives had done damage from time to time to crews of ships, or destroyed structures such as the mill, they dared not entertain the idea of attacking the fort itself. In fact, the walls of the fort were simple palisades, lacking inner ramparts and loopholes.

They passed the root house, a small, narrow structure where many of the vegetables grown in the gardens and fields were stored.

"Would you like to get a good view of the countryside, all around?" Not waiting for an answer, Smith led the way up a narrow set of steps running along the inside of the northern wall, ascending toward the northwest corner of the palisades. The two Americans emerged at the top of the steps to stand upon a small, rough-hewn landing.

Bass slowly turned, looking in each direction for long moments to marvel at the view he had of this wild, beautiful country. To the north and east, he could see his pilot peak—that single, snowy mountain that had helped guide him to Vancouver. To the west Bass watched the mighty Columbia fall away to the sea. And to the south he could see the Willamette as it fell into the Columbia, issuing forth from its beautiful valley.

"That fellow John Ball lives down that way," Smith said. "I told you about him. He was with Wyeth and me, too—came out with us. Last year when we all wandered in here, Ball began to fall in love with this land. More quickly than even I, it must be said. He himself was a New Englander, teacher—even said he was a lawyer, too." He saw Bass glance at him for a brief moment.

"Sours my milk!" Bass exclaimed. "Country gettin' too damned civilized when lawyers come trompin' 'round out here." He snorted in derision. "Law an' constables. Never would've thought there'd be that foofaraw out here. Time was, only one law for us: takin' care of yourself an' your companyeros. Man does that an' ain't nothin' else needed. Nigger can expect to be treated square by most, an' he can treat most coons the same way back. It's them few low, snaky bastards who make things bad for the rest of us."

Scratch chuckled lightly and shook his head. "Laws an' lawyers pushin' you around. An' if they ain't pushin' you around, they fool you with all the fancy foofaraw palaver. Lawyers an' gov'ment niggers—they be the same. Takin' what ain't theirs to begin with, an' live off'n a honest man's earnin's. Both of 'em the same: word-benders is what they is. Rattles my ass! Word-benders."

"I suppose you are right, Mister Bass," Soloman continued. "But Ball was a different sort of teacher, or lawyer, I think. He so enjoyed the spirited discussions and arguments held in Bachelors' Hall each evening after supper, 'til long into the night. He said he had not had so much intellectual stimulation in many a year until he arrived at what he called 'this bastion of civilized wilderness.' Also, we were all treated so kindly by McLoughlin as his guests that Ball was the first to leave Wyeth's service, offering to repay McLoughlin's kindness and generosity."

Bass turned and followed Smith down the steps to the compound once more. A pair of swallows whistled overhead, then darted from view like the shadows of leaves. "The doctor would not hear of a guest of his working, of course. But McLoughlin did suggest that if Ball wished to repay him, a school be formed to educate his own and the rest of the children. Since there had never been a real school out here, in eighteen hundred and twenty-six the doctor had to send his son John Jr. east to the Red River colony for an education. Well, Mister Bass—that was the perfect offer for a man like John Ball. He set up classes every morning, excepting Sundays, of course. The students came to his quarters in Bachelors' Hall for instruction, as they now come to my apartment. Ball quit serving the doctor back the first of March, and I took over the teaching chores. Ball told us he wanted to try his luck at farming. Got him a nice place started down the Willamette."

They strolled along the western wall of the fort, passing two large, high buildings that Smith explained were storage houses for trade goods and furs, as were the two others Bass had seen along the south wall the previous evening when he had entered the fort. They turned at the southwest corner near the small powder magazine and moved along the south wall, past the open gate and toward the wider gate, it being some fifteen feet in width when fully opened.

Smith smiled, shook his head. "I've taken on a tough job, Mister Bass—this teaching of the fort's children. Young ones from the village, too. May not seem like it to you, however. But my pupils speak a variety of tongues, so it not only makes it hard to get my lessons across, but also keeps things very, very lively—and interesting to boot!"

He chuckled. "The children can all get very excited about something and I can't make a hide or hair out of all the babble coming from so many tongues: Klickitat, Nez Perce, Chinook, Cree, and French. I'm slowly learning a little French, and I'm getting quite good at Chinook—the language used by most natives we see, it seems."

"Want someday to go back an' learn to read better," Bass remarked. "Knowed me how once. Didn't keep up with it, howsomever. Now it be just scratchin' on paper—cain't make no sign of it though." He snorted and shook his head. "Even got me some books I have read to me, I do. Shakespeare, one is—some plays . . ."

"Shakespeare, you say?" Smith was more than a little amazed. "Why, that comes as a bit of a surprise—I mean to say, no offense. But, to have a trapper here in this wilderness having read Shakespeare! Why . . ."

"I ain't read it my own self," Bass corrected. "Had me a play called *Macbeth* read to me 'round the evenin' fires by . . ." The memory tugged at a lump suddenly shooting into his throat. "It was a young fella what read it to me. Got me the book an 'nother—it called *Pilgrim's Progress*—back to my truck an' plunder, back on the Walla Walla at Fort Nez Perce. Where my ponies be."

"Somewhat an amazing character you are, Mister Titus Bass," Smith concluded. "You are ready to lift scalps," he said as his fingers flicked at some of the scalp locks that adorned the sleeves and quillwork of the trapper's shirt. "Yet, you have still found a place in your heart—nay, your very soul for . . . for Shakespeare—and other good reading! You truly are an astonishing man. Not at all like most I met down in Pierre's Hole, nor on my way here with Wyeth."

"Not all that dad-blamed differ'nt, really," Scratch protested.

"Yes, you are, Mister Bass," Soloman replied. "You are not like anyone else I have met before—or, likely to again." Smith stopped beside the long, tall structure. Its log walls, like the rest of those in the compound, had been plastered and whitewashed.

"This is the trading store. Some call it the Indian shop or the Indian store. Here the trading takes place with the natives of the surrounding areas. It was put here close to the main gate so that when the Indians come in for their trading, they would not be allowed any further access to the fort's interior."

They continued east along the southern palisade to the blacksmith shop, beside which stood the iron store in the southeastern corner of the fort walls. Stored inside were various sizes of the forged metal: standard strap, bar, plate and rod iron. A few men passed them and entered, only to emerge shortly, carrying strap iron into the blacksmith's shop where two other men were engaged in firing up the furnaces for the day's work. Bass listened to the alien sounds of metal banging on metal, the wheezing lungs of the bellows, the small wind blowing from its spout onto fiery coals. He turned away from the acrid smoke stinging his nostrils, let out a breath.

"I'll be damned if you don't have it all here, Soloman," Bass commented.

"They do . . . we do, here," he replied. "Besides the carpenters who make the furniture, some are coopers for barrels and such as that. Then we have these men here: the blacksmiths and tinsmiths who are constantly kept busy with work for this fort and many of the other posts. Work is already under way on another post, so these men have much to do—hinges, nails, frames, and all the iron goods necessary. A few of these men are gunsmiths, too. Up there"—he pointed past the dormitory—"by the kitchen, is the harness shop where the leathersmiths craft all sorts of things and repair the leather harness, saddles, and other goods we make from the cattle hides taken in the butchering." He turned to look at Scratch. "Is your outfit in good repair?"

"I be hopin' it'll make it through to ronnyvoo, son," Bass answered. "Good truck, it is. A saddle I got me down to Santee Fe, some time back. Injun pack saddles for the ponies. Best damned things I ever saw for such, too."

"I was just wondering if you might need some repairs on your outfit," Soloman said. "Some twenty craftsmen here—not counting clerks—who can repair anything you have need of fixing."

"Even if I did, ain't got it with me here, son," Bass said. "Back to Pambaroon's place. Stayed me one night afore comin' on downriver."

"With Thornbrugh."

"You knowed that, huh?"

"Yes. Not a man I would suppose doesn't know of you being here, having come in with Thornbrugh down on the supply barge."

"Thornbrugh tell ever'body?"

"Oh, no. Not Thornbrugh," Soloman said. "I was told by the doctor himself about your arrival."

"I know," Titus said matter-of-factly, "he come out to see just who Thornbrugh brung with 'im when we come in to the fort yesterday." He looked over at Smith again as they came around the back of Bachelors' Hall, moving toward the north wall. "He ask you—the doctor himself—to come meet me?"

"I would have done that myself, Mister Bass," Soloman replied. "You being American as I am, and all."

"Nawww, I mean McLoughlin ask you to . . . to check me over, huh?"

"Ah, well . . . er, to be honest, he did ask me to do that,"
Smith admitted. "Now this is the wash house, where all the
laundry is done: everything from clothing to bedding and
blankets. And there," he said, pointing to the well just behind
the east of the wash house, "is another source of water."

"I see you don't have to draw your water from the river,"
Bass observed wryly. "Just the same ways, I see you don't
wanna answer my question 'bout McLoughlin, son." He
looked at Soloman, who quickly averted his eyes. "You answered it a bit, son. But, not all of it. He wants you to read my
sign, right?"

"That's the bakery." Soloman pointed to the structure
nestled within the east wall of the fort, directly opposite the
wash house. "And north of the wash house here is the harness
shop where we can mend anything you might have need
of. . . ."

"I need my questions to have 'em some answers, damnit!"
Bass grumbled. "Why's it so damned, blue-blazes, gall-fisted,
bowlegged, bust-jawed hard for a man to get him some answers 'round this place?"

Smith stopped and looked squarely at Bass, surprised at the
sudden flash of anger in the trapper's response. "I suppose you
are owed some explanation, aren't you?"

"Damned right I am, son!"

Smith paused a moment to mull over his reply. "The doctor
was visited by Thornbrugh, after the Englishman left you last
night."

"He went straight to McLoughlin, huh?"

"Yes, but that is normal procedure, Mister Bass. The doctor
likes to know what is going on in other posts—*has* to know. He
is in charge . . ."

"An' he's in charge of all the folks 'round here, too," Bass
observed. "That it? So, he gets Jarrell to come up to his house
an' spill him his guts on me."

"To report on the status of the Walla Walla operations."

"To report on *me!*" Bass broke in. "Thornbrugh had to tell
him 'bout me . . . but now I think on it—that be just what I
wanted him to do, son. So, don't you worry none 'bout that,
now. I asked Jarrell to go see the doctor an' tell 'im I'm wantin'
to talk with 'im soon."

"I see."

"Ain't nothin' at all wrong with that, now, Soloman."

"Doesn't seem to be, if you asked Jarrell to do it." Smith was more than a little relieved.

"Jarrell's my friend, you see," Bass went on. "Got to know the man some on the way down the river. Like him, I do. Might even take a likin' to you, too, son." He grinned.

"Thornbrugh's a good man, that he is," Smith replied. "He works directly for McLough . . ." And he shut his lips.

"I thought he worked for Pambaroon—down to Walla Walla." Smith's evasiveness had not been lost on Bass.

"He does . . . Thornbrugh does work for Pambrun. Yes. You are right." Smith tried to smile. "It's stupid of me to get confused this way. He *used* to work for the doctor directly and now he works under Pambrun."

"I thought so," Bass commented. But he really felt there was something strange about it all. And strange, too—he began to sort through it now—that the Englishman was supposedly assigned to Walla Walla far away upriver, yet had a woman here at the fort, down in the village. Why, if he worked at Fort Nez Perce, why didn't Thornbrugh take her with him down to Pambrun's post?

"You had problems with Jarrell—Thornbrugh?" Bass inquired.

"No. Not in the least. Thornbrugh's a very nice fellow. Despite his size, one of the best of gentlemen I know. I don't know of a person who has had a bit of a problem with Thornbrugh. He doesn't seem to have a mean bone in that whole huge body of his, Mister Bass. Everyone, they have all been very kind to me since coming here."

"And now they want you to be repayin' that kindness by spyin' on this ol' boy, huh?"

"Not at all, sir!" Smith protested. "The doctor does not work in devious ways at all. And he would be highly offended if you accused him of such a thing!"

"Hold on, now." Bass put his hand up. "No one accusin' you or the doctor of doin' anything underhanded. Just meant to say that McLoughlin sent you to get to know me better afore he wants to see me. Right?"

"I suppose you must be right there," Smith agreed quickly.

Bass chewed on it a minute. It seemed to make sense to him. The Chief Factor was talking not only to Jarrell Thornbrugh about him, but also to Soloman Smith. This doctor wanted to know a lot about the American. So, he reasoned,

McLoughlin must be getting ready to call Bass in for a visit. That wasn't so bad, after all was said and done. Might just speed things up.

"You gonna talk with 'im 'bout me, right?" Scratch asked.

"Yes. But later. After classes this morning. I'll be having lunch with him, and others, in the Big House. Please feel free to go into the kitchen and get yourself something to eat whenever you get hungry again."

"Cain't have me lunch with the rest of the fellas?"

"Not all of us regularly eat there," Smith answered. "Just the clerks, officers, some of us others, you see. Seems I work directly for the doctor, too." He paused. "Teaching school, that is."

"Ain't nothin' to this, is there, Soloman?"

"Not at all, Mister Bass." He turned and walked back toward the dorm with Titus. "I must be getting to my wards now—the students, you know. Some already here, waiting for me," he said after they entered the dorm. He pointed to six children gathered outside his room in the hallway.

"You like children?" Bass inquired.

"Seems I have to. But—yes. I think I really do. I enjoy the job. Now you," he said, patting Bass on the upper arm. "You go and make yourself at home. Go down by the river, or stroll down to the village. Visit the Indian trading house. Anything you like. The place is open to you, Mister Bass. Anything you need, all you have to do is holler for it. Right?"

"Yep," Bass answered. "An' what I need is to talk with the doctor."

"And he will be visiting with you soon, I'm sure."

"I know. I know that, son," Titus replied. "I know he's gettin' himself all ready to have a lil' talk with this here child. Yes, sir. He knows him that this ol' boy got him some questions to ask him, right off." He moved away, then stopped and turned to look back at Smith, who was ushering the youngsters into his room. He nodded at the young school teacher and continued down the hallway between the other apartments, toward the large, open dorm room.

Smith lingered near the doorway, a bit confused in his own mind at why this American trapper was so much more important to the doctor than most others who had visited Vancouver. Why this hardened veteran of the Rocky Mountains, this man of many winters in the wilderness—why should McLoughlin take such an interest in him? Smith could not quite piece together why the doctor had sent for him late last night. Soloman had gone up to the Big House as the Chief Factor had requested of him.

The Chief Factor had gotten straight to the point in requesting the young teacher to acquaint himself with the visitor, who had come here requesting to talk with McLoughlin. It did not seem all that strange to him at first. Smith had agreed, saying he would enjoy the chance to meet the trapper. That was all there was to it, almost. McLoughlin, in his heavy robe, had escorted him to the porch. But since then, Smith had wondered about it. Especially what Thornbrugh had told the doctor about the trapper.

Now there was a bit of a mystery in itself. Jarrell Thornbrugh. Smith had often thought it strange how the Englishman had worked so closely with McLoughlin for a couple of years, so closely one would have believed he was grooming Thornbrugh to take his place at Vancouver. Then in 1830 James Douglas came on the scene to take the place of Edward Ermatinger. Douglas was not to be in charge of the company's accounts in the Columbia District. And Thornbrugh had been moved. Smith considered Jarrell Thornbrugh to be one of the men most loyal to McLoughlin, accepting the transfer to the Walla Walla post in early fall of 1831 without a grumble.

And yet he left his wife here at the village. Every chance the big Englishman had, he returned to Vancouver on this mission or that—very often at the personal request of the Chief Factor himself. Seemingly, too, to visit his wife. Thornbrugh returned so frequently, even in the harsh winter months. And he spent so many hours around the post—not just down in the village in his modest cabin. Instead, he spent hours with McLoughlin around his dining table, or in the doctor's office, or plopped comfortably in a soft chair in the Chief Factor's sitting room.

He walked over to the window and pushed open the shutters to allow the light to pour in. Perhaps more light would be shed on this whole matter very soon, too. And some fresh air. Then he would know why the good doctor had asked him to find out if the American trapper were going to the big rendezvous that coming summer. The Chief Factor wanted to know specifically about that. Smith had forgotten to ask that of Bass. But, as he turned to look into the clean, bright, expectant faces of the children, he knew he had time to find out.

* * *

The mountain lion paced back and forth along the rimrock, snarling and roaring with a grating, skirling sound. Suddenly there was another lion, and another, and finally a fourth—all setting up a horrible howl above him on the rocks over his small camp. They were poised above him, looking down on the old trapper, snarling and crying, each one crouched to leap on him at any moment. He twisted away a moment to grab his rifle, but it wasn't there. The howl suddenly increased and he turned quickly to see the four cats lifting off from the edge of the rimrock, flying through the air, straight toward him.

Bass just as suddenly awoke. He felt the thick, woolen blanket beneath him. His eyes adjusted to what dim, narrowing light slipped into the room through the windows. The trapper propped himself up on his elbows and only then realized where he was. It had been just a dream. He was on a bed in Bachelors' Hall, at Vancouver. He sighed and let his head plop back down again. But the howling mountain lions persisted.

He sat up on the side of the bed and slipped the moccasins onto his feet. He tied the whangs around his ankles and stood. Where was the noise coming from? It sounded like quite a passel of mountain cats fighting, howling—snarling-mad with one another, perhaps over some kill and how it was to be divided among them. Never before had he heard such a peculiar racket. Titus moved down the long room into the hallway between the apartments just as Soloman stepped from his door.

"Just what the hell is that?" Scratch asked.

"What is . . ."

"Sounds like a whole shitteree of cats settin' up a howl."

"Wha . . ." Soloman asked, "what did you say?"

Bass turned. "Sounds like'n you got some painter cats out there." He pointed. "Sounds like they got somethin' down an' now they's figurin' which of 'em gonna eat first."

"Surely you are joking?"

"I'm what?"

Smith came out into the hallway to face the trapper. "You . . . you surely are making a joke with me—thinking . . ." Then the look changed from one of confusion to sudden-found inspiration. "You don't know, do you?"

"I know 'bout mountain cats, all right," Bass retorted and stomped down the hall. "Painters be tricky critters, they is, for certain."

"No, no." Smith chuckled as they walked out to the compound. "I mean you don't know . . . you've never heard the kind of music . . . you've never heard bagpipes before, have you?"

"Bag . . . pipes?" Bass stopped and stared at Soloman. The sound was clearer now and he tried to discern where it was coming from. "What the blue blazes you talkin' 'bout, son?"

"A musical instrument," Smith replied. "Scottish. From the Scottish highlands."

"You mean to tell me all that caterwauling be somethin' you call music?"

"Yes." Smith chuckled. "I see now that you never have heard them before."

"I've heard such a racket afore, son," Bass bellowed. "Up to the mountains, them big cats get to . . ."

"No. No, Mister Bass. I'm asking if you've ever heard bagpipes?"

"You tellin' me you be certain that bo music? Real, honest-to-goodness, what-some-folks-call music?"

"Yes, sir."

"What the hell it playin' for?" he asked, still somewhat confused by the high, skirling sounds with the heavy, constant drone beneath the higher notes.

"Every evening the piper comes out to play before the supper meal," Smith replied.

"Then just tell me how come I ain't heard it last two nights, son." He squinted at the teacher.

"Of course." Soloman finally realized that Bass had not heard the piper before. "Of course you haven't. He's been sick—the bagpiper, that is. He was down with a touch of the fever, perhaps ague, for the last week or so. The doctor has sorely missed his piping."

"I ain't heard it 'cause he's been sick to now?" Bass inquired. "From the sound of things, fella still be pretty-some sick."

The teacher did not know if the trapper was serious or not until he saw a smile creep across Scratch's face. "That's a good one, Mister Bass," he finally agreed. "That is good. Come with me. You'll see."

Past them moved a small knot of workers, five dark-skinned men. Bass turned to watch them go into the dorm. "Them Injuns work here—mean to say, they live here?"

"Yes," Smith replied. "However, they are not Indians, Titus. Those men were Kanakas—from the Sandwich Islands."

"From where you say?"

"Sandwich Islands. Out in the Pacific Ocean. Hudson's Bay

trades out of some of the islands and those fellas were brought here to work at the fort. More of the islanders working at other western posts."

"I'll be go to hell an' et for the Devil's tater," he muttered. "You mean to tell me 'sides Frenchies, Englishers an' them natural Canadians—plus a American thrown in for good measure—you got niggers what come from a island out to the ocean workin' here, too?"

"Again you are right. But—come with me, and we'll show you the man who makes the mountain-lion music."

The two Americans ambled across the compound. They passed under the flagpole where one of the clerks was just retrieving the flag for the night, and began to circle behind the two large storehouses toward the powder magazine when the piper turned the corner and headed toward them.

The piper paced slowly, in rhythm with his music, a slow, plaintive dirge.

Utterly amazed, Bass stopped and stared at the piper.

"I ain't never . . . ," Bass stammered. "That nigger's got a skirt on!" He shook his head, as if to clear his vision of its odd image. "This infernal place is gone beaver! Man prancin' round here wearin' a dress—an' a real short'un, to boot!"

Soloman Smith laughed.

Bass turned and glared at the young teacher. "It's pretty goddamned funny, I gotta say that," he snarled at Smith. "This place does have it some funny . . ."

"No," Smith said, still chuckling. "No, Titus. That is not a dress . . ."

"Looks to be a dress to this here child's eyes, it does."

"I mean to say," Smith said, controlling his laughter, "that's what the Scots call a *kilt.*"

"Like . . . you kill't somethin'?" Bass asked. "Like you gone out an' kill't a animal?"

"No, no," Smith said with a new burst of laughter.

"McLoughlin make 'im do that? Just how can a fella let himself be caught out like that—wearin' women's clothes? Son, I just don't understand."

"The doctor is from Scotland himself . . ."

"Don't tell me he wears skirts, too?"

"Dear Lord!" Smith laughed. "I can't take this any more!"

Bass studied the piper's odd uniform, then stared at the baffling bagpipes.

The piper didn't even glance at the two Americans as he

paced up to them and marched on past them. He was dressed in the pleated kilt, the plaid running over his shoulder in thick folds, the bagpipe tucked securely beneath his left arm. Tall, knee-high stockings of gray ran up his legs and strapped to one leg was a sheath with a small knife in it. At the man's waist hung a small fur bag attached to his belt alongside a long, thin scabbard that held the highland weapon of choice, the Scottish dirk. His thick black leather boots that reached just over his ankles scuffed up little puffs of dust into the air with every step as he tromped away from the pair in time with his own music.

"McLoughlin, he's Scottish, Bass," Smith explained. "He had to have a piper from Scotland to play for him when he built Vancouver, you see."

"He don't wear him one of them skirts, too?" Bass asked again. "Big, big fella like him look even more stupider'n that'un there."

"He does not wear dresses—the doctor doesn't." Smith shook his head, trying to imagine how it would be to have spent almost a fourth of your life in the mountains, coming across that mountain spine to this refuge in the wilderness and finding someone playing a strange, howling instrument and wearing a short skirt that barely reached to his knees.

"The Chief Factor has the piper play each evening as a call to supper. See, Mister Bass?" He gestured toward the Big House where the tall man stood on the porch, wearing the same long, flowing, black frock coat, the white hair wisping across his shoulders in the evening breeze. "You see, he's not wearing a dress!"

"I can see that now, damnit!" Bass felt offended when Smith started laughing again.

"I'm sor . . . sorry," Smith stammered, his laughter fading.

"Well, you should be—you damned pup!" He grinned at Smith. "Things 'round here mighty queersome. Queersome, indeed."

He walked back toward the Bachelors' Hall with the young teacher. "First I meet the Doctor's boy down to the tradin' house. He tells me he be some twenty-five year old. Cain't rightly believe me that—the doctor cain't be old 'nough to be his pappy?"

"Yes," Smith answered. "McLoughlin is . . . he's about fifty-two as I was told."

The trapper shook his head. "Hard to believe—even with the white hair an' all. An' I thought I was gettin' on in the years." He shook his head again, then nodded to Smith. "Ain't seen the likes of all that foofaraw in some time, it's been. Even to ronnyvoo! They had 'em all the truck what comes with tradin' to the Injuns, blankets, beads an' such—but they also had 'em some fine an' pretty earthwares, glass dood-ja-dads, an' fancy clay pipes. Whoooeee! I was gettin' a eyeful of all the fancies when Jarrell come up to fetch me an' take me on down to his place, down to the village."

Bass glanced at the teacher. "Nice lil' place he has 'im there. Get down there an' I see what he wants me to do. Got him this big wood tub and got 'im his woman fillin' it with hot water—comin' outta big kettles she been warmin' in the fireplace. Well sir, that tub was smokin' an' steamin', like the mud pots down to the Land of Smokin' Waters. Just like it. An' this here child ain't had him nothin' like that in . . . it been many a robe season, it has. Jarrell tells this ol' boy to strip off my clothes an' climb in that lil' tub o' his. He says he's gonna scrub some on me."

Titus chuckled a little as they got near the dormitory, the wheezing sound of the bagpipes now faint in the air. "I got me some manners left an' asks him to have his woman leave the room. He up and tells me she's the one what's gonna do the scrubbin' on me! Now—if that don't take the circle! Man havin' me get naked in front of his woman an' havin' her scrub 'nother naked man right in front of him!"

Bass snorted. "Jarrell told me to get in the tub an' sit down, hangin' my feet outside, over the edge like, you see? I sat down, feelin' real squampshus 'bout the whole thing, an'—Lordee! That woman of his come up with a brush an' some real soap. Here"—he presented his arm to Smith, holding it just below the teacher's nose—"smell me now, son."

He waited for the young man to sniff. "I ain't smelled like this for a real long time, it's been." He dropped the arm. "Sat there in that hot water—ain't had my ass in hot water since I found me a nice lil' pool up to the Land of the Smokin' Waters. That be up where the Yallerstone River gets its birth. Been some long robe seasons since last I plopped my ol', ever-lovin' white ass into some hot water. Gotta say it did feel good to my ol' hide, howsomever. Today I must of washed off more grit an' shit from my skin than I would have ever knowed was possible to be wearin' on one nigger."

"You . . . you do smell . . . smell different," Smith began. "Not . . . not so much," he searched for tactful words. "Not so much like . . . You don't smell so much anymore like an animal of the forests and mountains."

"Gamy?" Bass responded as they got to the door of the Bachelors' Hall.

"Well . . ."

"I know," he interrupted, to ease the young man's self-inflicted discomfort. "Most time I ain't got no one smellin' me but me, son. An' the more like a animal I smell—all the better. Man got his own peculiar scent, you see. Differ'nt than any other animal. An' now!"—he sniffed at his own arm as they stopped just outside the doorway—"I smell like soap. Don't smell all that bad, I s'pose. But I roll my truck an' plunder an' plews into ronnyvoo—why, them niggers take 'em one whiff of this here ol' coon—they gonna laugh themselves all the way back to St. Lou. Gonna have to stink myself up some afore then. Won't be a hard thing to do, noways—not with a long trail to take me down afore gettin' to them ronnyvoo doin's."

"You are not heading straight from here? To rendezvous as you said?"

"Nawww. Like I tried to say it to you, Soloman," he said as he thumped down on the bench against the wall of the dorm. "I got me a cache of furs up north—well, east of here now. North of where we havin' ronnyvoo this year."

"Where is that?"

"Down to the Green River. They say it's to be near the Green an' Horse Crik."

"Yes, now I remember you mentioning that you were heading first to your cache—you mentioned that yesterday," Smith replied. He had inquired of Bass about his rendezvous plans. And had taken the information to the Chief Factor yesterday evening.

"Raise me that cache of furs, last fall's catch it be." He stared pensively at his toes a moment before he spoke again. "I s'pose my partner—my ex-partner—ain't gonna have no use for 'em, ain't gonna be needin' them furs leastways. I be the only one what's headin' to ronnyvoo. So"—he looked back up at Smith—"I take 'em an' trade 'em in for supplies for 'nother year in them mountains back there."

"Thirty-two, last year—it was my first. Awww, shit—you know that already," Smith apologized.

"That was a good'un, son," Bass replied. "A good one if'n it be your first." Then he thought of the young trapper who had been his partner at the last rendezvous. "A good'un if'n it be your last, too." He smiled. "I reckon Jarrell was a-wantin' me to be smellin' right—for when I was to be seein' the doctor himself this night."

"You'll see McLoughlin tonight?" Smith was surprised.

"Yes, sir," Bass replied. "I do, that." He rubbed the lower part of his neck. "Jarrell, he even shaved me a bit. Some shavin' lotion he got him up to the Injun Store—somethin' called *Ambrosial Shavin' Cream*—come in a small pomade jar."

"Does not look to be you shaved much at all," Smith commented. "And your hair is still over your shoulders."

"Said I let Jarrell just trim things a bit," Bass responded. "Wasn't 'bout to give up my warm beard an' the hair."

Scratch looked back down at the toes of his moccasins as his mind suddenly shifted to last summer and those early days with his ex-partner.

"Ain't got no reason to cut hair up here noways, son. You can let it grow down to your ass if you likes. Times was when Ashley didn't want no man with a beard an' long hair comin' upriver. You see, most Injuns don't take real kindly to a man with hair on his face. Just let it grow, son—your hair. All the better up here anyways. Keeps the sun off the back of a man's neck. Keeps his ears warm like some furrysome muffler when them winds get to growlin'. It's decoration, too! Just like them red nigger bucks decorate their hair: for lovin' or warrin'. 'Sides, man's got better things to do than be cuttin' hair back all the time."

The old trapper lifted his eyes to gaze at the young American, and snorted. "Thornbrugh even says McLoughlin likes things clean an' all—s'pose that be all right for him to think that way—him bein' a doctor an' all. Don't really see nothin' wrong with it. So, I don't mind me gettin' that hot bath, with all that scrubbin' 'til I thought me the woman was gonna wear off a couple layers of hide. Made my skin feel good, too. Just like a ol' grizz stroppin' at a tree. So good ol' Titus Bass went on up to that Injun Store an' buyed himself a brush. Yepper, I did. Got me a scrub brush now. When I go to cleanin' my ol' hide, ain't gonna have to scrape away with sand off the bottom of some stream where I'm ploppin' my ass down no more. Do it up right."

"I must say I'm surprised somewhat . . ."

"That I want to get me clean once't awhile?"

"I suppose so."

"Nothin' surprisin' 'bout a man that gets to where he cain't even stand to be with himself anymores." He rose from the bench. "You gonna feed this here nigger tonight—or you gonna stand there flappin' your jaws at me? I gotta fill my meat-bag afore I go over to meet this here doctor. Jarrell says me to watch out for the liquor the doctor might be civil an' offer me to drink. Says it be some strong stuff. Shit! I drink me all the time on some ol' John Barleycorn that be nothin' but harnessed thunder an' lightnin'. That chief of yours ain't got him nothin' what can turn this ol' belly of mine. But, afore I start drinkin', I takes me some grub—always better to have a full belly under your belt."

"The doctor serves the finest whiskeys, I've heard. Very old, aged in charred oaken casks."

"I ain't never had me ol' liquor afore. It gotta be smoother'n a young woman's ass, it does!" He smacked his lips. "This ol' nigger's just used to him drinkin' shit that's rougher'n five days' growth of beard on your face."

Soloman laughed. "Well, I am glad you will finally be seeing the Chief Factor. It came quickly—although, I know you feel it has been a long time." He led Bass into the dorm where they headed toward the main dining room of Bachelors' Hall.

"I do think on it bein' a long time, son," Bass said as they finally reached the long tables where other men were beginning to seat themselves. "Not long since I come here to your fort, that is." He sat down between Smith and one of the dark-skinned Kanakas.

Bass watched the kitchen help bring in steaming bowls and platters and set them down along the length of the table. "What seems like such a long, long time be . . . it be a long time gettin' to some answers. Long time waitin' for a ghost to . . . to stop his devilin' me, Mister Smith."

Jarrell Thornbrugh entered the dining hall as Bass was spearing a last slice of the rare roast beef from the large serving platter in front of him. Then he speared some more of the skinned, boiled potatoes and cut them with the edge of his fork into huge chunks that he stuffed into his mouth along with monstrous pieces of the slab of beef.

"You eat as if it were the last meal of a condemned man," Thornbrugh observed as he came up behind Bass.

Scratch looked at him and swallowed quickly. "Got me natural appetite back, goin' to visit the man what's gonna be able to answer some questions for me. Been lookin' forward to that for some time now, you know."

Thornbrugh placed a large hand on Bass's shoulder and held it there. "Yes, I know." He looked around the table at the few workers who were still eating. "You needn't hurry. I'm a little early. I have taken supper with the doctor himself, and others. The doctor should be ready when you are finished."

"I be ready right off." Bass started to rise from the chair, but Jarrell kept his hand on his shoulder.

"That is quite all right." He felt Bass relax back down onto the chair. "Please, finish your meal first off. There is no real rush. The good doctor has allowed himself the luxury of having the entire evening for your appointment."

"Sounds to this child like you're makin' out that I'm somethin' special." He stuffed another piece of meat into his mouth.

"And that you are." Jarrell took a seat next to Bass as the Kanaka rose and left the table. "I was sent to fetch you, but only when you're finished."

"Ain't right keepin' such as him waitin', is it?"

"Such should be the furthest thing from your mind now."

"You want you any?" Bass speared a piece of beef and presented it to Thornbrugh.

"Heavens no, sir." He held up an open palm to turn down the offer.

"You gonna be there, ain't you?" Bass pushed back from the table and started to wipe his mouth on the back of his arm. Then he stopped and picked up the linen napkin beside his table service. He swiped at his lips and then ran the napkin back and forth over his beard.

"Yes, friend," Thornbrugh responded. "McLoughlin has requested that I be included."

"That suits me just fine." Scratch rose from the table. "Some fine, fine vittles. That cow I just et, be pretty good for bein' slow elk. Cain't touch elk, howsomever—but that be the best cow I et in some long, long time."

Thornbrugh rose also. "If Lord Bass is ready"—he glanced down at Smith who quickly turned away—"I would be pleased to take him to meet Lord McLoughlin."

The two men left Bachelors' Hall and headed across the open compound toward the Big House, climbed the steps to the wide front porch. Bass stopped at the door, expecting Jarrell to knock. Instead, the Englishman put his hand on the large knob and opened the door for the trapper, allowing Bass to enter the house first.

He closed the door behind them and stood beside Bass in

the large foyer. Bass hesitated, then walked to the base of the stairs that led to the attic floor and looked up with a question in his eyes.

"No, Scratch," Thornbrugh said. "Only bedrooms are up there. Some storage room. Bedrooms for the children—the Doctor's children. Only two of his children left to him here. Joseph, whom I believe you met today at the trading house; and Eloisa. They room up there. David and John Jr. have both left for schooling. Here, this way." He steered Bass toward another door beside the stairs.

Jarrell opened the door and they entered the large, nearly square room. In the middle stood a long dining table. The kitchen help were clearing the dishes and removing the linen cloth from the table. Bass looked around at the large room and figured it comprised a quarter of the first floor of the house. A smooth wood floor lay beneath his dirty, worn moccasins. The highly polished mahogany gleamed as he stared down at his own diffused reflection.

Several kitchen workers scurried in and out through a doorway at the northeast corner of the room, a door that he supposed led into that passageway between the kitchen and the Big House. Bass glanced around the room. He stepped over to one of the highboys where the china, silverware and flat silver were stored. He leaned closer, peered through the etched-glass doors of the cabinet.

"The finest of English earthenware," Thornbrugh whispered. "Spode's most popular patterns, the *Italian* and the *Tower*."

Bass nodded. He had thought the earthenware at the Indian Store had been fancy. These dishes were altogether startling in their beauty, with colorful glazes of blue, green, puce, brown and pink. He stepped back from the highboy and continued his exploration of the room. Across all four walls was a wainscot: wood paneling that rose about three and half feet from the floor and was topped with a narrow, rounded molding. From the molding a patterned wallpaper began its climb to the ceiling where exposed wood beams raced across the top of the room.

The old trapper gazed around the room slowly, drinking in all the unexpected richness of the house. He edged toward the two large windows left of the huge, stone fireplace; east of the hearth, another large window offered a different outside view. The room, its natural colors now subdued in the pleasant, warm candlelight, would be fairly well lit during the day with such large windows, he mused.

Near the fireplace sat three men. They turned around to gaze at the newcomer. Each held a dainty glass in his hand. Thornbrugh headed toward them.

"Mister Bass"—he gestured toward the trapper—"would you be kind enough to step over here for a brief moment?"

Scratch padded toward the huge fireplace as the three men spread out of their tight knot. "I have the pleasure of introducing two of these gentlemen you do not yet know."

"I made this fella's 'quaintance today." Bass stuck his hand out toward Joseph McLoughlin. "Thank you for your help, son."

"It really is I who should thank you, Mister Bass," Joseph replied. "It was a genuine joy talking with you this afternoon. To hear of your travels and adventures . . . ah, it was what I myself dream of. It is I who longs to share such adventure and not be cooped up here behind the counter selling goods to Indians and what visitors happen onto us."

"Your lot is not that bad, dear Joseph," said another young man—a dark, tall, and slender fellow who looked to be about thirty years old. "Here you have all the riches one could really need." He raised his glass and drained it. "Out there"—his arm swept a semi-circle—"Mister Bass has to worry about the prime concern of all other Americans, do you not, Mister Bass?"

"'Fraid I don't catch your drift, sir," Scratch responded.

"The infernal Indians. In your case, out in your Rocky Mountains, they would be Piegan, the Blood—what you Americans commonly refer to as . . . Blackfeet. They likewise share no love for you Americans frisking about on their land, do they now?"

"Blackfoot got 'em a hard-on," Bass stammered. "Yes, sir. Them Blackfoot don't take to us Americans one whack. They like to trade with you fellas here." His head bobbed as he looked at each man in turn.

The stranger smiled slightly, the corner of one side of his lips turned upward. "And well it should stay that way, if I might say so. That confederation of tribes rules central Canada—quite a large territory—so you would not blame us at all for forming an alliance with them, now would you, Mister Bass?"

"It all be fair in love, war an' the trade, I s'pose."

"Aptly put." The man smiled. "Exactly my sentiments, sir."

"Titus," Thornbrugh suddenly broke in, "I have yet to introduce you to James Douglas. Titus Bass, Mister James Douglas: our post accountant, and . . . our Assistant Chief Factor."

Douglas stuck out a hand as Bass presented his. "Pleased to meet you, sir," Scratch said politely.

"I have met but few Americans," Douglas said. "Only those who have come to the post. It is always a pleasure to look over one's own competition, is it not, gentlemen?" He looked Bass over. The man to Douglas's left was the only one who nodded in agreement.

"And this gentleman," Jarrell announced as he turned toward the third man. "Elliot Morton, one of our clerks who works for Mister Douglas . . . and the doctor."

The two men shook hands. "When I get to meet the doctor?" Bass inquired of Thornbrugh.

"Gentlemen." Jarrell placed a hand on the trapper's arm. "Mister Bass has an audience with the Chief Factor. If you will excuse us."

"Perfectly all right," Douglas replied. "We were just going to retire to my sitting room." The two others headed toward a door on the east wall. "Mister Bass, believe me—it was indeed a pleasure meeting you. We must sit and talk at length some time soon. Perhaps tomorrow. There is much I wish to know about you Americans and your trapping operations here in the Northwest."

"I don't get up here a'tall, sir," Bass replied.

"Come now, sir," Douglas said. "Such a rich, vital fur area. And you have never trapped here before? You actually expect me to believe you?" He smiled wryly.

"You got that right, son." Bass spoke quietly, firmly. "Don't work for nobody but Titus Bass. An' I never set me a foot down 'round here'bouts afore in my life."

"Nevertheless," Douglas continued, "we must have us a chat. Nay, we should have us a nice long talk soon. There is much that you can teach me. And, I dare say—much I can teach Mister Titus Bass." He raised his empty glass in the form of a salute. "Titus. How quaint a name."

"Quaint?" Bass inquired.

"Shall I say *unusual*?"

"Maybeso," Scratch replied. "Sort of fella I be."

"All the more reason for us to have our talk, then, Titus," Douglas pressed on. "If you differ from the other Americans—all the more reason I would like to get to know you better."

James Douglas lowered his glass. "Please, Mister Thornbrugh, be good enough to get Mister Bass something to drink before you take him in to see the Chief Factor. Help yourself, gentlemen. The night is young and my wife refuses to afford me her company again. He turned and headed through the door, followed by Joseph McLoughlin and Elliot Morton.

Thornbrugh and Bass were alone. "We can pour ourselves a drink," Jarrell offered. He moved to a china closet and took down two large water goblets and set them down next to a crystal decanter. "No dainty drinking for us," he said, lifting one of the large goblets.

"I like you better an' better all the time, Jarrell."

Thornbrugh poured the two goblets full of the sherry and handed one to Bass. "Shall we see the doctor?"

"Ain't he drinkin'?" Scratch asked.

"McLoughlin does not imbibe in spirituous liquors often." He led the trapper toward a door along the west wall. "He does not mind those who do, but prefers not to drink much himself."

Thornbrugh knocked at the door. From inside, a deeply bass-sounding voice replied. "Come in, Jarrell."

"The Doctor," Thornbrugh whispered to Bass. "Perhaps now your questions will be answered," he said as he pushed the door open.

Seventeen

Bass looked about and could not see another person in the room with them. The light was dim, shed from only one candle. Then suddenly, the bulk loomed through the doorway at his left. Gone now was the heavy black frock coat he had seen the Chief Factor wearing before. In its place was a light robe that was sashed at the waist. His long, white hair billowed neatly over his shoulders as he lumbered into the room from his office.

"Make yourselves comfortable, gentlemen." His hands held candles and candle holders. "I will light these and be right with you."

Scratch was amazed at the sheer size of the man. He was a couple of inches taller than Thornbrugh. McLoughlin stood at least six feet seven inches tall. And his frame carried the mass of muscle and flesh as well as Jarrell's own gigantic, strong body. There was a rustle of cloth and Bass turned his attention to the office doorway once more as two women emerged.

"Good evening, Jarrell," the older woman said as the two stopped near the center of the room.

Thornbrugh bowed slightly from the waist. "Madame McLoughlin—allow me to introduce Lord . . . Mister Titus Bass, of America." He gestured to the trapper. "Mister Bass—Madame Margaret McLoughlin."

She stepped toward the trapper. "Pleased to make your acquaintance, sir." She presented her right hand to him.

Bass took the smooth flesh into his coarse paw and shook it slightly, gently—watching her gaze travel down to their hands with surprise before she quickly glanced over at Thornbrugh with a look of wonder on her face. "Pleased I am to meet you, ma'am."

She withdrew her hand and presented it to Thornbrugh. He brought it to his lips, kissed it lightly as he bowed from the waist again. Bass looked on with amused attention.

"I'm sorry, ma'am," he stammered with embarrassment. "I'm one dumb nig . . . I'm really stupid 'bout such things." He moved quickly over beside Thornbrugh. "I didn't know what you was offerin' your hand to me for—ain't used to such things."

She accepted his apology by offering her hand once again to Bass who raised it jerkily to his lips. "Mister Bass, you have no need of apology. I am the one who should apologize for expecting you to kiss my hand."

"Always the lady." McLoughlin had turned from lighting the candles that had gradually brightened up the room. "Always my lady." He came up beside her and put an arm around his wife's shoulders. She slipped her arm behind his waist. "And this beautiful young lady," he said, gesturing to the young fifteen-year-old girl near them, "is my daughter, Eloisa."

"Ma'am . . . er, Miss." Bass stepped toward her as she began to lift her hand.

She brought her hand up, her wrist limp in submissive presentation. Bass, in imitation of Thornbrugh, took her hand in his, bent his head and kissed it lightly. He stood up straight, stared into the young girl's eyes. So much she reminded him of

Waits-by-the-Water. And suddenly there was that peculiar pain inside him as he looked down at this young girl's face. The Crow woman would not be much older than this girl, he thought. Not much older at all—perhaps two summers, three maybe—at the most.

Staring at McLoughlin's daughter, he had to admit to himself that there were times when he still felt that young hunger, the youthful yearning for the smooth flesh beside him throughout the long night. There were those times when the thoughts of young fingers running over his tired body, massaging, kneading, and teasing all those tight places would weigh heavy on his mind.

But, he considered, perhaps it was better this way. Maybe a man didn't want to get close with a woman when there's medicine on him.

He suddenly felt embarrassed and let go of the girl's hand, averting his eyes from her strikingly beautiful features. For many, many weeks now he had been trying to picture Waits-by-the-Water in his mind. And then he would quickly push the vision from his thoughts. But now this young, striking girl made the memories rush in on him once more, causing him to draw upon that painful place in his heart where lived the wild, beautiful creature he had loved back in Absaroka.

"I forget myself, too." The doctor removed his arm from his wife's shoulder and presented a hand to Bass. "Please, do not kiss *my* hand, sir!" He gave a deep, gentle and pleasing laugh. Jarrell laughed too. Bass stepped forward and placed his hand inside the giant vise that held his hand with the kind of strong grip that told of a man with a gentle and powerful will.

"You two beautiful ladies run along now," McLoughlin said. "I would suppose Amelia is in need of company, also. Let us gentlemen have our talk together." He watched the women glide toward a door on the north side of the room.

"And dear—do not wait up for me," he added. "I have much to discuss and we might be late into the night."

The two women disappeared.

Bass took a moment to look about the room. At his back were several bookcases, boasting glass doors that shielded from dust, but not from view, part of the extensive library entrusted to the doctor's care. Beside the trapper was a small couch covered in rich velvet. Two matching chairs graced either side of one of the bookcases. In the southwest corner of the room sat a stove where McLoughlin now stirred the coals. From a box on the floor beside it, the doctor removed splintered wood and built a fire to a comfortable glow.

"There is still a chill to the evening air this time of year," McLoughlin commented. "But there also is much to be said about the warmth in the company of good men, strong men. Men both resolute and brave. A man who will not," he said, turning to face his two visitors, "be deterred from a singular purpose." He drew himself to full height, his bulk formidable in the play of darkness and candlelight.

"Jarrell, don't be so damned formal. Show Mister Bass a seat, will you?" He gestured toward some soft comfortable chairs.

Thornbrugh grabbed two chairs and brought them over near the stove where the doctor was already ensconced in a stuffed, well-worn chair of his own.

"You like the sherry?" McLoughlin asked.

"I ain't even tasted it yet, sir," the trapper answered as he sat down.

"Please, please do." He watched the trapper bring the goblet to his lips and sip slowly. "Yes, that is the way. Perfect! Slowly, for it is a drink to be cherished. I remember. Only remember those days. I have had to give up on much of my own drinking. How do you like it?"

"That be some smooth . . ." Bass sought out a proper word. "Fine, smooth drinkin' whiskey, sir."

"Oh, please, Mister Bass," he responded. "Don't call me *sir*. It has become quite an occupational hazard of this job for me—to be called 'sir.' I've become quite bored with it by now. My name is John. Please call me John. May I call you Titus?"

"He does not like the name himself," Thornbrugh interjected.

McLoughlin glanced over at Jarrell, who sat in a comfortably padded chair near the stove. "Oh?" He raised an eyebrow and looked back at the trapper. "You prefer the formality of *Mister Bass*?"

"Jarrell be talkin' 'bout my nickname, I s'pose, sir . . . John," Bass blurted out.

"Scratch," Thornbrugh offered.

"Scratch?"

"Yes, sir . . . John," Bass replied. "A name what was stuck on me some time back—in the mountains many robe seasons ago."

"You prefer to have your friends call you Scratch?"

"Yep." The fire crackled, popped as flames licked at the wood.

McLoughlin nodded once at Thornbrugh. "Then, if we are all to be friends—and you are in the company of friends, Scratch—then you must follow suit and call me John."

"Yes, John."

"Do you smoke, Scratch?"

"Occasional, I do . . . some of the time, that."

"Would you care for a pipe now?"

"If'n it ain't no trouble to . . ."

"No trouble at all." He gestured for Jarrell to get a pipe. "I understand you have come here from quite a distance, far away I am told." He watched Bass nod. "Likewise, I am told you come here to speak with me. That is correct?"

"Right again . . . John."

"Jarrell here"—he gestured as Thornbrugh handed Bass a large-bowled briar pipe and a brightly painted Chinese porcelain container that was commonly called a *ginger jar*, which McLoughlin used to hold tobacco—"tells me you have questions to ask me about a man called Asa McAfferty."

McLoughlin had said it. It was all out in the open now. "Yes," Bass said as he started to fill his pipe. "I come to you to find me out 'bout this fella McAfferty."

"A past partner of yours, I understand."

"Jarrell told you."

"Yes, Scratch. Jarrell has told me all. I am going to ask something from you out of perhaps nothing more than courtesy, if not out of our new friendship. There will be great confidences laid bare in this room this night. And I must ask you not to betray those confidences."

Jarrell turned slightly toward the doctor as Bass finished filling the pipe bowl. "Scratch is not a man to betray you, John. He, like you, has suffered many betrayals in his life—some in the recent past, as I take it. I, likewise, feel him to be a friend. A good friend."

McLoughlin nodded and raised an eyebrow. "Mister Ba . . . Scratch, you have been afforded a supreme compliment. This man, Jarrell Thornbrugh, is my best friend. I have had no finer companion in either business or my personal life than the fellow who now speaks on your behalf. Yes, indeed. To have him testify to your fidelity is a most valid testimonial indeed."

"He's teached me a few things, John," Bass replied. "Comin' down the river, he teached me 'bout not bein' 'fraid of somethin' just 'cause I wasn't one what could control what was happenin'. An' he's teached me 'bout havin' me faith in folks again."

"My friend here"—the doctor gestured—"never ceases to amaze me." He grew pensive for a moment. "Twice in the last few days, dear Thornbrugh has given you reason to hope, I see. And those two manifestations of hope both give rise to what I wish us to address this evening. I am in hopes that I will not bore my dear friend here with a recitation of my story, but I so wish to make certain you fully understand the entire framework into which you rode a few days ago, over the mountains and into our land, to . . . you brought back the ghost of this Asa McAfferty. To bring his ghost . . . hell, man. I can't really say that you brought the ghost back with you, either."

McLoughlin shook his head. "Nay, instead—what you did, Scratch, was open up a long-festering wound. A serious wound that needed that probing, that needed that purging of its foul infestation. This is what purpose you have served. We hope to begin the healing of this monstrous, noxious wound this night. And with your continued help, we both—you and I, Scratch—we both will be all the healthier for it."

Bass stared first at the throw rug beneath his chair, then somewhat nervously looked about the room. The walls were not wainscotted like the dining room. In the center of the west wall between two large windows, sat the tall, secretarial desk; on its open surface lay an odd assortment of medical instruments. Beside the desk stood a large, glass-fronted case containing medical supplies and more instruments. The four walls were plastered in the same manner as were all the exteriors of the fort's buildings, except that these interior walls were painted a light color, pleasing to the eye under the dancing light of the candles. A few paintings and engravings hung about the room.

"I . . . I ain't sure how I'm s'posed to be answerin' you, John," Bass stammered at last.

"No answer needed at this juncture, Scratch." McLoughlin settled deeper into his soft chair. "I was initially assigned to come west in twenty-four, but I didn't return east to bring Margaret and the children here until the next year. Four years later I was in charge of building this fort which now stands around you. Back in twenty-nine I decided to move the post from the coastal site, Fort George it was then, at the mouth of the Columbia. It had once been an old American post, built and owned by John Astor of the American Fur Company. I traveled upriver to this place, Belle Vue point in fact, and discovered this beautiful rise of land above the river. I formed the conclusion, from the mildness and salubrity of the climate, that this was the finest portion of North America that I had seen for the residence of civilized man. And, I wanted our fort to be just that: a piece of the Old World, or as much so as I could make it, here in the New World."

He watched Jarrell bring a lit twig over to help Bass light his pipe. "My Chief Trader at that time, Donald Manson—the man is a good Scot, too—remained at Fort George, our old site, to maintain contact with the Chinooks and to aid all of the vessels in navigating over the bar into the mouth of the river."

"Seems like he was the only one who stayed on, John," Thornbrugh commented. "Chief Cassino of the Multanomahs even moved his village to the south bank of the river, directly across from the new fort site. He considered himself such a good friend of the doctor that he would not allow John to leave Fort George without taking along his people."

"Yes. Cassino." The doctor seemed to lapse into reverie. "A good friend he was among the natives. But it seemed then in twenty-nine that our troubles began with the Indians of the area. Whereas before there had been a peaceful commerce, that singular year marked an unfortunate change in relations between white and red man that very nearly destroyed my plans at the outset."

He nodded to Thornbrugh, then returned his attention to the trapper. "There broke out an epidemic of fever and ague among the Indians of the surrounding region. And it just so happened that this outbreak coincided with the first tilling of our soil here at Vancouver. The natives, therefore, quickly came to believe that we whitemen had, through our cultivation of the soil around the new post, released some malevolent forces—*evil spirits*. These forces were said to have been freed when we first turned the soil to bring forth new life in this place. In consequence, they all watched the epidemic raging through their villages and were very much set against us continuing our construction here at Belle Vue."

McLoughlin shook his head as if saddened by the recollection. "The Indians, I am sorry to say, were the only ones to become ill at first. They took out their anger and frustration—nay, their very fears and rage—on our construction of the grist mill at the Falls of the Willamette."

"But, they were not the only ones to battle the fever," Thornbrugh added.

"But the ones to suffer the worst," the doctor replied, in his soft burr. "Oh, I know, my friend. You fought the fever off, as did Ogden. Peter Ogden. Both of you were strong enough to fight off its ravages. But the natives knew little to defend against it. I had quickly exhausted my supply of quinine used to calm the ravaging fever of the illness. Therefore, I was ultimately left to my own devices."

"And your resourcefulness, I might add," said Jarrell.

"That resourcefulness led me to try the bark of the dogwood tree, Scratch. By boiling down the bark I was able to manufacture my own quinine of sorts."

"Thereby saving not only Peter and myself—but the entire Northwest region from a major epidemic of disastrous proportions."

"I am afraid you flatter me much, dear friend," he said, looking at Thornbrugh. "I was almost driven mad by the inability to do as much as I wanted for the natives. From all around the area they came—whole villages. They encamped at the walls of our fort, those very walls so hastily thrown up for our protection. They came to those ramparts begging my help, soliciting the medicine, the cure that would save their peoples. They were sure I had in my power the magic to cure their ills as I had been the one to free the malevolent spirits from the soil."

The Chief Factor paused, heaved a deep sigh. It seemed to Bass that he could still hear the man's voice in the ensuing silence, a voice that rose and fell like soft music, a voice that was almost like singing, with the lilt of the Scottish highlands in its rhythms; its trilling "r" sounds, its crooked vowels, all sounding so strange and lyrical to his ears.

"Regrettably," McLoughlin continued, "there were far too many to cure with my home-made antidote. My feeble efforts produced barely enough for our own people here in the fort, while outside our walls were the dying sounds of so many. We became like prisoners confined in our own miniature world. The wailing and the beseeching nearly drove the women here mad in itself, besides the constant uncertainty of not knowing when an attack by those crazed natives might press itself upon us. I, myself, was driven to the formation of another terrible decision. I sent my own men, at least those strong enough to move about, to drive the natives away from our walls."

"Scratch," Thornbrugh remarked, "the air had become rotten itself with the foul stench of the dead and dying. We were sure that if we ourselves did not drive them away from our walls, we should all perish from what was borne on the winds coming from without our fort. There are grisly scenes etched horribly upon my memory—pictures I shall not soon forget, if ever."

"That was when Jarrell and I became close friends," McLoughlin commented.

"We both will find it very difficult to forget those scenes of the natives plunging headlong into the icy waters of the Columbia to cool their raging fevers. Few, damned few, survived the consequent colds that took a mighty grip on their already-weakened constitutions."

"Jarrell was a source of strength to me then. He helped to heal me spiritually from the burden of the whole ordeal pressed upon my private soul." McLoughlin lowered his head, shook it sadly. "Almost nine out of every ten persons living below the fort at that time perished in the epidemic. And it was at the height of the fever that the Clatsops attacked a company vessel that was stranded while crossing the bar into the mouth of the river. The *William & Anne* was spared, but not her crew. The natives butchered our men and stole the ship's cargo destined for our fort, some of the inland posts. Jarrell here stepped forward and volunteered his services once more. . . ."

"To head a strong detachment of our men in a campaign against the offending tribe," Thornbrugh picked up the account. "We severely chastised them, at John's strong command. However, we recovered but a small portion of the cargo. Most of the goods had either been buried in secret places or already traded off to other tribes by the time my force struck the Clatsop village. A pitiful, but necessary duty that was—the village itself . . ."

Jarrell muttered too quietly to hear; the memory a bitter picture to recall. "The warriors were already so weakened— they hardly resisted. So many fell before us, fell on their own accord, before we could even strike them. And with our own men afraid of being reinfested with the dreaded fever—we hurried out of their country without pursuing those who escaped. Not did we long pursue our search for the goods that had disappeared. We took what was ours from their village, and let the victims run away to spread their infection. The Lord is the only one now to judge our crime in allowing any of them to live—to survive only to spread the fever and its grisly death."

"We will all be answerable some day for our sins, Jarrell," McLoughlin said quietly. "We will all have to account for those sins which remain unatoned for upon our passing."

"Yet," Thornbrugh continued, "with that one act of omission, the Chief Factor became the undisputed ruler of all his domain."

"I believe it was more by the spread of the news among the various tribes," McLoughlin elaborated, "the spread of the word that this man would not take lightly an attack upon our people and property."

"And at that time they came to call him the *White-Headed Eagle*, with a fame that spread itself as surely as the fever raged through the tribes."

"I can see why they calls you the *White-Headed Eagle*, I can." Bass grasped his own long, dark hair for emphasis.

"With the Spring Express from back east that year, eighteen hundred and thirty," McLoughlin continued, "I believed I was receiving the help I so desperately needed here with the daily business affairs of the fort. While I had been looking forward to Jarrell himself receiving some more official, more worthy post at my side, and while I was disheartened when he was not selected after my nomination of him to the committee—I nonetheless was hopeful that the man they had sent me would truly share my vision for this land and our people here. Instead . . ." He slammed a huge hand down on the arm of the chair, then rose suddenly. "Instead, they sent me Douglas."

"The man you met in the dining room," Jarrell said.

"The one in the middle . . . that'un with the coal-black hair, huh?" Bass inquired. "The one what seems to want to have him a long talk with me real bad?"

"One and the same," Thornbrugh answered. "But we both would advise you never to attend a discussion with that one. *Black* Douglas, they call him. And he has taken to the name, believing we mean the coloring of his hair." He chuckled wryly. "If he only knew what the men really think of him, he would be a man who understands the truest meaning of his nickname. *Black* Douglas . . ."

"I trust my own soul to believe that the appellation refers to his mien, his cold, black demeanor," McLoughlin advised. "He is deliberate, and highly adept, a methodical businessman. . . ."

"But with a heart as dark as his name," Thornbrugh interrupted.

"Yet, a very quiet and reserved gentleman, is he not, Scratch?" John asked.

"Seems to be, that."

"I am sure." McLoughlin sat down, tired of his pacing before the stove. "However, Scratch—behind those cool eyes, that reserved exterior, I grew to see the darkness of his heart, his very soul. I came, in fact, to discern a plot—the subject of which we both find ourselves involved in, and the reason for your having arrived at Vancouver, I presume."

"I . . . I'm 'fraid I'm not followin' you fellas a'tall now," Bass admitted.

"You will," said Jarrell.

"Yes, Scratch. We will be certain that you understand. But, in due time," McLoughlin said. He glanced over at Thornbrugh. "The governor does not know the man I truly am, does he, my friend?"

"I would say not, John. But history will have the final verdict on His Excellency, Governor Simpson. His Arrogancy . . ."

"So we saw the plot," the Chief Factor broke in, "the year after Douglas came to Vancouver to be my assistant. The company sent Chief Factor Duncan Finlayson from the Red River to our Columbia District."

"That Red River of the north?" Bass asked.

"Yes," McLoughlin answered.

"Finlayson," said Jarrell, "carried a dispatch naming him as a replacement in the event John wanted to take his furlough that was coming up the next year. We both immediately became suspicious that Finlayson was sent to check upon the doctor, by none other than Simpson himself."

"I was not alone in this belief, mind you, Scratch," McLoughlin confided. "My closest friend shared the belief that Douglas had been reporting on his own to Simpson himself. And the culmination of those private reports to the governor was the dispatching of Finlayson to Vancouver."

"Perhaps Finlayson was not himself privy to those communications between the governor and Douglas," Jarrell speculated. "I choose to believe that he was not. . . ."

"And I likewise," McLoughlin agreed.

"I see him as merely a pawn used by the antagonist in Douglas's plot to undermine the doctor and all that he was attempting to accomplish out here."

"So much of it has to do with you Americans encroaching upon our territory out here," McLoughlin said.

"But I have told you, Scratch has his own ideas on what land belongs to whom," Thornbrugh reminded the Chief Factor.

"Be that as it may, the threat of the continuing American presence in territory both the company and Great Britain regard as their own, not only was judged to be an act of international significance, but signaled what the company saw as gross ineptitude on my part." The doctor cocked a thumb at his own chest.

"If I'm readin' all your trail-sign here . . ." Bass studied it a moment in his mind . . . "you both sayin' your bosses all thought you was the one to blame for us Americans comin' into this part of the country?"

"You grasp it, I see." McLoughlin smiled.

"Jumpin' Jehosophat! How the hell can they blame one man for them goddamned fur companies comin' in here to take 'em some beaver out?"

"They could not, would not, see it so simply." Jarrell leaned forward in his chair. "Or they might have—were it not for the devious mind and blackened heart of one James Douglas."

"So he was tellin' this here gov'nor that you was to blame for all the trouble with us Americans comin' in here, huh?"

"Yes, dear Scratch," McLoughlin said more softly now. "Yes, Douglas had much to report on regarding the Americans." He rose and stood with his back to the stove, pulling the robe more snugly about himself.

"There is a chill this evening," said the Chief Factor. "Jarrell? Would you be kind enough to fetch your old friend a small glass of the brandy? You know which decanter I prefer?"

Bass turned to watch the Englishman move out of the room, a little mystified that McLoughlin should feel a chill. The American felt fine: a little warm if anything. The stove was putting out a generous warmth. Yet the Chief Factor shivered slightly and rubbed his hands together over the top of the stove as he began speaking once again.

"It was in twenty-six, Scratch," he began, "some seven years ago now. It really does not seem to be that . . . that long ago. A group of American trappers with one of your companies first showed up in Flathead country. This company ran onto John Work's brigade. The men—our men, that is—were quite surprised to find your penetration that deep so early in your exploration of the Rocky Mountains. I later heard that the Americans were just as surprised to find us so far east, too."

He smiled a bit with the thought, then his lips turned downward in a grim frown once more. Bass watched his eyes. They were of a color so light that they almost seemed animal-like in their soul-piercing quality. Their pearl-like color reminded the trapper of the heat of what only appears to be dead ash: an ash that disguises the glow of scorching embers beneath it. Scratch turned as he heard the door close softly and watched Thornbrugh come across the sitting room to hand McLoughlin the small glass of brandy. The doctor took it without a word and sipped long at the thick liquid. After he set it aside, the Chief Factor continued.

"It was later that year, twenty-six, that Peter Ogden's brigade down in the Snake River country ran onto a group of Americans, also. It was Ogden's damnable misfortune, and mine along with his, to wake up one morning and find that twenty-three of his men had deserted to the Americans—with all their equipment, their horses, and their furs!"

"Twenty-six seems to be the year when it all began," Jarrell agreed. "We were not yet in Vancouver. We had yet to consolidate out power after merging with the Northwest Company. And the Americans were already on our front step, knocking at the very door to our kingdom."

"I never would have thought it'd been that long ago," Bass commented, then sipped at his sherry.

"The next year a young fellow named Jedediah Strong Smith came into our fort after his party had crossed the great southern desert, moved north through California suffering terrible, uncivil ignominies at the hands of Spanish officials, only to have his company of trappers fallen upon by Indians at the Umpqua River. They nearly wiped his party out. Smith stumbled north for many days, at last wandering into our post."

"Scratch, it was a mark of this man who stands before you, Doctor McLoughlin, that he took it upon himself to offer up an act of Christian charity to this Jedediah Smith. Yes, according to Governor Simpson, this Smith and his men should have been turned away. Instead, the doctor organized a command that would return to the site of the massacre and punish the offending tribe for their bloody-handed wrongdoing.

"It was during this time that the doctor and this Smith formed a close bond of sorts. Although relentless competitors—both were strong, able, courageous, and fiercely loyal to their own interests. I believe to this day this is something that is still lost upon his grace, Governor Simpson. I believe it is lost on his kind, and the James Douglas kind of man, that the Chief Factor here believed he could best serve the interests of the company in this region by spreading the felicity and gracious strength of one company through the offering of an able, mighty hand when needed. It bloody well angered His Grace, the governor, when he learned that John had not only helped Smith in many ways—but also resupplied the American, and on account, on credit, to boot!"

He and John chuckled a little at this. Bass smiled. "This child can see how just such a thing could be pissin' the gov'nor off some now!"

"Yes, Scratch," Jarrell continued. "I still believe this Jedediah Smith's own resolve, integrity and strength were traits with which the good doctor could readily identify."

"I think I heard Jed Smith gone under down on the water scrape," Bass said. "On the way down toward Taos—Santee Fe. That be as I 'member hearin' it."

"May I get you some more sherry?" Thornbrugh offered.

"No—no, my friend." He waved off the Englishman who started to rise from his chair. "I have me a nice, warm spot down to my belly now—an' that's just where I 'tend to keep it for now. But it were back to thirty-one as I recollect that I heard he went under."

"We had heard rumors drifting in and out of this area in regard to Smith's death, that he had been on his way to the Mexican provinces to establish a base of trade with those Mexican population centers," the doctor said. "We were not sure of the reports' validity, however. It is a shame. Such an honest, strong man, even though he worked against my own interests—I can say he would have been an asset to any employer in the fur trade. It is a shame to have him gone from the field for all eternity."

"Well, now," said Bass. "They be more to it than that, now, eh?"

Thornbrugh nodded and continued his account.

"It was in twenty-nine while this fort was under construction that an American ship, the first we had ever heard of along the coast, began to trade with the coastal tribes. The ship even dropped anchor near the mouth of the Columbia. I must say that Donald—Donald Manson—was frantic down at old Fort George." He chuckled.

"Indeed," said the Factor, chuckling himself. "Donald was frightened at this new turn of events. But he was given two peach trees as a peace offering by the captain of the ship—they were then to be given to me for my new orchard here at Belle Vue. A shame I cannot place the captain's name still."

"Twenty-nine also saw Jedediah Smith return to retrieve some of his men he had left behind. And he returned with an enlarged contingent of trappers and riflemen. This during Governor Simpson's visit to view the construction of the new post."

"Yes, as it had to be," McLoughlin muttered, clenching a fist and thumping it repeatedly on the arm of his chair. "Simpson saw firsthand the Americans on the grounds of Vancouver. From that point on, Simpson would be mere clay in the hands of the like of James Douglas—to be molded, shaped, guided, and goaded into underhanded, blackhearted deeds against my person and my position here."

"The governor met this Jedediah Smith and in fact traveled with Smith east on our annual Spring Express. Simpson had now seen firsthand the American incursion deep into the heart of the Columbia District." Jarrell finished his sherry and set his goblet aside.

"The governor, His Grace, harshly instructed me in no uncertain terms, as a schoolmaster would chastise a wayward student, to deal swiftly, and with all means necessary, with this American menace. That fall, in the annual supplies, Simpson's visit with Smith perhaps paid off."

"At first, John," Jarrell replied. "Yes, at first we believed all would be much quieter now that Simpson had viewed firsthand the American incursion into our district. For, as John already mentioned, in the fall supplies we began to receive more *luxuries*, as it were. These, John was told in a dispatch from Simpson, were to combat the trade the Americans might be having with the Indians. Little did His Grace understand that the Americans by and large were trapping on their own and very seldom traded with the natives."

"Our normal mark-up, Mister Bass," the Chief Factor said, "is a mere seventy percent. That was before the Americans were first seen in the region. Then the company saw a depression in the pricing structure following these repeated incursions by your countrymen. What had been at one time a table of trade that allowed for a rate of exchange of *five* large beaver for one four-point blanket, now gradually disintegrated until it took only *one* large beaver for that same blanket, about $7.62 in your American currency. I am most heartened that we have finally passed over the hill, so to speak, and some of the trade is once again turning itself around. Our current rate of exchange is approximately two beaver for one blanket, or about twenty beaver for a trade gun. So you will be able to understand what the bouncing, fluctuating rates of exchange meant to us when you realize we normally deal with about 30,000 pelts annually."

"I believe it was about that time that you began your fiery tirades against the unscrupulous practices of the American traders, in that they were using liquor in their Missouri River trade, and you were concerned that such a practice might eventually find its way over the mountains," Jarrell remarked.

"That is correct, my friend," McLoughlin answered. "Yes, I remained under orders to cut my rate of exchange, if necessary. I was to undercut the Americans' pricing *at all costs*. There were times that I traded many bundles of goods below cost, merely to cement our relations with the natives, to keep firm their bond with the company. Fortunately, my books still showed something in the way of a profit at the end of each fiscal period."

"You had to have been a magician, as you have heard me tell it before," Thornbrugh commented.

"You flatter your friend much more and his head will hardly fit on the pillow tonight," the Chief Factor replied. "But by eighteen-thirty the stage was set for the beginning of this dastardly plot that began to take shape with the arrival of James Douglas. He was followed, as I have mentioned, by the arrival of Duncan Finlayson, and my worst fears for my personal and professional integrity were confirmed. I knew I must react, not only to the rising American threat, but also to the encroachment of the Russian presence to our north. We had even been selling some of our wheat to the Russians in exchange for pelts. So in thirty-one I sent a ship with a large contingent of men northward to construct a new post to drain off some of the Russian's coastal trade."

"And John here"—Thornbrugh smiled as he turned to Bass—"he wisely christened the new post . . . *Fort Simpson* . . ."

The doctor responded to Jarrell's grin. "You make me out to be some devious, black-hearted bugger myself, my friend."

"Far be it, John," the Englishman answered. "Merely a wily businessman. Yes, wily you are. But your methods are unimpeachable."

"Perhaps that is why my star has been falling in the company committee rooms of late," he lamented. "I dared not—could not—utilize some of the tactics I was advised to pursue in answering the American threat. And well this James Douglas knew of my predicament. He waltzed right in and took advantage of me where I was most vulnerable: my own integrity . . ."

"But, there is a strength yet remaining in that integrity, friend."

"That winter of thirty-one, thirty-two, came and went, and with it, the departure of the spring brigades to the east. It was to be the last year for a profitable return on our Snake Country expeditions. The summer rushed in upon us here at Vancouver, and with it the arrival of another American ship, the *Llama*, under the command of one Captain William McNeill."

"You will not soon forget that Yankee, will you, John?"

"I should say not—the bastard." He smiled. "And I say that in an admiring sort of way, Mister Bass. Now there was a cagey competitor—or at least his backers were."

"Scratch," Jarrell began, "it seems McNeill arrived at the mouth of the Columbia with his cargo hold full of . . . of toys!"

"Toys, you said?" Bass cupped his ear. "What good be toys to them brownskins here'bouts?" He shook his head. "Cain't see why you'd get all squampshus an' fearsome over a fella what only got him toys to trade the Injuns with."

"Little wooden soldiers, tiny wagons, jumping jacks, and whistles—all brightly painted," Jarrell continued. "All to catch and mystify the eye and heart of the simple native. Indeed, McNeill's backers were wise men, too.

"I knew immediately that this McNeill would bear some close watching, but I was not sure just how much. Had I been perhaps more careful, it would not have cost me so much to wriggle myself out of that spot we were in with this Yankee and his ship full of toys.

"We quickly found out that with such brightly painted trinkets, the Yankee captain was trading for furs at rock-bottom prices. He was getting those pelts for next to nothing because, while we were offering essentials for their furs, this McNeill was offering the natives *fun!*"

"A master stroke of someone's genius, I must add," McLoughlin said as he shifted his position. "My hat came off to the procreator of that trading expedition. It quickly became apparent that I had little choice but to buy out the Yankee captain, which I did. . . ."

"Ship and all," Jarrell interrupted. "And at a price that was close to robbery itself!"

"I should never have let the man get started," McLoughlin grumbled. "Should have run his arse out of our district, swiping at it stoutly with my cane!"

"The bloody plot rolled on, picking up speed with every month," Jarrell confided. "Douglas—this damned James Douglas—sped on to consolidate his power and prestige with the company officials. Damn their hides! The lily-livered, soft-living, bloody, buggering fools!"

"Easy, man," McLoughlin quieted Thornbrugh. "It does one no good to agitate oneself needlessly."

The Chief Factor waited a moment until Thornbrugh had calmed himself. "Yet, Jarrell is speaking the truth. Last year saw much that hastened my demise here in the Columbia District. My dear friend," he said, turning to Thornbrugh, "although James Douglas is a bastard and a conniving snake, events have a way of sweeping us all up and carrying us headlong down the path of time with them." Now he returned his gaze to the American trapper. "Eighteen thirty-two was a year of reckoning for John McLoughlin and his future not only with the great Company of Adventurers . . ."

"I'll be damned to hell for a bloody eternity if they are a company of adventurers," Jarrell blurted. "The only adventure in their lives is what perfume to splash on, what slippers to wear to what party—perhaps their greatest adventure being whose wife they will bed next: just which of their friends and fellow adventurers they will try to out-cuckold!"

McLoughlin quaked gently with laughter at Jarrell's sudden anger, until Thornbrugh began to laugh with him. "Perhaps you are right, Jarrell. But, as I was saying, last year was a year of reckoning for me as concerns my future with Hudson's Bay, Vancouver, nay—even to having my mind torn in regards to staying on in this great land about us at this very moment. . . ."

Bass watched the Chief Factor turn somber. "Mister . . . Scratch," McLoughlin began, "you already know that Nathaniel Wyeth arrived at our fort last October."

"Lotta folks been tellin' me 'bout it—him, I mean," Scratch answered.

"I am sure you are aware of the fate of his attempted enterprise here in this part of North America?"

"I ain't too sure just what it is . . ."

"What I mean to say is"—McLoughlin pondered for a moment—"is that I am sure you know that Wyeth failed to establish this post of his dreams. Do you not know?"

"That's right," Scratch replied. "He come in here to have to find out after all that time an' work that this young fella's work . . . he be unable to finish what he'd set out to do."

"Precisely!" The doctor clapped his hands together. "Precisely, Scratch. Nathaniel arrived here at Vancouver only to learn his dreams had been shattered, his hopes side-tracked for the moment. He had to determine whether or not to continue to pursue his dream, or to lay that great vision aside in exchange for another."

McLoughlin leaned forward, brought his hands together, raised them to his mouth. "This last winter I had much time to gain a knowledge of the man. This young ice-merchant dreamer, you see, was not so different from myself. Although he was much more naive than I, we nonetheless share common qualities of character. I took a genuine liking to this sincere, gentlemanly soul, whose very naiveté seemed to wear off not long after he arrived here at Vancouver. At first, Wyeth wished to travel south to the Umpqua region to visit the site of the horrendous massacre of Jedediah Smith's men . . . I had no choice but to refuse, both for his own safety, and the future safety of my brigades in the area. It was my belief—and still is—that had Wyeth been allowed to journey south to the site, the Indians there would have believed that all had gone there solely to avenge the deaths of Smith's party.

"In addition," McLoughlin continued, "I could not allow Wyeth to venture south to Umpqua because of my already-weakening status here in the district. For if the natives did attack the party, word would quickly pass amongst the tribes and the power and prestige of our efforts here would be consequently lessened. We would have to redouble our efforts to reconsolidate our position amongst those southern tribes, for the future safety of our brigades venturing into California."

"You see, Scratch," Thornbrugh said, "by this time the doctor had determined the Snake Country expeditions were no longer profitable. We had stripped the country almost bare of beaver, forming a wasteland of sorts as a means of providing a buffer between us and the American companies trapping the Rocky Mountains. Therefore, John here determined that men and material would best be employed to the south toward California."

"Yet events were taking place outside the Columbia District over which I had no control whatsoever," McLoughlin said.

"You mean what this Douglas was sayin' 'bout you an' them bosses—your booshways—thinkin' 'bout you an' all the Americans comin' in here to your part of the country?" Bass inquired.

"That, too," McLoughlin answered, "but I am speaking specifically in regard to American events that would determine the shape of my future here in the Northwest—nay, the shape of that future for both the company and Great Britain here in this great land." He sagged back into the stuffed chair. "From Nathaniel Wyeth I learned of a firebrand back in your United States who was stirring interest and zeal in colonizing this Oregon country."

"Kelley," Thornbrugh offered.

"Yes. Hall J. Kelley. A fiery, philosophical type who was stirring up public sentiment once more for the rapid settlement and annexation of this country. In your houses of government, this Kelley was igniting fires that would not be tamed, fires continually exciting and aggravating the demarcation dispute between our two countries."

"I don't understand what you mean," Scratch said. "Demar . . ."

"The border question," McLoughlin explained, "between our two lands: the United States and Canada. Where the border itself will be drawn."

"And in the midst of all this news the doctor continued to receive dispatches from Simpson reciting that bloody fool's worry about American involvement here on the Columbia—his dread that eventually events would indeed overwhelm us and this land would become American territory."

"Jarrell and I have a real difference of minds on this point," McLoughlin confessed. "This is one time—perhaps the only occasion—where I find myself agreeing with Simpson. In this matter, I unfortunately have to put aside my philosophical difference with the governor and say that he may have legitimate reason for his concern."

"*We* are bloody here!" Thornbrugh protested strongly. "And it would take an army to remove us!" He slapped the arm of his chair. "They are playing with war!"

"Yes," McLoughlin agreed. "You are correct. The seriousness of this question cannot be underrated. However, there are men such as this Kelley who zealously bypass such considerations when foisting their own programs on the unsuspecting public."

Bass scratched at an itch on his leg, still studying the face of McLoughlin. The eyes: those light-colored eyes with a personal haunting all their own—one moment they were peaceful, like the surface of the snow on a quiet, cold morning; and the next instant they could fill with a strange, fiery intensity, like the wisps of wind-whipped foam on the surging waves of the Columbia.

"All of this was not lost on our friend, James Douglas, mind you," the Chief Factor went on. "It is here that I find Douglas and Jarrell Thornbrugh in a strange alliance—"

"I dare say not, sir!" Thornbrugh protested again.

"Albeit, unwitting on your part," John replied. "However, you believe as strongly as does Douglas that the American threat must be countered—and mightily, I must add."

"I would not have my name linked with that skinny, black-hearted bastard!"

"Yet you share the same concern, Jarrell," McLoughlin pressed. "Yes, Scratch—in so many ways, thirty-two was a pivotal point for us here at Vancouver. I frantically took certain measures to assure some future for both myself and the company."

"Finlayson?" Jarrell asked.

"Yes, Finlayson. Last summer I dispatched him to the Sandwich Islands to establish a trade station of sorts to trade away some of our furs, excess produce and salmon to the islanders."

"Keep the fox away from the henhouse," Jarrell commented. "Sending Finlayson on this mission or that—and all the while you could do nothing about the real seat of the problem: the stone that had been rolled into your garden."

"Agreed. I was suspicious of Finlayson. But Douglas was indeed the stone that had been rolled into my garden. I attempted to keep our enterprise moving forward here on the Columbia, for the company, of course. However, what I would do for the company would only assure me of a restitution of both power and favor in the eyes of the governor and his committee. I believed that I still had within my grasp some might to wield in staving off the doom to our enterprise. Late last fall I rushed John McLeod into the field along with French-Canadian trapper Michael LaFramboise and a detachment of men to finally establish a trade station to the south in Umpqua territory."

"And when Finlayson arrived back from the islands in early winter," Jarrell said, "you had laid plans that he would not tarry here at Vancouver."

"Exactly. So, this spring I dispatched Finlayson, along with Donald Manson from the old Fort George site, and Alexander Anderson to journey northward with Captain Kipling in his ship *Dryad*. They were to have their men construct a new post northward along the coast to check the penetration of the Russians into North America."

"In addition to naming this new post at Millbank Sound in honor of the man on whose ears fell so much of Douglas's scheming: Fort Simpson," Thornbrugh remarked. "And on Finlayson's heels another expedition was organized under Archibald McDonald, sent overland to the north to found a post on the Nisqually River, close to Puget Sound. The new site was to be along the northern route between Vancouver and McDonald's own northern post, Fort Langley. It was at this new post that horses and boats could be exchanged in the commerce of furs and supplies between Langley and Vancouver."

"So, you been buildin' forts an' tryin' to keep Finlayson busy an' all." Bass shook his head with the complexity of it all. "But, what I don't figure be just what all this gotta do with McAfferty?"

He looked first at McLoughlin, then at Thornbrugh, both of whom had fallen silent. Bass shifted in his chair and leaned forward expectantly. "Well?" he asked again. "Just how Asa McAfferty figure into all of this?"

"Aye, McAfferty is the answer to so many questions, Scratch," said the doctor. "The man was an instrument, affecting both of us. You do not ken it yet, but you will when this tale is told."

"Thornbrugh told me you knowed him," Bass said. "Really didn't have to tell—I just knew me you did."

McLoughlin nodded. "I made the acquaintance of this McAfferty back in the fall of thirty-one. A terrible misfortune had overtaken the man: he had lost his right hand, the upper wrist on down, from a rifle ball, he said."

"That be true," Bass commented. "Leastways, what he told me, too."

"He rode in here early that fall, on his own, and completely alone—just as you yourself have done," the doctor went on. "I ministered as best I could to clean up the healed flesh over the amputation he said he had begun on his own. He said that Crow Indians had completed the job for him when he had passed out from the pain. It must have been a horrendous ordeal."

"So you helped heal 'im up?" Bass inquired.

"Yes. But it was through his own ingenuity that he fashioned the hook to replace the missing hand."

"I've seen it," Scratch said.

"Then you have seen McAfferty since he left here, in the early winter of thirty-one, thirty-two?"

"Yes," Bass answered softly as he stretched his legs out. "S'pose that was when Asa gone an' went down to the Nepercy tribe. Even got himself hitched up to a daughter of some chief. Gal went by the name of Rain Feather. She died in birthin' a young'un not long back. That be when he went off an' done somethin' crazy. . . ."

"However, not the first crazy thing he had done, Scratch," Thornbrugh said.

"What you mean?"

"I want you to understand that this McAfferty was merely a pawn in a much larger plot."

"I got you," Bass answered. "Finlayson and Douglas, right?"

"No, sir," Thornbrugh said. "Only Douglas."

"Yes." McLoughlin nodded. "This was solely the doing of James Douglas."

"Black Douglas," Thornbrugh added. "He used McAfferty's Scottish heritage, and McAfferty's own grossly inflated self-righteousness, to create a pawn for his own ends."

"An' just how Douglas do that?"

"McAfferty was, of course, very grateful to me for the work I did on healing his wound," McLoughlin said. "He wished, in any way possible, to repay what he saw as a tremendous debt. And that was the beginning of my own undoing, Scratch. McAfferty went to Douglas, my assistant Chief Factor, to inquire as to how he might repay me for services rendered. He identified with me so closely, his heart and mind proved fertile ground indeed for Douglas's monstrous plot against me."

"McAfferty went to Douglas, as the doctor has said," Thornbrugh interjected, "unbeknownst to the doctor or myself until of late. Consequently, Douglas instructed McAfferty on how best to repay John here. He told McAfferty that the doctor would like to be assured not only that the Blackfeet Indians would constantly make war on the American companies and trappers, but also that they should be kept inflamed to wage constant war upon those tribes which were friendly to the Americans."

"That be why Asa up an' left me back last fall," Bass observed quietly. "Thought me it fit some way or 'nother. Found out that nigger left me 'round the Three Forks country to get north to the Blackfoot. Whilst I was still trappin' last fall, he was busy bringin' them red niggers down on the Crow. Arapooesh's folks—Kicked-in-Their-Bellies."

"I have heard Douglas played McAfferty's sanctimonious self-righteousness like a finely tuned violin—even to the extent of appointing this McAfferty as John's field commander for tribal harassment and extermination."

"What you mean by that? Field commander?" Bass asked.

"Douglas made McAfferty believe I had appointed him to be in charge of leading the Blackfeet, setting the various confederation tribes onto Indians who were themselves friendly to the Americans in the field."

"Why, I'll be go to hell right here an' et for the devil's own tater by a toothless nigger!" Bass exclaimed. "An' then he come dancin' right on into that same Crow winter camp some while later. Blackfoot down on Crow most time anyways," Bass mused. "Been that way for a damned long time, anyways."

"Yes, that much is true," McLoughlin agreed.

"It do all make the circle now." Bass stared at the toes of his moccasins. "My partner . . . my ex-partner, he told me what McAfferty said to him the night he killed a ol' Crow woman."

Bass stared directly into the white-light pearl eyes of McLoughlin. "Asa told him that you offered him a chance at riches to be got in the fur trade. But not as a trapper. Asa told him you was to send him into the Blackfoot country, seein' how he was one to know them Blackfoots—all to set them red niggers on the Crow, even to trackin' the American companies."

He waited a moment, watching as the doctor eased back in his chair, his gaze never leaving Bass's face. "Those Americans as he couldn't run out with them Bug's Boys bein' sorely troublesome, Asa was to see that them Blackfoots did some steady killin'. I couldn't believe it myself, not to the time I first heard the tale of it." Scratch shook his head sadly. "Hearin' that Asa was to see that them Blackfoots killed Americans. But McAfferty said he'd do just that if need be—to leave the English to this rich fur country all by your lonesome."

The doctor glanced over at Thornbrugh. "Perhaps 'tis more serious than we had allowed ourselves to believe at first."

"Might be, John," Thornbrugh agreed.

"If word is being spread by such as the like of this McAfferty, no telling upon just whose ears this odious plot has fallen." McLoughlin seemed to sink further into his chair.

"How McAfferty's part in this get to be so damned important to you fellas?"

"Scratch . . ."

"Let me answer this, John," Thornbrugh interrupted. "Douglas has his own vision of this Columbia District. Already you know that Douglas's vision does not include Doctor John McLoughlin. Right?"

He watched Bass nod his head. "And you agree that all this time McAfferty believed he was doing just as the good doctor had wanted him to do in his service to McLoughlin. In this manner, if Asa McAfferty were successful, Douglas could claim to the governor and the committee that he himself had orchestrated the brilliant maneuver to destroy the tribes that were aiding the American penetration in the Rocky Mountains and beyond."

"An' if McAfferty failed?" Bass stared at Thornbrugh.

"If he failed, and the whole matter became a diplomatic, political fireball of delicate proportions—namely the setting of one country, as the tribes are considered sovereign nations, against another country's citizens—in this case, American trappers—then Douglas was to have it known that McAfferty was acting under the strictest of orders from none other than John McLoughlin himself."

"Just when you go thinkin' you got a nigger figured out— that be when he up an' surprises you," Bass muttered.

John McLoughlin seemed to pick up in some way the thread of the American's thoughts. "You see, Scratch," he said, "I would therefore be held personally responsible for the consequences of all of McAfferty's actions in regard to northern plains warfare, perhaps even the harassment of American trapping parties." McLoughlin sagged again. "However, you say that Asa McAfferty is dead. Is this absolutely certain?"

"His body," Bass answered softly.

"I beg your pardon," John said. "I did not catch that."

"I said his body—his body's dead." He spoke almost in a hoarse whisper.

"I am afraid I do na' quite ken ye," McLoughlin said, lapsing into a thick Scot brogue. "What you are saying is that the man is dead."

"Just his. . . ."

"Let me try to explain this to the doctor," Thornbrugh broke in. "What Scratch here is trying to tell you is that McAfferty's ghost still haunts him, which is why he has come to see you. He was deeply hopeful that in some way you would be able to aid him in laying this ghost to rest."

"Aye," McLoughlin replied, glancing at Bass briefly.

"Scratch is saying that McAfferty's body may itself be dead, although he does not believe his soul to be. It has been a very private and personal haunting for him."

"No," McLoughlin said suddenly, "no, it has not been private at all. McAfferty and what he was sent to do has been a manner of haunting for me also."

"His ghost followin' you 'round, too?"

"In a manner of speaking, yes," the Chief Factor replied. "And it appears his ghost is going to haunt me the rest of my days."

"Then it be true what Jarrell told me that you really knowed Asa," Bass stated.

"That . . . is correct."

"An' it be the truth, too," he said, turning to Thornbrugh, "that you didn't know 'im, right?"

"Yes, I did not know the man myself," the Englishman answered.

"But, you knowed of 'im, just like you told me."

"As I promised, Scratch, there has been no deception on our part—neither John's nor mine."

"You two fellas . . . you're . . . you're good men," Bass said. "I think you two would sooner spit face on to the wind than tell a lie. I feel . . . I mean, I gotta believe that 'bout you two now," he stammered. "To think me that a ol' friend, a ol' partner got himself hooked up in such a way . . . it just don't make much sense to me that McAfferty . . . that he'd go an' be bringin' Blackfoot down on tribes what been good to us." He sighed as his body sagged with relief. "Turnin' his back on Americans— no offense meanin' to you fellas."

"There is none taken," McLoughlin said.

"I s'pose for a few of us fellas—like you two an' me, we all in this together, like it or not. Meanin' we all out here for the same thing, an' we watchin' it roll on away from us through no . . . power . . . of our own. Just them big stuffed-shirt niggers makin' all the plans: playin' the tune an' we each havin' to decide on dancin' to that tune or not."

"As much as I would have enjoyed thinking differently," McLoughlin answered, "I believe you are close to the real truth of it, Scratch. As much as I would have liked to believe I was the power out here, I have begun to see that I am not. And that realization is truly my haunting. Asa McAfferty's ghost, if you will, has brought home to me that I am truly like all of you. My feet are clay. Yet—what has been all the more difficult to admit to myself . . . is that . . . Great Britain and the company share my mortal affliction—and neither of them any longer possesses the might to hold on to this great land here."

"The Union Jack will not soon fall from the Columbia!" exclaimed Thornbrugh.

"Not soon," the Chief Factor agreed. "However, my friend— our day has passed its zenith. The Empire does not wield the power, either economic or political, that she once did. The sun is setting on our little empire out here in the Northwest." He began to nod his head. "Aye, the Union Jack will come down— here, at Vancouver."

"Never!" Thornbrugh protested.

"Do you see why I love this man so?" he asked of Scratch. "His loyalty and resolve are unshakable." Now he turned back to Jarrell. "We differ in opinion—so be it. But my vision of what this great land holds has been tarnished. That youthful vision lies rusting beneath a sky darkened with clouds of deceit, sloth, and duplicity. Vancouver is doomed—"

Thornbrugh leaned forward in his chair once more and started to speak, but the doctor raised a hand to silence him.

"Let me speak on, Jarrell," he instructed. "Vancouver is doomed. It was doomed from the moment the Company of Adventurers empowered a man such as Simpson, who is controlled by innuendo and deceit. Simpson will retire a man much impressed with his own worth. And I? I will merely retire. I cannot envision myself returning to Canada now. The torch is passing to new hands in this great land and I cannot envision myself being far from it. Fear not, dear Thornbrugh, I am not giving up, not yet. However, my efforts will be more wisely expended in the future. No more will I attempt to resuscitate the dying corpse that drew its own death upon itself through its very own blind, inept duplicity of purpose. The time is yet to arrive for John McLoughlin to leave Vancouver— but when that day comes, we will not leave vanquished. We will leave to travel a new trail, one of our own forging, alongside others who will forge that future for this land with us. We, Jarrell. We."

"I . . . I had thought several times of leaving the service of the company," Jarrell said. "But I . . . I had never really entertained the thought of leaving Vancouver. I suppose my vision always held John McLoughlin at the helm of this region. And I saw myself as his first mate, come whatever bastard storm to rock us." He reached over and placed his hand on McLoughlin's arm. "I am with you, John. Whatever be the course you set sail to, I'm with you."

"I never entertained a doubt as to that," the Chief Factor replied. He leaned back in his chair. For a long moment, the only sound in the room was the crackling of the wood in the stove. Then came the sound of the front door closing and a pair of feet shuffling off the porch and down the steps. A second pair of feet clambered slowly up the stairs.

"My son, Joseph," McLoughlin said. "He spends more and more time with the bastard himself. My greatest hope lies in David."

He gazed at Bass. "My youngest: David. With Ermatinger he left on March 3, with the Spring Express. I sent him east, on his way to Paris. My hopes are that he will complete medical school. Such a sad, melancholy parting that was. The last of my sons, moving away from the wharf, along with David Douglas, who had been out here collecting botanical samples."

He sighed once again. "And I am going to be bidding adieu to this new American friend also. Soon, I take it?"

"I gotta be gettin' back soon, yep," Bass answered.

"And where is it you are bound now, dear pilgrim?" McLoughlin inquired.

"Back over," he answered simply. "Back on over them mountains."

"Is there someone to whom you return—someone who is waiting for you?"

Bass dropped his eyes from the Chief Factor's gaze. "I . . . I ain't thinkin' so. Just . . . gotta move on back to my country."

"This is country for men such as you, Scratch," Thornbrugh said. "Make no mistake of that. This country and what is taking place out here are for the few such as yourself."

"I ain't so ready for things go changin' on me—like the doctor got himself ready for," he replied. "I like me things just the way they is now. Things back there," he said, gesturing with a thumb toward the east, "they ain't 'bout to change soon, like they is here. I'll be long gone afore I see any of them farmer folks this Kelley fella whips into comin' out here to settle. Damn the corn-crackers, sod-busters an' shop-keeps whilst there's still buffler in the hills yet! By God, I'll be long gone under afore I see their kind out here!"

He looked up at Thornbrugh, then at McLoughlin, and smiled. "This here fort be just 'bout as close to settlement doin's I care to get me close to. Things set by me just fine back there. Don't figure I'm ready for a roof an' four walls just yet. Things have a way of rushin' in on a nigger so fast, howsomever—might just find my walls be a hole in the ground an' my roof be six feet of dirt! If I'm lucky! But, nawww. I got me plenty time left afore I'm settlin' in somewheres. I thank you for the invite—if'n that what it be, fellas."

"Truly it was," Thornbrugh answered.

"Well, I thank you, most kindly, too. But . . . I gotta keep on movin' . . . movin' to find a healin' for my small heart now. Believe I can lay ol' Asa to rest now, I can. That be done—an' I gotta find rest for my ol' heart."

He rose from his chair and rubbed at his knees a few moments. They were getting stiffer and stiffer on him every day. "Gotta be movin' on—get me some shuteye. Figure me out a way to get back up to your Nepercy post next couple of days. Get on outta here an' get my heart right."

"I will see that you get back to Nez Perce," Jarrell said. "I'll take you myself."

"I was hopin' you'd be sayin' that." Scratch beamed at the big Englishman.

The trio strolled out of the sitting room and through the darkened office to the entrance hall. "And have you laid to rest the source of your haunting?" Jarrell inquired as they stopped at the front door McLoughlin opened.

"Believe so," Bass said quietly. "Believe so."

McLoughlin led the two others onto the porch into the cool night air. The fort was quiet. Wisps of smoke floated aimlessly across the compound from many stoves and finally drifted over the palisades to the forest beyond. The Chief Factor turned to the trapper. "McAfferty is dead," he stated. "McAfferty is dead for both of us now."

Bass looked up at him and laughed. "Asa's dead—yes."

"How did the man die?" McLoughlin leaned against the porch rail near the top of the steps.

"McAfferty didn't—he didn't *die*."

"He was killed, then?" John asked. "Perhaps in battle?"

"No, not rightly like that," Bass answered after a moment. "He was killed . . . by an ol' friend."

McLoughlin stood straight up. "You are . . . saying—"

"I killed him," Bass rasped. "I hunted McAfferty down in the snow this past winter. It come down to him an' me on . . . somethin'. Man chose his own time, his own place—an' I just come along to do the rest of it for him, I s'pose."

"Scratch," McLoughlin said, "that was not the beginning of your haunting . . ." He saw the trapper stare up at him. "That was the beginning of the *end* of your haunting. And a haunting for so many of us. No. You must be assured that your travail did not begin with you killing the madman. You had only taken into your hands the fire that needed to be extinguished. And it has been a long time in coming for you. The Lord will find his own rest for the madman. As he will find for all of us mad enough to believe there is something better, all of us who aren't content with the way things are, and for those of you who aren't content to rest in one place. The Lord will find peace for you. Yes, this haunting is over. The fire you took into your hands has died. The cold ash you must leave behind. Leave behind to begin seeking an answer to the fire in your heart. I pray you will find that answer—soon. My friend." He presented his hand to Bass. "I bid you a fond farewell, and—Godspeed."

Bass took the man's large hand and held it. The two did not shake hands, but only stood there in the darkness looking at each other. Scratch released his grip on McLoughlin and walked down the staircase two steps before he turned around.

"I'll not soon be forgettin' what you done for me this night, John."

"Nor I, Scratch. Nor I," Doctor McLoughlin answered quickly.

Bass walked on down the steps and into the dark. He walked quickly, loosely once more, as if he were again at peace with the darkness. There was a lightness in his frame, a weight gone from his shoulders. He stopped after the darkness had completely enveloped him, when he knew for certain that the two men could not see him any longer. Scratch turned around and gazed back at the Big House. There under the starlight and the silver of a new moon, against the whitewash of the porch woodwork, he could just barely make out the two tall figures, backlighted against the candlelit windows. The two men stood still, staring after him into the darkness, both perhaps even now yearning for the trapper's freedom. Perhaps, he thought.

I'll not soon be forgettin' what you done for me this night, John.

Nor I, Scratch. Nor I.

Eighteen

It was almost summer once more. Josiah lay there in the buffalo robes, his mind in that halfway place between sleep and wakefulness.

His time had come. Josiah had thought and thought many times on this day. He knew it would come. Lord knows he had tried—but he could deny it no longer.

Yesterday he had even walked down to check on the ponies in the compound where they were returned each night. Watching the animals with the spotted rumps had again made him restless. They were the animals acquired last summer at rendezvous when he had been with the Indian woman.

He remembered smelling her, nestling his head in that gentle valley of flesh where neck and shoulder blended so soft. Hers was not the sweet false musk of a St. Louis tavern maid, but the fragrant perfume of sage and earth and wildflower and wilderness. He had reached out to caress the firm mounds beneath her pliant buckskin blouse and felt his penis stir after more than a year of flaccid dormancy.

He looked down at the tattered ribbon lying across his pistol. Perhaps that deep wound had finally begun to ooze his poison. Perhaps he had begun the slow process of healing. Scratch had been right about him—he had been burying a deep pain within himself, holding it in, guarding it. And, now, a piece of him lingered in the valley west of the Tetons, across the river with the Indian woman.

It had been the first time for her, and she had filled a deep void with him. She had released the poison in him, brought light after so long a time of darkness and pain.

"We'll wash all the others away tonight, an' make it a first time for both of us."

Those were the words he had spoken that summer night in Pierre's Hole. Words she could not understand. Words he had made her understand in some primitive, fundamental way—with his gentle caress. Lord, he wanted to feel her flesh against his, to feel her soft fingers tending to his wounds. He ached for her. Yet hope was dimming that he would ever warm himself again with her intimate gift. Only the coals of memories remained for him now.

He was anxious to be moving once more. How quickly such a nomadic existence had become a way of life for him. And with the tribe now packing up to leave this winter camp, Paddock had finally come to a decision that night and discussed it in hushed tones with Arapooesh. He had spoken to Rotten Belly, telling the old chief that he did not want to migrate with the tribe.

Rotten Belly had already known in some way, already known that Josiah wished to move on by himself, for a while anyway. He had not asked the young trapper, but he was sure his young, adopted son would return again and again to the Sparrowhawks, just as *Pote Ani* had over the recent years.

What now seemed to be the hardest part for Josiah was pushing the robes aside and sitting up. Not that his chest still hurt. He had been gaining strength more and more over the weeks. In fact, Josiah had been riding some: out with a few of the young warriors, sometimes with Waits-by-the-Water, and many times with his adopted father. No, the hardest part was sitting up to get the day started by pulling his plunder together for the journey.

Arapooesh was awake. Paddock looked over at the old man in his robes, saw the chief smile back at him. The young trapper leaned forward to brush some dead ash to the side of the fire pit in search of some still-live coals. The small fire finally blossomed to life and he pulled his moccasins onto his feet.

The young woman stirred and rolled over in her bed. Paddock looked over at the beautiful creature with those big, round, sensual eyes that began to flutter awake with the growing early light that was creeping into the lodge. She smiled at the trapper. Looking at her now, it made him wonder again if he were doing the right thing, if he had chosen the right path. Yet, the strongest, most powerful part of him remained resolute in his decision. He would leave the Crow and undertake this journey. And he would be taking Waits-by-the-Water with him.

She pushed aside the blankets and rose to one elbow. This young woman had been patient with him over the months, finally coming to realize he could not get a full grasp of the Crow language. He had learned some words for important objects, animals and such—but Josiah had not been able to put thought and concept together enough to carry on a conversation with anyone else but these two: the old chief and the young woman. Whenever he had used one, perhaps two words, to express what he was wanting, they had always understood. Besides, Rotten Belly knew more of English than Josiah knew of the Crow tongue. And that helped immensely.

And Waits-by-the-Water, with her quick, bright mind, had picked up much of the language of the whiteman during the past three months. That was one of the reasons Josiah had decided to take her with him on the journey. She would be a big help in translating for him or signing with other Indians they might meet on the trail.

"Eat soon?" She pulled the edge of her dress back down below her knees when she sat up. She watched his eyes travel down the length of her brown legs and knew that he was studying her again—and knew, too, that he was studying himself. Over past weeks, their growing relationship had been one of testing. He had wanted her for himself—to fight off his loneliness, his need for warmth, perhaps to answer his need for closeness with another human being. Perhaps he was vulnerable. The testing had been hers to share, as she asked herself continually if what she really wanted for her heart would ever come to be. Or, if she were going to have to settle for something else, perhaps something less.

"Eat soon?" she inquired again, keeping her eyes on his as his gaze rose from her legs back to her face.

He nodded once and rose as Arapooesh pushed himself up on one elbow. "My son goes this day," the old chief observed.

Josiah stood by the warm cheerful fire and nodded. "Yes. I go today. I am ready."

"You decide it is good for you?"

"Yes," Josiah answered softly. "Yes. The trail may be long. But this one must see what waits at the end of that trail." He stared down at the flames for a moment. "When your bellies empty and you go to hunt the buffalo—do you worry how long the trail is?"

He watched the old man smile, then smiled back at the chief. "It is the same. The trail will be as long as it has to be, father-man."

Paddock edged around the firepit, between the flames and the young woman, and stopped at the door. "I am sad to be going away from you, Arapooesh." Then he quickly ducked outside.

He stood for a moment beside the bundled-up half-dome shelter of hides that belonged to the old trapper. It was wrapped and bound and ready for travel. The shelter was big enough. As big as a small lodge. So it would serve them well if they had need of it for refuge from the long, sudden spring storms that had been dotting the sky the last couple of weeks. He could always cut and strip branches for the short poles it required to set up, if the shelter were needed.

Paddock set out for the compound. Each morning, Waits-by-the-Water had helped him walk the ponies farther and farther away to forage along the river's bottomland, along with the tribe's horses. Each evening as the sun began to sink, she had gone with him to cut his ponies out of the herd and bring them back to the compound. Waits-by-the-Water had finally come to understand why he did not leave his ponies with the rest of the tribe's horses under the young Crows guarding the herd—why he preferred to return his to this compound. The whiteman did not steal horses. And that was strange to her mind. If a Sparrowhawk man lost his horses, he could always go out and steal some more to replace those gone from his herd. Eventually she had come to understand how special each of these eight animals were to him. Almost a year now he had owned them.

He leaned against a tree and watched the animals. Perhaps they would enjoy the journey, too. Perhaps they could again accustom themselves to the rhythm of the trail. It would be another long one. Nowhere near as long as the trip across the plains to get to the mountains two years ago, but at least longer than the tedious, circuitous route he and the older trapper had taken to get to this Crow winter camp.

Josiah ducked beneath the rope tied between the trees and moved toward the closest animal. The pony did not shy and prance away from him as the horses had weeks ago. They had not been ridden much, nor had they had that much contact

with a man for those long months of winter. They had grown
suspicious through the days and nights of white cold. It had
taken a few days of wrestling with them to get the ponies used
to his touch once more, used to his smell, and once again accustomed to being ridden.

He dropped the rest of the lead ropes and slipped a halter
over the muzzle of the first pony. That done, Josiah moved to
the rest of the horses in turn until each was strung to the pony
in front of it. Then he went to the tree and untied the rope,
moving from one tree to the next until the rope had been
coiled and the bundle circled over his shoulder. He picked up
the halter rope and led the animals out of the compound that
had been their home for the past months.

The two trappers had owned eight ponies when they came
here to Absaroka. Those, along with the horses Asa had left
behind late last winter, made a total of thirteen. One of the
animals had been killed in the winter manhunt for McAfferty.
Bass had taken four along with him when he had pulled out
suddenly last winter. Now there was one each for him and the
young woman, leaving more than enough to pack all the plunder he had readied for the journey. And the shelter. One pony
would carry the shelter on its back.

"*Bu-aka kanna,*" an older warrior greeted Josiah.

Paddock nodded and continued to the chief's lodge. There
he tied a few of the ponies off to the cover pegs and ducked
back inside. After allowing his eyes to become adjusted to the
light, the young trapper seated himself on the robes near the
back of the lodge with his adopted father. Arapooesh handed
him a flat, wooden bowl. Waits-by-the-Water rose from the fire
with her kettle and served him some of last night's elk stew. He
tucked the bowl between his knees and was handed a spoon.
He had to admit he was pretty damned hungry. Hadn't had
much to eat. Didn't have an appetite at all yesterday. Perhaps
some pre-trail jitters.

"You have eaten?" he asked, glancing over at the young
woman and the chief and seeing that they had no bowls in their
laps.

"We are done, my son," Arapooesh answered. "You eat.
Awu'xtpe. We finish work." He motioned for the young woman
to leave with him and the two ducked out of the lodge.

Awu'xtpe. Sun Runner. He heard some of the ponies snort
and the sounds of their hooves stomping the ground. It

seemed he was always being named after another. After someone else or something else.

His mind suddenly flooded with the memory of the Whitehair telling him of the young King Josiah in the Bible—knowing he had been as foolish as the man his mother had chosen
for his namesake.

*"There be a tale of a young King Josiah in the Good Book,
lad. He was a likely youth, as ye be yourself—at first sure to
set what was right with the Lord God."*

Hunting the Whitehair down. He had been just like that
young king in the Bible. Figuring on going after McAfferty
himself.

*"This young king of Judah named Josiah was so wantin' of
gettin' a name for himself in battle that when some older king
of ol' Egypt come to his land to do battle with some other one,
this Josiah made him up a plan to trick the older man. Ye see,
that Egypt king was not wantin' to fight Josiah, but the young
king of Judah was itchin' for the fight an' dressed himself up to
look just like the one the Egypt king was wantin' to fight. He
come on down into the valley they called Megiddo, then called
out for the Egypt king to come out an' fight him, makin' it look
like he was some other one. Bad doin's it were, for the Egypt
king was never a man to be dealin' fair. When the man he
thought was the king he was wantin' come down in the valley,
he just had his men kill him. And the archers shot at King
Josiah; and the king said to his servants, 'Have me away, for I
am sore wounded.'"*

The ponies snorted again. Then Waits-by-the-Water came
back inside the lodge to pick up a bundle which she carried
outside.

It was then that he noticed that his things were no longer
hanging from the dew-cloth rope and the poles inside the
lodge. He stopped chewing a moment, studying the place
about him. She had completed their packing, stuffing everything into blanket-wrapped bundles, everything she did not
have space for in parfleches and rawhide cases. All that remained was laid out near him: his old, worn blanket coat, his
rifle, and the otter medicine bag. All were stacked neatly on
the bed where Arapooesh had been sleeping.

He started to chew again. Both on the meat and on the
thought that the old chief must have finally accepted that he
was leaving, that this was indeed something he had to do to

complete his own healing. Paddock continued to eat as he watched the young woman duck in and out of the lodge, carrying the baggage to Arapooesh, he supposed. His old man must be packing the horses.

He was wiping his mouth on the back of his sleeve when the young woman knelt by the doorway and looked in at him. "Go soon?" she inquired.

"Yes." Paddock rose from the bed and set the bowl aside. He stood motionless for a moment, letting the lodge itself speak to him now in their parting. So much had taken place here. So much good, so much evil—so much he wished could be changed through some magical wave of his hand. But he felt all the older for it, all the smarter—maybe even wiser.

He was not the same person he'd been when he had first come here last freeze-up to sit with the old men as they welcomed the two whitemen to the Crow winter camp. Neither was he the same man who had been carried back inside after a cold-winter manhunt to heal his serious wound. And, he reflected, he was not even the same man who had left this lodge in late winter for a sweat-lodge ceremony: carried out but able to walk back under his own power.

Josiah sighed and looked up at the sky through the wide smoke-hole. Clouds danced across the opening. Might yet rain this afternoon, he mused. Bass had taught him that much. Hell, the old man had taught him so much more. And that was perhaps why his soul had continued its healing process after the sweat-lodge ceremony. It must be finished between them. That much he knew.

Paddock reached over and picked up his old coat, pulled it over his arms and shoulders. Then he stopped a moment to pull his shooting pouch over his shoulder. The lodge had seemed to speak in some mystical, whispering way to him. He knelt again by the fire and scooped up a small handful of the ashes from the edge. Holding the warm ashes in his hand, he studied them for a few moments.

His adopted father had told him the difference would someday make itself known: that difference between the finality of ash and the ever-lasting quality of the earth itself. Then, Arapooesh had instructed, and only then, would his adopted son know the true nature of the difference between the man who had come to the Crow last freeze-up and the man who was leaving that camp this morning. Yes.

Quickly he dumped the ash back into the firepit and dusted

his hand off as he scanned the lodge, his glance taking in the bed and the dew-cloth rope. Then he spotted something he could use. Near the doorway, hanging from the rope, was a small pouch, almost unnoticed because it was so small. He slipped over and untied it from the rope. It was empty. Yet in studying it, he was gently washed with the feeling that he had seen it someplace before, in another time almost. He scooped up another handful of ashes and dumped what he could into the top of the brain-tanned pouch he held open with his finger-tips.

When the small pouch was about half-full, he leaned down and scraped at the earth that was hard-packed from the many feet that had trampled over it. He pulled out his knife and scraped at the soil, loosening some of the dark, rich earth. Then he scooped up the earth and placed it within the pouch along with the ashes. When the pouch was full, he sheathed his knife.

His fingers fumbled at his greasy leggings until he found some long fringe. He yanked the fringe loose until he had enough to tie into a cord that would circle his neck loosely. When he was done, the new pouch rested on his chest against the other small, soft-skinned pouch. Josiah stared down at the two of them: the new, with its medicine of this time and place held within it; the older he had carried for almost a year.

She had given it to him last summer.

The woman beyond the Tetons. The woman of memory, her image tugging at him now in the silence of the lodge.

She had finally spoken to him as they cradled each other before dressing, teaching him a few Flathead words for those objects he pointed out. Paddock had walked the young squaw back to her people's village later that morning. But beyond the edge of the lodges, she had stopped him. There she had turned and lifted from her neck the small pouch she had tied to the skin blouse the evening before. She had held it against her breasts, then put the short loop over Josiah's head as he bent forward. Before he could say anything more, before he could touch her, she had fled into the village, turning only once to remind him, with a wave of her hand, not to follow. In the late moments of the afternoon he had ridden to the edge of the village to seek a glimpse of the elusive plain-faced woman.

The two pouches together. Now, he thought, he was ready. He picked up the shooting pouch and the rifle. Scratch had bought it for him last summer, trading those cold-won beaver pelts. He felt the warm security of its wood and metal, its solid heft as he delicately ran a finger over the huge flintlock.

"*Heavier'n my rifle*," he had remarked to Bass at last summer's trading counter. "*Why don't you like percussion?*"

"*What you gonna do when you run outta them nipple huggers? Your life ain't gonna be worth a grizzly shit then, son,*" Bass had answered. "*You run outta spare flints with that rifle, well—most men can find themselves somethin' work 'bout as good.*"

A J. J. Henry, it was. Sublette's clerk had told the trappers the gun was built for the mountain trade. Henry had been putting the weapons together for more than sixteen years, on contract with the American Fur Company.

Damned sturdy it was. Built to take whatever a man dished out. And they bought it for the inflated mountain price of $110 with Bass insisting that the clerk throw in a mold, a couple of screws and patch worms. The wood was suddenly damp beneath his palm.

Paddock pulled on the otter-fur cap he had won at rendezvous in a knife-throwing contest. He lifted the otter-skin medicine bundle. The two old men had taught him much. First the trapper—damned ass that he could be sometimes. And the old chief, his adopted father. He drew a deep breath; he was ready.

Josiah hunched through the doorway and was greeted by more light than when he'd gone out to fetch the horses earlier. The village was beginning to stir. Tiny knots of people stood in small, separate groups some distance away, watching the young trapper stride to the ponies where the chief and the young woman stood waiting. Josiah scanned the curious onlookers, then went to his pony. He tied the medicine pouch to the saddle, behind the cantle. Asa's old saddle. Much like Scratch's Santa Fe saddle. He had been glad these last few weeks of riding and healing that the old trapper had brought the dead man's saddle back.

He was glad that he had the Whitehair's saddle. Paddock could not stand the pad saddles the Crow used: stuffed with thick, coarse buffalo hair. He smiled, glanced at the pony Waits-by-the-Water had chosen to ride.

Long trip as this was going to be, no way his ass would take sitting on some flimsy pad. From horse to horse he stepped slowly, inspecting the work the young woman and Arapooesh had done in packing the baggage. He turned and found Arapooesh and the girl watching him expectantly.

"It is good." He smiled. "You done good." Josiah slapped his pony on the rump gently.

"You wait, my son," the old chief said. He turned, entered the lodge, rummaged through his belongings. A short time later he emerged, carrying a blue woolen blanket folded across his arms. Arapooesh stepped close to the tall youth before speaking.

"Your coat," he said.

"What about my coat?" Paddock fingered his old blanket garment that had seen him through two winters, countless rains, and many cold days and nights when he lay helpless on a travois.

"Give me," the chief said. "Make trade." He thrust the blanket toward Josiah.

"You want it?" Paddock asked, taking off the shooting pouch and handing it to the young woman. "Not sure why you do, father-man. But you can have it." He pulled his arms from the sleeves and handed the red and black coat to the chief.

Arapooesh took the garment, presented the blue blanket to Josiah. "We trade." He smiled as Paddock unfolded the blanket.

It was actually a capote, hood and all. The light blue wool was set off by the black stripes near the bottom of the coat and near the base of the long sleeves which were turned back into cuffs.

"Put on," the young woman instructed.

"Sure!" he said, excited about his new gift. He slipped into it and saw that it was a good fit.

The chief stepped back to look him over, then nodded. "Look good, son."

Paddock ran his hands over the arms of the capote, feeling the newness of the material. "You make this capote?" he asked Waits-by-the-Water.

She shook her head and lowered her eyes. He did not quite understand. A new blanket fashioned into a coat. If she did not make it . . . "Yours?" He looked up at the chief.

"Yes," Arapooesh answered. "No. Yours now." He smiled at the young trapper.

"Mine now. Thank you."

"Wife—Sleeps-by-the Door—make me come last winter—

time," he explained as he slowly bowed his head. "Last thing give me then she killed by Whitehair in *Moon When Trees Pop*. My heart on the ground. I tell her she give coat I no wear."

"Why didn't you wear the coat?"

"I say her it much . . . Heap much . . ." He sought for the English word for the expression. ". . . pretty for me. I warrior. No need pretty coat."

"I see."

"It make her heart small for some suns me no wear coat. Never wear coat. You wear coat now, my son." He grinned broadly at Josiah.

"Yes." He placed a hand on the old chief's shoulder. "I am very happy with this pretty coat. A very pretty—fancy coat from my father-man."

Paddock, with his other arm, encircled Rotton Belly's shoulders, giving the older man a firm, warm hug. He felt the old Indian's arms come around his waist and return the gesture with an intimate fierceness, a surprising strength in one of his advanced years. The old man's hug told him much.

At the side of the lodge Josiah noticed Buffalo-Tail-Scares-the-Fly. She stood apart from the other spectators, watching silently. Paddock smiled and nodded to her. The older woman smiled lamely at him, then swiped at her cheeks. He supposed there were tears in this parting after all.

Waits-by-the-Water ran to her mother and the two women embraced for long moments without saying a word. It was then that the girl's brother appeared.

Strikes-in-Camp stood to the side, his arms crossed, his blanket wrapped about him. His face wore a blank expression. His sister turned to say something to him, but he jerked his head, turning his face away. Waits-by-the-Water pursed her lips in frustration, anger perhaps, and embraced her mother one last time before scurrying back to the ponies. The young woman climbed easily onto the animal and adjusted her thick capote around her legs.

"What . . . what of him?" Josiah gestured toward the chief's nephew.

"I know not what you mean."

"Trouble from him?" Josiah asked, always conscious of having to phrase his questions carefully.

"Yes, I think," Rotton Belly responded.

"This one I will watch carefully, father-man." Paddock

stepped to his pony with Arapooesh at his side. He hauled himself up into the old Sante Fe saddle. He feet rested comfortably in the stirrups adjusted for his long legs.

"No . . . in Absaroka." The chief gazed intently at the young trapper.

"You mean . . . not in Absaroka," Josiah said patiently. "You mean I will not have to worry about trouble from him while I am in Crow country."

"Yes." Arapooesh nodded. "When you go from land of Sparrowhawks—he say you no more Sparrowhawk. This one you have wounded his pride. Pride a bad thing. It hurt more than body. Yes?"

"Yes, father-man. Pride a very, very bad thing."

"You know that," Arapooesh said, "you all time be stronger than him."

"I do not want to fight with this one, her brother." He saw the chief nod knowingly. "You already know that, don't you? Yes—you do. But, I will not walk away from a fight with this one. You can't figure I would."

"If Strikes-in-Camp come after me—after us, you tell him—you say to all Sparrowhawk here—your son will not run from that fight. If it is my day to die, my father—then I will die having drawn his blood first."

Arapooesh looked up into Paddock's face with melancholy eyes. "A bad heart he has for you. Him bad heart for all *masta sheela*—all whiteman now. I send you away with present—that make his heart trouble for you. You take his sister away—that make his heart trouble for you. You go on hunt for killer *masta sheela* when winter-man comes—that make his heart trouble for you."

Finally the old man reached out a hand and placed it on Paddock's thigh. "You *masta sheela*—Pote Ani and you—come Sparrowhawk with white hair. Make his heart bad, bad trouble medicine for two *masta sheela*. For two, *Pote Ani* and my son."

"Got him bad heart for both of us, eh?" Paddock said. "Well, *Pote Ani* is gone now. And I am near to his bad medicine heart. I suppose I got my own problems to worry about, father-man."

Josiah shifted his rifle, patted the back of the old man's hand. Arapooesh squeezed Paddock's fingers, then dropped his arm and stepped back.

"Know where find him?" Rotten Belly inquired, squinting up into the morning sun.

"Who?" Paddock asked.

"Friend. Uncle to you now. *Pote Ani.*" The chief watched the young trapper sit back in the saddle and study the ground for a moment. "Know where go find? This journey not for great circle, my son," he said as he swung his arm in a wide arc. "This journey"—his gesture was now a straight extension of his arm—"go straight to heart of trouble. You find—make heart strong again."

So the old man knew. Josiah realized he had not been able to keep a secret from the cagey old fart after all. He had to smile at his adopted father. Rotten Belly smiled back warmly.

"You fool me"—Josiah chuckled lightly—"thinking I was fooling you. Come over here, father-man."

Arapooesh stepped forward to stand directly beneath Paddock. Quickly Josiah bent to the side and planted a kiss on the old man's wrinkled cheek, then sat back up straight.

"What is this?" Arapooesh touched his cheek. "Not for women to kiss?"

Josiah chuckled again. "No . . . not just for women do I kiss, father-man. Also kiss all I love. I love you, father-man." He looked up at the sky a moment, then met the eyes of the Crow chief. "I have two men who teach me many things—many things about the heart." His left hand tapped his chest for emphasis. "You finish job *Pote Ani* start. Both men big in my heart, father-man."

"Yes," the chief replied. "Both men big in heart." He tapped his own chest with a bony finger. "You stay big in my heart. *Pote Ani* stay big in my heart, too. You find."

"Yes, my father. I find."

Arapooesh squinted into the sun before his eyes found Paddock once more. His smile was brave, though his heart was saddened by the parting. "*Awu'xtpe* . . . Sun Runner, your medicine races over the sky." He lifted an open palm toward the bright globe climbing into the early-morning spring blue. "You must follow and take this trail—find *Pote Ani* for your heart, for her heart. My heart waits for you. My body is tired. I go now. You go now, too. Run on the sun, your heart. Find brother-man. Bring home."

"My father . . ." Josiah started, then felt the hot lump in his throat begin to choke him. He swallowed hard against it. "I find him. I talk with him. I make things straight between us. I make things straight between them." He nodded toward the young woman beside him. "Then I bring him home to you."

"Not long I live more," Arapooesh said.

"You will live many winters, father-man, many winters yet."
Josiah smiled.

"Perhaps. But time is short now. Bring *Pote Ani* home see
brother-man before I go over." Arapooesh brushed his fingers
along the fringes of Paddock's leggings.

Josiah thumped a fist against his chest as he kicked the pony
gently. He could not say anything more as the ponies headed
into the trees toward the river crossing, toward the turbulent,
snow-melt-swollen waters. He finally stopped and looked
back. The old man stood in the center of the lodge-circle,
watching them leave, his right arm raised high.

"Say a prayer for me, father-man!" he called back to Rotten
Belly. "Say a prayer for *Awu'xtpe* and *Pote Ani!*"

When he saw the old chief nod, Josiah turned back in the
saddle and heaved a big sigh.

On Tuesday, May 7, the caravan pulled out of Lexington,
beginning its long march across the flat, grass-filled land toward the Rocky Mountains. The nights were still cool and
damp and each man was thankful to have been assigned his
bedding of two three-point blankets.

The keel-boat *Gallant* pushed itself out into the current of
the river and began its trip north, towed by the steamboat *Otto*
as far as Fort Pierre.

After the caravan passed the old Shawnee Mission, messes
were organized, with approximately nine men to each mess.
These groups each elected their own mess captain and determined their rotation of guard duty for the caravan. Campbell,
Stewart, Brotherton, Edmund Christy, and Doctor Harrison
messed together with trader Louis Vasquez and clerk Antonine
Jeunesse among others. Redman and Nute found their mess
augmented with Charles Larpenter and some French voyageurs, men who found this overland travel something novel.
However, the food that was offered to the groups huddled
around the fires each morning and evening was not novel. The
voyageurs had come to know well the fare of such a journey.
Each man was sparingly given his daily ration of bacon, hard-
tack and cornmeal, at least until the caravan reached buffalo
country. And each day the men eyed the twenty head of sheep.

It was a three-day march from Muddy Creek along the Missouri River on to the Kaw River where stood the shanties of the
Kaw Indian Agency, short sod hovels that looked as if they had

been pushed up from the ground, rather then built of earth themselves. They were an anticlimax after having passed the empty buildings of what remained of old abandoned Fort Osage. At the Kaw Agency the great muddy river rolled off on her climb to the north. The men crossed the junction of the Blue River and the Republican, a coming together that formed the Kaw, and began their trek to the northwest, following the Republican. When that watershed twisted almost directly west away from them, the caravan struck out overland toward the Platte River.

On the afternoon of Thursday, May 23, the men finally reached the forks of the Platte. Some were jubilant—for in the hazy, shimmering distance, they believed they could at last make out the low blue belt that promised the Rocky Mountains. That night the men camped in small groupings around fires built with buffalo wood, and cooked their meals before the sun ran from the sky. Most of the men turned in early as they had become accustomed to doing on the journey. The five men of the first watch took up their stations as the camp grew quiet with the rhythmic waves of snoring. After about two hours the second watch was awakened by the first and assumed its solitary vigil. These men later awakened their counterparts and the third watch began.

Sir William accepted every duty assigned him by Campbell, including the task of acting as Captain of the Guard. To him fell the lot of watching over those men who had been elected by each watch to be their officer. Each night he would awaken and take a stroll through the darkness to check upon the five men who guarded the camp during each watch. They could not move about here in Indian country. Such movement would make a man an easy target for a sniper. Instead, each of the guards on each watch had to sit in one place during his duty. Every half hour the watch officer would sing out with "All's well!" and would wait for the same response from the four other men to assure himself of their wakefulness.

Stewart awoke, restless and anxious. They were closing in on the great mountains. The shimmering sunset behind the faint blue line on the horizon had told him that the evening before. And yet, Campbell had told him they were still a little less than half the distance to rendezvous. With each day there was a growing excitement among the men as well as for Stewart himself. This great, boundless land was where he had come to taste freedom again, that freedom in answer to what he saw as a kind of slavery, a slavery he was escaping, a slavery imposed upon him by his family back in Scotland.

William slowly pulled the blankets back and stood. Moving as quietly as possible, he brushed Brotherton and stopped. His friend merely rolled over and continued his peaceful snoring. Stewart smiled, then stepped out of the tent. The sky was black, without much of a moon to brighten the canopy of stars. He sucked in a long breath of the chill late-night air. He wondered if the water in those mountain streams would taste as good as this air.

Silently he pushed toward the first post. As he drew near the man sitting near some of the animals, William saw the figure turn at the sound of his approach. "Good morning," his whispered.

"Good mornin'," came the quiet response.

"Perhaps I should say, 'good night,'" Stewart said.

"Yes, sir," the man replied. "A black'un it is."

Stewart stalked on toward the next station, where the officer of the guard should be. He could see the dark form before he heard the man singing to himself, singing softly, perhaps to ward off the sleep that always seemed to come like a thief to men who must sit still for so long. William stopped and listened carefully so that he would not disturb the man's song.

Down in the cane-brake, close by the mill,
There lived a yellow girl, her name was Nancy Till.
She knew that I loved her, she knew it long,
I'm going to serenade her and I'll sing this song.

Come, love, come—the boat lies low.
She lies high and dry on the Ohio.
Come, love, come—won't you come along with me?
I'll take you down to Tennessee.

The guard stopped singing after the verses and merely hummed the tune. Stewart eased toward him and was almost on the man before the hunter turned in his direction. "Good night," William whispered.

"Hello, sir." The young man looked a little embarrassed. "I didn't hear you comin' 'til you was close-up on me. Sorry."

"That is quite all right, son," William responded. "I don't

mind finding a man awake on his watch, no matter how he keeps himself awake." He knelt beside the big youth. "Are you from this place called Tennessee?"

"Oh, no, sir," he whispered hoarsely. "I'm from Cain-Tuck—Kentucky, that is."

"A beautiful place, I imagine."

"Oh, yes, sir. Very beautiful. Hills all wooded an' just waitin' for a fella what to come 'long an' hunt hisself somethin' to eat." He looked upward. "Sky out here nice an' purty—but back in Cain-Tuck, sky even purtier, sir."

"Sounds much like my own home, son," William observed. "The rolling, wooded hills."

"Yes, sir. I'm sure your home is purty as the one I remember my own self."

"Sounds as if you miss it, home I mean to say."

He looked down at his knees. "Yes, sir. That I do."

Stewart swallowed hard. "These are times I sorely miss my own home, son."

"Good night, sir," said the Kentuckian, as William walked away.

"Good night."

Stewart penetrated farther into the inky darkness, trying to pick out the clumps of sage and bunch-grass so that he would not stub his toe or make any noise. A large lump loomed in front of him, at first almost inseparable from the clumps of vegetation across the plain. Then the Scotsman discerned that the lump was the form of a man sitting on the ground. As he drew nearer it looked as it the man's head was slung between his shoulders. Stewart stopped suddenly and listened. Then he was certain.

"The goddamned bugger is asleep!" he muttered angrily.

Stewart stomped up to the guard and began to tap the man on the small of his back with the toe of his boot. Still the sleeping guard did not awaken, merely muttering something groggily before he went back to snoring. Now the Scotsman was angry and gave the man a swift, sound kick.

Hickerson Nute rolled to the side with the force of the blow and jerked to his feet. "Goddamn you bastard!" he shouted.

"I see now that you have awakened," William remarked calmly.

"Just who the hell are you to come an' kick a man?" Nute demanded, bristling forward.

Stewart was not to be bullied. He stepped forward until he was

almost at the large man's chest. "I am the Captain of the Guard, sir."
He watched the man's shoulders sag a little, but was still watchful of
the mule-tender. "And you, you have been caught sleeping on duty.
A grievous error on your part, young man."

He pointed back to the ring of tents up the rise, watching
Hickerson rub his ass where the boot had landed. "I suggest
you take your sore arse and go sleep where you are supposed
to sleep. Back there in camp. Not out here where all our lives
depend on your wakefulness."

"Yeah," Nute responded. "I'll do just that. An' I'll settle this
with you come daylight."

"We will talk of this in the morning, sir," William said flatly.

"No goddamned fancy rich bastard gonna tell Hickerson
Nute what he gonna do or ain't gonna do."

"I am afraid that I might become angry should you stay here
any longer." Stewart began to circle the American. "I suggest
you return to camp now and continue your slumber."

"I'll see you to the mornin'," Nute snarled.

"Yes. Then we shall talk about your three walks—and the
monetary penalty to be imposed upon you."

"You gonna do what?"

"As I have said," Stewart began, "we shall see in the morning. Good night, sir."

"Goddamned fancy, bastard assholes." Nute finally
stomped away, grumbling. "Thinkin' they better'n us anyways . . ."

William watched the tall man disappear into the edge of
darkness and sat down on the spot left by the sleeping guard.
The ground was still a little warm. He would assume the rest of
the watch, and he would take up the matter of penalty enforce-
ment with the offender in the morning. He smiled. If these
men only knew the discipline needed in battle. That Kentucky
boy probably had some idea. And through Stewart's head
strolled the words of the song.

Come, love, come—the boat lies low.
She lies high and dry on the Ohio.
Come, love, come—won't you come along with me?
I'll take you down to Tennessee.

He was groggy when Brotherton nudged him awake. Stewart opened his eyes wearily and looked out the flaps of the tent.
"Another long night, friend?"

"Yes, my dear Brotherton," he replied. "Found one asleep on his watch." He rose and sat on the edge of his blankets. "It feels as if I just put my head down on the pillow."

"Perhaps you did," Brotherton remarked. "Breakfast is ready. If you tarry, the rest of the mess won't leave you much to eat."

"That is quite all right." He rubbed at his eyes and yawned. "I do not have much of an appetite this morning."

"Come on, at least have some coffee."

"Now that, my friend, does sound like an inviting offer."

They ambled out to the small, smoky fire and sat on the ground with the rest of their messmates. Christy handed Stewart a steaming mug of black coffee. The Scotsman held it between his hands, savoring both the aroma and the blazing warmth it gave to his hands to fight off the damp, morning chill. Finally he began to sip at the thick brew. Over the edge of the cup his gaze wandered about the camp, almost with a purpose. Then he spotted the one whom he believed was the offender.

"I will be right back," he excused himself.

"Problems?" Campbell inquired as Stewart walked toward the sleepy guard.

"No, sir," he responded. "No problem I can't handle."

William strode purposefully over to the group of hunkered, huddled men gathered about the smoky remnants of their breakfast fire. He peered closely at the men's faces in the gray predawn light.

He circled, watching each man in turn look up at him, then gaze back down at his tin cup full of morning coffee. Finally Stewart stopped opposite the guard he had found asleep.

"You, sir," he said quietly. "You!"

Nute raised his head, feeling the others' eyes fixed in curious stares upon him, and let the blanket fall back away from his head. "You talkin' to me?"

"That I am." Stewart stepped forward so that he was right behind another of the offender's messmates. "You were found asleep on watch last night."

"So . . . what of it?" Nute guffawed. "Man needs a little sleep. Ridin' all day—pullin' them goddamned mules along. Man needs himself a little sleep."

"Yeah," laughed Obahdiah Redman, who sat next to his friend. He glared up at Stewart. "What you got to say to that, Cap'ain?"

"I would say simply that such a man is a coward . . ."

Nute shot to his feet with Redman at his side. Obahdiah held his friend's arm tightly. "Hick don't like bein' called a coward, Cap'ain."

"Such a man is no better than a coward," Stewart persisted. "He would sacrifice his own life and the lives of all of his fellow travelers for the sake of a little extra sleep." He watched Nute wrestle slightly with Redman who was holding him back.

"Hickerson don't like bein' called a coward," Obahdiah repeated. "He just got sleepy." He grinned. His face sobered when he saw the look of anger on Nute's face. "You want a piece of this fancy one's ass, eh?"

Redman watched Nute nod silently. "I wonder if he's any good with a knife, Hick?" He turned to look at the Scotsman. "You any good with a knife, Cap'ain?"

"A dirk, perhaps." Stewart saw some of the other men quickly spread away from the circle. "And after I am finished, and if you are still alive, you will walk for three days!"

"I ain't walkin' nowhere but over you!" Nute roared. "Just 'cause I was sleepin', you ain't made me think you can make me walk."

"Walk you will," Stewart said firmly.

"I'll gut you first before I have to walk," Nute spat.

Stewart pulled aside the left flap of his coat to expose the handle of the long dirk. "Perhaps you should reconsider this. You will walk for three days—and forfeit five dollars of your pay."

"Won't do no such thing!" Nute shouted. He lunged at Stewart, but Redman yanked him back.

Stewart's right hand shot to the handle of the dirk and waited for a cue to pull it free from its sheath. "Three walks, sir. Beginning today. No man's sleep is worth the life of his fellows. No man—"

"Just what the hell is going on here?" Campbell demanded as he rushed up with Christy and Brotherton at his side. Vasquez was close behind them.

"I am forced to discipline a guard who was caught asleep last night," Stewart answered quietly.

Campbell looked about him, noticed the rest of the men swarming into a tight circle. "You say this man was sleeping on his watch?"

"That is correct, sir," William answered, his eyes never leaving Nute's.

"Is that true?" Campbell turned to address Hickerson.

Redman turned to Nute and saw the anger in Hickerson's eyes. He knew his friend's temper.

"Hick," he whispered. "You gotta let it be. Just let it drop for now. We gotta get to the mountains. Got us a job to be doin'." He continued to watch his friend until Nute finally looked over at him. "That's right. Just simmer down an' we make it to the mountains first."

"Then I have 'im?" Hickerson snarled, in a whisper.

"Yeah, then you can have 'im."

"Is it true that you fell asleep during your watch?" Campbell demanded, his voice more powerful.

"Make him walk," grumbled a mule-tender named Holmes. "I don't want no man goin' to sleep watchin' out for my ass."

Other men muttered their disapproval of Nute's actions.

Nute stared wildly at the more than forty irritated men, hoping he would find some support among them. But there was no hope of that. He would have to wait until they reached the mountains. Until the rendezvous. He wanted to gut the son of a bitch here and now. But he would never make it to Stewart. He would have to wait.

"I s'pose I was dozin' off some," he mumbled.

"And what fine have you imposed, William?" Campbell inquired.

"What was declared to be the penalty when we undertook this journey," Stewart said, glaring at Hickerson Nute. "Three days' walk—and five dollars forfeiture of pay."

"So be it," Campbell declared, and turned to walk away.

"Sir!" Redman called out to Campbell. He waited until Robert Campbell turned to face him. "Don't you think that penalty be a lil' stiff for a man's first crime?" He smiled politely at the caravan leader.

"No," Campbell answered flatly. "If I had been Captain of the Guard, the man might be walking all the way to rendezvous!"

Redman felt suddenly deflated. His appeal had not worked. He saw Campbell turn away again. "Sir! I'm thinkin' it be just a lil' unfair this here greenhorn noble-fella givin' orders—tellin' us what to do an' orderin' a man to walk for three days. We all good hands out here. An' we don't have to take none of this shit from no greenhorn fancy fella."

"You're saying you are not going to take orders from a *greenhorn*?" Campbell inquired, stepping close to Redman.

"That's right." He backed up a step and lamely tried to smile. "Cain't see how we should. We all better'n him out here anyways. Know what's what out here. Him bein' just some for-eign-fella anyways."

"A *greenhorn*, you say?" Campbell said mockingly.

"That's right." Redman looked around at the gathered men for approval. Some of them nodded.

"A *greenhorn* he might be to some," Campbell snapped, and took another step forward until he was almost on top of Red-man. He gestured toward the expanse of rolling hills to the west. "A *greenhorn* in prairie travel, perhaps." Then his arm dropped. "But this *greenhorn*, as you call him, is a veteran of many commands, many battles on the continent of Europe. A true hero of the battle of Waterloo, where time and again he rode into the face of stout rifle and cannon fire to lead his men into battle himself. He was not content to stay behind and di-rect his men. Never did he ask of a man something he himself would not do."

Campbell watched a lot of the men turn to stare at Stewart. "A hero of that battle that spelled the end to Napoleon in France. A *greenhorn?*" He peered closely at Redman. "He has faced death more often than you have taken a piss, I'd wager!"

Laughter rippled through the crowd of men. Redman ner-vously eyed the crowd, glanced up at Stewart, then over at Nute before his gaze dropped to the ground.

Watching Redman, Campbell waited until the laughter sub-sided before he addressed the man again. "And I dare say, had your friend here pulled his knife on Sir William, there would have been much blood shed—your friend's."

"Maybe he ain't a greenhorn after all, sir. But that still don't give him the right—"

"He has my orders!" Campbell snapped. "My orders! And what he says in regard to the guard of this camp each night—whatever Sir William says—is law! Any man who disagrees, any man who has problems with that, he can start walking now! All the way back to St. Louis!" He glared at all of the men in the circled throng. "Do I make myself clear?"

He waited until there were murmurs of assent. "Sir William has commanded men on the field of battle. He has watched many fine young men die around him. And he has killed many a man on that field of battle. He well knows the need for disci-pline—and if we are to arrive at rendezvous for those trappers with our supplies and hair intact, then this camp will be run with such military discipline. Do I make myself understood?"

Campbell again scanned the group of men, most of whom were no older than he. Most were bigger than he was, perhaps stronger.

"He won't have no trouble from me," one of Redman's messmates remarked.

"Me neither," another commented as the throng of men began to voice their general agreement.

"Then I see we have no argument with the penalty for sleeping on guard duty?" Campbell said.

"No, sir," several of the workers answered.

"That's good." His voice was somewhat quieter, but remained firm. "I would hate to think of someone falling asleep who has to watch out for my hair!"

"Won't happen again, will it, fellas?" the man named Holmes asked of those around him. "Will it, now?" He glanced at Redman and Nute. "Don't think none of us wants a fella what goes off to sleep when he's s'posed to be watchin' the camp. Can't have that happenin'."

"Won't happen again," Redman finally said, feeling himself overwhelmed. "Will it, Hick?" he said to his silent partner.

"No," Nute whispered, glaring at the Scotsman. "It won't happen again." He wondered if the nobleman was really any good with the dirk. If Stewart was indeed good with the weapon, it would have been a good test of Hickerson's skill. It had been a long time since he'd had a good fight with sharp blades. Most of the time, his type of killing required him to sneak up on someone and slit the man's throat. Not a real fight of steel and cunning and strength and blood.

"Then we are in full agreement," Campbell said. "We have wasted much time here. Finish your breakfast and coffee, then get the animals rounded up and packed. Thirty minutes and we're breaking camp!"

Campbell turned on his heel and stalked off toward his tent. Stewart remained a moment more to stare at Nute. He knew it was not finished between him and the big American. Hickerson pushed Redman's hands away from his arm. "Ain't gonna pack no animals today—"

"You will pack them," William interrupted, "and walk beside them for the day. Tonight you will unpack them. Tomorrow you will pack them again and walk beside them. For three days you will walk while the men you might have sacrificed ride."

"Right," added Holmes. "We'll be watching you, Nute. You're a lucky man it wasn't Campbell who caught you sleeping. He'd have made you walk all the way into rendezvous camp."

Stewart turned and walked back to his tent with Brotherton and Christy.

Vasquez looked at Holmes. "You have things in your hands, all right?" he asked in his thick accent.

"Yeah," Holmes said. "We got things under control over here now. Things be fine with all of us here."

Nineteen

The giant felt the land change as the days stretched long, the rivers ran full and muddy, the streams thrashed with snowmelt. He squinted at the glare of sun burning through the morning mist and drew a clean breath, the air fresh with the changes in the land, scented with the mountains. He was running lean now, like the deer, avoiding people, eating up miles, living off the land as though he owned it.

The young one he sought must be like himself, going wherever he wanted. With whomever he wanted. Not answering any call but his own, working for no man but himself. Emile Sharpe smiled as he broke into a run just to feel his muscles flex, his sinews stretch and contract with the freedom of movement. His moccasins seemed to make him lightfooted and he knew he was quieter than a deer as he ran, quieter than an antelope. Was his prey as good a woodsman, was he strong now with the freedom? He must be strong, yes. Ezra's son, yanking and tearing his existence out of the brutal wilderness. Perhaps young Paddock was some better than those Frenchmen who had contracted for his death. Men like LeClerc lined their silk purses with the profits brought them by the toil and deaths of other men.

The giant stopped and leaned on his long rifle, his breath coming heavy now in his lungs. The scent of the mountains was strong now, laced with pine-bark and spruce, the evergreen aroma he remembered. Strong now in his nostrils, almost as strong as the fear he had smelled in many of those he had killed. Young Paddock would be a particular victory for him.

Perhaps he would be able to smell the fragrance of real nobility on the lone, mountain trapper he hunted. Not the perfume of the rich dandies and noblemen of St. Louis, but the true and unmistakable fragrance of a man in his element, answering to no other—a king over his life and destiny.

At least until he, Emile, found him. The young had been lord over his own destiny. Until now. For the giant knew where Josiah would be this fine spring. He would find him and smother that noble flame. Perhaps, he smiled, as his breathing smoothed, the real pleasure of victory would be in smelling the lordly fragrance for a moment before he replaced it with the foul stench of fear and death.

Yes, that was the moment he sought, as he hefted his rifle and loped toward the mountains, to the place where he knew Josiah Paddock would be, to the place by the river where Ezra's son would draw his last breath. There, in that shining mountain wilderness he would blow out that single candle, snuff out the flame that had glowed for so long in those high and terrible places.

May. Thornbrugh had said it was May already. May and with it the longer days, shorter nights. The big Englishman always kept track of such things. Bass smiled, thinking about those pleasant days at Fort Vancouver.

Thornbrugh asked Bass to lay over one more day while he arranged for horses for the trip back to Fort Nez Perce on the Walla Walla. It was one more day running through his fingers like the sands through an hourglass. Time with each grain, lost and never to be recovered. There was always the unsettling feeling, like a slow nausea, that told him he had to seek relief. The pain in his soul seemed healed now. But the gaping wound in his heart still ached. It must be salved. Rendezvous and shining times would take care of that, he thought. There he would no longer be tormented by the aching loneliness for her. Could he, would he, ever be able to return to the Crow? To his brother-man, Arapooesh? Ultimately, he decided, it would not matter. He would have to make it so that it just did not matter.

Thornbrugh came up with three horses McLoughlin let them use for the trip back up the Columbia. Three small Indian ponies which they placed on the barge and ferried over to the south bank of the river along with four other men. On the brief trip across the waters of the mighty river, Thornbrugh told Bass of the magnificence of these spring brigades: the spectacle as they left for the wilderness beyond; the pageantry McLoughlin enjoyed in the annual dispatching of those men to the far reaches of the Northwest.

"Those French, these voyageurs—a very, very merry lot they appear to be," Thornbrugh said as the waters lapped at the sides of the barge. He stood at the railing with Titus, watching the fortress slowly drop away behind them. Vancouver, on its high ground above the river, rising from the center of a small pain that overlooked the river, presenting a commanding view of the waters and the barge some two thousand feet back from the Columbia. From down here on the river, the fort looked all the more awesome, all the more powerful and imposing as the barge bobbed and swayed on its line toward the south shore.

"As soon as the oars in the *bateaux* touch the water, those merry little voyageurs set themselves up in song," Jarrell continued. "McLoughlin loves his music. We have stood on the platform in the lagoon, the piper above us on the hill, the notes of the bagpipe washing over the party there for the leave-taking. Then those strong men break into song." He smiled over at Bass. "It was always a joy to McLoughlin, and never ceases to raise his spirits. There seems so little these days to raise those spirits any more."

Jarrell sighed. "When the boats are taking their leave, there is a genuine smile on the good doctor's face. He is a Canadian, after all. He has always enjoyed the colorful leave-taking of the bright flotillas."

As they neared the south shore, Thornbrugh looked back at the fort. "In earlier years, John was wont to ride out with the northern, overland brigades for a few days—some hundred miles or so, Scratch. He did so enjoy those brief sojourns. Such a beautiful sight—the doctor with his dark-skinned Margaret at his side atop our finest horses, she arrayed in her very finest, brightest colors. Ah!"

He leaned against the railing, reminiscing. "The French and their little boats. I, sir—prefer the full rigging of a fast schooner that plies the oceans. A matter of man against the water and wind. At full sail, running close-hauled before the wind—that is a sight for a man's eyes."

"Never seen the ocean," Bass commented. "Didn't know me

no better, thinkin' I heard Vancouver was on the ocean. Thought I'd see the ocean this trip west."

"Aye," Jarrell continued, his eyes wistful, "a man needs to see the ocean at least once before he dies." His deep voice burst into song.

'Tis advertised in Boston, New York and Buffalo,
Five hundred brave Americans, a-whaling for to go.

Singing, blow, ye winds in the morning,
And blow, ye winds, high-o!
Clear away your running gear,
And blow, ye winds, high-o!

They send you to New Bedford, that famous whaling port,
And give you to some land-sharks—to board and fit you out.

They tell you of the clipper ships a-going in and out,
And say you'll have five hundred sperm before you're six months out.

It's now we're out to sea, my boys, the wind begins to blow,
One half the watch is sick on deck, the other half below.

Then comes the running rigging which you're all supposed to know.
'Tis "Lay aloft, you son of a bitch, or overboard you go!"

The skipper's on the quarter-deck a-squintin' at the sails.
When up aloft the look-out sights a school of whales.

Now clear away the boats, my boys, and after him we'll travel,
But if you get too near his fluke, he'll kick you to the devil!

Now we've got him turned up, we tow him alongside;
We over with our blubber hooks and rob him of his hide.

Next comes the stowing down, my boys 'twill take both night and day.
And you'll all have fifty cents apiece on the 190th lay.

*And when our old ship is full, my boys, and we don't give a
damn,
We'll bend on all our stu'nsails and sail for Yankeeland.*

*When we get home, our ship made fast, and we get through
our sailing.
A winding glass around we'll pass and damn this blubber-
whaling.*

"Sounds to me like'n there be a good bunch of niggers to
stand at your side. Somethin' I'll have to see me afore I pass on
over," Bass commented.

"There is something I myself have to see before I . . . before
I, too, pass on," Jarrell said.

"What's that?"

"Your rendezvous. From all that I have heard, that occasion
must be something to behold. To be in the company of good,
strong men—who daily face the possibility of death. As were
those seamen of the great ships. Yes! Rendezvous must be
quite some experience. With as much noise, and color, and
excitement as a man could want."

"A child's gotta cache him up a full year's worth to ronnyvoo," Bass said. "Get him a full year's worth in his belly afore
he has to take off for the high an' lonesome again."

"After you left the governor's house that night," Jarrell confided, "while John and I stood on the porch watching you leave
for the Hall, he commented to me that the Company would
some day have to attend this rendezvous as a regular practice.
He has been considering this for some time now, and evidently
is formulating some plans in that regard: that one day the Company of Adventurers will indeed come to rendezvous. There,
he said, to meet the American competition head-on, eye to
eye, on that competition's own ground, so to speak. Perhaps as
early as next year."

"Hudson's Bay down to ronnyvoo." Bass clucked. "Now
that'd be somethin' for this child's eyes to be seein'. Jumpin'
Jehosophat! How things is changin' quick 'round 'bout me."

Bass thought about the rendezvous many times on the ride
across the Columbia. It lifted his heart just to think of those
shining times yet to come. There were years left in him yet.
The prospect of living that life few others had chosen gripped
him and gave him strength for the journey ahead. A journey

through the days and weeks that would take him south and east along the Snake River, plotting out in his mind those rivers and landmarks about which Jarrell had instructed him. The old Snake would take him back to his beloved Rockies, the big Stonies of his youth.

Thornbrugh chattered those three days of travel back to the post on the Walla Walla. It was almost as if the Englishman were trying to store up his experiences with this American trapper, neither one knowing if he would ever see the other again.

That evening in the quiet of the Nez Perce sleeping dorm, the two friends talked for a long time, sharing some of their last thoughts before they were to part. Thornbrugh again attempted to entice Scratch into returning to the Vancouver area, perhaps even to settle down along with the others who were leaving the fur trade and setting themselves up on small farms.

"I ain't cut out for it, damnit," Bass muttered, exasperated by Thornbrugh's tenacity.

"Perhaps not yet," Jarrell replied. "But you would not be the first to leave the fur trade to settle down and live the rest of your years in one place."

"It just ain't for me, Jarrell."

"Perhaps not yet. As it has been for others. Such beautiful land—a spot I myself might choose for my final home, where my wife and I could live out our days."

Thornbrugh sighed. "It would be down on the French Prairie, some fifty miles south of the Willamette's mouth, near the falls of the river. The place has earned its name from being first settled by a French ex-employee of the Company. In eighteen hundred and thirty Louis LaBonte left us after some six years of service to settle in that beautiful valley. Soon thereafter, Etienne Lucier also left to stake a farm near LaBonte's. Then in thirty-one Joseph Gervais settled down there. He had been up north at Fort Colville until thirty. They make out all right, farming very little, really. It seems they live off the land to feed their families, trapping when they can to buy things at the fort. An easy, comfortable, enviable existence, yes?"

"Maybeso, for some it be."

"But, not for you. Not yet, anyway." Jarrell turned over on his bed and sighed in the darkness. "I can see myself becoming quite the country gentleman before too long. I would grow peas and wheat and barley. Perhaps some Indian corn. Even grapes and apples. We have apples and peaches here. Those beautiful, budding trees in the fort's orchard. The seeds were brought to us from halfway around the world. Apple seeds themselves were brought to us from a young lady in London back in 1826. She wished to have her apples grown in the New World. Captain John Pearson of the good ship, a tall ship, *Cadboro*, had the honor of handing over the precious seeds to Robert Bruce, our Vancouver gardener. John has told me he would stake me to some beef cattle and a milk cow, two brood mares, also. Why, I could even raise some hogs, goats and sheep. Might even talk John out of some of his chickens. What do you think of it?"

Jarrell waited a few silent moments. There was no reply. The Englishman assumed Bass was asleep, and rolled over, closed his eyes.

Scratch smiled in the darkness. Perhaps someday he would settle. Not soon. There was still so much wandering to do, so many different winds blowing him this way and that.

Scratch thought about that in the darkness of the small dorm at Nez Perce. Maybe things could be different. No longer was he being chased by the ghost. Asa had been put to rest. But now the trapper was running after something he could not quite describe, could not quite grasp at yet. Where the haunting of his soul had been something tangible, something to taste and feel and experience, this elusive something was a sought-after vision he held secretly inside his most private place.

Bass was no longer being chased by McAfferty's ghost. Instead, he was the hunter, running after something even more elusive than the ghost, something that haunted his heart. Something that had no name.

On that final, melancholy morning at the Walla Walla post, Jarrell Thornbrugh gripped the trapper's shoulders, making Bass repeat the route he would take east and south toward the Rockies. Then suddenly, the big Englishman hugged him fiercely before he took a step back from the trapper. Thornbrugh smiled somewhat lamely and sped away, leaving Bass alone to mount his pony and pull the other animals behind him out of the gate.

Those first days out of Fort Nez Perce, Scratch traveled

faster, easier than he had when he'd arrived. He was able to cover more ground each day, the earth now clear of snow, the daylight hours becoming longer and longer with each passing sun.

Many times those first days, toiling up the Snake River, his mind played on the route plotted for him by the friend he'd left behind. Bass would follow the Snake River south past the Clearwater, on south past the Salmon, south past the Weiser and the Payette. When the Snake finally curved back east, he would pass the Malade before the river curved north and he would reach the Blackfoot River. There he would take that sixth river north and east until it ran out. From there he would ride overland, east toward the Green River and the rendezvous at its confluence with Horse Creek.

French names for some of those water courses. Named after company trappers. The rest just named by company trappers. The long arm of those Britishers, extending so far to the east, at least until he got to the Green and Horse Creek. Back to the real Rockies, back to American territory.

So, so long ago he had first come to the Rockies, and those three trappers had taken him under their wing. Taught him a lot about the ways of the mountains. Much about the ways of men. When was it? The last time he had seen them? Years gone by so quickly.

Last time seemed to be up near the Three Forks as Bud, Billy and Silas were fixing to head down to trade for whiskey and women at the first post they came to on the big river. He had given the trio his own plews. And never saw them again.

"Others'd tell me as them three made off to St. Louie with my catch an' quit the mountains," he had said often, with a sad shake of his head. *"They must of lost hair down the Missouri or somethin' such."*

There had always been that hidden part of him that couldn't bring itself to admit they had gone under. That tight, hard, guarded place deep within him that kept telling him they had abandoned him and stolen his furs. Only once, when he could finally deny it no longer, had the old trapper finally spoken of one day looking for the three.

"If'n the truth be knowed 'bout it, a time or two I thought real hard on it. Then got me thinkin' 'bout other whatnot. But that ain't to say it ain't been in the back of my head all the time, right there. Thinkin' some day of lookin' them fellas up."

Back there. East. Where it would never be home again.

Never really could be now. But the Rockies. There it was, after all. Back home again. There was still some magic left in those words. He only wished that he would have more to return home to—something more. Someone, perhaps.

Damn! If it hadn't grown into an actual physical ache inside himself by the evening when he reached the Clearwater and decided to camp there. Perhaps it had been a little early to end the day's travel. But there was a restlessness that was not easily salved with the trail. A great, deep empty that yawned open, gaping and bloody—a pain still only a little duller than it had been more than three months before.

It was a young man's world out here. And he, like so many others, had come out here to cling to the richness of his youth, as if those early years in the mountains were something personal, something private, something to be carefully guarded. Where did it say a man had to age before his time?

Titus shook his head again, feeling the braid brush against the side of his cheek. Two fingertips went up to touch the hills and valleys of the crusted hair. Here was youth, he thought. Wearing his hair like this for years. When had he first put it up this way? Something else he could not remember—the same spring he had first taken the Snake gal to his lodge. Again he sighed.

As Scratch stood with his back toward the setting sun, he stared into the east, into the land whence he had come, the land where he had felt that special comfort that comes from a singular love and wholeness. And there was for him a realization that it was a *feeling* as much as it had been a place. It had been a dream he held tightly within himself, a dream as much as it was the soil and the rocks and the trees and the waters. He had tried. Lord knows he had tried, damnit. Tried to turn that feeling, that dream, into reality. And just as he had thought it was about to become real for him—things had come crashing down around his shoulders.

It was so hard to make sense of it all. How a man could hope and pray and wish so much for something—then see it all taken from him. All that time, all those years of cold, lonely nights and bitter, blazing days had told him, had convinced him, he was not asking too much. So he had kept on hoping through the years. Then Bass had found first the boy, and in him found someone he thought would be the first real, true friend who would not desert him. A person he could rely upon until death.

And when Scratch had thought that Josiah had been killed—that hope began to wither inside him. But Josiah had lived. And Bass had found reason to hope once more.

Had he come to want too much? Was it in having his prayers answered with Josiah that Bass came to believe that his prayers would be answered for a woman? She had come to him, the beautiful Indian girl, wanting him, loving him, making him feel strong and young again. And for a while, he thought he had everything that mattered. Yet, in one fell swoop of the axe, it had all come crashing down. Perhaps so: he had wanted too much.

The boy had grown to be like a son to him. A son he had never had. Bass had finally learned patience in the time he had shared with Josiah. Most of all, the need for patience with himself.

And, Waits-by-the-Water. Oh, there had been one woman before—but Scratch had not been ready to love her. The settler's daughter back east had loved him. But he had moved on, those many years ago. He had not been ready until the Crow woman stepped up and took control of that void, that empty place in his heart.

Like poultices, those two people had been for the two noxious wounds in his life. The friend he had never had, and the love he had searched for when he was finally ready, the love that had found him. Son and friend. Woman and friend. The poultices that would draw out the poison in his heart. But where had it gone so wrong? Where was it said to be just or fair that both people would be wrenched out of his life through one single act? Both gone at once. And with both, just about everything else worth living for.

He turned to see that the sun had fallen completely from the sky. Bass went to his robes and stretched out upon them in the cool evening air. It was then that he began to sob quietly, softly, most of the racking pain still held tightly inside. And with the sobbing eventually came the relief of knowing where his trail would lie. The tears finally slowed. And Bass felt a relief from the pain in his knowing that with the coming morning, his trail would no longer take him to rendezvous.

Instead, Scratch would follow this Clearwater east from here, head over the Bitterroots and on east. Forever east until he got back to Absaroka. Home: and always in the right place. There it would remain. In his heart. As the tears dried, the certainty became all the stronger. And with its strength grew his resolve.

He was man enough, his heart was big enough. He could—and he would—forgive the two of them. Perhaps it was to be all the better, he decided that night. He could live out the rest of his days with the two of them, knowing they were happy together. He was strong enough for that. He needed both of them more than he needed his stupid, childish pride. It was such a thing that had driven him away from them. But he was so much more now than that person who had ridden off that dark winter day months ago.

The words began to pour gently over him now. Those words from the old song Hatcher loved so dearly. Ol' Jack Hatcher. His voice quivered and crackled in the darkness as he sang. Last summer when they had the Blackfoot at bay and forted up, Hatcher had died singing the song that seemed so fitting now. So right as the words poured over him.

> I'm just a poor, wayfaring stranger,
> Traveling through this world of woe.
> Yet, there's no sickness, no toil, no danger
> In that bright land to which I go.
>
> I'm going there to see my brother,
> Who's gone before me, that good one.
> I'm just going over Jordan.
> I'm only going over home.
>
> I know dark clouds will gather 'round me,
> I know my way is rough and steep.
> Yet, beautiful fields lie just before me,
> Where God's redeemed their vigils keep.
>
> I'm going there to see my brother,
> Who's gone before me, that good one.
> I'm just going over Jordan.
> I'm only going over home.

His eyes were dry as he finally closed them. The low flames of the small fire licked at the darkness around his camp. There was such a new-found strength that came in knowing that what he was going to do would be the right thing for all of them. If they would take him back as a friend. It was all he could ask anymore of anyone. He could forgive. Truly and without reservations, he could forgive. If they would only forgive him, too.

He would push on in the morning. A faster trail, perhaps a longer trail now. But he knew it would be a more peaceful trail. The sleep that came to overtake Bass was a gentle, rocking peace that he had been lacking in so many, many weeks. Since last he had been in Absaroka. Since last he had been with the both of them. Since last he had felt whole.

For now, the fact that he had finally forgiven himself was enough to carry him on over and back to them. The strength that came from forgiving himself—the one person he would ultimately have to live with all his days—that strength was enough to give him peace.

That night, for the first time in a long time, there came no bad dreams to rob Bass of sleep. No. No more dreams to disturb his slumber. His heart was at peace.

His heart had forgiven him.

It took Bass less than two weeks to climb up the Clearwater and over the mountains down toward the long, north-south valley. He had been here before, he remembered, through the years gone by. Back into his Rockies where there was comfort at being home. By evening he would be down from these foothills and into that valley where he would camp for the night, and in the morning he would strike south and east over the next range until he was south of the Land of Smoking Waters, there to turn east and climb again. Then he would push north into the land of the Sparrowhawk.

"That's God's country, ever there was one, Josiah," he recalled saying to his young partner. *"That be the place God lay claim to if'n he had to settle down."*

He smiled with the warmth of it and nodded his head unconsciously. Comfort washed over him once more. Yes, sir. That was God's country.

"Only most think God stays on t'other side of the Missouri. Some say He's got no place out here. Titus Bass don't feel that way. No, sir. God made this here country for Himself and the likes of us, He did. Sure, there ain't no churches pushin' steeples an' bell towers toward the sky down that valley or any other out here. Damn! Look at them mountains! Them are the house of God He made with His own hand for the likes of us!"

He had cleared the Bitterroots and was on his side of the mountains now. Coming back into familiar territory and heading home. Out of the hills, down into the rich bottomland along the river. And that was when he smelled the smoke.

Bass slid his left leg over and dropped from his pony before tying the string of horses in the trees. Then he crept to the top of the rise. There in the bottom, along the river, were the lodges. Damn! If his luck wasn't getting worse all the time. First he ran onto Blackfeet going west. Now he had to run into them again heading back home.

His fist slammed into the grass. The frustration of it almost made a man want to cry, if not damn near give up. But he could not let himself do that. His heart had cried out in pain far too long to allow him to just give up his ghost now. Not this way.

"Goddamned Blackfeet!" he muttered. "Why them sons of bitches Bug's Boys this far south?"

Bass continued to study the camp, as if something were out of place, something on which he could not place a finger. Something disturbing and unsettling about the camp. Perhaps the horse herd nearby, maybe the way the lodges were thrown up. Something was damned sure off of plumb center here.

The sun would slip behind him in less than an hour. Bass shook his head and thought of another all-night ride to hightail it out of dangerous country. Such seemed to be his lot once more. The cards dealt him now were the same. Blackfeet then. Blackfeet now.

"Damn all the luck!" he muttered, and slammed his fist into the same smashed clump of grass out of sheer fatigue and frustration.

Only reason those Blackfeet down this far south, penetrating this far into these hills, he mused, be the search for buffalo.

"Goddamn!" he repeated the oath. "Maybeso the same sons of bitches I run onto comin' west! If'n that don't take the circle! That'd be the turn of it! Same goddamned redskins again."

Less'n they were Flathead. Yes. The Blackfeet could be driving the Flathead south for the season. Long had they been bitter enemies. Yes. Moving the Flathead . . .

Then something clicked in his head and he rose to his knees within the thick underbrush. That was it! That was what was so damned disturbing to him. He knew something had been wrong. Getting old, you bastard!

Scratch scooted back to his ponies and untied them. He vaulted onto the horse and gave it his heels. As weary as they were, the pack animals followed obediently at a quickened pace. Over that last rise and down the hill toward the camp. He could see some figures turning to look at him in his zig-zagging approach down the slope. Some pointed in his direction now. Some scurried back among the lodges. Others walked slowly out to meet him. Damn, he was addled. Pretty soon he would be able to carry his brains around in a priming horn.

Lord, was he happy to see these brownskins. Flathead! Bass pulled up on the reins some fifty feet from the warriors who had swarmed out to greet him. He stopped his animals and waited until the Indians were close enough to read his sign. *Friend.* He laid the rifle across the tops of his thighs and raised both arms in the air so they could see that his hands were empty, palms out. Now he became sure as he signed for them. Now he could see the way those braves fixed their hair. They were Flathead all right. The lodges had finally made him realize it. They were not set up the way the Blackfeet erected theirs. Blackfoot lodges did not have as much of a slope to the rear of the lodge as these here in the valley.

The warrior in front finally signaled that he, too, was a friend and signed for the trapper to come on in, slowly. Bass tapped the pony's flanks with his heels and was soon surrounded by the escort for the rest of the ride into the encampment.

Near the center of the lodges Scratch slipped from the pony's back and waited for the head man to come greet him. Maybe things weren't going to be all that bad after all. Perhaps his luck was going to get better from here on out. Lord knows, it was about time.

He turned at the sound of the approach of many feet. Bass watched the head man move through the assembled crowd. The chief was tall, almost as tall as Josiah would be. And he looked distantly familiar, too. He could not place him—but this old boy looked like someone he had run onto before.

The chief came up and presented a hand to Bass, who realized that this Indian had been around whitemen to have picked up that particular custom. The chief spoke in his native tongue until Bass finally put a hand up to stop him.

"Hold on," Bass said. "Don't know me no Flathead. Never did. Not that I ain't willin' to try some. But . . . you talk you any English—any white talk?"

"We talk good," the chief answered.

"Well, now." Bass was surprised. "You talk somethin' we can understand ourselves with. Good."

"Yes, I know some so of your tongue," the chief said. "Other whitemen call me Big Blue. My paint. You American. Not French like many others. It is good. Like English. Better on my mouth than this French. Jocco . . . I like American talk better. You welcome to camp. We make home for you."

"Why, I thank you kindly. I was hopin' you was gonna be sayin' that. Could use me some supper an' a place to set my ponies out for grass. We eat an' then we can palaver. Make big talk. Maybeso, a good smoke, too. Been some time since last I had me a good smoke. Damn!"

"What this *damn*?"

"Hell, it's cussin'." Bass grinned. "Don't suppose you Flathead ever cuss, now do you? Talk good English, an' you don't know how to blow a blue streak? Cuss—I mean?"

"Don't know this damn cuss, I don't," the chief said. "Damn is what?"

"Damn—it's good to see me some friendly Injuns again!" Bass smiled widely now.

The chief smiled along with him. "We eat and smoke. We talk, too. Then we damn and cuss!"

"Sounds just fine with this ol' boy," Bass remarked as the crowd behind the chief parted.

A young woman appeared at the Indian's shoulder, perhaps no older than Waits-by-the-Water. No more than seventeen summers. And her presence suddenly twisted something inside him. She was studying him closely and making him all the more nervous for it. But there was something strangely familiar about her.

Finally she stepped closer to Bass and peered into his eyes. Another older warrior came up behind her to scrutinize the whiteman's face. Then this second warrior talked some Flathead with the chief.

Bass felt uncomfortable. He wondered just what the hell was going on now. Here was this young woman studying him, measuring him, and the old boy behind her talking Flathead with the chief.

"What's?" He waited until the two warriors had finished talking and the chief had turned back to the trapper. "What's goin' on here? Don't know me . . ."

"I know now I see you before."

"That right? Where's that? You see me before—I mean?"

"Valley of fight with *Pieds Noir*. Last season of dry grass. South of here. We fight. Whitemen fight. Kill many *Pieds Noir*."

"*Pieds* . . . Blackfeet?"

"Yes. Blackfeet how you say. Many we kill with whiteman."

"Ronnyvoo? You was down to ronnyvoo?"

"Yes. How you say big white camp in season of dry grass. This . . . *ronnyvoo*?"

"Yeah! You was there? I'll be damned!" Maybe all this was going to make sense after all. "You seen me down there, huh?"

"I think," the chief answered. "I not only one see you there."

"Oh?" he asked. "Some of your fellas here . . . braves down there for the big fight see me, too?"

"No. Not them. Her."

The chief slipped an arm over the young woman's shoulders. She stepped forward and continued to gaze into Scratch's eyes.

"Her?"

"She say her father she know you from big camp."

Bass peered down into her face. The features were not extra noticeable. He had seen so many young women over all the years—but, still, there was something disturbing about her eyes.

"She say I know her?"

"She say she know you," the chief answered.

"How she know me?"

"She say know you—and your *friend*. Last season to big white camp. Your friend—she . . . she say her man."

"Now—hold on a minute!" It was buzzing too quickly for him to make sense of it all. "She sayin' a friend of mine she knows from ronnyvoo. Right?"

"That is right."

"An' she say my friend is her man?" Bass looked down into the wide eyes and images rose up in his memory.

"Yes. She say your friend her man."

"I know. I know what she sayin' now," Bass said.

He remembered her now. A bright, moonlit night beneath the Tetons in Pierre's Hole last summer. The boy had been sliced up a bit in a fracas over some stupid horseplay that almost cost another man his life. Then some young girl—this young girl—had come looking for him.

It was a foggy memory at first. Foggy at best. Everything was out of focus because Bass had been damned near dead drunk that night. But the girl's eyes had finally reminded him of that evening when she had come looking for Josiah. This was the one who had taken Paddock back to their place in the trees that night. Bass had merely passed out. But he remembered those eyes.

"What she say of you, it is right?" the chief asked.

"Yeah. She's right. I know her."

"And what she say about your friend. He is her man?"

"I don't know about that now." Bass was confused.

The chief turned to address the young woman. Without hesitation or a word spoken in reply, she dashed through the crowd. Her father stayed with the chief.

"She says this friend of mine be her man," Bass continued. "I don't know 'bout that, not rightly. I only know she knowed my friend back to ronnyvoo."

He dropped his gaze to stare at his moccasins. He was hoping Josiah hadn't gotten himself into a bunch of trouble with these folks. Maybe the young gal was married up to some warrior, something like that. Indian morality had some mighty strange bends, like the twisting, tortured course of the Snake River. But one thing a man could hold to though: that morality would not be violated, no matter how strong or how sweet the temptation. Hell! And all he was wanting was a little grub, some grass for the ponies, and a fire to curl up beside.

"She say she sure 'bout all this, huh?" He was sure already.

"She sure." The chief turned as the crowd behind him bustled and jostled again, making way once more for the young woman. "She say you be sure when you see."

"See what?"

Then he knew. Bass knew what she was going to show him. "Oh . . . Lordee!" he exclaimed softly as she came up to present the cradleboard to the white trapper. "It . . . be a . . . baby."

Scratch took the cradleboard and turned it clumsily in his arms. He was awkward at such a thing. Gently he pulled a flap of the deerskin back from the infant's face. There were the same curly locks. The locks not as dark as its mother's black hair. More brown than anything. And with all them curls, too. Just like Josiah's. At last it was making complete sense, coming home to him now. The child's skin was not as bronze as his mother's either. Chances were pretty damned good this baby did have a white father. He already knew for sure before he asked the question.

"She say who?"

"She say your friend." The chief looked over at Bass and smiled. "She say your friend her man. His child."

"My friend's, huh?" he repeated quietly. "A girl, or boy?"

"Man-child, this one."

"A boy, huh?" Bass was suddenly filled with the joy of it all. A real, honest-to-goodness, genuine joy that made his heart giddily leap and dance while holding this infant who was not more than two months old.

"A boy," he repeated. "Yes. Josiah has him a *boy.*" Now Paddock had him two wives and a child.

Bass smiled widely and pulled the deerskin further from the child's face. His old partner now had everything Bass had ever wanted for himself. A wife and a son of his own. Damn! What a lucky bastard Paddock was. But, Titus could be genuinely happy for him. That he could do.

"A *boy,*" he spoke quietly, almost reverently as the tears welled in his eyes.

"Josiah has him a *boy!*"

Twenty

Scratch pulled out of the Flathead camp as their lodges were coming down for the day's travel. He was not alone in the early light of the new day. Behind him, with the pack animals, were the woman and the child, Looks Far Woman and her son. Josiah's son.

They climbed south and east over the hills into that big hole of a valley, following a river that would run into the Jefferson before it raced toward its junction at the Three Forks. He calculated this would be the shortest route—although the most dangerous. From the Jefferson he would move east, avoiding the Blackfeet, ever moving toward Absaroka. Over the days and nights, Bass began to learn the Flathead tongue so that he could teach her what she could learn of English.

"Joze-ze-awww."

She kept repeating that young man's name since the night he

had come onto the Flathead camp. She had been catching on to the whiteman's tongue quickly over the last few days. Better than a week since she had turned on her pony to wave a final farewell to her parents and sisters, and the Flathead band moving south toward rendezvous.

Rendezvous—where a small part of him itched to be headed. But that larger, more urgent, more immediate part of him drove him on east, east along a trail of uncertainty. Not the first time he'd taken such a trail. He smiled, knowing it would probably not be the last. Whereas the way west to Vancouver had been a trail taken for the soul, this one had become a trail traversed for his heart.

"Joze-ze-awww."

The boy had him an instant family now. Two wives and a son. Pretty good work for a fella's second winter in the mountains. Bass could be happy for him. He had forgiven himself and could be happy for Josiah. In some way, Scratch was a member of that family, too. That had already happened in his heart weeks before Looks Far Woman had recognized the old trapper. She knew the two were tied to each other in some way.

"Pawww-duck."

She had eventually learned the rest of the young trapper's name. Bass taught by saying a word and making Looks Far Woman repeat it. Scratch spoke it again slowly, and she repeated it just as slowly in imitation. The chief had told Bass the young gal's name, both in English and in Flathead, so Titus had begun to teach the girl her own name—in English.

"Looooks Fawwr Wooman."

The words sounded strange on her tongue. Sitting in the warm light of the small fire they shared each evening after the long trail, she repeated the words he taught her. She nuzzled the young infant, let the boy suckle at her swollen breast. Josiah's boy. Titus watched with a peaceful glow spreading inside him each time. The young woman was not ashamed before the whiteman. For her, it was natural to untie the side of her dress or deerskin blouse and bare her firm, milk-laden breasts.

Scratch watched the mother and child, his own amazement never ceasing at this life-giving feast, his own wonder never diminished at this miracle of life passing from her body to the infant's.

She often watched those eyes of the old trapper, with their own soft glow of peace and contentment behind them. And she patiently repeated the English words for him, making the sounds as best she could. Repeating the words for camp gear, horse trappings, and clothing.

At times Bass would watch her unnoticed as she murmured quietly to the infant while suckling the child through the night or at their morning breakfast fire. Other times he would sit where he could not be seen to watch Looks Far take the cradleboard to the streams each day to wash the excrement off the child and his deerskin wrappings. The young woman cooed and murmured to the child happily as she bathed the boy, cleaned the cradleboard, and packed new moss around the child's genitals before re-wrapping the ties that securely bound the infant. Sometimes she sang softly to him as the cradleboard swung and rocked gently in the early summer breezes from its place in a tree above her.

She was good with a knife, good at butchering the game Bass brought in for their meals. The old trapper would sit by the fire, sharpening the knives he carried, or cleaning the rifles and pistols, watching her cook and scamper about the campsite, all the time chattering to him or the infant. What a warming sense of completeness it gave him to watch this young mother and her infant—Josiah's son.

Bass favored a route south of the Land of Smoking Waters, hoping to avoid the Blackfeet and their roving bands of thieves and war parties. For their safety—the two he watched over—he led them south and east. Up into the thick stands of pine and alder, then across the snows until the valley finally lay before them. Here the Snake River began its mighty race to the Columbia and the western ocean. The three beasts, the pilot knobs, were no longer to his right, steering him, guiding him onward. Now they lay at his back as he led his small party toward the rising sun into the mountains that formed the eastern border of the beautiful hole. As soon as they broke over these hills, it would seem all downhill as they headed almost due north again to Absaroka and the home of the Sparrowhawks.

There would be so many old friends, at least familiar faces, getting close to rendezvous by now. But it ceased to itch at him any more. Bass only thought about it through the days, into the nights. Those men, the great numbers who had hired on with the companies. The fewer still, like himself, who worked for no man, laboring through the mountains and down into the valleys toward rendezvous where they would be resupplied for the coming year, paying with the profit of a hard year's labor in the freezing waters, after fighting the mind-numbing cold and the flesh-raking grizzlies and the Indians, to extract their beaver dollars from these western mountains.

There would come another year for him, for him and the young trapper. They could go to rendezvous in 'thirty-four. He hadn't missed one in . . . it was many years, anyway. But the two of them would trap this fall and then again into the spring. And the partners would just have to make sure they had enough lead and powder to make it through two years now. They would just have to do without the sugar, and coffee, and . . . raisins.

He smiled in the remembering —warm with the memory of '32 and raisins. The small, shriveled fruit he had given to Arapooesh that night late last fall when the whole tin disappeared very quickly with the child-like appetites of the Crow. Yes, he figured. He and the young trapper would just have to make it for another year. And he was certain they could in Absaroka.

From the position of the sun behind them, Bass calculated they had been riding about four hours since they had taken a short, midday break. Looks Far had gone into the bushes and he had sat with his back against a tree, holding the cradleboard. So much had he wanted to ask her to unwrap the child, to take the infant out of its restricting cradle—so he could hold this little miracle of life. He wanted to bounce the boy on his knee and study his tiny fingers and toes. So many times Bass had wished to ask her to hold the infant himself after the child had finished suckling at her breast. But, he had stayed his words. Josiah should be the first to hold his child, to hold his son. Scratch would wait.

They topped the ridge and came to the edge of the trees where he signaled the young woman to halt behind him. There below was a wide, open meadow, stretching away from the bordering trees. The creeks raced toward the small river below him. Perhaps on the other side of this draw, down and across this valley, up and into the trees and the higher ground once more, perhaps there he would choose a place for camp. He did not have to push now. There was no particular rush when you were going home at last. He could enjoy another evening by the cheery fire watching the young mother play and cuddle and give her son suckle.

Something caught his eye. He studied the valley closely. Something moved. Something was down there.

He dropped to the right side of the pony, then began nudging and coaxing the animals backward into the trees. He signaled for the woman to stay put and to remain quiet. He hoped the infant was asleep. The baby's cry now would alert whoever was down there.

Along the top of the ridge he scooted in his prairie-hen waddle, staying to the timber. Then he stopped after about seventy yards and poked through the branches and limbs. Out of the corner of his right eye he caught the movement again and turned in its direction. There they were. The black shapes moving through the trees, heading down—down toward the water. Black shadows back in the dark timber. Pieces of brief light and color between the play of sun and shadow—back in the trees.

Elk. Gotta be elk down there. Heading from their beds down to water. Out for some early evening feeding perhaps. Get to the water and feed some before the night comes on. Had to be elk. How many where there? Looked to be a small herd. Maybe a bull and some cows. Maybe some calves, too.

He counted them slowly as the light dappled the shadowy shapes back in the timber. One, two . . . three. . . . He watched them cross the hillside. Four, five, six. . . . They continued down into the bottom of the valley. Seven . . . was there eight? He was not sure. There was meat down there. Good meat.

"Prime doin's for a man," he whispered. And the woman with her baby. They'd have elk for supper. His mouth watered.

The elk would come out of the trees soon. He would just have to stalk carefully and drop a young, tender cow. There—they were just about to come out of the darkness, from the safety of the trees. The old bull would be wary, however. The old bull who carried such a harem with him would have to be a good-sized fella.

Damn! If it . . .

"Goddamn!" he muttered quietly. "They ain't elk!"

He squinted into the late-afternoon sunlight. The first one emerged. No dull colors there—no blond and brown. The first one wore a pale blue coat instead of a furry hide. He had the

cap pulled down over his head. And behind his saddle was a
spotted rump.

Bass shook his head. It just did not figure for him. The first
rider turned and motioned now for the second to come out of
the trees. From the shadows emerged the second horseman,
this one with long, black hair. Indian, for sure. But, it was not a
man at all. There along the side of the pony the second figure
was riding, there below the edge of the capote was the bottom
of her dress and the leggings emerging beneath it. This woman
also rode a spotted-rump pony.

The old trapper was confused with it. What would Nez
Perce be doing this far to the east and south? He could not
imagine that a small group of them would be heading to rendezvous. And they were coming from the wrong direction anyway. They should be coming along from the west, the direction
from which he and the woman and the baby had come. This
was all wrong. They were coming out of Absaroka country.

He stood at the edge of the trees and studied the figures as
they crossed below him, stopped at the wide creek. The man
swung his left leg over and dropped from his pony, looking
around quickly. The woman dismounted and joined the man at
the creek bank. He kept his head up, alert, while the woman
knelt to drink. When she had taken her fill, only then did the
man drop to his knees to taste the cold water.

Bass studied the scene below him. He watched the way the
two of them handled the ponies as they brought the animals to
the bank to drink. He was becoming more and more certain
with every moment. The woman walked as no other woman
could. He had learned her habits, the way she moved, the way
she held herself among the animals, the way she held her head
in the sunlight.

Waits-by-the-Water.

The coat was new. Something she would have made for him,
he supposed. But, it had to be Josiah. The man finally rose to
his feet and removed the fur hat.

Paddock.

He seemed to be walking around well enough now. He had
healed—Bass smiled with the thought. He had healed, and the
young son of a bitch was able to ride again. He watched them
for only a moment more before scooting back into the trees and
skittering along the ridge. What a surprise he would make for
the two of them!

Scratch reached the ponies and the woman, almost bursting

with the news. But he would wait a few minutes to tell her. She would be part of the surprise he planned for Paddock. He gestured for her to remain quiet, then motioned for her to follow him on horseback. They began to pull the animals down through the trees.

When he neared the border of the pines, Bass signaled for her to halt and come alongside him. He motioned toward the figures a couple hundred yards below them and signed for her not to move.

"Stay," he whispered. "I call—you come then. Maybe I come get you."

She nodded obediently atop her pony, shifting the weight of the cradleboard on her shoulders. He smiled at her.

Bass touched the sides of the pony lightly with his heels and set the animal into motion out of the trees. As soon as he shot into the sunlight, he began whooping and hollering at the top of his lungs. "Hoooraw!" he bellowed.

He saw Josiah and the woman suddenly dart back into the circle of ponies. Paddock swung the rifle up and over the back of one of the pack animals. Waits-by-the-Water used the animals for cover, staying within the small group of ponies that milled nervously about her.

The old trapper watched Josiah's head drop as he placed his cheek against the riflestock and swung the muzzle up the hill toward the intruder. Bass knew the joke was over. The boy was a good enough shot at this range.

"*JOSIAH!*" he shouted.

He continued his headlong rush down the hill, holding his rifle aloft with a full extension of his right arm.

"*JOSIAH PADDOCK!*"

He saw the young trapper's head rise from the cheek-piece and study him as he raced toward the circle of animals across the stream.

"*DON'T KILL ME, YOU YOUNG NIGGER!*"

"Bass?"

"You ain't stupid 'nough to shoot your ol' partner, is you?" He brought the pony to a dust-showering halt across the stream from the young man and woman.

"Wh . . . why, no." Josiah pulled the weapon off the pony's back and came around in front of the animal. "That really you, Bass? It truly you?"

"Ain't none t'other, son!"

"Lord! I can't believe it! I mean—I gotta believe it! It's . . . it's really you!" Josiah started to race toward the old trapper.

Bass turned to watch Waits-by-the-Water emerge from the circle of animals some ten feet away from the young trapper. Paddock studied Scratch's eyes and then glanced over at the Crow woman.

"Well, now—son." Bass looked back at Paddock. "You best be believin' it. For sure! Here I is in the stinkin' flesh an' you was ready to put a ball to my meatbag—"

Suddenly Josiah leapt forward and grabbed for the old trapper. Paddock yanked Bass out of the saddle and both of them fell to the ground. It all happened so suddenly that Bass did not have time to recover as Josiah rolled him on over across the grass. Scratch felt the young man's bulk moving atop him, pinning him to the ground, as the confusion mounted in his own heart. He had come to tell Josiah and the woman that he had forgiven them. He had come to let them know that his love for both of them was strong enough to allow them to be together— if they would only allow him to be together with them both. He needed them both more than he needed either one singly. And, he needed to tell them.

But the air was squeezed out of his lungs as Paddock sat atop him. Bass fought to rise.

"Stop it!" Paddock hollered down at the struggling man beneath him. "Got yourself worked up into some fine froshus fittle!"

"Arrrghhh!" Bass growled through clenched teeth, his arms flailing beneath Paddock's grip on his wrists.

"Said simmer down!" He tried to quiet the trapper. "You gotta listen to me. Get yourself all worked up to a fine blue funk, don't you? Damnit! Now, Bass. Damnit! Stop fightin' me!"

Josiah realized he had to soothe. He could expect Bass to act like this. His former partner believed he had stolen his woman from him. It was understandable. And he had rushed the old trapper in his own excitement, surely confusing the old man with his intentions.

"Maybe I should've gut-shot you," Paddock said.

"Better'n wraslin' me to the ground!"

"Maybe should have taken you to the lights, ol' man."

"Been better'n this!" Scratch barked as he arched his back off the ground in an attempt to free himself.

Finally he simmered down, breathing hard and raspy from

the weight on his chest, from the exertion. His arms arched from the struggle. He dropped them to the ground.

"That's better, Scratch. Better."

"You . . . you learned a lot, son," Bass said quietly.

"I wanna talk to you, ol' man—"

"You come a long way, Josiah Paddock. Able to pin Titus Bass to the ground—"

"Will you just shut your yap!"

Bass tried to raise his arms again, but they were quickly pinned. His shoulders went limp as his muscles relaxed. "Awwww . . . all right."

"I wanna talk." The words burst from Josiah's lips. "We gotta talk . . . you and me . . . we gotta talk 'bout . . . 'bout some things between us."

"It . . . it's all right, son. I understand. It be all right with me. I understand 'bout you an'. . . ." His eyes rolled in their sockets as he tilted his head toward the Crow woman a few feet away, "you an' her—"

"You don't understand a goddamned thing!" Josiah snapped. Then, more softly: "You don't really understand a thing 'bout it all. What I wanna tell you—what I need to tell you."

"It's over 'tween us—me an' her." He looked back up at Paddock. "That somethin' I wanna tell you both. But it be all right 'bout you two bein' together like—"

"Just shut up and let me 'splain things, will you?" he pleaded with a softness in his voice, a tone that already asked forgiveness of the old man. "You gonna be quiet while I talk it out to you?"

Bass studied his face, gazing into the young eyes for a long moment, not sure what all this meant. "Yeah—I'll let you speak your piece, son. If'n you let me explain that it be all right 'tween the two—"

"There ain't a damned thing 'tween her and me, ol' man," Paddock said. "You gonna keep your mouth shut while I tell you 'bout how stupid I feel?"

"You ain't the stupid one—"

"You gonna keep your yap closed?"

Bass nodded. "If'n you let me get this goddamned carcass off me first."

Josiah rolled to the side slightly onto his right knee to come off the older trapper. Then he sighed. He watched Bass sit up and rub his hands back and forth across his ribs where they had been squeezed under the young trapper's weight. It was the moment for which Paddock had planned all the words, all the things to say to settle the rift between them, heal the raw, gaping wound that tore at him when he thought about what he had done to the older man.

"Well?" Bass rose, brushed off his clothes. "You wantin' me to shut up—so, talk."

Paddock stood and glanced at the Crow woman. Then he dashed over to her and yanked her back over to the older trapper. He pushed her at Bass.

"There!" Josiah said with a tone of finality. "There, now. She's yours."

"Nawww, son," Scratch replied. "I come—"

"Just be quiet while I tell you."

Bass stared down at the girl. Tears began to pool at the edges of his lower lids as the feelings washed over him again. "I. . . ."

"Just hush up!" Josiah held up a palm toward the old man to signal silence. "That's where the two of you belong—with each other. I know that. Known it all 'long, too. Even since the day you come in on me and her in the lodge." Bass looked down at the woman's face.

"Now . . ." Josiah continued, "now you gotta make it right for her. Make some good medicine outta all this for her."

Scratch studied the woman a moment before he gazed back into the brimming eyes of the young man. "Wha . . . what you mean, son?"

"Her," he answered simply. "She's the one you gotta make it right with, ol' man. She's the one who you run out on."

Bass looked at the woman again, then to Josiah with eyes squinted to shield out the afternoon light. "Near as I can recollect, I ran out 'cause I found my woman an' my partner—in the robes together," he said. "But, it ain't what you thought it was."

"Seems to me I wasn't thinkin' back then. Ought'n been differ'nt," Bass said.

"You didn't give me a chance to talk to you 'bout it. You just run." Josiah shook his head and stared at the ground. "Didn't give me—didn't give us—a chance to talk 'bout it with you."

"Then, talk . . ."

Paddock sighed. "All right. You . . . you found us . . . together—right?"

"That's right, son."

"And what you saw . . . well, it weren't what was really happenin'."

"Just how that be now?" he asked quickly. "I got me my own two eyes, Josiah. Ain't I? Got me my own eyes to see what was happenin'."

"But . . . but what you saw happenin' weren't the way things was really goin' on."

"You can spare the words, all them words, son." He let the breath out of his lungs. "No need for us bringin' it back up again, Josiah. Let's just be shed of it. Just let it be. I wanna be with the two of you . . ."

"And you will be, Scratch," he broke in. "Just let me get this all said, will you?"

The old trapper nodded.

"We was . . ." he started, then came to an abrupt halt. Paddock searched for the words. All those words he had put in proper order had suddenly flown from him and now he felt at a loss. "I was . . . was . . . it were cold that day—"

"Yeah?"

"Cold that day and I was havin' some bad, real bad chills— got the shakes so bad I couldn't stand it no more, Bass. She"— he nodded quickly at the Crow woman—"she seen me in such a bad shape and come over to tell me 'bout how she was kept warm as a lil' girl. Folks who was not shiverin', was not cold like her, stripped off their clothes and climbed in the robes with her to warm her up. She said she could do that for me— get me warm that way."

"You was really naked in them robes with her then," he replied softly.

"Yes—damnit!" Josiah snapped, hating to admit it. "Oh, goddamn, ol' man. Lord knows I was ready to take her if the chance come up—and of a sudden, there was the chance. She and me in the robes. Her naked body layin' up 'side mine like that. Damn! I'd thought and thought 'bout gettin' her under them blankets with me—but when I was gettin' rid of the shakes, when my body was gettin' warmer from her own skin, you see—"

"Yeah?"

"I . . . I was ready." Josiah hung his head as he felt the older man's stare boring into him. "Get my hands on her . . . on her . . ." He paused. "Thought maybe she'd want me, too."

"An'?"

"And . . . she pushed me away from her!" He lifted his head to meet Scratch's hard gaze. "Damn! But the gal's strong, Scratch!" He smiled lamely. "And she was pushin' me off her, knowin' what I was fixin' to do with her—when you come roarin' in on us. See?" He begged, the pitch in his voice rising.

"See what?"

"Can't . . . you see that she didn't want to have no part of me?" He shook his head and stared directly into Titus's eyes again. "She's yours. The woman is yours!"

Scratch measured the young trapper for long moments, watching Paddock's eyes gaze back into his unflinchingly. Then Bass turned his head to look at the young woman. She held her head high and without shame beneath his assessing gaze, her eyes mirroring a gentle, unspoken challenge.

"Waits-by-the-Water?" He spoke her name in English.

"Yes?"

"You know," he began, then thought of what he was going to say in Crow. "You know what we have been talking about?"

"Some. Yes. Not all do I understand of your white talk. Some. You talk about him . . . and me. When you found us . . . together. Is this not so?"

"You are right," he answered. "What have you to say to all of this?"

"I came after you."

"I do not understand what you mean."

"*Pote Ani*, I came after you when you went away with the horses and your bad heart for so long a time, for so many moons. After you came and found us together. Your mind was not right on it. What you see is not always what is. It was this way with the young one. We all were wrong, each of us. And I came after you, followed you to the edge of the river to scream—scream out my love for you."

She suddenly took a step, turned and pressed herself into him. "Would you have me do such a thing in front of my people had I not truly loved you? Would I come after you had I not loved you very much?"

He felt her cheek move against his chest, the caress of her hair against the bare flesh below his neck. And he could easily see the sense in all of it now. The only thing that made it all the more difficult was that he had been such a damned fool—putting himself through all that pain, over what he thought was such an ugly betrayal. Instead, she had pushed Josiah away, had been faithful to him when he had come into the lodge.

Bass watched her lift her cheek away from his chest and look up at him. The woman's eyes were strong in their reassurance for him. And he could draw the strength he needed from them now. Lord knows he wanted to be sure. To be sure this time around. He had made a mistake before.

"She . . . she didn't make that there capote for you, huh?" he asked. "Back up on the hill yonder, thought me she'd made it for a love present—"

"Ain't no love present from her," Josiah answered. "She loves *you*, ol' man. It's you she keeps talkin' 'bout all the time. Chatterin' away in that Crow talk I can't keep pinned down in my head. All the time talkin' 'bout you. The woman didn't give this present to me."

"How you get it then? Who it come from—brand new an' all?"

"Your brother-man."

"Rotten Belly . . . Arapooesh?"

"Yep," Josiah answered softly. "If it were a love present, it's 'cause I'm his son now."

Bass whistled low. "I 'member that now, Josiah. Arapooesh said he was gonna be doin' that—told all us in the lodge when we had the night of that big red-stick eat, comin' back off the trail. Yepper. You be his son now, huh? For real? It were done up right by the ol' boy?"

"Yes."

"Then, that make me your Sparrowhawk—"

"Uncle."

"I'll be damned, Josiah." He shook his head. "Got me . . . I got me my woman back an' . . . an' a nephew-boy all at once't."

"She always been your woman, Bass. Nothin' she done to ever change that. And you oughta known you'd have some trouble gettin' rid of me so easy, right?"

"Yeah," Bass said with a toothy grin.

Bass looked from Josiah to the Crow woman. He tried to smile wider, feeling foolish—much like a young child who had thrown a temper tantrum. "Waits-by-the-Water?"

"Yes?"

"You still love me like you did back then?" he asked in Crow.

"No," she answered clearly in English.

"Wha . . . what do you mean—'no'?"

She started to smile first with her eyes, then her lips curled up at the corners. "I don't love you as I did then. I love *Pote Ani* more!"

Suddenly she flung herself against the old trapper, catching him by surprise. Her cheek went into his neck, her arms locked around his waist fiercely. It was but a moment before he

responded. He began to crush her shoulders as if he feared he
would fall if it were not for her support. At the same time he
began to sob, unashamed.

"Why . . . ah, what the hell you two doin' down here'bouts,
anyway?" He sniffled out the words. "You headin' toward ronnyvoo?"

"Nope," Paddock answered. "Comin' to find you."

"Nawww. You wasn't comin' to find me," Bass replied. "I was
comin' . . . comin' back for you, Josiah."

"You ain't headin' to rendezvous?" Josiah swiped at his own
runny nose.

"Hell, no." He smiled across at the younger trapper.
"Headin' toward Absaroka, first-off, son."

"Really was comin' back for me? Your hard feelin's and all?"
Paddock looked down at the ground a moment as the knot
seared his throat.

Scratch knew, finally. And it warmed that special place inside him where both of them were held. "You hurt me bad—
thought you hurt me bad, son."

"I was the stupid nigger—but you didn't give me no
chance—"

"I were the dumb one—hurtin' too bad to let you say anythin' to me back then, Josiah. But, the hurtin' gone now. I
come back 'cause I miss you both. I wanted the both of you to
know."

"I've missed you . . ." Josiah snorted, against the tears he
felt welling up in his eyes, spilling over into a flood across his
cheeks. "Missed you somethin' bad, ol' man."

Scratch suddenly dropped his arm from the woman's shoulders and roughly embraced the young trapper. Josiah was
caught off guard, his arms dangling uselessly at his sides. Then
he quickly answered the hug with a ferocity of his own.

Bass felt his own eyes beginning to gush. This was what he
had been planning for so many weeks now. Standing here with
his arms around Paddock, he could not recall ever having
hugged the young man before. He could remember only cradling him in his arms on one occasion: in the snow, with a dark,
red circle spreading over the boy's chest, as he had wept when
he had thought he'd lost Paddock. And over these last months,
the old trapper had come to believe that he'd lost Paddock
again.

Paddock felt the older man begin to sob, Bass's upper body
shaking with the struggle against the tears. He was dumb-

founded again. First the old man had come and put his arms around him, as if he were asking for forgiveness of Josiah—if not also granting forgiveness. And now the old man was weeping. It was too much, more than Josiah could handle, and he began to sob quietly along with the older trapper.

Finally, Bass stepped back. "Damn!" He shook his head slightly and sniffled. "Look at us, will you? Bawlin' like a couple of young pups, ain't we now?"

"Yeah . . ."

"Goddamn, Josiah! It's good to see you, boy!"

"And it's damn good to see you too, ol' man!"

The older trapper snorted to clear his freely running nose and looked over at the Crow woman. He held his right arm out for her, beckoning for her to slip within his embrace once more. She quickly wrapped her arms around his waist. He looked down at her, then nuzzled his chin into her dark tresses. He smelled of her hair, the scent that could belong to no other woman. The remembrance of her special fragrance had obsessed him for all these weeks.

Then he remembered. His head jerked back up toward the hillside he had raced down long minutes before. "Yeah! Whoooeee! Boy! Have we all got us surprises comin' this day, son!"

Scratch moved quickly from the woman's arms to the side of his pony again and put a foot in the stirrup. "Just you wait you here a bit. I got me a surprise for you, Josiah!" He swung up into the saddle and started to pull the pony hard around.

"What the blue devil you talkin' 'bout?"

"Just you be the patient one now, young'un!" He nudged the pony down the slippery bank into the stream.

The pony splashed across the stream. When the animal reached the opposite bank, Scratch gave his heels to the pony's flanks. The animal exploded up the opposite slope at full tilt, Scratch hollering and whooping in glee.

"Damn!"

What a glorious feeling this gave him. To have his friend and his woman returned to his heart in one fell swoop. And he was going to return the gift!

"Jumpin' Jehosophat!"

He yanked the reins back hard and felt the animal skidding to an abrupt halt. Bass flew off the pony before the animal stopped moving. There she was, some thirty feet back in the trees, pointing a rifle at his chest. The young thing seemed to be trembling some, too.

"Hold on, now," he said quietly, breathlessly, with a hand outstretced toward her. "You ain't fixin' to shoot me, is you?"

"Shoot, I do," she answered in the words she had learned. "Scared they come get me—bad ones."

"Just me, Looks Far."

"See me now. I hear . . . I hear. Not see before."

"Just me whoopin' it up, lil' gal!" He turned as she lowered the rifle. "Where be the boy?"

"He over there . . . in tree," she answered. "No good him killed, Skatch."

"Scrrraaatch!" he chortled. "Damn! You never will get the hang of it, will you?" He shook his head in sheer exasperation with the young girl. "Get the boy—an' be quick 'bout it. Now!"

"We go?" she asked.

"We go an' show you a big surprise! Big!" He gestured with his arms to show her how expansive a joy he hoped it would be. "Come on, damnit! Get your lil' ass galloping!"

She scurried off to retrieve the cradleboard. She slipped the straps on the board over her arms and shoulders as he packed McAfferty's old rifle away.

"That's good. That's good!" He was breathless with excitement. "C'mon! Let's be goin'!"

She climbed aboard her saddle and watched patiently as he fussed with her capote and dress, straightening them out so that they flowed neatly over her leggings. He stepped back to admire his frantic work. "Gotta make you look just some for meetin' strangers." Bass looked up and smiled. She grinned uneasily.

"Me look good?"

"You lookin' just fine, honey!" he whooped. "Just fine. Let's go."

He grabbed up the long lead rope for the pack string and sprang upon his horse. They headed out of the trees and down the slope.

Even from a distance, Bass could see Josiah's puzzlement—and Waits-by-the-Water's uneasiness as she realized Bass had a woman in the pack train with him.

The prancing, tugging ponies crossed the stream and Josiah pulled his animals back from the edge of the water to allow Scratch's animals to climb and jolt up the bank.

"Why, you ol' bastard," Paddock whispered as he came up alongside Bass. "You got two women now."

"What the hell you mean?" Scratch barked as he slid from his pony.

"Her." Josiah nodded toward the young woman who rode down the opposite bank and into the stream behind the pack animals.

"Her?" Bass grinned. "That other gal? Nawww. Josiah, I brung her 'long as a present for my new nephew." He slapped the younger trapper on the shoulder.

"You—you can't go givin' people away like they was . . ." Josiah stopped abruptly, looked at the newcomer.

Scratch watched Paddock's face, studied his eyes. Almost unconsciously, Paddock's fingers began caressing the pouch around his neck.

"That ain't?" Josiah began.

"Yep!" Scratch grinned proudly.

"I . . . I don't . . . I can't believe it!" He stepped forward as Looks Far Woman's pony bolted up the bank. "It . . . it is her!" He smiled broadly at Scratch, then at Waits-by-the-Water.

"An' that ain't the half of it," added Titus merrily as he saw Looks Far smiling down at Paddock.

Josiah raced over to her pony, to help her down. "What you mean?"

Then Paddock saw the cradleboard. Quickly he looked over at Bass. His eyes flickered with the shadows of unspoken questions.

"Don't look at me, boy!" Bass chirped.

"Ain't my young'un!" Josiah snorted in protest.

"How you so damned sure?"

"It ain't . . . ain't been long 'nough!"

"It has too. Long 'nough since ronnyvoo."

"But . . . but," Josiah stammered. "Don't mean it's mine. She had many a man afore—"

Bass let the young man's voice trail off before he spoke. "You really thinkin' that, son?"

"S'pose, I am."

"Your brains is addled, Josiah. This 'un an' me—we get us chance to palaver some on the trail over. This gal, well now—you was her first."

"Me?" Josiah said, pointing to his own chest.

"That's right, nigger. You was." He pointed at Paddock.

"Then—then, that mean . . ."

"You right again, Josiah. That be your boy."

"A boy?" He suddenly grinned widely.

"Yep."

Paddock looked up at the young woman. "I don't—don't even know her name."

"Looks Far Woman," Bass announced.

"Looks Far Woman?" Paddock looked up into the girl's eyes.

"Joze-ze-aww," she responded quietly.

"That my son?"

"Yes, Joze-ze-aww. I amb yer woooman." She spoke the words she had been practicing for so many weeks, the words Bass had taught her.

Paddock put his arms up to her again and she slid into them, coming off the horse a little clumsily with the cradleboard strapped to her back. Paddock held her at arms' length a moment, looking into her wide, doe-like eyes. Then he slowly embraced her, pulling her into him gently. She closed her eyes and nuzzled against his chest. As he slid his arms around her, his hands touched the cradle. Josiah gently pushed Looks Far away from him and turned her around.

"My son?"

"Yes." She watched him stoop to peer into the shadowy cradleboard.

"My son," he repeated as he pulled a piece of the deerskin covering from the boy's face. "He's . . . he's beautiful!" Josiah turned as Waits-by-the-Water slipped up beside him to peer within the cradleboard's shadows.

"Good," said the Crow woman to Scratch. He nodded and smiled at her "Good for man-child. Knows his father now."

Bass signaled for Waits-by-the-Water to come over to his side. He slipped an arm around her shoulder and looked down into her face before he brushed his lips against hers for a brief moment. He watched her eyes close slightly with the sudden embrace.

"You give me son?"

"I give *Pote Ani* many sons," she spoke in English.

"I'll be damned," he exclaimed. "If'n that don't take the circle! You get to speakin' white talk real good without me, huh?"

"Some good now. Yes."

"I'll be damned!"

"Know when you cuss me good, *Pote Ani!*"

He drew his head back and his chin sank into his chest. "I'll be go to hell an' et for the devil's tater right here! Josiah?"

He looked over and saw that Paddock and Looks Far were cuddled against each other. "Josiah?" Titus asked again.

Paddock looked up. "You ain't changed one bit, ol' man. Still don't know when to mind your manners and let a fella do a lil courtin' with his woman."

"Plenty time for that, son." Bass smiled and pulled Waits-by-the-Water along with him toward the other couple. "We got us a camp to be settin' up, son. Get them women-folk get us a fire goin'. Have us a real feed this night! Whoooeee! Ain't this some, now. Some shinin' times we got comin'! We gonna sing an' dance this night, Josiah Paddock!"

"You sure an ol' man like you can put up with so much o' singin' and dancin'—then get in the robes with your woman, too?"

"Shiiit!" He grinned. "I can out-wrestle any nigger in these here hills." He gestured broadly. "If'n that nigger don't sit on me first! An' you think I'm gonna be whipped by this lil' ga here?"

"Yep, I do." Josiah winked at the older man.

"Only when I'm ready, boy! Only when I'm ready!"

"So, let's do it—right here."

"Fine by me, Josiah."

"Later on we can talk 'bout why you ain't goin' to rendezvous."

"Like I was sayin'—comin' back for you. To make things right between us, if'n we could do that," Bass said. "Give up on makin' it to ronnyvoo this year. Had to come get it straight with you first, son."

"Yeah," Paddock agreed. "That's just what I had in mind too."

Paddock swung a hand up on the old man's shoulder. "Why you down here lookin' for me, you ol' shit? You should be lookin' for me up toward Yellowstone country, shouldn't you?"

"Headin' there."

"This way?" Josiah asked. "Take you a sure-'nough round-'bout way to get up to them Sparrowhawk, you do."

"Like to keep what lil' hair I got me left."

"Blackfoot?"

"Yep. Run smack into gaggle of 'em comin' out west. Had me chance to take on two of them bucks, I did."

"Still wearin' all your hair," Josiah said, glancing at the side of Scratch's head.

"That I am, you damned pup. Too ornery to go under yet.

Wanted me to be sure I made it back to Absaroka to . . . to talk with you first—afore I gone under. Couldn't let the bad medicine between us sit on my heart like it was."

Paddock dropped his hand. "All the time I was as certain as I could be that I'd be findin' you down to rendezvous."

"You'd been plumb center there," Bass commented. "Any other time but now—with me comin' to find you first. Good calculatin', howsomever. You've come some long way, Josiah Paddock."

"Sometimes, feels a lot farther than others," he answered.

"Yes, it truly do," he said, his words soft and wistful as he gazed into the hills. "We can talk 'bout ronnyvoo some—'though there ain't that much to be talkin' 'bout, son. We headin' there now, ain't we?"

"You damned bet we are!" Josiah grinned. "I remember an ol' man tellin' me 'bout the two shinin' times of a year. Rendezvous trampin' and headin' for winter diggin's. He said them was the times a mountain nigger's in the clover, too. The prime squeezin's of a man's life, he told me. Everything else just makes it so a man can have himself such a time twice a year. The way that ol' man said it to me, sounded like he just loved the livin'!"

"Sounds to me like somethin' I'd be sayin'."

"It were you, ol' man!"

"Thought me so." Bass had to grin. "Ronnyvoo. Ummmm! We can set us our truck down 'longside other skin trappers, maybeso. Sell us our plews to one of them big companies, then get us some gewgaws, girlews an' foofaraw for the women here!"

"These women here gonna shine!" Paddock beamed.

"They'll be some now!"

"Damned if they won't!"

"We get us some whiskey down there"—Bass raised an empty hand as if holding up a large mug in his fingers—"sit 'round with them other fellas to yarn an' tip a cup or two of Billy Sublette's liquor all day long."

"You told me I'd be bug-eyed to take a horn of medicine water come rendezvous time," Paddock said.

"I'll swear to that float-stick, I will."

"Said to me that a man swallers fire down to rendezvous 'cause he won't get it for 'nother year—maybe never 'gain for some fellas."

"Yeah, true that be." Bass nodded his head sadly. "Man swal-

lers whiskey-fire to forget them coons as'll never be drinkin'
with him 'gain. Drinks to forget all he's come through just to
get himself that drink to ronnyvoo."

"We got us enough pelts to be doin' all this buyin' of fancy
stuff for the women, an' have us some left over for whiskey,
too?"

"You damned betcha!" Bass grinned broadly and slapped the
younger trapper atop the shoulder. "Hudson's Bay tried to talk
me outta my plews—a pretty penny they was offerin', too. But,
I like sellin' them beaver pelts we pulled down to rendezvous
on this here side of the mountains."

Scratch pointed toward the pack horses. "Only money we
got us be right there, son. Yours an' mine together. Furs we
done us both. Beaver dollars to buy us good times an' 'nother
year in the mountains 'til next ronnyvoo. Then we gonna bust
our asses earnin' that other ronnyvoo. Bust our asses tryin' to
save our hair. Many's the coon what comes away from them
shinin' times, headin' out for the season—leavin' with a headache from the cups, maybe the clap to boot. If'n niggers like us
come away from ronnyvoo broke, what's it all count anyway,
son?"

"Not a damned thing, Scratch," he answered. "Last year it
bought you what you wanted. S'pose them pelts always will.
Gettin' a man whiskey an' the women. Got me a set of skins an'
a real mountain rifle, too. With some cups thrown in for ol'
Titus Bass."

"Told you I'd work the devil outta you for the debt, I did."

"You did it to, ol' man!" He chuckled. "Worked my ass hard!"

"You earned you a good spree, boy," Bass replied. "Earned it
proper. Have you learned why you come to these here Stoney
Mountains, Josiah? 'Tweren't for the money."

"'Tweren't for the beaver, neither!" He could feel the tears
welling against his lower lids. "I know why I come to the
mountains now, Scratch. It was for you, ol' friend. For you—
an' them women there." He nodded toward the Indian
women.

"An' for bein' a pappy, Josiah!" He once again raised an imaginary mug filled with trader's whiskey. "We'll be drinkin' us a
toast to Josiah Paddock's new son."

"Lotta whiskey to that!" Paddock replied merrily.

"We drink—we fall down—we get back up an' drink some
mores." Bass smiled. "We drink to your new son . . . what—
what you gonna name him anyway?"

"He . . . he don't have a name?" Paddock looked at Bass seriously a moment before he turned to Looks Far.

"Nope," Scratch answered. "Flathead boy-folk only get theys first name from the men-folk of the tribe, Josiah." Bass glanced over at Looks Far, then looked back at Paddock. "What's it gonna be?"

Josiah studied the three faces in turn, finally holding his eyes on Looks Far for a long time before he figured this really was his alone to do. A hawk suddenly circled off the ridge to the west, dipping on the wing overhead before it cried out as if to protest in its screech that the human beings were disturbing his hunting across the wide, stream-fed meadow. Paddock was immediately drawn to the large bird, watching its stalking flight pattern. Then he looked into the face of Looks Far.

"Joshua."

"Joshua," Bass responded quietly, having also witnessed the wide-winged hawk circle back over the ridge.

"Joshua?" Paddock asked with his voice and with his eyes as he searched into Looks Far Woman's.

She smiled and nodded her head. "Jozshuwaa."

"Joshua it is!" He clapped his hands, then put them alongside the Flathead girl's cheeks to kiss her quickly on the lips. He brought his hands down to grasp her waist and raised both the woman and his new son into the air to swing them around and around in a tight circle.

"For Joshua Paddock! For the one who carries the sun across the sky!" he bellowed to the ceiling overhead. "For Sun-Boy! For Joshua!"

The grumpy, irritable men had been asked by Campbell to practice a little patience—to wait until the caravan reached buffalo country. There they would all be fattened on the lean meat of the big shaggy beasts. Until then, however, the clerks, laborers and mule-tenders had to satisfy themselves with salt-pork and hardtack and cornmeal and rabbit.

They ate their scanty fare and pushed past the Little Blue and the Big Blue and on to the south bank of the Platte River. And three days later the brigade finally came into buffalo country. From there on out, the men were instructed by the few veterans of western travel, the fare at each meal would be buffalo. So for long weeks the men experimented with various ways to cook the lean meat after their first experiences proved disappointing. Following all the build-up of expectations, all the monotonous wait for the flavorful, lean, red meat, the men were not able to see why buffalo was so highly praised by those veteran travelers.

Only problem was, once the caravan reached buffalo country in earnest, they also ran out of easily obtained supplies of wood for their cooking fires each morning and evening. The men took to cooking over the smelly fires, using dried buffalo chips, sunflower stalks, sage and bunch-grass. Smoky, flaring fires were created with such tinder—but without much heat. So their first experiences with the meat of the plains were totally disappointing. The cuts were not cooked well at all. Each man had to chew and chew to masticate the tough, barely warmed, fairly uncooked meat. Even when they waded into some cows that had fattened themselves up that spring for the nursing of their calves, the men still continued to question why buffalo was so highly praised.

They crossed the South Platte not far from the forks of that river, then moved from the north bank of the river to the south bank of the North Platte. The caravan labored west, ever onward until they reached LaRamie's River, where its mouth poured into the North Platte. It was at LaRamie's Fork that Campbell called the men to construct bull boats out of willow and buffalo hides to cross the swirling torrent to the north bank of the Platte. While some of the men cut the thick willow limbs, others heated tallow and still others tied and sewed the hides over the small, domed structures that would serve as bobbing, bouncing boats to cross the run-off-swollen river.

Just above the mouth of LaRamie's River, Campbell ordered a two-day halt to dry out what goods had taken on water in the crossing. A week before, Campbell had dispatched Louis Vasquez and two others to ride on west ahead of them, to see if they could determine for certain where rendezvous would be held on the Green in little more than a month. Campbell put Sir William Drummond Stewart in charge of the drying-out process for those trade goods soaked in the ferry-crossing and to set the animals out for a relaxed two-day grazing sojourn. Campbell sent six others south and west along LaRamie's Fork in search of honey.

The six returned the next day with quite a prize: several large tin containers and iron kettles filled with the sweet, thick syrup. The caravan commander immediately set some of the workers to preparing *metheglin:* a hastily mixed concoction of pure grain alcohol and river-water sweetened with the honey. Every man was most gratified to let the sweet, alcoholic drink swirl and slip past his tongue that evening around the smoky, smelly fires. The men were told that they were close. Perhaps a month more of travel, most likely less, before they made it to rendezvous. But, here they would wait until word arrived as to the exact location chosen for this year's celebration and trade fair.

Early the next afternoon Vasquez and his two men rode in with Tom Fitzpatrick, who was still sporting his white hair earned after a harrowing escape from Gros Ventre Indians the previous summer. He and Henry Fraeb had been sent out this year, as Fitzpatrick had been last summer, to locate the supply caravan and spur them on. Last year the hapless Fitz had unluckily happened onto that band of Gros Ventres that had been south for a few years visiting their distant cousins, the Arapaho. Fitz had had to run for his life from those Indians, who were considered one of the three branches of the Blackfoot confederation. He had been forced to leave his horse and most of his plunder behind, including his weapons. For days he had stumbled about before he had been found half-dead and picked up by two Delaware scouts sent out to search for him. Ol' Fitz had been brought back into Pierre's Hole riding behind one of the Delawares, badly sun-burned, scratched and bloodied from his wilderness ordeal, and with his hair and beard turned a blazing white.

Fitzpatrick and Fraeb negotiated that evening with Robert Campbell, the trade talk whetted with the *metheglin* and reminiscences of the previous year's rendezvous in that valley west of the magnificent Tetons. Most of those who had been there in '32 agreed it had been the most glorious rendezvous yet, with more of everything—including a battle with the Blackfeet—to wrap up the trade fair. This year it would be even better.

Early in the evening the three hunters who had been sent out in search of game came back in to tell of finding three dead buffalo not far from camp. Their news caused no small alarm as Campbell and Fitzpatrick knew such evidence usually spelled the presence of Indians in the surrounding area. The brigade was camped, after all, on the main north-south route of the shaggy beasts of the plains. And where the buffalo moved, so moved the Indian. Fitzpatrick rode out with the hunters to inspect the carcasses in hopes of solving the mystery, only to find that the three buffalo had been killed by lightning. It proved to be a good laugh on the three greenhorn hunters.

A little later there came a second alarm when gunshots were heard south of camp, up the LaRamie's Fork. Several men raced to the scene to find some hunters had cornered a sow grizzly, fattening herself up after a long winter's nap. She had no cubs with her so the greenhorns had taken sport in finding out if all they had heard about the great strength of the blond beasts was indeed true.

Sir William arrived on the scene to find the men teasing the enraged, bellowing, snorting and much-bloodied monster. He was told that more than fifty balls had been sent crashing into her body. Still, she rushed at her tormentors, then paused to scratch and paw at a new sting in her flesh as another ball tore through her thick hide. After a moment she pounced up and down clumsily on all fours and tried to rush the fun-loving hunters. Stewart dropped from his horse, calmly aiming his custom-made, big-bored Manton rifle, steadied atop a wiping stick, at the wildly gyrating, confused beast. His first ball brought the sow to the ground, but it took a second ball, well placed below and behind the animal's ear, to kill the huge bear.

Slowly the men ventured from their hiding places, gradually working up courage enough to approach the prostrate bear. She had been feeding on the wild currants that grew abundantly around LaRamie's Fork, the delicious red berries on bushes flocked with tiny, delicate, white blossoms. Stewart rose from his one-knee stance and approached the dead animal. He was very interested in having the animal butchered and some of the choicer cuts brought back to camp for supper. William had suffered, along with many others weeks before, what was called *le mal de vache*, known to the American prairie travelers as "cow sickness," that peculiar ache in the bowels and the belly from eating too much lean meat. The bear meat had fat, and the Scotsman wanted it.

The rumbling, aching dysentery he suffered seemed to dissipate the next morning when Campbell gave the marching orders. They were going to push on over the Continental Divide and rush to the confluence of the Green River and a stream called Horse Creek. There, Fitzpatrick and Fraeb told Campbell, the trappers were already gathering.

On westward they marched, climbing up the Continental Divide on so slight a grade that the newcomers and greenhorns could not believe they were actually crossing the great spine. On Tuesday, July 2, the caravan reached the top of South Pass, the high, sagebrush flats and rolling hills belying the fact that they now would be following waters that flowed eventually into the Pacific Ocean.

On the morning of July 3 they awoke to find ice in their water buckets. Most were surprised that here in the middle of summer, here on what appeared to be no more than rolling hill country, there would be ice frozen in their kettles.

The caravan made good time over the next two days, driving their mules and animals down the western slope. As near as Campbell could tell, they would reach the rendezvous site that afternoon. At least by tomorrow. With the joyful, long-awaited news, each man set about his own toilet, preparing himself for the long-overdue arrival at the great summer fair of the mountain man.

That Friday morning, July 5, Stewart set his small cloudy mirror atop the bundles and began to shave himself as he had done every morning of the long journey. It had become a much-loved ritual for him to set out the ivory razor, soap mug and ivory-framed mirror with which he had kept his face shaven with a military neatness. A former barber, now a mule-tender with the caravan, had from time to time trimmed William's hair to keep the dark-brown locks from becoming too unruly. The Scotsman looked himself over in the mirror, proud of his appearance and his military bearing. Perhaps, just perhaps, these lords of the wilderness that he would meet this day could appreciate him. He knew he would be one of the very few groomed men in the camp.

While most of the men washed their long-used, smelly, well-worn shirts and britches in a cold stream, beating them with rocks to agitate the dirt from the cloth, others had their hair trimmed and their faces shaved for the first time in months of travel. Each was preparing for his grand entrance to rendezvous, those last hours of the long march, enduring the final minutes before their arrival, keenly anticipating the assortments of supplies and the whiskey they would lay out for their buckskinned customers at the end of their journey.

Stewart watched Brotherton and Christy puttering about their own toilets as he wiped the remaining soap from his chin. He would always leave the mustache, he told himself again as he glanced briefly at the mirror. He liked what it added to the sallow contours of his face. Unable to grow an attractive beard, even sideburns, Stewart wore his hair a little longer than was fashionable at the time on the Continent. Yet, he was very proud of this long, bushy mustache that he fought to keep groomed.

William smiled at his reflection. He fairly glowed inside at the prospect for the day. They would finally arrive. All the anticipation, all the planning, all the disappointments suffered with the arrival of that final letter just before he had launched himself into this journey—they would all be gone within a few hours. Carefully he packed the shaving set away, placing the mug, brush, mirror and ivory razor away in his small toilet bag.

Then he reached for a large leather valise that had not once been opened since he had closed it the evening before they had pulled out of St. Louis. The satchel had been lashed with rain and wind, drenched with blazing sun all along the journey. He fumbled with the buckles and straps that resisted his expectant fingers. Finally he pulled the leather straps free of the brass buckles as some of the men set themselves into song around the camp in a festive mood of celebration and homecoming.

> Come all you fair and tender ladies,
> Be careful how you court young men,
> They're like a star of a summer's morning,
> They'll first appear and then they're gone.
>
> They'll tell to you some loving story,
> They'll declare to you their love is true;
> Straightway they'll go and court some other,
> And that's the love they have for you.
>
> I wish I was some little sparrow,
> That I had wings, could fly so high;
> I'd fly away to my false true lover,
> And when he's talkin' I'd be by.
>
> But I am not a little sparrow,
> And neither have I wings to fly;
> I'll sit down here in grief and sorrow,
> To weep and pass my troubles by.
>
> If I'd a-known before I courted,
> I never would have courted none;

I'd have locked my heart in a box of golden,
And pinned it up with a silver pin.

First he pulled out the white leather hunting jacket. The garment, with innumerable pockets, was set aside for later use. Next he drew forth a pair of snug trousers, the Scottish *trews*, tailored of the Stewart family tartan, a hunting plaid of green, royal blue, red and yellow. As he slipped into them, he once again admired the work of his favorite London tailor. He put on a clean, ruffled, heavy shirt. After he donned the white hunting jacket, he pulled the flat, low-crowned panama-styled hat from the valise and positioned it atop his head. He turned to find many of the other men staring open-mouthed at his outfit which, he knew, was a strange mixture of style and color for the western mountains. Some of the Americans might have felt William to be dressed in a ridiculous, gaudy manner for their arrival at rendezvous. Yet not a word crossed a lip. The silence perhaps spoke most loudly as a mark of the singular respect held for Stewart among those men who had, after all these months, come to respect the Scotsman's diligence, steadfastness, resolve, and courage. In a word, he had become somewhat one of their own.

Stewart turned and appraised himself in Brotherton's mirror. No more were the men staring at him. Each had his own tasks to complete this last morning on the trail. Campbell flitted about from one knot of workers to another like some nervous prairie hen. He waited until they were finished rounding up the horses and mules and packing the animals before he gave the long-awaited orders.

"Men!" Campbell shouted from atop his pony, amidst the braying of mules and the cursing of the handlers. "It's on to rendezvous!"

There were shouts and shoving, along with good-natured, profane exchanges among the men who had come to know each other so well over the past months. And then the caravan plunged west for its last hours before they reached the valley of the Green.

After only a few hours of travel, a dozen horsemen roared from around the brow of a wide, low hill. They appeared suddenly out of the shimmering afternoon haze and headed straight toward the head of the caravan column. Campbell immediately recognized the fanciful Joe Meek at the head of the welcoming party, as well as several others of the Rocky Mountain Fur Company men.

"Hyar ye now!" Meek hollered as the men behind him discharged their weapons into the air. Their shots were answered by a thunderous exchange of volleys from the caravan's weapons. Some of the trappers circled the caravan wildly, showing off their riding skills with crazy stunts from horseback for the amazed greenhorns and mule-tenders. Meek drove directly for Robert Campbell and yanked back on the reins to send up a showering cascade of dust over those in the vanguard.

"Howdy, Joe!" Campbell yelled above the noise of gunfire and whooping.

"How be ye, Bob?" Meek wiped the dust from his eyes and steadied his horse as it pranced alongside the caravan leader.

"Fine!" Campbell exclaimed. "And all the better for seeing this damned trail behind me!" He reached over and slapped Meek on the shoulder, sending up a small cloud of fine dust.

"It be some punkins to see your whiskey a-bobbin' back thar', too!" Meek said. "Yer lookin' purely some, Bobby! Some punkins to see ye, 'gain!"

"I see you're still wearin' your hair, Joe!"

"Ain't been so lucky to have some red nigger wantin' it bad 'nough for his lodgepole, I s'pose."

They both laughed as Fitzpatrick rode up beside them. Fitz had taken of from LaRamie's Fork after settling terms with Campbell and had sped back to rendezvous to tell of their impending arrival, having arrived only a day ahead of the caravan. He had been pushing constantly for more than a month now and looked tired. But a smile broke across his face, which was caked with dust and sweat from his wild ride around the supply caravan moments before.

"Good to see you again!" He nodded to Campbell and dusted off his hat across his thigh.

"See you had the boys ready for us, Fitz!" Robert replied.

"Yeah. They was some ready for that news, too—they was. An' when we saw your dust comin' off all them hooves, why— every man knew it could be only one fella an' his whiskey! Bob Campbell's best! Joe an' me spread the word an' some of these others come 'long with us to greet you to camp. Rest of 'em back to camp already practicin' gettin' rid of a year-long dry. They layin' in the grass playin' dead drunk! They ready for you, Bob. Real ready!"

"So am I," Campbell agreed. "So am I. Let's get these mules on into camp so I can get my poor ass outta this saddle for a few weeks. Hell! It's good to see you boys! Almost as good as it will be to see that camp."

"She be over the next couple of hills," Meek directed.

"What are we waiting for?"

"Only you, ye nigger!" Meek grinned. "Yer the booshway what's gotta make his grand entrance to them shinin' times! We only the ones what's been waitin' on you, Bobby!"

"Let's go to rendezvous!" Fitz hollered as he gave his pony his heels.

"Let's go!" Campbell shouted as he roared off behind Fitzpatrick and Meek. "Let's go to rendezvous!"

Twenty-one

"Son, that's what we worked our ever-livin' asses off for a year to see." Bass pulled up his pony and watched the others as they looked down at the scene. "This here's the best of times— what a mountain man lives for! We come to ronnyvoo! That there be the Seeds-kee-dee Agie!"

"The Green River, Looks Far." Josiah smiled over at his Flathead woman.

"Big white camp," Waits-by-the-Water commented.

"Looks to be the biggest ever, too," Bass answered. "C'mon, let's go to ronnyvoo!"

They had been following the high ground most of the day as they rode directly south toward the Seeds-kee-dee. Up and down over the rolling hills. Finally, from the long, low hill, Bass gazed down to his right to watch the Green River drift and flow around in front of him. There it was, being lazily fed by two large streams almost directly below them, one flowing into the Green from the northeast, the other from the northwest.

It was green enough down there, with trees and brush, willow and some sage. Up here on the hill there were no trees. Bass glowed inside as they descended the slope. Good grass for all the horses. Plenty of water, too. An adequate supply of firewood. Booshways picked them a good site for the rendezvous, he mused, as he stared down at the fertile benchland below them.

Looking down at the fortress situated some three hundred feet back from the west bank of the river. Bass wondered who would be foolish enough to establish a post here. Sure, the geography and weather looked pleasant enough at this time of year. But at this elevation of better than seven thousand feet, with the winds and open plains all around, this would be some cold winter doin's. Some goddamned fool must have thought he could make a right nice home here.

From the west bank the wide, lush grasslands spread around the fort. From the distance the fort itself looked to be some fifty to sixty feet along each side. There were blockhouses on the southwest and northwest corners. The pickets surrounding the fortress were some fifteen feet high and were each about a foot in diameter. Built sturdy enough, he figured. But what really held his eye was how far the encampments seemed to spread down the valley along the river. All about the fort itself were tiny knots of structures: canvas tents, blanket lean-tos and brush bowers thrown up by the trappers gathering in the valley. Further downstream from the fort were the lodges of some several hundred Snakes. The fifty or sixty Shoshone lodges pointed their cones to the late afternoon sky as if in offering, each one pouring forth smoke that told of the preparation of an evening meal. Beyond the Indian camp was a large pasture where the hundreds of Snake ponies were being tended by young guards who moved slowly through the herd.

Scratch wondered if this were Slays-in-the-Night's band. The old Injun friend who had insulted him last summer after the battle of Pierre's Hole. Perhaps this year they could settle the matter, he thought. He hoped the Shoshone warrior harbored no resentment for him. If he did, so be it.

His gaze roved to the white tents and lean-tos thrown up among the willows and trees as far as he could see, all down the Green. Some big camp, he thought. Spread out along the river, much as was the rendezvous of '32. This already promised to be bigger, perhaps better.

They came to the bottom of the hill and rode onto the narrow bench lapped by the lazy river. Across the water some men dangled their feet in the cooling waters and looked over the recent arrivals as Bass and his party splashed across a shallow ford. They slogged onto the wide western bank of the Green and plodded slowly through the willow, passing groups of men who were heading for the river: for water, for bathing, for washing clothes, for cooling off. Scratch did not recognize a single

one of them. Somewhere, off in the trees, a man in his cups
sang an off-key lament.

Come all you sporting bachelors,
Who wish to get good wives,
And never be deceived as I am,
For I married me a wife makes me weary of my life,
Let me strive and do all that I can, can, can,
Let me strive and do all that I can.

She dresses me in rags,
In the very worst of rags,
While she dresses like a queen so fine;
She goes to the town by day and by night,
Where the gentlemen do drink wine, wine, wine,
Where the gentlemen do drink wine.

When I come home,
I am just like one alone;
My poor jaw is trembling with fear.
She'll pout and she'll lower, she'll frown and look sour,
Till I dare not stir for my life, life, life.
Till I dare not stir for my life.

When supper is done,
She just tosses me a bone,
And swears I'm obliged to maintain her;
Oh, sad the day I married; Oh, that I longer tarried,
Till I to the altar was led, led, led.
Till I to the altar was led.

The ponies carried them through the blanket lean-tos and
brush bowers while Bass searched for familiar faces. They rode
slowly through the assembled structures around Bonneville's
Fort. There seemed to be a little activity in the fort itself so
Scratch figured the traders had set up inside the walls. He
decided to stop and check on the going rate for beaver before
they set up camp.

Bass pulled on the reins and signaled the others to wait as he
handed the lead rope for the pack string over to Waits-by-the-
Water. He kicked his left leg over the saddle horn and plopped
to the ground. It took a brief moment to steady himself before
he could walk. The knees again. Maybe just stiff from being too

long in the saddle. They were wobbly as he took the first few steps. He looked up at the Crow woman, only to find her staring at him with a worried look on her face.

"Nothin' to worry 'bout, lil' darlin'," he muttered as he rubbed each knee in turn. "Just sore from a long trail gettin' here. Nothin' to be worryin' 'bout now."

Scratch walked off, conscious that the others were staring at him. He planted each foot before transferring weight to the next leg in the peculiar, prairie-hen walk that seemed to mark a man who spent much of his life on horseback.

Small groups of trappers passed through the gate, coming and going. Some carried huge tin cups, while others lugged small iron kettles sloshing with liquid. This seemed odd to Bass. They stumbled as if they had been drinking liquor.

Against the pickets in the shadows near the gate squatted a large man whose monstrous hands dwarfed an otherwise large tin cup of whiskey.

"Howdy, friend!" Bass exclaimed as he approached the big man.

The man looked Bass over quickly, then took a long drink from his cup. "Hello," he said in a deep voice after he swallowed. "Squat."

"How's beaver?" Scratch asked, as he knelt on crackling knees. "Goin' per pound, I mean."

"Don't know that," the man said with an accent that was hard for Bass to place.

"You ain't done you no tradin' yet?"

The stranger looked over at Bass with eyes that appeared to burn with the same intensity as the grain alcohol he was drinking. "No, mister. I do not do any trapping."

Bass thought that one over a moment. What the hell could this fella be doing here at rendezvous if he were not a trapper? Clerk—yeah, a clerk maybeso. "Trader got him some business goin' inside, huh?" he asked.

"No trader inside," the stranger answered, then took another drink. "Whiskey only. Trappers come in. Trappers go away. Get good drunk here in fort."

"Ain't no traders here yet?"

"Only whiskey here, I say," the big man answered brusquely.

"Ahhh," Bass crooned as he watched another group of men walk into the compound.

"Trader you want, he down south—of here, some way."

"Trader's down there?" Bass said, looking off to the south. "Why? Ain't this ronnyvoo here?"

"Many camps," the stranger said. "Many camps there is. Down river. South, mister."

"Trader's down south, huh. S'pose that be where I need to go then, friend. Got me plews to be tradin', you see. You ain't a trapper, then you ain't got anythin' for tradin'. How you get your whiskey?"

"I have money to drink. Is no trouble. I have good money, plenty money. I drink on no man."

"S'pose you let me buy you a drink here sometime," Scratch offered. "One on the prairie—for free, I mean. I thank you for your help, friend." He rose on the sore knees and wobbly legs once more.

"Thank you, no," the stranger said simply.

"You ain't a trapper—how come you here? A clerk maybe?"

"Clerk, no," the big man said. "I work for no man."

"Just the way I like it, too," Scratch said.

"I no trap."

"What you doin' to ronnyvoo?"

"I come visit rendezvous."

"Huh," Bass snorted. He could not imagine a man just coming to visit a trappers' rendezvous.

"I sit and watch—all men come in and all men go out," the stranger said. "Like to watch men, this one. Bonneville's trappers here."

"You . . . you just watch fellas, huh?"

"Yes. That is right. Like just watch—and drink."

"Yoah!" Bass exclaimed. "And drink! That's some now. I could do some of that, I could. Just sit an' watch an' drink. Been a long one for this here nigger, it's been." He pursed his lips. "Your words, they's differ'nt. Where 'bouts you hail from, friend?"

The big man brought his eyes up slowly. "North. Far away. Red River of the North."

"Canada? You come a long way."

"You know Red River of North?"

"Yepper," Bass said. "Know of it. Never been there. Never been me nowhere near the Canadas. Only heard of it, friend. You must be Hudson's Bay. Heard they—"

"No!" the stranger snapped. "Not Hudson's Bay! They murdering devils—I cut their hearts out!"

"Sorry," Bass apologized. "Just knowed Red River and Hud-

son's Bay seem to be somethin'—seem to this here child to be
tied up together—"

"Hudson's Bay bastard-devils up to Red River, yes. But I no
Hudson's Bay."

"Sorry to rile you so, friend."

"Me just carry bad blood for company."

"This nigger's sorry he brung it up on you." Bass stuck out a
hand. "Name's Bass. T. Bass, it be."

The stranger glanced at Bass's hand, then unfolded the fingers of one hand from around the tin cup to present his huge
paw. Bass felt the vise-like grip grind at the bones of his right
hand.

"Sharpe, I am. Emile is Christian name. Emile Sharpe
whole name, Bass."

"Pleased makin' your 'quaintance," Bass gritted, feeling the
burning in his hand.

The Canadian finally realized he was causing the American
real pain. He looked down at the coupled hands and released
his grip. "You miss finger. Trap bite off?"

"Nawww. Grizz got that from me." Scratch laughed.

"*Grizz?* What this *grizz* you talk of?"

"Grizz . . . grizz is a bear. Big, big bear out here in the
mountains." He thought it strange that a man would not know
about grizzlies. "Hell, you almost as big as the grizz come after
me. Had her a lil' bite of me—but didn't like the taste of this
poor ol' bull—so, she moved on."

"You not kill?"

"Yeah, I kill," Bass answered. "It come down either her or
me, it were."

"You good man. Good man it take to kill this grizzly."

"They big—grizz is." Scratch agreed. "Smart, too. Know 'em
how to fight. Hide's tough, friend. Stop most any ball you can
thunk against it, for certain. Tough critter to kill—just won't go
down for most of nothin'."

"I like find me a grizz before I go home," Sharpe reflected.
"They out here."

"First—I drink and watch," Emile said.

"Yeah. First you drink an' watch men, right?" Bass smiled.
He looked back toward his partner and the two Indian women.
"Best get my outfit movin' an' set up for the night."

Scratch signaled to Josiah and the women to join him. He
watched Paddock nudge the animals forward, then looked up
at the sky. The sun was dropping behind the fort walls. Perhaps

as much as another hour of daylight left. No more than that. They would set up their camp nearby and wait until morning to look for the traders.

"We gotta do us some tradin' first-off," Bass said. "Then I can be buyin' whiskey. Buy you a drink, my friend—for your help. Me an' my partner, Josiah—we buy you—"

"Josiah?" the stranger asked suddenly. He leaned forward ever so slightly to watch the approaching trio and the string of pack animals.

"That's right. Josiah. Said me that. Josiah Paddock. My partner got him a new son." Bass beamed.

Bass saw the Canadian's face lift slowly out of the dark shadows into the fading light of dusk. Emile's right eye was scarred almost entirely shut, the old wound showing white against the dark, tanned skin as it ran its ragged course down from the forehead across the eyelid and onto the cheek. Scratch had seen that scar someplace before. He was certain of it. Deadly certain. He watched the way Sharpe studied Josiah.

"You know him?" Bass asked.

"No." The word came out softly as Emile leaned back and the shadows fell across him again. "I do not know this Josiah."

"Thinkin' you did," Bass remarked, "way you was lookin' at him."

"Don't know this Josiah Paddock."

"Leastways—we owe you a drink, on us. How 'bout it?"

"Yes," Sharpe said as he reconsidered. "Yes, I take your drink, some time, some place. Emile Sharpe like to drink."

"I see me that, friend." Bass walked over to his buffalo runner and placed his foot in the stirrup.

"How—how long you go to mountains?" Sharpe suddenly asked.

"How long afore I go back to the mountains? Be after we finish ronnyvoo."

"No, no—this question, Bass. How long you be to the mountains, I ask."

"How long I been in the mountains? Been better'n some nine seasons now, as close as I can recollect. Some nine robe seasons. Why?"

"You fight that she-grizz."

"Not the first neither, friend."

"You fight this she-grizz, hmmm." He seemed to chew on the thought with a growing degree of respect for this American trapper. "You up this mountains so long a time. You some man,

Bass. *Oui*. Yes, you some man fight she-grizz and Indians. Be alive still."

"Why, thank you kindly, Sharpe." Bass grinned. "Such kind words as them there'll get you 'nother free drink on Titus Bass. You take me up on it—you will, huh?"

"Yes," Emile said. "Yes, I drink your whiskey, Bass. I drink whiskey from Titus Bass and Josiah Paddock."

Scratch and the others rode south of the fort to choose a site for their camp. The two trappers dropped the baggage from their pack animals, then picketed them out to pasture near the camp. They drove the picket pins deep into the soil and hobbled their four riding horses so they would not wander off to graze with the ponies in other herds.

Titus and Josiah set about separating the baggage until Looks Far came up to Paddock and removed the cradleboard straps from her shoulders. She handed the infant to Josiah.

"Look on Jozshuwaaa," she requested quietly.

Paddock grinned. "You mean, look *after* Joshua."

She nodded her head and returned his grin. "Yes. Look after Jozshuwaaa."

"Be glad to look after my boy." He smiled as he gazed into the infant's face. Looks Far motioned to the Crow woman and together they took off for the timber, each carrying a blanket.

"Well, now," Bass sighed. "Can see me now I ain't gonna get nothin' done 'round here." He plopped against some of the beaver packs as Josiah slowly lowered himself and the cradleboard to the ground.

"Got them women-folk off traipsin' 'round in the bushes for devil knows what, I don't," the older trapper continued.

"Probably gone to take a pee," Josiah commented.

"They best be gettin' 'em some firewood," Scratch grumbled. "My meat bag hollerin' for fodder an' needs it somethin' to eat. Want me some supper, I do."

"Seems I remember an ol' trapper tellin' me 'bout when a man takes a Crow squaw to pack 'round with him, he don't have much of a say 'bout most everything then."

"You talkin' 'bout me again, boy?"

"Don't know any other ol' trappers. That I don't." Josiah grinned. "That ol' fella told me the squaw runs the lodge—runs him, just about. Told me you give a squaw so much say over a man—why, you might just as well give that woman the right to take a pee standin' up!"

"I say that?" Bass smiled.

"Yeah," Josiah answered. "You did. Sayin' Crow women make the best robe-warmers. Damned sight better'n them bangtailed whores back to St. Louis what always want a man's money, an' a good time thrown in, too!"

The old trapper gazed toward the timber where the women were. "Crow women always been best in the robes. Not meanin' nothin' again' the Flathead, you know. Just want me some supper, I do. Best they be gettin' 'em some firewood."

"Will you quit bein' so goddamned fussy all the time?" Josiah chided his partner. "You're just like a ol' mother hen."

"What's bein' fussy 'bout wantin' a fire an' some warm vittles, huh?"

"Just . . . just them two is here for a good time, too," Paddock said. "We all here for a good time. The same as us. They ain't gotta work all the time, Scratch."

"Why you so all-fired high an' mighty 'bout what they gonna do an' what they ain't gonna do?"

"Just thinkin' we come to play some—been some time since we last played, hasn't it?"

"It has, that—"

"So I'm thinkin' we should let them women-folk be playin' some here to rendezvous, too."

"Long's the fire keeps goin' an' the vittles cooked an' the coffee's always hot—"

"Ain't got us any coffee."

"We gonna have," Bass blurted. "Just as soon's I get some beaver traded off."

"An' whiskey?"

"Goddamned right, boy. We get us some whiskey—drink us a few goodly toasts to Joshua."

Paddock leaned back against some baggage, his knees drawn up and the cradleboard laid against his thighs. "You wanna hold him?"

"Thought you'd never ask." Bass grinned as he took the cradleboard. "Gettin' pretty good at holdin' on to this lil' pup, I am."

Bass leaned back against the beaver pack and pushed the soft deerskin wrapping from the sleeping infant's face. Joshua stirred a little but kept his eyes closed. Bass never asked: he always waited for an invitation to hold the infant. He didn't want his eagerness to show. But, damn! If it didn't give him all the warmer a place inside to hold on to the infant strapped in his cradleboard.

Paddock smacked his lips. "Come to think of it—coffee does sound good." Then Paddock smiled at the older trapper. "Whiskey even sounds better."

"Ain't no doubt to that, son."

"We go tradin' tomorrow?"

"Should do us some of that, yes."

"Buy us some pretties for them two women."

"If'n they ain't up an' runned off with some other niggers by now."

"Awww, c'mon, Scratch. You know better than that. Way that woman feels 'bout you? Why, Waits-by-the-Water just pined and pined for you after you left. Woman's got her a strong heart for you, she does. Back then, seemed like she was gonna die of a broken heart."

"You sayin' the true?"

"Nothin' but, Scratch."

The older trapper was quiet for long moments before he spoke again, looking from the infant in the cradleboard to the dropping sun, then back at Joshua sleeping. "Want to have me a pup some day," he muttered.

"Got you a good wife now. Why don't you have a baby?"

"Yeah," Bass said quietly. "Like to have lots of pups."

"You never been a father before?"

"Leastways, I ain't a pappy as I knows of."

Josiah read the expression on Bass's face. "'Til you got a pup of your own—you can hold Joshua as much as you want, ol' man."

"Really?"

"Really. As much as you want. 'Cept when he's feedin'—somethin' like that. Hell, you can't hold him all the time: his mama and me gotta hold him sometimes, too."

"I know, I know. I 'preciate it, son. Want lil' Joshua to know what's what 'bout his ol' Uncle Scratch, I do."

"You'd be his *great*-uncle."

"That's right. I be your uncle 'cause Rotten Belly be your pap an' I be his brother-man." Scratch looked back down at the infant's face as it began to screw up. "That makes me Joshua's grand-uncle, wouldn't it now?"

Suddenly Joshua began to wail. Bass bounced the infant on

his thighs to quiet the boy but when the crying grew louder, he thrust the cradleboard at Josiah. "Here—you take the boy."

Josiah shrugged. "I can't do nothin' special for him. You keep him. You're doin' just fine. Good as me."

"Just fine, huh?" Bass snorted. "I can't get 'im to stop his bawlin'!" He glanced over at Paddock with panic in his old eyes. "Here. You just gotta take 'im, Josiah."

"Told you, I can't do a thing for him." Josiah grinned.

Scratch rose clumsily, balancing the cradleboard in his arms. He rocked the baby, but it didn't help to calm the infant.

"I . . . I cain't get 'im stop cryin', son—"

"Give me." Looks Far suddenly appeared with Waits-by-the-Water at her side.

Bass eagerly presented the cradleboard to Looks Far Woman. "I couldn't do nothin' to stop him cryin'."

"You couldn't." Josiah smiled. "Least when he gets hungry. You know 'bout gettin' hungry, don't you, ol' man?"

"Pup cain't suck on this ol' tit!" Bass cupped a hand beneath one side of his chest. He watched Looks Far settle herself against some baggage and untie the thongs along the side of her blouse. She pulled one swollen breast out and moved the infant toward the nipple. The baby began to suckle happily.

"You two gals come back at just the right time," Bass said.

"Get wood," Waits-by-the-Water said as she gestured toward the two blankets loaded with squaw-wood. "Not much."

"But 'nough there, lil' darlin'," he answered, and put his arm around her shoulders. "Camp's too big here. Gotta spread it out, or we just gotta move. How 'bout us movin' on down a ways in the mornin' afore we go to tradin'?"

"Sounds fair to me," Paddock answered. "'Nough folks 'round as it is."

"Don't know who set up in that fort there." Bass nodded at Bonneville's fortress. "It don't sound to me it'd be Campbell an' the Rocky Mountain Fur. Didn't recognize a one of the fellas comin' in an' goin' outta that gate."

"Looked like you knew that big fella you was talkin' to," Josiah remarked.

"Nawww. Never seen him afore in my life—least, near as I can tell. Somethin' . . . 'bout a scar on his face, howsomever. Nawww. I'm just . . . dreamin'. Never seen him afore. Name of Sharpe. Told 'im we'd buy him a drink of Campbell's whiskey."

"Hell, you'd buy anyone a drink of whiskey," Paddock said, "just as long as you got the chance to drink along with him."

"You be right there, boy. You be right there."

"We gotta wait afore we start buyin' drinks for other niggers 'til we get us supplies. And get some gewgaws and pretties for the women here. Get the 'portant things first, Scratch. Then, what's left over, we buy us some whiskey for any nigger wants a drink with us. Fair 'nough?"

"Where'd you get such a idea now?" Bass asked. "Buyin' the 'portant things first afore you go an' drink your plews away in whiskey?"

"You—skinhead!" Paddock grinned. "It was from you. Titus Bass taught me that last year, you ol' bastard."

"Why, I'll be damned. Cain't rightly 'member doin' such a thing now.. Seems I only 'member gettin' drunk a lot with Hatcher an' them others—'round a kettle. This nigger's smarter'n he thought he was," Bass said proudly. "Really teached you that, huh?"

"Yep," Josiah answered. "But—sometimes—you ain't all-fired smart as you think you are."

"Just what you mean by that?"

"Look for yourself." Josiah nodded over at the two women and the infant.

"You mean 'cause I couldn't get Joshua to stop his cryin'?"

"No, no." Josiah chuckled. "Not 'cause of Joshua, ol' man. 'Cause of her. Waits-by-the-Water."

Scratch looked over at Waits-by-the-Water, who was getting the fire started. He knew what Josiah meant.

"Yeah," he agreed. "Sometimes this ol' child real glad to find out he's been wrong 'bout somethin'. Real glad sometimes to be wrong."

The words to the old eighteenth-century song carried on the gentle night breezes that rustled and nudged the blankets of the shelter, drifted to Scratch's ears.

Black, black, black is the color
Of my true love's hair.
Her lips are like some rosy fair,
The prettiest face and the neatest hands.
I love the ground whereon she stands.

I love my love and well she knows,
I love the grass whereon she goes.

If she on earth no more I see,
My life will quickly fade away.

I go to troublesome to mourn and weep.
But satisfied I ne'er could sleep.
I'll write to you in a few little lines,
I'll suffer death ten thousand times.

So fare you well, my own true love,
The time has passed and I wish you well.
But still I hope the time will come,
When you and I will be as one.

Black, black, black is the color
Of my true love's hair.
Her lips are like some rosy fair,
The prettiest face and the neatest hands.
I love the ground whereon she stands.

He felt her before he even heard her, much less saw her shadow slip around the side of the blanket-and-brush bower he had thrown up for the two of them. He supposed that was what it meant, after all was said and done. Knowing she was near even when he couldn't see her, couldn't hear her, couldn't even smell her own special fragrance.

Then Scratch thought he felt his ears tickled with the soft padding of feet behind the shelter, just before his eyes caught the change of light that grew into her shadow creeping around the side of the blanket walls. Waits-by-the-Water was there, the moonlight framing her as she slowly knelt before him. Bass had been leaning back against some folded robes and now raised an arm toward her. She gave him her hand and he held it gently, without saying a word.

The Crow woman put out a hand to tell him not to move. He relaxed back against the coarse, sensual buffalo fur. Her hand gently slipped from his.

"We have not really been alone since . . . since Absaroka." He spoke quietly in Crow.

"Yes, *Pote Ani*," she answered in a whisper, kneeling before him in the moonlight.

He could not make out her features in shadow. Yet, he thought, if he were blinded at this instant, never again to see her face, he could nonetheless tell her from all others. He closed his eyes a moment to test himself, and drank in her sensual musk. Yes, he thought, he would forever be able to know her by her smell. There was no other who had ever made him rigid and ready just in the smelling of her fragrance. And he was hard now.

He thought back to that first night after being reunited with Waits-by-the-Water in those mountains east of Davy Jackson's Hole. A frantic, furtive, hurried coupling off away from camp and Josiah and Looks Far and the infant.

It was among the aspen and the grasses that he had pulled open her blanket coat and inched her dress above her waist, pushing her back against a tree roughly before he had begun to slow down. Waits-by-the-Water had taken his rigid member into her hand and guided it into herself: at the same time she had nudged a thigh along each side of his hips. He had forced her back against the tree, rocked her back and forth, moved in and out of her. She had kept her heels locked behind his buttocks until he had been spent in unison with her. Scratch's legs had shaken from the after-shocks, trembled until he could no longer support her. One leg at a time she had deserted her perch atop his pelvis until his softened member fell from her.

They had collapsed against the tree, cradled each other for long minutes before either one spoke. She had grabbed some fresh damp grass and held it against herself to soak up the part of him that spilled when he had shot into her.

There had been so few words that night. Much the same as the other nights in their travel south to the Green River and rendezvous. There had been no words necessary. Each was moving toward the other out of a pent-up hunger. Words would only have intruded upon what they shared, away from the others, away from the rest of the world into one of their own making.

Remembering now made him twitch with readiness. Lord, he hadn't known he could perform night after night with such power. And she had always answered him with a cat-like ferocity.

She rose and he watched her untie the leggings at her waist and let them slither down along her beautiful legs. She had gone to the bushes barefoot moments before, perhaps to assure herself that there was no one around to disturb them on this, their first real night alone together after so many moons of loneliness, and desperation, and desire.

Bass, shirtless, felt a slight tingle, like a chill that needed warming, surge over his arms and chest. At this elevation, he thought, they would need the robes before morning. Perhaps the chill was not solely from the breeze that made the leaves dance at the edge of their bower. Perhaps it was more the tingle of excitement in seeing her finally naked before him for the first time in all those months.

Waits-by-the-Water knelt again and began to untie some of the thongs at her waist that held the sides of her buckskin dress together. Bass went to his knees and gently nudged her hands aside.

"Let me," he whispered hoarsely.

"Why? I can do."

"I want to, sweetheart."

"What is this—*sweetheart*?"

He stopped, realizing what he had called her. "It . . . it is someone who is very big in my heart. The biggest." He tried to explain the white term in the Crow tongue. "Someone my heart is sweet on. Sweet like our sugar, good to my mouth, you see. It is how I feel for you: my heart is the biggest when I am around you. As I love the taste of sugar in my mouth, I love the taste of you in my heart."

"Sweetheart." She placed her hands gently alongside his cheeks and knelt to kiss his forehead as he continued to untie her dress.

Bass could feel the impetuousness of his penis, buried in and straining against the breechclout. Lord knows he wanted to rush his hands inside the gaps at the sides of her dress, to put his hands on the mounds of flesh and push her down, push himself into her. But something else stayed him. That something else made him suffer the agony of expectation, the waiting to make the final climax all the sweeter for them both. She pulled back a little and anxiously grabbed at the bottom of the leather dress to begin moving it up her thighs.

"No," he whispered. "I told you, let me do it for you—for us."

Her hands relaxed beneath his and then floated away from the bottom of the dress. Bass slowly inched the leather garment up while she slithered out of it. She shuddered slightly in the night breeze as she knelt, naked, before him. His gaze pored over her form, over the play of shadow and twilight in every contour.

Bass grasped her firm, soft breasts. He could see the outline of the breasts against the moonlight. His member strained against the leather breechclout as his hands fondled and kneaded her breasts.

He heard her moan low, moan softly, the sound rising from deep in her throat. She was sensitive there and he remembered it well. He slid a hand down the firm, flat plane of her belly, down into the hair and beyond. There a finger wandered back and forth in rhythm with the hand that stroked and kneaded the breast.

She began to weave slightly, in time with his rhythm, moaning and whimpering. Then Waits-by-the-Water wriggled her fingers into the side of his breechclout, tugging the leather free of the belt. Her fingers lightly caressed his penis and she felt it jerk in her hand.

"You are ready for me," she whispered as her lips lightly brushed his ear.

He was breathing heavily now, as he pressed his lips against hers, his tongue forcing them apart until he could taste her tongue. When the kiss ended, he looked down at her shadowy face.

"You know I have been ready for so long." His voice was low, hoarse.

"And I am ready for you—sweetheart."

He leaned back to pull at his belt, but she grabbed at his hands. "I do this."

Her fingers glided over the belt, pushed the leather breechclout aside and worked at the buckle. The breechclout fell from his waist. She took his rigid member in her hands and gently kneaded the flesh.

"You . . . do that too much . . . an' I won't have nothin' left for you," he moaned.

She withdrew her hands obediently and knelt at his bare feet. Waits-by-the-Water tugged at the bottom of both leggings, pulled them free. Then she spidered her fingers up his legs, delicately tickling his thighs. She cupped him, felt him jerk.

"I'm warnin' you—you lil' she-cat," he said playfully.

"Then I want you inside me now." She turned away from him, arched her back as she presented herself. "Come into me as the stud comes to the mare in heat, my love."

"Yes." He went to his knees behind her, his hand wandering over the globes of her buttocks, sliding around the slimness of her waist.

"Put *that which grows* inside me before I scream to have it!"

she breathed. "I . . . have waited so long for this. Have . . . have dreamed . . . so many times . . . of this . . . with you, *Pote Ani.*"

"So have I, sweetheart," he rasped. "I have dreamed so much on this, being with you like this . . ."

Waits-by-the-Water reached between her legs to guide his member into her. Both of them moaned as she plunged it into her deepest recesses. She was well-ready for him: hot and wet. She squirmed, her buttocks wriggling back into him, to drive him all the deeper inside her.

She felt him move slowly at first, little thrusts and with-drawals until his movements were no longer tentative. He pushed against her, and with hands gripping her shoulders, pulled her back into him with every forward thrust of his hips.

Her legs began to quiver, her thighs began to shake. Her arms trembled until they could no longer support her weight and her upper torso slumped to the robes. He sank still deeper inside her. Her stomach turned at the joy of his deep penetra-tion. He touched parts of her that had never been touched before, even by this whiteman in their previous love-making. He was rigid and trembling inside her, ready to explode.

She answered his thrusts with the force of her own body as she rose on his crescendo. Then the explosion rocked her. He burrowed into a place deep inside her that she had felt could never be touched by anyone. Her soul seemed to leave her body and look down on her as she rocked against him. It seemed her body was on fire, the flame spreading out of her groin to crawl up her belly to her breasts where the nipples grew rigid and tender.

Then the dam burst and the relief washed over. Her spirit came back into her body just as he finished his final thrust. The side of her face against the buffalo robe was damp with her sweat. Her thighs trembled against his quaking legs.

"Lay down," he whispered behind her ear. His breath made her shudder.

She dropped to the robes, and he rolled with her so that his penis would not drop out. Waits-by-the-Water slipped a hand beneath her belly, past her groin to his scrotum. There her fingertips gently kneaded the soft flesh where his explosions originated.

The Crow woman felt his breathing become more rhythmic over the long minutes. So, too, did her own slow.

"This is what I wait for," she murmured.

"Just like your name," he answered. "You waited for me beside the waters of the Yellowstone."

"Yes."

"You waited until you had to come down to the river—to get me to believe you loved me only."

"Yes."

"The same river where you waited after I left you," he whispered again. "Waited for me."

"Yes, *Pote Ani.*"

"And you waited for me beside this river tonight." He nuzzled against her neck where it met the shoulder. "Waited until it could be right for us by the river."

She felt his softened member drop from her and she rolled over to take him into her arms. Bass resisted her pull a moment to kiss both her nipples and gently bite at them before he allowed his head to rest in the crook of her neck.

"Yes, my man," she murmured softly.

"It were worth the wait for you, pretty one."

"Why did you choose me?" she asked in Crow.

"As I remember, you chose me." He chuckled.

"Yes, I did."

"I don't want you making the mistake of blaming me for what has happened between us."

"I blame no one."

"That is as it should be," he said. "We both have been caught up in this—together."

"For the rest of our lives?" she asked.

"I would like that."

"I, too," she sighed. Her cheek brushed against the blue bandanna. "Why do you wear this?"

"I was scalped," he said. "Left for dead. The cloth now holds the scalplock of the warrior who did this to me."

"Does it hurt you often?"

"Almost never, no," he answered. "Not any more now."

"May I take . . . off you?"

"No." He was quick with the word. "I mean, it is probably better that I leave it on."

"But, if it does not hurt you, then you should not be ashamed."

He realized that through all these years, he had been ashamed. Not just because of the loss of hair, for he had been losing enough of that the last few years anyway. He had watched his hairline receding further and further on either side of his forehead. So it was not just the hair. It was more the humiliation from having been scalped. It was like admitting a weakness.

"You are right," he whispered. He felt the lump grow in his throat: so hot, so large that he did not know if he could speak at first. "Why . . . why is it that you love me so much?" he choked.

"It is so big—this love I have for you."

"And I do love you so."

She cradled him tenderly. "It does not matter now. It does not matter that you wear the blue cloth. It does not matter that you were scalped. You were strong enough to rise from it."

Her cheek brushed against the bandanna again and she kissed the side of his temple. "That is why I love you. Your strength. Your quiet, deep strength. Like a fire that will not die—so deep inside you. You pull me to you, to be warmed by that strong fire deep within you. A strong fire it makes in my heart for you. I could not deny what you did to my heart with your power. *Pote Ani* became a ruler there, in my heart. Like a lord." She tapped her finger against her breast.

"That is truly where I wish to be a lord," he answered in Crow.

"And I wish be this sweetheart of yours, my love," she replied. "To be a good taste in your mouth. You taste good. Taste sweet my mouth."

"That is my love for you."

She shifted his body, slid out from beneath him. After a moment of staring down at this man in the moonlight, Waits-by-the-Water let her fingertips glide down his chest and belly, down to his soft member. She took hold of it lightly and kneaded the flesh gently. The Crow woman felt it twitch beneath her caress.

"*That which grows*," she began, then looked up into his eyes, "grows all the stronger with my touch."

He groaned, fully under the spell of her gentle caress. "I . . . am not . . . do not know . . . how you do that to me—"

"Sh-h-h-h," she whispered.

Her fingertips roamed across his lower belly, then wandered down along the inside of his thigh before she grasped his penis again. He felt it jerk with the sensation that shot through him. It was not at all a localized pleasure. The burning began low in the belly and spread across his chest like liquid fire the more she stroked him. He could feel himself stretching, hardening, growing every second now as she continued gently to knead him the full length of his growing member.

He moaned low and let his head fall back as Waits-by-the-Water grew more excited herself. It stimulated some secret place down within her own body to caress his most private part, to feel him grow with her touch, to hear him moan.

"You like this . . . this touch?" she asked.

"Jumpin' . . . Lord, yes!" he murmured, and shuddered with her stimulation. "This . . . this is very good."

"I like to feel you grow strong . . . grow big—under the power of my touch," she said. "I want to show love for you. Want to give you much pleasure—get much pleasure back from the man I love."

"You . . . you like this, too?"

"Yes."

She lay a palm lightly across his lower belly. The Crow woman could feel the muscles twitch and dance in spasms as he moved closer to explosion. Too, the muscles in his member wriggled and gyrated more and more the further she took him to climax. Finally, Waits-by-the-Water heard his breathing become heavy and grow into an audible moan that throbbed at her ears.

"I want you to finish in me," she whispered as she rose to her knees above him.

"Yes," was all he could whisper.

Waits-by-the-Water rose from her hands and knees and squatted over his abdomen, letting herself descend while her hands guided his penis into her. Never before had she sat atop a man like this. Those two before had come to rob her of any joy, of any explosion, to take from her any opportunity for her own pleasure. But this whiteman, he was a part of her, and she a big part of him. They each could pull much pleasure from the other simply by giving and granting that pleasure to the other.

Bass slid his hands up her thighs, his fingertips climbing across the flat of her belly, then up to cup the firm mounds. He pulled her shoulders toward him and raised his head so that he could suck on her breasts. He was so close now. She gyrated faster with the stimulation of her breasts. Her moving for him, on him, with him, pushed Scratch to those final moments before climax as her bucking dance topped a fiery crescendo.

He moaned as he exploded within her, feeling her close tightly about him as he expended himself. The Crow woman threw her head back with her own ecstasy and nearly lost her balance. They rocked on together, his hips pushing upward into her like some yet-to-be-broken pony would gyrate to throw its rider. They rocked on through it, her heels dug into the back of his knees so that he could not throw her with the strength of his climax. Finally, their dance began to slow.

She gasped twice and fell across him, keeping his member firmly planted within her moistness. Her breathing began to slow and become more rhythmic. She sighed as he began to stroke her hair. She sensed his heart next to her chest, heard the pumping of the blood in her ears.

"You are more than Waits-by-the-Water remember," she whispered hoarsely. "*Pote Ani* is all the bigger in my heart than when he left me, to go away for a long time."

Waits-by-the-Water became silent, feeling and listening to the man beneath her. The trapper began to snore lightly. She cocked her head to look at him. His head had fallen to the side as he slipped into sleep. She smiled and eased off from him. Rising to her knees in the chill night air, Waits-by-the-Water gazed down at her man. Her loving gaze caressed him much as her hair and lips had brushed across his flesh. Those sharp lines denoting where the sun had stopped and the white flesh began stood out dimly in the moonlight. She let her fingers lightly touch and circle within the little hair in the center of his chest.

She reached out and pulled the front of the bandanna down more securely over his forehead, then let her fingertips brush his cheek. The Crow woman bent over to kiss his cheek above the whiskers and then she pulled at the blankets near the foot of their bed. Waits-by-the-Water was filled with so much of him, with his love and with his power.

As she lay beside him to snuggle into the fetal curve made by his sleeping body, the woman rested her cheek against the coarse buffalo robe and nuzzled her nose into his chest, to smell of his musk. The smoke, and tobacco and pine. The sweat and the blood and the pain. Leather and damp wool. And excitement. They were all there for her in his smell.

She had chosen well, she thought. She had believed her life had nearly ended the evening he had left her. But she had somehow kept that flame within her alive for him. If she lost him again, there would never be another. No one else had his own peculiar, peaceful strength. If she lost him now . . . she did not want to think. She would just have to do everything she could to ensure that she would never be without him.

She heard him snore more loudly, more restfully as he turned in his sleep, snuggled into her. Waits-by-the-Water smiled and closed her eyes. She wanted to grow old listening to his peaceful snores.

The weariness of the trail finally began to slip from her mind and her body. The waiting was over. The beginning was at hand once more. They would venture into that tomorrow-place together, as unafraid as she could be.

She would not lose him again.

Twenty-two

"Jumpin' Jehosophat! C'mon, boy!" Bass hollered. "Let's get these women all prettied up with some gewgaws, girlews an' foofaraw!"

He swung up into the saddle, tied off the lead rope for the four pack animals carrying the beaver packs. Josiah and the two women mounted their ponies and trotted alongside the older trapper.

"Red," said Waits-by-the-Water.

"Red?" Scratch asked. "What you mean by that?"

"Red cloth," she explained, rubbing her hand across her breasts and down the front of her dress. "Get red cloth of trader."

"Ahhh," he answered knowingly. "You want me to get you some red tradecloth from the trader, huh?"

"Yes."

"Why, you damn betcha, lil' lady. You damn betcha, I will."

"I'll get some blue for Looks Far," Josiah added. "They make 'em up some fine dresses for struttin' 'round rendezvous."

"That wool be warm for 'em, too." Bass nudged his pony forward with the others. "Keep 'em warm come winter."

"Where you headin' for winter?" Paddock inquired. "Figure to head back to Absaroka and the Crow again?"

"Give myself some thought to that, I have of recent," Bass replied. "Been some long time since't last I was down to Bayou Salade, down to South Park. Fair bit of winterin' down to that place, it is."

"Ain't gonna go back to see Arapooesh?"

"S'pose I could do me that."

"He wanted to know if I'd found you all right. Wanted to know you was all right and have me bring you back to Absaroka."

"He did, huh?" Bass looked straight ahead into the distance. "Ol' brother-man. Love 'im, I surely does. Have to think on that. Been wantin' to head down toward Taos for winter doin's for last few years. Maybeso, it's time for that to get done."

Bass looked over at his friend. "We can send us some word to Rotten Belly that we see him next year—that ever'thing be all right. We gonna be seein' him this time next year—after ronnyvoo, next year."

"Where'bouts you plannin' on trappin' this fall?" the younger man asked. "And come next spring?"

"Headin' down toward South Park, that be where we trap for the fall. So damned close to there now, I can feel it in my bones. Feel it ticklin' my blood to come on down there. Trap our way in an' outta Park Kyack, then in an' outta Middle Park, right on down to the Bayou Salade. Like I was sayin'—maybeso we even take these here ladies on down for some fandango at Taos. Drink some of that *lightnin'* I hear tell is gotten better over the years. Hell! Was good 'nough when first I had me some!"

"*Lightnin'?*"

"The whiskey they make 'em down to Taos, up to the Arroyo Hondo," Bass said.

"Better than trader's whiskey?"

"Wagh!" he snorted with a quiet grizzly battle-cry. "Traders always dump shit in their whiskey: put red peppers, tobaccy an' molasses in the whiskey here to ronnyvoo. They water down the alcohol so much they gotta add that stuff to give it the whiskey color, give it back the bite of real whiskey, you see. Down to Taos, Josiah, that *lightnin'* be pure whiskey. Ain't gotta have it cut with nothin'."

"Maybe," Josiah said thoughtfully, "maybe you're right. Might be a good thing for us to get on down south for the winter. We can both send word to Arapooesh we all right and we be seein' him come next year. Wanna see this South Park–Bayou Salade you always talkin' 'bout. Even on down to this Mex'can town you say is some now."

"It is," Bass replied. "Truly is. Many's the man what winters down there. Many's the free trapper what works outta Taos, an'

down to Santee Fee. Maybeso, we even trade off some plews
from the fall trappin' down there whilst we at it, son."

"Let's do it."

"Does sound some good, don't it?"

"Damn if it don't!"

"You're on, son." Bass winked as they rode into a scattering
of tents, lean-tos, and other improvised shelters.

Men ambled about on foot, others rode horses through the
camp a little more than two miles south of Bonneville's Fort.
More men lounged in the shade of their shelters, drinking and
watching the rendezvous activities swirling around them. Most
nodded back to Scratch as he nodded to them in passing.

"Skin-trappers," Bass muttered out of the corner of his
mouth.

"What you mean, *skin-trappers?*"

"They work for the comp'ny, see," he replied. "They ain't
like us. They ain't cocks of the walk, son. We the best. No man
holds a candle to us." He sat straight and proud in the saddle.

He stared at Waits-by-the-Water. Damn, if he wasn't proud
of this woman. She was some now, and getting a few glances
from the men they were passing by.

"None better than us, eh?" Paddock said.

"You got it, son," Bass boasted. "We work for no man. No
goddamned booshway tellin' this here nigger where to throw
his bed-robes come night. No nigger tellin' this child where he
can set his traps an' then tellin' me what I made for the year.
No, sir, Josiah Paddock. Ain't no man like a free trapper."

"These here fellas don't seem to be doin' all that bad, now."
Josiah grinned.

"These boys?" Bass snorted. "They ain't got 'em no outfit like
what we got, now do they?"

"No, it don't appear to be they got 'em—"

"That's right. They don't. They get what they can get from
the booshway an' the comp'ny trader. They ain't got 'em no
wives, neither, Josiah."

"I see that."

"Ain't got 'em a chance to," Bass said. "Maybeso, the booshway knows a woman might'n just take a man's mind off'n trappin' an' be puttin' his mind onto other things, huh?" He
winked over at his young partner.

"Could be." Josiah nodded.

"Maybeso, these here fellas only get themselves laid 'bout
once't a year, son," Bass concluded. "They gotta find them-

selves a squaw down to ronnyvoo to get their wipin' stick wet in—some woman what's gettin' sold by her buck. Maybeso if'n she's lucky 'nough, that buck buy her somethin' pretty, too. Yep"—he nodded as he looked around—"these here fellas gotta get themselves a hurried job of lovin' whilst they can."

Bass watched the approach of a man on foot tugging a string of three ponies toward the southern edge of the encampment. Bass drew up.

"Howdy, friend!" he hollered.

"How do!"

"Been tradin', I see," Scratch observed.

"Yep, I have." The man smiled up at Bass.

"Campbell's outfit?"

"Nope. Down just a piece to American Fur this time."

"They ain't far?"

"Nawww." The stranger pointed. "Just past them trees."

"American Fur, huh? You with 'em?"

"Wouldn't have nothin' to do with a comp'ny booshway, this nigger wouldn't," the man commented sourly. "I'm a free trapper. Me an' five others wintered over on the Snake west of here. Spent two seasons over that part of the country."

"Nez Perce doin's, huh?" Scratch said. "You got somethin' to feel right proud 'bout 'round here. Bein' a free trapper, like us here."

"See that," the stranger said, glancing at the two women. "We come in to get us some plunder, drink their bad whiskey an' have a song or two before we head back west an' north some for fall trappin'."

"Campbell an' Sublette's train in yet?"

"Yeah," the stranger said. "He beat American Fur in to rendezvous by some three days. We was all waitin' for 'em both. See which one come in first.

"Last year, American didn't get in to rendezvous a'tall." The man spit some tobacco juice on the ground near his foot. "Sublette had the whole trade to himself."

"I know," Bass said.

"Things be lil' differ'nt this year, it seems," the stranger went on. "Drips was here waitin' an' Font'nelle finally come in last Monday, the eighth, with all his goods. They set up just back there." He pointed.

"Campbell on down?"

"That's right. They down on Horse Crik. Campbell seems to have lil' better prices, appears to me."

"Horse Creek? How far?"

"Just some two, maybe three mile. No more'n that. Gets its name from 'twenty-four when ol' Tom Fitzpatrick had some ponies stoled by Crows down near there. He named it Horse Crik in honor of the occasion."

The stranger smiled. "You been up doin' some tradin' with Bonneville up at his Fort Nonsense?"

"*Nonsense?*"

"Yep." He smiled broader. "We call it that—cain't see why a man build a fort out here on the high prairie."

"Really didn't see no sense in that neither," Bass agreed. "Nawww, we ain't been tradin'. Don't think this Bonneville's here. Looked to be not much tradin' goin' on."

"Oh, he's there all right. An' for certain he ain't doin' much tradin'. Just got some whiskey for his men. That be what they mostly doin' up there. I'm camped nearby."

"We spended us a night not far from that fort," Bass said. "The handle do fit it, don't it? *Fort Nonsense.* This Bonneville got to be some stupid booshway."

"Ever you see a smart booshway?"

"Come to think of it, I ain't now!" He and Josiah laughed with the stranger.

"Yeah, that Bonneville come in some three days back, on Friday the twelfth, packin' 'long some hundred or so men, an' a big herd of ponies. Better than three hundred of them animals. Near as I could tell, anyway. From the looks of it, a fella would figger Cap'ain Bonneville would have had him a good year."

"He didn't fare all that well?"

"That he didn't, for certain," the stranger replied. "Even though he's got some real, hard-knot boys workin' the field for him: Joe Walker, lil' Michael Cerre—like them. They good boys, too. How they got hooked up to that slicker, I ain't never gonna know."

"Free trappin' best, ain't it, friend?" Bass said as he presented a hand to the stranger.

"That it be," he replied, and brought up his hand to shake with Bass. "Name's Frye Teeter, friend."

"Titus Bass, recent of the Columbia by way of the Yellowstone."

"Whoooo," Teeter exclaimed with a short, low whistle. "You done some travelin', Bass."

"This here's my partner, Josiah Paddock. That be Josiah's

woman, she called Looks Far Woman. An' this here be the apple of this ol' nigger's eye—Waits-by-the-Water. My Crow gal."

Teeter nodded politely to each of the women and touched the brim of his hat. "Some fine lookin' women you got there, fellas. Some of us got Nez Perce wives. Mine a Digger. That be a workin' fool there, that woman. I'm thinkin' she be so damned grateful to have her a warm robe to sleep under an' a full belly all the time. She do her share of the work in camp, that'un. My woman, an' proud of her."

"As it should be, man," Bass said.

"Best be gettin' back to her an' the others up to camp." Frye tugged at the pack animals' lead rope.

"An' we best be to tradin'."

"You come on up an' have a drink on Frye Teeter!" he hollered over his shoulder.

"Same go for you, Frye," Bass yelled back.

Bass and his group moved into the expanse of open land south of the American Fur Company camp, heading toward the Campbell supply tents and the camp of Rocky Mountain Fur Company. The tents were thrown up on the point of land formed by the junction of Horse Creek and the Green River. A pretty site, with the lean-tos and shelters nestled back in the evergreens and among the willows.

Four large canvas tarps were strung out from the giant wall tent Campbell had erected. The sides of the tent had been rolled up to allow the breezes to move in and out of the saloon. There seemed to be more activity around the saloon tent than beneath the canvas awnings where trade goods were laid out on the crude, rough-hewn counters. A few men leaned against the counters, negotiating with the clerks.

Bass pulled up on the reins as the others brought their ponies to a halt. Waits-by-the-Water immediately slipped off her horse and began unloading the beaver packs from the horses.

"First we do this." Scratch nodded toward the crude trading counters. "Then we get us some of that." He nodded toward the saloon where a noisy celebration was going on in the middle of the day.

"Sounds like they're havin' a good time."

"Just like we gonna, son."

The two trappers studied the saloon, with its complement of comatose drunks stretched out on the ground. Some men wandered in and out carrying mugs of all sizes, stumbling back and forth between the drunks on the ground. Others merely leaned back against the huge tree limbs that served as poles for the tent and awnings.

Looks Far helped the Crow woman drag the beaver bundles to the counter. Bass and Paddock joined in, then went back to picket four of the ponies and tie the three pack animals off. Bass stepped up to the trading counter, his eyes on the saloon tent.

"Can I help you?" a clerk asked. "I suppose you wish to cash in some furs for credit, then step over to the watering hole?"

"Nawww, son," Scratch replied, now turning to study the clerk. The old man knew that each year it was automatically an adversary relationship with these employees of the trader. Fine, he thought. Long as I know how it's gonna be—it's just fine then.

"Wanna get us some truck first-off, mister." The old trapper studied the spare, wiry man. Probably a Frenchy, he thought.

"What can we help you with first, sir?" the twenty-six-year-old Charles Larpenter inquired.

"How be your lead an' powder, son? The pound?"

"Lead be Galena's finest and the best American powder is some three-eighty the pound."

"I'll have me a look-see over your goods here." Bass bowed to look closely over the trays of goods containing the small items. Then he peered into the back of the structure at the barrels and tins of hidden treasures.

The young clerk swept around the end of the counter. "I'll have a look at your skins." He headed for the bundles the two trappers had dragged up. "Free trappers?" he asked as he eyed the two Indian women.

"That's right," Josiah answered, watching the clerk's gaze drift back down to the beaver bales. "Why do you ask?"

"I just supposed you were," Larpenter answered. "Packing squaws along."

"They ain't our squaws," Josiah snapped. "They our wives, man!"

Larpenter glanced up from the cutting he was doing on the thick rawhide strips that held the heavy bundles together. "Lots of free trappers have Indian *wives*, is why I asked."

"We need some extra traps, son," Scratch said.

"Sacks behind the counter." Charles nodded toward the back of the awning. "Help yourselves."

"Believe we will." Scratch led Josiah around the end of the counter and each opened a heavy leather sack. Bass pulled out an iron trap and set it on the ground. Deftly, the old trapper placed a foot upon each spring and watched the two square jaws flop open. He bounced up and down on the trap-springs, then finally knelt with the balls of his feet on the trap to set the pan and the trigger. Metal groaned under the strain. Then he looked up at Josiah, who watched him with amusement.

"What you think?" Paddock asked.

"They good. Tough." Bass looked up at his younger partner. "They do us."

"How much?" Josiah turned toward Larpenter as the clerk straightened himself.

"The traps are twenty dollars the half-dozen," Larpenter replied, reaching for a tall, narrow, leather-bound ledger.

"How many we need?" Josiah asked Bass.

"Maybe a dozen," Bass said. "That be 'nough for you to work 'long with what we already got."

"That's some bit of money, Scratch."

"Ain't no way we gonna make us money less'n we spend some money on traps, noways." He glanced over at the clerk who had sorted the plews into three stacks. "We gotta spend some of our plews to make us some more."

"Maybe we oughta just settle on me usin' Asa's traps," Paddock suggested.

"No tellin' how long it been since last he set any of 'em in water," Bass said. "They need work for sure."

"I'd rather repair them traps than pay all that money for these new ones, ol' man."

"I'll think on your idea, son. I'll think on it."

Bass went on to look over some more of the items in the tin containers and the small wooden barrels. He sifted through flints that clattered together like coins and poked around at wiping sticks and spare locks that made soft clicks as he tested them; let his fingers toy with the selection of small strung beads and the larger Venetian trade beads. Finally he came to what looked to be bundles of blankets."

"How your blankets?"

"They are by the point, sir," Larpenter said. "Haven't got many left, however. It seems everyone needed an extra blanket this year. Go ahead and take a look at what we have left."

Scratch pulled back the blanket that draped over several of

the hidden bundles. "Come here," he said in Crow to Waits-by-the-Water. "You like you any of these?"

"This one." She pointed to a blanket that was white with light blue and bright red stripes at either end.

Bass held it up and unfolded it for her. The cloth whispered like wind through aspen leaves. "Four point: it's some pretty, all right," he commented. "Yeah. Just for you." He turned his head. "Josiah, your woman needs her 'nother blanket to keep her warm—the boy needs one, too."

Bass glanced quickly at the Flathead woman. "Looks Far, come here."

She came over, beaming happily. "I like this one." She pointed toward a bright red blanket with a black stripe at either end.

Josiah unfolded the blanket and held it up for her inspection. "Don't know why you think Looks Far needs 'nother blanket, ol' man. She got me to keep her warm."

"In that case, young'un," Bass said with a wide grin, "better be gettin' your woman *two* blankets!"

Paddock groaned. "You like this one, eh?" he said to his woman.

"Yes," Looks Far answered with a wide smile.

"It's yours, lil' woman," he replied as he handed it to her.

Looks Far took the heavy, woolen blanket and draped it around her shoulders as Waits-by-the-Water had done, each admiring the other's choice. They sniffed the cloth, smelling the musty scent of newly woven wool. They turned and curvetted friskily, like young colts. They made little cooing sounds of pleasure as they performed for each other.

"You gotta get 'nother, Looks Far," Bass said. "That boy of your'n be gettin' too big real soon an' gonna need a blanket of his own."

"C'mere and pick 'nother one out." Josiah waved her back to the counter. "What one for Joshua?"

Looks Far studied all of the blankets, trying to make up her mind. She had always wanted a red blanket and now she had it. But to choose another one, even if for their son—this was beyond her wildest dreams. Finally she pointed toward the forest-green blankets near Bass. "This one."

"Green one, huh?"

"Yes," she answered Bass. "Green one for Jozshuwaaa."

Bass picked the folded blanket off the top of the stack and

handed it to the younger trapper. "There you be, son. For you an' the boy."

"Glad you thought of that, Scratch," Josiah said. "Joshua be gettin' too big for his cradle soon and we gotta be keepin' him warm someway this comin' winter."

"Don't want the lil' pup freezin' come robe season, son. Just makes sense to me to be gettin' them all warm blankets now. The warmer we keep our womenfolk, after all, the warmer they gonna keep us." He winked at Josiah. "Right?"

"You right there, ol' man!" Josiah smiled widely. "Looks Far asked me for some cloth to make a dress from. Where you find it? They got anything like that here?" He glanced around at the stacks of trade goods.

"You got any cloth—for dresses, shirts, an' such?" Scratch called to Charles Larpenter.

"Yes, sir," said Campbell's clerk. "Keep on going down the stacks of blankets. Cloth hasn't been moving too well last few days. Most men are drinking. It's under the blankets." He went back to separating the plews.

"Lotta drinkin', huh?" Bass said.

"That's right. In fact, I was not supposed to work the tent here. But the fellow who was, Redman, has gotten himself so drunk every day, that Fitzpatrick turned the trade-clerking over to me while Campbell was over to Pierre's Hole to raise a cache of furs. That's him, Redman, over there. As you can see, he's not worth a tinker's damn right now."

Bass glanced over at the saloon tent. One man, apparently passed out or sleeping it off, leaned against another, who silently watched the trading. Flies buzzed around the drunk man's whiskered chin, the dried vomit caked on his shirt. The watchful second man's glazed, sullen eyes flickered as he dropped his gaze to look back into his tin cup before he brought it to his lips to drink.

"They trappers, I bet," Scratch commented as he turned back toward Charles. "Get a good drunk on myself, I'm plannin'."

"No," said Larpenter. "They came with the pack train. The one who's out cold was supposed to clerk—but obviously can't. Hasn't been able to for many days. Robert Campbell's going to be docking his pay some."

"Boys should learn to get their work done first—then comes the play," said Scratch. "Be needin' some sugar, coffee, flour. . . ." His gaze drifted to the canvas awning above his head as he continued through his mental checklist. "Get some flints, powder, lead."

"Beads," Josiah added.

"Yepper—some beads, too," Bass agreed. "Some trade cloth!" He pulled the blankets away to get to the bolts of cloth. He grabbed a bolt of bright red cloth and another of royal blue, set them both on the counter top with a muffled thump.

"What you think of them, ladies?" Scratch smiled at the two women.

The Indian women rushed to the counter and fingered the coarse, wool cloth, each one caressing first the blue, then the red.

"I take this one," Looks Far said, holding the edge of the blue cloth.

"That's blue," Josiah told her.

"Red?" Waits-by-the-Water asked of Josiah as she held up the cloth for him.

"Yes. Red, that one is," he answered.

"Yes. Red one I like." She nodded at Bass now.

"How much the cloth?" Bass asked Larpenter.

"The trade cloth is ten dollars per yard."

"Hmmm," Bass considered. "Ain't never buyed me none of that afore. Three feet to the yard . . . how many you s'posin' we need for them women, Josiah?"

"What you askin' me for?" Josiah countered. "I don't know a thing 'bout womenfolk's clothes."

"Let's just try it on for size."

Bass grabbed the large bolt of cloth, unwrapped it until he thought he had enough strung out. Then he unfolded it and held the cloth up for the Crow woman.

"Come, step in here," he directed.

Waits-by-the-Water waltzed into the semi-circle he had made of the cloth. He wrapped it around her twice, then marked the spot with his two fingertips.

"That be 'nough, I s'pose."

Carefully he unwrapped the Crow woman, keeping his fingers tightly on the spot where he wanted the cloth cut. "How you want us to mark this, son?"

"Just cut it yourself, sir," Larpenter replied. "Scissors on a chain at the back of the counter."

"Get 'em for me," Bass asked Josiah.

Paddock hunted around until he located the scissors and

then handed them to the old trapper. Still marking the spot with his fingers, Scratch spread the cloth out across the counter top. After smoothing the cloth out, Bass slipped his fingers into the handles of the large scissors and hacked raggedly across the cloth. When he was done, he looked up proudly.

"You're next," he said to Looks Far.

"Just cut it same size," Josiah suggested. "Be all right, won't it?"

"I s'pose," Bass answered as he wrestled the blue bolt out across the counter. He measured it with the red, and hacked off a long piece. The two women folded their choices and set them atop the three folded blankets.

"You gonna tell us how much credit we got, son?" Bass asked Larpenter, who was behind the counter where a crude scale was set up.

"That is the next order of business," the clerk said, "once I see how many pounds of each grade you have here."

"This be where the screwin' starts, boy," Bass mumbled, as he nudged Josiah.

"I know that," Josiah replied. "I learned all 'bout that last year, 'member?"

Josiah's thoughts flew back to the bright mental images of his first rendezvous in Pierre's Hole west of the Tetons. And his first instruction from Titus Bass about the intricacies of barter. Scratch had smiled broadly with those twinkling, merry, wrinkled eyes as he had spoken.

"I laugh at a red nigger I'm tradin' with, tellin' him he's stupid for givin' me a few plews, maybe even a buffler robe, for a handful of shiny, blue beads. That nigger, you know, goes an' laughs right at me then. Tellin' me I'm the dumb shit in the tradin'. Givin' him some blue beads he can have his squaw put on a new pair of mokersons, maybe a war shirt—an' me askin' in trade only them skins. He's laughin' at me for givin' him somethin' what come all the way from St. Louie, sayin' he's givin' me what comes right outta these here hills. Furs any man can get, he says. I s'pose we both walk 'way from the tradin' thinkin' the other's a dumb-shit, no-mind nigger. S'pose that's what tradin's all 'bout anyways, when you looks at it. Both of us happy, thinkin' we got the best of the deal, thinkin' we did the screwin' on the other nigger."

"Yeah, ol' friend," Josiah continued, "I learned all 'bout that last year."

"Then I tell someone what doesn't know yet." Bass looked

over at Looks Far and the Crow woman. "Lemme talk with Joshua."

The two women glanced at each other, not at all sure the old trapper was in his right mind. Finally the Flathead woman turned so that the cradleboard faced Bass.

"Now, son," he began, leaning into the infant's face, "I know I'm startin' you early 'nough. An' I know your mama may not want you to be a trapper. But, this here is a 'portant lesson for any young pup of a trapper to be learnin'. This fella here"—he gestured toward Larpenter—"he's gonna try screwin' me now: sayin' what my plews be worth, you see. The worst he can make it for me, Joshua—the better he make it for the trader."

The two Indian women glanced at one another again. Josiah clapped a hand over his mouth to keep from chuckling too loudly.

"That be your first lesson, Joshua," Bass concluded. "You pay close 'tention to what's goin' on here—you'll be a master trapper like your ol' Uncle Scratch—your grand-uncle Scratch, that is. Thank you, Joshua—for your kind 'tention." He lifted a flap of deerskin from the boy's face.

"I'll be damned. The boy was 'sleep all the time I was teachin' him!" he snorted. "Pups these days. What the world comin' to when a pup won't pay 'tention to his elders!"

Josiah laughed, then turned to the clerk. "What beaver be worth, anyway?"

"Four dollar the pound on beaver plew," Larpenter said.

"Four dollar! Whooooeeeee!" Bass exclaimed. "Mother of whores—bless me on Sundays! Was only three just last year. That's some now!"

"I hear the market has gotten itself healthier," Charles commented.

"Dollar a pound healthier—wagh!" Bass roared. "We just gonna see how much healthier when we get to the pricin' on your trade goods, son. Market gone up on what beaver brings—trader gets a mind to raise his prices all in the same, too."

He moved up to Larpenter. "What these blankets bringin' a point?"

"Six dollar a point," Larpenter answered without looking up from his ledger. "Those are four-point, heavy ones. That comes to twenty-four dollars a blanket."

"Ooooh!" Bass exclaimed, and slapped a hand across his belly. "Josiah! I been gut-shot by Bobby Campbell, I have."

"Would you rather have the three-point? That can save you some six dollars a blanket."

"Nawww. Them ladies already picked 'em their blankets, an' one for the boy there," Bass said. "We keep them heavy four-pointers, for winter doin's."

"A wise choice, sir," Charles replied. "You have quite a credit here. Looks as if you will net about six dollars a plew for your work, gentlemen."

"That's some, ain't it, Josiah?"

"I s'pose," Paddock agreed, still somewhat confused by the beaver market and his niche in that marketplace.

"So, how much we got?" Scratch inquired.

"You have netted three-hundred, fifty-five pounds of beaver here," Larpenter answered. "In my grading of them—"

"Watch out, Josiah," Bass interrupted, "this boy's 'bout ready to put it to us! 'Bout ready to skin us 'live!"

"That's not part of my job, sir," Larpenter retorted testily.

"Just a joke, son," Bass said. "Now, how 'bout tellin' me what you come up with?"

"Just leave the man alone, will you, Scratch?"

"I am," said the old trapper, a little subdued. "I am. Just want him to tell us what he come up to with his cipherin'."

"I have arrived at a total of two-hundred, thirty-two pelts. Of those beaver, fifty-eight are poor for some three-hundred, fifty-six dollars. The poor come to a little over eighty-nine pounds."

"You boys always say a passel of a man's furs be poor," Bass commented. "Well, son—they didn't look poor to me when I was the freezin' nigger to pull 'em out of the water, grain 'em an' stretch 'em afore I packed the mothers' sons up for ron-nyvoo."

"It is merely what I have been trained to do, sir," Charles said politely. "Mister Campbell himself taught me how to grade the beaver for him."

"I'm sure he trained you some good, too."

"That he did, sir. Next: your good grade amounts to ninety-two pelts at one-hundred, forty-two pounds. That puts you in at five-hundred, sixty-eight more dollars. Your subtotal is now nine-hundred, twenty-four dollars."

"That's more than last year's take, Scratch," Josiah whispered.

"Beaver gone up, boy," he whispered hoarsely. "'Sides, we should have us all the more plews—you workin' them streams with me, son."

"And finally, your prime plews amount to eighty-two pelts at some one-hundred, twenty-four pounds, or some four-hundred, ninety-six dollars."

"What that make my total come to?"

"Your three-hundred, fifty-five skins amount to some fourteen-hundred and twenty dollars in credit, sir. Now, if you will just tell me your names?"

"Wagh!" Bass roared. "That be a lotta plew, Josiah!"

"'Bout six-hundred better than last year."

"You right, boy. Oh"—he turned back to the clerk—"my name be Bass. Titus Bass. That spelled T-I-T-U-S."

"Titus Bass," he repeated as he wrote. "Very good. Now, you sir?" He eyed Josiah.

"Paddock."

"First name?"

"Josiah."

"Josiah Paddock," Larpenter intoned.

Behind them against the poles of the saloon tent, one of the two mule-tenders sat up a little straighter. Hickerson Nute rose to his feet clumsily. His head spun with the effects of his hangover. He was groggy; he knew that. But he was sure he had heard the name right. He wandered over toward the awnings and counters, as casually as he could. He wanted to take it slow now. Perhaps the long wait was over.

"Now, with a sizable credit such as this," Larpenter went on, "what do you two gentlemen feel like buying—before the whiskey, that is?"

"How much we got in that cloth here?" Bass slapped a hand back down on the stack of blankets and trade cloth.

"Coarse cloth is ten dollars a yard," Larpenter said. "Fine cloth like the linens and calicoes comes to twenty dollars a yard."

"How much we got here?" He tapped the cloth.

Larpenter pulled at the bundles of trade cloth and began to measure them against marks along the top of the counter, while Bass and Paddock went back to digging through the treasures behind the counter.

Nute approached the two trappers slowly.

"You fellas drinkin'?" he slurred.

Scratch turned around first to find the stranger's attention fixed on Paddock. "No, friend. Not yet, we ain't."

"How 'bout havin' you a drink on Hickerson Nute then?" He

offered Paddock a large tin cup he held unsteadily. The liquid sloshed around in miniature amber waves.

Josiah stared into the stranger's eyes. He looked down into the tin cup, saw it was about half-full of the discolored grain alcohol, with bits of grass and hair floating on the surface.

"No thanks, friend." Josiah smiled slightly and turned back to the trade goods.

"You ain't gonna drink with me?" Nute snarled.

"No thanks, friend." Bass responded this time. "We got us some business to be dealin' with right now. Maybe later."

"You too good to drink with me? Just who the hell you sons of bitches think you are, anyway?" Nute exploded.

Bass slowly examined his antagonist, then glanced over Nute's shoulder at the saloon tent where it had gotten suddenly quiet. "Us?" He tapped a finger against his own chest. "You wanna know just who the hell mother-whore-sons you talkin' to, boy?" His voice had a controlled, finely honed edge to it now.

From the corner of his eye, Scratch watched Paddock move away slightly. "You wanna know, boy? I asked you the question, son."

"Yeah," Nute said hoarsely. "I wanna know—know why you ain't gonna drink with me, Paddock."

The younger trapper swung around to face Hickerson. "How you know my name?"

"I heard you tell it to Charlie here." He pointed to Larpenter, who began to edge toward the three men.

"Hickerson." Charles reached out for Nute's arm. "I think you had best sit down and finish your drinking."

"Don't touch me, you asshole weasel-face!" Nute spit toward Charles, and knocked the clerk's hand off his arm.

"Hey, son," Bass said, moving between the clerk and Nute. "The young fella said he thought it best for you to go back an' finish up your drinkin' now."

"You goddamned, all-roarin'-mighty mountain men!" Nute snarled. "What's that you got in your ear there, ol' mountain man? Wearin' a earring, like a woman, eh?" His upper lip curled in a derisive sneer. "Thinkin' you so tough—maybe you ain't so—"

"Maybe you just better shut your mouth afore it gets you in trouble any deeper," Josiah warned.

Nute started to weave, then looked up into Paddock's face

and, with a flick of his wrist, lashed the warm whiskey into the young trapper's eyes. Josiah jerked backward as he fought to see, the image of Hickerson lunging at him now only a hazy blur.

Scratch dove toward the big man and laid a shoulder into the drunk's belly, sending the mule-tender sprawling. Then he sprang to the balls of his feet near the prostrate drunk, waiting for him to recover.

"I've seen me some real asshole muleheads afore—but you take the circle!" Bass said. "Son, it best be you leave my partner alone. You best read me and read me good. What I 'bout to say ain't no baldface, ain't no baldface 'tall, boy! You gotta come through me to get to him." The voice was as calm as he could make it.

Josiah had heard this razor's edge to the old man's words few times before.

Nute struggled to his feet, staggering sideways a couple of times before he crouched low to maintain his balance. His right hand darted to his waist where he yanked free a big knife. But just as suddenly it was kicked out of his hand and sent sailing, sliding in the grass toward Scratch's feet. The young stranger who had kicked at Nute's hand stepped right up to the drunk.

"What the hell's going on here, Nute?" Robert Campbell asked, pushing his way in between Nute and the older trapper. "You're making a goddamned spectacle of yourself! What the hell's gotten into you, man?"

"I . . ." A sheepish look crawled across his face. "I just wanted 'em to have a drink with me is all—an' these bastards didn't wanna drink with Hickerson Nute."

"Maybe they've trading to do." Campbell looked at Bass and Paddock. "Perhaps they aren't interested in having a drink. Goddamnit, man! Behave yourself! Maybe—Lord knows—just maybe I should have let Stewart cut your liver out back there along the Platte. But I saved you then. And I've always got to come along and save you from getting yourself cut up. You get back over there." He pointed to the saloon tent.

Campbell waited a long moment until he saw that Nute was not going to move. "Now!" he yelled. "You go and finish your drunk and leave the trading tent. It's off bounds to you from now on out. Move, man!"

Nute glared at him before he slinked back to his place beside Redman.

Obahdiah had snored through the whole thing. Nute crumpled to the ground beside his partner and roughly shoved Redman aside, jostling his head and making Obahdiah awaken. The second man looked about sleepily, as if in a dense fog, to see why he had been so rudely awakened. Then his head plopped back down on Nute's shoulder. Hickerson shoved it alongside roughly.

"What the hell you do that for?" Obahdiah asked as he raised his head.

"Mind your own goddamned business!"

"What . . . what the hell goin' on with you?"

"Tell you later, goddamnit. Go back to sleep."

Redman fell asleep and Campbell knelt down to pick Nute's knife off the ground. He slipped it into his belt while the mule-tender watched him, so that Hickerson would know where it was. Campbell turned then to Larpenter. "Let's just all go back to work, boys. It's all in a day's fun, this is. Let's just be going back to our business."

Campbell headed for his tent on the other side of the saloon, while Larpenter returned to the counter. "You have seventy-two dollars in the three four-point blankets. Along with three yards apiece on the cloth. That comes to sixty dollars plus the seventy-two, a subtotal of one-hundred, thirty-two dollars."

"How much your red paint?"

"The vermilion? Eight dollars the pound."

"Chinee?"

"Yes, sir."

"Six pounds," he ordered, as Larpenter went to measure the powdered pigment. Bass turned to Josiah. "Them women do like their red paint, don't they?"

"But—six pounds of it?" Josiah asked.

"We promised to get 'em all the gewgaws we could, son. Right?" He turned back to Charles. "Tell me what the damage be on these here pretties." His fingers played with the bracelets, rings and necklaces resting in several wooden trays.

"Finger rings be seventy-five cents per dozen; dollar the dozen for bracelets. Those necklaces in the last box are one-dollar-ten apiece."

"Son, you pick out two dozen of them bracelets, couple dozen of the rings an' 'bout three of them real pretty necklaces with a lotta hangy-downs on 'em for the ladies each."

Paddock set to work pulling the items out of the wooden trays while Bass ambled down the counter toward more displays, glancing up once to see Nute glowering at him. "How much these mirrors?" He held up a small mirror with a soft, lead border around it. "This pretty ribbon, too?"

"That ribbon is ten cents a yard," said Larpenter as he finished wrapping the vermilion in small, folded, waxed papers, "and the hand mirrors are sixty cents a dozen."

"I'm gonna set two dozen these mirrors out for you an' the clerk, son," Bass explained to Paddock. "Then you get us measured some fifty yards of this here ribbon. There be five real pretty colors here for the women—get 'em ten yard of each color."

"You gonna wrap yourself up for a pretty present—for your woman, eh?" Paddock winked.

"Wouldn't need no fifty yard, I wouldn't!" Bass laughed. "Close, but not quite. How much that come to, Mister Clerk?"

Larpenter was bent over the ledger page, trying to keep up with Bass's instructions to the younger trapper. He jerked his hand back and forth between the paper and the inkwell, racing his quill across the page. Finally he raised his head. "Your subtotal is now one-hundred, ninety-six and thirty cents."

"Good." Bass smiled. "We rollin' now, son. Need lead. How much the mark on Galena?"

"Galena is dollar-sixty per pound."

"If'n you be sure it come from the Galena mines—gimme two hundred pounds."

"*Two hundred* pounds?" Josiah almost choked. "Why so damned much?"

"Got more rifles—two more ladies—two more guns we might be usin' some times." He turned back to the clerk. "Make that two hundred pounds, son."

"Three-hundred, twenty dollars." Larpenter stroked the number on the ledger page.

"Powder?"

"American?"

"Nawww," Bass replied. "English."

"Four-sixty a pound."

"Hmmm." Bass considered and calculated, staring at and moving his fingers slightly in his projections. "Seventy-five pounds of the shootin' stuff an' some fifteen pounds of the primin' grade."

Larpenter stroked some more ink on the paper before he looked up again. "The powder comes to four-hundred, fourteen."

"How you doin', son?" Bass watched Josiah going through the bracelets and rings, making them jingle, picking out the prettiest among the many wide and narrow brass bands. Paddock held up six long necklaces, three strung across each hand. The necklaces had blue and red chevrons, colored beads and tiny brass balls hanging from each of their strings.

"They look good, Josiah. Them'll do." He turned back to Charles. "Wipin' sticks?"

"One dollar twenty-five each."

"Straight-grained hick'ry, I take it."

"Nothing but, sir."

"Three dozen."

"Three   ," Paddock started.

"We got us more guns now." Bass quieted him instantly. "Gotta have us more wipin' sticks gettin' broken. What's your flints?"

"American?"

"Nawww, son. I want the best you got. You have any French ambers?"

"Yes, sir. Right over here," he said, motioning toward a small keg that had its top pulled off. "Pretty lil' things they are, too."

"Josiah, you finish with them gewgaws, get us three dozen of them wipin' sticks, straightest ones you can find. Then get us some twelve dozen of them amber flints."

"They are sixty-five cents a dozen," Larpenter commented.

"Don't make no never mind to me," Bass replied. "They the best. You gettin' all this down? How much we up to now?"

Campbell's clerk went back to his calculating. When he raised his head, he said, "All of that comes to seven-hundred, ninety-one and sixty-five cents, bringing your total now to nine-hundred, eighty-seven and ninety-five cents, sir."

"We rollin' some now, Josiah. How much credit we still got left?"

"Something in the way of four hundred dollars," Larpenter said.

"Two of them square axes there." He pointed to the axes hanging from a post that supported a section of the canvas awning. "Three of them big butcher knives, an' three of them skinnin' knives there. How much are they?"

"Axes are three dollars each," the clerk answered. "Knives are ninety-cents each."

"Nails? Brass?"

"Yes. Sixty cents per dozen."

"Four dozen we need for nailin' repairs and decoration. Them firesteels an' awls? What they?"

"Firesteels and awls both are two-fifty a dozen." He wrote furiously as Scratch was placing his order.

"Four dozen of each, then. How we set on the numbers, son?"

"That little run cost you only thirty-three and eighty cents, bringing your total to—hmmm: one-thousand, twenty-one dollars and seventy-five cents, Mister Bass."

"We almost there, now," Bass said. He looked around the tent. "Don't see no coffee, flour. Maybe some pepper, salts an' sugar."

"Coffee right here." Larpenter gestured behind him at the burlap sacks full of beans. "The rest over here, too."

"Coffee?"

"Three dollars the pound."

"Twenty-five pound. Flour?"

"Two and sixty-five cents."

"Just ten pound'll do us for that. Sugar?"

"Three dollars the pint."

"Take some fifteen pint of that—"

"What?" Paddock suddenly lifted his head from counting out the amber flints. "What we needin' so much sugar for? You sudden got a sweet-tooth, ol' man?"

"Might say that, son," Bass replied. "Might say that. The woman I'm so sweet on likes her coffee with a lil' sugar to it."

"Way you make coffee, I'd say she needs a lotta sugar."

"You sayin' I make bad coffee? Never heard you complain 'bout it afore."

"Don't take it so hard." Josiah chuckled and returned to his counting. "Get the sugar, Scratch."

"Plannin' on it, son. Plannin' on it." Bass eyed Larpenter. "Forget the salt. Do with the pepper only. How's it?"

"Seven-fifty the pound."

"Five pounds'll do of that," Bass decided. "You got some numbers so far?"

Larpenter raised his head. "You are getting there, sir. That was one-hundred, eighty-four dollars, even—and now you are up to twelve-hundred, five dollars and seventy-five cents."

"You ain't gonna forget tobaccy, are you?" Paddock asked the older trapper.

"How's your 'baccy?"

"Two-eighty per pound."

"Give us some thirty pound of the honey-dew. Josiah, you pick us out some carrots an' twists. Best to smell it up good afore you choose it. Don't want to be gettin' sick off bad tobaccy like I done one year." He craned his neck toward the counter.

"S'pose we needin' some of these beads on them strings there—for tradin' an' for them womenfolk makin' up some things. We want 'em to be prettied up with fancy beadwork. An' we cain't forget Joshua's clothes. Won't be long, he won't be havin' to ride in that cradleboard there. He gonna need some right fancy duds, too. What the damage on the beads, Mister Clerk?"

"Six dollars per pound."

"Five pounds and give me the total." Bass sighed. "I think I better call it quits for now."

"Tobacco comes to eighty-four dollars and the beads come to thirty dollars." Larpenter burrowed down to calculate his grand total.

"Them beads give our women lotta winter work, wherever we be come freeze-up. Wherever we plan on puttin' down robes for the season, son."

"Your grand total comes to thirteen-hundred, nineteen dollars and seventy-five cents."

"Well," Bass drawled, "what that leave us credit?"

"Credit?"

"Yeah, credit. For the whiskey tent, son."

"Credit," the clerk stated matter-of-factly. "Afraid there isn't much of that left you, sir."

"Just how much ain't left us, Mister Clerk?"

"Only one-hundred dollars and twenty-five cents."

"Ain't much to wet my dry, Josiah."

"'Bout as much as you had to drink on last year—some ninety-five dollars got you pretty drunk last year."

"Things have a funny way of evenin' themselves right on out. Beaver's got up to four dollar a pound. So the trader marks his own prices up to match. Keeps a fella 'bout even. An' it seems this nigger always only got 'bout a hundred dollar left to get drunk an' hungover with each an' ever' year."

Paddock grinned wide.

"So be it," Bass said. "Let's get the ponies loaded with all this plunder. We gonna have to walk, us two, it looks to be, son. Use six of 'em to carry all the truck. Maybeso, the women still got 'nough room to ride with them other ponies all loaded.

We get that done, we get us our paper from Mister Clerk here to say we got that hundred dollar of drinkin' over to Campbell's waterin' hole."

"I bet I've got a thirsty that comes close to matchin' yours, ol' man!" Josiah said, as he started dragging the bundles of newly traded goods over to the horses.

The women were already loading the things as Scratch concluded his negotiations with the clerk. They had wrapped up the smaller items inside the pieces of trade cloth, while other items had been secured inside the three blankets. They lashed these to the ponies. Then the sacks of flour, lead, coffee and sugar, along with the tins of powder, they strapped on top for the short walk back to their camp.

Joshua began to whimper quietly.

"Feed to camp," said Looks Far as she mounted.

"Yeah," Josiah replied as he swung the last load atop a pack animal and cinched the bundle down. "The boy ain't the only one who's hungry. We all get us somethin' to eat—get back to camp."

"You ready?" Bass asked his Crow woman.

"Yes," she said. "We walk slow."

"If you ain't gonna be outrunnin' us, you're gonna have to walk them ponies slow." He turned back to the clerk beneath the shade of the awning.

"Thank you, son," he hollered cheerfully at Larpenter. "We be back. Most like, not 'til tomorrow. Then we stoppin' in to spend some of the rest of that credit with Mister Campbell over there." He nodded toward the saloon tent.

Bass squinted in that direction and the wide smile disappeared from his lips. The drunk was still passed out against the post. But the loud-mouthed big man was gone. Redman was alone. Nute was nowhere to be seen.

He looked over at Josiah. "Let's be makin' tracks, son. We got us lotta work to do sortin' an' packin' away all this plunder an' truck for travelin'. We'll make supper this night for the women. They can be makin' their dresses an' we fix dinner. Even have us some coffee, too!"

"That sounds good now."

"Saw them red wool shirts they was sellin'. Better idea be to get some pretty cloth for to make a new shirt," Bass mused.

"For the one you tore up last year?"

"Yep. But get them womenfolk all decked out like we gonna first. We just get 'em all the gewgaws an' finery on, we take us a stroll back down here tomorrow an' do some drinkin' with Bobby Campbell. Nigger like me don't need a new shirt. Hell, I got me a woman to do some fine sewin' for me now!"

"And besides, if the women got any cloth left after they cut out the dresses, you can be usin' it for a shirt."

"Sounds to be a handsome idea, son." Bass nodded. "Damn! If this ain't gonna be the best goddamned ronnyvoo for this child!"

"Looks to be," Josiah agreed.

"Best by a long chalk, Josiah." Bass sighed. "Both got our women here with us. Got us 'nough plews for tradin' plunder for 'nother year—'sides a lil' drinkin', to boot. Be the best damned ronnyvoo for this child ever! Bigger an' better!"

Some distance behind the small party, a large shadow slipped through the trees. He stayed in the darkness of the shadows as he skittered from tree to tree, following the trappers and the two women. He would come back to tell Redman later. When Obahdiah was sober.

Tonight. Yes, tonight they would collect their prize. And with the pistol in hand, they were assured of a small treasure upon their return to St. Louis.

But for now he would follow to see where the two trappers camped. Memorize the location, and study the other tents nearby so he could bring Redman directly to it after they had made plans for their . . . their job.

Nute smiled. This was getting easier all the time. Get this young fella out of the way and then he could wrap up all the celebrating by going after that Scot. Finish it. Settle the score with that fancy son of a bitch.

But tonight he wanted to get his hands on that French dueling pistol. Tonight he would hold on to the pistol and wipe the blood from his knife. That thought made him smile more broadly as he slid quickly and quietly from tree to tree.

Blood on his knife.

Twenty-three

"You sure this is their camp?" Redman whispered into his partner's ear, his breath stale, whiskey-sodden.

"Sure, I'm sure."

"Well, I ain't so damned sure, Hick." Redman shook his head, the movement almost imperceptible in the darkness of the undergrowth where they huddled, and waited. "All I seen for close to an hour is them two squaws 'round that fire. I ain't so damned sure as you."

"I was the one that saw 'em," Nute replied. "Was the one that saw *him*. I stood right next to the son of a bitch Paddock. And I follered 'em here this afternoon—right here."

"You're sure—you're sure?"

"I'm certain as I can be," Nute answered irritably.

"Damn!" Obahdiah cursed. "Wish I knew where them two sons of bitches was. Make this whole thing all so easy."

"Why don't we just go in and take them women?" Nute suggested.

"What for?" Obahdiah shot back. "Ain't you had 'nough women since you got here?" He shook his head. "Jesus Christ! You still got a hankerin' to wet your stinger in them red sluts, eh?"

"Might say that—"

"Well, out with it," Obahdiah prodded. "What's your plan?"

"Ain't really got much of a plan, but way I see it—we take them women, maybe get 'em tied up. Tie 'em down so they cain't fight us much. Then we wait 'til the men get back and finish the job up slick. You like the sound of that?"

"Don't know," Redman considered. "Don't like not knowin' where the men are."

"They off drinkin', most like."

"How can you be so damned sure, you buckle-brain?"

"I was the one saw 'em tradin' this afternoon, wasn't I?" Nute asked. "I know they was plannin' on gettin' some drinkin' done with the money left after buyin' all them supplies. You

426

wouldn't know—you was damned near plowed under there."

"Still my head's ringin'," Redman said in some little misery. "Not in the best shape to be cuttin' a man up."

"I ain't the best neither," Hickerson whispered. "But I come all this way to cut this sapsucker's heart out and get me a pistol to take back to St. Lou," he said hoarsely. "I ain't 'bout to let a little headache go botherin' me now."

"I ain't backin' out on you now." Obahdiah felt chastised. "I . . . I just wish I could get my mind on somethin' else."

"That's just what I was talkin' 'bout—goin' in an' gettin' them women." He twisted a smile toward his partner. "Make me feel all relaxed and loose for when them menfolk come back home tonight. Be ready for 'em both myself then."

"Maybe a lil' fun with them bang-tail squaws make me feel lil' better. Maybe you're right, Hick."

"'Course I am."

"You fixin' on goin' in just as you please?"

"Nope. Them two'll set up a real caterwaulin' somethin' fierce. Nope. We just gotta wait 'til one of 'em goes out to the woods. Then we slip in on the one in camp. Get her tied down an' get the other one when she comes back."

"Sounds good," Redman had to admit. "You gettin' smarter and smarter the longer I know you."

The two Missouri rivermen did not have to wait long. The Crow woman rose and walked out of the dancing firelight toward the shadows. Redman nodded for Hickerson to slip toward the right. He himself would head to the left around the back of the blanket-and-brush bowers.

Looks Far had grown tired. She did not wish to wait any longer for Josiah. He would just have to find her asleep when he returned. She rose slowly, carrying the baby into their lean-to. After she had placed Joshua on his blanket and covered him with the deerhide, she rose from her knees and looked down at his peaceful, smiling face in the dim firelight. Suddenly a shadow crossed behind her without a sound and the light disappeared from Joshua's face.

Looks Far spun around, sensing the danger before she even got a look at the man. He stood between her and the fire. Her gaze dropped to the blankets where she had put her knives and the camp axe they had purchased that afternoon. Then she raised her eyes to stare back at the shadow-maker. He just stood there, grinning at her with those missing teeth. And his smile told her all she needed to know. He was not there to steal

from her. He had come after something else. Something far
more precious than material objects. Looks Far glanced down
at the axe again and began to inch toward that side of the shelter.

Suddenly, a greasy hand clamped over her mouth to stifle
her surprised, pained scream. Another arm came around behind her and pinned her two arms together, arching her shoulders and making her yelp in discomfort. The first stranger
started toward her. She was scared. Deep in the pit of her
belly—she was truly scared. Looks Far hoped they would not
hurt her son. Take whatever they wanted and just go. But not
hurt the boy. The first man came into the light.

"This'un no more than a girl," Redman said.

"Strong one for a lil' girl," Hickerson observed. "Get me
somethin' to tie her up with."

"She don't look like she's gonna be a fighter, Hick," Redman
whispered low as his eyes gleamed in the dance of light and
shadow. "You just take her now, like it is. I get her second. I'll
wait and watch for the other gal. I get that other'un first."

"Do sound fair to me, Obahdiah. More than fair."

Looks Far felt the hot, stale-whiskey, smell-of-death odor of
his breath on her skin as he brought his lips down onto the
place where her neck and shoulder met. He licked at the bare
skin and smacked his lips. Then he bit hard into her shoulder.
She tried to scream but the strong fingers clamped a smelly
vise over her mouth.

"This'un got more fight to her than I thought, maybe." Nute
pushed the Flathead woman toward the grass beside the lean-
to.

Looks Far resisted, twisting and turning, despite the pain in
her arms and shoulders, to free herself from his powerful grip.
Finally the man who had locked her arms kicked viciously at
her ankles. The blows knocked her off-balance, sent her
sprawling. The young woman landed on her knees, the jolt
shooting slivers of pain up through her thighs, into her belly.

He pushed her on over. Looks Far Woman's glance shifted
from the man on top of her to the one who stood beside them
and leered down at her. The one on top of her grabbed the
neckline of her new wool dress that she had laced up that afternoon. His fingers reached inside to the milk-swollen breasts,
then brutally ripped the cloth. The blue wool sundered with a
sound like steam hissing to expose her breasts.

"I'm gonna suck some young mama's milk here, Obahdiah!"

he exclaimed, bending his head down onto the crook of her neck. He bit her hard again.

Looks Far struggled, the pain coursing through her. She tossed her head from side to side to fight him as best she could, to loosen the clamp his teeth had on her.

"Go 'head—get it over with." Redman husked, his voice a nervous rasp. Lust flooded him as he watched his partner toy with the attractive Indian woman. Her breasts thrust up firm in the moonlight, the nipples erect. Obahdiah felt himself getting hard.

"Goddamned right," Nute growled as he rose on his knees, straddling the prostrate woman.

Hickerson Nute pressed hard against her, pinning her arms beneath her. He eased his hand down to unbutton the flap on his pants: five buttons before the flap fell. His member swelled in anticipation of violent conquest. He grasped his swollen flesh and shook it for her as he rose back on his knees.

"See this, you red slut?" he rasped. "You gonna get the best of Hickerson Nute an' then you gonna want some more, ain't you?"

"Just get it over with, damnit!" Redman insisted.

"I am!" Nute glared up at Obahdiah. "You just shut your mouth an' let me do this the way I wanna do it."

"Just get it done, will you?"

Nute let go of his penis and screwed his hands down onto one of her breasts. Then he dipped his head down and savagely bit at her nipple until she felt he would bite it off. Instead, he withdrew and looked down at the blood he had started flowing from the breast.

"That so you can 'member this night with Hickerson Nute," he whispered lustfully. "'Member me with your scar, you red-whore slut!"

"You gonna fuck her—or sit there talkin' to her?"

"You bet I'm gonna fuck her!"

Nute yanked savagely at her dress, ripped it down the middle. He brushed the remnants off her body and let his right hand wander down her quivering flesh.

"That's good! Real good! I like it when they cry. Go 'head. Cry some more. Cry some louder. I like that! C'mon, you goddamned slut—cry!" He slapped her across the mouth. Blood began to trickle down her chin onto her neck. He backhanded her, driving her head to the other side. Again she did not cry out.

Something inside Looks Far told her this was what the man wanted. He wanted her to fight back. He wanted her to cry out for mercy, cry out for compassion. That was his real lust; more than lust for her body. She bit her tongue as he lashed back and forth across her face, pounding her head against the ground. Each time he struck her she bit her tongue to keep from crying out. She felt blood welling up at the back of her throat. She coughed, sprayed a crimson cloud over Hickerson as he bent over to try to kiss her lips.

"You lil' bitch!" He slapped her one more time. "I'm gonna show you! You don't spit nothin' on Hickerson Nute—cheap Injun slut!"

He shoved her onto her side, then pushed her over onto her belly. He yanked the torn dress out of the way to expose the rounded globes of her bottom.

"Gonna fuck you in the ass, the way any good Injun whore likes it, right?"

He took his penis in his hand as he knelt between her legs. Looks Far had an idea what was coming and tried to put her mind someplace else. Perhaps if she thought of her man, her mind would not know what was happening to her. It would not remember what had happened to her this night. She felt the tip of his organ spread the globes apart and begin to force itself against her anus. Then she felt him jerk suddenly and twitch off of her.

"Goddamn! Goddamn! Goddamn!" he hollered as he rolled off of Looks Far. "It's a goddamned knife, Obahdiah!"

He grabbed at the handle of the small camp butcher knife imbedded partway in his rear. "Stuck me in the ass! I'm stuck in the ass!"

"Hush up!" Redman commanded as he scanned the perimeter of the camp for the one who had wielded the knife out of the darkness. "Keep her down. We got somebody out there!"

"I'm bleedin', Obahdiah! I'm bleedin' to death! Oh, goddamnit! I'm stuck in the goddamned ass!"

"Told you—be quiet! Hush now!" he ordered. "I gotta hear—"

But it was too late. She was on his back, her arms around his neck and her legs straddling his waist, at the same time pinning his arms to his sides as he struggled to rise again with her weight atop him. Redman twisted and turned, trying to throw her off, trying to wrench an arm free to grab at his tormentor. He stumbled and twisted toward the firepit.

The Crow woman spun violently, then began to fall, along with her attacker. Downward, on down until the sparks shot up all around them.

Redman landed in the firepit with most of his weight on top of her, which jolted the breath from her lungs. He twisted and grabbed the Indian woman, yanking her to her feet. The sparks hung in the air as she shook the dizziness from her head. It hurt where she had banged it against a log. Her hair and cloth dress smoldered, sending puffs of acrid smoke into the dim light.

"I ain't gonna burn you up yet, honey," he whispered to her as he wrenched her around, forcing an arm up her back until she started to whimper. She bit her lip, the pain almost more than she could bear.

"You ain't gonna cry neither, eh?" He grabbed her other wrist. "We just see how much pain you take afore you cry out, slut!"

"Forget 'bout her!" Nute said, still whimpering. "Come get this goddamned knife outta me first."

"Pull the goddamned thing out yourself an' quit cryin' like a stuck pig!"

"I'm gonna bleed to death I do that!"

"No you ain't! You keep that bitch down there an' pull that sticker out. You keep your hand over the hole 'til I get this'un tied. Then we wrap up your bleedin'."

He looked around the camp until he saw what he was looking for, some rawhide strips which were used to tie the baggage together. The strips hung from one of the cross-members of a lean-to near him. He dragged the dazed Crow woman along with him, twisting and shoving her arm up her back every time she faltered.

"I'm gonna teach you pain, bitch!" he snarled as he yanked one of the strips down and tied her hand behind her. Her wrists bound, he ripped down another strip and used it to pull her elbows together. Then he stepped around in front of her.

Redman reached out with both hands open and chopped savagely along both sides of Waits-by-the-Water's head. She felt an explosion in her skull, felt herself falling. And then she felt nothing. He jerked her legs around and brought down another rawhide thong and tied it around her ankles.

He glanced over at his partner. Nute was leaning against the Flathead woman, holding her down with one arm while his

free hand clamped the handle of the camp knife. He rocked
back and forth, shuddering with pain.

Redman turned back to the Crow woman. He grabbed the
red trade cloth that decorated the hem around her neck with a
thin leather thong, and wrenched it. Her neck snapped as the
cloth gave way, and her head flew back against the grass with
an audible thud. He tore savagely at the remaining rags until
she was fully exposed to him. He felt himself grow harder as he
looked at her in the firelight, the great expanses of golden skin
laid bare and waiting for him to plunge himself into her. He
started to unbutton the fly on his britches.

"You ain't gonna fuck her 'fore you help me!" Hickerson
pleaded. "You gotta get this knife outta me. Get me somethin'
stop this bleedin'—then you can fuck 'er—do what you want
with her then."

"Ahhh, goddamn!" Redman murmured almost under his
breath as he stuffed his rigid member back inside his britches.

He walked over to his partner. He untied the dirty red scarf
on his neck. He stuffed it around the knifeguard and down the
blade, then began slowly to pull the steel out of Nute's but-
tock.

"Arrrggggh!" Nute gritted in pain. "Just pull it out now!"

Redman yanked on the blade with one, swift motion, shoving the dirty neckerchief over the ragged hole as the tip of the
sharp steel tore from the flesh.

"Goddamn, goddamn, goddamn!" Nute whined as he rolled
off the Flathead woman. "You get done with that'un over
there," he said, nodding his head toward Waits-by-the-Water,
"I want her."

"She's mine, damnit!"

"Don't wanna fuck her—I want to watch her die!" he
snarled. "For this!"

"You ain't touchin' her," Redman commanded. "This'un
yours." He scooted past his partner and grabbed the back of
the Flathead woman's hair to shake her head.

Looks Far regained consciousness. She looked up fearfully
toward the big whiteman who held her hair gathered in his
hand. Then her eyes rolled wildly until they focused on Waits-
by-the-Water. She saw that her friend was tied and unconscious on the ground near the lean-to. Suddenly the pain at the
back of her head increased and she realized he was dragging
her across the ground.

Redman slammed her head down, then kicked at her jaw

viciously. Looks Far saw sparks flash in her brain before she slipped back into the dark void of unconsciousness.

When she came to, the world was blurred. A shadow moved over her face. She saw Waits-by-the-Water nearby, her flesh bruised, her dress ripped as hers was. She looked up to see the man called Redman standing over the two of them, looking back and forth between them with a greasy sneer. Her gaze wandered down his body, saw his member rigid and stiff in his hands.

"You're first, lil' mama," he whispered. "Since this other bitch made it so my partner cain't give you what you need."

Redman addressed the Crow woman: "I'm gonna give you both what you deservin' tonight. Then, when I'm finished with you both, we all just sit back an' wait 'til them men of yours get back to camp. We gonna have a lil' more fun later on when they come back all liquored up. Ain't gonna be expectin' a thing—hey ain't."

He rolled Looks Far onto her back and knelt between her knees, shoving her thighs apart with his left hand while his right gripped his organ like a knife. He began to rock forward, thrusting to penetrate her.

The Flathead woman felt the head of his penis begin to ram against her flesh. How much fight did she have left in her now, he wondered. It didn't matter. She had no fight left. She would push her mind away as this thing was taken from her, as his brutal act was forced upon her.

She felt her flesh give way as his rigid member burst past the entrance to her most private self.

"Gettin' late, son," Bass suggested, looking across the fire at the younger trapper. "Maybe best we headin' back to camp an' the women now."

"S'pose you're right, ol' man," Paddock replied. Then he looked over at Frye Teeter. "We gotta make sure these ol' folks get their sleep, you know."

Paddock and Teeter chuckled as Bass rose to his feet. Teeter's wife had long since gone to bed, having tired of listening to the whitemen's stories, their friendly bravado and profane humor. She did not like to see Frye drinking that much, either. She always scolded him for being worthless when he was drunk. But tonight, he had behaved himself, by and large. Teeter had put down enough to give himself a rosy glow and then

quit, from that point on sipping at the whiskey from the kettl
only as some of the warm spot inside him began to wear off

"You'll think old," Bass said, "when I take to whippin' th
both of you young—"

The first rumbling blast of rifle-fire slashed through th
night. There had been the usual shouts, the loud laughter an
off-key songs all night long. But, the low, bass boom of the gur
shot stopped everything else. A second and a third sh(
sounded close on its heels. Bass looked quickly at the othe
two men across the fire and scooped up his rifle before settin
off toward the fading echo. Behind the trio ran more of thos
free trappers who had set up their shelters near the America
Fur Company campsite.

All night between the choruses of good-natured, fun-lovin
songs and the roaring of belly-felt laughter, there had been th
cries of the sentries, singing out "All's Well!" from their post;
But now the shouts were not of those guards watching over th
camp and the horse herd. The words that sprang from the trap
pers' throats as the trio ran into the camp were of a differer
tone. "There the son of a bitch goes!"

Then, "Shoot 'im, Caleb!"

"Dear God, I'm bit!"

Followed quickly by another strident voice shouting, "He b
me! He bit me! The son-of-a-goddamned-bitch bit me!"

Bass and the others scrambled into the melee of runnin
darting bodies, some carrying rifles, others brandishing liml
from the various fires for use as torches as they scurried bac
and forth through the tents in search of something. They a
hollered instructions, suggestions, orders and curses back an
forth in the wild confusion. Some of those who were not ru
ning were sitting on the ground beside their blankets as man
men had chosen to sleep in the open on this warm, pleasar
night. Then one of the guards could be heard barking his o
ders.

"He's in the horses!"

The animals whinnied and cried out in their confusion an
fright, rearing back against their picket pins. There was th
distinct staccato thudding of hundreds of hooves stomping th
ground, giving a rhythmic backdrop to the horses' cries (
panic and the herd guards shouting orders to one another.

"He's over here now, Micah!"

"I see 'im! I see 'im!"

"Don't shoot the goddamned horses, you idjit!"

"I see 'im, damnit!"

And then another blast from a rifle, the muzzle fire briefly brightening a piece of sky against the wide pasture where the horses milled. Bass tore off in that direction, catching up to one of the American Fur Company trappers who was running in his longhandles, a shooting pouch and powder horn hastily slung over his shoulder, a rifle ready in his hand.

"What's all the goddamned ruckus 'bout?" Scratch rasped.

"Wolf . . ." wheezed the man beside him.

"Wolf, huh?"

"Rabid wolf!" The stranger skidded to a halt near three of the guards who stalked slowly into the midst of the swirling, stamping horses.

"Rabid?"

"Yeah."

"What that mean—rabid?"

"Mad. A *mad* wolf."

"How you fellas know it's *rabid*?"

"Goddamned bastard bit three men back to American Fur just a shake ago."

"That you, Davey?"

"Sure be," the stranger replied to one of the guards in front of them.

"Critter got three of the boys, eh?"

"Yeah, three of 'em." The guards halted to await the telling of the rest of the story.

"Go on, damnit!"

"The son-bitch just strolls on in from the dark like some Injun dog—so most of us don't give the ugly critter no never mind. Couldn't really see him good with the lil' fires an' all," he continued. "Then all of a sudden, the bastard jumps over on them by Henry's fire. Takes on ol' Neil Bottoms first an' then goes right on down the line—finishin' by rippin' up ol' Henry's face."

"Told you." One of the guards shoved an elbow into the ribs of another.

"You told me nothin'," he snarled back. "We gotta get that goddamned wolf outta the ponies—an' fast!" He looked over at the trio of free trappers. "Who you fellas?"

"We come 'long to help," Teeter answered.

"You with American Fur?"

"Nope—we help anyways," Bass answered this time.

"Looks like we can use some of that. Let's go!" He led the

men into the panic-stricken herd of horses and mules. Whinnies and brays mingled with the sound of stamping hooves.

"Here!" yelled a guard who was running toward them. "Bring me that torch!" he instructed another of the guards. "Over here!"

The small knot of men rushed to follow the one who had requested the torch. They soon stopped near a pony which had been bitten several times around the throat and muzzle by the wolf. It kept dipping its head between its forelegs and rubbed at the bloody, gaping wounds.

"That's one," Teeter commented sourly.

"Figure more?"

"Sure," Frye answered. "Wolf just workin' his way through camp an' the herd, too. 'Less we get 'im. 'Less we stop 'im now."

"We fixin' to do just that," the first guard replied as he plunged off into the darkness. The horses' shadows swallowed him whole. Then the rest of the men bolted off behind him, their small group illuminated by the dashing torch held overhead by one of the guards.

"Mad wolf!" The cry came from their right just before more gunshots racketed through the night.

The men shoved their way past the ponies toward the sound of the gunfire and shouting. Soon they encountered four more men from camp, all standing in the darkness reloading their rifles.

"Font'nelle's gonna be some pissed 'bout this!"

"Drips, too," another added. "Losin' some ponies to a goddamned mad wolf!"

"You bet I'm pissed!" a voice bellowed. "You kill the son of a bitch yet?"

Then the disembodied voice merged with a growing shadow as the field commander of the American Fur Company pushed through the ponies toward the group of men. He had been in command of the mountain brigades of the American Fur Company ever since the previous fall when Vanderburgh had been killed by the Blackfeet. He was a small, wiry and feisty sort who naturally waded right into the danger.

"No, we ain't, sir."

"But, we gonna, Mister Drips," a guard added.

"Not like this, you ain't," he scolded. "Get your asses out into them horses! Now! You can hear where the son of a bitch is by listening to the ponies. Get that bastard!"

Most of the guards took off in the direction where the animals were in an uproar, to the north, toward the free trappers' camp and their horse herd.

"You fellas gonna stand there with your thumbs up your butts?" Drips barked at the three who remained behind.

"We don't work for you," Bass quietly answered.

Drips drew closer to inspect the three strangers in the moonlight. "I'll be damned—you don't work for me." He chuckled shortly. "Who you with?"

"Nobody," Teeter replied. "We free trappers, Mister Drips. Don't work for no one."

"You fellas can go to work for me anytime," Drips remarked. "Need good men—good hands with the traps and Injuns all the time."

The horses whinnied wildly again behind Drips. "In fact, you can go to work for me right now—on the payroll right now—you go get that goddamned wolf."

"Sounds to be he's headin' toward our camp." Frye nodded toward Bass and Paddock.

"It does, that," Bass replied.

"The beast chewed up three of my men in camp while ago." There was an edge of desperation to his voice.

"I think your boys gonna get 'im," Teeter responded.

"We headin' back to watch our own ponies," Bass said.

"Passin' up to fifteen-hundred dollars a year right on by," Drips offered. "We been payin' such for a master trapper to hire on for a year. Supplies and goods up front, too, fellas."

"That's some good money," Paddock responded. "But we like payin' ourselves. Takin' care of ourselves, too, Mister Drips. Thanks just the same. You keep your money, and your wolf. We gotta go take care of our own now." Paddock started to step away with the two other free trappers.

"I'm gonna be losin' three of them boys back there." Drips jerked a thumb back toward the American Fur Company campsite. "Three of 'em bit—an' they ain't gonna make it. Could use three more good hands."

"Mister," Bass began, "think the young fella here just told you we take care of our own. We thank you kindly for the offer. But—we just don't cotton to no man sayin' he's booshway over us. We like playin' on our own hook, we do."

Bass started walking to the northwest, toward the free trappers' camp and Teeter's group of tents. The two others shrugged and followed Scratch.

"You be sorry, fellas," Drips hollered after them in the darkness. "Fifteen-hundred dollars be more than you'll see in a few seasons!"

Scratch and the others heard hoofbeats before they saw the horsemen bearing down on them. The riders came out of the darkness and pulled up their horses in a swirling, snorting fury beside the men on foot.

"You seen 'im?" one half-dressed man yelled breathlessly.

"Nawww," Bass answered simply. "We ain't none of us seen the wolf—just hear of 'im movin' through the herd, there."

"You American Fur?"

"Why's ever'body wanna know if we work for American Fur!" Teeter exclaimed.

"No we ain't," Josiah answered. "You with 'em?"

"No—Rocky Mountain," said a second rider who pranced up to the trio on horseback. "Scurvy critter started off in our camp, down to the herd. Got him the herd bull, too. Billy Sublette's finest; from Sublette's own farm, he was. That fine animal surely be a goner now."

"Cows ain't belongin' out here anyway," Frye commented dryly.

"Just the same," the fellow on the horse offered, "the bastard bit some men in Rocky Mountain before he come up to the American Fur Company camp."

"It figures," said Josiah.

"You goin' after 'im?" the first rider asked.

"We goin' to check up on our own ponies," Teeter answered.

"Fare you well, boys." He kicked his pony and twisted into a run, followed by the other horsemen. They all dashed toward the shouts and gunfire that were growing more distant with every passing moment.

"Seems they've run the critter off for the time bein'," Teeter observed.

"Seems so," Bass replied.

"They don't get 'im," Josiah said, "he come back?"

"Sure will, son," Scratch answered. "Critter knows there be flesh down here. Mad wolf needs some flesh to chew on, he does."

There was thoughtful silence among the trio for the rest of the short walk back to Teeter's camp. The women and the rest of the men of his group were up and eager for news. A few sat around Frye's kettle of whiskey. Someone was putting a pot of coffee on to boil over the rekindled flames.

"Care to stay for a cup?" Frye offered.

"'Fraid not," Bass answered.

"Yeah—we best be gettin' back to our own camp. See how the ponies and women are," Paddock begged off.

"Want me to come with you?" Frye asked. "Case you need 'nother rifle—you run onto that mad wolf?"

"Nawww," Bass said. "We be just fine, Frye. Much 'bliged to you, we are. Real fine time this evenin', jawin' and drinkin' some. We do it next time down to our diggin's. All right?"

"You're on, fellas." Teeter smiled again and nodded as the two trappers traipsed out of the circle of firelight into the darkness.

Bass and Paddock clambered aboard their saddleless mounts, headed south.

"I'll take the horses," Josiah offered as they neared their tents. "You go and check on the womenfolk, Scratch. I'll see if we had anything botherin' the animals."

Bass nodded. He slipped from his horse and handed the reins up to his younger partner. "You need help out there, you holler. See you back to camp."

Josiah slipped into the shadows toward the pasture where their stock was picketed.

Scratch watched him disappear and then set off toward the two dimly lit huts. The fire was low, looking almost unattended. The fire pit seemed oddly disturbed, ashes strewn around it.

He gazed into the shadows of the tents and the surrounding vegetation. Looks to be the women went to bed, he thought.

With the shadows so thick and dark, he could not tell for sure, but it looked as if the women were sleeping over beside Looks Far Woman's lean-to.

But—there was something strange here. The way they were lying down; the way the two were stretched out. Flat on their backs with their legs together.

He felt it suddenly in the pit of his stomach and lurched into a run, tightening his grip on the rifle. Something was terribly wrong.

Goddamn!

The wolf had come right on through their camp and got the women! *Goddamn!* He cursed himself for being away when the wolf went roaring through. He was sure the women were dead as he came to the firelight and skidded to a halt.

His heart hung still in his chest. They were lying there, very still, their arms by their sides, their legs close together. That was odd. He sucked in against the lump in his throat, against the fiery knot of fear in his belly. He knew they were dead. He could feel the tears starting to well in his eyes.

Damn!

Oh, damnit! Why had they gone to Teeter's?

Then he saw Waits-by-the-Water raise her head to stare at him a brief moment and then twist toward Looks Far. In the glow of the embers he thought he saw a gag in the Crow woman's mouth. He saw that their clothes had been torn, were barely hanging from their bodies.

He stepped hesitantly, not sure of any of this at all. He was totally confused. The wolf could not have done all this. The Crow woman was not at all bloody. There was a little blood on Looks Far Woman's bare breast. He took another tentative step forward and saw Waits-by-the-Water lift her head again. She shook it violently, trying to tell him something. But only muffled, indistinct sounds escaped the gag over her mouth.

Scratch stepped toward the women to sort this all out when the figure stepped from behind Josiah's lean-to. Bass was not sure in the dim light, but he thought he had seen the face before. Only recently, too. There was a smile on that face. A wild, crazy, twisted and perverted smile. And in his hands, a rifle—pointed directly at Bass.

Scratch quickly glanced down at the women and put it all together. They had been raped! The women were tied down and raped! Both of them. Maybe the boy might even be dead!

He wanted to shout for help but he knew he was all the women had for a little while anyway—until Josiah walked back from the pasture. He was all they had. It was just him and this fella here. But how could one man get both of them down? Tie both of them up like that? There had to be another. . . .

The old trapper turned at the sound of the Crow woman's muffled scream, moving his gaze from the distorted, wild expression on the one man's face, at the same time feeling the approach of another, sensing there was another man close by.

Scratch's mind suddenly brought up the words Josiah had spoken the year before.

"You know I might be havin' some fellers come huntin' me."

Bass felt the air suddenly shift around his body and along his neck before he really saw the second man. And then everything went black.

Twenty-four

Josiah lifted the rawhide rein over the horse's head, let it dangle while he played out the rope. He took out a picket pin from his bag. He drove the pin into the soil with a rock and tied the pony to it. He secured Bass's mount to another rope picket, stripped both animals of their halters.

Josiah touched the pistol in his waistband, checked the lock on his rifle. Just in case. He listened, scanned the wide pasture, saw nothing amiss. The other horses grazed peacefully. Evidently the wolf had not ranged here this evening. Horses belonging to the other free trappers whickered at him from across the pasture. There was no fear in the sound. Moonlight dusted the meadow, and he listened to the sound of teeth tearing at fodder, the rustle of ropes snaking across the still-dry grass.

Satisfied, Josiah headed back toward their camp, toward their lean-tos and the robes. Back to his woman and their child. He continually marveled at what a warm, secure place Looks Far occupied within his heart. It still amazed him that he could feel this way about one woman, about this sense of family, about having it all wrapped up in this beautiful wilderness.

A man could get lucky, he thought to himself. And he was one of those few. Some men really could be lucky and have it all, without a care in the world, perhaps, except where the next meal might come from or the next camp might be.

Josiah reflected on the healing that had occurred many weeks before. He had been shown the way by Arapooesh and the Sparrowhawk people. He had been shown that he was the only one who could truly heal himself. And it was down that long, tortuous path his own soul had taken him. He had come finally to realize the worth of those small things: the love of a good woman, a beautiful man-child to call his own and raise here in the wilderness as he saw fit, and the best friend a man could want.

He took the shortcut through the trees. He was weary. And what few steps the shortcut saved him would be worth both the stumbling and the bruised toes.

As he emerged from the trees, he bent over a moment to pick a twig out of the side of his moccasin. He was home again. And home was back with his family. For sure, his home could move and he was not at all ready to set down real roots. But, for now, his woman and their son proved to be the embodiment of *home* to him. It made that warm spot inside him shimmer all the brighter.

There was the sound of a muffled voice. Then the first voice was answered by another. Josiah held his breath. He stood at the edge of the trees, only some ten yards from the back of their camp.

Neither of the voices belonged to Bass. He could not place it, but the deeper of the two voices sounded vaguely familiar to him. He let his breath out slowly.

He drew in a quick breath, held it, as he saw the profile of a stranger over the top of the lean-to. Paddock studied the man as he turned in the dim firelight, looking down at something. Then he saw another head above the lean-to. The two strangers jerked the slumped, unconscious body of a third man upright, roughly jostled him back and forth between them.

It was Bass. And Paddock could see that the older trapper was missing his bandanna. And the scalp-lock. Josiah saw the pale skull between the two strangers' faces as they whispered to one another.

Josiah dropped to all fours, tightened his fingers around the stock of his rifle. He kept the men in view as he slid from his hiding place to hear what the two strangers were saying. Bass was out. Unconscious. He could not see the women. He did not know where the boy was.

He crawled toward the men, feeling his way ahead of him with the empty left hand. Did not want to snap a dry twig or rustle the grass too much. The young trapper stopped behind his own lean-to, held his breath.

He watched one of the men wrap a rawhide cord around Bass's neck. Then they dragged the old trapper toward a tree off to their right. They yanked the unconscious man up against the trunk and tied the neck cord around the trunk.

Josiah felt for the pistol at his waist. A beautiful thing it was. Damascus steel barrel and hardware. Then his tensing fingers wandered around the belt to his sheath where they touched the handle of the one knife he carried now. He wished he had two.

". . . get 'nother," one of the strangers said loudly enough for Josiah to make out the words.

The other man scampered back over to Paddock's lean-to and grabbed more of the rawhide thongs. He took them back to the tree.

Josiah crept around the edge of the lean-to. Could there be more of them? More than just the two? He wanted to know the odds before he dove into this blind. They tied Bass's hands and one man lashed the old man's feet to the bottom of the trunk. Scratch's body slumped against the trunk, the wide rawhide thong at his neck cutting into his flesh as his head hung limply in the shadows.

"Then we have the son of a bitch to ourselves," the one standing said clearly.

"Yeah," the other answered. "What we come for. This been too damned easy, Obahdiah. Too goddamned easy."

"It ain't over yet," the first replied. "We ain't got back to St. Lou and got the money for the job yet."

"Get that pistol," the first one continued, "we get us that money from that Frenchy."

Paddock's mind snapped and his breath caught. What the hell now? Could it be the same Frenchman? No. Couldn't be. He had killed him back in St. Louis in what started as a duel. Back to 'thirty-one. More than two years ago now. But the Frenchman he had killed surely had family. How would these men know about . . .

His fingers felt for the pistol at his waist. Could they be talking of this same pistol? The weapon he had taken from the scene of the duel on Bloody Island out in the Mississippi River?

Where were the women?

He crept on all fours to his left. He would go around the far side of the lean-to and find out what had happened to the women.

". . . want him to die slow," one of the two large men was saying.

"Have him watch me fuck his red slut while he's dyin'," the second joked.

Josiah slipped to the edge of the lean-to and peered around the side. He could barely see the feet and legs of one of the women not far from him. He could tell there had been some struggle there, the way the ground was torn up. He dared to stick his head out a little more. It was Waits-by-the-Water. At least, he thought it was, because of the red cloth dress.

Then Josiah saw Looks Far Woman's legs and let his gaze creep up the bodies of the two women. They were nearly naked. They were tied and bound. And both were gagged. Their heads were turned slightly so they could watch what was being done to Bass.

". . . one bragged that I'd have to come through him to get to Paddock." The voice drifted to Paddock again.

"You come through him all right?" one voice chortled. "You come through him and now you just got the other murderin' son of a bitch to go, Hick."

Hick?

The name stung like some bite at his memory.

Josiah looked again at the women and for the first time he realized what must have happened. The women had been raped. They were tied down, all but naked, their bodies cut and battered.

Paddock's belly twisted, began to smolder with a slow-burning rage.

The smoulder burst into flame and he burned inside for the women, for Bass. And for himself. These bastards were not going to . . .

". . . cut his cock off and stuff it in his mouth so he can't holler while he watches me fuck his red slut—right in front of his eyes." One man, a dim figure in the shadows, stood and turned. "Then I cut her up real slow, too. Like that other'n. Both of 'em. Real slow. Watch 'em die by first light. Then we get outta here afore anyone knows."

"I like watchin' the blood." The second man spit into the grass. "Almost as much as I'll like hearin' that lil' bitch cry out in pain."

Josiah jerked to his feet at the edge of the lean-to.

"Almost as much as I'll like watchin' his eyes when I cut his cock off an' stuff it in his mouth."

Paddock strode into the light.

"You wantin' me, you bastards?" Josiah's rifle muzzle came up as he stepped into the firelight.

Josiah watched their heads jerk around. He heard the two women stir as he passed by them. And he knew they saw him.

"It's him!" Redman shouted.

Josiah rammed the muzzle of the rifle toward Redman as

Obahdiah dove for his weapon. Paddock squeezed off the shot and thought he heard the stranger grunt in pain. Josiah turned his head as Hickerson scampered off.

The young trapper dropped the rifle and reached for the pistol. He pulled it from his belt and yanked back the hammer with one smooth motion. He saw Hickerson Nute coming back into the light with a rifle in his hand. Paddock dove to the side and began to roll as he saw the muzzle-flash exploding out of the blackness. The sound boomed in his ear as something tore at the top of his shoulder.

He rolled on over and sprang to his feet. Paddock felt as if he were going to lose his stomach as the pain scorched along his left shoulder. The arm hung numbed and almost useless. His right hand fought the capote aside and whipped to the back of his belt for the big knife. He wrenched it loose from the sheath and crouched lower.

"Redman?" Nute hollered.

He did not get an answer at first.

"Hey, Redman! You hit?"

"Bastard got me, Hick." The answer came from the darkness.

Damn! Josiah thought he had hit him pretty square. But the bastard had been moving. Shit! Now he had just the pistol and the knife. One for each. Then it would be over.

"You got your gun, Redman?"

"I can get it."

"I cain't reload on him," Nute hollered. "You take 'im!"

"He got my goddamned leg!"

"Now you the one hurtin', huh?" Hickerson asked. "Quit your cryin', damnit! Can you take 'im?"

"Yeah."

Paddock jerked his head back and forth, from the grinning, firelit face of Hickerson Nute to the disembodied voice from the darkness. If the first man did find his rifle it would be all over. He would have to do something fast. He watched Nute reach behind him and pull out a large, double-edged knife. So that was the way it was going to be.

"You just cover 'im," Nute commanded.

"I take 'im."

"No!" Hickerson barked. "He's mine! I'm gonna cut 'im up some."

"All right," Obahdiah said. "All right. Just cut him an' let's get on with it so we can finish with them squaws."

Nute began to stalk Paddock slowly, a graceful, choreographed dance of death and blood. Out of the corner of his eye Josiah saw Bass's head shake, as if trying to knock loose the cobwebs clouding his mind. From the old trapper's left came the first man out of the shadows, dragging a leg behind him. Josiah could see the wide, dark stain on the man's pants where the rifle ball had hit him squarely in the thigh. Up high, near the groin. He turned his head to see Nute approaching, then looked back at Scratch.

The old man was coming to now. Josiah could see that. And he knew neither of the strangers could see the old trapper's head move. He watched Bass's leg twitch and a foot move. His gaze flashed to Nute, and again to Bass, who had worked a foot out of the loose rawhide thongs just as Redman passed the tree where Scratch was tied.

Redman slowly dragged the wounded, painful leg behind him, his rifle pointed in Paddock's general direction. He started to cross in front of the old man and that was his mistake.

"I cover 'im for you while I get this bleedin' stopped," Redman called. "You just go 'head an' cut . . ."

His words were chopped short as Bass stabbed out with the freed leg and tripped the wounded murderer. Redman sprawled onto his face as the one strong leg crumpled under him.

Nute heard the crash. He spun around as his partner fell to the ground. Paddock struck like a blast of lightning over the firepit.

Nute didn't have time to recover as Paddock neared him. He couldn't even bring the knife up. Instead, he let Paddock hit him, and whipped over on his back, pulling the young trapper down with him.

Looks Far Woman slid and twisted, slid and twisted again across the grassy, rocky ground. Slowly she inched her agony-raked body toward the Crow woman. When at last she touched Waits-by-the-Water, Looks Far gazed into the woman's eyes momentarily with her message. The Crow woman nodded and rolled onto her side, away from Looks Far. The Flathead woman squirmed backward until her bound hands reached those of Waits-by-the-Water. Then her bloodied, dirty hands began their work on the knots. She closed her eyes tightly— shutting out the snarling scene whirling around her so she could concentrate on this single, desperate act. Her aching fingers fought frantically against the stiff rawhide thong that held Waits-by-the-Water's hands behind her.

Bass lashed out at the second man, kicking as Redman attempted to roll out of the way of that one lethal leg. At least he didn't have the rifle anymore. Obahdiah rolled out of Bass's range, knelt on the one good leg and pulled out his knife. He smiled crookedly at the old trapper.

Bass wasn't smiling. He knew what the odds were for a man with a knife against a man tied to a tree with only one leg free.

Paddock rolled onto his sore shoulder and grunted with pain as he sprang to the balls of his feet. He crouched as Nute bore in slowly, the blade in his hand glinting. Hickerson eased around the side of the fire, the light playing off the twisted smile smeared across his face. Paddock held the pistol up. Nute stopped moving. He stopped smiling for a moment.

"Gonna blow you straight back to hell," Paddock hissed low, almost too quiet to be heard.

"Go 'head."

"Josiah!" Scratch yelled when he saw Redman coming toward him, knife in hand.

Josiah glanced away from Hickerson to the knife-wielding Redman, who was bearing down on Bass. He saw Scratch kick, lashing out wildly with his freed leg. Obahdiah Redman merely stumbled back and forth on his good leg to stay out of the way of the wild kicks.

Redman suddenly slipped past the moccasined foot. He turned to jab the knife into the old trapper. Bass twisted away as far as the rawhide thongs would allow him. In that instant Paddock saw the old man's neck stretch and bind against the rawhide strip as he tore at it to duck from the oncoming blade. Paddock fired.

The shock of the ball only hastened the knife on its path, as the lead tore into Redman's back. The knife plunged straight toward Obahdiah's chosen target: the meat of Bass's thigh, high on his left leg. Redman jerked with the force of the ball and his hand released its grip on the blade. His pain-glazed eyes saw that the knife was imbedded partway in the flesh of Scratch's thigh before his gaze climbed back up to the old trapper's face.

Bass gritted against the pain he felt throughout his tired body. His head ached where Nute had smashed him with the rifle butt. His neck burned where he strained it against the wide thong. And now his leg stung with the knife wound in his thigh. He stared at Redman and saw the smile fade from the attacker's lips. Redman slumped to the ground, dead before he hit the grass. And Bass's thigh began to flow blood.

"Ain't got a gun now!" Hickerson snarled.

"I don't need one for you." Paddock jerked his head to glare at the big man across the firepit from him.

"First I'm gonna stick you," Hickerson snarled. "Then I'm gonna let you watch while I finish stickin' that red slut of yours. Ain't nothin' you can do 'bout it."

Paddock edged forward again, this time advancing on Nute. He saw Hickerson's smug smile.

"C'mon," Nute whispered. "Come an' get it," he beckoned. Teased. Challenged. "Just like your woman. C'mon an' get yours now. What you got comin'—"

"Who are you?" Paddock asked.

"Name's Nute." The sneer grew across his face. He knew the advantage of being unknown.

"What you want with us?"

"Your pistol."

Paddock glanced down at the empty pistol in his right hand and realized the knife was worthless in his left. He quickly switched them.

"More'n that—" Josiah prodded.

"Right!" Nute said. "More'n that. Your woman first. Then your heart. I'm gonna carry your heart back to St. Lou."

"Why? Why you come from St. Lou?" But Josiah already knew.

"I been sent to kill you."

"Who sent you?"

The words had barely cleared Josiah's lips when Nute lunged toward him, striking Paddock squarely in the chest. Josiah felt the breath suddenly knocked out of him as he staggered under the force of the blow. He fought to keep from falling as the pistol went spinning out of his grasp. Hickerson was right on top of him, carrying him down. Paddock clawed the fleshy neck and felt the soft skin give under his fingernails.

Josiah's fingers found the semi-circle of the windpipe and he clamped down on it. Nute jerked and shifted his weight, freeing Josiah for an instant. Josiah twisted to the side and rolled out from beneath Nute. He brought his knee up into Nute's groin. Hickerson doubled up in pain, one hand seeking to cover himself from another blow. Paddock slammed his knee up into the groin another time, then up under the man's jaw, jerking the attacker backwards to the ground with a loud thud.

Paddock straddled him instantly, his right arm drawn back, the left locked and straight, pinning down his enemy's knife-wielding arm.

"Who?" Josiah wheezed.

The eyes just stared up at his, glazed with pain. But not defeat.

"Who? Goddamnit!" His knife arm shook.

Still Nute did not answer.

Bass leaned against the tree, winced from the pain in his leg. "Don't kill 'im, son," he called out. "Leave 'im be—we kill the cocksucker slow!"

Paddock turned to glance at Bass. And that was all Nute needed. Hickerson rammed his legs up and around Paddock's neck, then snapped the legs back down to spring Josiah off of him.

The young trapper writhed in the grip of the mighty, muscular legs, but it seemed useless. He had lost so much strength already. And this man outweighed him by some fifty pounds. He groaned as he felt the big man's weight roll over him. Suddenly there was a knee on his right arm, crushing the flesh and muscle against the bone of his upper arm with such an excruciating pain he lost the grip on his knife. Then he felt his hair being ripped back, jerking his head toward the sky. Paddock felt the tip of the knife prick his flesh at the side of his forehead and the warm blood begin to dribble.

"Gonna scalp you, boy—you God-Almighty tough mountain man! Gonna scalp you while you still alive!" The rancid breath steamed into Josiah's ear with the hoarse whisper.

"Then I'm gonna fuck your squaw while you watch. An' then while your blood's drippin' away, I'm gonna tell you who sended me to do this to you."

Josiah felt the knife cut across his forehead until it was about at the center. Suddenly the pain faded away and his attacker jerked spastically and slipped to the side. The blade dropped from Nute's hand, hit the ground with a dull thud. He stared at it a moment. The steel was covered with his own blood. He could rake air into his lungs. Fluid dribbled into his eyes and he blinked against the salty sting of sweat and blood.

He twisted sideways and watched Nute drifting, falling, falling as if in slow motion. The roar of the rifle-blast rolled over him now as he studied Hickerson's contorted face. And at the edge of the firelight stood the half-naked shivering woman.

Waits-by-the-Water!

He felt his mind cry the name out, even though his mouth could not say it. The smoke from the Crow woman's rifle muzzle drifted away as she stepped forward, then stopped at the edge of the gray curtain. Nute twisted on the ground. The ball had torn through his body low in back, exiting from his abdomen with a spray of splintered bone and pulverized flesh. Paddock saw the knife. He was going to finish the job the lead ball had started.

His fingers clamped over the handle as he brought the knife up into the firelight. With his free hand he yanked the greasy, matted hair, lifting the wounded man's head off the ground, and lashed across it with the handle of the knife.

The flesh across Nute's cheek and nose split apart below the handle's raking path. Josiah watched the blood ooze from the jagged, raw line as he brought the knife back up.

At that moment another shadow appeared at the edge of the firelight. Josiah twisted, growling low in his throat, the blood lust upon him. Then the figure eased from the shadows and slowly dropped the muzzle of the weapon held ready at the waist. The pale flicker of firelight danced across the man's face, pushing away the dark night's shadows.

"Easy," Teeter whispered to Paddock. "It's me, Josiah. Teeter. Frye Teeter. Easy now." The tall, gangling, lodgepole of a trapper took another step and halted, fully in the firelight now.

Josiah slowly dropped his eyes to stare down at his attacker. His shoulders shook with the rage so long pent up, for the outrages to the women, to his partner, to his own self. He struggled to control his being, to control his body.

Paddock stared down into the bloodshot eyes, glassy in approaching death. They were fixed upon Josiah's. There seemed to be a tenacity there which the specter of death could not defeat. This Hickerson Nute in some way clung to life as long as he could to show that he had not been defeated by Josiah Paddock.

"Who sent you?"

Nute's eyes blinked but the lips did not move.

"Who the hell sent you to kill me?"

The eyes blinked once more. But again the dying man offered no words.

"What's it all for?" Josiah demanded. He gripped the collar of the man's greasy wool shirt. "What you wanna kill me for?"

Nute spat at him, then smiled. Quickly the smile faded and the eyelids fluttered briefly.

"NO!" Paddock roared. "YOU AIN'T GONNA DIE!" He yanked the man's shoulders up and shook them savagely.

"You gonna tell me! Who sent you to kill me? Who was it, you goddamned bastard?"

He shook the limp body with all the unspent rage left in him.

"Josiah." Teeter touched the young trapper's shoulders. "He cain't tell you now. We'll never know why he come to kill you. Never know who sent him."

The tall trapper's fingers gripped Paddock's good shoulder a moment. "Let it be for now. Just let it be, friend."

Paddock glared down at the man below him. Slowly the eyes fluttered open into half slits, staring back into Josiah's. Nute's lips curled into a sneer as Paddock brought his knife up.

"TELL ME!"

"That'un still alive?" Bass asked from the tree where Waits-by-the-Water was untying him.

Teeter glanced at Bass. "Looks to be he is . . . still is."

Titus saw that Paddock was frozen. The young trapper did not jerk the knife down. Nor did he drop it slowly. Josiah kept the weapon ready, hanging in the air, poised.

"Don't," Bass said simply. "You can kill 'im later, son."

Paddock let his gaze wander up from Hickerson's face to Frye Teeter standing above him. He glanced over at the tree at Bass. Then he looked up to his own raised arm, which seemed almost disembodied from him. Slowly, Josiah brought his gaze once more to Nute's eyes. And suddenly the knife arced downward, plunging into the attacker's heart. The body twitched and then lay still.

The young trapper heard the air escape from Teeter's lungs. Bass moaned. Frye raced to Scratch at the tree, slicing the rawhide that Waits-by-the-Water couldn't untie. Scratch crumpled slowly to the ground, turning to spare his wounded leg. He looked up at Teeter, then down at the knife jutting out of his leg. "Think we should get rid of this damned thing?" He clamped his fingers around the handle above the guard.

"S'pose we should," Teeter answered just as matter-of-factly, as he knelt.

Scratch pulled on the knife slowly, his eyes squinting and his teeth gritting against the pain. Then he dropped the weapon on the ground. Teeter loosened the dirty bandanna he wore around his neck and tied it around Bass's thigh.

"That'll do," said Bass when the cloth was tight. "Ain't much blood," he gasped. "Just got a lotta meat, is all."

The baby began to squawl. Josiah ran toward Looks Far. He cut the strips holding the Flathead woman's ankles together, then knelt before her and gazed down into her eyes. In them were strength and resolve. He thought that strange. He had expected shame. Instead, there was only relief, and a hidden strength showing there. He cut her bonds and pulled the gag from her face. Then he tenderly covered her with the torn shreds of her dress.

Waits-by-the-Water sat near Bass, unmoving, for those long moments, shivering slightly, as much from the cool night breeze as from the events of the last hours.

Scratch pushed his back up against the tree and forced himself to stand upright. Looking toward Waits-by-the-Water, he felt the love come moving from her to envelope him. The leg hurt, but the wound was not disabling. Hell, he thought—I walked many a day with an arrow hole through my other leg. This ain't much at all.

Teeter rose silently with him, not reaching out to help, knowing such an offer of assistance might offend the older trapper. Scratch hobbled to his woman, favoring that left leg.

Josiah pushed the lump back down in his throat as he stared at the bloody teeth marks around the nipple of Looks Far's breast. He had to fight back the tears. She had been raped. Would she ever be as open to him as she had been up to this point? When he touched her, would she respond?

Much of his question was answered as she sat up and threw her arms around him. Paddock was startled. Truly startled by the sunburst of her love. Perhaps it was relief; perhaps gratitude for saving them. She finally let go and scooted on her hands and knees into the lean-to to pick up the crying infant. Looks Far pulled aside a torn flap of her new dress and placed the boy to suckle at the right nipple.

Waits-by-the-Water rose to her feet shakily and self-consciously rubbed at her wrists as Bass came up to her. She hugged him, her cheek resting against the hollow of his shoulder. Teeter turned away to stare at Nute's body lying a few yards from the fire.

"It's gonna be all right," Bass said as he slowly pulled the woman away from him. "Gonna be all right now."

"They not . . ." She sought for the words in English, but her mind was too numb with all that had happened. It was just too difficult. "The two," she began in Crow, "they did not . . . touch us."

"I thought . . ." Bass began in English as he looked back into her eyes.

"No." She put a flat palm out to touch his chest lightly. "They wanted to . . . they start . . . we fight bad men. I . . ." Waits-by-the-Water whimpered. Bass pulled her back into his arms, caressing her hair with his fingers.

He hugged her and looked over at Teeter, who was kneeling over Redman. Bass squeezed the Crow woman's hand and hobbled toward Frye.

"That'un still alive?" he asked.

"Nawww," Teeter replied. "Josiah done a good job on him."

"I was hopin' the nigger might still have a spark left in 'im," Bass said quietly.

"You know him?" Frye asked.

Scratch studied the face. "Seen him somewheres afore. But . . . but, I don't know him."

"How 'bout that other'un?"

"I think we do," Bass said. "Josiah an' me." He shook his head slightly. "Nigger wanted us to drink with him down to Campbell's place—while we was tradin'. Got in a bit of a ruckus 'cause we didn't want to. Son of a bitch was pretty roostered. Campbell his own self had to come break it up."

"This . . ." Frye puzzled. "This all can't be over you not wantin' to have a drink of whiskey with him."

"I s'pose that's all I can figure on, how—"

"No," Paddock interrupted as he approached. "It wasn't over us not drinkin' with him, Scratch."

"What you mean?"

"More than that, Scratch," Josiah answered softly. "It's a lot more than that, I figure. He was tellin' me someone sent him to kill me."

"Someone here at ronnyvoo?"

"St. Louis."

"Someone from St. Louie sent him here . . . all the way out here to kill you?"

"Someone sent them both to kill me. Yes." He looked down at the face smeared with blood and dirt and began to feel the pain across his shoulder where the bullet had grazed him. His forehead hurt where Nute had begun to scalp him alive. He put two fingertips up to touch the wound. It was tender at the hairline, where his curls fell over the long slice. But he knew he would heal.

"Seems that woman," Josiah said, motioning toward Waits-by-the-Water, "saved my hair for me."

"Been a-teachin' her 'bout a rifle."

"She learn't 'nough, it appears to me," Teeter said.

"Yeah." Josiah sighed and looked back down at the body. "That be two times now she saved me."

"How you mean?" Bass asked.

"Way I look at it," Josiah said, "first time she saved me was back to Absaroka. Prob'ly never would've growed the way I did less'n it been for you findin' . . . less'n you'd never took off last winter. S'pose in a way, she saved my life for me there. The whole thing makin' me . . . makin' it so I could . . ."

"I think I know what you're meanin', son," Bass said gently. "An' the gal shoots good 'nough to save your hair for certain this time. He tell you who sended them two out for you?"

"No."

"Looks to me like you never gonna know," observed Teeter.

"Never know who now," Josiah replied. "But I got me . . . got me some idea."

Bass's old fingers gripped Paddock's shoulder. "We just gonna have to let it be, son. Move on. Both of us. The five of us now."

He felt Paddock's tense muscles begin to relax, then Josiah sagged a little more in relief. "Let it be, son," Bass repeated. "Our women wasn't raped."

Looks Far Woman was nestling Joshua in his blankets. A full belly had quieted his squawling. Waits-by-the-Water sat nearby, her blanket around her shoulders, shivering slightly from the cool night breeze, shivering perhaps from the after-shocks of all that had happened, and her deadly part in it.

Scratch lifted his hand from his young partner's shoulder and looked over to Frye. "How come you happen 'long when you did?"

"Lil' while after I got back to camp," Teeter said, "got to thinkin' more an' more 'bout that wolf movin' up this way. How I'd like to be the one what kill't him. Got back on my pony an' started real easy-like back up this way. Then I heard the shots. Just figgered you or somebody had that wolf at bay again. So, I come ridin' in a lil' faster. 'Tweren't much light, least 'til the woman blowed that ball into this nigger. Wished I got here soon 'nough to do it myself."

"S'pose we . . . we real lucky you come lookin' for that wolf,

Frye. That woman missed—s'pose we'd both gone under then."

"Good 'nough shot it was. Done the job," Teeter said.

"I owe her a lot now," said Josiah.

"Son, we both do." Bass sighed.

"Would've done the same for you my own self." Teeter grinned. "Seein' how I cain't stand to see a man get scalped the second time."

"Wha-a-a?" Scratch felt back of his head. "Oh, yeah," he smiled slightly. "Didn't even know the scalplock got knocked off with all the scufflin'."

"Don't matter none," Frye said. "Just goes to show ever'body else a free trapper got the hair of the bear in 'im. Nigger like you can even take bein' scalped." Teeter eyed the bodies. "Don't like fellas get so nasty drunk they cain't have 'em no fun no more, anyways. Looks to be them two been havin' it comin' for some time, too. They just been lucky up to now, is all. Afore they run onto Titus Bass and Josiah Paddock, recent of the Yellowstone."

"An' . . . Waits-by-the-Water," Josiah replied, "recent of the Yellowstone."

"What you gonna do with them two?"

Paddock stared at Bass.

"I ain't gonna bury 'em," Bass said. "Bein' left for wolf-bait still too good for these here niggers."

"What you gonna do with the bodies then?"

"We take 'em back to Campbell." Josiah made the decision.

"Yes, son," Bass agreed. "They his niggers. We take them bodies back to Bobby Campbell an' leave 'em with him."

"In the mornin'." Josiah suddenly felt very tired.

"In the mornin'," Bass repeated. "First off, we gonna drag this bastard over with that'un by the tree. Get 'im outta my camp 'til mornin'—"

"No." Josiah's tone stopped Bass.

"No? What you mean by that?"

"Not yet. Gimme your knife, Scratch."

Bass pulled a knife from one of the sheaths at his back and passed it to Paddock.

Josiah knelt beside Hickerson's head. "Not 'til I scalp 'em. They came after me. I think these belong to me, then."

"They yours, son." Bass stepped back to allow more of the firelight to pour across the dead man. "They both yours, Josiah."

They were both his. Won in battle. Josiah had already proven himself in combat last year. Not only in the Gros Ventre fight at rendezvous, but also later, on their way north. Josiah had taken Indian blood.

Teeter and Bass watched Josiah circle the full scalp with the tip of the knife blade. He twisted the head to the side to complete the bloody incision before jamming a knee on the dead man's neck and ripping the hair. It gave way with a sucking pop.

Josiah rose to his feet shakily. He tromped to the edge of the trees where Redman's body lay in the brush. There, too, he knelt and pulled free the scalp.

"Looks like you done that afore," Teeter observed as he and Bass dropped Nute's body near Redman's.

"Never have."

"That be hard to believe."

"It really be the boy's first scalpin'," Bass said.

"Ain't you killed Injuns afore?"

"I killed some, yes," Josiah said. "But I never got me a scalp."

"Whooo!" Teeter whistled. "Your first scalps—an' they be white niggers. That's some now!"

"Think he can wear them scalps just as proud as any Blackfoot nigger's scalp," Bass said, praising Josiah in his own way.

"That I will." Josiah shook off the blood and gore from the flesh.

"I let you fellas get some sleep now," said Teeter. "I'll be lookin' for you to come by in the morning. I wanna go in with you when you drop those niggers off at Campbell's doorstep. If'n you don't mind."

"We don't mind," Bass said.

"Wanna let that goddamned booshway know none of his men stand up to a free trapper—even one what's already been scalped."

"We'll look for you on the way south to Rocky Mountain," Scratch said, gazing up at the dark sky and its sugar-dusting of stars. "Won't be all that long 'til light, Frye."

"No," he whispered. "Not that long at all."

"Thank you, again."

Teeter stood there a moment, and then drifted away into the darkness. In a few minutes Bass heard the quiet plodding of a horse's hooves fade away.

Bass looked over at Josiah. "Let's get these women some sleep afore first light, young'un."

"Need us some sleep, too."

"Both us do, Josiah. Been a long night already."

"Damn," Josiah muttered. "I wish I knew who sent them two to kill me."

The only one he could figure would do it, who hated him enough . . . but, how could that be? Still, the two assassins had come for the pistol. Come to kill him and take back the pistol to the man he had taken it from.

A dead man.

Twenty-five

"Are you going to hire those men?" Stewart asked as he watched Harris walk to a small knot of trappers by the trading canopies.

"They look to be good ones," Campbell replied. "Yes. I think I will. The rest of his group have decided to stay here in the mountains. They've already talked with Fitz. And Christy. Those two will take them on. Those not staying can help in the trip north to meet up with Bill on the Big Horn."

"I like the cut of that Antoine Clement," William commented.

"You met him, too, eh?"

"Aye, Bob," William said. "Half Cree, half French-Canadian. He seems just the bonnie sort I would have working under my command were I in the field."

"Well, Sir William," Campbell said, "Clement is now working for the new firm of Fitzpatrick, Fraeb, Gervais and Christy."

"Sounds like a group of London solicitors. I thought it was called, um . . . Rocky Mountain Fur Company?"

"It is." Campbell laughed. "It is. That's the legal name; those are its present partners. Changing partners year in and year out, makes for confusion it seems. Easier for everyone concerned just to call it Rocky Mountain Fur."

William Stewart, his countenance soft in the mid-morning shade of the awning overhead, drew a breath as he looked at the surrounding mountains, the slopes bristled with stately trees. "I wish to return here, to the mountains someday, Campbell. Someday soon. There are a few of these fellows I have grown quite fond of, frankly. Such bonnie friends they could become. In fact, if the truth be known, I envy their life out here among the forests and the rivers. It appeals to me no end, Bob."

Campbell nodded. "Yes, I know what you mean. If it weren't for me wanting to make money—needing that money back home for the plans and dreams I have—I would not have chosen for myself the path I've taken. Back and forth, back and forth."

"But you and Bill have your own company."

"Yes, true." Campbell looked to his left at the rolling pasture falling away from him. "But, it is not as if I were in the field myself anymore. Neither Bill nor I, for that matter. Seems to be the price one pays."

"The burden of the entrepreneur?"

"You might say that. At least the weight of that cross the businessman must bear."

"You are so young," said Stewart.

"And quick I must grab at it, then." Campbell smiled at the Scotsman. "While with you—you had your wealth the moment you sucked in your first ragged breath of life."

"You will never let me forget my family's money, will you?" Stewart asked peevishly.

"I apologize," the trader asserted. "I promised I would never do that to you again. It is just so different here, William. We have no rich lords and ladies in America—as you do back in Europe, and England, and the home you have in Scotland. We have none of that nobility with—"

"Ah," Stewart interrupted, "but that is where you are truly short-sighted. That is where you are truly wrong, my American friend. Here in your country, once you have passed the reaches of your settlements, once you are into those borderlands of boundless wilderness—then one begins to trod upon the regal domain of your American lords." He gestured with a wide sweep of his arm.

"This?"

"Exactly, Robert. Exactly. This place, your Rocky Mountains and these men who come to drink your whiskey, come to purchase your supplies and outfits. These are the noblest in spirit. If they are not the noblest in habit and dress—and I will grant you that—they still possess something stronger, something more at the bedrock of nobility. These few men have a nobility of spirit that will not be denied."

"These fellas?" Campbell was incredulous. "These are noble of spirit?" He gestured toward the saloon tent not far from them, indicating the men who drank from early morning until late in the evening, consuming so much whiskey that they either threw up and drank some more, or passed out. "You call that crew and those drunkards noble in spirit?"

"I believe you miss the point, dear Robert." Stewart smiled. "While their habits might leave something to be desired, I grant you, it is so true that the drinking to excess merely proves their inherent nobility of spirit. Most will not have a drink for yet another year, you tell me. Is this right?"

"Yes."

"And a few will never have another drink at all," Stewart continued. "They will fall victim to one calamity or another. A man's life is ofttimes short out here."

Campbell shook his head, smiled. "I am afraid I am not with you on this particular description of these men."

"It is only fitting that their noble spirits cause them to pursue excess in almost everything, Bob. They realize—truly realize—their time is fleeting. So they grab at life with all the vigor they can muster."

"I think I might understand that someday," Campbell finally replied. "I will have to consider that."

"But you have other things on your mind, I know." Stewart shifted on his stool as he leaned back against the tent post. "The trading has gone well for you, has it not?"

"Yes. It has."

"Then you could call this rendezvous a success for Rocky Mountain Fur?"

"Yes," Campbell said. "But, you have heard me say so before. That Harris party that came in on foot—some of those fellas going back east with me—they had between them only seven packs of beaver."

"Yet that small group accounted for some seven hundred pounds of beaver, true?"

"Yes," Campbell admitted. "That's unusually good for a small group. That Captain Bonneville, who had no means of supplying himself and his men, accounted for another twenty-two and a half packs. The free trappers gathered and scattered across the valley have brought some thirty packs of beaver. Over three thousand pounds from your noble souls."

"Then you come to the big fellows in the trade, have you not?" Stewart asked.

"Drips came in with over one-hundred-fifty men behind him, yet had taken only some fifty-one packs from the streams. Astor will not be pleased at all."

"Astor cares what his mountain brigades do?"

"I suppose you're right, William." Campbell sighed. "Astor is really concerned about the river trade. This venture of his is merely to keep the rest of us at bay for a while, while he consolidates his control of the western trade for himself and American Fur. With our new post, Bill and I will do what we can to stall him off."

"And what pleases you about your friends in this Rocky Mountain Fur Company so much?"

"What really pleases me is that they do far more with far less than those reaching out from Astor's empire. Rocky Mountain has had less than sixty men in the field this past season, yet they came in with some fifty-five packs. You see, with less than a third of the men, they still managed to pull more beaver from the streams than all of Astor's outfit."

"There will be a lot of fur heading for the eastern markets, and perhaps on to Europe."

"Yes, William," Campbell agreed. "Your noblemen have done well for themselves this past year. It seems that as the price of beaver rises or falls, and it matters little which direction the market takes, the men work all the harder year after year. They bring in a bigger catch each succeeding year."

"And this Yankee Wyeth who is here?" Stewart asked. "He is not a threat?"

"Nawww." Campbell shook his head. "He had those grand plans of building a fort out here someplace to drain the trade off from companies like ours. The trappers would not have to rely upon the supply trains such as mine and a summer rendezvous. Grand plans, fine plans—but a stronger man it would take to put them into motion. No, Wyeth is a dreamer. A dreamer who has had his vision crushed beneath the heel of weather, and adversity, and desertion, not to mention the mighty boot of the Hudson's Bay Company. He'll never build himself a fort out west, to compete either with us, or with the British company."

"That's an impressive dream," William responded after a moment. "Taking on Astor and American Fur, besides you and Rocky Mountain Fur. Not to mention knocking on the door of that empire the English have established in your northwest."

"Your countrymen have quite a foothold—"

"They are not *my* countrymen," Stewart flared. "The English are damnable bastards against which my family fought for many, interminable years. So do not characterize them as being my *countrymen*. Scots do not relish the idea of English rule. Much less English anything, actually."

"Sounds to me as if I have hit a nerve, dear William."

"Aye, you have, Robert."

"You need not fear the long arm of the English Hudson's Bay Company reaching this far east. They would never come into the heart of the Rocky Mountains to compete head on with us. No, the company would never be able. . . ."

His voice wandered off into silence as he rose from the stool, studying something. Stewart rose too, to watch the approach of three horsemen.

The calicoed and buckskinned trappers rode defiantly through the Rocky Mountain Fur Company camp toward the trading canopies and the saloon, where voices suddenly became hushed. It was not the three riders, but the two pack animals behind them, carrying the wrapped bodies of two men with the boots protruding from the elk-hide shrouds, that quieted them all.

Drunks careened toward the oncoming procession until there was a cluster of men gathered where the riders pulled their ponies to a halt. Campbell and Stewart hurried across the trampled grass toward the trading canopies.

"I need to see Campbell," Bass announced from atop his pony. He stared unblinkingly at the trappers who had been drinking or trading moments before.

"I'm here," came Campbell's voice as he fought his way through the crowd. "Who wants to see me?"

"I do," Scratch said. "The three of us." He nodded toward Teeter and Paddock.

"We got something to return to you, Campbell." Bass spoke quietly as if the words had been rehearsed.

Bass motioned and the two other men dropped to the ground. Josiah and Teeter untied the wrapped bodies and let them slam to the earth.

"Who are they?" Campbell asked.

"Yours, Campbell."

"Wh . . . why?" Campbell stammered.

"Them bodies is yours," Bass repeated. The crowd around them shifted and jostled against one another, each man trying to see what was going on.

Campbell pulled back the elk hide from one face. He started to say something, but held his tongue until he stepped over to the second body.

"They . . . they are mine," he said.

"Said his name was Nute," said Josiah.

"The one what caused a ruckus with us to your tradin' tent here yesterday," Bass said.

"This the one you had trouble with?" Campbell asked.

"Yep. This one. How the other'un figure in all of this?"

"His name is—was—Redman. A common riverside drunk." Campbell shook his head. "Nute's partner. But this, this can't all be over that single incident in the tent yesterday?"

"It isn't," Paddock snapped.

"What then?"

"Nute talked some afore he was . . . afore he went under," Bass broke in. "Afore my partner killed 'im, he told Paddock he was sent here to kill him. You know anythin' 'bout that, Mister Campbell?"

"Hell, no! I don't know a thing about these two being sent out here to kill anyone. And if I had, I surely would not have hired them."

Bass could read the man's face. Out here you had to learn to read a man quickly and well. And what he saw in Robert Campbell was the truth.

"Thought we might get your help in figurin' all this business out." Bass squinted at Campbell.

"Told me someone in St. Louis sent him here to kill me," Josiah offered.

"Why you?" asked Campbell as he studied Josiah's face.

"That's what I can't sort out," Paddock replied. "Somethin' 'bout me an' this pistol." He patted the weapon's handle at his waist.

"So it weren't just some goddamned noisy, pushy drunk what threw whiskey in my friend's face here yesterday," Bass growled.

"Doesn't appear to be," Campbell allowed. "This Nute was trouble almost all the way out here. Even had a row with Stewart after getting caught sleeping on guard duty back near the forks of the Platte. Figure that's one less worry for you now, William."

"I was never concerned about his kind," Stewart replied.

"Be that as it may, the two are dead and off my hands now." Campbell turned to leave.

"Them bodies is yours now, Campbell," Bass emphasized. "Felt like leavin' 'em for wolf-bait. Maybe that mad wolf chew the bodies up."

"Been too good for 'em," Teeter added.

"And who are you?" Campbell requested.

"A friend," Paddock explained, "a friend who come to help out."

"Got there just after that one got his lights blowed out," said Bass.

"And what have you got to do with all of this?" Campbell asked Frye Teeter.

"Nothin'," Teeter said. "Nothin' at all, 'ceptin' it sours my milk to see your scum tryin' to kill off some good trappers, is all. And they tried to rape these fellas' women, afore the bastards got scared and stopped to wait for Paddock and Bass to come back to camp."

"Bass?" Campbell looked over at Titus. "Your name Bass? You was down to the fight in Pierre's Hole last summer. Thought I recognized your face, man."

"Yep, I waded into that fight, too," Scratch answered.

Campbell turned to Paddock. "You were there, too— weren't you?"

"Yeah," Josiah replied. "A ball whistled between your legs not long after Billy Sublette took some lead in his shoulder."

The trader snapped his fingers. "I knew I had seen you somewhere before. What was your name?"

"Josiah Paddock."

"Seems as if you two wade into almost every good fight," said Stewart.

"Try not to," Paddock said.

"On occasions, things have a way of catching up with a man," Stewart said. "Testing his mettle. You seem to be that sort— both of you."

"Catches in my craw, it does. Don't like bein' tested, I don't," Scratch retorted irritably. "Wanna be left alone. That's all. Just leave me be."

He glared at the crowd gathered around them. "Any more of you figurin' on tryin' to lay into my partner here, want you just to think 'bout it some. We both just want to be left alone. We don't cause no harm to no man—he don't come messin' with us. Any more of you come pullin' my tail, I cain't help it you get the horn."

Scratch turned to leave.

"You were the one who scalped them?" the trader asked.

"I was," Paddock said as he settled in his saddle. "I scalped 'em."

Campbell stared up at the young trapper. "Why? Why the scalps?"

"Same as we'd do to any nigger," Bass answered. "Any nigger what comes after us."

"I don't think anyone else will be bothering you now," Campbell said after he glanced around the crowd.

"Don't want us no more trouble," Scratch said.

"I don't think you'll have any more of it, Bass," Campbell assured him. "It's all over with now."

"Get them robes," Bass grumbled, nodding at the wrapped corpses.

Teeter and Paddock dismounted again and cut the rawhide bonds, spinning the elk robes into the air. The two stiffened bodies rolled out of the hides across the ground, forcing some of the spectators back.

"It's over now," said Bass.

"It's over," Campbell repeated. "But ever you want a job working for me, you have one."

"Already I work for someone."

"American Fur?"

"Titus Bass," he retorted. "We be back later for some of your whiskey."

"You'll have a drink on me," Campbell called as the three horsemen bisected the large crowd and rode away.

Robert Campbell stared at the corpses sprawled across the grass. "Don't look like those boys have much of a sense of humor about things," he observed wryly.

"I don't believe you would either, had there been someone sent to kill you," Stewart responded.

"No, you're right. They have every reason to feel the way they do," Campbell had to admit.

"They've come to the mountains to live their life in as much peace as circumstance will allow," Stewart said.

"Man can't be guaranteed peace and quiet, William," the trader answered. "Especially out here."

"Out here, a man does not figure on others conspiring against him," Stewart demurred.

"I suppose you're right," Campbell muttered. "Want a few of you men to take these bodies across the river. Downstream some few miles. Dig some shallow holes for 'em." His eyes scanned the group that was beginning to break up.

A few of the assassin's trail-mates came forward to pick up the corpses and drag them away. Campbell watched as some men slung the bodies across horseback for the trip across the Green River.

"Man can't be guaranteed much of anything out here," Campbell said as he and Stewart headed back to the tents.

Into the void left by the crowd stepped a huge shadow of a man. His one good eye squinted into the sun toward the disappearing riders. Slowly he turned to watch the bodies being moved down the bank toward the sluggish river. Finally the giant assessed Campbell and Stewart thoughtfully as the two men walked away.

Emile Sharpe smiled and headed back to the saloon. He still had some time to drink before nightfall. Lots of time. And he was going to enjoy himself before he would glide through the darkness. Lots of time left for him. So, perhaps—all the less time for Josiah Paddock.

Alas, my love, you do me wrong,
To cast me off discourteously,
And I have loved you so long,
Delighting in your company.

Greensleeves was all my joy,
Greensleeves was my delight.
Greensleeves was my heart of gold,
And who but my Lady Greensleeves.

I have been ready at your hand,
To grant whatever you would crave;
I have both waged life and land
Your love and good-will for to have.

I bought thee kerchers to thy head,
That were wrought fine and gallantly;
I kept thee both at board and bed,
Which cost my purse well favour'dly.

I bought thee petticoats of the best,
The cloth so fine as might be;
I gave thee jewels for thy chest,
And all this cost I spent on thee.

My men were clothed all in green,
And they did ever wait on thee;
All this was gallant to be seen,
And yet thou wouldst not love me.

They set thee up, they took thee down,
They served thee with humility;
Thy foot might not once touch the ground,
And yet thou wouldst not love me.

Well I will pray to God on high,
That thou my constancy mayst see,
And that yet once before I die,
Thou will vouchsafe to love me.

Greensleeves, now farewell, adieu!
God I pray to prosper thee!
For I am still thy lover true,
Come once again and love me.

Campbell was moody as he sat down on the ground and leaned back against the canvas tent. "More of 'em gone. Those trappers from Harris's group will really come in handy now. Keep losing men the way I have."

"Drips lost nine men last night," Stewart said.

"I suppose you want me to admit we were lucky losing only three men to that bastard wolf?"

"One is never lucky when the fates turn against him."

"No. No one is ever lucky, such as that comes to pass." Campbell shook his head. "I was led to believe some of Fontenelle's men had killed the bastard last night when it got into American Fur's camp."

"They did not kill the wolf?"

"No," Campbell answered sourly. "Found out this morning they did not. The animal could have been shot last night while he was in our camp, but Fitzpatrick gave the orders not to shoot in camp, for fear of killing someone."

"A . . . a man would be correct in that command, Bob," Stewart reminded him. "Had there been a wholesale shooting in camp, no telling how many men might have been killed." He paused. "As it was, poor George will surely succumb to the madness."

"Holmes?" Campbell inquired. "He was bitten, too?"

Stewart sighed. "Aye, and much of the blame lies at my doorstep."

"How do you figure that?"

"He shares the bower with me—"

"I know that," Campbell said. "But how can you blame yourself for Holmes being bit?"

"I . . . I asked him to sleep elsewhere last night," Stewart confessed. "I told him . . . I had a . . . visitor coming—that I was expecting a guest last evening."

"You had a lady coming to visit you, so you asked Holmes to bed down somewhere else."

"Exactly." Stewart felt shame. "She was there when the excitement aroused the camp. There came to my ears the sounds, those confused, wild sounds of both man and animal. The shouts and orders. The wild, frantic discharge of firearms. And through it all, the bellowing and roar of Sublette's bull, crying out in hideous terror and rage at his attacker."

"Sublette is going to be pissed that his bull was killed," Campbell said. "By a rabid wolf, no less."

"I took up a blanket, leaving my guest to herself in the bower," Stewart explained. "Upon rising from our bed I belted the blanket securely about me and raced out into that confusion. I had not traveled far until I found dear Holmes seated on the ground."

There was grief on Stewart's face now. "He was bleeding profusely, the right ear, the side of his head. The flesh laid open—so ghastly. So utterly ghastly. An efficient assassin the mad wolf proved to be."

"Many of the others called him *beauty*," Campbell offered, in the silence that followed. "His sunny smile and good looks had earned him everyone's praise."

"And I was his undoing. It weighs heavily upon me, Bob. For from that very hour of the attack, his sunny disposition has seemed to change itself into something ugly. He is not the same bright, beautiful, young man that I sent away from our bower so that I could . . . could meet . . . with . . . have a guest for the evening."

"You must not take it all this hard," Campbell tried to console the Scotsman.

"But I do, Bob. I do place the blame at my own feet."

"You are being entirely unfair to yourself," Campbell said vehemently. "Everything that can be done is being done for the men who were bitten. Holmes and the others. We have dispatched men to search for a certain stone believed to cure the madness that follows an attack."

"Hydrophobia?" Stewart gazed up with a wan smile. "You believe a magic stone will cure the madness?" He laughed disconsolately. "There is no cure, Bob. No magic potion, nor magic stone will cure them."

"Alcohol is said to combat its worst effects," Campbell said.

"Indeed. And you have been giving the victims copious quantities of your very best diluted spirits."

"We must do what we can. Even to searching for that particular stone that may yet prove a cure."

"You are as superstitious as the natives gathered about us in the wilderness," Stewart said.

"Perhaps not a superstition," Campbell replied. "For who is to say that if a man believes something will cure him, that he will not be cured?"

Stewart shook off his melancholia. "Perhaps you are right, Bob. If the men believe some stone has magical powers to cure them, perhaps the power they hold within them will effect a cure. Yet, I still cannot help blaming myself. You see, it was not Fitz who gave the order against shooting in camp—"

"You did," Campbell said quietly as he looked at Stewart. "I would have issued the same order had I thought of it, William. And you did what you could for Holmes, our *beauty*."

"How he utterly despised that name," Stewart replied bitterly. "All I could do to comfort him was to bathe the wounds and let him drink from my flask."

"Ah, yes, the one emblazoned with the Stewart crest, yes," Campbell said. "Little more any of us can do now."

"The shamed Stewart crest! I should have killed that wolf!"

"You saw the bastard?"

"Yes," Stewart answered, "as I came upon poor Holmes. Sitting there, bleeding. Moaning. Crying out for someone's help. He already knew the great cost! And the beast with his baleful eye staring at me. Larpenter came up beside me at that moment and raised his rifle to shoot. But . . . I pushed the weapon down and allowed the wolf to slink into the darkness."

"Harrison stayed with Holmes through the rest of the evening and night, didn't he?"

"Yes, he did." He looked up at Campbell. "Holmes was one of the few to get some sleep after the excitement of the attack."

"Except Meek," Campbell said.

"Damn his ass!" Stewart snapped. "He slept through it all."

"You mean he was passed out through it all."

"Yes." Stewart grinned. "This morning I gave Meek what I believe to be justified hell for being so drunk at the time of the attack. I blistered his ears, but it didn't sink into his brain. He was passed out cold last night—would have been bitten had the wolf found his useless carcass stretched out on the ground."

"What did Joe have to say about you raking him up?"

Stewart chuckled, a brighter thought crossing his mind. "He told me solemnly that he might have cured the wolf!"

Both Stewart and Campbell laughed. "He thought all the booze would cure the mad beast?"

"Yes."

"Well, dear William," Campbell said, his laughter fading, "the campfires have a new legend now."

"Meek?"

"Not just Meek and his curing of the wolf, exactly. More the whole story of the wolf attack."

"Do you think the danger has passed?"

"I think so, yes," Campbell mused. "I don't think the wolf will be back."

"I am not so sure," the Scotsman asserted.

"We have better things to consider than rabid wolves this evening." Campbell smiled.

"And, what is that, Robert?"

"I have been invited to supper," he replied. "With a powerful Shoshone chief. And you, my dear William, are going with me!"

"Aha! Food and diplomacy!" Stewart exclaimed. "What will we dine on this evening?"

"Perhaps . . . perhaps your belly cannot take the main course, and that is why I thought I had better warn you first. So that you have time to beg off if you choose. I would not want to embarrass you or the chief by having you turn up your nose at the main course."

"Well?" Stewart waited for a moment. "Are you going to tell me what the fare is?"

"Dog."

"D . . . dog?"

"A puppy roast, you might say. Maybe even boiled," Campbell answered. "I received the invitation from the chief,· and asked him if I could bring you along. He was most happy about the prospect of having a lord of Scotland at his dinner table, as it were."

"Then, I see I have no other choice but to accept his invitation." William smiled. "Dog, you say. How utterly . . . interesting."

"And tomorrow we move camp," Campbell said.

"The pasturage is growing sparse nearby."

"Yes. We must select a site farther to the south to continue our trading."

"That will not be all that much trouble, I suppose."

"I don't believe so," Campbell said. "Trouble is something I can do without anymore."

William Stewart sighed and listened to the song someone sang while a concertina squeezebox gently carried the melody.

Greensleeves, now farewell, adieu!
God I pray to prosper thee!
For I am still thy lover true,
Come once again and love me.

Twenty-six

The evening's meal settled warmly in their bellies. Coffee steamed into the cooling air as each of them sat back and stuck his feet out toward the fire. Bass sipped at the scalding liquid, then blew across its surface. He looked over the brim of his cup at Josiah.

"Never told me how your winter was with the Crow."

"You was there for part of it, Scratch."

"You know what I mean, son."

"I s'pose I do. Weren't much of a winter at first," he said, "layin' on my back all day and then all night in Rotten Belly's lodge. Got so I could close my eyes and still see them drawin's he had painted on the lodgecover. My mind fairly remembers 'em still. The sunlight comin' through the hides strong as if they was scraped thin as parchment."

"You know much 'bout ol' Arapooesh: the greatest of all Crow chiefs?"

"I know some of what he's done," Josiah answered, "but not all that much. How come you call him the greatest of all Crow chiefs?"

"Simple, Josiah. 'Cause he is. Simple as that." Bass dug around in the pouch beside him until he fished out the old pipe. "I know there's Long Hair with his own band of Sparrowhawks, an' there's Little White Bear—but, to them Crow, there ain't never been no chief like Rotten Belly afore, an' to the way some look at it, not likely to be again."

Josiah stared into the fire a few moments before responding. "He's got some strong medicine, my father-man."

Bass stuffed tobacco from a little pouch around his neck into his pipe bowl. "Yes. Some strong medicine. His lodge got strong medicine, too. You got healed there, son."

"Not . . . not rightly, Scratch. Had a sweat to do that."

"You had you a sweat with the ol' boy?"

"Him," Josiah said, "and some other old men."

"Wagh!" Bass snorted, with a smile. "That's some now, it is! You got the royal treatment, Josiah. Don't you see? That special sweat held for you by the chief his own self. An' he gave the invite to his most powerful ol' warriors an' . . . an'—oh, hell. What's the word I'm lookin' for now?"

"Counselors?"

"That's it, son!" He clapped the pipe between both palms. "Counselors. Had you a sweat with the top boys, you did. Tell me 'bout it." He finished stuffing tobacco into the pipe bowl.

"Ain't all that much to be tellin', really."

"Now, don't be stingy with your words, son. Open your hand an' give it out to the ol' man."

"Well," Josiah began thoughtfully, recalling the vivid memory of that bright, sparkling mid-winter day. "It was near a mid-mornin' as I can recall now. An old warrior come into the lodge and scooted Waits-by-the-Water out of the way, then called in a couple young fellas. This old warrior, Stands in Heavy Timber—as I come to know him later—gets me to take my clothes off." He started to chuckle. "I was really thinkin' they was gonna give me a bath."

"Yeah?" Bass plucked a small twig from the flames to light his pipe. He puffed to get the pipe started.

"Didn't know they was gonna give me 'nother kind of bath right then," Josiah continued. "I got out of my clothes—"

"All of 'em?"

"Nope, they let me have my breechclout here." He flipped it up briefly. "Then ol' Stands in Heavy Timber showed me he wanted to have me lie down on this travois set-up they'd rigged up for me. I did and he had the two young fellas carry me outta that lodge through the village."

"Ever'body there, I s'pose."

"Seemed to be, plus some!" Josiah smiled at the vivid recollection. "People lined the whole way, to where I was goin'—I didn't know where that was. Just out for the ride in the sun, an' let me tell you it was some good to feel that sun on my body after layin' in them robes all them weeks."

"So," Bass said as he tossed the twig into the flames, "go on."

"Got to the place and I turned over to see this . . . this thing built on the snow. Didn't know it then, but it was the lodge—just the willow sticks for it. Some fellas come over and helped me to the lodge and sat me down. They made me real comfortable to lean back on an old buffalo robe but I was gettin' kinda cold by then. 'Bout that time them other boys came into that willow frame and took off their coats—"

"An' you found out they wasn't wearin' nothin' underneath, right?"

"You know it." Josiah grinned. "Didn't know for sure what I was in for then: the whole village out there singin' and playin' little drums while these ol' fellas was droppin' down to their birthday suits."

"It come as a surprise first time for me, too, Josiah." Bass leaned back against a saddle and stared at the sky a moment. "Good 'baccy you picked us, son. Fresh as it can be, gettin' out here, I s'pose. Good honey-dew, it is."

"Finally they started coverin' the frame with blankets and robes, then stuffed rocks into the pit. The warm felt good for a while there, 'til Arapooesh started droppin' water on them hot rocks to make it steamy inside."

"Gets some hot, don't it?"

"You ain't said nothin' there, Scratch." He shook his head. "Thought I was 'bout to go under some of the times through the whole damned ceremony."

"That'd been some now!" Bass pulled the smoking stem from

his teeth. "They have this big ceremony for you an' they go to pull the robes back off the lodge—there lays the dead body of the man they wanna honor. Some now, wagh!"

"I was close to it as I care to be again," Josiah said. "A kind of feelin' like no other feelin' I ever had. Not like when I was shot and you thought I was dead. That was all different from the sweat-dyin'—'cause I was awake through it all. And when them two bastards come into camp last night, thought me near death at least once there, too. That was somethin' different from the sweat. It's like . . . it's like it had to get so hot that it pulled the poisons right on outta me."

"An' what was you thinkin' 'bout while it was happenin'?"

"Gettin' outta there as fast as I could crawl!"

"Nawww," Bass chided. "C'mon now. When you finally come round an' figured out what was goin' on with you?"

"When that time come, they'd had the blankets pulled off couple times already, as I recall. Lotta singin' and rattles and drums. Arapooesh prayed to the sun, offerin' a prayer for his people and himself, then one special one for me, he explained to me later."

"You ain't never gonna get the hang of the Crow tongue, is you, son?"

"Why should I now?" he asked. "Got me a Flathead woman. Learn her Flathead. Right?"

"I s'pose." Bass stared into the flames dancing before him. "We ever get back up there next year, you gonna have to go back to school on it—just so you can get along understandin' the folks you livin' with—them Sparrowhawks."

"I'm doin' some good with Flathead now," Josiah replied, "but that Crow gives my tongue an ache that won't quit. Just ain't cut out for it—ain't cut out for speakin' it."

"So, you gonna tell me 'bout the rest of it—after the prayers an' all?"

"Yeah," he answered. "Somethin' strange happened to me as I thought I was dyin' in there." His voice wandered off in the telling of the bright memory. "My father-man's medicine took me close to dyin' afore I was allowed to live again. I hadn't really been livin' all those weeks while I was layin' back in that bed in his lodge. Feelin' sorry for myself afore you left. Feelin' all the sorrier and madder at you after you left me."

"Ain't never gonna happen again, son."

"I know it won't." Josiah glanced over at Bass and smiled warmly. "But I was took on down as far as I thought I could go, then somethin'—maybe all the magic and that medicine of Rotten Belly—took me right back on up higher than I ever been afore."

"Or, likely to be again."

"Or—to be again," Josiah agreed. "You been through all this, too—ain't you?"

"Might say." Bass blew a smoke ring in the cool air. "Not wounded, I weren't. Not like you. Weren't so far down as you an' in the need of the healin' as you, neither."

"Sounded like you knew what was goin' on," Josiah said. "On that road back up, it was then I come to know I was the only one gonna help me. Wasn't anyone else ever gonna help me until I was ready to go healin' myself first. And that was when ol' Rotten Belly had the blanket pulled off."

"Blanket?" Bass asked. "Just one?"

"Yep," was the answer. "Just one blanket—pulled off right across from me. And the sun come pourin' in all over me. Warm the light was, but I wasn't really cold anymore. There were more shouts and singin' as the rest of them robes and blankets come off. Then them two young fellas come over to help me to that litter. I hadn't walked in many weeks by that time, you see. Not since McAfferty nearly blew my candle out."

"You sayin"—he leaned closer across the flames—"that you walked then?"

"I didn't know it at first," Josiah said. "But I was standin' on my own when them two fellas let go of me. And Arapooesh came to make me part of his clan, the Otter Clan. He give me that special medicine bundle." He gazed toward the bundle that hung from the lean-to pole.

"Powerful medicine there to watch over you," Bass said quietly, and leaned back on the saddle again.

"Then Rotten Belly give me my name—my Crow name."

"Yeah?"

"What?"

"What the hell's your Sparrowhawk name?"

"*Awu'xtpe.*"

"You speak that Sparrowhawk pretty damned good for one what doesn't know him much more of it, son. They tell you what it means?"

"They tried to, best they could. Somethin' like Runner with the Sun, like that."

"Not exactly, Josiah." Bass shifted against the saddle and

sucked on the pipe. "You speak it short-like, it do mean *Sun Runner.*"

"That's what—I got no idea what it means."

"You hush your yapper a minute an' you'll find out. It be a type of a blessin', I s'pose—you given that name."

"How's that?"

"The sun. The Sparrowhawk believe 'em strong in the sun. That one god runs across the sky each day—movin' faster an' farther than any man could. 'Sides, the sun makes ever'thing grow strong and green—they know 'em that. Cain't live without the sun makin' its run 'cross the sky ever' day."

"So, how that fit with me? Bein' a blessin' and all?"

"Come to that, you give this ol' man time, son." He inspected the burnt tobacco in his pipe bowl. "Seems to me like they was tellin' you some real medicine things when you was named *Awu'xtpe.* First of all, you named after the sun itself what races 'cross the sky each day. Each an' ever' day. That seems to be a blessin' for a long life for you."

"Hope that comes to be," Josiah said quietly.

Bass nodded. "Then they always believed the sun had some real special healin' powers—powerful medicine like no other."

Bass thought back to the previous winter when he had believed his own life was going to come to a bloody end. And all he had wanted was to get to the light. If he could only make it to the sunlight pouring across the snow before him, his medicine would be strong once more.

"You mean the most powerful healin' power they named me after?"

"Looks to be, son."

Josiah leaned back suddenly. "That's some now, ain't it? I got myself healed in that sweat and . . ."—he considered his thoughts a moment—". . . and I come to know I healed myself same time, too. I got the sun's power in me—don't I?"

"'Spect you do, Josiah," Bass answered with a toothy smile. "You always had. I always seen it in you. Rotten Belly did too. Seems to be you was the last one to find out."

"I s'pose so." Josiah turned sheepish, felt like a little kid again.

"Even that woman over there that give you your son, she knowed it afore you. That you had that power. You was the last one to own up to it."

"What do you mean—own up to it?"

"I mean, you not only have to figure out you got a power,

son—but, you also gotta know what your duties is with that power, an' how to use it. Just knowin' you got it ain't 'nough." He shook his head. "You gotta know how to use it."

"Do . . . do I know that?" he asked of Bass at the same time he was asking it of himself.

"S'pose you already started learnin' 'bout usin' that power you been given—you healed up your own self, didn't you?"

"I . . . I did."

"Then, you be on down the trail a ways already."

"And a big part of what happened inside me after that day was thinkin' on what you meant to me, Titus Bass."

Paddock looked across the fire at the old man. "That's right, Scratch. Part of my healin' come from finally knowin' what a blue-ball pain in the ass I'd been to you through all them months."

"Yep," Bass answered. "You got that plumb center there, son. You was some kind of asshole back then."

"I know, I know," he muttered. "Don't need for you to be remindin' me of it. Been hard 'nough on myself." He smiled.

"Sorry, Josiah. No offense meant."

"No real offense taken, you ol' fart!" He chuckled before he continued. "I come to realize just how much you meant to me, ol' man. How you was the . . . ," and the lump suddenly grew hot in his throat, ". . . the best friend I'd ever have."

"I want me to be, son."

"The way it's gonna be from now on, Titus." Josiah looked up at Scratch. "Can't remember when I ever called you Titus. Don't mind it, do you?"

"Nawww. Sounds good comin' from a friend."

"Started ridin' some every day not long after that," Josiah said. "That always give me reason to wonder, too. How just a few days afore that I was layin' in my bed, feelin' this powerful hurt from myself and knowin' it was gonna be a long time afore I could ever stand up. Not even wantin' to think 'bout walkin'. And a few days after the sweat, I took a short ride with Arapooesh."

"You got you some powerful medicine," Bass responded. "Just what I saw me in you."

"Waits-by-the-Water helped me care for all them ponies—them ponies of ours. Takin' 'em out to feed and all. And I growed healthier every day. My muscles ached to be movin' more and more all the time. Then I finally decided to come lookin' for you, ol' man."

"Sounds to me your healin' reached down an' touched your own soul, too."

"Believe it did, that." Josiah nodded. "Yes. It did."

"Arapooesh some powerful medicine man for you, son. For us both."

"You was gonna tell me more 'bout him, wasn't you?"

"Yeah, I was," Scratch said. "Your step-papa was quite the warrior his own self—back to his younger days. Crow always liked to steal horses, an' Arapooesh was no differ'nt there, Josiah. He put together horse-stealin' parties to go into Cheyenne, Blackfoot, Arapaho, Sioux, Bannock—even Blackfoot country."

"Them Bannocks—wasn't they the ones we run onto comin' north outta Pierre's Hole country last year, after rendezvous?"

"Believe your memory serves you well, son," he answered. "Think you're right. Well, now. Rotten Belly got to be a right popular fellow in the Crow tribes: seein' how he always was bringin' in horses an' most times nary losin' a scalp to the enemy in doin' it."

"He never got caught by them other tribes he was stealin' ponies from?"

"Not rightly." Bass grinned. "Your papa did get followed an' on a few times had to prove he could be just as good a leader in battle as he was in stealin' horses. So, Arapooesh always made sure he took with him the best men, on the best ponies they could ride, carryin' the best weapons to use. An' he always chose places to hightail it to where he could run to if'n he was followed an' chased by them they was stealin' horses from. Many's the time he's told me he an' his men had to fort themselves up in the trees, throwin' up the best defense they could. An' he had been pretty good at it. For a long time there, Rotten Belly always come home with lots of ponies an' some goodly scalps. Why, by the time your father-man was some thirty years old, them Sparrowhawk had made him their chief."

"Ain't that pretty young—to be a chief?"

"Not at all, Josiah," Bass said. "Crow boys start pretty early goin' out to steal horses. Then they start by takin' care of horses on a scalp raid, an' later on start growin' to be a warrior pretty young. Makin' war be a young fella's job—for young pups, such as you." He smiled. "Us ol' horses get age in our bones an' it's not so easy makin' war any more. So, Rotten Belly weren't really all that young to be made a chief."

Bass re-ignited his pipe and tossed the twig into the firepit thoughtfully.

"The ol' boy was a good leader, son. Besides him bein' thought to have some special medicine. He made no big show of it all, not prancin' up an' down like some men might have done if'n they'd been as good as him. Nope. Arapooesh wasn't that kind. He was just the quiet sort, always prayin' to his own special medicine, the thunder, for all the help he needed in decidin' on things."

Scratch stared up at the smoke curling out of the pipe bowl. "He had a good head on them shoulders back then, too. Always pickin' good spots for the whole Crow tribe to camp—you see, this was when there was just one tribe of Crow. Afore they broke up into more camps, Josiah. Yep, them ol' men say Rotten Belly always picked him good places to camp, where the water an' wood an' pasture was good. An' where they could put up a good fight if'n they was attacked by their enemies. Rotten Belly got them Crow to trade for more guns, too. He knew that if the Crow was to make it, they'd need the whiteman's guns."

Bass leaned forward a bit to emphasize a point. "You see, young'un, them Crow was really not all that big a tribe, if'n you look at the other tribes—their enemies—set up all 'round Absaroka. So them Crow had to be some fierce warriors to survive. They was set on by the Sioux from the east all the time. An' them Sioux outnumbered them Crow by some terrible odds. To the south there was always Cheyenne an' Arapaho. On to the west of Absaroka were them Bannocks. An' always—as always—to the west an' north there was Blackfoot. So Absaroka was surrounded with enemies. They had to be some mighty warriors to fight all them enemies off an' keep them tribes outta Absaroka country. That be why Rotten Belly knowed they needed the whiteman's guns, they needed the whiteman's tradin' to help fight off the enemies. In fact, Josiah, Arapooesh was the first chief of the Sparrowhawk to start usin' camp an' herd guards them many years back now. He got his people them guns from tradin' with the whitemen a long way off from Absaroka, long way to the big river in the early days of the trade, see? An' started guards to watch over the camp an' the ponies in case they was attacked."

"What happened then last winter?" Josiah asked. "Last winter when McAfferty brought them Blackfeet down on the Crow winter camp afore we got there? How come them guards didn't do no good then?"

"Arapooesh was some sad 'bout that," Bass said, "sayin' that Whitehead was a better fighter than some of his young Crow warriors. Sneakier anyway. McAfferty had them Blackfoot creep up an' rub out most of them guards just afore first light that mornin'. Then there was nary a warrior to give the warnin' when the rest of them Bug's Boys come roarin' into that camp."

"Rotten Belly feel bad bein' outsmarted by McAfferty?"

"Not near as bad 'bout that as him losin' so many folks that day," Bass commented. "Not all that many really—just some twenty or so. But to have it happen right in your own camp. That's what still makes him burn 'bout it. He hates them Blackfoot almost as much as I do."

"You really ain't got no use for them niggers at all, do you?"

"You right there," Bass answered. "An' Arapooesh back then stopped makin' only them little raids into Blackfoot country when he was made chief. What he started doin' then was makin' big attacks into the enemy's homeland. No more hit an' run for ponies. Nope. Rotten Belly was takin' the big war right on into the enemies' lands. Same thing McAfferty done last winter."

Scratch watched Josiah dip a tin cup into the kettle and sip at what remained of the strong liquid before he went on. "Yepper, Josiah—the first big battle he brung right into Blackfoot land was when he found some eighty or better lodges up to the Musselshell River. The ol' boy had his spies out watchin' the camp for weeks afore an all, seein' just where they was headin' an' all. All that time he'd been movin' the Crow camps to make it look to them Blackfoot like he was headin' on outta Blackfoot country. Them stupid Blackfoot didn't know the ol' boy was really surroundin' 'em, bidin' his time, 'til he was ready for to attack."

"Then he jumped 'em an' rubbed 'em out, right?"

"You jumpin' ahead of me quick, son," Bass answered. "But you right. One night he had him better'n some four-hundred warriors get down close to the enemy camp so when them Blackfoot pulled out the next mornin' across a flat, open plain—he give the word to attack. Whoooeee! Them Bug's Boys didn't have no idea what was comin', an' them Sparrowhawks laid into 'em somethin' fierce. Most of them Blackfoot warriors was in the lead of that march the way they always does, so they had to come back to fight the Crows attackin' the middle. But they soon saw they was outnumbered bad. Them warriors what stayed to fight—to defend their women and chil-

dren—was rubbed out quick. The women was took to marry
Crow warriors who captured them, to have more children. An'
the Blackfoot children was gonna be raised as Sparrowhawks.
All that to help fill the holes in the tribe for havin' their own
children an' women killed or took from 'em. So only a few of
them Blackfoot warriors got away with their lives. Better'n a
hundred of 'em was killed, an' only some twenty Crow. Almost
three times as many women an' children took prisoner as was
Blackfoot men killed, 'long with better'n five hundred head of
horses, all that camp gear an' truck, what have you, them
Blackfoot was totin' 'long."

Bass chuckled. "They couldn't even begin to finish scalpin'
all them Blackfoot—they got so tired of it! So, from that battle
Rotten Belly got to be some bigger man in the tribe. There was
scalps hangin' from his lodgepoles, from his shield an' rifle
case. The hair hung heavy off his shirt an' leggin's. 'Sides, few
men can make a whole robe of scalps—an' such a robe was
made by Sleeps by the Door for her husband."

"A whole robe of them Blackfoot scalps?"

"An' that was just what was left over after the rest of 'em had
been used on his lodge an' his clothes. That be when he
painted that ol' lodge of his with pictures of the battle an' how
he had led them to rub that Blackfoot camp out. But it weren't
long afore them Crow got the big heart 'bout it all. They
thought they wasn't to be gettin' beat by no one at all. So they
broke up into smaller bands then—some goin' this way an'
some headin' that."

"An' one of them groups run into trouble. That what happened?"

"You jumpin' on ahead of me again, son," Bass chided, and
then smiled. "Some thirty lodges or so of Sparrowhawks had
headed south an' east some to visit some new country down by
the South Fork of the Platte. Cheyenne country. But them
Cheyenne had left that country some time afore that to move
south. An' they'd found they didn't like always havin' to fight
off them Comanches all the time. So they up an' figured on
comin' back to their home country. An' run smack onto that
small group of Crow. They bushed 'em good, them Cheyenne
did. Attackin' 'em at night so only a handful of warriors got
outta there with their hair. An' them few warriors carried the
sad tale of that slaughter to the rest of the tribe some weeks
later when they finally made it back to Absaroka."

He looked up at the stars thoughtfully. "They all knew that

all the women an' children what wasn't killed right off was took prisoner, an' them Cheyenne ain't at all nice to prisoners. Them Crow knowed their relations was tortured in some terrible ways by them Cheyenne. Now the job was to go for revenge. But for 'em to do that, they figured they'd have to bring all them bands together again an' get 'em a good leader to head up the fight. They looked up ol' Arapooesh again. They found him visitin' the Flatheads, on west of the Three Forks."

"Arapooesh get along with the Flathead, eh?" Josiah inquired.

"Yep, he does like 'em: them Flathead folks."

"Been kinda wonderin' how he'd take to Looks Far when we get up there to Absaroka next year."

"Don't see no problem with that a'tall," the older trapper said. "Rotten Belly likes the Flathead, he does. Good friends with 'em, an' goes visitin' 'em all the time. So, they rounded up all the tribe an' get Arapooesh to lead the tribe. Well, sir—this was the time for that ol' boy to really shine, it was. There was some other goodly chiefs amongst the Crow by this time: Long Hair, Two Face, Little White Bear, Yellow Belly an' others. But—Rotten Belly was the best. Like I said while ago, probably the best chief they ever had 'em, likely to ever have. Them other chiefs was Rotten Belly's council of war an' Arapooesh had better'n some seven, maybe eight, hundred warriors ready an' saddled. He made sure they was all on the best mounts, takin' two extra ponies along, an' makin' sure they carried all the best weapons for the trip. They took off for the south an' east to lift some Cheyenne scalps an' wash away the dishonor they'd been handed when that band of Crow was nearly rubbed out."

"Bet that was some sight to see," Josiah commented wistfully. "Seein' all them warriors an' all them ponies. All of 'em painted up for battle."

"An' their ponies painted up too," Bass said. "Arapooesh must have been some. That ol' boy wearin' his long bonnet—that'un he keeps to his lodge you seen. Feathers reached clear down to the ground even when he's on top of a pony. Wearin' that robe made all of Blackfoot scalps an' pictures of the time they rubbed them Blackfoot out. Ever'body singin' his own war song, their own medicine, 'sides those who was cryin' in loss for their relations killed by them Cheyennes. He rounded up them other chiefs, that war council of his, an' made 'em all a personal-like promise, Josiah. Rotten Belly told 'em they would not return until they had the full revenge on them Cheyenne. Then he told the camp they had two days before they was leavin', to make medicine an' to get all the weapons an' ponies ready for the long trip."

"They wipe them Cheyenne out pretty quick, eh?"

"Not afore they crossed the train their relations had made in headin' south. They come up on where the Cheyenne had wiped that camp out, findin' the bones not drug off by wolves an' coyotes an' such. They sang their death songs over them bones, then buried 'em in the ground."

"Don't Crow bury 'em in trees?"

"Usual they does. But you gotta 'member they was down to enemy country then. An' they didn't want the bones of their relations bein' bothered again by the enemy. So they put the bones in large holes in the ground, makin' strong promises for revenge, an' covered the holes up afore leavin'. Run all them ponies over the spot, too. An' Arapooesh knowed how them warriors felt 'bout the bones of all their relations. He gave 'em a good speech an' whipped 'em up into a real fightin' funk. Somethin' good! They took out after the Cheyenne, followin' the trail of that big village."

"Then they come on 'em an' wiped 'em out?"

"You wanna tell this story, or you gonna let me?"

Josiah smiled at the older trapper. "I s'pose I'm gettin' ahead of you again."

"That you are, son," he said. "A sorry listener you gotten to be, too."

"I'll just shut my yap an' listen, then." Paddock leaned back against his saddle.

"Was 'bout two weeks later they'd been followin' that trail an' got down to the Bayou Salade country."

"Where we headin' for fall trappin'?"

"That's right," Bass said. "There was two lil' creeks flowin' down into the park an' camped right between 'em was them Cheyenne. Them Crow stayed back that night in some timber 'bout a mile back. Rotten Belly divided his men into two groups, one under him an' the other under Little White Bear. One line went on one side of the Cheyenne camp; Arapooesh put his warriors on the other. All them warriors was put out in long lines some ten paces apart. An' when it was all ready, Arapooesh sent a handful of warriors down to the camp with orders to wait until first light to attack."

He signed and smiled in the telling of the battle. "Come the first gray of mornin', them few Crow warriors drove the Cheyenne horses off toward the waitin' Sparrowhawk warriors. Them Cheyenne jumped outta their robes an' seein' just a small handful of Crow they started chasin' 'em—thinkin' this was gonna be some easy pickin's. Some hundred or so Cheyenne braves come runnin' down between them two lines of Sparrowhawks, who waited for Arapooesh to give the signal. Then they come roarin' outta the woods an' timber an' rubbed them Cheyenne out, just like that." He snapped his fingers.

"Not a enemy lived. Wiped out all at once. But some others come out from camp to see what was goin' on now—an' they was killed, too. Now there weren't many warriors left in them lodges so the Sparrowhawks rushed the camp. Some few warriors escaped, but most of the whole number of fightin' men was killed off quick—better'n two, maybe three hundred Cheyenne warriors. Women an' children was took prisoner an' some thousand or better ponies to add to the Crow herds."

"How many Crow as there killed?"

"Just one." Bass held up a single finger. "An' some 'nother handful wounded."

"Why didn't they just rub out the women an' children? Like them Cheyenne had done to the Crow people back up on the South Fork of the Platte?"

"Arapooesh had a differ'nt idea 'bout war," Scratch explained. "Not like other Injuns at all. He figured it better to make wives outta the women so they could have more children to fight their enemies. Also figured that the children grow up to be Crow warriors to fight off the enemies."

"Didn't he figure some would escape?"

"Some few always did, son," Bass agreed. "But most of them prisoners the Crow always took in battle—most of 'em stayed with the Crow. They found things better with the Sparrowhawk, found life better an' easier with a new life in Absaroka."

"So, my father-man just killed warriors, an' brung the women an' children home with him."

"Right. Not like them Cheyenne that laid into Dangling Foot's camp an' wiped 'em out."

"Dangling Foot?"

"Crow chief what had his camp rubbed out by the Cheyenne. The battle that brought the Crow back together again."

"Ahhh." Josiah nodded.

"Rotten Belly's medicine was all the stronger for the big

showin' in wipin' out them Cheyenne down there toward the Arkansas River. You see, Arapooesh had told all the warriors not to kill any birds on the march south to find the Cheyenne. His thunder medicine had told him not to do such a thing. But this one young, big-mouth warrior made big talk 'bout killin' a magpie on the trip, sayin' nothin' wrong with killin' such a bird."

"An' that warrior the only one killed by the Cheyenne?"

"Yep," Bass replied. "That made Arapooesh some big medicine. The only one who didn't do what the chief ordered was the only one killed in the battle."

"So now there be just two bands of Crow," Josiah said.

"That's right. They know they won't get wiped out if'n they keep big numbers like that. One band under Arapooesh now, and the other'n under Long Hair since Little White Bear died just few years back now."

"How many Crow there be now?"

"I ain't good at countin', son. You know that."

"How many lodges then?" Josiah asked.

"I hear tell they got 'em some eight hundred lodges between the two camps. Maybe little better'n that."

"Then, how many is the count to a lodge? I remember you told me once."

"You can always figure 'bout some eight folks to a lodge," Bass said, watching Josiah across the fire. The younger trapper was scratching at the dirt beside the firepit with a twig. "You been a store clerk, help you cipher like that, huh?"

"It does," Paddock answered. Then he brought his head up. "That be better than six thousand, four hundred Crow!" There was real astonishment in his voice.

"In both camps," Bass added.

"So, in one camp, maybe just in Arapooesh's, there be better than three thousand folks. That's some now!"

"Wagh! Lotta folks to be findin' water an' wood an' good horse pasture for each an' ever' time you move your camp."

"I think this child gonna move off to the robes now," said Josiah as he rose slowly to stretch. "Didn't get much sleep last night, ol' man."

"No, we didn't, son," Bass agreed. He gazed over at the two lean-tos beside them. He saw the sleeping form of Waits-by-the-Water, then looked over at Looks Far Woman and Joshua, who were sleeping at the edge of the dim firelight.

Josiah watched the old man's eyes. "You happy, Scratch?"

"Yeah, I'm pretty happy. Got all I need to be happy 'bout now."

"Maybe have some children of your own?"

"Like to do that, yes," Bass answered, looking down into the flames. "Some kids to grow up while I'm growin' old."

"Didn't think you was gonna make it—gettin' old, I mean. Last night—with them two fixin' to gut you."

"All that matters is they didn't." The fire crackled and he watched the sparks ascend into the darkness overhead. "Our women wasn't raped an' Joshua weren't touched at all through the whole damned thing."

"I s'pose we come out of it in fine shape." Josiah nodded.

"Looks to be, son."

"'Ceptin' me not knowin' for sure exactly who sent them to kill me, all the way from St. Louis."

"Never know now, Josiah," Bass said. "Just sounds like you left some real bad blood back to St. Lou."

"All the trouble has come to me, Scratch."

"I know that. I know." Bass nodded. "Just like it is for me at times. The trouble come lookin' for you when you ain't expectin' it a'tall. That be the real shame of it. Man just wants to be left alone, don't want folks messin' with his life—an' that be when it just come jumpin' right outta the dark on you."

"You sayin' you think it don't do no good to try?"

"You jokin', ain't you, son?" He smiled at the young trapper. "My whole life been stayin' ahead of trouble that always come to find me. Keep it at bay. Just like you keep a wolf at bay."

"That wolf run off now," Josiah said.

"Don't think so," Bass demurred. "Figure he keep comin' back until he gets himself killed. The way of sick, crazy critters like that. They got a death wish, they do. They just keep comin' back to attack 'til they gonna get themselves killed."

"How you so sure of that?"

"Saw 'im."

"The wolf?" Josiah looked up suddenly. "You saw the mad wolf?"

"I did, that," Bass answered. "Tonight, just after dark. Not long back. Down by the river. I was gettin' water. Scared shit outta me. He come across the trail just lopin' 'long easy-like an' seen me an' stopped. I stopped myself right there an' then, an' started gettin' the willies from lookin' at that ugly hoodoo thing. The look he had to his eye was somethin' evil, it was, Josiah. Some real evil there, son."

"You didn't shoot him?"

"Weren't carryin' a gun, a'tall, young'un."

"Figure I'd been scared, too."

"All I had me was a knife I pulled outta my belt real slow-like an' got ready. But the evil beast just stared at me long an' hard, like he . . . like he was tryin' to tell me somethin'. His eyes all bloodied up an' borin' holes into me the way he was. Tryin' to tell me somethin'."

"You gonna have some bad dreams tonight, Scratch, you go thinkin' like that."

"Nawww." Bass passed it off quickly. "Won't have me no trouble sleepin' all the way 'til first light, son. This nigger gonna hit the robes here early an' not get up 'til it's a bright new day."

He rose wearily to stand over the flames. "Night, son."

Bass watched Paddock head to his lean-to. He stood a moment more at the fire and played with some limbs, tapping at them with a toe. Then he turned toward the robes himself. No bad dreams this night, he promised himself. He would sleep good this night. He needed it.

And no dreams, no mad wolf, no evil medicine from that beast was going to keep him from that sleep.

Twenty-seven

Josiah rolled over in his sleep. Those few inches of movement saved his life. He felt the cold steel slide off his skin as he turned, the warm trickle of blood where the sharp blade had broken the flesh.

He bolted awake and erupted out of the blankets, charged the huge shadow that blocked off the light outside the lean-to. Josiah crashed into the figure, felt the man give way, saw him rise from his knees to stand, blocking out the rest of the thin predawn light. It was as if the giant was holding back the sun itself, staying it from rising above the mist that hung in the valley like smoke. Paddock rocked to his feet, kicked free of the blankets.

The shadow drew himself up to full height, taking in a long, slow breath. He smiled down at the young trapper. Josiah had never seen anyone so big. It wasn't the twisted, perverted smile of Hickerson, or of his other attacker, Redman. This smile told of someone who was deadly serious. Paddock's fear twitched deep within his bowels.

Josiah, shaking off the grogginess of sleep, looked down at his fingertips. They were red. His own blood again. So damned many wanting it.

The giant's smile widened across great, white teeth. Even his smile was big. Paddock's gaze coursed down the giant's arm to the knife. The big man held it poised in front of him. The last shreds of sleep fell away and Josiah pulled his own blade, the steel hissing against leather as it slid from its sheath. The remnants of last night's fire raised lazy curls of smoke into the mist-shrouded morning air. IIe thought it strange that some-one would come just before daybreak. Why not at night, under cover of darkness?

"Ahhh, Monsieur." The grin opened and the big man-shadow spoke to him. "You wish to dance?"

"D . . . da . . . dance?"

"Yes, Monsieur Paddock," came the answer. "Move in the dance of death with me. I have waited long to hold you close."

Paddock shook his head. He could not make any sense of the words. Perhaps he was still in the robes asleep—dreaming all of this. He shook his head again, and felt more warm, red blood trickle down his shoulder. No. He was not asleep.

The shadow-man had tried to slit his throat. Only his move-ment had saved him from a deeper, perhaps fatal, wound. Whoever he was, this shadow-man had crept all the way to the lean-to on cat's feet. He was not like the blundering riverfront assassins who had come for him the night before last. This one moved with the stealth and silence of a wilderness cat.

The giant gazed down at the knife in Josiah's hand, then looked into Josiah's eyes again.

"Dance?" Josiah asked.

"Ahhh, little one. I have waited long time to hold you close. The knife you pull tells me you wish to dance with Emile."

"Dance?" he uttered again. Then Josiah realized what the giant meant. The huge shadow was talking of a duel with knives. Two partners waltzing in and away from each other, parrying and thrusting, lunging and dropping back. A dance.

"Yes," Josiah whispered as some movement caught his eye. "Let's dance."

He glanced to the left. Waits-by-the-Water had come out of her robes. Looks Far was suddenly sitting up at the entrance to their blanket lean-to. Both women seemed frozen and motionless, watching as the young trapper faced off the huge attacker.

"Where's Bass?" Josiah rasped.

"Gone," said the Crow woman.

"Where, damnit?"

"Whiskey. Gone early, he tell me," Bass's woman replied. Take kettle. Tell me not wake up. Go for whiskey. Be back."

Fine time for the goddamned old man to be heading to Campbell's for whiskey. Wants to get drunk so damned early in the day. Fine time."

"I wait long time for that one to leave." The huge man grinned. "Just you—me now."

Paddock sighed. It was his alone to do now. Much again as that night with the two who came into their camp. Josiah's mind filled with the vivid, flashing montage of scenes flush with Bass tied to the tree, the half-naked women, and the flash of bright muzzle-lightning in the dark, cool air.

This one had come for him too. But he was not here to dally with the women. He had come for just one thing.

"Why . . . why you—"

"Why do I want you, Monsieur Paddock?" The man straightened a little. "Why do I want you and not Monsieur Bass? This is what you ask?"

"I already figured it's me you want. Figure this ain't got nothin' to do with Bass."

The giant nodded slowly. "You are right, little one. You are right. This has not to do with Bass. It has only to do with—"

"Me."

"Yes."

"Why?" Josiah felt the hot rush of adrenaline begin to charge the taut muscles along his arms and pour into his legs to burn away his drowsiness.

"Why do I come to kill you?" The one good eye peered out of the shadows. "Yes. This you are owed. This you should be told before I kill you. Every man should know why he dies. And know whose hand kills him."

Paddock stared from the man's good eye to the long scar nearly closing the other one. It sent a cold shiver along his spine, as blood dribbled down his back. "Tell me."

"My name is Emile. Sharpe. The name mean anything to you?"

"Emile. Emile Sharpe. No," Josiah replied steadily. "Should it?"

"Perhaps no." He shook his head. "What does the name Henri LeClerc do for your courage, little one?"

LeClerc!

"I . . . I ain't heard the name in a long time."

"Yes." The giant inched forward, rotating the knife slightly in his hand. "But—you do remember?"

"I remember LeClerc. Yeah."

"I like the way you kill him. Good. It was good. You duel. But do not kill him with a pistol. You kill him with your feet, you did. Good. Emile Sharpe like that."

"How—how you know 'bout all that?"

"It is for another, one who lives, that I come kill you."

"They sent you out here to find me—to kill me. His folks. That it?"

"You catch onto it quick, little one."

Paddock studied the big man, considering, measuring. He had been fool enough to think it could all be left behind him in St. Louis. That the long arm of the past would not reach out to the mountains. He had been fool enough for the past two years to think that he might be able to breathe easier. But there had been three sent after him already. If they did not return, perhaps the price would be lifted from his head. Perhaps no others would take up the challenge of the long journey to the mountains to kill him. Perhaps. If he was able to rid himself of this Emile Sharpe. If.

But what if the price on his head were raised—and there were more next year? And the year after that? And the year. . . .

"You ain't the first," Josiah said.

"I know," Emile replied. "Two others." Then the smile broadened. "But they no good like Emile. They stupid river men. Fast on knife. Slow on brain. They think all too much on the women. Think too little on the killing. They fail where Emile is to win."

"They know 'bout you?"

He shook his head. "No, Monsieur Paddock. They know not of Emile Sharpe. *C'est si bon.*"

"You come out with the supply train, too?" Paddock asked,

perhaps to stall, hoping the shape of things would change. Perhaps Bass would make it back.

"No," Sharpe answered simply. "Emile Sharpe come on own to mountains. I born in wilderness. *Pays sauvage*. I little boy in wilderness. I grow in wilderness. Now I man in wilderness all over. Not like whiskey boys from river you kill. I better. No better than Emile Sharpe. Wilderness and me—we are one. Yes. You can be afraid of this one." He tapped his chest with a finger.

The shadow-man was right. Josiah could be afraid of Sharpe. If it were true that he was born and raised in the wilderness, he already had another edge. Besides his size. Josiah dropped his gaze to the man's huge moccasins, then let it drift slowly back up the tall frame. Perhaps not all that big. Six and a half feet. A half a foot taller than Josiah. But the sheer bulk of the muscle and sinew, that was where the size of the man became frightening. He looked older than Scratch. In his forties, probably. Hard to tell with the scars and the wrinkles. The wilderness could mark a man.

"I weren't afraid of them other two," Paddock muttered. "An' I'm just gonna have to deal with you now. Same way I done with them."

Sharpe watched Paddock move a couple of steps toward him. "*Ici*," the trapper snapped, "*et maintenant*." Here and now.

Paddock sighed. "What they payin' you for killin' me?"

"They pay me much for you," Emile said. "But, it is not all the money. I like the rich folks to—how you say it—be in the hock to me. Yes. Emile Sharpe likes to know the rich ones owe me. First they pay me their money. But I do not always stop there. Sharpe needs money. Sharpe goes to old customer he get money. Old customer never refuse Sharpe the coins. Yes." He nodded. "The money is there when I need it. They all time pay Emile Sharpe."

"How you gonna convince 'em I'm dead?"

"I bring LeClerc his pistol."

Josiah should have remembered that. The pistol was his link with the past. The last thread linking him to the duel, and the killing, the escape from St. Louis. That damned pistol—and he didn't even have it on him. Lotta good the goddamned thing was to him now.

"Lotta pistols like that." Paddock smiled. "Maybe they won't believe you—won't believe you killed me. You won't get your money."

"They believe me. They pay me. Emile Sharpe get his money." Sharpe eased forward, the knife sliding up in front of him. "I bring them something make them believe Emile Sharpe."

"How they gonna believe you for sure?"

"Little one—I bring them your head."

The picture loomed across his mind. He saw Sharpe entering one of the fancy French drawing rooms with its brocaded furniture and polished walnut, crystal goblets holding the red wine they would drink in celebration for the successful completion of the prescribed task. Then Sharpe opening the large sack he had slung over his shoulder, slowly pulling at the knots and loosening the draw string. As he pulls up the end of the sack over the table loaded with china and crystal goblets, the large object rolls across the sparkling walnut, scattering the tableware. The battered object comes to a stop and Paddock recognizes what it is. The eyes stare open in sudden death. The mouth and tongue frozen and gaping in violent death. His own head comes to a stop among the fine dinnerware. His head causes the French in the room to recoil and gag. Then Sharpe is told to take his gruesome trophy and leave the room, leave the house with his money.

His mind snapped back to the present. He glanced over at Waits-by-the-Water and Looks Far Woman. After all they had been through, they would have to endure this, too. In a way he was glad they had not pulled up a rifle and tried to shoot. Better this way. He would take on the specter of death on death's own terms. Steel and blood and flesh. His gaze left Looks Far Woman's frightened, pinched face and glanced at the medicine bundle hanging from a pole of the shelter.

His father-man's bundle. No. Paddock's now. *Awu'xtpe.* Sun Runner. Once the sun came up this morning, it would race across the sky to chase the haze and clouds from the canopy overhead. The day would become warmer. Brighter. And he suddenly realized that if he did not live to see the passing of another day, then it was still all right. He realized what Bass had often attempted to teach him. Paddock felt at his core what the old Sparrowhawk chief had truly been trying to teach him.

If he was not around to see the falling of another sun from another sky, it was still all right. Only that sky and the hills and the grass and the rocks last forever. Man was never meant to. Man should never attempt to. It was all right now. He had shared real happiness with the woman. He had fathered a man-child to carry on in the world. So if this were to be his time, then it was truly a good day to die. Paddock smiled and looked back at Sharpe to see the giant studying him.

"*Bia tsimbic da-sasua.*" Paddock spoke quietly, firmly, as he stared back at the giant. He was surprised he remembered the words in the Sparrowhawk tongue. Before, he had never been able to remember the Crow words. But now they flowed from his lips like a cooling refreshment against a parched, drying, blazing-sun day.

"*Bia?*" Sharpe asked. "What is this talk you tell me?"

"*Bia tsimbic da-sasua,*" Josiah repeated in Crow. And felt the power surging through his muscles, a power that came from finally knowing. And with it the peace that came from finally knowing. He remembered that he had learned all there was to know about a knife. The power was there now.

He glanced quickly at the medicine bundle, the beaded and festooned otter pouch hanging from the blanket tower. He knew he had the power now.

He smiled broadly at the giant, whose smile had quickly faded. "It is a good day to die, monsur," Paddock proclaimed. "You, or me—whatever one—it is a good day to die."

"This is this *bia?*"

"No," Josiah answered. "It is much, much more'n you'll ever understand, Sharpe. Much more."

Paddock eased forward a step and saw Sharpe jerk his knife up. Josiah crouched and slid his own knife up in front of his chest.

"It is a good day for you to die," Sharpe whispered as he began to glide to the side, circling toward Paddock.

Josiah shook his head. "You'll never know, you bastard. You'll just never know."

When I come from behind,
I will carry two songs with me.

The words the two old men had taught him last winter slipped through his mind as his hand tightened around the knife. Rotten Belly had taught the words to Scratch before the manhunt for the Whitehair. And Bass had rehearsed them with Josiah through the cold, blazing-white days of the winter hunt for a murderer. But Paddock was considered the murderer now.

I will have my medicine here upon my chest.
You I am hunting—you are poor now.
Look to me!

Paddock glanced down as the soft caress against his skin made itself known again. The pouch. She had given it to him last summer in the valley below the Tetons. Pierre's Hole and the start of their life together. He had worn the pouch ever since that morning. Truly—that was his medicine: the love of this woman for him. The love he held forever in his heart for her.

"Look to me," Josiah repeated in English.

"What you say?"

"Look to me—for I will kill you." He smiled broadly at Sharpe.

"Little one . . ." Sharpe leaned back from his crouch and put both hands on his hips, mockingly. "You have all this wrong. I kill you today. It is your good day to die."

Beyond the hills I have stayed,
From there I have come here now.

The song rose up high on this last part, soaring as if upon wings with the eagles and hawks into the high places. Where his heart began to soar.

Long time will I be the eagle.
Long time have I been coming here.

He had been a long time in coming to this place. Better than two years now.

I shall ride after the wolf in the mountains.

He would not run from the wolf any longer. There would always be wolves. This giant was but one more. And he would not run from him. He knew he must go after the wolves. One at a time—so be it. He would ride after the wolves.

Paddock's scars heated up with the flush of hot adrenaline to his muscles: the pony tracks across the tops of his arms where Rotten Belly had ripped flesh off before his hunt of the White-hair. The tight skin across the holes on his chest and back, where the Whitehair had shot him last winter, in the Cold-Maker's time. They burned now. The slice across his belly from last year's rendezvous and a stupid drunk's knife. And she had come to him that night to heal much more than the torn flesh.

Finally at the side of his head, hidden beneath the curls where few ever saw, the deep, white furrow where the ball had raked along his skull that misty, gray morning on Bloody Island out in the Mississippi River. The Frenchman's bullet had missed. But it had stunned him for a few moments. Slowly he had risen to march on his attacker, and had tossed his loaded pistol aside. Then kicked young LeClerc to death.

Strong of leg. That's what Rotten Belly called it. The old Indian chief had seen Josiah kick and flail at the ponies as the younger trapper had been healing. He called it strong of leg. Ever since he was a kid, Josiah had been able to jump and kick like few others. Paddock smiled more broadly and rocked to the balls of his feet. He was ready. If it were to be here and now that the past was laid to rest—so be it. If it were to be here and now that he were to die, so be it. It gave him a good feeling inside knowing Emile Sharpe would never know the strength that knowledge gave him at this moment.

"Little one," Sharpe spoke abruptly. "Come here to me. I kill you now."

Josiah thought on it a moment. "Yes, you have come after me, Sharpe," he replied. "But, this is where your hunt ends, you bastard. This is where I come after you."

"Come to me, Paddock."

Emile edged in toward the young trapper, the knife weaving back and forth in front of his vast body like a pendulum. He feinted to feel Paddock out. But Josiah did not flinch.

"Ahhh, little one." Emile smiled. "You do not move. You know knives, eh?"

"I know knives, yes."

"It is good." Emile stepped forward again and feinted. "Make this better fight then for me. Make this more fun for Emile."

"You will never know now."

Paddock leapt to one side and spun in midair, raking the edge of his knife along the giant's upper arm as he came back down and waltzed past the big man.

"Unnnnhhh!" Sharpe grunted at the sudden pain in his left arm. He looked quickly to his upper arm and the torn sleeve with the blood pouring from the slice across the thick muscle.

"The little one moves like a cat, I see. This is good. I cut a cat today."

Josiah feinted, then whipped the knife back in, striking lower.

Sharpe raked the tip of his huge knife across Josiah's shoulder, ripping at the huge scab and healing flesh where Nute's ball had hit the young trapper.

Paddock jerked from the pain and stumbled back a few steps. He could feel the blood flowing from the wound. It had only recently begun to dry, but now it was ugly and gaping again, oozing blood down his bare chest.

"Old wounds sometimes bleed more." Sharpe smiled as he eased the knife up higher and looked down at the blade. "See?" He turned the knife toward Paddock. "Your blood. There will be more, little one." He dabbed his finger into the blood on the blade, and licked it.

Paddock watched in tickling anticipation, rotating his wounded shoulder as Sharpe smacked his lips.

"You taste good on my tongue, little one." Emile lifted the blade to his mouth and licked the rest of the blood. "Give me some more of you to taste."

"You tasted my steel, too," Paddock said.

Sharpe looked at his own torn left arm. "Yes, I tasted your steel. Lucky one you are, little one. Lucky. The last you have taste of Emile Sharpe."

The *metis* thrust again, circling the younger trapper. Josiah feinted, then danced to the left. A sudden pull on his left arm almost unbalanced him. Sharpe had snagged him, catching Paddock's left wrist as the trapper slid past.

Josiah gripped the big man's lower arm with his left hand, digging in with the nails. They waltzed slowly in a small circle away from the lean-tos.

"Now, we dance, Paddock." Emile beamed. "Now we truly dance!"

Josiah slashed out with his knife, but his reach was not long enough. Sharpe leapt backward, out of the way.

"Good, little one." Sharpe continued smiling, continued goading. "Come for me now."

"You come taste me again," said Paddock easily.

"Yes, I come to taste more of your blood." Sharpe jerked the knife forward, slicing the tip of the blade across the wide belt that held Paddock's leggings and breechclout around his waist.

Josiah felt the pressure instantly and jerked back against the mighty arm yanking him close as Sharpe lunged with his blade. The tip of the steel slid up across the muscles of his belly, opening a gash that became a thin red line. Then the flesh finally began to ooze. Paddock looked down at his belly, then back into the eyes of the *metis*.

"More blood, little one. I taste you good soon."

Paddock slashed downward, jamming his right arm up as if to jab down at the halfbreed. He watched only Sharpe's eyes now, seeing their gaze climb to the raised arm and the knife poised high. The giant slipped his right arm up to parry the intended blow, but the trapper's right arm was no longer high. Josiah had watched the attacker's eyes to see when to spring and he had slipped his arm down as Sharpe had brought his up.

As Josiah whipped his right arm down, he rotated the knife to another position in his palm. In one fluid motion his right arm struck forward. Paddock felt the tip of the blade pierce into the flesh and Sharpe's body jerk backward, his mighty left arm tugging him away. With nothing but the awesome strength of his body, the *metis* threw Josiah to the side as if he were a child's doll, halting the knife's thrust.

Sharpe glanced down at his abdomen. The young trapper's steel had pierced the flesh and blood began to grow in an ever-widening ring down toward the groin. He wanted to touch the wound he could not see beneath the soiled breeches; instead, he looked back into Paddock's eyes.

"You taste Sharpe good there, little one," he breathed. "This is good fight, no? I like good fight. Most fight for Sharpe no fight. No fight at all. Over too soon. No fun, over too soon. You good with knife. More blood to come, eh, little one?"

"Likely," Josiah whispered.

Paddock jammed the knife up suddenly, straight through the wrist that bound his left arm to Sharpe. He felt the blade rake past the bones as it twisted on out the top of the lower arm, slicing along the side of his own wrist in the process.

Sharpe jerked his hand loose and ripped his arm free in one motion, backing away. His eyes changed. The light, gray color mutated into a dark thunderhead.

"You real good." Sharpe no longer grinned. "You good fight for Emile. I quit playing with you. Enough fun for now. I taste your heart now."

He shook his left wrist, slinging the dripping blood from his arm where it billowed brightly over his hand. The man was mpervious to pain. If he could not feel that an artery had been ut, if he could not feel the seriousness of that wound. . . .

"I'm glad you gettin' serious now," Paddock rasped from the ack of his throat. "Let's finish this now."

He rushed the 'breed, watching the big man raise both arms s if to catch the young trapper as he flew toward him. But at he last moment, Paddock dropped to the ground and slid on is back. Paddock's bare feet caught the big man squarely, just elow the knees. At that instant Josiah kicked out with both ighty legs.

Sharpe sprawled backward as his great bulk toppled. Padock watched him hurtle off-balance, flailing through the air, hen hammer the earth. The young trapper sprang to his feet riumphantly, rushed toward the *metis*.

But the huge legs lashed out as the young man dashed forard, tripping Paddock, catapulting him down into the dirt nd grass. The *metis* was on him even before he met the earth. he huge, bloody left hand gripped Paddock by the throat and rced his head back, smashing it against the ground. His huge ght arm flew to the sky and the knife turned in it, the tip tating down toward its target.

Paddock coughed and choked against the pain, unable to reathe. He watched the eyes above him, those cloudy thunerhead eyes, grow darker as the right arm whipped downard. He knew it was over in that instant. And for a moment siah was ready for it to end, feeling the *metis*'s blood from the ounded left arm mingling warmly with his own at the raw eck wound.

But instead, the monstrous fist smashed against his jaw, ending slivers of pain and bright light exploding across his rehead. The giant had slammed the mallet-sized fist against im instead of the steel. Then Josiah could think of nothing ore.

Waits-by-the-Water pulled back the hammer on the rifle. he had seen Bass go through each step many times. She ushed the frizzen forward and checked the powder in the an. She snapped it back over the pan and pulled the hammer ack to full cock. The old trapper had shown her to put the utt-plate into the crook of her shoulder first before lifting the fle up to her cheek. It was difficult. The weapon was so heavy ad she could not hold it steadily. She could not even nestle e butt-plate in the crook of her shoulder. The stock was too ng for her to reach the trigger. Instead she slipped the top of

the butt beneath her armpit and brought the wobbling weapo
up to her cheek.

Now there were two triggers to contend with. She got th
big man centered on the front blade and pulled. Nothing ha
pened. No fire. No spitting of smoke. No big explosion. I
front of the muzzle she watched the intruder grip Josiah
throat once more in that mighty vise. With the one arm l
brought the young, strong trapper up into the air to hang wit
his feet dangling and helpless. It did not matter now. Paddo
was unconscious. She pulled the trigger again.

Once again no fire nor explosion. She continued to watch
the giant raised Paddock into the air like a limp doll and smas
him to the ground. At that moment she remembered son
obscure words about the two triggers and looked down to th
trigger guard. There was another trigger. Her forefinger curle
around the front trigger and she suddenly remembered not
put any pressure on it until she was ready.

Down the muzzle she watched the big man reach out fe
Josiah again and toss him into the air the way a wolf would pla
with a dead rabbit. Playfully, Sharpe smashed the young tra
per to the ground once more as Waits-by-the-Water lined th
front blade up on the middle of his back. Wobbling, shak
trembling, swaying from side to side, she pulled the trigge
The spit of smoke burst from the pan and the touchhole ar
then came the explosion at her shoulder that slammed he
backward. Her rifle fell to the ground as she stumbled. Sh
didn't know if she had hit her target.

Sharpe felt the burn along his left side as the lead ball to
into it. He looked down, the pain searing his flesh where th
ball exited, and stared at the blood on the front of his shir
Instead of being hypnotized by the ragged, gaping hole, I
raised his face to the heavens and clenched his eyes shut. Ar
roared.

"Arrruuugggghhhh!" The cry burst from his throat. And th
pain was instantly gone. He opened his eyes and turne
bringing his gaze down to the two women behind him at th
lean-tos. The smaller woman held out a large butcher knife ar
tossed it to the other woman as the second one came to her fee

That must be the one who shot me, he decided.

Waits-by-the-Water tightly gripped the knife, her kne
quaking. She glanced quickly at Looks Far to see that she, to
had taken up one of the large skinning knives. At least if I

came for either of them, the other could torment the attacker from the back. Slashing, stabbing, making him weaker and bloodier with every blow.

Emile stalked toward her slowly. Quick work of the two young women and then finish with the little one on the ground. On he came.

Waits-by-the-Water scooted away from the lean-to and motioned for Looks Far to do the same. He would not be able to attack them both at the same time. But in the next instant she knew he was coming for her.

His head sank down into those massive shoulders as he snorted and bellowed. The crunch of each step he took across the dirt and grass seemed to ring in her ears. He moved too slowly. He was toying with her now.

Paddock blinked his eyes, struggling in the grip of the thick, painful dream. Some of the blackness slipped away as slivers of light shot back and forth across his eyelids. He blinked again. His cheek against the ground felt the vibrations as he opened his eyes more fully to stare at the giant advancing on the Crow woman. The ground trembled. It shook from his every step. But the trembling and pounding Josiah felt beneath his cheek beat faster and pulsed more strongly than the *metis* stomped toward the women.

Behind the giant, from the edge of the trees, Waits-by-the-Water saw the man coming. He rode tall in the saddle, standing in his stirrups.

The rider, empty rifle across his saddle, thundered toward the giant, as Paddock raised his head to look. Emile, startled, turned to face this new adversary.

It was too late for Sharpe to do anything but watch the tall stranger swing the dark, walnut butt of the rifle. The cheekpiece smashed full force against the *metis*'s face.

The horseman bolted on past, then yanked on the reins savagely. The horse answered as it skidded to a dust-billowing stop. Almost in the same motion, he wheeled the animal around, pushing and prodding the horse into furious motion for another run at the giant.

The big man rose from the ground, shrugging off the pain from the bone-crushing rifle butt. Emile grinned crookedly. The blood poured out of his nose and flowed across his mouth, dripped from his chin. The *metis* hulked there like a massive tree, waiting for the stranger to ride down on him.

The rider swung his weapon at Emile's mouth with its sickening, bloody grin. But the rifle struck no bone nor flesh.

Sharpe ducked at the last moment and grabbed upward, snaring something in a huge, meaty hand. It was the stranger's belt. The half-breed's fingers ripped into the rider's back and clamped onto the wide leather band. Then he yanked. And the horseman flew off the back of the horse as it raced on by the giant.

The stranger's rifle sailed through the air, striking the horse on its back as it came down, causing the animal to skitter into a blanket lean-to. The horse whinnied as it stumbled and slid to the ground on its side. It snorted and cried out against the tangle of ropes and blankets, attempting to stand. Looks Far Woman dashed into her lean-to and scooped the infant into her arms. Then she watched Waits-by-the-Water pull at the reins of the downed horse, trying to get the big animal up and out of her way.

Paddock rose to his hands and knees as he watched the giant drop to a crouch over the prostrate stranger. The dehorsed rider was a large man himself. Josiah knew it wasn't Teeter. The man was too big.

The horseman, groggy, blinked at Sharpe. He suddenly snapped onto his side, throwing the *metis* off him and rose shakily to his feet. He shook his head from side to side slowly as if testing it, then focused his eyes on the half-breed. Emile charged, crashed into the stranger. Their monstrous bodies resounded with a crack as loud as the boom of trees in a mountain freeze.

Over and over they rolled through the dust and the grass. The *metis* pulled and yanked at the hair of the stranger's head while the rider pushed upward against the half-breed's lower jaw. Finally Sharpe released his grip on the hair and brought a thumb slashing down into the corner of the stranger's eye socket, at the same time jabbing a knee up into the big man's groin. The rider immediately released his grip on Emile.

This was all Sharpe needed. He struck the man again and again, pummeling the stranger's face and head with huge hammer-like fists. Then he rolled the horseman over on his stomach. The half-breed pulled the large knife from the stranger's sheath and held it aloft. The bloodied left hand clamped the back of the stranger's head to the ground, grinding the right cheek into the grass and dirt and bits of broken kindling wood.

"NO!"

Sharpe turned to see Paddock rise to his knees by the firepit a few yards away. Emile smiled, his face a bloodied mess. His grin boasted of a triumph soon to be his.

"You be next, little one," he thundered, bellowing almost like a huge grizzly in battle. "Him first I kill. Then it is you I come for next!"

"NO!" Josiah screamed again. "You come after ME! It is *me* you must kill. *My* medicine you must take!"

"Soon enough, little one." The giant's voice was soft. "Soon—"

Suddenly Emile turned his head at the pounding of more hooves. Another rider thundered down upon the camp. Almost like troublesome insects these mounted intruders were to him. Nothing more than annoying, meddlesome bugs to be squashed.

The bail of the large, cast-iron kettle full of whiskey hung from his left hand.

He rode down on the giant, swung the black kettle. It glanced off the monster's shoulder and knocked him off his knees, slammed him down atop the stranger's body. The buffalo pony dashed on by, only to be brought up short by a savage pull on the rawhide rope around his jaw.

The *metis* began to rise and turn toward Bass. The old trapper's hands were empty now. The kettle was gone. All that was left was the knife. Scratch pulled his left leg over the back of the pony and dropped to the ground as he slipped the large knife from the back of his belt.

Sharpe grinned that huge, toothy smile. "The one who fights the she-bear," he grunted with satisfaction as Scratch went into a fighting crouch.

"This time it is different—eh, my friend?" The giant grinned.

"How's that?" Scratch inquired.

"This time"—Emile shook the large knife out in front of his body—"this time the bear she has some bite, eh?"

"Could be," Bass answered, then rocked forward onto the balls of his feet. "Could be."

He dashed toward the half-breed but Sharpe caught the trapper short, each man's arms locked against the other's body. They stumbled in a tight circle, imprisoned against one another, each man struggling in the wild dance to free his own knife hand while holding down his opponent's.

Bass began to feel himself weaken against the stronger,

taller, more powerful enemy. His arms were being forced
downward, and the knife was being pushed away from Emile's
body. Then Sharpe struck out with a powerful kick, swinging
his foot from the side to knock Scratch's ankles together, sending the trapper falling to his back. Sharpe jumped on top of
him.

Bass's huge knife spun out of his grip toward the firepit
where Josiah came to his feet. Josiah winced almost unconsciously as the two men collided. There was a sudden expul-
sion of air, and blood flew, as the two men crashed to the
ground.

Waits-by-the-Water stood frozen, the breath caught at the
back of her throat. Josiah staggered to his feet and blinked his
eyes against the dust in them. Then as his vision began to clear
he saw the huge half-breed rise off the old trapper.

"No-o-o-o," Paddock almost whimpered, and dropped his
gaze.

Sharpe rocked backward, then slowly pushed himself to his
feet. He stood there, almost triumphant over the trappers. The
huge smile was still there on his face. He had beaten them all.
Three of them. And now he would have the one he had come
for all those miles.

The sound caught in the Crow woman's throat as she realized
it was not her man who had risen from the ground. A muffled
sob was all that finally broke from her lips. The young trapper
heard that desperate sound—felt that woman's pain as an answer to his own grief.

Now his gaze climbed from the knife he had picked up from
the ground, to fix on the Crow woman as if his look was drawn
magically toward her as a reminder of Absaroka. And he saw it
once more.

The otter medicine bundle. Given to him by his adopted
father. But the real gift had been the healing. The supreme gift
from Arapooesh had been the power within that he had earned
through the pain of a long and deep healing. That medicine gift
Josiah had earned in a battle with his own mortality. And not
until a few minutes ago did he really understand the true
meaning of that gift.

All that his adopted father had taught him came flooding
over him once again: the meaning of the pain, the ascension of
his spirit, the tortured growth of his soul—it was all captured
in that medicine bundle.

It was a good day to die. He was ultimately a warrior. And it was a good day to die.

Emile Sharpe would never know of the power in that very private medicine. The giant would never know what power that knowledge gave the young trapper. Paddock glanced down at the stranger, then over to Bass, and knew this day was his to hold fiercely—to wrench from the fabric of life everything that was a warrior's right. There suddenly came a surge of power flushing through Josiah's body in that knowledge. He was on the half-breed like a mountain cat.

The *metis* began to turn as he heard the padding steps coming his way, finished just as Paddock collided with him. They fell, and rolled, until the huge man's weight rested on top of the young trapper.

Looks Far cried out as she watched her man struggle beneath the giant, then struggle no more. The two men were suddenly motionless. After a frozen moment, Emile Sharpe jerked and rose to his hands and knees. He staggered to his feet and stood over the young American he had been sent to kill.

Slowly, Emile dropped his gaze to his belly. His empty hand climbed slowly to grasp the torn, bloody shirt that hid his abdomen. The cloth was ripped aside to expose the knife buried to the guard beneath his ribs. The *metis* stared transfixed at the protruding handle—all that could be seen. Slowly, like a tall, heavy tree cut down in the forest, he fell to his knees and gazed up at the young man's face.

"You . . ." He gushed up a mouthful of blood. "You leave knife . . . knife in bear . . . this is good."

Sharpe gurgled and frothed red bubbles at his lips. "Good . . . good in fight . . . the little one . . . with the bear."

Josiah finally rose unsteadily to one elbow, still keeping his gaze fixed on the giant before him. The *metis* now put his empty hand on the bloody handle to let the red fluid billow from trembling, frantic fingers. The young American could not be certain that the large knife had found the aorta as that vessel trunked its way toward the lower body.

"Good in fight . . . little one—"

The giant fell over forward onto the grass.

There seemed little sense to it. Such waste and futility— Paddock shook his head. Finally he looked about him. The stranger and the giant both sprawled across the bloodied ground. Then Bass came up on his hands and knees, snapping his head groggily. Weaving, Scratch crawled over to the half-breed's body and rolled it over.

Titus placed a hand on the man's chest, over the heart, and could not feel it beating. He had been fooled before. Back last winter when he thought Josiah was dead. And he was not going to take any chances this time. Bass tugged at the lapels of the half-breed's bloody shirt and tore the cloth the rest of the way from the chest. There in the belly rested the huge knife. It had pushed up from the abdomen into the chest cavity with Josiah's last, desperate thrust of steel and muscle and sinew.

Bass finally turned to see Paddock rise enough to sit, his shoulders sagging in weariness. And the other huge bulk of a man crumpled in the grass nearby. The old trapper squinted against the first shocking rays of sunlight pouring across the pasture through the leafy tendrils of the tree branches. Sweat and dirt mixed in his eyes to sting with a salty burn, creating a mystical, unreal haze to everything he looked upon.

Then the stranger moved a little, and rose slowly, unsteadily to his hands and knees. And groaned. Bass looked over at the newcomer in the shadows before he scooted over to help the stranger climb to his feet.

It couldn't be!

Bass stood there frozen, his hand outstretched.

He was surely dreaming!

It just couldn't be!

But it was. Somehow.

It was Thornbrugh!

Twenty-eight

"I see that. . . ." Jarrell Thornbrugh spit some dirt and grit from his lips. ". . . you have not lost your manners, my friend." He accepted the hand Bass offered.

Scratch, still speechless at the shock of seeing Thornbrugh, shook his head.

"I suppose I am one to be thanking you, Mister . . .

Scratch," Jarrell said as he looked down at the body of the half-breed.

"L . . . Lord knows this gotta be a dream, Jarrell."

"I am afraid I must differ with you again, dear friend." Thornbrugh's words flowed as softly as the sunlight spreading across the pasture. "It . . . this has not been a dream. There, you see the reality of it all." He pointed at the body of Emile Sharpe.

"Ain't no dream—not this," Paddock muttered, feeling pain radiating through his pummeled body.

"I . . . have to know for sure," the Englishman said as he plodded toward the *metis*'s body.

"His name was Sharpe," Bass began.

"Emile Sharpe," Jarrell nodded in conclusion.

"How you know?" Josiah asked.

"Emile Sharpe—at last, we meet again," Jarrell said, shaking his head. "It has been many . . . many years. I wondered if I would ever run onto this bloody bastard again."

"You knowed him?" Scratch turned to Thornbrugh, amazed at the Englishman's declaration.

"No . . . not exactly, Scratch. Not exactly. Mostly by reputation. We met once—under far different circumstances. Ah, this is a bad one. Truly evil. A thorn in the side of the Company back to the days of the war with the Nor'westers. Not your common grade of murderer, this Monsieur Sharpe. More the ilk of a very professional assassin."

"You're gonna have to explain that to me an' Josiah here." Bass turned to Waits-by-the-Water. "Bring me my medicines, woman. I got me some mendin' to do. Looks to be Josiah been out playin' with knives again." He chuckled along with the two other men as the Crow woman brought two pouches to the trio, then retreated to sit with Looks Far once more.

Thornbrugh's eyes narrowed. "Josiah? You said: Josiah?" he asked, almost as an afterthought. "This young man is your trapping partner then—Josiah Paddock?"

"Yeah. Almost come close to not havin' each other as partners last few days." His lips bowed in a wry smile.

"Jarrell Thornbrugh." The big Englishman presented his hand. "I've forgotten my manners, Josiah. Here I have forgotten to introduce myself. It is a pleasure to meet you at last, young fellow."

"I'm pretty goddamned happy to be meetin' you," Josiah

replied. "Seems like you run onto a mess of trouble when you come callin' this mornin'." He shook his head. "Sure glad you come along when you did." He forced a smile before he turned and hobbled off.

"Indeed, Josiah. And who would the two ladies be?" He turned to Bass as he gestured toward the remnants of what had been Bass's lean-to.

"They be our women, Jarrell," Bass answered, watching Josiah tramp over to Looks Far to embrace both her and Joshua.

Josiah led Looks Far over to Thornbrugh, Joshua curled within an arm.

"This here's my wife, Looks Far Woman."

"And this would be your child?"

"My son, Joshua. Yes," Josiah replied as he slowly sank to the ground.

Bass motioned to his wife. She tugged at the rawhide halter on the still-skittish Indian pony.

"My Crow woman: Waits-by-the-Water."

Thornbrugh looked at the striking Indian woman, then turned to Bass. "You mentioned something a moment ago—something to the effect that you and young Paddock here had come very close during these last few days to not having one another as partners. I . . . I take that to mean, this . . . this here is not an isolated circumstance?"

"Sharpe ain't the first," Bass blurted out, then sighed. "Josiah an' me seem to be gettin' set on at these doin's—this ronnyvoo."

"Sharpe is not the first. That must mean . . . rather, I take it to mean, there have been others?"

"Yes," Josiah interjected.

"Two others, mule-tenders, come out from St. Louie with Campbell's supply train to raise Josiah's scalp. Couple days back."

"I take it they were not successful, then?" Jarrell grinned as he winked one eye.

"Us niggers wouldn't be standin' here jawin' with you if'n they'd raised some hair." Bass knelt beside Josiah to begin work on the young trapper's wounds.

"And why . . . why all this interest in young Josiah Paddock here?" The Englishman watched the older trapper begin to sort through the medicine pouches. "Why is it I was nearly killed helping the young fellow? Why all the bloody, deadly interest?"

"You mean why they sended out to kill him?" Bass said. "That we don't know us."

"I do now," Josiah replied quietly. He gazed over at the dead body briefly, then looked up at Scratch.

"You find out from Sharpe?" The older trapper daubed a sticky substance across the belly wound.

"No." Josiah motioned to the Flathead woman to leave, then looked back at the questioning face of his partner. "Really knowed all along."

Bass nodded for Waits-by-the-Water to follow the Flathead woman. The trio waited silently while the women retreated to the lean-to. Joshua suddenly fussed and Looks Far began to nurse the infant before the three men continued their quiet conversation.

"How come they come gunnin' for to lift your hair, son?" Bass studied the shoulder wound. "You find out who sended 'em?"

"I know who. S'pose I always knowed that, too." Josiah sighed. "A fella name of LeClerc."

"That family of the one you killed back to St. Lou?"

"The same, seems to be—"

"Wait just a minute here." Thornbrugh held up a hand. "You two will just have to explain what you are talking about. I am afraid I am not following any of this at all." He eased to the ground near the two trappers and laid his big smoothbore across his thighs.

"I . . . I killed a man back to St. Louis," Josiah began, ". . . some two years ago." Then he winced at Scratch's probing of the tender shoulder wound.

"You murdered him?"

"Not rightly," Josiah answered as he grit his teeth. "It was a duel—"

"Then it was not murder, young fellow," Thornbrugh stated flatly.

"Looks to be, the family of the dead one thinks it was murder," Paddock said after a moment of thought.

"What reason would the LeClerc family have to believe you murdered this fellow when it was a prescribed duel?"

"I . . . I didn't kill him with a pistol," Josiah explained. "I . . . ah, killed him . . . kicked him 'til he was dead."

Thornbrugh leaned back. "I see, Josiah. Even though it was a duel, you did not kill your antagonist honorably."

"I killed 'im fair and square—and there ain't nothin' wrong with the way I done it!" Josiah broke in, eyes flashing.

"I am afraid you misunderstood my statement," Jarrèll explained. "If the man had been killed with a pistol ball in that duel, all would have been according to the code of honor regarding a duel. Instead, you killed your opponent in a different manner. And there the family's great anger arises. That anger, I suppose, has caused that family to send out these murderers to kill you."

Bass wrapped a swathe of trade cloth around Paddock's midsection.

Thornbrugh looked thoughtful. "Who were the first two who came for you, Josiah?"

"Like we said, they was just mule-tenders on Campbell's supply brigade."

"Hired to ride along with this Campbell and kill themselves a Josiah Paddock here at rendezvous. Exactly." It began to fit in the Englishman's mind. "Were they American, such as yourself?"

"Yeah," the young trapper answered. "I mean, I s'pose they was."

"They wasn't Canadian, like that'un." Bass threw a thumb over his shoulder in the direction of the body.

"Two common thugs, then, gentlemen," Thornbrugh said. "Most likely, they were nothing more than hired murderers. This one, however," he said as he rose to move over to the body of the *métis*, "is a different case."

"Just what makes him so differ'nt?" Bass asked.

"If this truly is Emile Sharpe, then we have done a great service to many people. Many, many more than just yourselves."

"Yeah?" Bass looked up at the big Englishman and squinted one eye.

"Yes, my friend. If this truly be Emile Sharpe, it would explain a lot of things—would explain much as to his coming out here to kill you. He is, in every sense of the word, a dangerous killer, an assassin to be feared."

"Killer's a killer. All the same." Bass tied a knot in Josiah's belly bandage. "Don't see no difference 'tween one what's drawin' pay and 'nother what does it for free."

"A hired killer," Thornbrugh mused, as if thinking out loud.

"The two Americans were hired killers. No—Sharpe was a professional killer. That is the way an assassin makes his living—by killing people. Clean. Neat. Tidy in all respects."

The Englishman watched as the two American trappers turned their heads to stare at the dead body. "And it makes sense to me that this LeClerc family of St. Louis would hire only the best to accomplish the task—sparing no expense to see the job done right."

"Most all them French in St. Louis got enough money," Josiah said.

"The LeClercs happen to be one of the richest and most powerful families along the great rivers of your country," Thornbrugh said. "Ranking in wealth and influence and power right beside the Chouteaus and Bertholds. Their money has been a force in the river trade for generations. And the Company has often run up against their influence and wealth. Because of what happened in Canada—being now under English rule after the defeat of the French many, many years ago—there would still be long-held rancor for the Company. They, too—just like this Sharpe fellow—have long been a thorn in the Company's side."

"A professional killer, huh?" Bass pondered that as he brought his gaze back to Thornbrugh's face. "S'pose we all the more grateful Josiah was the one to gut an' bleed that son of a bitch."

"There is a justice"—Jarrell sighed—"perhaps slow at times. But there comes a day when punishment is meted out for one's crimes. This one has spilled much blood—across the borders and out in the wild places."

Through the trees, in the distance, a harmonica took up the melancholy strains of the old song in a nearby camp, the plaintive melody drifting toward the trio on the early-morning breezes. In a moment, another trapper began to sing the words.

Oh, Shenandoah, I want to hear you!
Away! You rolling river!
I'll come to you across the water.
Away! I'm bound away.
Across the wide Missouri!

The old Missouri's a mighty river.
Away! You rolling river!

The Indians camp along her border.
Away! We're bound away.
Across the wide Missouri.

"Just why the hell you way out here, Jarrell? I cain't figure why you'd come walkin' in right outta the blue to rendez-vous."

"John sent me. The doctor."

"He figured I needed some lookin' after, huh?" Bass snorted as he stuffed several small pouches back into the two rawhide parfleches. "Maybeso he were right again."

"No." Jarrell grinned. "On the contrary, dear friend. I was asked by John to be the advance scout for the legion of his army."

"You gonna have to say—"

"I will explain," Jarrell interrupted. "John has decided to have his brigades attend your rendezvous here in the Rocky Mountains. We have been penetrating the mountains from the west for some time now—and at last the time has come to send brigades to those rendezvous."

"You got Hudson's Bay Company trappers here?"

"Heavens no, friend!" He slapped Scratch on the shoulder. "John wishes to send a brigade here next summer, and to do so, I am to scout the field."

"You come here alone then?"

"Quite alone."

Bass snorted.

"Is that so hard to believe?" Thornbrugh paused. "I see that it is, even for you, who journeyed all alone to Vancouver."

"But . . . but, Jarrell . . . Jarrell." He sought for the words he could use without offending. ". . . you just . . . you ain't—"

"A mountain man?" he finished for Bass. "A lord of the wil-derness? Perhaps not, dear friend. But I have learned much on my journey. It has been a long, lonely trek—but a rewarding one for me. John will receive my report with great excitement. And he will be able to send his men to rendezvous in 'thirty-four. I am considerably stronger for my solitary sojourn, too. I am not yet a mountain man—as are the two of you gentlemen. But by the time I return to Vancouver with my report for John, I believe I will be long down that road to becoming ac-customed to the wilderness. Partly anyway. Perhaps one day I, too, shall be a lord in this border wilderness—such as you two are."

"There you go again. An' after you promised me, too," Bass protested. "You said you wasn't gonna be callin' me Lord Bass no more." There was mock pain in his voice.

"And I have not, Scratch," Jarrell answered with a grin. "Nevertheless, no matter what you wish me to call you—you are truly a lord out here. I have jolly good reason to believe that, especially after this trip."

He and Bass helped Paddock to his feet. "I am hungry, friends. What do you have to feed a weary and beaten traveler who arrived so late last night that none of the fires in the camps below yours had anything cooking over them?"

"You come in last night, huh?"

"Late. And inquired as to anyone's knowledge of this old fellow, Titus Bass."

"Ol' fella, huh?" Bass grinned. "You older'n me, Jarrell."

"Ah—but in many ways very young compared to you, friend," he answered. "You see before you one who is very young in the ways of the wilderness. While you, dear Scratch, are an old man—and very much at home here—in the ways of this wildness which surrounds us. That wildness you have chosen for your home. A wildness on the border between the civilization you shun and shy away from, between it and the wildness and freedom after which you yearn so mightily with all your heart."

"Who told you how to make it up to our camp?" Titus asked.

"Robert Campbell said you were up this way. But Nathaniel Wyeth showed up about the time I was ready to come here and diverted me last evening."

"He's that Yankee slicker what had him plans to build a fort to work again' the Company?"

"Right you are, Bass," he answered. "And no love he shares for you American trappers, fellow countrymen notwithstanding. A paradox—but he told me of a letter he had written here at rendezvous to Edward Ermatinger, a letter he asked me to deliver to McLoughlin for him. Wyeth warns of great personal danger to any Company personnel who would come to rendezvous, saying, too, that our beaver would be in danger of robbery, as well as our bodily safety. He says this even though this Green River is on the west side of the mountains and empties into the western ocean—making a substantial claim for the Company's rights to this very area."

"None of that got nothin' to do with me," Bass protested a little testily, "goin' where I please, trappin' where I may."

"On the contrary, it does have some to do with you—both of you," Jarrell said. "He has little regard for you American fur trappers."

"You just gonna have to get off your high English there, Mister Thornbrugh."

"Wyeth has written Ermatinger and the doctor his opinion that you American trappers are a rabble; indeed, he said you all comprise *a great majority of scoundrels.*"

"I . . . I don't know me if'n I oughta be flattered, or 'shamed of myself." Bass grinned widely.

"I would never put much credence in Wyeth myself—knowing he even considered throwing in with this Captain Bonneville for a time, to head a brigade to California that will soon be leaving this rendezvous."

"I think me I'm still proud to be called a scoundrel!" Bass studied the sun raking through the trees. "Fella like Wyeth call me a scoundrel—somethin' to be proud of then."

"And Mister Wyeth didn't even feed me." Jarrell patted his stomach. "He merely talked both my ears off about his grand plans. Still hungry. Have to admit I hurt, too. Hungry, mostly—"

"I s'pose we better feed this man." Bass turned from the sunlit trees back to the Englishman. "Then we gotta be buyin' a heap of a hangover down to Bobby Campbell's saloon."

"Whiskey?"

"Yeah."

"I have never had this . . . liquor you call your trader's whiskey. I hear tell it tastes absolutely bloody rotten."

"Not so bad really." Then Bass thought a moment. "Come to think of it, the shit does taste *bloody* rotten."

"Good!" Jarrell put his hand on Scratch's shoulder. "My palate awaits your hot breakfast and then we shall attempt to swallow that poor excuse for proper drinking spirits."

"Gotta do somethin' with this nigger's body, first." The old trapper cocked a thumb toward the dead *metis.*

"Bury him?" Jarrell asked.

"No," Josiah replied quietly.

"That be too good for him," Bass agreed.

"How did you dispose of the other two?" Thornbrugh asked.

"Took 'em down to Bobby Campbell," Bass said. "But them two had worked for that trader. They was his niggers. So we dumped the bodies off at Campbell's feet."

"This one would have come out by himself." Thornbrugh stared down at the wet, reddened earth around the corpse.

"Another of your lords of the wilderness, Jarrell?"

"Truly," he answered. "A lord of the borderlands." Jarrell finally raised his eyes to gaze at Bass. "At least until he met up with some lords who were stronger."

"You come along to help." Josiah turned toward Thornbrugh.

"I was merely fortunate enough to have a hand in it," he answered quietly. "Young man, you finished what many I know would have given half their lives to have had the chance to do—kill Emile Sharpe. Many have given much more for the opportunity to kill him. What . . ."—he mused a moment before he continued—"what would seem fitting for disposing of the body?"

Bass considered it, looking from Jarrell's face to Josiah's, then finally to the body. He strode over to the shambles of his lean-to and brought his buffalo runner alongside the dead man.

"Would you gimme a hand, Jarrell?" he asked quietly as he started to lift the heavy corpse.

Thornbrugh dropped his rifle and stepped up to help the two trappers lift the body across the horse's back. It was difficult even for the three of them to get the dead man across the animal, but at last they slung the cadaver over the pony. Thornbrugh looked up at Bass and Paddock.

"You have decided?" the Englishman inquired. "What would be a fitting disposal of the body?"

"We give him back to the wolf."

"Yes," Josiah answered with a soft rush of air from his lungs.

"Wolf?" Jarrell said, looking first at Paddock, then at Titus.

"A mad wolf," Bass answered.

"He come 'round the camps for a couple of nights back," Josiah added.

"Ah, yes," Jarrell said. "I heard of that incident. Seems he made a foray into the herds last night, too. Do you believe he's still in the region?"

"Yeah." Bass nodded. "He's still around. Where there be meat—there be a wolf."

"Then, it is fitting that you dispose of the body for this mad wolf," the big Englishman said. "A mad wolf to feed on another mad wolf."

"In the end, as it should be," Bass decided.

"You want us come along—" Josiah began.

"No," Bass answered quickly, then looked up into his young partner's eyes. "No, son. You killed the bastard. Now I'll be the one what's got to do this part—by my own self." He sighed. "That too, in the end, as it should be."

Scratch tugged on the rawhide halter to pull the pony behind him. "I take him back to the wolf," he almost whispered as he headed out of camp toward the hills to the southwest.

"Breakfast for your belly when you get back, my friend," Jarrell called after him.

"We'll have it ready for you," Paddock called.

Bass did not answer. He tramped across the pasture and began the climb up the first slope into the rolling hills and ridges. The old trapper did not stop until he felt the sun hot, piercing, on his bare neck. He pulled on the pony's rawhide rope and the animal halted.

He turned. He raised his head to look up to that half-circle of the sun just breaking over the tops of the trees down in the valley. Soon the smoke from countless morning fires would smudge the clear, morning air.

"We give him back to the wolf."

It was almost like a prayer. Bass gazed at the new-born globe, its pristine light crawling thick and blood-like across the deep-red soil of the valley floor.

"An' that is as it should be," he told the sun. "As it should be."

Scratch turned to the north and west, his gaze slowly following each new hill as it rose away from him until he finally stared at the dim, hazy peaks in the distance. Away to the high, and the lonely, and the terrible places.

The great western land stretched before him, vaulting itself beyond him into those serene and soul-soothing places in the high country. Gradually the old trapper closed his eyes and drew in a long breath, pulling the sun's light and warmth deeply into his lungs. It was almost like a prayer, this too, taking the sun into his body.

"As it should be," he whispered.

Eventually the old man opened his eyes again to gaze once more at the high places out there beyond him—those lonely, terrible places that beckoned, and eternally called out to his soul.

ABOUT THE AUTHOR

TERRY C. JOHNSTON was born in 1947 on the plains of Kansas and has lived a varied life as a roustabout, history teacher, printer, paramedic, dog catcher, and car salesman, all the while immersing himself in the history of the early American West. His first novel, *Carry the Wind*, won the Medicine Pipe Bearer's Award from the Western Writers of America, and his subsequent books, among them *Borderlords* and the Son of the Plains trilogy, have appeared on bestseller lists throughout the country. Terry C. Johnston lives and writes in Big Sky country near Billings, Montana.